ELIZABETH WAITE
OMNIBUS

KINGSTON KATE
COCKNEY COURAGE

Elizabeth Waite Omnibus

KINGSTON KATE
COCKNEY COURAGE

ELIZABETH WAITE

timewarner
paperbacks

A Time Warner Paperback

This omnibus edition first published in Great Britain by
Time Warner Paperbacks in 2003
Elizabeth Waite Omnibus Copyright © Elizabeth Waite 2003

Previously published separately:
Kingston Kate first published in Great Britain in 1998 by
Little, Brown and Company
Published by Warner Books in 1999
Reprinted 2000, 2001
Copyright © Elizabeth Waite 1998

Cockney Courage first published in Great Britain in 1999 by
Little, Brown and Company
Published by Warner Books in 2000
Reprinted by Time Warner Paperbacks in 2002
Copyright © Elizabeth Waite 1999

The moral right of the author has been asserted.

A CIP catalogue record for this book is available from the British Library.

ISBN 0 7515 3503 6

Printed and bound in Great Britain by Mackays of Chatham Ltd, Kent

Time Warner Paperbacks
An imprint of
Time Warner Books UK
Brettenham House
Lancaster Place
London WC2E 7EN

www.TimeWarnerBooks.co.uk

KINGSTON KATE

A Childhood Memory

IN 1930 OUR Sunday-school summer outing was a trip from Tooting to Hampton Court Palace and gardens. The charabanc was outside our church hall by nine o'clock. Twenty-eight excited children scrambled aboard and squabbled over who was to have the seats by the windows. Eight already harassed Sunday-school teachers accompanied us. After a short coach ride, which took us over Vauxhall Bridge, we arrived at the Embankment. There we boarded what seemed to us an extremely big riverboat, which would take us all the way down the mighty river Thames to disembark at Hampton Court Bridge.

It was a beautiful sunny August day. The whistles blew, wisps of steam could be seen coming from the funnel and then we were going downriver, passing under Chelsea Bridge and on to Putney, Hammersmith and Richmond, under Chiswick Bridge and through Teddington. By then we had left behind all the sights and sounds of busy

London and were steaming slowly through Kingston upon Thames.

To me, an eight-year-old child, it was like entering another world. Green fields, tall trees and tiny villages all set alongside the river. Cottages that were so pretty it had us London kiddies gasping with envy. Music was being played on board our boat and the sound brought folk to their cottage doors and men came to stand in the doorways of the inns. Children lined the towpath waving to us, and we all waved back and, to this day, I remember thinking how lucky they were to live in such a clean and wonderful place.

From that day's outing, all those years ago, has come the setting I have used for this book. Littleton Green and its inhabitants are purely ficticious, though I haven't the slightest doubt that such a place did exist albeit under another name. Whether or not the same could be said today is an entirely different matter.

Of one thing we can always be sure, no one can take our memories away from us.

Chapter One

'DON'T CRY, KATE, it's nowhere near as bad as it seems.'

Kate Kearsley dashed away her tears, fell to her knees and laid her head in her mother's lap.

'Why have you got up? How ever did you manage to wash and dress yourself? You should have stayed in bed, you really should have,' she said, her voice no more than a whisper.

Hilda Kearsley wriggled to sit in a more comfortable position on the side of the bed, put her hand into the pocket of her long dark skirt and drew out a white handkerchief which she used to dab at the tears still dribbling down Kate's cheeks. 'Your father's been good for a long time, Kate. Try to remember that.'

'That doesn't in any way excuse him. Just look at your face! One eye is almost closed up. He must have been well and truly drunk last night. He's usually far more clever – doesn't leave a mark on you where it shows.'

'Oh, pet, I'll bathe me eye. The swelling will soon go down.'

'Mother! Stop being so forgiving. Why can't you see him for the bully he is rather than keep making allowances for him?'

Kate was distressed to see the state her mother was in and so angry with her father that all she could think of was it was a damn good job he'd had the sense to leave the house so early that morning, otherwise she would not have been responsible for her own actions. The way she felt she could easily do him an injury. What a business, she thought bitterly, inwardly shuddering at what her mother had endured this time.

She had long given up trying to fathom her own father. When he was sober he was a lovely man; a wonderful father and a good provider and that was as it should be seeing he owned his own boat yard. She knew full well she was the apple of his eye and, to be truthful, she adored him in return – most of the time. He had never laid a finger on her. But there was a dark side to him which frightened her and with the demon drink inside him it was a different story. She would lay in bed with only a thin wall between her and her parents' room and try not to imagine what was going on in their bedroom.

It was so unfair to her mother.

Why does she let him get away with it? Why can't she stand up to him? Tell him enough is enough. I suppose she must do just that from time to time, Kate reflected, because there would be weeks, even months sometimes, when everything between her parents would be fine and life enjoyable, even happy. Then her father would go off on a drinking spree, neglect his work and give no thought to anyone but himself. Whatever it was that took over within him, it was always her mother who he took it out on. She had to bear the brunt.

Kate shivered, raised herself to a sitting position and did her best to smile at her mother. 'I'll make a fresh pot of tea and boil you an egg with some thin brown bread and butter. Could you manage that, Mum? I'll lay it out nice on a tray and bring it up here to you. Come on now, lift your legs up an' I'll settle all the pillows behind your shoulders.'

Hilda took one of her daughter's hands in hers and gently squeezed it.

'You're a good girl, Kate, you shouldn't have to be living this dull life with just your father and me, let alone take on problems that are none of your concern. You'll be eighteen in a few weeks' time, you must start giving a thought to what you want to do with your life. If only your brother . . .' her voice trailed off and Kate knew she was overcome with emotion.

Kate had made the tea, covering the pot with the pretty blue cosy her mother had hand-stitched. She was buttering bread, warm from the oven, when the door to the kitchen opened and Hilda stood there. The stairs had been too much for her and, as she drew in a deep, rasping breath, the tears came.

Kate dropped the knife she had been using and ran to her mother's side. 'You shouldn't have come down. Here, sit here.' She pushed the big high-backed wooden armchair until it was against her mother's knees, then helped her to sit back in the chair. She didn't know

3

what to do. Her mother never cried, at least she couldn't remember ever seeing her do so before. But she was crying now; great sobs which left her gasping for breath.

Kate busied herself pouring tea into willow-pattern cups and when Hilda's sobs finally subsided, and she was quiet, she placed a cup and saucer on the end of the hob within her reach and patted her shoulder.

'Try and sip that before it gets cold. Are you warm enough?' Touching her hand, Kate realised she was freezing. 'Hang on. I'll only be a moment,' she murmured, making for the stairs. She came down carrying the big double patchwork quilt that had been on her parents' bed. 'Here, let me wrap this around your shoulders and tuck it in tight round your knees.'

Her mother's hands were shaking so badly, that she couldn't hold the cup.

'Shock. I'll have to leave you and go for the doctor.'

'No! Please, Kate! I'll be all right. I'm just cold. No doctor, please.'

'We'll see,' Kate said, as she crouched down at the grate. Opening up the top of the range she piled a shovelful of coal onto the glowing embers, adding two small logs which caught quickly, cracking and flaming and giving out a warm glow.

A little later they were both dipping fingers of bread into their soft-boiled eggs and drinking their tea.

Kate sighed deeply as she watched her mother put a hand to her side and flinch more than once; her ribs must be badly bruised. Why, oh why, did her father have these terrible outbursts? He was so big. A powerfully built six-footer with brown eyes, craggy features and a deep voice.

Her mother wasn't small. In fact, as she herself had often told Kate, she was too tall and large-boned to be called a beautiful woman. But she certainly did have character; graceful in all she did, with her head held high on a beautiful neck, loving and kind, mindful of those less fortunate than herself. She was not a commonplace woman; any emotion she showed was both deep and true.

Kate had heard the bare bones of the story that had been so tragic for her parents, but she thought it should never have been allowed to fester and eat away into their lives like some horrible incurable disease. She had only been two years of age when it had happened.

'Kate, dear, I do wish you would try and stop worrying. A few days and I'll be right as ninepence, you'll see.' Hilda's voice held a note of pleading.

'Yes, till the next time.'

'Don't harp on it, please. Your father will be really sorry when he sobers up.'

'True, but as I said, only until the next time.'

'You were deep in thought when I broke the silence, what were you thinking about?'

'Nothing really. Daydreaming I suppose.'

'That's not quite true, is it?'

Kate looked her mother directly in the eye. 'No. If you must know I was thinking about David. My brother who no one is allowed to mention. A subject that is entirely forbidden in this house.'

Hilda turned her glance away from her daughter as tears welled up in her eyes. She felt totally confused. She turned her head back to look at her daughter.

'Old story,' she said. 'Best forgotten.'

'Oh, no, Mum! No. That's more than half the trouble. Dad blames himself, you blame him as well. I know you do. I just can't understand why you've never brought it out into the open. Talked about it. Surely losing a son is best not forgotten? All these years you've both lived with the heartache of that day and it doesn't get any better, does it?'

'No, I can't say that it does. Sixteen years ago it was. Do you remember anything about it?'

'Not really.'

'No, you were only just two. Your grandma took you off to live with her for a while afterwards. A Sunday it was. Summer. A really lovely day. Crowds of people on the riverbank, families, lots of kiddies. Folk had brought picnics. There were loads of small boats on the river. Your father couldn't get his near the bank and David so badly wanted to get into it and be with his dad. I tucked up my skirt and petticoats, picked him up and waded out – it wasn't too deep where we were sitting – and handed him into your father's arms.' Hilda put a hand to her face and covered her eyes as if trying to blot out the memory.

Kate felt the urge to wrap her arms around her mother, hush her, soothe her, tell her everything was all right. But it wasn't, was it? Once in the early hours of the morning she had heard her mother round on her father and cry out, 'David was my son, too, you know. I've felt his death every bit as badly as you have, but I haven't spurned my responsibilities, nor have I tried to drown my sorrow with alcohol.' Her voice, so full of sadness, had made Kate miserable for days.

Now that her mother had started to talk, she sat quietly

and listened. It was probably the best thing that could have happened, her bringing up the subject of David. Kate knew full well that the tragic consequences of that day on the river were never very far from her mother's mind.

'David was such a beautiful child,' Hilda said, still speaking very quietly. 'I stood on the bank and watched your father steer the boat until it turned at a bend in the river. David was waving to me, his eyes alight with excitement, his curly hair blown about in the breeze. Half a mile down the river they were when your father saw that little girl in the water being swept away by the current. He didn't hesitate for a moment. No doubt about it, he saved her life. David must have been frightened when he saw his dad go into the water. He stood up, he shouldn't have but he didn't understand what was happening and he fell over the side. There was some barbed wire on the riverbed. His little feet were still tangled in it when your father got to him. Your dad couldn't save him.'

'Dad wasn't entirely to blame.'

'Most of the time I would agree with you and I do know the guilt of not having saved his own son still plays heavily on his mind, but I just cannot bring myself to forgive him. Not altogether I can't.'

'Didn't Dad hurt his back saving that child?'

'Yes. He damaged his spine. That's why he's not able to lift heavy objects, some days he has a job to straighten up. It's made working very difficult for him.'

'Poor Dad,' Kate mumbled.

'To tell the truth, Kate, you're right. Poor Dad. That boat yard has been his pride and joy since he was a mere lad. Left to him by his father and by his father before him.' Hilda broke off and shrugged. 'I suppose neither of us have coped all that well.'

Kate was thrown off balance by her mother's admission. Now her loyalties were divided. Her father had to rely on his employees to do boat repairs that he would much prefer to tackle himself. Frustation probably had a lot to do with his bouts of drinking which, in turn, led to his horrible temper. Still, it was wholly unfair that he should offload his frustrations onto her mother. There was no reason in this world for him to treat her so badly.

'Mum, I think we've talked for long enough, you look ready to drop. I'll fill the hot-water bottle and take it up, remake your bed and then I'll come down an' help you up the stairs, see you into bed and you can stay there for the rest of the day. How does that sound?'

Hilda nodded her agreement, smiling at Kate in gratitude.

With a lump in her throat Kate removed the sheets from the bed and fetched clean ones, smelling of lavender, from the linen cupboard on the landing. There wasn't a photograph of her brother anywhere in the house, at least not to her knowledge. She kept trying to imagine what he had looked like as a child. What would he look like now? He'd be a man. She tried to put him from her mind as she went back downstairs to tend to her mother, but still her thoughts were full of him.

David had been just four years old when he died. Such a small boy to be the unwitting cause of so much grief.

Chapter Two

KATE LET GO of the shafts of the wheelbarrow she was pushing and opened the front gate which led to the towpath. She was off to make her monthly visit to Melbourne Lodge; a visit she looked forward to with great pleasure. This small barrow was lined with brown paper to protect the fine linen that lay in the bottom, the top protected by a white starched cloth. By a long-standing arrangement her mother repaired the fine linen and quality shirts that belonged to the Collier household.

At times it didn't seem right to Kate that her mother should have to do this kind of work while her father squandered his money. To outsiders Fred Kearsley was a prosperous businessman. Only those close to him knew his weakness for gambling and drinking.

That was her mother all over. A fierce streak of independence made her refuse to beg her father for more housekeeping money. Besides which, she let it be known that she hadn't enough to do to fill the hours of the day and the offer to repair fine linen was as much a hobby as a means of earning money. In addition, she was a very fine needlewoman.

Kate closed the gate behind her and glanced upwards. Her mother, who was standing at the bedroom window, raised her hand to wave goodbye. She watched her daughter set off along the towpath with mixed feelings.

Kate was a beautiful young woman. In fact, that was the one thing that she and her husband were entirely in agreement about, and because she was such a lovely, trusting young girl they feared for her. Tall and slim but shapely, laughing, sparkling, full of spirit, seeing good in everyone, she had so far led a sheltered life. She should have had brothers and sisters as companions to grow up with instead of spending all her time with adults.

Kate's hair was her crowning glory. She had her father's colouring; Fred had a thick head of reddish hair, now shot through with grey. Kate's hair was also thick and heavy, and almost reached her waist. It was the exact colour of a rich ripe chestnut, and unruly was the best way to describe it. No matter how many slides or combs she used it had a will of its own, refusing to be restrained. Dangling ringlets always seemed to escape to bob free about her cheeks and ears. Beneath that mop of hair she had arched eyebrows, deep-brown eyes, cheeks and skin that were like a soft ripe peach and full lips that were always smiling. Oh yes, one look at Kate and men were impressed.

Letting out a deep sigh Hilda closed her eyes. Things couldn't go on as they were, she told herself. Life had held out such promise when Fred Kearsley had brought her home, as his young bride, to this lovely hamlet of

Littleton Green, not very far from the market town of Kingston upon Thames. Bramble Cottage had taken her breath away on sight. Fred had carried her over the threshold and she had immediately fallen in love with it. It had been like a real-life fairy story she had thought then.

Born in Bermondsey, she had been one of nine children, all of them brought up in a two-bedroomed flat, the like of which folk, who had never been outside this beautiful part of Surrey, would not believe. Seven brothers but only one sister. Five of those great strapping brothers had worked in Covent Garden. It was there they had met Fred Kearsley. He had gone to Bermondsey to purchase a quantity of leather for the inside upholstery of a boat he was building and had been directed to Covent Garden as a place where he could kill spare time and also get a good breakfast. Her brothers had brought him home and Hilda's fate had been sealed from the moment he set eyes on her.

Suddenly she felt dizzy. 'I feel so sick,' she murmured out loud. She moved back to the side of the window and leaned her head against the wall, one hand covering her mouth, the other wrapped across her sore ribs. Outside, a weak February sun showed up the frost still lingering under the hedges in the front garden. Beyond, standing beneath the huge oak tree, she could see the big wooden picnic table that Fred, with the help of his neighbours, had constructed a good many years ago. Around another mature tree he had built a seat. Her blue eyes filled with tears, and she ran her fingers through her tangled hair. They had had such happy times out there when David had been little.

Beyond the towpath lay the river. The dear old Thames. Always moving, always busy, it had a life of its own and a good many men depended on that river for their livelihood.

God in heaven, she and Fred had loved each other so much during those first five years of their married life. Why had everything had to go so wrong?

Hilda stared at the floor. Where had the time gone?

Moving away from the window she crossed the room to her chest of drawers, knelt and opened the bottom drawer. She took out two silver-framed photographs. She brought one of a small, smiling, curly haired boy to her lips and kissed the glass. The other photo was of Fred and herself. He had been twenty-five and she seventeen on the day in 1901 that they were married.

What a year that had turned out to be. In January she had become a bride, two weeks later Queen Victoria had died and come October, David had been born.

Angry at herself for harping back on matters that no amount of tears would alter, she put the two silver frames right at the very back of the drawer, underneath the clothes and shut it again.

She stared out of the window again for a few seconds, then made for the bed. 'I'll have to have a lie down,' she muttered to herself. Last night Fred had been brutal, hurting her far more than she had admitted to Kate. Things between them were getting worse, not better, and if she wasn't careful one night he might end up doing her a really serious injury.

I should do something about the way we live our lives, she chided herself. But what? With her head resting back against the pillows, her eyes closed and she thankfully dozed off. Even so, there was a frown on her wan haggard face. It seemed sleep didn't blot out the troubles from her mind.

Kate had been glad to get out of the house. She hoped her mother would at least have a rest. She wouldn't let herself dwell on exactly what had gone on last night between her parents. She wasn't totally naive and thought sex was probably half the trouble. Over the years she had drawn her own conclusions: she thought her mother probably never refused her father but neither did she show him any outward signs of love; more than likely she was revolted at the thought of him touching her; unable to bear the idea of becoming pregnant again after losing David.

The saddest part of it all was they were such decent people. She loved them both. Dearly. Hated having to take sides. Such a pity that the tragedy of losing their young son had embittered them so early on in their married life.

She pushed the loose strands of her long hair back from her face, tossed one end of her plaid shawl over her left shoulder and quickened her pace. There was a very cold nip in the air even though the sun was doing its best to shine.

Not much further and she would be able to see Melbourne Lodge, so called, it was rumoured, because the first gentleman to have lived there had been an Australian. Whether that was true or not, she didn't know and didn't really care. She loved the place. The house was set on a hill, with gardens running down almost to the river. From the top windows you could see right downriver to Appleton's boat yard. Kate smiled at that thought. Her father hoped that she would marry Victor Appleton because the Appleton yard was similiar to his. She was friendly enough with Victor, but no more than that. In Kate's mind he didn't have a lot going for him. A bit of a dull plodder was how she saw him.

From the back windows of Melbourne Lodge there was a great view of the Surrey countryside. Not that I've been over the whole of the house, she said to herself. On hot days Mary Kennedy, who was cook-housekeeper there, always gave her a glass of lemonade and a piece of her home-made cake. In wintertime it would more likely be a bowl of soup taken in that huge kitchen where big shiny copper pans hung from hooks high up on the wall and a great fire burned in the black-leaded grate.

There had been the odd occasion when she had gone upstairs with Mary collecting linen and such like from the various landing cupboards. Her tendency to stand and stare in awe at the beautiful furnishings always brought a smile to the housekeeper's face and she would playfully tell her that curiosity killed the cat. She had never been allowed to enter the main bedroom, but she was truly envious of the washing facilities in all the other bedrooms. Glazed white earthenware wash-hand basins were fixed to the walls, with pretty splashbacks, sporting pictures of pheasants and fruit. Each basin had a brass plug and chain although there was no running water. Large pitchers were supplied to carry it up from the kitchen. Dirty water drained away into large floral pots which were, in reality, buckets but not shaped as such. Difficult to handle when emptying, Kate supposed, but very decorative for all that.

You wouldn't think anyone who lived in a house like

that could possibly be discontented, but that was how Kate saw Mr Collier. Or, to give him his full name, Mr Charles Christopher Collier, referred to by local folk as 'the Squire'. He was a big man in every sense of the word. Held in awe by some, but revered and respected by the whole of Surrey, though there were many who didn't know of the double life he led, and those who did did not always approve.

Kate turned into the long driveway, trundling her wheelbarrow behind her and immediately saw Mary Kennedy, who had the side door of the house wide open and was waving her welcome. She had a plump face, big breasts, and short brown hair which was only just beginning to go grey. Kate waved back, a happy smile spreading across the whole of her face.

'I knew you'd be on time,' Mary said as Kate drew near. 'As I always say, Kingston Kate always reliable, never late.'

Kate laughed loudly. Every time she came to the house she was greeted with the same saying. Mary had known her from the time she had been a shy toddler holding onto her mother's long skirts. She had a lot of time for young Kate and had grown to love her very much. Kate's well-fitting clothes and strong, good leather boots set her apart from the poorer local children. Her innocence and pleasant attitude, not to mention her well-pronounced speech, made her stand out from the badly spoken kiddies one found begging along the riverbanks.

The name Kingston Kate had come about because, as a child, Kate had been unable to pronounce her surname Kearsley, and she could never remember that she lived at Littleton Green, only that her nan lived at Kingston.

So, to a good many folk, she had become known as Kingston Kate.

She propped her wheelbarrow against the passage wall and hurried into the kitchen. The warmth and cheer that greeted her was always a joy. Afternoon tea was set out on the enormous scrubbed table, as Kate had known it would be. The big brown teapot was beside the range to keep warm and Mary presided over her own home-made scones with strawberry jam and a rich fruit cake.

There were two staircases to the house: the main one, broad and sweeping, carpeted all the way to the top; the other, running up from the kitchen, used only by staff. Dark and narrow, the wooden treads were uncovered. At the foot of these stairs there was a door from which Mrs Bates now stepped out.

''Allo, Kate. I guessed there'd be a cup of tea going seeing as it was your day to vist.'

'Hallo, Mrs Bates. You're here late today, aren't you?'

'Yeah, I am an' all. His floozie . . .' she paused and nodded her head towards the ceiling '. . . she's worked herself into a right uppity mood. Seems 'is lordship ain't been near nor by for two days now and though she'd deny it if you were t'ask 'er, I'm telling yer straight that lass is worried sick.'

Mrs Bates was the cleaner who came each day to 'do' at Melbourne Lodge. Try as Kate might she didn't like the woman though she would have been hard pushed to say exactly why. Perhaps it was because she was rather intimidating, a whole head taller than her own husband and more than half as broad. She always wore a man's flat cap, indoors as well as out. 'I bet she even wears it in bed,' Kate had whispered to her mother when once

16

they had met Mr and Mrs Bates in Kingston market. 'An ill-matched pair if ever I saw one,' had been her mother's comment.

'Put your cleaning things away, Mrs Bates, an' come an' sit up to the table.' Mary's voice was sharp. 'We can't be sending you off home on this cold day without offering you tea and a scone – they are still warm from the oven.'

When both Kate and Mrs Bates had been served, Mary sat down at the head of the table and crossed her arms over her ample chest.

'Mrs Bates,' she began and her tone was so serious that Mrs Bates paused, her mouth wide open, half a scone in her hand halfway to being bitten. 'You would do well to remember that there is a vast difference between a mistress and a floozie. Especially if you value your job in this house.' Mrs Bates' mouth snapped shut and Kate, sitting next to her, heard her teeth grind.

'That's nothing to what they say about the pair of them in the Boar's 'Ead,' she hissed in reply. 'You wanna 'ear them some nights an' I can't say that I blame them. Be honest, Mrs Kennedy, he's well over forty, nearer to fifty if you ask me, an' even out in public he treats her ever so gentle like, you'd think she was some kind of a princess. Bet he never treats his wife like that.'

'Will you stop it, Mrs Bates. I've listened to you spout off about Mr Collier far too often.' Mary spat the words out.

The colour drained from Mrs Bates' cheeks and a brief look passed between her and the housekeeper, but it was Mrs Bates who dropped her eyes first.

'Let me put you straight on a few details,' Mary began.

'Jane Mortimer is mistress in this house, no matter what you might think. I agree with you that she is much younger than Mr Collier but I have always found her to be a lovely, shy, young lady. And I mean lady. There is nothing wicked or shameful about her.'

The hostility between Mary and Mrs Bates rocked Kate to the core. She knew quite a lot about Mr Collier and was aware that many people, her own mother included, were curious about him but never had she heard his affairs discussed so openly. She would have like to have told Mrs Bates that she was a spiteful woman and Mr Collier didn't deserve to be spoken about in such an insolent manner. Warning bells were going off in Kate's head. Keep quiet, keep out of it, she chided herself, remembering what her father was always telling her, 'Your tongue's too sharp for your own good, Kate, and one day you'll say the wrong thing to the wrong person.' He could well be right; there were times when he could be so wise!

Mr Collier's main house was a few miles away from Melbourne Lodge, bordering Hampton Court, and it was there that he and his wife hosted grand parties and balls. There were no children and it was perhaps for that reason that those who knew of Jane Mortimer and this more humble house cast no criticism, even though Mr Collier let it be known that she had taken up permanent residence. It was only the likes of Mrs Bates who thought they had the right to comment on matters that were nothing whatsoever to do with them.

'Is there anything else you would like to bring out into the open?' Mary asked Mrs Bates as she reached for the woman's teacup in order to refill it.

'Well, yes, there is, as a matter of fact.' Mrs Bates' expression was one of defiance. 'What about his wife? 'T'ain't the poor woman's fault she couldn't carry a child full term. Who knows what might 'ave 'appened t'cause her to drop 'em?'

'How dare you!' exclaimed Mary.

Suddenly a deep shadow flitted past the kitchen window, and Charles Collier came in through the back door. His entry into the kitchen caused all three women to jump in surprise.

His shoulders were draped with a heavy velvet-collared cape which he quickly removed laying it across the back of a chair close to the door. As usual he was dressed in the height of fashion. Always a fastidious man he was wearing a double-breasted coat, a perfectly ironed shirt with snow-white frilled cuffs, a silk cravat, heavy corded breeches and knee-high polished boots.

Kate liked him. He was tall with a wide chest, brown eyes and dark hair. She thought of him as a strikingly good-looking gentleman. To some folk he was a miserable man. Not so to Kate. To her he was the grand lord of the manor who lived in a mansion with his wife and took his responsibilities seriously, most of the time. The fact that he owned this riverside house which he used for his lady friend only intrigued her. She saw it as a great, romantic love affair, although sometimes she suffered from a tormenting curiosity as to what the outcome might be. Still, you wouldn't get a bad word about him from me, Kate thought, tossing her head and glaring at Mrs Bates. Mr Collier had always been exceedingly kind to her as far back as she could remember.

'A tray of tea and perhaps some of that rich-looking

fruit cake would be nice, if you please, Mary.' Mr Collier gave Mrs Bates a friendly nod, and sat down to remove his boots. He smiled at Kate, whose hair had broken loose from the ribbon that was meant to be holding it back. 'Like to give me a hand, young Kate?' he asked, thinking how young and fresh she looked.

'Of course.' She smiled back, crossed to where he sat and cupped her hands around one foot, tugging for all she was worth.

'Thank you,' he said when both boots were off and standing side by side against the wall. 'So, how are you, Kate? And your parents?'

'Fine, thank you, sir,'

'Well, give them both my regards.'

'Phew!' Mrs Bates let out a great gasp of breath as they watched him leave the room, making for the main staircase, in his stockinged feet. 'D'you think he 'eard me talking as he came in?'

'You can thank your lucky stars that he didn't, my lady. If he had, your feet wouldn't have touched the gravel as you went down that driveway. Now I think it is time you were gone. But just remember my warning, Mrs Bates. You have a kind employer who pays you fair wages, doesn't interfere in your business, and does not expect you to concern yourself with his.'

'All right,' she answered sullenly, 'what d'yer take me for? I do know when it's best t'keep me mouth shut.'

'Do you? Well it's a pity nobody ever told you that a still tongue makes a wise head.'

'No need for you to be so nasty,' she mumbled. 'I'll gather up me things and be on me way. See you on yer next visit, Kate.'

'Yes, all right, Mrs Bates.'

Both Kate and Mary heaved a sigh of relief as they watched Mrs Bates pull her cap down hard, put on her coat, pick up her shopping bag and leave by the side door.

Mary came back downstairs, having taken tea up for Mr Collier and Jane. She sighed very deeply and very sadly, as she flopped into a chair.

'I'm blowed if I know what the outcome will be. They're both such nice people. You only have to look at them to feel the attraction and the love they have for each other. It shines through their eyes, it really does.' She held her hands up in the air. 'But I can't stop myself from wondering whether there can be a lasting happiness for either of them.'

Kate didn't know the answer any more than Mary.

Mary glanced up at the clock on the wall. 'I'd better not keep you too late today, it turns really cold as soon as it gets dark.'

'Yes, it does,' Kate agreed, rising and going into the passage to lift the repaired linen out from her wheelbarrow and to collect her heavy cloak from the peg on which she had hung it.

'There's a parcel over there on the dresser. I've put a note inside for your mother. It's a couple of Mr Collier's dress shirts that need new frills for the cuffs, not much else at the moment,' Mary said, as she came back into the kitchen.

'Well they won't take my mum long, so I'll bring them back soon without waiting for the whole month to slip by,' Kate declared, a happy smile lighting up her face.

'Right then.' Mary took her arm as they walked to the side door. 'You know you don't need an excuse to come down and see me. I've told you often enough I'm always glad of your company.' She smiled at Kate, whose face was framed by loose strands of hair blowing in the wind.

Although Mary was called 'Mrs' Kennedy, it was a courtesy title given to unmarried housekeepers in gentlemen's residences. At that moment she was thinking what she had missed; she would give the world to have had a daughter such as Kate.

'I'd better get off then.'

Mary's lower lip trembled as she put her arms around Kate. 'You take care now. Look after yourself.'

'I will. And I'll see you soon.'

At the bottom of the drive Kate turned to wave, knowing full well that Mary would stand there watching her until she was out of sight.

Chapter Three

KATE GLANCED AT the clock as she swung her legs over the side of her bed. It was just five thirty on Monday morning, the day of the week she loved best. For this was the day that she spent with her gran. Grandma Kearsley, her father's mother.

Tiptoeing across the linoleum she gently pulled the curtains open. Outside, the May dawn already held the promise of a day that would be warm and dry.

It was three months since her father had last knocked her mother about. Kate didn't delude herself that he had turned over a new leaf; that was too much to hope for. Still, the last few weeks had been nice: no raised voices, the three of them eating dinner together every night. Conversation had flowed, with her dad telling them of the work that was rolling into his boat yard, which was sited near old Hampton Court Bridge. It was three years now since the war had ended and the yard was back to running normally. He employed three full-time craftsmen, and at the moment he was cock-a-hoop because he had landed an order for a very special type of boat to be built for a local brewer.

Success usually depended on whether or not the coming summer would turn out to be a long hot one. The saloon steamers had already started to run daily between Kingston, Hampton Court and Windsor. Passengers sat on the decks sipping long, cool drinks, eating sandwiches and fresh fruit, squinting over the sides of the boat at the rippling water, thinking how lovely it must be to live on the riverfront.

They should come back and see it on a really bad winter's day.

Kate slipped her nightdress over her head, filled the washing bowl from the matching jug which stood on top of her marble-topped washstand. She shuddered. 'This water is freezing,' she moaned, rubbing Lifebuoy soap onto her pretty face flannel.

She washed her body quickly and when she was dry, sat down to pull on her long-legged bloomers, then her chemise, then her dark stockings and garters. Today she was to wear a dress laid out ready by her mother last night. It was navy blue and one which her gran had made for her, quite plain really, just two rows of pearl buttons down the front and a lace collar, hand-crocheted by her mother.

She brushed her hair briskly, combed and pinned it into a bun at the nape of her neck. Much good all the pins will do, she thought, barbed wire wouldn't keep my mop in place. Taking a last look in the piece of mirror fixed to the wall she wasn't over-pleased with what she saw. 'Dull-looking, that's what you are, Kate Kearsley,' she said out loud. 'Brown eyes, brown hair. Good job you've got those glints of red in amongst those thick tresses otherwise you'd look even worse.'

That wasn't how Hilda Kearsley saw her daughter as she sat at the kitchen table, watching her drink her tea and eat a slice of toast. Kate had crossed her legs causing the hem of her skirt to ride up, almost to her right knee. She had lovely legs, in fact she was beautiful in every way. With the return of the young men from France young ladies seemed to be . . . well . . . not so modest as they should be, and it was rumoured in the papers that hemlines were to become shorter. Hilda hoped not. She liked the way her girl dressed, the way she acted and, most of all, the way she spoke. She herself had talked with a cockney twang when first she had met Fred. Living here, away from London where life was quieter, slower, more gentle, she took the trouble to pronounce her words properly. Well, at least she tried.

There was a catch in her voice as she bid Kate goodbye. 'Give my love t'yer Gran,' she called after her.

'I will, Mum. See you tonight. Bye.'

Kate set out to walk the three miles to Kingston with a lightness in her step. The birds were singing their hearts out, as if by chorusing their songs they were sharing this lovely, bright spring morning. She turned a bend and saw a great carthorse coming towards her, towing a barge. It was brightly painted and was towing another boat, the second one heavily laden with timber. Two scruffy lads about her own age were balanced on top of the timber, one steering with a long pole-like rudder. She knew who they were; part of the Wilson family who she and her parents met up with from time to time, particularly when the river was busy or Hampton Court was holding its annual fair.

The boys, one blond the other dark haired, spotted her and raised their hands.

''Ow y'doing, Kate?' the tallest of the two yelled.

'I'm fine, Mickey. Good t'see you, and you, Bertie,' she called back, laughing at them both. 'Where are you making for?'

'East Molesey, 'Arry Burton's yard, not far from yer father's place.'

Kate resisted the temptation to stand and watch the gaily coloured barges stream down the river. 'See you,' she shouted, waving like mad and walking backwards for several steps before turning to continue on her way.

Alice Kearsley wore a shapeless dress under a long white apron, the front of which was dominated by two enormous pockets. She lived in a house her husband had built himself when they were a pair of starry-eyed newly-weds. It was a flat-roofed, long, low, part-timbered building. She was a widow now, content with her own company and able to live largely on what she grew in her half-acre of land. She also kept chickens, ducks and rabbits.

The very sight of her grandmother wearing a floppy straw hat on her head and brown button-up boots on her feet brought a smile to the face of her only grandchild.

'Hallo, Gran!' Kate called enthusiastically as she opened the wicker gate. Alice covered the ground between them in a few strides. 'Hallo, my luv,' she said, as she gave Kate a hug.

Kate reached up to straighten her steel-rimmed spectacles. 'I don't know how you manage to see, Gran, your glasses are always crooked. Whatever am I going to do with you?'

Alice took the spectacles off and put them into one of her pockets. 'To tell you the truth, I don't know why your father insisted I had them; I can still see the difference in a halfcrown an' a florin, so why should I bother?'

Kate laughed loudly.

'Up an' about early this morning an' sharp with it, aren't you?'

'Well I don't need no alarm clock to wake me these bright mornings, do I? My big cockerel makes sure everyone hereabouts is awake good an' early.'

'So are we going to sell a load of stuff today and make a lot of money?'

'Well, we better, by golly, 'cause I near broke me back digging up a load of new potatoes and there's some tomatoes that I have had under glass, an' if I do say so myself they are real good. Taste lovely they do. Go on out back, will you, luv, there's two baskets ready, one full of ducks' eggs, the other one is me chickens' eggs. I've packed plenty of straw round them because you know how mad Jack Dawson drives his horse an' cart – don't want no cracked ones, do we?'

'You're always knocking Jack, yet he comes week in week out, no matter what the weather, just to cart you and your produce into Kingston.'

Alice had the grace to mutter, 'Sorry,' then quickly added, 'He's going to market anyway and I sees he don't lose by it. I always buys him a pint in the Griffin an' he don't go home empty-handed.'

Kate shook her head, Alice had an answer for everything. She came back through the kitchen carrying the two baskets of eggs just as Jack Dawson shouted 'whoa' to his horse, bringing it to a halt in the lane outside the house.

'Morning, Mrs Kearsley. 'Allo, young Kate. I've left the right side of me cart free, so put those baskets on and I'll give you an 'and to fetch whatever else your gran has got ready to go.' Jack Dawson, looking as swarthy as ever, let go of the reins and jumped down. Grinning at Kate he said, 'An' 'ow's the old lady today? Still giving out 'er orders left right an' centre, is she?'

Alice sucked in her breath, and fixed him with a beady eye. 'I heard that, young man, just pay attention t'what you're doing and stop asking my granddaughter silly questions!'

'I can see for meself, Mrs Kearsley, you're in fine fettle, an' no mistake.'

'Fit enough to keep you in yer place, me lad,' she teased him solemnly.

Kate was thoroughly enjoying listening to them bait each other. Amid much laughter they sorted everything out, making several trips from the house and garden to the cart.

'That's the lot,' Alice told Jack as she led the procession out to the roadway.

In less than a quarter of an hour they were setting up the stall in Kingston market. All about them other stalls were piled high with vegetables and salad stuff, mostly straight from local smallholdings or allotments. What was that gorgeous smell? Strawberries. Nothing like the scent of the first strawberries of the season. Someone must have a greenhouse to be able to pick them so early. And one farmer's wife had had the good sense to bring a bowl of clotted cream. She's sure to sell that quickly today, Kate thought as she watched the woman cover the bowl with a fine mesh cloth, weighted down by dangling glass beads.

The market wasn't populated entirely by well-fed, prosperous-looking people. There were women with painfully thin children clutching at their skirts. For some of them there was no longer a man in the family; so many men had been killed in the War. Those who had come home had soon found out that the promise of a land fit for heroes had been an empty one.

Kate was well aware that in parts of Kingston living conditions were utterly apalling. Streets where back-to-back houses had three or even four families living in a few cramped rooms. In the hot weather they stank; with one shared lavatory out in the backyard and no proper sanitation, the Lord alone knew how these folk kept themselves clean. Most of the men had no jobs to go to, just the endless daily drudgery of searching for work.

Alice finished serving a young mother with an assortment of pot-herbs and held out a great big, green cabbage. 'How will this do yer, luv? Give us a penny an' it's yours.'

'Aw, thanks, Mrs Kearsley,' the neat young woman whispered. 'Every week you're ever so good t'me.'

'Go on with you, t'ain't everybody can be doing with a cabbage as big as that one. An' wait a minute – 'ere, give the kiddies one of these new carrots to gnaw. You'll need to give them a wipe, but a bit of clean earth never hurt no one.'

Small hands reached up quickly and each child's face

had a wide grin as their mother shared out the fresh young carrots.

'Thanks, Mrs Kearsley,' the children chorused.

'You're welcome,' Alice said lovingly.

Kate smiled warmly. 'You're a right old softie, you know that, Gran, don't you? A real right softie.'

'I'll give you softie, Kate Kearsley, if you don't start pulling your weight round here. Those empty boxes need stacking up. Me feet are killing me and me throat is begging for a drink.'

'Humph,' Kate grunted. 'I wondered how much longer you were going to stand there seeing as how the Griffin has been open for the last hour or more.'

'You cheeky young beggar!' Alice cried, swinging round towards her. Then her voice took on a cooing note, 'You don't mind if yer old gran goes for a drink, do you? I'll bring you back a hot pie.'

'No, you go. We've not much left to sell anyway. Only a few eggs.'

Kate set about packing up the stall. As she worked, she mused, 'I'm so lucky to live in such a lovely place as Littleton Green and even more lucky to have a mum and a dad who love me, never mind dear old gran. Can't be many of her sort left in this world.'

Kate was feeling content as she sat at one end of the kitchen table while Alice sat at the other. When Jack Dawson had brought all the empty baskets and boxes through to the backyard and gone back to lift Alice down from the cart she had seen him kiss her goodbye before he got back up and set off home.

Gran was so special. She had always been there for

Kate with hugs and kisses and help when her mum had been so ill that time. Hilda had been struck down with a terrible flu and Alice had moved in, staying for three weeks. Cooking, washing and ironing for her and her dad, making a lovely dinner every night and special broth for her mum because her throat was too sore to eat solids. Many an afternoon she had walked all the way back to her own house just to see that her neighbours were keeping their promises and looking after her animals. She was also the only person who knew that her dad treated her mum so badly at times.

She looked so different now. Since returning from the market she had changed her clothes, had a wash, and combed and fluffed out her snow-white hair until it formed a halo around her face. On her small feet she wore a pair of red velvet slippers.

'How's your mother?'

Kate looked up, puzzled. 'Why are you suddenly asking?'

'Because I haven't seen your father for a couple of weeks and that's not like him. He usually drops in at least once during a working week, more often than not, twice. Has everything been all right between him and your mother?'

'Yes, but it frightens me.'

'Frightens you? What does?'

'The calmness. They're even acting as if they're friends for a change.'

'And what's wrong with that?'

'Nothing at all. But as you know, it isn't normal. Sometimes you can cut the atmosphere in our house with a knife. At the moment it's like the calm before a storm.'

'Oh, luv.' Alice put out a trembling hand. 'Don't say that. For God's sake, don't even think it. Just let's be grateful that things are so much better between them.'

'Can I ask you a question?'

'Since when did you need permission? What is it? Go on, fire away.'

'Does my dad always come and tell you when they've had a bust up?'

'Yes.'

'Always?'

'Well, I'm pretty sure he does. You see, Kate, when he comes to his senses he's absolutely guilt-ridden. I know that's of no help one way or another to your mother, and I feel for them both. Have done for years. Still, I have to say that there are times when I think it's half a dozen of one and six of the other.'

'Oh, no! No, gran. You can't blame Mum! She's the one that ends up with the black eyes, sore ribs and bruises that turn her body black and blue. Surely you can't believe she deserves it?'

'I never said that, lass. Let's go back to the start of all this trouble. You were far too young to remember. It was a terrible out-and-out tragedy them losing their dear little boy. And, of course, it was made worse by the fact that your father saved the life of someone else's child and in a roundabout way caused young David's death.'

Kate sat with her eyes downcast, saying nothing.

Her grandma got to her feet, and poured them each a glass of home-made lemonade.

'Thank you,' Kate said as she took hold of her glass, then quietly added, 'I don't see why you don't have more to say to dad when he tells you about what he's done. I mean . . . well . . . you don't think it's right for a man to hit his wife, do you?'

Alice sighed heavily, crossed the room and perched herself on the wide window sill so that she was facing Kate.

'I'll tell you what I've come to know over the years, because I think you're old enough to hear it, and I'll tell you, lass, as honestly as I can. Most men have their needs, and when two people get married that gives the man the right to expect that those needs will be satisfied by his wife. As far as I know, my son has not gone looking for other women. Your mother is a good woman and I could not have asked for a better daughter-in-law, but what she has seen fit to tell me has lead me to believe that all your parents' troubles started in the marriage bed. Your dad once said it was like sleeping with a stuffed dummy and your mother on one occasion admitted to me that she cringed whenever my Fred came near her.

'To my way of thinking, a little forgiveness on her part wouldn't go amiss. Sixteen years is a long time to bear a grudge. Your dad did what he thought was right when he went into the river to save that little girl. Perhaps he did make the wrong decision. But he wasn't to know that David, left on his own in the boat, would stand up, topple the boat and fall into the water. Your mother has always said he should have thought of that.

'No one blamed her at the time for turning on her husband. She was distraught – as any mother would have been. I can say only now that with hindsight we can all be clever. Your mother has held bitterness in her heart for so long she doesn't know how to forgive any more.'

Neither of them moved until Kate let out a deep breath.

'All my life I've hated being an only child, at times it's been very lonely, especially when we went to London, to see Mum's sister, Aunt Dolly. Up there I've got so many cousins yet I can't remember when we last visited any of them. Oh, I don't know. I'm eighteen years old, you'd think I'd have got used to it by now.'

'Kate, luv, there are some things in life that you never get used to no matter how hard you try.'

Look at me, Alice Kearsley almost said to her granddaughter, but decided against it. Poor lass had enough to cope with already. There was, however, no one more able to tell her that life never went as you wanted or even expected it to. She and her Jack had started out reaching for the moon and Jack, a young man of nineteen then, had promised her the stars to go with it. And he was well on his way to giving her all that when, in the prime of life, he'd suffered a stroke and died. Three children they'd had. A right good little family. Just the one boy and two girls, and both girls had caught scarlet fever and died before they even reached school age. Life could be a bitch sometimes, but these memories didn't help either of them.

As if sensing the sadness in each other, their eyes met and Alice got to her feet and crossed the room, to put her arm around Kate's shoulders.

'Come on, luv. Take it a day at a time. At least yer mum an' dad are doin' all right at the moment. Don't let's start looking for trouble.'

Kate sighed and tilted her lips up to kiss Alice's soft cheek. 'What would I do without you?'

'Silly question, girl. You haven't even got to think about that, 'cos you have got me. Now, how about going through to me scullery, filling the kettle, puting it on the gas an' making yer poor ole gran a good strong cup of tea while I fix us some scrambled eggs and bacon.'

'You don't have to go t'all that trouble.'

'I know I don't, but I am. Eating a meal with you, lass, every Monday, before you set off home, is the highlight of my week. Oh, an' I forgot to tell you, I've made you the biggest bread pudding you've ever seen. It's full of spices and raisins, so what you don't eat you can take home for your mum an' dad.'

When it was time for Kate to go, Alice kissed her and, before releasing her, whispered, 'Take care, an' remember I'm always here.'

'Thanks, Gran. God bless you.'

Alice stood in the lane and didn't go back inside until she'd seen her granddaughter turn and wave before stepping out of sight. Long after Kate had left, her mind was filled with confusion. That lovely girl obviously felt that the burden on her shoulders was too heavy to bear at times. And so it was. She would like to beat the daylights out of her own son when he came to unburden his soul, blurting out how hateful he had been to Hilda.

But there again, he was not entirely to blame. She was not blind to the fact that he had had no reasonable married life for the last sixteen years. There had to be a breaking point somewhere. Her Fred was a man and no man could go on living and suffering the way Hilda made him. Enough ought to be enough for the pair of them. What would the outcome be?

If the way they were acting at the moment, according

to Kate, was anything to go by, perhaps at last there might be some happiness there for both of them in the future. I can't see it though, they've hurt each other too much, she thought.

She dropped down into her armchair, bent and took off her slippers, replacing them with the old boots she wore only in the garden. When she had them laced up, she went through to the scullery, found her sacking apron and tied it round her waist. Then, with a sigh, she went wearily out through the back door to feed and water her animals and see they were settled down for the night.

Chapter Four

KATE STUDIED HER mother, who was standing on the
towpath gazing out across the river. Her feelings were
mixed. Her father had been away on business for three
days, and since his return her parents seemed to be
doing their best to avoid each other, as if their brief
truce had never happened. At dinner the night before
she had felt they were struggling to be polite, glancing
occasionally at each other, but determinedly refraining
from speaking.

It had been left to her to break the silence. 'Did you
have a good trip, Dad?'

Her father had shrugged. 'Did a bit of business, Kate.'

A terrible expression had spread over her mother's
face, and she had let out a snarl. 'You're not man
enough t'tell her what kind of business, are you?' Then
she'd left the table.

Kate's stomach had twisted itself into knots. She
had lain awake half the night telling herself that open

hostility was obviously going to be the order of the day once again. You'd have had to be blind not to see and feel the animosity between her parents at breakfast this morning.

She glanced over at her mother and found she was watching her. Gran's right, Kate thought, she's so bitter. It's such a shame she's so unhappy. She opened the front gate and crossed to where Hilda stood.

'Do you feel better now?'

Hilda studied her daughter, then did her best to smile. 'I'm fine. There's nothing wrong with me.'

'I lay awake last night, Mum, wondering what's going on now between you an' Dad.'

'Nothing's going on. There's nothing for you to worry about.'

Kate shocked her by replying, 'I wish you'd tell me the truth for once.'

Hilda flushed and quickly turned away, making for the house.

In the kitchen, Kate resisted the impulse to put her arms around her.

'Don't be so hard on Dad, please, Mum.'

'He's hateful to me.'

'I know. You're hateful to him, too. Why can't you both try to be a little more . . . well . . . gentle with each other?'

Hilda reached up and took two cups down from the dresser. 'I'm sorry, Kate, I'm beginning to see what harm your father an' I have done to you by letting you witness our long-standing bitterness.' She set the cups down on the table and sunk down onto a chair. 'All right, I'll speak to your father. I'll try.'

'Thanks, Mum.' Kate smiled broadly, feeling hopeful.
'I'll make the tea and then do you want me to take the
shirts back to Mr Collier?'

'Yes, they should go back today. I couldn't get the
lace locally as you know, I had to send a special order to
London, so what with one thing an' another I've been a
long time doing the repairs, though I did write to Mary
and ask her to explain to Mr Collier.'

'It wasn't your fault. I'll tell you what. Why don't you
come with me to Melbourne Lodge? It's a lovely day,
the walk would do you good and you know how pleased
Mary would be to see you.'

'No, luv. It's a nice thought, but I'm tired. I'll have
a cup of tea and a bite to eat with you now, an' then
I'm going to have a lie down.'

Hilda made them each a cheese sandwich while Kate
poured out the tea, but it was a sad, somehow lonely
lunch with very little conversation from either of them.
Kate left as soon as she had finished eating, saying she
wouldn't be late back and for her mother to have a
nice nap.

When she was gone the house suddenly felt awful.
Silent and unfriendly.

Hilda cleared up the kitchen, washed her face and
hands and went to sit in the front room. The bright
sunshine was dazzling, shining directly through the bay
window. She set out her sewing basket beside the sofa
and settled herself down to do some work, but found
concentrating difficult and finally laid it aside. She had
come so near to telling Kate that her father had another
woman and that in all probability he and she had been
off on holiday together. Business trip! Never in your life!

She shouldn't blame him and there were times when she didn't. Their marriage had been a sham since the day David had died.

She sat stock still, wondering. She was not a person to shed many tears, she knew herself to be too hard for that. It was her own fault that Fred had turned to another woman, and at least he had the decency to be discreet. Even his own mother had never cottoned on, and he would sell his soul rather than let his beloved Kate find out. What made her blood boil was that, when full of drink, he would come home and demand his rights from her. She hated the whole performance: the touch of his hands roaming over her body, his wet lips and beery breath. If he kept to someone else and left her alone she would be more than happy to live a life of routine respectability, put on a show for their relations and neighbours. But that wasn't enough for him. How could he come from another woman's bed and into hers?

Yes, she had been hard, laying all the blame for David's death on him. She couldn't help it, that's how she felt. It *had* been his fault, no one else's. She had lost her first born, her son, because of him. David had drowned because his father was too busy looking after another mother's child.

But still . . . Her thoughts trailed off and she made herself remember that she had promised Kate to try and adopt a more friendly attitude towards her father. God give me the strength, she said to herself. She had her doubts but try she would. Whether she or Fred could somehow put a stop to this wretched existence, show respect and learn to treat each other as ordinary, decent human beings was another matter entirely.

*   *   *

Kate did a little hop, skip, and jump. Now, in sunny warm June, the river was a sight to behold. A passing steamer blew its whistle, folk on board waved and Kate waved back. Everything outdoors today looked and smelled wonderful. The air rang with the squeals of half a dozen children playing down by the river. She stood for a moment watching them. Their bare legs were brown, their hair bedraggled, their feet dirty, but they were having a grand time. Why hadn't her mother made the effort and come for a walk? Perhaps the sight of small boys playing by the water would have brought memories rushing back. Even after all this time her mother could not forget, let alone forgive.

The thought suddenly angered her. Her mother had no right to bear such a grudge against her father and her father had no right to hit her mother no matter what cause she gave him.

'I'm always the one in the middle! I don't deserve to have to live with all this pent-up anger!' she muttered.

She moved on, taking deep breaths as she glanced round her. How could anyone be miserable when they were lucky enough to live in such beautiful surroundings?

A grin spread over her face as she heard the trot of a horse's hooves.

'Morning, Mr Baldwin.' Kate greeted the local miller.

'You daydreaming or something, young Kate? It's almost two o'clock so I think we can safely assume that it's now afternoon,' he said as he pulled his horse to a halt.

Mr Baldwin had iron-grey hair, steel-rimmed glasses and huge hands covered with black hairs. His voice was loud and hearty. He looked well pleased with himself as he added, 'Want to know something else?'

Kate put out a hand to pat his horse. She had known the miller ever since she could remember and liked him a lot; you couldn't have a kinder man. A jolly man was how most would describe him.

'And what would that be?'

'You're looking, well . . . sort of tempting this morning, Kate Kearsley, and I think there should be a law against allowing young women who look as beautiful as you do from roaming the lanes.'

'Still full of flattery, or is flannel the better word? You know, when next I come up to the mill I think I shall have a little talk to Mrs Baldwin about you.'

The miller threw back his head and his roar of laughter rang out loudly. 'There is nothing about me that you or a dozen others could tell my Bessie that she doesn't already know. By the way, lass, how's your mother? I saw your dad yesterday but I haven't set eyes on your mum for ages.'

'Mother's not too well. She doesn't go out a lot, but she sits in the garden and gets the air.'

'Well, tell her I was asking after her and that my Bessie would be only too pleased to see her when she fancies a walk.'

'I will, and I'll try and get her to pay Mrs Baldwin a visit.'

'Good. You take care, Kate.'

He flicked the reins and told the horse to walk on.

'I wonder if the Kearsleys really know what they put that girl through?' Ken Baldwin exclaimed angrily to himself. 'Bad enough that they make life hell for each other, but I reckon it's time that someone told them a few home truths.'

The whole village knew that Fred Kearsley laid into his wife when the mood took him, and one night in the pub when he'd had a skinful the customers had been forced to listen to him wallow on about how his wife didn't understand him. Nothing but self-pity! It had been degrading!

Like a lot of the men who had been in the bar that evening he'd felt the urge to smash him in the face. That wouldn't have done anyone any good – least of all young Kate – but he had been sorely tempted.

The thought of seeing Mary and having tea in that happy household made Kate quicken her footsteps.

She had taken such pains with her hair this morning but still strands had torn free and were dangling down over her ears as she walked up the drive. Never mind, she grinned to herself, Mary is well-used to seeing my hair in an unruly state.

Mary answered her knock dressed in a very nice dress the colour of the clear sky, pale blue with white daisies all strung together round the neck and each cuff. Her hair must have been newly washed; it looked shiny and fluffy.

'Hallo there, Kingston Kate, always reliable, never late, in fact I think you're early today.'

'Something smells delicious,' Kate commented, having planted a kiss on Mary's cheek.

'It's a cherry cake baking in the oven and those fruit pies on the dresser aren't cold yet, but it's not quite teatime, so would you like a cold drink? There's milk in the larder.'

43

'Milk would be lovely. I'll get it.'

She felt at home as she cleared a pile of knitting to one end of the dresser and placed the neat parcel containing Mr Collier's two shirts beside a bag of wool.

Mary was busy wiping away all signs of flour from the kitchen table when she came back into the room sipping a glass of creamy milk.

'What's all the white wool for? What are you knitting?'

Mary looked at Kate and raised her eyebrows, her expression cagey. 'That's what I'm dying to tell you.'

Kate propped herself up against the front of the dresser. 'Oh, that sounds interesting. Has Mrs Bates been given her marching orders?'

Mary laughed. 'No, nothing like that. Jane Mortimer is pregnant.'

Kate drew in her breath sharply and her eyebrows shot up.

'Really?'

'Yes, really. The baby's due about Christmas time, and I'm trying my hand at baby clothes.'

'Well, after all this time! Miss Mortimer pregnant! Imagine that. What does Mr Collier think about it? Does he want the baby?'

'Yes, both of them do. Very much so, by all accounts.'

'Bet that was a relief for her and for you, Mary, when you heard. Otherwise it could have been a sticky situation.'

'Don't I know it. But guess what?'

'You mean there's more?'

'Only that it was the squire himself who came and told me. Over the moon he was. Fetched Jane down,

44

brought a bottle of wine up from the cellar, opened it, and here in the kichen, we three together toasted the new baby. 'To my first born' is what he said, an' oh, Kate, you should have seen the look on his face as he stared at Jane. If ever a man was in love, then he is. He adores her. You can tell just by watching him.'

Kate was fascinated.

'Does Mrs Bates know about this?'

Mary shook her head. 'We've managed to keep it from her so far. You can guess at the rumours she'd soon have flying about.'

Kate put her glass down on the table and smiled at Mary. 'I'm so happy for them.'

'Me too. But it won't be all plain sailing. On the quiet, Mr Collier asked me to take extra care of Miss Jane. As if I needed asking! What he really wanted was to hear me pledge that I would remain on here as housekeeper after the baby is born. Even went as far as promising me an increase in my wages.'

Kate went and patted her on the shoulder and giggled. 'No need for you to tell me what your answer was. You'll be like a mother hen with a new chick.'

Mary's face suddenly lost its colour and her eyes glistened with unshed tears.

'What's the matter? You look as if you're going to faint. Are you all right?' Kate asked, full of concern.

'Yes,' she whispered, sitting in an armchair. 'I'm really pleased for them both, of course I am, but I'm not sure how it will affect me. I've been in this house a lot longer than Miss Jane has. Mr Collier engaged me when he first acquired this property. In those days it was hardly used, only for entertaining business gentlemen, and some of his guests were very distinguished, I can tell you. Some even from foreign countries. It remains to be seen what kind of duties I will be called on to perform now. I've come to love Miss Jane, no one could say different, and the baby well . . . just so long as they don't install any toffee-nosed, stiff and starched nurse in this house to give me orders and expect me to wait on her hand, foot an' finger.'

Mary's outburst startled Kate. She wanted to reassure her but wasn't sure how to go about it. 'Come on. It's not like you to trouble trouble before it troubles you. Mr Collier won't let anyone upset you, he values you too much; he's already proved that by coming to you directly and asking you to stay.'

'I know I'm being daft. Pity though, everything here goes so smoothly and now there will be disruptions, bound to be, and that's putting it mildly.' Mary got up and finished her clearing up, rinsed her cloths out under the tap and filled the kettle.

'To be honest, Kate, I don't relish the prospect, but then they do say all babies bring their love with them.'

'Course they do.'

'We'll just have to wait an' see, won't we? Now, my kitchen is all straight an' tidy so I think I've earned a cup of tea and you can save my legs by taking a tray upstairs to Miss Jane.'

Kate made no reply.

'Well?' Mary demanded.

'I will if you want me too,' she said half-heartedly.

'I wouldn't have asked if I hadn't wanted you to.' In fact, it was Jane herself who had asked that Kate be sent up to see her.

Kate laid the table and set out a tray for one, while Mary made two pots of tea. Coming back from the larder Mary set a plate of butter shortbread down onto the tray beside the bone-china cup and saucer.

'Miss Jane likes shortbread. And I think we'll tempt her with a slice of apple pie.'

'You're sure you want me to take her tea up to her? I mean, she won't mind, will she?'

'I'm sure she'll be more than glad to see you. Doesn't get much young company. I expect she will be glad of the opportunity to tell you about the baby herself.'

'I hope you're right,' Kate mumbled as she picked up the tray and went out into the hall.

Outside the first-floor front room, which Jane used as a sitting room, Kate paused for a moment and gripped the handles of the tray more tightly before giving a gentle knock. She had barely taken her hand away from the wood panel when the door was opened by Jane.

'Oh, Kate, how kind of you to bring tea up for me. Here, set the tray down and come and sit by the window.'

Kate swallowed hard. This was too much. Miss Jane was treating her as if she were a friend come to pay a visit.

She did as she was bid and, as soon as she was seated, Jane came to stand beside her, and laid a palm on her right arm. 'Has Mary told you about the baby?'

'Yes, she has. Congratulations.' She was unable to think of another word to say.

'Thank you, Kate. I'll pour the tea.' A moment later she protested, 'But you've only brought one cup, aren't you going to join me?'

Kate felt her cheeks redden, 'Oh, Miss Jane, I shall have tea downstairs with Mary.'

'I see,' Jane murmured sadly. 'You don't mind if I have mine?'

'I'll come back later and fetch the tray, Miss Jane.'

'Will you do two things for me?'

'I will if I can.'

Jane clicked her tongue against the inside of her cheek. 'Please stop calling me Miss Jane; Jane will do nicely, if it's all right by you. And the second thing is, please stay a while with me.'

Kate gaped at her and then nodded, and while Jane busied herself with the tea tray Kate watched her closely. She was such a pretty young woman and her movements were so gentle. Her face had a delicate look, framed by her blond hair, which was swept up into neat curls. Her body was slim. She caught Kate's eye and smiled.

There was something else about Jane that Kate couldn't fathom. She was from humble origins, or so the gossips said. But her affair with Charles Collier had gone from strength to strength, despite that most had warned it would not last. Each time Kate saw them together they appeared to love each other more dearly. The fact that their relationship had lasted so long had become the talk of Surrey. Now a baby was on the way. Well! That would certainly put the cat among the pigeons.

Jane had taken the chair opposite her. The big wide windows were open and the bright afternoon sunshine filtered in through the long lace curtains and shone on Jane's fair hair making it look like spun gold. She was wearing a pale-pink chiffon dress, with a high stand-up collar, the embroidered bodice falling loosely down over her waistline.

Her blue eyes lit up as she suddenly announced, 'Having you here, Kate, calls for a celebration. I have a bottle of wine, I'll open it.'

'No, please don't.'

'Why ever not? I want you to drink a toast to my unborn baby. Say you will, please. You are happy for me, aren't you?'

'Oh, yes, Miss Jane. Really I am.'

'There you go again. You promised you'd call me Jane.'

'It doesn't seem proper,' she said firmly.

'And why not? We can be friends, surely.'

'You're being very kind.'

'Anyway, we're not going to argue about it now. I'll fetch the bottle.'

Kate gazed round while Jane went to the sideboard. It was a lovely room, furnished with sofas, deep armchairs and side tables on which stood small lamps. The colourings were mostly beige with soft peach overtones and the carpet pile was deep enough to bury your toes in. How many happy hours Jane and Mr Collier must have spent here together.

'Here we are,' Jane declared happily, setting down a bottle and two glasses on the small table which stood between them.

Kate had to smile; at that moment Jane looked like a little girl having an unexpected treat. She opened the bottle without difficulty and poured some of the sparkling white wine into each of their glasses.

'You name the toast, Kate. What shall we drink to?'

Kate shot her a sideways glance, got to her feet and

held up her own glass. 'Here's to you, Mr Collier, and your baby. May you all three have a healthy and happy life.'

'Thank you, thank you very much,' Jane said softly. 'I'll drink to that.'

They drank their wine in silence and Kate watched as Jane nibbled at her shortbread. When their glasses were empty she rose to go.

'I do wish you well, Jane,' she murmured as they stood together in the doorway.

'I know you do, dear Kate. Will you come and see me whenever you can? Say you will.'

'I will,' Kate promised, and she meant it.

She breathed a sigh of relief as she entered the kitchen.

'Well?' Mary asked even before she had a chance to sit down. 'What d'you think. How was she?'

'Happy and excited. Pleased. Hoping to give Mr Collier the son he has always wanted, she confided to me. And she gave me a glass of wine. I hope and pray everything works out well for both of them.'

Mary let out a deep breath. 'Come on, lass, I've had the cosy on the pot, let's have our tea now.'

They sat opposite each other at the kitchen table. Kate was eating a slice of blackberry and apple pie, over which Mary had poured a generous amount of thick cream, when out of the blue Mary said, 'About Jane and the baby, you sound as if you're doubtful.'

Kate swallowed what was left in her mouth, wiped her lips with a napkin and raised her eyes to Mary's.

'Not everyone in the world outside this house will smile when this news gets out, will they?'

'Oh, Kate, you've got an old head on your young shoulders.'

'Be that as it may, I'm right, aren't I?'

'They deserve some happiness.' Mary's voice had grown defensive. 'They'll soon find out who their true friends are.'

The remarkable day ended with Kate giving her mother a full account of what she had learnt at Melbourne Lodge.

'A baby for his mistress when his wife has never been able to bear him a child. How sad for poor Mrs Collier.'

In many ways Kate agreed, but she did not say so out loud. 'Miss Mortimer and Mr Collier have been together a long time. It isn't as if it's a five-minute fling.'

'That's hardly the point. You mustn't be heard taking sides, not out in the village at any rate. Say what you like, he does still have a legal wife.'

'Miss Jane opened a bottle of wine and she and I drank a toast to the baby.'

Hilda started to laugh. 'It's funny when you think about it. His wife lives in that great mansion, they have every single thing that money can buy and still he turns to another woman, in this case, a young woman. Men! There's not a lot to choose between any of them when it comes down to it.'

Kate sucked in a deep breath and merely shrugged.

If she had spoken at that moment it would have been to tell her mother that she hoped to God the day would never dawn when she became as embittered as she.

Chapter Five

THE HEAT WAS unbearable.

'I think we've both had enough for one day,' Alice complained to Kate. 'We've been standing in this market since half-past seven this morning and I think we should make tracks for home so's I can put me feet up.'

'I'm all for that. But we'll have to walk because it's not yet two and Jack said he wouldn't come back for us until four.'

'Never mind, I'll leave word for him with Ben over at the Griffin, we can take it slowly, anything is better than standing about here in the heat and we've practically sold out what little we had, anyway.'

Kate smiled to herself. Of all the places to leave a message for Jack it had to be in the Griffin!

'Go on, Gran, I'll clear up here. You might as well have a drink before we set off, and I wouldn't mind a bottle of something myself.'

Kate watched as Alice made her way between the stalls. In her long black skirt and white blouse adorned with a narrow black ribbon tied in a bow at the neck, she looked smart, even elegant. On top of her fluffy white hair she wore a shiny black straw hat with a wide brim which helped to shield her face from the sun. She might be small, but she held her back straight and she certainly was not the typical type of old woman who frequented Kingston market.

A huge dray cart, laden with barrels of beer and pulled by two enormous shire horses, barged its way round the corner making for the Griffin, at the same time as Kate decided she might as well join her gran inside. She gave the dray a wide berth and breathed a thankful sigh as she entered the dim, cool saloon bar and headed for where Alice was seated.

'Everyone seems to have the same idea today,' Kate said as soon as she had taken a long drink from the glass of shandy Alice had ordered for her.

'Can't blame them, can you? We're going to have a storm, an' God knows we need it to clear the air. Best we drink up, lass, and start out on our walk.'

'Well, we've nothing to carry. I've piled the bowls and cloths into one of the bigger boxes and I've tied the handles of the baskets together. They're all out in the yard and Mrs Hodgeson said she'll see that Jack loads them up and brings them home for you.'

'Ah, you're a good girl, Kate, and Dolly Hodgeson is a good landlady. It's all the thoughtful little things she does for her customers that help t'make the Griffin such a great pub.'

And the fact that they serve you a great pint of

Guinness, Kate thought, but wisely she said nothing as she helped her grandmother to her feet.

They walked slowly, keeping to the shade as much as possible.

July and August had been lovely months, but as the weeks had progressed, unrelenting sunshine had brought drought. The fields were so dusty they seemed to be shrouded in mist. Cows and sheep searched in desperation for patches of shade and even the birds stayed on the branches of the trees or in the hedgerows as if longing for a breeze. The Thames seemed to have stopped flowing and the water near to the bank appeared still and scum-coated. We'll keep to the tow-path, Kate decided.

Her throat was dry despite the fact that she had had that drink before leaving the market and Alice was sweating visibly.

Her gran was marvellous, the way she had coped during all this hot weather; tending her chickens, and all the other animals she seemed to acquire. Then there were her flowerbeds and the vegetable garden. Cans and cans of water she must lug about to keep the plants from shrivelling up.

Alice let go of Kate's arm and took a deep breath of the dry hot air. 'Let's stop for a minute,' she pleaded.

'Undo the neck of your blouse, that might help,' Kate suggested, as she dragged her hair further back away from her face.

The sky darkened so suddenly it was as if someone had turned off the light. Within seconds a deafening peal of thunder split the sky and blobs of rain, heavy and stinging, fell onto the parched ground.

Kate didn't know whether to look for shelter or to carry

on and get Alice home as fast as possible. Another thing was nagging her; her mother was at home on her own and she'd be terrified of the storm. At the best of times she would tremble at the first rumble of thunder, and lightning would send her scurrying to hide beneath the staircase. For days now she hadn't been well. I shouldn't have left her on her own this morning, Kate rebuked herself.

'Come on, Gran, we've come too far to turn back now. If we hurry we can be home in about ten minutes.'

Forked lightning streaked across the sky. The rain was coming down straight, like stair-rods. They had no choice; to stand beneath trees would be too dangerous. Holding on tight to each other's arm they tucked their heads down until their chins were resting on their chests and did their best to quicken their footsteps, hampered by their long wet skirts.

Alice pushed open her front door. It was never locked, and she stood a moment to thank God that she and her granddaughter had safely reached the shelter of her home.

'Undo your skirt. Come on, step out of it,' she ordered Kate, as she herself did the same thing. 'Everything off, it won't do to leave those wet underclothes on, you'll catch your death. I'll nip upstairs and fetch us some bath towels and we'll see about getting you something to wear home after we've had something to eat.'

More blasts of thunder shook the doors and caused the windows to rattle as the storm grew fiercer by the minute.

With one arm full of towels and a thick woolly dressing

gown draped over the other, Alice smiled at Kate. 'Here, put this on for now. This storm can't last much longer, it will soon pass over,' she said with more conviction than she felt.

But the storm did not pass over. It went on and on for the next hour while Alice prepared some sandwiches and Kate busied herself making a pot of tea.

'I'll have to go home soon, Mum will be half out of her wits by now. You know how she is whenever we have a storm.'

Alice sighed heavily as she went to stand near the window and peered outside. There was no let up in the rain, though it had been some time since sheet lightning had lit up the sky.

'It's been a long time since I've seen anything like this. In fact, I can't remember anything remotely like it and God knows I've seen some storms.'

'All the same, Gran, I'm going to have to go soon.'

Kate was feeling warm and dry now, wrapped up snugly in the enormous woolly dressing gown, which, if Alice ever wore it, must have covered her small frame ten times over.

Looking up, Kate saw an expression of sorrow on Alice's face. 'What's the matter, Gran?' she asked anxiously.

'I was thinking of your mother. I do know how storms affect her. Poor Hilda, she'll be really frightened by this lot I shouldn't wonder.' She shook herself, much as a wet dog might, then pulling her massive fringed black shawl even more tightly around her, she tied the two ends of it in a knot across her belly to keep it secure. 'I'll have a rummage through me cupboards and see what I can find that's fit for you to wear. I know what will cover you an' keep you a bit dry. D'you remember that big black mackintosh cape I keep down in the shed, I'll get that in, that'll cover you from head . . . I was going to say from head t'toe, but seeing as you're lanky, like it will only reach as far as your knees.'

Kate laughed loudly. 'By the time you've finished with me I'll be going home looking like a scarecrow.'

'Better that than a drowned rat,' her grandmother told her sternly.

On impulse Kate bent and kissed her gran on the cheek. 'You're a lovely lady, an' I'm glad you're my gran.'

'And you're a lovely lass,' Alice answered softly, turning away to fetch the dry clothes, thinking as she left the room, and you deserve a far happier life than you've been living these past years. My son and that wife of his! One is no better than the other. They both need their heads banging together, though to be honest I think it's a bit late in the day for that now. Too much bitterness between the pair of them.

Kate didn't feel at all comfortable in the clothes Alice had fitted her out with but she kept quiet. The tweed skirt came barely past her knees and she looked like a bedraggled policeman with the shiny cape hanging from her shoulders. The hat was the funniest. It must have been dug up out of the ark. Still it was close fitting, and at least she had managed to tuck some of her hair up inside it.

'Your mum will be relieved to see you,' Alice observed as she came to the front door to see Kate off. 'You're a tower of strength to her, Kate, she's always telling me that.'

'Really?' Kate asked, feeling pleased.

'Yes, really. Now off you go. Keep your head down and mind you don't slip, 'cos the paths will be treacherous.'

'Bye, Gran.' She turned away quickly so as to hide her amusement. There were times when her gran treated her as if she were eight years old instead of eighteen.

Fate was kind. The skies lightened and the rain ceased to fall so heavily. By the time Kate had left Kingston behind the air was beginning to feel much fresher and she was taking regular deep breaths. It must have been almost six o'clock when she walked by the George and Dragon public house, on the outskirts of Thames Ditton. The doors to both the public and the saloon bars were propped open and Kate could see men grouped together at the bars.

''Allo there, Kate,' a middle-aged woman who had a weekly stall in the market close by her gran's greeted her. 'I've just been inside trying t'persuade me 'usband t'come home for his tea. Didn't have much luck. Can't say as I blame him. Right proper storm, wasn't it? When my Frank didn't come to pick me up I guessed where he was. The men have all got an excuse today, what with all that heavy rain. Bob Bateman says he hadn't the heart to turn them out an' so he let them stay drinking all the afternoon. One way of lining his pockets still further, isn't it?'

Given half a chance Kate would have kept walking; what happened in the George and Dragon was none of her business, plus she felt very foolish, looking as she did.

The stall holder, whose name was Martha, had other ideas. She wasn't finished with Kate yet. Not by a long chalk. 'Your father was just leaving the pub when I arrived here and he wasn't going of his own free will neither.'

Kate clenched her fists, the colour rising in her face. You malicious old busybody, she wanted to yell at the woman, but all she managed to say was, 'Really?'

'Yep, see it all, I did. Bob Bateman helped your dad to the door, not too gently I might add. Yer dad would have fallen flat on his face if it hadn't been for Chris Wilson. She led him away. Or to tell you the truth, she half dragged him down the road, not that he was putting up much resistance.'

'Thanks,' Kate managed to murmur. 'I know where Mrs Wilson lives, I'll see to it my father gets home all right.'

Martha gave her a look of sheer pity, which only served to make Kate feel even more cross.

'Some hopes you got, my luv. It'll take more than a slip of a girl like you to get your dad free if Chris Wilson has got her claws into him, and from what I've heard tell, you're too late. Years too late. Chris is no fool, she knows when she's onto a good thing.'

'Yes, well, thank you.' Kate managed to make her goodbye sound polite, and, deep in thought, she carried on walking.

Everyone knew of Mrs Wilson. Some of the tales told about her were good, others . . . well, as Gran would say when Mrs Wilson came to buy eggs from her, 'Live an' let live has always been my motto. Right common she might be but she ain't never done me no harm, an' until she does I'll mind me own business and leave her to get on with hers.' Dear old Gran saw good in everyone, but she was right about one thing, Mrs Wilson did look common. She was a brassy young widow who had been pampered by her much older husband. Not so well off since his death, she now made a living by filling her house with male lodgers. Not that any of them stayed for any length of time, by all accounts.

Kate didn't have to close her eyes to picture her. Chris Wilson would stand out in any crowd. She was a plump, henna redhead with her cheeks always heavily rouged and her lips brightly painted. Very outspoken. On the other hand, Kate knew her to be kind-hearted. More than once she had seen her buy an extra half-dozen eggs and give them to some old woman or to a young mother with a crowd of kiddies to feed. That was another thing Gran said about her: that if she took to someone there was nothing she wouldn't do for them, but God help anyone that got on the wrong side of her. How she had come to that conclusion Kate didn't know, and she had never yet found the courage to ask.

Kate approached the cluster of cottages with caution, mainly because the pathway was slippery, just as Gran had warned it would be. She was also not exactly sure where Mrs Wilson lived. There were just four cottages, all very old, with stone walls and tiled roofs, very sturdy dwellings in an idealistic setting. Each one detached, set in its own small plot of land, open fields to the back and a wooded area to the front.

What shall I do? Shall I knock at the first door and ask for her by name? Kate was tingling all over, was it fear? She hadn't got anything to be frightened of, had she? Every instinct warned that she had. If her father was in such a state, how was she going to get him home? Oh, for goodness' sake, pull yourself together, she scolded herself.

Suddenly she stopped dead in her tracks. She couldn't believe what she was seeing! It couldn't be happening! But it was! Right there in front of her eyes, in the very first cottage she came to.

The evening being balmy after the storm, the curtains had not been drawn and the sash window was thrown up, open as wide as it would go. There was very little front garden to the cottage and only a low stone wall separated it from the public pathway. A few yards lay between Kate and the two occupants of that small front room. Mrs Wilson and her father were both standing up, arms locked around each other and neither of them had a stitch of clothing on.

Kate watched as her father kissed and fondled the woman. His actions appeared to be gentle, even reverent, and hot burning tears stung the back of Kate's eyes. Oh, dear God, it's not fair. Why in heaven's name didn't he treat her mother like that? She stood as if made of stone and stared. She watched as her father grabbed Mrs Wilson by the waist and swung her round. 'Whoopee! There's never been a better lover than you, my beauty. Fit for any king you are.' His speech was slurred, but Kate heard every word.

When he finally let her feet touch the floor she was giggling helplessly. 'You're my king, yer daft bugger,' Chris Wilson said.

Kate could never clearly remember what happened next. Although she wanted to leave it was as if she were rooted to the spot. Afterwards she supposed she must have screamed. Her father, almost in slow motion, released his grip on Mrs Wilson and took a step towards the open window.

His good humour vanished abruptly. 'Damn you, Kate. What sort of a daughter spies on her father?'

Minutes must have passed and still she hadn't moved, but her father, now wearing a long raincoat, was outside, confronting her. He reached for her, grabbing her spitefully by the arms. She smelt the whisky on his breath. Oh God! Why had she lingered? Why had she watched? Why hadn't she just run? She struggled, using her elbows to try to push him away, all the time pleading, 'Dad, calm down, please, Dad, you'll regret this when you're sober.'

Her words never got through to his drink-fuddled mind. In fact they made him worse. He was wild-eyed as he grabbed her hair and, knocking the ridiculous hat flying, pulled her head back hard.

'Stop it!' She brought the heel of her boot down on his foot with all her strength.

Releasing his hold on her he yelled in pain, 'I'll kill you, you little bitch!'

Kate took a deep breath and ran, stumbling, but he was quickly after her. His clenched fist lashed out, smashing against her jaw, hard. With a piercing cry she pitched backwards, hitting the ground with such force she split the back of her head open. She saw stars and felt sick and dizzy; when she put her hand to her head, she felt warm blood matting her hair and trickling down over the back of Gran's rain cape.

'Serves you right! You're deceitful, cowardly, horrible.

You deserve everything you get, and I ain't finished with you yet,' her father bawled at her, shaking his fist in front of her face.

This wasn't her father, it was a drunken madman, and he was going to kill her. Terror gave her strength, made her voice loud, 'Go away, Dad, leave me alone. You don't know what you're doing.'

She managed to get to her knees. On all fours she crawled away from him, then toppled, and rolled over and over down an embankment, into a clump of bushes. Branches lashed her, prickles scratched her hands and face. At last she came to a halt. For what seemed ages, she lay very still.

Where her father was, she had no idea and at that moment she didn't care. He was foul. A drunken beast. She had seen him – him and her. Both of them, naked! She closed her eyes trying to blot out the shameful, unforgettable sight.

Her head hurt and her body felt as if it were on fire, yet Kate knew she had to keep going. If she were to lay down now she might fall asleep and never again wake up.

Home. At last. It took a tremendous effort just to get the front door of the house open.

'What on earth . . . ?' Hilda Kearsley's hands flew to cover her mouth. She had never seen such a sight. From where she stood, in the doorway of the living room, Kate looked filthy. And the clothes she was wearing!

Kate stumbled, putting out a hand towards her, the very gesture was a plea for help. In two strides her mother was at her side. Grabbing hold of Kate's hand she bent and took a close look at her face.

'Jesus! Holy Mary! Were you out in the storm? Did you get struck by lightning? Whatever happened to your own clothes?'

It was beyond Kate to form any answers. Her body sagged and she would have slipped to the floor had her mother not caught her up in her arms. Hilda half dragged her into the living room and laid her down on the carpet, placing a pillow under her head and a blanket over her body, then she fetched a bowl of warm water and some soft white rags.

She was grateful that, for the moment, Kate was unconscious, but terrified when she began to thrash about, murmuring words that at first she couldn't put a meaning too.

'No, Dad. Leave me alone. Dad!'

Hilda was horrified. The state Kate was in was bad enough. The implication of what she was muttering went beyond all else! Huge bruises were showing on her arms, the side of her face was badly swollen and her hair was sticky with blood. Because of the blood and hair it was impossible for Hilda to see how bad the head wound was, but from the dark stains already showing on the pillowcase she knew Kate needed urgent attention.

'Oh, Kate, Kate, don't try to tell me what happened, just lie still, I'll get the doctor.' Hilda's voice was thick with suppressed anger, and hatred flamed in her eyes.

'Well now. You are in a mess, young Kate, and no mistake.' Dr Pearson removed his jacket and handed it to Hilda, saying softly, 'You did right not to move her.'

He dropped down onto his knees, moving his hands gently over Kate's limbs. Looking up at Hilda, he said,

'Thankfully, no bones broken. Must see to her head first. May I have two bowls, one filled with really hot water, the other with cold?'

Hilda nodded and left the room to do his bidding.

Gently raising Kate's head from the pillow, he examined the wound, smiled, and said, 'I'm going to have to cut some of that lovely hair away.'

Kate didn't even open her eyes.

'These bruises and cuts on your face and hands, how did you get them?' he asked.

'I fell and stumbled down a bank into some bramble bushes,' she replied faintly.

'Did you indeed?' he muttered, asking himself what kind of a man would attack such a lovely slip of a lass. 'Well, I'll try not to hurt you.' Taking a gleaming pair of scissors, a pot of ointment and a dark-green bottle of disinfectant from his medical bag, he set to work.

Some time later he helped Hilda get Kate up the stairs and onto her bed. 'I'll leave you to get the rest of her clothes off, just make sure she takes these two tablets – with some warm milk would be best – and I'll look in again some time tomorrow.'

'Thanks, Dr Pearson, I'll come down and see you out.'

'No need, Mrs Kearsley, it's not the first time I've been up and down these stairs now, is it?'

Hilda managed a weak smile. 'All right, but I really am grateful.'

'Kate will be fine,' he hastened to assure her.

Fine! It'll take a lot more than iodine and ointment to make Kate forget whatever it is that has happened to her tonight, Hilda thought bitterly as she straightened the bedcovers and went downstairs to warm some milk.

She never left Kate's bedside all night.

The sky was light and the sun just peeping through a crack in the curtains when Kate turned her head and manoeuvred herself to the edge of the bed until she was able to grasp her mother's hand.

'Mum?'

'I'm here, Kate, go back to sleep,' she whispered.

That afternoon there was a banging on the door and, looking out of the window, Hilda saw her husband. She had been expecting him to turn up and had shot the bolts, top and bottom, on the inside of the front door.

Looking up he saw Hilda. Still very drunk and realising that she had deliberately locked him out, he started to rant and rave.

'It's all your fault, woman. You sent our girl to spy on me. I'm gonna . . . I'm gonna teach her a lesson . . . an' you.'

Hilda looked back to where Kate lay so still in her bed. She must stop Fred from making such a racket. Kate's eyes were closed but her face wore a frown, as if she could see and hear things she didn't understand.

'Your glass is empty, luv,' Hilda whispered, smoothing Kate's hair back from her forehead. 'I'll get you some more water, be back in a couple of minutes.'

She wasn't sure whether Kate had heard her or not, she only knew she had to get herself downstairs and try and talk some sense into her husband. She gave a harsh laugh. A good talking to is the last thing he needs, especially from me. I know what I'd like to do to him, but that would be against the law. But then it isn't exactly lawful what he's done to his own daughter, and come hell or high water he's going to pay for that.

Slowly, she opened the door just a crack. Before Hilda knew what was happening, Fred put his shoulder to the frame and shoved hard. Hilda was thrown back against the wall, hitting it with a heavy thud.

'No one, least of all you, is going to keep me out of my own house. It's my house, I'm telling you, an' don't you ever damn well forget that!' His voice had risen to a shriek, his eyes staring. 'You've made my life an absolute hell and, up till now, I've done bugger all about it. Now you've gone too far. You've set our daughter against me. The one good thing that's come out of my marrying you and you had to make sure that she finished up hating me as much as you do. Didn't you?' He spluttered the last two words thrusting his face forward until it was only inches from her own.

Hilda could feel his hot beery breath; she was rapidly becoming more and more alarmed both for Kate and herself. In the state of mind Fred was in there was no telling what he might do. She made to turn her head to the wall.

'Oh, no, you don't.' Fred was a big man, and today, with his belly full of booze, he had the strength of ten men. He grabbed his wife's chin in a vice-like grip with one hand and wagged her face from side to side. 'You, Hilda, can rot in hell as far as I'm concerned but you'll leave our Kate alone. I love that girl an' I'm not gonna have you turn her against me. Do you hear me?' he roared.

'I should think you can be heard as far away as Kingston, Mr Kearsley.'

Fred lowered his arm, backed away from his wife and turned to look into the face of Dr Pearson who had entered the hallway without being heard.

'What's it got t'do with you?' Fred tried to bluff, but his voice was much quieter.

'We'll discuss that later. For now, you're coming home with me. My wife and housekeeper between them ought to be able to clean and sober you up.'

Dr Pearson was not as tall as Fred but he had a military background and, as he roughly took hold of Fred's elbow, he barked out an order, 'Get in my car.'

Fred hesitated, frowning deeply.

'Do as you're told, man, or I'll send for the police.'

'But . . .'

'No buts, wait in the car. I'll have a word with your wife and then we'll be off.'

Still Fred didn't move. 'I want t'know how my Kate is.'

'She's as well as can be expected,' Dr Pearson replied.

'No thanks to you,' Hilda shot back at him.

Fred clutched the doctor's arm. He swallowed hard. 'She will be all right, won't she? I never meant . . .'

The doctor's manner softened. 'Come along, man. I'll help you.'

Two minutes later the doctor was back. 'He's feeling very guilty, Mrs Kearsley. When we get him sobered up he's going to be full of remorse.'

'That's as may be but him having a guilty conscience isn't going to help Kate, is it?'

'No, of course it isn't. But both of you are going to

have to come to terms with what has happened and get on with your lives. You, and Mr Kearsley more so. It is how you two react that is going to affect young Kate.'

Earlier that day, quite by chance, he had met up with the landlord of the George and Dragon and between them they had pieced together the whole sorry story.

'Now, let's go upstairs and see how my patient is.'

At the foot of the stairs he turned and faced Hilda squarely.

'I will do what I can for your husband because, basically, I think he's a good, hard-working man. One thing though I will promise you, if I can prevent it he will not come back to live under this roof until he is well and truly sober and settled down. One more thing. He's right, you know. You, I, or anyone else for that matter, cannot keep him out if he decides otherwise. It *is* his house.'

Chapter Six

THE DRESS KATE was wearing was one of the nicest she had ever owned, sage-green brocade silk, perfectly simple, fitting really well. Its only trimmings were an edging of beige lace at the cuffs and collar. Her mother had made it for her in the last three weeks, during which Kate hadn't set foot outside the house.

The idea of a new dress to cheer her up had been a kind thought and she was grateful. But the belief that new clothes could make matters better was beyond her. The dress felt good. It made her look good. But it also made her feel guilty. Of what she wasn't sure.

Her father and mother seemed, once again, to have called a truce. The worst thing was that they only spoke to each other when the occasion demanded it. Not one word of regret, sorrow or remorse had her father uttered to her. He was gentle towards her but, somehow, nothing rang true. Kate felt the peace in the household was as fragile as a sheet of tissue paper. It could be blown away at any moment.

The door to the front room opened and Hilda came in pushing a tea trolley over to where Kate sat by the window.

'It's a lovely day out, cold but bright, you should make an effort an' go for a walk, Kate.'

'I've told you, Mum, I don't want to go out, not yet.'

'You're better now, luv. You can't go on burying your head in the sand for ever,' Hilda coaxed, laying out the cups and pouring a little milk into each of them.

'I know that, but do you?'

'It's best forgotten,' her mother muttered beneath her breath.

'Really, Mother! You're no more able to forget it than fly to the moon. You're just waiting for your chance to get your own back on Dad, only you won't admit it.' Kate sounded as she felt: bitter. 'You know what happened, don't you?'

Hilda busied herself cutting a Victoria sponge into sections, making no answer to her question.

'I don't know how you found out what happened to me but you have, I know full well you have. You won't even let me talk about it, never mind tell you the details.'

'I keep telling you, luv. We all have t'live together and it's best forgotten. As soon as you feel able, why don't you go and stay with your gran for a while?'

Kate's head jerked upwards. 'And leave you and Dad to fly at each other's throats again?' A sudden thought flashed through her mind. 'God! Why did it never occur to me before now? Look at me. You know all about Mrs Wilson, don't you? You've known all along! For just how long, Mum?'

'Don't judge me too harshly,' Hilda pleaded. 'I've done what most women in my position would have done. I've turned a blind eye. Your father and me, well, we never felt the same after David died, and a man has his needs. That's the way it goes.'

'You didn't think what Dad was doing was . . . wrong?'

Her mother thought about that for a while. 'When I first found out, I minded.'

At that moment Kate felt something unlock inside her. The sight of her father and that woman together had replayed itself over and over in her mind so many times that she had wanted to scream. Now she wanted to talk, to tell her mother exactly what had happened, how she had felt when her own father had come towards her with hate in his eyes. The words, which until now she had not been able to utter, came tumbling from her lips and Hilda could only sit there, helpless to stop the flow or mend the hurt that was eating away at her daughter.

'I saw him, Mum! Through the open window in that house with that woman! She was . . . she had no clothes on an' neither did Dad. I stood an' watched what they were doing. I should have run. I know I should have but I couldn't move. I don't know why, I just couldn't. Then Dad saw me. He caught me looking in.'

Kate's outburst came to an abrupt end as a sob caught in her throat and angry tears fell from her eyes.

'Oh, my goodness! My poor Kate. Neither your Dad nor me ever wanted you to find out. Certainly not this way.'

'I'll never forget. I keep dreaming of the way he stared at me. He hated me. He wanted to kill me.'

Hilda looked at her sadly. 'No, luv. You've got it

73

wrong. He was so upset because you'd found out. You of all people! He still feels so guilty, I know he does.'

'But he knocked me to the ground. Started hitting me. Said I was spying on him.'

'There now, luv, leave it be. Truly, it was guilty conscience that drove your father to do what he did. And I'm so sorry,' she whispered, 'so sorry you had to be brought into it.'

Tears, unstoppable now, trickled down Hilda's face. She got to her feet, pushed the tea trolley to one side and opened her arms. Kate stood up and went into them. Both were crying softly.

Hilda rocked her daughter back and forth, hushing her, whispering against her hair, 'It will be all right, you'll see.'

When at last Kate seemed to relax, Hilda used her forefinger to tilt her daughter's chin upwards and looked into her eyes. 'Your dad has never hit you before an' he never will again, that I promise.'

'It wasn't the blows that were so awful, not even the pain really. It was . . . well . . . first seeing him . . . like that . . . with her. Then, when he came at me – to see him in that state. He was, I don't know, mad I suppose. I'm sure he hated me.'

'Come on, dear, this won't solve anything. Let's have our tea,' Hilda said.

Kate nodded her agreement and they sat down.

'In so many ways your father is a good man. It's the drink that sets him off.'

To herself she said, but he's overstepped the mark this time. I've taken his brutal lovemaking and, yes, even blows he's struck in anger. I've always told myself that kind of behaviour was my punishment for not hiding the fact that I did not and could not love him. I couldn't pretend feelings that just weren't there. Not after he let David die.

But to hit Kate! That wasn't right. Kate was the one good thing in her life. The only reason she had stayed with Fred. On the day they had lowered their baby son's tiny coffin into the ground she would have done away with herself had it not been for Kate. That sweet dark-eyed little girl, as innocent of evil as an angel. Both she and Fred had been so wrong. They had allowed her to be the invisible cord that bound them, keeping them together even though the hatred had festered and grown with the years. It was sinful what, between them, they had done to their only daughter.

It was true that they had given her a secure, sheltered upbringing; she had been well fed, given nice clothes and had a lovely warm house in which to live. The only real poverty she had ever seen was when she'd been taken to the East End to visit her aunt. It was a vastly different picture up there. The way Dolly and her husband Bert struggled to bring up their children in a small house, which was cramped, dark and squalid. Hilda shook her head at the memory. It didn't bear thinking about, yet it was home to dozens of families, where women fought an endless battle against poverty. Filthy children, tawdry prostitutes earning a few shillings by selling their bodies. Bug-ridden tenements, all in shocking disrepair, inside walls where the dampness ran in rivulets. Kate had only ever had a glimpse of that part of the world.

Had Kate been fortunate? In dozens of ways, yes. But because of the hatred between Fred and herself there had been no brothers or sisters for her to play with or to fight and squabble with, let alone to stand alongside against the rest of the world. I suppose most of the blame for that must rest on my shoulders, Hilda told herself grimly. I hope she finds a decent lad and gets married soon; I wouldn't want her to be on her own when Fred and I die. She'll probably be very cautious and choosy having seen the way our married life has turned out. There was that Victor Appleton who'd come calling on Kate quite a few times and Fred was still doing his best to encourage that match. Well, he would, wouldn't he? And old Jack Appleton, Victor's father, was of the same mind. Amalgamate the two boat yards and they'd have almost complete control of this section of the river.

Hilda shook herself, and sat upright. She looked at her daughter's sweet face. If there was one worthwhile thing she had done in this life it was to rear Kate. She loved her daughter dearly and Kate, in turn, was a credit to her. I wish there was some way I could ensure that she had a happy future, Hilda said to herself.

Fred and herself were doing their best to appear friendly towards each other, but how long would that last? Things between them had been dreadful before and now, since Kate had found out about her father, they'd become desperate. Neither of them willing to forgive the other.

And perhaps the worst thing of all was that Fred was unable to forgive himself. Every time his gaze settled on Kate's bruised face, Hilda was aware of his torment. It'll not be long before he turns to the drink again, she thought sadly, never mind what assurances he's given to the doctor and his wife. Men used to drinking couldn't suddenly give it up, no matter how hard they tried. And Fred was never going to be the exception.

Chapter Seven

'ARE YOU IN, Mum?' Kate called standing in the centre of the empty living room. She had been staying at her grandmother's for the past week.

'Yes, luv, I'm upstairs,' came the faint reply.

Fear rose in Kate's throat as she made for the stairs; there had been something odd in her mother's tone. She crossed the room to stand at the side of the bed. Hilda had the bedclothes pulled tight up under her chin and, as Kate bent over her, she saw tears glistening in her mother's eyes, though she was doing her best to smile.

'Are you all right? That's a silly question. You wouldn't be in bed in the afternoon if you were. Pull the clothes back, Mum, I want to have a look at you.'

Hilda winced as Kate gave the top sheet a tug.

'It's only my arm.' Hilda bit her bottom lip hard.

Tenderly, Kate moved her fingers along the line of Hilda's shoulder; she felt jagged bone and knew it was broken. Very, very gently she took the pillows from the other side of the double bed, raised her mother as best she could, and made a padded seat around her shoulders giving support to her neck. Hilda looked weak and her face was a funny colour.

'I'm going downstairs to make you a hot drink and then I'm going along to Dr Pearson's to find out how I can get you to hospital. Lie as still as you can, I won't be long.' She softly kissed her mother's forehead.

Once out of the bedroom, Kate's mouth straightened into a thin, angry line. This time was once too often. She was going to threaten her father with the police. He couldn't be allowed to use her mum as a punching bag every time he felt like it. She had to find a way to put a stop to it.

Dr Pearson was goodness itself. He quickly confirmed that Hilda's collarbone was broken and, brooking no argument, said, 'Give me about a quarter of an hour and then I can be free to run you both into Kingston Hospital. That will be the best and quickest way of getting you there.'

Following an X-ray, Hilda was admitted to the hospital. She had been given an injection to ease the pain and Kate sat by the bed until, at last, Hilda's eyelids began to droop. Kate looked at her mother's lovely brown hair, free of pins and combs, fanned out over the pillow. Her face was a deathly white, though there were no dark bruises, thank God. She looked desperately tired.

Kate leant across the bed and kissed Hilda's cheek. 'I'll be back to see you tomorrow. I love you.'

As she left the ward she asked herself how it was that two good people, who must have loved each other dearly at one time, could go on hurting each other day after day, year after year, making their lives a living hell.

What had set her father off this time? By the look of her mother it must have been quite a beating. She was probably alive only by the grace of God. One day he might end up killing her and then where would they all be?

The next afternoon, Kate stopped outside the hospital and bought a sweet-smelling bunch of freesias from an old lady who wished her luck. From the next barrow she chose a huge bunch of black grapes and was rewarded with a cheeky grin and a sly wink as the young man pressed her change into the palm of her hand while holding onto her fingers for much longer than he needed to. These friendly gestures told her she was looking nice and it was with a smile on her face that she entered the ward.

'Oh, Mum, you look miles better,' she exclaimed, laying her gifts down on the counterpane.

That wasn't quite true, but Kate felt there was some improvement, even though there were dark rings around Hilda's eyes. The nurse brought her a cup of tea and while she was sipping it her mother suddenly asked, 'Have you seen your father?'

No point in telling the truth, Kate decided. Her mother would only lay there and worry herself sick. 'No, he hasn't been home while I've been there.'

'It was my own fault, you know, Kate.'

'Mother, don't be so daft.'

'It was,' she insisted, 'I shouldn't have answered him back.'

'For goodness' sake, what are you? A dimwit who has to keep their tongue between their teeth?' Anger welled up inside Kate and she didn't know how to cope with it.

'Kate, you know how things are between yer dad an' me. Just as soon as the doctor says I can get up I'm coming home and everything will be all right. You'll see. I won't be in here all that long. A few days at the most.'

Kate turned away, not wanting her mother to see the doubtful expression on her face. The day that everything was all right between her parents was a day she wished she could live to see.

'Are you sure you'll be fit enough to come home so quickly?'

'I'll be fine once I get on my feet again,' her mother replied bravely, attempting a smile that didn't quite come off.

They fell silent. Neither of them able to voice what they were thinking.

When the bell rang to signal that visiting time was over, it was on the tip of Kate's tongue to tell her mother that when she had got up that morning she'd found her father sitting at the kitchen table, eating his breakfast as if nothing had happened to interrupt their daily lives. She fought back the impulse. Perhaps when her mother did return home, things *would* be different – after all, it was the first time that her mother had ended up in hospital, and it might just act as the warning her father so badly needed. Would he take heed of it? He might if he stayed sober, Kate thought dolefully as she kissed her mother goodbye.

*   *   *

It was the second week in October before Kate was allowed to bring her mother home to Bramble Cottage. The front door was closed even though Alice had been staying while Hilda was in hospital; Kate had expected her to be at the door to welcome them.

Both Hilda and Kate smiled as they set foot in the living room. The old lady was sitting by the fire dozing, with her needlework in her lap, her glasses resting on the very tip of her nose. She woke with a start, staggered to her feet, and kissed her daughter-in-law on the cheek.

'Welcome home, lass, I've put a rabbit and loads of vegetables into your big black pot, it's all in the oven, won't be ready for ages yet, but I've made a few rock cakes an' I'm sure you can be doing with a cup of tea.'

'Thanks, Ma, I'm ever so grateful t'you. Kate's told me all you've done an' that Fred has been the soul of discretion.'

'Never mind about all that now, Hilda, I'm only sorry I couldn't get him to visit you . . . but perhaps it's just as well he stayed away.'

Alice pushed her glasses further up her nose sizing up her son's wife. She looked ill, there was no getting away from that. Until now she had always maintained that it was six of one an' half a dozen of the other where right an' wrong was being handed out between her Fred and this wife of his. This time she wasn't so sure. But, she thought as she watched Hilda take off her coat, there's no getting away from the fact that you drove my son into the arms of Chris Wilson, more's the pity, the cold frigid way you've treated him. And if it hadn't been her it would have been someone else.

81

Something didn't seem right, Kate decided. Her gran and her mother were being cagey with each other. When was the atmosphere in this house ever going to feel normal?

Her thoughts turned to her father. When he didn't come home she worried, and when he *was* at home she worried even more. Time was when she had no doubt that he loved her. Always had and always would. She'd have sworn that to be true up until the day she had caught him with that woman. She'd have given anything to be able to turn the clock back, but that was impossible.

Now my father doesn't even like me, she told herself, sadly. Sometimes he looks at me with such a terrible expression. I'm not imagining it – some days there's hate in his eyes. Gran keeps telling me I'm wrong and that time will ease the situation. She says my father is to be pitied because of the shame and humiliation he has suffered.

He should be pitied! All this was of his making!

What about *me*, Gran? she would like to have asked but hadn't dared. I'm eighteen years old! I never go out with young people. I want to dance, be happy, have fun. There's certainly never any fun in this house. And if and when I get married, I want a lad to fall in love with me because he likes me. Not because my dad owns a boat yard.

'You're deep in thought, lass,' Alice said, bringing Kate back with a start. 'You might put the kettle on, and while you're out in the scullery have a look at the copper for me, will you? I put some sheets in t'boil.'

Hilda put out a hand to stay Kate. 'I'll go. I can

manage, I don't want you or your gran to treat me like an invalid.'

Alice looked dubiously at Hilda. 'You always were too independent. Still, if that's the way you want it, I'll have a cup of tea with you and then I'll be on me way.'

'Oh, Mum, I didn't mean it like that.'

'It's all right, lass, don't fret yerself. No kitchen has ever been built that's big enough for two women to work in. Besides I want to get off home. Neighbours are very good an' kind but I worry about me animals, and there's no bed like yer own.'

Hilda did her best to smile. 'You're right there. Be a treat for me to get into my bed an' not have to feel a rubber sheet underneath me. Hospital beds are horrible.'

Kate had made the tea and the three of them ate and drunk in an atmosphere that was edgy to say the least.

'I'm going upstairs to have a little rest,' Hilda said, her voice little more than a whisper. 'Kate, why don't you walk part of the way with your gran?'

'If you're sure you'll be all right, I'll do that.'

'You don't like my mum all that much, do you, Gran?' Kate asked as they wandered along the towpath.

'I have my reasons, or more likely you could call them regrets.'

'I don't understand.'

'Don't you?'

'No, I don't.'

'It doesn't matter,' Alice said dismissively. 'Let's just leave sleeping dogs lie.'

They paused to watch two young men carry a small boat down towards the river.

'Peaceful out here, ain't it?' Alice said out of the blue. 'The more time I spend outdoors the better I like it.'

'You're deliberately changing the subject,' Kate accused her but a smile spread across her face.

Alice chuckled. 'True. When it comes to your parents I think the least said between you an' me the better. Unless, of course, there comes a time when you really feel things are getting on top of you and then . . . well, you know where to find me. Day or night you know that my door's never locked.'

'Can I tell you one thing, Gran?'

'What's that?'

'I'll be glad when tonight's over. You know what I mean, the two of them coming face to face like.'

Alice wanted to fling her arms round her grand-daughter, to comfort and reassure her. Poor girl, she thought, she's been robbed of the joy of having brothers and sisters, brought up in a terrible atmosphere and, if I'm honest, part of the blame has to be laid at my door. I should have knocked her parents' heads together years ago!

'When your dad comes home, try to act normal. Dinner's all ready, I told you, nice rabbit stew. So, you lay the table and set a few flowers in a jug and you'll see, you'll have yer dad twisted round your little finger before it's time for bed.'

'Wish I could be as sure as you are.'

'Yes, well, it's about time you turned back an' I continued on my way. Come on, give yer old gran a kiss, and for God's sake don't leave me looking like that. Stop frowning an' let me see you smile.'

Kate hesitated, then said, 'There are times when it seems as if everything is fine and then it all blows up. If you weren't around, I wouldn't know who to turn to.'

'Would you like to move out, live with me?'

'I don't know. To tell you the truth, I've thought about it before now.'

'You've never mentioned it. I think your mum and dad would understand if you should decide that's what you want to do.'

'Thanks, Gran. I'll see how things go. You're a wise old bird and I do love you.'

They spent a few moments enfolded in each other's arms and when they finally turned to go their different ways they were closer than they'd ever been.

Chapter Eight

IT WAS NEARLY midnight on the last Saturday in October, and Kate had been fast asleep for the past three hours.

What on earth was that noise? She half raised her head from the pillow. There was another almighty crash! She shook herself fully awake. Somebody was breaking down the front door. But why? If it was her father he knew full well that a spare key hung from inside the letterbox on a string. Surely he wasn't drunk!

Since her mother had come home he had been very docile. His eyes had often filled with suffering, showing just how much he regretted having hurt both his wife and his daughter.

The days hadn't been easy. Kate still worried about her mother; she always looked so tired and her shiny brown hair, worn in a tight bun at the nape of her neck, was becoming increasingly mixed with grey. Small wonder when you considered what she'd been through.

At times Kate almost hated her father, then he would raise his head and look at her, pleading for understanding and, against her better judgement, she would find herself feeling sorry for him, biting back any angry words.

There was no doubt it was her father downstairs; he was kicking up an awful commotion. What should she do? Go first and see if her mother was all right or venture downstairs to see what he was up to? The living room was probably a right old shambles by now. Suddenly the racket stopped and the silence that followed seemed more menacing than the din. Perhaps he had fallen down. If so he could lay there and sleep it off until the morning.

However, Kate finally reached for her dressing gown, stretching her arms above her head to loosen her shoulder-blades. Pushing her feet into her slippers she glanced around her bedroom. It was a small, square, low-ceilinged room. The walls were papered with a pretty pink paper and on the polished floorboards soft rugs had been placed on each side and at the foot of the bed. It was a comfortable, cheerful little room by daylight; a room where Kate felt happy and safe. Now, with only a glimmer of moonlight showing through the edge of the curtains she suddenly felt terribly afraid.

Someone was staggering up the stairs. The noise was enough to wake the dead. Kate hesitated and that was her undoing; her father must have sensed she was standing behind the door.

He pushed open the door and, scarcely inside the room, he reached out and grabbed his daughter round the throat with one large fist. Kate stared at him, terror and disbelief blazing from her eyes.

'I'm gonna teach you a lesson, you dirty little sneak. You deliberately followed me.'

Fred's face was red with anger and he forced the words out through clenched teeth. His hands now gripped her shoulders, pressing her down onto the mattress. Kate twisted and turned, fighting to get away from him. He wasn't going to give in that easily. He gripped her more tightly, his fingertips digging into her flesh.

God help me, Kate prayed as, now towering above her, he brought his arm back and gave her a stinging blow on the side of her head. His face was inches from her own. His breathing was heavy and his breath hot and foul.

She gave up struggling; gasping with the pain in her head. She knew her father didn't realise what he was doing but she was helpless against his great strength and, with the amount of whisky he must have drunk, he was a very dangerous man.

The only thought going through Fred Kearsley's mind at that moment was that he needed to teach his daughter a lesson. He had to let her know that what he got up to was none of her business. It was bad enough that for years his wife had led him a dog's life, he wasn't going to let a slip of a girl dictate to him what he could do and who he could see. She had humiliated him once. Well, she wouldn't get the chance to do it again.

He clenched his fist. Kate saw the blow coming and flinched from it. His hand struck her jaw but the blow had no force behind it. She felt her father shudder, his fingers opened and his fist uncurled. He reeled sideways, his whole body now full-length on top of her, his arms stretched forward, either side of her head. He made a noise, a horrible sort of groan, shuddered again and then lay still, his full weight bearing down on her.

Kate turned her head to one side and, with amazement, saw her mother standing there, dressed only in her long thin cotton nightdress, her hair hanging free over her shoulders. Her face showed no trace of emotion, but her eyes were gleaming. It was almost as if she were gloating. She heard her mother's intake of breath, watched as she leant forward and with a mighty effort pulled Fred's heavy body to one side.

There wasn't a sound in the room.

Relief flooded through Kate. The removal of her father's weight was sheer blessed deliverance.

'Are you all right?' her mother asked, her voice sounding strange.

Kate nodded. Big tears welled up in her eyes as she struggled to sit up. She took the hand her mother was holding out to her and the minute she was up on her feet she began to cry in earnest.

Hilda took her in her arms, whispering soft words. 'It's all right. Calm down, my darling, he won't hurt you any more.'

'What will we do? We can't leave him there like that, we should call a doctor, shouldn't we?'

It was then, as she turned towards the bed, that she saw the knife sticking out from between his shoulderblades and the dark, sticky red blood staining her bedspread. Bile rose in her throat. 'Oh my God, I'm going to be sick!'

Her mother pushed her aside and bent over her father. Suddenly Hilda let out a weird eerie sound, then, drawing swiftly back, she began to scream. Kate couldn't bear to listen. She covered her ears with her hands. Every bad thing about her father was wiped from her mind as she walked towards the bed. Perching herself on the edge she raised her father's head and cradled it in her lap.

Her mother stumbled from the room, her piercing screams vibrating in the air behind her.

Kate's mind went blank. She didn't speak, just sat there, swaying back and forth.

She only realised that strange men were in her bedroom when Dr Pearson endeavoured to free her hands from her father's body and she heard his soft voice urging her to stand up. There was a steady hum of male voices but the actual words went over Kate's head, until she heard the word mortuary.

'What?' she heard herself scream, but even she knew it was more like a wail. 'Why isn't my father going to hospital?' She directed the question to Dr Pearson, the only friendly face she could focus on.

'Come, Kate, I'm going to take you home with me, tuck you up nice and warm, Mrs Pearson will.'

'I don't want to go home with you. My father has been hurt an' I want to go in the ambulance with him. Please, doctor, let me do that.'

God in heaven! The doctor sighed heavily, he'd had some tasks to perform in his life but surely never one as distasteful as this. He took hold of her hands and firmly turned her until she was standing facing him. 'Kate, listen to me. Your father is dead. I am so very sorry but there is nothing we can do for him now. Your mother is not at all well and she is being looked after. So, please, be a good girl and do as you're told.'

Kate's face was set in a deep frown, she uttered no words, just let out a long, low moan as she withdrew her hands from the doctor's grasp and walked from her bedroom and down the stairs.

Dr Pearson picked up his case, nodded to the police officers, and followed her from the house.

How the hell had this come about? he asked himself. It just goes to show that a woman, if pushed too far, is capable of anything.

Chapter Nine

KATE WAS SITTING with the Reverend James Hutchinson and her grandmother, still feeling bewildered and shocked. The past three weeks had been a living nightmare.

She had been given only the briefest information as to what was happening to her mother, but now Reverend Hutchinson was taking great pains to make sure she understood what would take place now that the police had released her father's body for burial. Kate was only too willing to let others take complete charge of the proceedings. She listened, saying nothing, until the vicar said, 'Do you agree, Kate?'

She looked across to where Alice sat.

'It's the best we can do, Kate, just say you agree,' her gran instructed.

The Reverend Hutchinson stared at Alice in open admiration. She had been like the Rock of Gibraltar, sustaining her young granddaughter day and night.

When you took into consideration that it was her only son that had been murdered, one wondered how it was that the old lady had been able to bear up so well.

'Well, Kate?' The vicar's voice was gentle.

She nodded her head and agreed to the date and time of the funeral. 'Please, Reverend Hutchinson, may we keep it as private as possible?'

With a bleak smile, he said, 'Of course, Kate, the private service will be held in the small chapel.'

God forgive me, he prayed silently. It would take more powers than I possess to keep the sightseers away on that day. The circumstances in which the poor man had died and the date having been set for his wife's trial was enough to bring inquisitive busybodies out in droves. There was also the press! They would have a field day.

Three days to go until they could lay her father to rest.

Kate was in Bramble Cottage, on her own for the very first time since that awful night. Alice had gone to buy black for the two of them to wear.

Despite her gran's pleading, Kate had steadfastly refused to leave the house. Her cup, saucer and porridge bowl remained on the kitchen table and she sat still, staring into space. Nothing but silence. This is how it will be from now on, she thought, just me, no one else. Strangely, at this moment she felt quite calm about it, which amazed her. Perhaps it had all been a dream, simply some horrible nightmare, but the picture in her mind was vivid: her father lying on her bed, she cradling his head while his life's blood trickled from his body, her mother, screaming. It was no nightmare, it was grim reality and the repercussions had hardly started. There was so much more heartache to come.

Of that there was no doubt!

Her feeling of calm gave way to a terror that escalated until it threatened to crush her.

'Mum! Dad!' she called. Her voice, resounding through the empty house, brought no response. 'Help me, God! Help me, someone!' she wailed.

A sudden pounding on the front door had her almost jumping out of her skin. Such a racket, she muttered, rising and going to answer it.

As an assortment of voices called, ''Allo, Kate,' she had to blink away the tears.

How good of them all! She hadn't been expecting Aunt Dolly and her three children. Didn't look as if Uncle Bert was with them though.

Her four relations crowded into the narrow hallway and Kate led the way into the living room. Awkward minutes ticked away until Aunt Dolly pushed forward her twin boys, Tom and Stan, now fifteen and already working on the docks. Each in turn wrapped Kate in their arms. It was an affectionate gesture.

''Ow ar yer, Kate?' Tom queried.

'You're gonna be all right,' Stan chipped in. 'Me Dad says t'tell yer he'll be down for yer dad's funeral an' that you're t'remember there's always a 'ome for yer with us.'

Hilda, Dolly's only girl, named after Kate's mother, and almost the same age as Kate, yanked Stan away and she, too, gripped Kate affectionately. 'See! You ain't alone. No matter what, you got family. You just remember that.'

Aunt Dolly squeezed Kate's shoulder and in a voice strong with emotion announced, 'We're taking you back wiv us t'day, luv. But not before you've put the kettle on an' we've all 'ad a cuppa. Jesus, the journey down 'ere seemed t'take forever, an' me feet are killing me. Ye don't mind if I take me boots off, d'you, luv?'

'Stop moaning, Mum,' Hilda rebuked her. 'Yer can take off yer 'at, yer shawl, yer boots, an' any thing else yer like just so long as yer stop complaining.'

'I expect yer want to loosen yer stays as well, don't yer?' Tom threw in for good measure.

A few chuckles eased the strain, more so when his mother's hand whizzed about his head, but didn't make contact as the lanky lad ducked with the ease of a trained boxer.

Hilda went out to the scullery and took charge of making the tea.

Dolly, now comfortably settled in an armchair, leant towards Kate and laid a hand on her knee. ''Ow 'ave yer bin really, my luv? We ain't stayed away 'cos we didn't care. It's just bin . . . such a shock. Yer uncle Bert did come down an' 'ave a talk wiv yer gran. You were out for the count that night.'

'I know, Auntie, Gran told me Uncle Bert had been, and you're here now, and it's very good of you.'

'Nonsense, an' you know it. Yer mum is me only sister an' though she went off and left London, we always knew we only 'ad to shout an' the other would be there like a flash. In times of trouble real families cling together. Pity two of me brothers were killed in the war, an' the rest of them married stuck-up bitches.' Lowering her voice, Aunt Dolly said seriously, 'Me and my Bert, we've tried

twice t'see yer mum. Nothing doing. They said they'd
let us know when we can go.'

Kate's head was lowered; she made no comment.

'Come on, luv,' Dolly pleaded. 'Talk t'me. Let it out.
I can be a good listener yer know.'

Kate straightened up and made a decision to tell her
aunt the unvarnished truth.

'I think I'm going mad,' she began. 'I can't sleep, I can't
eat, everything sticks in my throat and I feel I'm going
to choke. I feel sick all the time. Gran keeps telling me,
what's done is done, there's no bringing Dad back. I know
that's true but I can't look her in the eye. After all, he was
her son. Her only son. And my mum killed him. She's a
lovely old lady. I love her dearly, she knows I do, but she
didn't really like Mum and I can't help wondering how
she feels about her now. She doesn't say much.'

'Oh, you poor lamb.' Aunt Dolly whipped a handkerchief out of her pocket and rubbed at her eyes. 'What a
mess. What a Goddam awful mess!'

Kate stifled a sob and stared at her aunt. 'I never
meant to upset you. I'm sorry.'

Dolly shook her head, hard. 'Never mind being sorry,
an' don't you go taking yer gran's troubles on your
shoulders. Christ knows it's bad enough for her, but
none of it was of your making, so just you remember
that. Yer gran will survive it all. You'll see.'

'What about Dad's funeral? That will be bad enough,
and then there's everything else to get through.' Kate's
voice was little more than a whisper.

Dolly's heart ached for her. Kate was so young, and
unworldly. This was a terrible business an' no mistake.

'Nobody seems to be thinking about my mum.' The

accusation came harshly from Kate's lips and once started she couldn't stop. 'Oh, Aunt Dolly, they let me see her. She was worried about me! Can you believe that? It was a nice room they brought her to so we could talk, but what about the rest of the time? Is she alone in a cell? Is she allowed to do anything? Read a book? Talk to anyone? Or does she just sit and stare into space? What's happening to her doesn't bear thinking about.'

Later in the afternoon, when the twins came back from a walk along the riverbank, Dolly said it was nearly time for them to set off for home so Kate had better put a few things into a bag. Kate didn't respond.

'I'll do it for you,' Dolly said, heading for the stairs. ''Cos I'm not taking no for an answer. You're coming 'ome with us whether you like it or not.'

'Kate, let's go outside for a minute,' Hilda suggested and the two cousins put on coats and went out into the front garden.

The wind swept in from the river, tangling Kate's long hair. A longboat glided into view and the man at the tiller, seeing the two girls, tugged hard on a rope sending out a loud whistle from the steamhorn. They waved in answer. Then a strained silence descended.

Hilda kicked at the grass and Kate thought that already the garden had a neglected look.

'You don't mind coming home with us, do you, Kate?' Hilda asked.

'I don't care one way or the other,' was the despondent reply.

'Hell, even our noisy home has t'be better than staying here on yer own. We're yer family, we want you with us, you know that.'

'Yes, I know.' Kate stared at the toes of her shoes.

Unexpectedly Hilda grinned. 'You don't 'ave much choice, Kate. If me mum says you're coming with us, she means it.'

Under her breath Kate mumbled, 'I still can't believe it.' It sounded as if she were still in shock.

'Neither can any of us, luv,' Hilda said sympathetically, 'so I reckon it must be a thousand times worse for you. I've always been jealous of you, did you know that, Kate? I always thought you had it made, living down 'ere in the country, just you, Aunt Hilda an' Uncle Fred. 'Ole 'ouse, by the river all t'yerselves. Everything so clean, nice an' fresh. Wanting for nothing. You've never even had t'go out t'work let alone slave hours on end in a dirty dark factory like I do. I just can't believe it 'as all gone so wrong for you.'

Kate made no answer.

Finally Hilda draped an arm across Kate's shoulders. 'Come on, time t'make a move. Nothing we say or do will turn the clock back. I'll be with you as much as I can. You'll not be lonely, you'll 'ave me mum for company, an' I expect she'll show you bits of London you've never set eyes on.'

Kate knew she had to make a stand and speak up for herself. She said, 'It was really good of Aunt Dolly to fetch you all down here today. I haven't been able to find words to tell her that yet, but I want her to know that I really do appreciate it.'

Impulsively Hilda threw her arms around Kate, hugging her close. 'So you'll come indoors an' get yerself ready t'leave?'

'I didn't say that.' Kate backed away, blinking hard, turning towards the house that no longer felt like a home. 'I need time. I can't leave Gran, not now, not until after my dad's funeral. I will come an' stay with you then. I promise. But this next three days – God how I wish they were over – Gran and I have so many things to do.'

'There's no moving you, is there?'

'Afraid not. I do think at the moment Gran needs me as much as I need her.'

'All right then, luv. I'll tell me mum. As long as you tell her you will come to London as soon as the funeral is over I don't suppose she'll carry on too much at us.'

Linking arms they walked inside, and in the doorway Hilda turned, 'Dad will do everything he can, I promise you that, Kate.'

'I know he will. Uncle Bert's a good man,' Kate answered, all the while asking herself what there was that anyone could do?

They had done her father proud. After all, he was a well-respected businessman and his yard had built boats to order for more than half of the dignitaries who were here to attend his funeral.

The glass-sided hearse and black horses with black-feathered plumes drew the coffin slowly towards his last resting place.

'Throw that rose down onto his coffin,' Alice, standing close beside Kate, ordered in a tight voice.

Kate took a step forward but her legs were shaking so badly they nearly collapsed beneath her.

'Steady. Hold on t'me. There's a good girl.' Uncle Bert was there beside her, his warmth and strength reassuring, as he led her to the side of the gaping hole.

Kate tried to smile at him but her chest tightened. It wasn't possible. Neither could she cry. She was past tears. The father she had adored, who had loved and cherished her, had turned into a man of whom she was afraid. Well, at least that part was over now. He was at peace. Some day soon, if God were good, her mother might also be able to find peace.

As she turned she saw Alice wipe away her tears, and went to her. Dear Gran, she reflected, how hard it must be for her.

Dr Pearson stood at the edge of the crowd, hoping against hope that his services would not be needed. He nodded as Kate's relations passed by, making their way back to the carriages. He stepped forward to shake hands with Alice, then he shook hands with Kate.

There was still Hilda Kearsley's trial to be got through. What a mess, he thought as, shoulders hunched against the cold, he returned to his car. What a bloody awful mess.

Chapter Ten

BY THE TIME her mother's trial came to Kingston Assizes, nearly four months after that terrible night, Kate had become used to people recognising her in the street. When she walked into a shop, folk whispered. She hated the notoriety.

The trial was halfway through its second morning and Adam Wright, one of the Kearsleys' neighbours, had taken the stand.

'I am a neighbour of Mrs Kearsley and live at Tumble Weed cottage, Hitchin Lane, Littleton Green,' he told the court. 'About two in the morning of the last day of October last year I heard a terrified screaming coming from the Kearsley cottage. I ran the few yards along the towpath, and all the while the screaming went on and on.

'The front door had been smashed open and the gas light at the top of the stairs was lit. I entered the house, taking the stairs two at a time. Hilda Kearsley was standing on the landing staring through the open door of the small bedroom. My main concern was to stop her screaming and this I did by taking her by the shoulders and shaking her.

'The daughter, Kate Kearsley, was in the bedroom with her father who was stretched out, full-length, on the bed and I asked her if her dad had had a heart attack but she shook her head. I then asked her to tell me what had happened and if I could help in any way.

'"Don't touch him, don't touch him," she said in a most piteous way. About a minute after that, Jack Seymour, the Kearsleys' neighbour on the other side, burst into the room, he was breathless and panting hard. "The doctor is on his way," he gasped.'

The man dressed in a long black gown and wearing a wig on his head, whom Kate had been told was a barrister, now asked Adam Wright a question.

'All this time Mr Kearsley had not moved?'

'No, sir. He just lay on the bed. I think I knew he was dead.'

'Mr Wright, did you say anything else to the daughter?'

'Yes, I asked if she thought her father had suffered a stroke.'

'What answer did she give you?'

'None. It was Mrs Kearsley who said, "Maybe . . . No . . . I don't know."'

'So, it was quite evident, was it not, that Hilda Kearsley was in a very agitated state at that time?'

'Oh, yes, sir, definitely. In my opinion she was distraught.'

'Thank you, Mr Wright.'

The barrister sat down and Adam was told he could leave the stand.

Next it was the doctor's turn to be cross-examined.

'Dr James Pearson. I live at 24 Oaklands Way, Littleton Green, which is approximately five minutes' walk from the towpath. I was called up by Mr Seymour in the early hours of the morning on October the 31st and I went to the Kearsley's house. Upstairs, in what I knew to be the daughter's bedroom, I found Frederick Kearsley lying on the bed, with his daughter, Kate, rocking back and forth by his side.

'I first felt for his pulse, and found that there wasn't one, the man was dead. I should think that about twenty-five minutes had elapsed from the time I was woken up to the time I actually got to the body. When I examined the man I should say he had been dead somewhere between forty and forty-five minutes. Mrs Kearsley could not give me a coherent version of what had happened, she was totally confused, hysterical almost. When I told her that her husband was dead she nodded her head vigorously, muttering, "He'd gone too far, I wasn't going to stand by and let him hurt Kate. No . . . I wasn't going to let that happen, not again."'

At this point the barrister held up his hand.

'You think Mrs Kearsley was aware of what she had done?'

Dr Pearson turned to face the judge, and asked, 'Do I have to answer that question?'

'Yes, I'm afraid you do,' came the stern reply.

'Then my answer has to be yes.'

'Thank you, Dr Pearson, please continue.'

'I leant over the body and saw a knife had been plunged into his back, just the one wound, no other bleeding points, but the blood had welled out, saturating the bedclothes he was lying on. I did not see any indications of a struggle having taken place.'

Dr Pearson was thanked and told he, too, could stand down.

Next came a gentleman who identified himself to the court as being the Senior Pathologist to the Home Office.

'I made a post-mortem examination of the body of Frederick Kearsley on the 2nd of November last. The body was that of a well-nourished and well-built man. I found one deep cut, delivered from behind. The knife had penetrated deep into the man's chest and that one blow was enough to have caused his death.'

The following day Kate was called upon to take the witness stand. Having given her full name and address she was asked to take her time and give her version of what had happened to cause her father's death.

'. . . I think matters came to a head when my father became aware that I knew he was having an affair with another woman. It was the day we had a terrible storm, my father was the worse for drink and in a terrible rage when he realised I had seen the two of them together.'

'You hadn't known about this association previous to this day?'

'No, sir, I had not.'

'Please go on, Miss Kearsley.'

'My father came racing out of Mrs Wilson's house, accusing me of spying on them. He bellowed at me, saying it was disgraceful that a girl should follow her father to find out what he was doing.' Kate's voice ended on a sob.

'Had you been keeping a constant watch on your father?'

'No, I hadn't. It was pure chance I came upon him and Mrs Wilson as I walked home from my grandma's.'

The barrister gave Kate a smile of encouragement before prompting her by saying, 'And then?'

'My father just went berserk. I'm sure he didn't know what he was doing. If he had been sober at the time he would not have hit me. He seemed to roar like a lion and . . . well, rush at me.'

'Miss Kearsley, are you telling the court that on this occasion, your father actually did you physical harm?'

'Yes, sir. Until I lost my footing and rolled down the bank he just went on hitting me.'

'And?'

She was tired and very near to tears.

'My father was full of remorse. For the next few weeks he was kindness itself to both me and my mother. Kind, but sort of edgy all the time.'

'That was how you would describe his behaviour up until the night of his death? Kind, remorseful, but on edge.'

'Yes, that's the best way I can put it.'

'Very well, Miss Kearsley, at this stage we won't put you through the ordeal of what happened on that fateful night. Thank you.'

Kate turned her gaze to meet the eyes of the grim-faced judge.

'You may leave the witness box, Miss Kearsley,' he said, in what it seemed to Kate was a very kindly manner. 'But please remember you may be required to give further evidence.'

Examinations continued until the name of Mrs Christine Wilson was called. Kate watched her mother closely. Her big frame had lost its firm look and she no longer held her head high. Most of the time her hands lay clenched in her lap, her head so low that her face was not to be seen, only her greying hair which was drawn back severely into a tight knot at the nape of her neck. This was the first time during the whole of the proceedings that she had seen any reaction from her mother.

As Mrs Wilson entered the witness box, her whole frame moved as she shuddered and Kate felt a longing to rise from her seat, rush across the floor of the court-room and throw her arms around her. How long since anyone had shown her the slightest affection? She wasn't a bad person. Of course she wasn't. Frosty, embittered. Yes, both of those things. But wicked? No. What she had done had been in her daughter's defence. Kate was hard pushed to keep back her tears.

Chris Wilson was in fine form.

Her hennaed hair looked as brassy as ever but she had taken pains with her make-up, going easy on the bright red lipstick. She wore a brown costume with a fawn blouse showing beneath it, which Kate thought suited her plump figure very well.

'I well remember the 31st of October,' Chris Wilson began her evidence, her voice strong and very assured. 'Fred Kearsley had spent the whole day with me, took me out an' about and during the late part of the evening we were together in my house. I should think it must have been going on for two o'clock in the morning when he left to go home.'

'Are we to take it that Mr Kearsley was a regular visitor to your home?'

Mrs Wilson drew herself up to her full height, stared straight into the barrister's eyes and took her time before answering his question.

'Mr Kearsley had been in the habit of visiting me at least once a week for the past eight years. I will tell you what his last words to me were. As I let him out of the door, he said, "I'll see you again soon, my love."'

'So, would it be true to say that you entertained men at your house and in return they gave you money?'

The forthright question seemed to shock Mrs Wilson and some few seconds passed before she was able to answer.

'That's not how it was at all,' she replied indignantly.

'You are telling the court there is no truth in that?'

By now Mrs Wilson was a very disgruntled witness.

'No, there's not,' she said, raising her voice to a much higher pitch. 'I'll have you know Fred Kearsley was my only gentleman friend, and God alone knows there were times when he sorely needed a friend and I like to think I was that friend.'

'Very well. Mrs Wilson will you please tell the court something of what you and Mr Kearsley did on that fateful day.'

'Well, I suppose seeing as how I'm on oath I've got to admit we drank far too much. Started at lunchtime we did, had a bit of a sleep in the afternoon, then went on a pub crawl in the evening and at turning-out time Fred bought a bottle of whisky to take back to my place. It was nearing midnight when he started to get argumentative and I annoyed him by taking the whisky bottle from him, going into the scullery and pouring what was left down the sink. That's when he tried to lay into me.'

'Are you telling the court that Mr Kearsley actually struck you?'

'He would have if I hadn't kicked him. The din he set up could have been heard yards away. It wouldn't be the first time he'd belted me, but that's not to say that Mr Kearsley was always violent, cos he wasn't. When he wasn't in drink he was a lovely man. Ever so kind an' generous.'

Just as Kate felt she could bear no more the judge said he was adjourning the proceedings until the next day.

Inwardly sobbing with rage and weakness Kate pushed aside the detective sitting beside her. She wanted to get out of the building, breathe some fresh air into her lungs. This portrayal of her father was absolutely dreadful. No one, least of all the likes of Chris Wilson, should be allowed to stand up in open court and tell the world that her father was a drunken, violent bully. If her mother had never said that much aloud, and she was the one who had cause, it wasn't right that a woman of that sort should be permitted to do so.

Kate hesitated outside the court, her head drooping with weariness. She couldn't go straight home to face her gran, although she asked no questions and had stead-fastly refused to accompany her to the court. What the old lady's thoughts were or even her intentions for the future, Kate had not the slightest idea.

She began to cry, as she slowly walked towards the river. No matter how hard she tried there was no getting away from the stark truth. Her mother had killed her father and it seemed very likely that the law of the land was going to decide that her mother should pay the price and die also.

Leaving the pathway, Kate sat down on the ground. Laying the flat of her hands on the cool, damp earth, she wished that all the pain and misery was over and done with.

'Are you awake, Kate?' Alice called softly in the darkness, sensing that she still was. She couldn't sleep either, the guilt she was feeling was stopping her from dropping off.

'Yes, Gran.'

Alice crossed the room to stand beside the bed. 'Are you all right, luv?'

Kate struggled to sit up. 'I keep thinking about tomorrow.'

'Yes, I know. Be all wrapped up, won't it?'

'So I've been told.'

Alice reached out and touched her arm. 'Do you hate me for not having been to the court with you?'

'No, 'course I don't. I've done my best to see your side in all of this. It can't have been easy for you.'

'Come to that, Kate my luv, it hasn't been easy for any of us. I thought it would break my heart losing my son, and it nearly did, but I've tried to keep going for your sake. There was an awful time when I could willingly have killed your mother myself, but now . . .' She started to sob.

It was the first time Kate had seen her cry.

'Imagine me feeling like that. Wanting to kill my own daughter-in-law. Pretty messy state of affairs all round.' Her words were muffled by her sobs.

'Please don't take on so,' Kate murmured, trying to comfort her.

Alice pulled Kate to her, held her tight, and began stroking her hair. 'It's what this mess is doing to you, that worries me. God knows what the long-term effect will be. I love you so much, lass. I would do anything to help you through it all, but I just couldn't bring myself to sit through those proceedings, hear all the details, face your mother. I just couldn't do it. I shan't blame you if you do end up hating me.'

'Stop saying that! You've been wonderful to me all my life. How things got to this pitch we'll never know, but whatever happens tomorrow, well, we'll have to live with it. I don't know how, but somehow I suppose we'll carry on. Have too, won't we?'

Alice had no answer to that, so she continued to stroke her granddaughter's hair. Then she said 'I think perhaps it would be better if I went back to live in my own place. You ought to think about going to stay with your aunt and uncle in London.'

Kate wriggled free from her arms. She knew her gran couldn't stay with her for ever.

'You're right, of course. I've kept you away from your animals for far too long and it is about time I began to stand on my own two feet.'

'Hmmh. We're not going to fall out over this, are we? I shan't be doing you any favours if I stay on here indefinitely. It's some young company you need around you not some old woman like me holding you back all the time. When the dust settles you have to look around you, start making decisions, live your life as you want to while you're still young enough to enjoy it. Anyway, since both of us are so

112

wide awake I'm going downstairs to make us a cup of tea. You tuck down in bed and I'll bring the tray up here.'

Alice still felt very guilty as she made her way down the stairs, ashamed of her cowardice in not going to the court. But she knew her decision had been the right one. Her daughter-in-law had no one to blame but herself for the predicament she was in. God help her. More to the point, God help young Kate, for it was she that was going to have to live the rest of her life with the aftermath of all this hanging over her.

Kate looked up at the stone steps leading to the court and began to feel light-headed. She didn't want to go in there today. Frowning, she stood still and took a deep breath.

The policeman at her side, glanced at her. 'You feeling all right, miss? You've gone very pale.'

Kate brushed a hand over her forehead and managed a weak smile. 'I'll be fine,' she said.

The burly copper nodded his head. He had a great deal of admiration for this young woman. She had stood up to the ordeal remarkably well. He sighed heavily, today would be different. Should be all over and as far as he could tell the outcome was a foregone conclusion.

'Come along, Miss Kearsley,' he said kindly. Taking hold of her arm he directed her towards the side door of the court. The crowds waiting to be admitted round the front seemed even greater today and she could surely do without any more harassment.

They had hardly settled in their seats when an usher called the court to order and the day's proceedings commenced once more.

*　　*　　*

Closing speech for the defence.

'May it please your lordship, members of the jury, the time has now arrived for me to perform the last part of the duty that has been assigned to me in presenting to you the defence to this charge of wilful murder against Hilda Kearsley. There is, and never has been, any dispute that Frederick Kearsley met his death because of one blow inflicted on him by his wife. That being the case, the facts are straight and simple. The only question for the jury is whether, from the facts placed before them, they are justified in bringing in a verdict of wilful murder or one of manslaughter, or some other verdict.

'Let us return to the night of the murder. I contend that everything points to the killing of Frederick Kearsley being an unpremeditated act by his wife.

'Everything that Frederick Kearsley did and said on the night of his murder indicates that he put his daughter in fear of her life. Hilda Kearsley heard her husband's frenzied attack on their daughter and did what any other mother would have done. She was horrified when she realised that in trying to ward off this drunken man she had, instead, killed him.

'What happened to her husband was a tragedy but it was in no way premeditated.

'This lady suffered intense loneliness and frustration. Her husband spent large sums of money on his mistress, Mrs Wilson, and was frequently drunk and violent. Hilda Kearsley is a lady; not one to complain. Her one aim in life was to see her only daughter happy. She bore in silence her husband's beatings – until he turned on Kate Kearsley.

'That ladies and gentlemen of the jury was one blow too far.

'It is for you to say whether the arguments I have put forward for your consideration are well founded. You must decide whether, beyond all reasonable doubt, Hilda Kearsley is guilty of murder. Or was her act unpremeditated, in which case, you must find her guilty of manslaughter.'

A drawn-out silence was followed by a shuffling of feet and a clearing of throats. Then another gentleman rose to his feet to give the closing speech for the prosecution.

'Your lordship, members of the jury, you have listened to an impressive and powerful speech from my learned friend. Now I ask that you treat this case as a straightforward murder. Do not be impressed or swayed by the fact that the prisoner is a woman. It is an indisputable fact that Mr Kearsley was killed in his own home, by his wife. Killed with a knife that she had ready to hand, which she had placed beneath a pillow days before. I have to tell you that it was a case of deliberate, premeditated murder. It will be for each of you to decide whether any of the arguments that have been put before you justify you in finding a lesser verdict than murder. It has been suggested that Hilda Kearsley acted, not with any intention to kill but purely in the defence of her daughter, and, therefore, the verdict ought to be one of manslaughter.

'It has also been suggested that this is a justifiable homicide on the part of Mrs Kearsley, which means that she acted in self-defence.

'Members of the jury, Frederick Kearsley was stabbed in the back. Therefore I put it to you that there is no evidence upon which you can reasonably or possibly come to the conclusion that the prisoner was acting in self-defence when she killed her husband. Your verdict has to be guilty of murder.'

As the judge made ready to sum up, Kate couldn't bear the pain as she looked at her mother. She had made no move to defend herself. Despite encouragement from all sources she had refused to make a single statement. Now she seemed to pull herself up to sit straight and face the judge. Her head was high almost as if it were an act of defiance. But her face was the colour of parchment and her eyes as they met Kate's for the first time since the trial had begun, held a look of sheer despair.

'My charge to you, members of the jury, is that there is only one indictment in this case, and that is the indictment of Hilda Kearsley for wilful murder. If you are satisfied that she intended to murder, then, of course you will find her guilty. You have to study the evidence very carefully, patiently and sensibly and acquit the prisoner unless you are satisfied that the case against her is proved beyond doubt.

'Her whole case is that she did not intend to kill. Ask yourselves then, why take a knife upstairs to the bedroom? Does one need a knife to frighten a drunken man into keeping his distance? She was shocked that just one blow, delivered in the heat of the moment, was enough to kill her husband. Could she have delivered that blow had the knife not been to hand?

'You will not convict unless you are satisfied that there was intent to kill. If you are not satisfied of that it will be your duty to acquit Hilda Kearsley. Will you please retire and consider your verdict.'

How much longer? Kate wondered as she watched the

men standing outside on the steps light up yet more cigarettes. For three hours now she had been in a quandary. Should she or shouldn't she stay to hear the verdict? Whatever the outcome she must hold her emotions in check. On no account must she scream.

'The jury is coming back!' someone shouted.

If her legs could have carried her, Kate would have run a mile at that moment.

'Come on, Miss Kearsley, soon be over now.' She felt her elbow taken in a strong grip and she was propelled back into the courtroom.

Soon be all over! For whom?

Whichever way the verdict has gone, it will never be all over for me, Kate told herself ruefully. This was a nightmare that would go on for as long as she lived.

The twelve good and true members of the community sat upright in the jury box, their faces blank. The clerk of the court faced them, his question directed at the foreman.

'Have you reached a verdict?'

'Yes, sir, we have.'

'And is it the verdict of you all?'

'Yes, sir, it is a unanimous verdict,' he answered, handing a slip of paper to the clerk, which he in turn handed up to the judge.

The judge scanned the paper in silence. Then, looking at the foreman of the jury he asked, 'Do you find the prisoner, Hilda Kearsley, guilty or not guilty of the murder of Frederick Kearsley?'

The foreman cleared his throat before making his reply, 'Guilty, sir.'

As if in a trance Kate watched as someone placed a

square of black cloth over the top of the judge's wig.

'Hilda Ellen Kearsley, you have been found guilty of murder. The sentence of the court upon you is that you be taken from this place to a lawful prison, where you will be held . . .'

Kate could bear no more. 'Oh dear Jesus!' She clenched her hands, tightening them until the knuckles were white. She had to get out of here. She struggled to stand up, her head spinning, her breath coming in short hard gasps. She put one foot forward, the room was spinning. Then mercifully, blackness.

When she came round she was sitting on the ground propped up against the stone wall of the Court House at the top of the steps. Her head throbbed and she could taste blood where she had bitten her lip so hard. She wiped her mouth with the sleeve of her coat and just sat staring into space.

'Come along, Miss Kearsley, we'll find someone to take you home.' The kindly police officer who had carried her from the court would have wrapped his arms around her shaking body if there hadn't been so many people around. It would be a wonder if she didn't lose her reason! First her father was murdered and now her mother was to hang. Just how much trouble could the good Lord heap on the shoulders of such a young girl?

'Come on, let's get you home,' he urged her more strongly.

'Home,' she repeated, parrot-fashion. 'Home to what?'

If only he had an answer for her. What this lass had to look forward to didn't bear thinking about.

Chapter Eleven

ON THE FIRST Monday in April, Kate walked slowly down the aisle of the lovely old Saint Peter's Church holding onto the arm of her Aunt Dolly. Reverend Hutchinson had suggested that she came to church on this morning; the morning her mother was to be hanged.

At this early hour there was no one else there. Alice had still refused even to talk about the outcome of her mother's trial, let alone come to church.

Kate thought it was good of her aunt to have come. No sign of Uncle Bert or her cousins but then she hadn't been expecting them.

'Much as I liked yer sister, you can't expect me t'go to the governor an' ask for time off t'attend me sister-in-law's funeral, now can yer, Dolly? Be fair. It ain't a funeral, is it? God rest 'er soul, it's a bloody 'anging!'

That was how Bert had argued his point.

Kate had half guessed at what had taken place as she listened to her aunt making her uncle's excuses.

119

Rough-and-ready Joe Blunt was Bert Hopkins. Different as chalk and cheese had been her parents' marriage and that of her aunt's. Time had proved which sister had experienced the happiest years. For all the pinching and scraping to make ends meet you'd hardly ever see Dolly and Bert Hopkins without a smile on their faces. The same could never have been said about her parents.

This morning Dolly looked different. Huge dark eyes in a pale white face. Her clothes didn't help. Thick black skirt, black blouse, black coat, thick black stockings and black button-up boots. On top of her straggly hair she wore a wide-brimmed, black felt hat anchored down by two enormous hatpins.

Kate was wearing a simple fitted dark-grey coat which had a small cape fastened beneath the collar allowing it to flow around her shoulders. Alice had shown good taste when buying it. Kate also had on a black felt hat pushed to the back of her head. It had a broad, high brim with narrow black ribbons as its only adornment. Beneath it, her face was also the colour of chalk. She had tucked her unruly hair tightly beneath the brim of the hat, but as usual odd strands had broken loose and lay on her white forehead and around her ears. A door opening made her look up, and Reverend Hutchinson came to stand in front of the pew where they were sitting. Kate stole a glance at her watch. It wanted just two minutes till eight o'clock.

Quietly the vicar began to pray. 'Though I shall walk through the valley of the shadow of death I shall fear no evil, for thou art with me. Thy rod and thy staff they comfort me.'

Kate put her finger into her mouth, and bit it so hard that she drew blood.

Two days ago they had allowed her to see her mother. Calm, utterly composed, Hilda had not spoken one word. Just held onto Kate's hand, her thumb moving in circles across the back of it the whole time. Not even a goodbye when the wardress had told Kate it was time for her to go. Just one last, long hug and then her mother had gently pushed her away. There had been a smile on her face as she had turned at the doorway to look back. The most sweet and loving smile. It had seemed filled with longing.

And now . . . it was time!

Somewhere, far off, a clock chimed eight.

She was no longer even sure how she felt; it was as if her insides were frozen. There was a sense of loss, of broken promises, of utter, deep despair.

Her mother was dead. She and her father were both gone.

Kate swallowed, stopping herself by force from being sick. Slowly she sank down onto her knees. She was crying now, her tears dripped onto the hassock on which she knelt. She moved her right hand, seeking comfort. Aunt Dolly, herself now crying profusely, took hold and held on tightly as though she too was finding it all too much to bear.

James Hutchinson put his hand on Kate's shoulder. 'The horror will lessen, Kate, the memory will fade.'

'Will it?' she asked pitifully.

Would it ever? She very much doubted it. This day, this hour, this exact minute would stay with her, imprinted on her mind for the rest of her life. A beam of sunlight hit the stained glass window high above the altar, sending down into the well of the church a ray that could almost be called a rainbow. Or perhaps, she thought wistfully, a stairway to heaven. Emotion stronger than any she'd ever previously experienced welled up inside her, rendering her speechless. For a while time stood still and she felt at peace . . .

Aunt Dolly was pulling her to her feet, 'Come on, pet, time t'go.'

Reverend Hutchinson shook hands with each of them in turn.

'God bless you both. I'll remember you in my prayers, Kate,' he said, praying that this young girl would survive the ordeal she had been forced to suffer and that happier times lay ahead.

Dry-eyed and utterly miserable Kate allowed Dolly to hold her close and kiss her on both cheeks.

'Now you promise, luv. Two weeks to sort things out. Listen t'what yer dad's solicitor 'as t'say, then shut the front door an' come t'London. You'll be right surprised as t'what good a change of scenery will do for you.'

'All right, Aunt Dolly. I promise. Two weeks and then I'll arrive on your doorstep.'

'Good girl. Meanwhile, you do yer best to set things right with yer gran. Just try an' remember, luv, it's been damned 'ard for 'er as well. Like every mother she idolised 'er son. Now he's gone an' you're all she's got left, apart from some wonderful neighbours so she tells me.'

'I'll do my best,' Kate promised meekly.

The tram came rattling into view. Dolly kissed her

again. 'Do try an' put the past behind you, luv,' she murmured.

Kate made no promise as she handed her aunt's shopping bag up to where she stood on the outside platform of the tram. 'Bye, auntie, thank you for coming, and . . . thanks for everything.'

'Just get yerself sorted, pet. An' I'll be expecting yer. Two weeks mind, no longer.'

Kate waved until the tram was out of sight. Then, taking a scarf from out of her coat pocket she wound it round her neck, pulled her hat down harder over her ears, and her gloves onto her hands before setting off to walk beside her beloved river Thames.

She didn't have any idea what she was going to do next, never mind with the rest of her life and, more to the point, she didn't really care.

Chapter Twelve

'AUNT DOLLY.' KATE stood at the kitchen door, waiting. 'It's Saturday. You said we were going to the market. If we don't hurry surely we'll be too late?'

Dolly threw back her head and laughed loudly.

'You're in the East End now, my love, the stalls in the markets will be doing business till ten o'clock tonight. They probably do a third of their trade when the pubs turn out.'

Kate had been staying with her aunt and uncle for almost a week now. Try as she would she didn't like being there one little bit. The houses and tenements were horrible, soot blackened and identical, huddled together in rows, front doors opening directly onto the pavement. Her aunt and uncle were better off than most. They lived in a funny little house, which had no inside toilet and no bathroom whatsoever. It was at the end of a narrow street which backed onto a yard belonging to the Sunlight Laundry. The yard was used for the vans that came in and out from morning till night.

The day she had arrived a long-legged young man with a saucy smile had swung down from the back of a white van and actually asked if she wanted to go up to the pub with him to have a drink. She could not believe the cheek of the man. The next day she had been standing in the street, trying to get a breath of air, for it was stifling inside her aunt's house, when the same young lad with the cheeky smile and a mop of brown wavy hair, had come out of the yard and walked up to her. Before she could return his greeting, he had put an arm around her shoulders and planted a wet kiss on her cheek.

'He don't mean no 'arm.' A middle-aged woman who lived next door grinned as Kate pushed the lad away. She looked a kind, cheerful woman. Her top front teeth stuck out over her bottom lip and they were badly discoloured. She wore a sack apron over her flowered dress and what looked like men's lace-up boots on her feet and a man's flat cap stuck on her head. For a moment Kate was reminded of Mrs Bates who did the cleaning at Melbourne Lodge. No, that was unfair, Kate chided herself, Mrs Bates never looked as rough as this cheery London woman did.

The thought of Melbourne Lodge had Kate yearning for those days. It seemed almost another lifetime since she had walked the leafy lanes and taken tea with dear Mary. So much had happened since then! She had received letters of condolence both from Mary and from Mr Collier for which she was very grateful. So many so-called friends and acquaintances had crossed the road rather than speak to her since her father had died. Who could blame them? What does one say to a girl whose mother has killed her father?

Victor Appleton didn't court her any more, which was very funny when she came to think about it. After all, she had never been under any illusions about his feelings. Victor's and his father's main interest had always been in the Kearsley Boat Yard; being on the part of the river that ran so close to Hampton Court made it a very valuable site. Now it seemed she was tainted. Not good enough for Victor Appleton, because of the notorious reputation attached to her by her mother. What difference that made to the business she had yet to fathom out.

Oh dear! Kate shook her head, how could I have been so thoughtless? Thinking of Melbourne Lodge brought Jane Mortimer to her mind. Her baby had been due at Christmas! God, I hope she was delivered safely. Whatever must they think of me never to have been in touch? The very least I could have done was enquire from Mary as to how Jane was managing. Christmas had come and gone in Bramble Cottage with both Gran and me too mixed up to have anything to celebrate.

'You sitting in there daydreaming, Kate?' Dolly's sharp voice made her jump.

'No, just thinking,' she answered with a sigh.

'Never a day passes but what I don't think about your mother,' Dolly shouted from the scullery. 'There's not many sisters got on as well as me an' her did.'

You never came near her for months on end, Kate muttered under her breath. Aloud she asked, 'Where's Uncle Bert?'

'Where he always is on Saturday mornings. Up the

flaming pub. If I 'ad me way he'd take his bed up there an' give me a bit of peace.'

Dolly passed Kate a cup of tea, so strong it looked more like prune juice. That seemed to be the way folk liked to drink their tea in London. Hot and strong, even stewed, as long as the spoon stood up in the cup. That was another thing. She had never seen anyone put so many spoonfuls of sugar into one cup as her twin cousins did.

''Elps it stick to yer ribs,' Stan had teased her when she had passed comment.

'Thanks,' Kate said as she sipped at the tea from the thick, heavy cup. 'Am I stopping you from getting on?'

'No, course you ain't, luv. You don't know 'ow 'appy I am to 'ave you.' She stretched out her arms and Kate went into them. 'You ain't altogether 'appy 'ere though, are you, Kate?' Dolly sounded serious for once as she softly stroked her niece's long hair.

Kate coughed to cover the sudden rush of tears, telling herself she should feel glad to be here. Those two weeks in Bramble Cottage had been so lonely and terrifying. When she did manage to get off to sleep it was never very long before she was sitting bolt upright again, covered in a cold sweat, her chest heaving. To her embarrassment it had happened twice since she'd been here in London. The first time it had frightened Hilda out of her wits. Aunt Dolly had rushed in, telling both girls that it was only a nightmare. Only a nightmare! Her aunt had no idea how unbearably real it always seemed.

Awake or asleep the screaming was the worst. If she lived to be a hundred she knew there would never be a time when she would be able to blot from her mind entirely the sound of her mother's shrill, piercing, agonised screams which had seemed to go on for ever after she had struck that fatal blow. And there was always the image of her father! A big hefty man to be struck down by one single stab from a knife.

Daytimes, alone in the cottage, had been almost as bad. No one to talk to, to share a pot of tea with. No one to give her a bit of a cuddle when she was feeling down. Here, it was the exact opposite. The little house was teeming with people, young and old, morning, noon and night. The boys were on opposite shifts, which meant meals on the table at all odd hours. Hilda came home at lunchtime, bringing mates with her everyday. Neighbours were in and out, calling over the wall, shouting down the passageway from the street. There wasn't a moment's peace to be had.

The nicest rooms in this funny house were the kitchen and the scullery that adjoined it. At least that's how Kate saw it. Whitewashed walls, deep brownstone sink with a brass tap and a great wooden plate rack above it which Uncle Bert had made.

'Mind you, that's why the plates 'ave so many chips out of them,' Dolly complained. 'No one puts them in the rack gently, in too much of a ruddy 'urry to worry about being careful.'

The kitchen floor was covered in cracked lino, red in colour, and the pans hanging from the wall over the fireplace were enamel not copper as they were back home. Still, the black-leaded range was lovely. A fire was kept going all the time and a huge black kettle, always full, sang away. In the centre of the room was the kitchen table, the top scrubbed till it was as white as any butcher's block. Only on Sundays, high days and holidays was it covered with Dolly's best tablecloth.

Many a tale could be told of what went on when the whole family gathered around that table. It was an experience Kate had never known in her life before. And some evenings the loud chatter, the merriment and the jovial teasing made her feel so sad. There was no getting away from it, she was an outsider, she didn't belong here in London and no matter how hard she might try she knew she would never entirely fit in.

'Aunt Dolly, I would like to go home soon. Not that . . . I . . .' Kate's voice trailed off in embarrassment.

Dolly took her hands out of the bowl of soapy water and turned to face Kate. 'Now you don't mean that, luv. You've not given yourself a chance to settle in. There's our 'ilda's wedding t'think about and you know she's put in a word for you to 'ave a job alongside her. You'd like working with a load of other young girls, you'd 'ave a laugh – go out together. Especially weekends, maybe meet a few lads. God knows you've lived a sheltered life for far too long. It's 'igh time you went out into the world, see 'ow the other 'alf live.'

'Oh, Aunt Dolly! Please, I don't want to sound ungrateful but that kind of life is not for me. I don't need to work in a factory. My father has left me well provided for. Our house is bought and paid for and the boat yard is being sorted out.'

'What d'yer mean by being sorted out? Is it t'be sold?'

'No. The solicitor said Dad was very wise when he made his will. Everything would have gone to my mother, but in the event that I was the one to inherit,

I could dispose of nothing until I reach the age of twenty-five.'

''Ow the 'ell can a slip of a girl like you be expected to run a boat yard? It's only men that work there, ain't it?'

Kate found herself laughing. 'What difference does that make, Auntie?'

'A ruddy lot in my book. Can't 'ave you scrambling about in an' out over sides of boats. Wouldn't be decent, not with men looking on.'

'There's never been any intention of me working there. Dad has employed a foreman cum manager for years. Jack Stuart his name is and the firm of solicitors stand by Dad's judgement. They say he's a sound worker, happily married with three kiddies, and that under his management there will be enough income to keep me in comfort.'

'But you'll go barmy! Sitting alone in that cottage, nothing t'do, no one t'look after yer. Never going out t'work, t'aint natural. That's been more than 'alf the trouble with my sister all these years. If she 'ad 'ad t'get up off 'er backside an' do a 'ard day's work she wouldn't 'ave 'ad time t'dwell on all her supposed troubles.'

Kate sighed. She would have liked to stand up for her mother, telling how well she kept the house, all the baking she did, providing wonderful meals and spending time doing exquisite needlework. Better to keep quiet. After all, she was in her aunt's house and as such she should keep her opinions to herself.

'No, I'm not 'aving you going back 'ome, at least not yet.' Dolly flopped down in a chair to sit opposite her. 'You ain't given yerself a chance t'see whether you like living up 'ere or not. Besides you must be 'ere for your cousin's wedding. Our 'ilda can't possibly get married without you being there. Tell yer what, luv, I bet she's just waiting for a chance t'ask yer t'be 'er bridesmaid.'

Kate did her best to smile, touched as always by her aunt's intensity. She knew she was trying to impress on her the fact that she was part and parcel of their family, even if they were only her poor relations.

'It'll be a proper do. 'Onest it will, Kate. A real East End turn out.' Dolly's eyes sparkled with amusement, then suddenly darkened. 'Kate, I 'ope our 'ilda is doing the right thing. Benny Withers is a real catch, there's no doubt about that. You 'aven't 'ad a chance to meet 'im yet, but you will. He's got a finger in more pies than I could ever keep count of, not much in the way of social graces – been too busy making money to take much bother over his manners. There's always rumours going round about him, folk love to gossip, still he swears our 'ilda is the first girl he's ever asked to marry 'im. Suppose that's something in his favour.' Suddenly the excitement in Dolly bubbled up again and she wrapped her arms over her flat chest and grinned at Kate. 'Reckons he's gonna buy an 'ouse up 'Amstead way. Can you imagine it!'

Kate made no reply. She was thinking of the first night she'd been here when Hilda had been getting ready to go out with Ben Withers and Uncle Bert had complained about the amount of rouge she had put on her cheeks. Hilda had said her goodbyes and made her escape.

Once she had gone, Dolly, doing her best to keep the peace, had said to Bert, 'Don't know why you don't like

Benny, he's never done us any 'arm. A bit of a rough diamond maybe, but he's all right.'

'Hmm. He's rough all right,' Uncle Bert had declared, stomping out of the room, muttering fiercely to himself.

Kate had stayed quiet on that occasion, and she stayed quiet now, her head hanging low, her fingers fidgeting nervously in her lap. She didn't want to meet this Ben Withers, and as to being a bridesmaid at her cousin's wedding, the very thought terrified her.

Dolly's conscience came to the fore as she gazed at this lovely niece of hers. Kate wasn't right. Each day she should be getting a bit better, putting the past behind her, but she wasn't. The girl was never at ease. Jittery was the only word that came to mind and, God help her, she felt useless just looking at her. Kate needed help, there was no getting away from that fact. The kind of help that neither she nor any member of her family seemed able to give her. Oh Kate! she thought, whatever is to become of you?

Aloud, she said, 'You miss your mum an' dad.' It was a statement not a question.

Kate nodded her head and sighed deeply.

'Course y'do, luv. But life 'as t'go on.'

'That's all everyone seems to be telling me these days. But what life is there for me? That's what I'd like to know.'

'Why don't yer try and settle down 'ere, amongst yer own family? After all yer mum were me only sister. In time you'd get used to going out to work, once you met up with girls of yer own age.'

Just for a moment Kate felt awful. Why couldn't she be more grateful. Do as her aunt wanted her to? Stay here for ever. She cringed at the thought. This tiny cramped house got her down. Going with Bert to his allotment was the best part. There he toiled endlessly to grow vegetables and even some flowers in the poor dusty soil.

'I'm ever so grateful to you and Uncle Bert, really I am,' Kate murmured in appreciation, 'and I will try a bit harder. Do you mind if I go for a walk now?'

''Course not, luv, I'll be finished 'ere shortly, then I'll get meself ready an' we'll go shopping. Just don't go too far. Hang about up by the corner. You should meet our 'Ilda coming 'ome; she finishes at twelve on a Saturday.'

They smiled at each other, both secretly relieved that Kate had made the decision to leave the house for a while.

Kate had walked a lot further than she had intended. She paused to stare up at several blocks of tenements. How dirty and dingy they looked, she thought. Each level had a corridor that ran right outside people's front doors and was criss-crossed with washing lines. She supposed that the washing had to be dried somewhere, but how awful to have to live like that. She couldn't imagine getting up in the morning and never being able to walk out into a garden. However small, a garden provided so many things to do and see. She lowered her eyes to the entrance of these buildings. Gosh, what a shambles! She could only gape, wide eyed. A long line of what looked to be coal sheds; did folk really have to come down several floors with a bucket and shovel to get their coal? How, for goodness' sake, did they manage to carry the heavy bucket all the way back up to where they lived? Besides that, look at the junk! There were prams, pushchairs, bikes and barrows of all shapes and sizes. The whole place was strewn with litter, cats and dogs roaming free, not to mention the hordes of yelling, grubby-looking children, and hoarse-voiced vendors hawking their wares.

Two old women in tattered coats and greasy felt hats slouched by. They looked dirty and they certainly smelt funny. They never even sent a glance in Kate's direction. At home in Littleton Green no one passed without a cheery greeting and, as for the river folk, well . . . that very thought brought a lump to Kate's throat and tears to her eyes, and with shoulders drooping, she retraced her footsteps.

Come Monday morning, Dolly watched as Kate packed her clothes neatly into the small case she had brought with her.

'Kate, we none of us want you t'go back t'live on yer own.'

'I won't be on my own all the time. You mustn't worry about me. Gran only lives in Kingston, which isn't so far away. And then I've plenty of neighbours, besides I've made up my mind to call in at Melbourne Lodge. Mary Kennedy's always been a good friend, she might even find me some work to do, just to keep my mind occupied.'

Dolly nodded, admitting defeat.

When it came time to say goodbye she had the feeling that her aunt was, in some ways, relieved to see her go. She didn't blame her one little bit; after all she hadn't exactly been the best of company.

Chapter Thirteen

KATE COULDN'T BELIEVE it. She had only been home for four days and here was Mr Collier sitting opposite her in what had been her mother's front parlour. He was the last person she had expected to find when she opened her front door in answer to his knock.

'So how are you, Kate?' he asked.

Kate's reply was a slight shrug.

'You're looking very thoughtful.'

'To tell you the truth, Mr Collier, at this moment I'm feeling very guilty. I haven't enquired as to how any of you at Melbourne Lodge have been faring.'

'That's very understandable. You have had so much to cope with, but you have constantly been in our thoughts and Mary sends you her love and said to make sure I let you know how much she is looking forward to seeing you.'

Kate's face lit up with pleasure. 'Oh, please thank her. And what of Miss Jane, and the baby, did she have a boy or a girl?'

'Jane gave birth to a little boy three days before Christmas. He's doing remarkably well. We've named him Joshua.'

Kate's smile broadened. 'Oh, how lovely, I can't wait to see him. And is Miss Jane all right? She must be very happy.'

There was a long-drawn-out pause and Kate raised her eyes to meet Mr Collier's. She knew straight off that something was dreadfully wrong.

'Jane died . . . of a haemorrhage,' he said quietly.

Kate sucked her breath in sharply. How terrible! What could she say? She had been so wrapped up in her own affairs that she hadn't given these kind friends a thought.

'I am so sorry.' The few words she managed came out as little more than a whisper. 'I just can't find words . . .'

Mr Collier nodded wretchedly. 'There's nothing one can say. No one knows that better than you do, Kate. I found writing that short note to you one of the hardest tasks I've ever had to do.'

'How have you been managing with the baby?'

'Getting by. But only just.'

'Mr Collier, may I ask you a question?'

'Certainly, ask away.'

'You said 'we' named the baby Joshua.'

'Yes. This is a bit awkward. I rather feel I have relied far too much on Mary since Jane died. Mary is more than just a housekeeper, she's become, over the years, a very good friend and it was she who came up with the name. Since both of Jane's parents are dead there was no one else for me to confer with. Mary also helped me to find a daytime nurse for the baby but it has fallen to her to cope with the nights. May I be perfectly frank with you, Kate?'

'Yes, of course.'

'You know the circumstances of my relationship with Jane so you must realise the stigma that will be attached to Joshua. Through no fault of his own, disgrace will inevitably follow him throughout his entire life. I shall do my utmost to relieve at least some of that handicap. With my wife still alive it is impossible for me to acknowledge him as my son. To the outside world that is.' Mr Collier paused, a deep frown creasing his forehead.

Kate groaned inwardly, not knowing how she could help.

'If you will bear with me I will set out the main reason for my being here today. But before I put it to you I would like you to know that the proposal came from Mary Kennedy herself. Would you consider moving into Melbourne Lodge and taking charge of Joshua on a long-term basis?'

'Oh, I couldn't,' Kate protested, 'I've had no training to be a nurse.'

'Training is not what is needed, my dear Kate. Common sense and a loving, caring attitude is going to be of more importance to Joshua as time goes on than all the authoritative approach of an official nanny. Please, Kate, will you consider it?'

Kate nodded but didn't reply. This was a bolt out of the blue.

'I would make adequate and binding arrangements, both for you and my son. You would need have no fear of the future. I am not a young man; chances are I shall not live to see Joshua grow into manhood. His education and his well-being will be provided for and should you do me the honour of taking on the task of bringing him up as if he were your own, you too will be protected.'

Kate was utterly lost and it showed on her face.

'You do like babies, don't you?'

This sudden question made her smile. 'Yes, doesn't everyone?'

'Indeed they do not,' Mr Collier replied and he too was smiling. 'I'll tell you what, why don't you give yourself time to think about my proposal and in the meantime come along and meet Joshua, have tea with Mary. She will be so pleased to see you.'

'I'd like to do that, but I'm not sure I want to give up this cottage and move into Melbourne Lodge.'

'My dear Kate, no one is asking you to give up your home. That would be foolish. If you do agree to take care of my son, you will still have time off, time to lead your own life and Bramble Cottage could be a bolt-hole for you if ever Joshua has a day when he never stops crying.'

'Oh, Mr Collier, you're teasing me now. As if I'd come away from the house if the baby were in a fretful mood.'

He beamed. 'Ahh, so you *are* considering coming to share the Lodge with Mary and taking care of the baby?'

'I didn't say that.' But she was finding it difficult not to be swept along by his enthusiasm.

'Believe me, Kate, I have spent long hours giving this matter a great deal of thought. There will be a number of prejudiced people from all walks of life who will turn against Joshua because he happened to be born out of wedlock. I am doing my best to protect him from such folk.

'Luckily enough, my financial situation is such that I am able, in a somewhat limited way, to ensure that these slights will not affect him too much. Money talks all languages, Kate. You will do well to remember that. But, and it is a very big but, there isn't enough money in the world to provide my son with the love and affection he would have had had his mother lived. I do believe, however, should you decide to become Joshua's guardian, he will be getting the best substitute for Jane that I could possibly find.'

'Oh, Mr Collier! I'm only nineteen years old, surely the law would not allow me to become a child's guardian. Besides . . .' she paused and took a deep breath, 'I still need time, time to come to terms with the fact that both my parents are dead, time to really think about what I want to do.'

'I don't mean to rush you into making a decision, I appreciate what you say and as for you becoming Joshua's guardian let me reassure you.' He leant forward and took Kate's hand between his. 'All the time I am alive I shall be his legal custodian, there's no two ways about that. When I am no longer around . . . Well, as I've already said, ample provision will be made both for you and for Joshua. No one, and I mean no one, would have the power to remove him from your care if you did decide to take him on.'

'You seem to have thought of everything, but what I don't understand is, why me?'

'To be honest, many professional nurses would be reluctant to take on an illegitimate child, more so to take charge when there is not even one parent living in the same house.'

'I see,' Kate murmured, sounding very doubtful.

'I don't think you do, my dear. Mary is loathe to have a stranger move into the Lodge, especially as they would be at liberty to leave at will. I owe Mary a lot and my plans have to include her long-term well-being as much as Joshua's. When she put it to me that since the death of Jane she felt very much alone living in that big house and she felt you must also be in need of company, she didn't need to elaborate further. I thought of it as a God-sent solution. You really would be doing me a great kindness.'

Kate made no reply, and a minute or two passed before he added, 'One answer might be for you to visit Mary and meet the baby as we have already decided you would, and then before you commit yourself to any long-term arrangements pack a few things and stay at the Lodge for a few days. A trial run might help you to make a decision, don't you think?' He looked at his watch. 'I have to be going. I've taken up quite enough of your time.'

Time is what I have plenty of, Kate told herself, it's company I lack.

'Just promise me you will give a lot of thought to what I'm asking. There is no hurry. I wouldn't expect you to move in to Melbourne Lodge until you are absolutely sure that it was right for you to do so.'

Kate took the hand he held out. 'I'd hoped to find work of some kind, but . . .'

'Well, there we are. God moves in a mysterious way.'

They left it at that. But it was a very thoughtful Kate who watched as Mr Collier doffed his tall hat to her before walking off along the towpath.

Chapter Fourteen

I DO MISS Mum and Dad, Kate thought, as she dusted the china which stood on the dresser. She missed them more than she cared to admit even to herself. But she wasn't going to let her loneliness influence her decision as to whether or not she would go and live in Melbourne Lodge.

Gran had told her she would be daft not to. Poor Gran! She had aged terribly since they had buried her son. She hardly ever came out to Littleton Green these days, but she was always pleased to see Kate when she appeared in Kingston unannounced.

She reached up to replace a tiny figurine and, as she did so, she smiled. Her father had taken her and her mother to the Derby at Epsom and she had bought the statuette as a present for her mum. Derby Day wouldn't be the same without the Epsom Fair.

Kate sighed. All these memories she was left with.

Whenever she opened a cupboard or a drawer she had to blink back tears. Between her mother's underclothes she had found silver-framed photographs of her parents' wedding and of her brother David. The big old chest on the landing contained stacks of winter woollies, mostly hand-knitted by her mother. In the spare bedroom stood a tall lightweight set of drawers, used by her father as a filing cabinet, full of documents to do with the boat yard going back more than two generations.

I suppose I ought to invite Jack Stuart up to the house and let him go through that lot. She mulled the matter over. After all he was in charge of the business now.

Then there were her father's suits and the lovely dresses belonging to her mother, many of which had hung for so long unworn at the back of her wardrobe. What, she wondered, should she do with all these items? As she went from room to room, sometimes she found something that had her laughing outright, other times she was reduced to tears.

Yesterday she had gone berserk. Scrubbing and scouring the house from top to bottom. Chucking out so much stuff that she'd come to the conclusion she'd have to find a totter with a big cart to take away the mound that was now blocking the back gate.

The trouble was, every decision made had to be hers. There was no one else.

During the days that followed Mr Collier's visit, Kate spent a lot of her time walking by the river. Although May was almost out, the nights were still a little chilly, but it made no difference. Sometimes she did not return to Bramble Cottage until it was quite dark. Wearing a scarf over her head, an old mackintosh and proper walking shoes, she trudged miles.

By the first week of June Kate's decision whether or not

to live at Melbourne Lodge had become slightly easier. She had woken early one morning with a very sore throat and realised that, for the very first time in her life, she was virtually alone. There was no one near who would know whether she was sick or well except Dr Pearson and the Reverend Hutchinson who had repeatedly checked on her. It was then that she made her decision. She would take up Mr Collier's kind offer. Suddenly she very much wanted to go and live at Melbourne Lodge.

I've been very selfish, she chided herself, not giving a moment's thought how Mary feels about all of this. She was a bit long in the tooth to be having to take charge of a young baby during the night, and she must be feeling lonely. Taking care of Mr Collier and Jane had filled her life. Kate found herself wondering whether Mr Collier spent as much time at the Lodge as he used to. Poor Mary's life had been turned upside down.

I really must make the effort and at least pay her a visit before anything is finally decided, Kate rebuked herself, picturing the plump, homely face of her dear friend. Mary was the kindest, most decent person she knew. She did not have a bad bone in her body, was always considerate, and generous to a fault. She had never heard her say an unkind word about anyone, and knew that she spent a great deal of her time helping those less fortunate than herself.

Kate felt she couldn't stand being on her own in the cottage for a moment longer. Abruptly, she jumped up and started to get herself ready. Twenty minutes later, she closed the front door behind her and hurried off down the garden path.

* * *

It was a gorgeous morning. The sky was clear blue, without a cloud in sight, and although it had only just turned nine o'clock the sun was really warm. She walked quickly, turning off the towpath into the leafy green lanes which held so many memories – most of them good – and felt she was about to solve some of her problems.

Because it was such a nice day Kate had left her coat at home and was wearing a white dress patterned with tiny blue flowers, with a darker blue shawl thrown round her shoulders. On her feet she had her favourite sandals, made of a wonderful soft brown leather.

As Kate approached the Lodge, she saw Mary setting the baby's pram outside in the sunshine. The moment Kate set foot on the drive Mary looked up and saw her. Kate flew the yards that separated them, straight into the older woman's arms and they held each other tightly, each taking comfort from the other's presence. Kate let out a contented sigh, feeling more secure than she had done for a very long time.

Finally they drew apart, and Mary looked up into Kate's pretty face. 'My God, Kate, you're a sight for sore eyes. I can't tell you how pleased, and, yes, relieved I am to see you.'

'Me too,' Kate managed to murmer, hastily sniffing away her tears.

Nothing much had changed in Melbourne Lodge since she had last been here almost a year ago. The instant Kate stepped inside the large, familiar kitchen she felt at home.

'Take your shawl off, and go and put it in my sitting room,' Mary said. It was on the tip of her tongue to say, you're as thin as a rake, but she thought better of it.

To Kate, Mary's sitting room had always been one of the prettiest rooms in the Lodge, decorated by Mary herself many years ago when she had first come here as housekeeper. The walls were a soft peach, the carpet beige, while the chairs and sofa that gave some bright colour to the room were floral chintz. One wall was covered with white painted shelves which held many books and a stack of magazines. Instantly Kate imagined herself and Mary on cold winter's nights sitting in this room, the log fire blazing in the grate and the two of them peacefully reading.

'What would you like to drink?' Mary asked as she came back into the kitchen.

'Tea will be fine, please,' she answered, smiling because Mary had already set out the tray and a big home-made cake.

'Oh, Kate!' Mary took hold of her arm. 'I've worried myself sick over you.'

It was true, she had longed to go to Kate and time after time she had set out only to turn back again. Now her relief that Kate was safe and well and, more to the point, here in the flesh, so overwhelmed her that she was near to tears.

They sat at the table, drinking their tea and catching up as best they could without going into sad details, so happy to be in each other's company the time just flew by.

'I'm so comforted by the thought that you will be coming to live here. I'm not jumping the gun, am I? You being here today does mean that you have agreed to Mr Collier's proposal, doesn't it? I don't think I could manage the baby on my own during the night time, not for much longer, I couldn't.'

Kate gave her time to get her breath back before looking across the table. 'I'm looking forward now, Mary, to being with you and to taking care of Joshua. By the way, where is he?'

As if on cue, the kitchen door opened and a woman dressed in a nurse's uniform stepped in, a bonny baby, looking every inch a boy, bouncing in her arms.

'This is Miss Parker, Kate. Come along it's high time you two met.' Mary beamed, taking six-month-old Joshua into her arms and leaving the nurse free to shake Kate's hand.

Miss Parker was a tall, thin lady, her back was as straight as a ramrod and she held her head so high, that when she faced Kate, it appeared as if she were looking down her nose at her. It was only when she said, 'Hallo, Kate, I'm Ethel,' and, smiling gently, sat herself down opposite her, that Kate began to think she had been too quick in jumping to the wrong conclusion where Miss Parker was concerned.

Kate rose and went round the table to where Mary was holding the baby. She stared, long and hard, totally captivated. 'Oh, he's absolutely delightful,' she whispered. Her hand sought his tiny fingers and when they curled round her forefinger she stood still, mesmerised by his perfection. Such clear skin, soft blond downy hair and blue eyes the likes of which she had not seen before. 'He has his mother's colouring, don't you think so?'

'Why not let Kate hold him?' Ethel Parker suggested.

'I hadn't better, he's not used to me, he might cry.'

'What could you do to him that would make him cry?' Miss Parker asked, pretending innocence.

'Get on with you, she's teasing you. We both know this is the best-behaved baby there ever was. He'll go to anyone, doesn't seem to give a fig just so long as someone is taking notice of him. He won Mrs Bates over before he was a week old.'

'Is Mrs Bates still working here?' Kate asked, suppressing a giggle.

'Yes, still comes three times a week, still putting the world to rights, as she sees it. Only yesterday she was saying she hoped you were going to come and live here. Mr Collier told her what he had in mind and even he was astounded when she told him she heartily approved.'

Mary gently placed Joshua in Kate's arms and Miss Parker looked on with a smile on her lips. 'There, you see, it's not so difficult. A baby knows how to snuggle up and it also knows when loving care is being showered on it. Joshua will take to you like a duck to water.'

Mary gave Kate a faint smile, and she smiled back. But there was sadness in her smile and Mary thought again of the amount of pain she had suffered. There must have been times when the sorrow had been almost unbearable. Who knew what scars would be left on her? She suppressed a sigh. She would do everything within her power to make Kate's life a happier one. Coming here to live and taking charge of the tiny infant she was nursing so gently, might be just what she needed. A blessing in disguise that's what it was!

'This calls for a celebration,' she declared. 'How about we have a glass of sherry before I start on the lunch?'

'That would be lovely,' Miss Parker answered.

Kate raised her head but still kept her tight hold on the baby. 'Yes please, Mary, I'd like that.'

Handing them each a brimming glass, Mary said, 'Here's to friendship and a long and happy life to this young man.' She nodded her head towards the baby and raised her glass in a toast.

'Friendship and the baby's well-being,' Kate and Miss Parker chorused.

'You two sit there and get to know each other while I prepare a few vegetables,' Mary instructed.

Kate was more than happy to do as she was told just so long as she was allowed to keep hold of Joshua. And after only a short while she realised what Mary had already discovered, that Ethel Parker was a kind woman who only held back because of her shyness.

That wasn't the only reason Kate was smiling to herself. She had the distinct feeling she had made the right decision. She would care for this baby as if he were her own. It would be a hard struggle to put the past behind her, but if she didn't succeed it wouldn't be for want of trying. The past had to be just that. Life was for living and, today, she felt better than she had in a long time. Somehow the future no longer looked quite so bleak.

'I'd better see about taking Joshua for his walk. Would you like to come with me? You can push the pram if you like.' Miss Parker broke into Kate's thoughts.

'Oh, yes, please.'

Mary stared after them as they set off down the drive. Then she gazed up at the sky and prayed, 'Please God let it all work out. Let this house ring with some happiness before too long.'

Then with a mischievous glint in her eye she went back

inside to finish drinking her glass of sherry. Already she was planning what room she would make look fresh and pretty for Kate to move into. It had to be near to the nursery. There was no doubt she would insist on that.

Chapter Fifteen

KATE BREATHED IN deeply. There wasn't a smell quite like it in all the world. Hay. Newly scythed, lying in the fields, almost dry enough to be stacked. Security, for the farmers, winter fodder for the animals.

She looked out once more across the rolling fields. She had so much to be grateful for. Coming to live here at Melbourne Lodge had saved her reason, she was in no doubt about that.

The months following her parents' death had not been easy, most of the time she had felt crushed, lost. For so long the daily routine of her mother and herself had revolved around her father and his needs. His death had left a vacuum that no amount of hard work could fill. But she had somehow got through each day, trying not to show how bewildered she actually was. One thing puzzled her, and that was how well Alice had coped. She seemed to have found some great strength which Kate could not fathom. How lonely she must have been.

After those first few months life had changed so fast that she sometimes felt it was all a bit unreal. She hadn't minded working hard and taking care of Jane's adorable little son. He'd been such a dear and so helpless. The constant attention Joshua had needed had helped to dull the pain of having no parents to turn to. Her dad had always given her a hug when he came home of an evening, encouraged her to talk of the day's events, and it was those good times that she did her best to keep alive. She hadn't realised just how lucky she had been. Her mother had loved her just as much, of course she had, but hers had been a practical love.

Then, after all the turmoil and the pain and the tragedy and the utter despair, Charles Collier had come to her rescue. Moving into Melbourne Lodge, having baby Joshua put into her arms, being with him, feeding him, changing his nappies, singing him to sleep, watching him grow, his first smile, his first tooth, taking his first unsteady steps, knowing that he was hers to care for, that nobody could take him from her had been like slipping into another, much happier world. And that's how it had stayed for the last nine years.

Joshua knew she was not his mother. He had been told the full facts just as soon as he was able to grasp their meaning. No son was ever more loved by his father than Joshua. He was a lively child with Jane's colouring, blue eyes and tight curly fair hair. When he smiled it was often with a wicked grin which would melt your heart to see. Many a day Kate had stood waiting for him at the school gate, watching him come stomping along with his hands in his pockets, socks falling down and the belt of his raincoat trailing down at one side, and thanked God that she had been given the privilege of caring for him.

It was by his own choice that he called her Mum and Mary Nanna. Both women had guessed the reason; it made it so much easier for him at school.

Now his father was dead and soon Joshua would have to go to a different school, most probably as a boarder. In three months' time it would be Christmas and Joshua would have his tenth birthday. The years would turn him into a handsome youth, but come what may he would still be her baby.

'You spoil him rotten,' Mary was fond of saying. 'That boy can twist you round his little finger.'

'And of course you don't.' Kate would laugh.

Kate found herself wishing that Charles could have lived just a few more years until Joshua was old enough to face the world on his own. His wife had died when Joshua was two years old and from that day he had devoted his life to his son; taking him to places of interest, spending time with him, attending every school function in which he was involved. He was always there whenever Joshua needed him. It had done Kate's heart good to see them together. She sighed softly. Charles Collier had been the dearest, most loving and most generous man in the world.

Telling Joshua the news of his father's death had been one of the worst things Kate had ever had to do. She had taken a deep breath and said, 'Joshua, your father has died. He didn't suffer, he wasn't ill or anything. He died peacefully in his sleep.'

Joshua hadn't said a word, but his face had crumpled and, child that he was, he had reached out and she had taken him into her arms, smoothed his hair and kissed the top of his head, rocking him to and fro as if he were still a baby. With tear-stained cheeks and blurry eyes he had pulled away and looked into her face. 'I don't want him to be dead. I love him. The days when he doesn't come here I miss him an' now he won't ever come here again, will he?'

'Shh . . .'

'Oh, Mum . . .'

'Shh . . . There now . . .' was all she had been able to murmur.

Life was so cruel, Kate thought, and perhaps now without Charles to defend him Joshua was about to find that out for himself. She would fight tooth and nail for him, always be there for him. He was her life. She had made him so and she had no regrets. Would that be enough? How could she possibly know?

'Come on, son, we don't have to be brave,' she had soothed him and together they had given way to a bout of weeping.

The solicitors had sent a message, that they would deal with the funeral arrangements and would notify her of the time and place in due course.

'Will I have to go to the funeral?' Joshua had asked.

'Only if you want to,' Kate told him.

'Will you be there?'

'Of course.'

'And will you hold my hand all the time?'

'All the time. You'll be close by my side.'

'Then I shall go and take him some flowers from the garden.'

And that is what he'd done. Daisies, cornflowers

and roses, hand-picked by Joshua himself and, with the help of his beloved nanna, they had been woven into a tight posy.

Mr Collier had been buried very quietly although quite a crowd of dark-suited men filled the front pews of the church.

Joshua had sat between Kate and Mary, and Mrs Bates had sat on Kate's left. They had taken seats about halfway down the aisle because Kate thought it best to distance themselves from Charles's relations and business friends. Most of the villagers stood at the back of the church.

They heard Reverend Hutchinson praise Charles Collier for having done so much for others less fortunate than himself.

'So moving,' Mrs Bates had sighed, her flat cap exchanged for a wide-brimmed felt hat in honour of her past employer.

'Yes,' Mary had quietly replied, 'nice to hear that people didn't take for granted the fact that Mr Collier toiled endlessly to improve the lot of the poor.'

After the service was over Kate had told Mary she was taking Joshua for a walk, there was no need to put him through the ordeal of standing by the open graveside.

It had been no surprise when, three weeks after the burial, Kate received a letter summoning her to the offices of Hawhurst and Weatherford, Mr Collier's solicitors. The day of reckoning had arrived!

Kate took one more look out over the green fields, then turned away, telling herself she must get ready to keep her appointment. It had been a long night in which she had lain awake tormenting herself, feeling very uneasy as to what the situation would now be not only for Joshua but also for herself.

Could the powers that be take Joshua away from her? What ever would she do if they did?

She gave herself a mental shake. Stop it, she chided herself, you'll get nowhere meeting trouble before you even know what the outcome is going to be. Shoulders back, head held high and with a grim, determined look on her face she left the sitting room and went upstairs to get ready to do battle. Joshua had been her charge for as long as he could remember, to all intents and purposes she had moulded his young life. He needed her and God in heaven knew that she needed him as much, if not more.

She wouldn't give him up! Not without a fight she wouldn't.

Kate wore a tailored pale-grey suit with black velvet collar and cuffs and a matching hat which had a small brim adorned with a single band of corded ribbon. Her hair was still a bother and it had taken her some time to secure it, with the help of many pins, into a tight pleat she could tuck away out of sight. Still, a few curly strands hung down over her ears. Oh well, she shrugged, it will have to do.

She felt apprehensive as she walked the length of Kingston High Street. Over the years, Mr Collier had many times sought the opportunity to reassure her that both she and Mary would be provided for in his will. And, more to the point, that she would always have sole charge of Joshua so long as he was a minor. Well, she was about to find out exactly where she and the boy stood now.

Polite gestures were over and Kate was seated facing a massive desk littered with legal documents. Mr Weatherford was a large man, with iron-grey hair and heavy horn-rimmed spectacles, and in his dark well-cut suit and white shirt with a stiff collar he looked every inch a successful partner of this old, established firm of solicitors.

He cleared his throat, and gazed at the young lady he knew so much about but had never met before today. Her clear dark eyes were looking at him with frankness, she looked fresh and cool, and he noticed the good summer's sun had left her with a lot of freckles. He smiled at her, which made him seem younger, coughed again and began to speak.

'Mr Collier had only a couple of distant relatives and he has left them, and his favourite charities, well provided for,' he began, shuffling a host of papers into some kind of order. Raising his eyes to meet Kate's, he said, 'I presume you knew that Charles Collier was an exceedingly wealthy man?'

Kate made no answer. If she had, she would have told him he had no right to presume any such thing. It was not a matter that had ever been discussed between them. Of course, I knew he had money, Kate indignantly said to herself, how else could he have lived as he did, and run two homes into the bargain?

'Melbourne Lodge he has bequeathed to you, Miss Kearsley, including all the contents therein, together with the adjoining land. This is freehold and outright.' Mr Weatherford ignored the hiss of Kate's indrawn breath and continued. 'He wished to make sure that it would be a safe haven for you and his natural-born son until such time as his son is of age to inherit his own bequests. You, Miss Kearsley, are to be Joshua's legal guardian until he comes of age at twenty-one. Sufficient monies have been invested for the upkeep of the property, and to give you a monthly income that should well meet your needs. You may also set your mind at rest about Mr Collier's housekeeper, Mary Kennedy. A very generous annuity has been arranged and he has also set aside a tidy sum for her which she will inherit outright.'

Kate said nothing. Relief flooded through her veins so swiftly it was making her feel dizzy. She couldn't speak, but her eyes blazed with brightness. Joshua was to stay with her! Still be her son, at least until he became of age. Charles Collier had been as good as his word.

The sheer relief of knowing their strange relationship was not to be undone had her heart thumping with joy. The money didn't matter, she didn't need it. She still owned Bramble Cottage and she and Mary often spent the day there, opening the windows and letting in the fresh air. And the beauty of it was, that all the bad memories had dimmed over the years; only happy memories were allowed to be brought out and thought about. She also owned the Kearsley Boat Yard; under Jack Stuart's management the business had continued to do well and the accountant saw to it that she received an ample income.

'Well,' Kate said at last, 'and how about Joshua?'

Mr Weatherford allowed himself a smile as he took off his glasses. His eyes, without them, seemed to screw up as he peered at her. Across the desk, she met his stare.

'Miss Kearsley, you need never fear on Joshua's account. His father has seen to it that he is a wealthy young man and the icing on the cake is that Hampton Place now belongs to him, together with the remainder of all his father's worldly possessions.'

'It doesn't seem right that I should be given so much.'

'Matters are exactly as Mr Collier wished them to be,' Mr Weatherford said gently.

'I don't need more money, I . . .' She knew that she was behaving stupidly, yet Mr Weatherford was being very kind.

'Does the prospect of money and owning property alarm you?'

'A bit. But not half as much as having to decide what's best for Joshua in the future.'

'Ahh! That is a matter for a great deal of discussion, but it can wait for another day. Our firm will still hold young Joshua's interest as being of paramount importance, and his inheritance will be held in trust and administered by trustees who have been named in Mr Collier's will.'

'Oh, thank you.' Kate really did feel most grateful.

'My partners and I will set up another meeting with you. The first thing to be sorted out will be the question of the boy's education. Again, Mr Collier has set out his preferences so it shouldn't be too difficult.' He started to gather together his documents. 'Mr Collier left a letter in my charge, Miss Kearsley,' Mr Weatherford said, holding it out across the leather-topped desk. 'No doubt you will wish to read it when you are alone. Have you any more questions you would like to put to me?'

'I don't think so.'

'If you do think of anything don't hesitate to contact me, or if I'm not available my partner will be only too happy to help. In any case we shall certainly see each other again before too long.'

'Will you discuss Joshua's new school with him?'

'My dear Miss Kearsley, you are not to worry yourself, I shall make sure that Joshua is present at every meeting that not only affects his education but his entire future.'

At that moment the office door opened and they were joined by a well-dressed man. Younger than Mr Weatherford, he had fair hair, a happy, smiling face and tucked underneath his arm was a bundle of legal documents. 'This is my partner, Mr Hawhurst.' Mr Weatherford rose to his feet as the introductions were made.

'I'm happy to meet you, Miss Kearsley, though I must say your reputation has preceded you.'

'Oh dear, I don't like the sound of that,' Kate told him, her face looking quite stern.

'All good, I do assure you, young lady. According to our late client, Charles Collier, you are a paragon and I am truly pleased to meet you.'

Mr Weatherford coughed. 'Yes, well, I think we have covered enough ground for today. Are you happy with things as they are, Miss Kearsley?'

'A darn sight more happy that when I came in. Oh . . .' Kate's hand flew to cover her mouth; she had said the words without thinking.

Both men looked at each other and burst out laughing.

'I think you'll agree, she'll do,' Mr Weatherford used

162

a stage whisper to make this statement to his partner as he came round from behind his desk. 'Goodbye then, Miss Kearsley.' He held out his hand, smiling benevolently at her.

'Goodbye, Mr Weatherford, and thank you for everything.'

It was Mr Hawhurst who opened the door for her and, as he said goodbye, he was smiling broadly.

Out in the street Kate stood still, took a deep breath and said a silent prayer. Whether she was thanking God or just Charles Collier she wasn't too sure.

All she had been told! She needed time to sort it all out in her mind.

Wait till she told Mary that their boy, their Joshua, was to stay with them. No one was going to take him away. Even if he did have to go to boarding school, he would be home during the holidays, even weekends maybe.

We'll celebrate tonight. I bet Mary will give Josh all his very favourite things for his tea this afternoon, she thought.

She had stood on this spot for long enough. Her feet started to move then, casting caution to the wind, she began to run. She couldn't wait to get home.

Oh, the future was full of promise.

It was much later that night before Kate, having made sure that Joshua was well settled and that Mary was happily reading a book, finally made herself a cup of cocoa and settled down to read Mr Collier's letter.

The first few sentences had her in tears. What a kind man he was, and so lonely since Jane had died. He too, had made Joshua a great part of his life. What a pity things couldn't have been different between him and his wife.

She put aside her cup and continued to read.

Charles had covered two pages explaining why he had decided that she alone should be the owner of Melbourne Lodge. He wrote that he felt that, whether she married or stayed single, she would keep her promise to bring up Joshua in a just and proper way.

The next part of his letter surprised her even more. He suggested that if she cared to, she could put the unused bedrooms in the house to good use. She could allow needy families from the towns to stay for short periods; sick mothers who needed a rest; children, whose parents would be grateful for a short respite from trying to make ends meet.

Kate's emotions were in a whirl. Was there ever a more caring man? What a wonderful idea! If only he were here to help her get it off the ground. Perhaps he had thought it was a way for her finally to put all the black deeds of her parents behind her. Give back to others a little of the happiness he had made available to her.

Folding the letter and replacing it in the long envelope, Kate lay back in the chair, folded her arms across her chest and was no longer able to hold back the tears. Her grief was for her parents, for Jane, who had never known the joy of bringing up her little son, and now for Charles Collier, who had completely transformed her life.

She cried and cried until there were no more tears left.

*   *   *

During the days that followed, Mr Collier's idea never left her. Would she be capable of doing as he had suggested?

She knew that too many children didn't get enough to eat. Whenever possible she still helped Alice on her stall at Kingston market. Going into Kingston was an eye-opener, and on the rare occasion she paid a vist to her aunt and uncle, she always came home counting her blessings and thanking God for the way she was able to live her own life. The East End was awful, at least where Aunt Dolly lived it was. Men unable to find employment. Whole families living in rat-infested tenement blocks where landlords ignored the damp and rotting walls, the leaking roofs and the total lack of sanitation. No wonder so many kiddies had rickets and suffered scurvy. And this was 1931!

From listening to the tales Aunt Dolly told she knew too many young girls had their first baby before they were barely sixteen years old. By the age of thirty they not only looked nearer fifty but were worn out by years of child bearing, producing huge families for whom there was never enough food to go round. Maybe, just maybe, she could provide a holiday and a few necessities that these poor families must yearn for.

Mary was full of approval. 'It will keep us occupied while Joshua is away at school,' she wisely pointed out to Kate.

I'll do it, Kate decided. At least I'll do my best.

A sudden inspiration came to her. Mr Weatherford had said she could call on him for help at any time. Well, he was her solicitor, wasn't he? He knew the law. What rules would cover such a venture and so on. I bet he didn't deal with Charles's estate without getting well paid for it. And for the administration of Joshua's inheritance, he would be getting a fee. She laughed aloud, let's see that he earns those payments.

Chapter Sixteen

JOSHUA CHRISTOPHER COLLIER looked around his room. He couldn't say it was just a bedroom, more a bed-sitting room. Whatever it was, he loved it. It had an open fireplace and on this November day a fire roared halfway up the chimney, the tall fireguard, with its polished brass rail, set firmly in place. He smiled to himself. Nanna, and Mum too come to that, still thought he was a little boy, always telling him to be careful and not to play with the fire. A whole wall of shelves crammed with books and jigsaw puzzles, a big double bed all to himself, two armchairs with flowery loose covers which Nanna was forever taking off for washing. A thick dark-blue carpet, and a table covered with more books, pens and ink, blotters, rubbers, pencils and, best of all, a shiny geometry set, for it was here that he did his homework. This room was entirely his own. Set at the front of the house it boasted a huge bow window and because the house was built on a hill, the gardens ran down almost to the river. He never tired of watching the river. So much went on there and river folk were the most friendly types you could possibly wish to meet. If he had his way he would work on the river when he was older, at least have something to do with boats. And there he was lucky because his mum owned a boat yard and some of his most enjoyable days were spent down at the Kearsley Boat Yard.

He knew his own mother had died on the day he was born, which was very sad. But he loved Kate, she was the only mum he had ever known and the only mum he ever wanted. He had never lacked for anything, not material things, nor for loving people to take care of him.

One of the teachers at his local school had remarked that he was a special and very lucky little boy, even if circumstances had put an old head on his young shoulders. He hadn't really understood the meaning of that statement.

He was happy at home and at school and had plenty of boys with whom he was friendly. His particular friend was Peter Bradley, who knew that whenever he decided to call at Melbourne Lodge or come home with Josh straight from school he would get a fine welcome and good things to eat. His mum and his nan were great like that.

Life would never be quite the same again now his father had died.

He was to stay at home until Christmas, though even Christmas this year was going to be different. Mum and Nanna were having some poor people with children to come to stay for the holiday; he hoped they would be nice and friendly. If they were boys he might even let them have a turn at running his railway set. It went all the way around the walls of one of the spare bedrooms. His Dad and Dr Pearson had set it up. After Christmas he was going to boarding school. The 10th January to be exact. So much was changing in his small world and he wasn't sure that he would like any of it.

For the last two weeks Nanna and his mum had been flying around the house, opening up rooms that were never used, making beds, and a cot, which they told him had been his, was dragged out of a landing cupboard, reassembled and set up beside a double bed in one of the back bedrooms. He'd first heard about these people coming for Christmas when the three of them had been sitting round the huge scrubbed table in the kitchen having a midday meal.

'Josh, are you listening?' his mum had asked in a stern voice, which told him her patience was running out.

'Yes, Mum, but you did say that after we had eaten you were going to take me to Hampton Court and let me spend the afternoon at the boat yard with Mr Stuart.'

Kate had told him she wasn't about to break her promise but that he had to get used to the idea that they were all going to share this house, at different times of the year, with young children and perhaps their mothers, who were not so well off as they were. At first he had listened to this news with considerable alarm. How he wished his father was here. He would be able to tell him whether this was a good idea or not.

'Josh! Josh, will you please answer me.'

His nan, calling him from the bottom of the stairs, brought his thoughts back to today. He bent down, tied his shoelaces, picked up his jacket from where it lay on the chair and made for the door.

Mary watched him descend and, smiling to herself, decided he was a charming little boy. But then that had been her way of thinking from the moment he had been born. To this day it was still impossible for her to see him without becoming emotional. The way he looked, sometimes like a scruffy urchin, other times like a well-scrubbed cherub, but always adorable. The house was never the same when he wasn't in it. The sound of his voice, his laughter, and his tight curly hair which never would lay flat, everything about him filled her with delight and daily she thanked God that she had been allowed to be part of his life. It was just so unfair that his mother had had to die. She had been such a lovely person and so young.

Her thoughts turned to Kate. She had never married herself and now, well into her fifties, she never would. It didn't matter because in her day if one had the chance of a good position that was sufficient.

But Kate was another matter altogether. What a hell of a life she had endured in her younger days! Still, it had all worked out absolutely marvellously with her coming here to care for Joshua. Kate had become a daughter to her, Joshua was a son to each of them and Charles Collier had been their benefactor in, oh, so many ways.

But what of the future? Joshua would be all right. Money wouldn't buy happiness, but the provision his father had made for him would certainly ease his way through boarding school and hopefully on to university. By the time he became twenty-one he'd be a very wealthy young man.

That still left Kate. For the last ten years she had wrapped herself in the role of mother to Joshua. But now what? Every day she hoped and prayed that some nice gentleman would come along and see Kate for the wonderful, kind person she was. So much of her life had been devoted to others; she needed someone to take care of her, to love her, marry her, before it was too late.

'Joshua, for heaven's sake! What have you been doing up there? You know you're supposed to meet your mother in Kingston at twelve.'

'I'd better get going then.'

Mary put her arms about him. 'Have a good time and I'll have dinner ready when you get back.'

'What's it to be tonight?'

'What would you like it to be?'

'Shepherd's pie. And could you kind of burn all the top of the potatoes so that they're all crisp an' crunchy like?'

'Anything for you, sir. You've always been able to get round me and get your own way with your mother. You're not as daft as you make out.'

'Thank you, Nanna. I shall buy you some chocolates for being so kind.'

'Same old charmer. Get off with you, you'll never change.'

She watched him go down the drive.

Yes, that boy had been the best thing that had happened to her. They had been so happy. A good trio. She wondered where their lives would go from here. There was no telling was there.

As Joshua climbed down from the tram he spied his

mother standing with her back against the wall of the chemist's shop, surrounded by brown carrier bags and gaily wrapped parcels. 'Are these all yours?' he asked, disbelief in his voice.

'Well, yes. A bit of Christmas shopping and a few little things for a young man I know who has a birthday coming up.'

'Oh, Mum, what have you bought me?'

'Wait an' see.'

'I can't wait, Mum. Please.'

'Curiosity killed the cat. Anyway, I've finished most of what I wanted to do. Shall we have lunch before we start searching for whatever it is you've decided you'd like to buy?'

'Nanna's going to have dinner ready when we get home this evening so I'd better not eat too much, though I am hungry now.'

Kate threw back her head and laughed. 'I'd like to know when you're not hungry. Hollow legs, that's what you've got. Come on, pick up some of my shopping an' let's go.'

'Where to?'

'How about Bentalls? Isn't that where you say they do the best chips?'

'Cor, that big restaurant upstairs does a fabulous Knickerbocker Glory, can I have one of those?'

'All right then, but . . .'

Josh hadn't stopped to hear any more. He had gathered up his mother's packages and, with both hands filled, made his way towards the kerb. Swiftly, Kate collected up the few items he had left on the ground, and hurried after him.

Kingston's largest department store was only a few minutes' walk. Joshua heaved his shoulder against the heavy glass door and stood waiting until his mother had gone through. Inside he paused, his eyes darting all round. Everything was wonderful. Christmassy. All shiny silver and gold decorations with lots of red balloons hanging from the ceiling.

Kate watched him, her heart bursting with love. Almost ten years old – how the time had flown. He was such a happy boy and it showed. His cheeks were rosy from the wind and his eyes as bright as stars.

They took the main staircase up to the restaurant and looked around for somewhere to sit. A waitress returning to the kitchen with a tray laden with dirty crockery nodded her head towards a window table. 'That table is free now, madam.'

Kate smiled her thanks.

Joshua piled all the packages in a neat pile on the floor and with this done his mother said, 'Take your coat off, hang it on the back of your chair, look at the menu and decide what you are going to have to eat.'

'Mum . . .'

Kate looked across the table. 'Well, what is it?'

'I only had porridge for breakfast this morning.'

'Josh, you're telling me fibs. I left early because I had so much to do, but I know full well your nanna was there to get your breakfast.'

'I am not telling fibs,' he said, doing his best to sound indignant, 'and it wasn't Nan's fault . . . I didn't have time.'

'Aah! Now we're getting to the truth. You, my lad,

didn't get up when I called you. You went back to sleep, didn't you?'

Josh tried to look sheepish, his lips twiched and they both laughed.

'All right. You don't deserve it but, come on, decide what you want.'

Joshua never even glanced at the menu. 'Bacon, egg, sausage and chips, please, and please may I have at least a milkshake to follow?'

'You're naughty, you know that, but all right, I give in.' Kate turned to give her order to the friendly waitress who was standing, smiling, at her side. 'And I'll have a pot of tea and two toasted muffins, please.'

'Would you like a preserve to go with the muffins, madam?'

'Yes, please, make it apricot.'

'Bless my soul, you made short work of that,' Kate said as she watched her son clear the plate.

'It was a super breakfast, thanks, Mum. But you're only halfway through your muffins an' you haven't drunk your tea.'

'I'm doing fine, the tea's still scalding hot. Of course, you're waiting for your second course of whatever gooey stuff it is you've decided to have,' she teased him. 'And while you're waiting perhaps you might give me a few suggestions as to what you would really like for your birthday.'

There was no hesitation on Joshua's part.

'I'd really like a boat.'

Kate wasn't in the least surprised by this request. Josh had been mad about boats ever since he could walk. Sometimes, when they were at the boat yard, she would stand back and watch Jack Stuart outlining some intricate part of the boat the men were working on while Josh hung on his every word. Her own imagination would run riot. What if her dad were still alive? What if Josh were her own true son? His grandson. Oh, if only!

Josh was busy drawing strawberry-flavoured milk up from the tall glass by means of two straws and, pausing for breath, he did not wait to hear what answer his mother was going to give. 'I thought as it would be such a big present you could give it to me for my birthday and for my Christmas present as well.'

'Josh, slow down, and take your time to drink that milkshake. The way you're going on you'll choke yourself. Even if I do agree that you may have a boat we certainly won't be buying one. What we could do is rope Mr Stuart in on this, kind of give him a commission to build you one.'

'Really?' Joshua could scarcely believe that his mother had given in so readily. 'When can we go and see him?'

'Oh, don't rush me along so. There's a lot to talk about. Size for one thing. It can only be a small one and Mr Stuart will decide if it's to be just a row boat or whether he thinks fit to add a small outboard motor.' Kate frowned as her thoughts turned to her little brother who had drowned. Sounding flustered, she added, 'And there's the safety angle to be considered. I'm not having you out on the river on your own. Definitely not.'

'Oh, Mum, you're not going to start fussing me, are you?'

'No, but how about for your birthday I buy you all the safety trappings and pay someone to give you lessons on how to take care when out on the river and how to maintain your own boat and keep it in good order?'

'I can learn all that from Mr Stuart, I know most of it anyhow and, besides, when would I get the boat?'

'Just you listen to me, Joshua, if we agree, we'll have all of the arrangements on a proper businesslike footing and, as to when you can have the boat, perhaps Mr Stuart will give us a date. If you're lucky, maybe, and it is only a maybe, he and his men could have it ready by the time you come home for your summer holidays.'

'Mum, you're smashing, honest you are, but couldn't it be ready by Easter?'

In spite of herself Kate was laughing as she told him firmly, 'If I were you, young man, I wouldn't push my luck. I have been known to change my mind.'

'Cor! You wouldn't do that to me, I know you wouldn't.'

He was right. Kate knew she could no more disappoint him than fly in the air. If he had asked for the sky and the stars to go with it she would have done her very best to get them for him.

'A boat of my own! Can't wait to tell Peter,' Josh mused.

Kate couldn't keep the smile off her face as she watched him but she wasn't about to totally commit herself.

'It all depends on what Mr Stuart has to say about it,' she said, forcing herself to be stern. 'If he thinks you're old enough and is confident you wouldn't do anything reckless, then we'll ask him to go ahead and build you a boat that, in his opinion, would be suitable.'

She looked at her watch, gathered up her handbag and pulled herself up onto her feet. 'Is there anything special you want to buy today or did you just intend to have a look round the shops – get some ideas?'

'Nothing really special, except I promised Nan I would buy her some chocolates.'

'Bribery now, is it?' Kate teased him. 'And one more thing, Josh, whatever we decide, you are not to rush Mr Stuart. If he says he could have a small boat ready for you by the beginning of the summer I think that should suit you fine. You won't need it before then anyway.'

No, Josh thought sadly as he loaded himself up with his mother's purchases, you and my father's solicitors have settled that I am to be sent away to boarding school and there doesn't seem very much that I can do about it.

Chapter Seventeen

'UNBELIEVABLE, ISN'T IT? Ten years old today.' Mary wiped her eyes with the corner of the pinafore she was wearing.

'Yes, the years have simply flown by, haven't they?'

The two women were standing in the doorway watching Josh and his friend Peter Bradley tear the wrappings off Joshua's birthday presents.

Peter was short and dumpy compared with Josh, and as dark as Josh was fair. Nevertheless, as Kate watched their open smiling faces she was grateful that these two boys were such good friends.

'I have a present for each of you,' Mary informed them.

'Really?' Josh smiled his thanks. 'May we open them now?'

Peter flicked a strand of dark hair away from his face as he took the bulky parcel from Mary. He grinned. 'It's not my birthday, Mrs Kennedy, but thanks anyway.' Turning to Josh and seeing that his parcel was exactly the same shape and size, he asked, 'What do you think it is?'

'Haven't a clue. Has to be something to do with the boat. Any ideas?' Josh asked.

'I don't believe you two,' Mary said, making a funny face, 'the only way you'll find out is to open them!'

Both lads laughed and raced to see who could get the string undone and the paper off first.

'Good gracious!' Peter exclaimed. 'It's a life jacket.'

Josh had his out of the wrapping paper, and slung the brightly coloured jacket over his shoulder and hugged Mary. 'Thanks, Nan, it's a super present and thanks for buying one for Peter as well. You're wonderful, you really are.'

'Cor yes, Mrs Kennedy, thanks ever so much.' Turning to face her, Peter asked, 'Does this mean that I shall be allowed to go out with Josh in his boat?'

'If your parents give their permission of course you'll go out together, but only with an adult to begin with.'

Josh hugged her a second time. 'You couldn't have given us anything better. I love you. And you, Mum, the waders and everything else you've given me are great.'

'I'm glad you're pleased with your presents. Wait a minute though, you're not to pester Jack Stuart. He'll do his best to give you a good, strong boat but it will take time. Meanwhile, he's going to arrange for both you and Peter to be taken out on the river whenever he gets the chance. If you listen to all the instructions and pay attention to all the rules then, please God, you'll enjoy yourselves and be relatively safe.'

'So,' Mary said, rubbing her hands together, 'we've a hell of a lot to do today what with our Christmas guests arriving this evening. You'd better tell me now what time you would like your tea.'

Josh glanced at his mother. 'Am I getting a cake?'

'I don't know,' she teased. 'You'd better ask your Nan about that.'

'I am, aren't I, Nan? And candles.' Without waiting to hear her reply he tugged at Peter's arm. 'Come on, Pete, let's take all my presents upstairs. If we stay down here you know what will happen, they'll rope us into helping with all the jobs.'

Mary and Kate stood still for a minute listening to the boys' footsteps as they clattered up the uncarpeted back stairs. Suddenly they heard Joshua let out a yell, 'I'm gonna get my own boat!' His voice rang with excitement.

'Does your heart good to see them together, doesn't it?' Mary exclaimed.

'It sure does.'

When the two of them had finished picking up all the torn wrapping paper, Kate straightened the chairs and smoothed the creases from the tablecloth.

'Right then,' she said briskly. 'Let's get ourselves ready for this invasion.'

At the end of Joshua's birthday there were five adults and five children sleeping in Melbourne Lodge.

Kate, despite being tired out, was sitting in an arm-chair in her bedroom. It was past midnight. The curtains hadn't been drawn and the sky was bright with stars. There was no wind and a bright moon showed up the outline of the trees. It was so quiet that when, somewhere in the distance, a dog barked it split the silence. About time you got into bed, she chided herself, the house won't be quiet in the morning; it will be noisy, full of children's chatter.

Kate was never to forget how her visitors had looked when they arrived. First to step over the threshold was Mrs Holt and her three-year-old daughter Peggy. She looked little more than a teenager herself. Pale faced and thin as a rake she was wearing a long, faded dark dress beneath a coat so worn Kate was sure you could shoot peas through the material. Peggy was not too badly turned out, though the coat she wore, while being clean and of good quality, was several sizes too big for her tiny little body. The pair of them looked as if they hadn't eaten a good meal in ages. The other family was a middle-aged mother, Mrs Flynn, her married daughter, Jean Brown and Jean's three sons, Tommy aged five, John aged seven and Stanley who was eight. A terrible sight, those young boys, shocking. Not a decent bit of clothing on any of them. First thing in the morning she would have to go into Kingston and see what she could rustle up. Thank God there were two more shopping days before Christmas.

Wondering what the hell she had let herself in for, she climbed into bed, telling herself there was little to be gained by staying awake and worrying herself sick.

Kate wasn't prepared for the noise that hit her as she opened the kitchen door. Grey-haired Mrs Flynn and her daughter were facing each other like two spitting cats.

'Mrs Flynn! Whatever it is that is wrong, surely there's no need to shout.'

The angry woman shot Kate a look to kill.

'It's 'er eldest boy, Stanley. Cheeky little sod, says he

ain't staying down 'ere where there ain't nuffin t'do, an' no shops. An' my Jean, would yer believe it, is all for giving in t'him, packing up an' clearing off back to London. I told 'er, I'm staying put! There ain't a thing in our 'ouse t'eat, this is the first chance we've 'ad in years to 'ave a good Christmas an' I ain't gonna stand by an' see that little tike spoil it for the rest of us.'

Kate caught her breath and swallowed, taking a minute to make sure she stayed calm. Then, turning, she faced Stanley, all the time wondering how she could ask his grandmother to curb her language. It was difficult to believe that this whole arrangement had been set up with the help of Reverend Hutchinson through the London Church Association.

'Stanley, you haven't given yourself or us a chance, have you? I promise you that after we have all had breakfast there will be lots of things for you to see and do.'

The spotty-faced lad, who acted as if he were years older than he really was, stuck his nose in the air and sniffed deliberately. 'I ain't seen no signs of a proper breakfast. I don't want none of that porridge muck.'

Mary turned from the stove where she was busy frying rashers of bacon. Kate had never seen her look so angry. She heaved a sigh and said, 'If you would all sit up at the table there is plenty of toast ready and your fried breakfast won't be long.' She raised her eyebrows and with a note of pleading in her voice said to Kate, 'Would you please make two pots of tea? Kettle is boiling.'

Standing side by side at the stove, Kate asked in a whisper, 'Where's Joshua?'

Mary tutted. 'No need to whisper.' She nodded her

head to where the seven visitors were now busy stuffing their faces. 'Eating doesn't seem to stop them talking, they all speak with their mouths full. Josh heard the beginning of the rumpus and disappeared. He'll be back when the coast is clear, or at least when he's hungry. Going to be a great Christmas, don't you think?'

Kate was about to answer when Mary lifted the corner of her apron and wiped the sweat from her forehead, in doing so her elbow nudged Kate quite hard.

'Taking it out on me, are you? I'm beginning to think we must have needed our brains tested. I bet Mr Collier didn't know what he was letting us in for when he made this suggestion.'

'I bet he never! And we're only at the start of it. I can't help wondering what the next few days are going to bring.'

Their eyes met and they had to smother their giggles.

'Oh, well.' Mary grinned as she handed Kate a cloth. 'You can be waitress and take their breakfasts to the table. Mind, the plates are very hot.'

'In for a penny, in for a pound,' Kate muttered as she made the third trip from the stove to the table.

'Did you threaten them or was it something you put in their tea?'

Mary gave Kate a sideways look. 'I know what you mean. Funny ain't it, the difference three hours has made. Come to the front door, you can hear more of what's going on from there.'

As Kate opened the front door, the sharp cold air hit them. It was a bright day with weak sunshine. There had been a frost during the night and signs of it still lingered beneath the shrubs. Pulling their cardigans tight round their chests they walked down the front lawn until they were able to view the children in the distance. Kate was surprised at how much noise they were making; it looked as if they were splashing each other and they were certainly screaming with laughter. Thinking back, she remembered the time she had spent in London with her aunt. The awful smell of too many people living close together, their sweaty bodies, the big tin bath hanging in the coal shed and dragged into the house only once a week for each to use in turn. The coalman in his soot-covered clothes and cap, delivering the sacks of coal by walking right through the house, brushing against the walls as he went. No wonder Mrs Brown's eldest boy had wanted to go home. Fresh air was something he wasn't used to, and the silence all around must have seemed frightening.

'I have a feeling we're in for a hellva lot more surprises before this week is out. That poor thin woman, Mrs Holt, doesn't have much to say for herself, but the other lot make up for her and then some.'

'I can't help feeling sorry for them,' Kate murmured as they turned to go back into the warmth of the house.

'Yes, I know what you mean, right bedraggled looking lot, aren't they? They need some warm clothes if it's only a jersey each and scarves and gloves. I could take to that little one, Tommy. The way he looks at me, well . . .'

'He gets to me just the same. He's so tiny and chubby and what with his cheeky face and blue eyes he could bring out the maternal instincts in any woman without even trying. Wonder where the father is?'

'Best if we don't start asking awkward questions like that. I think we've taken on as much as we can cope with now without looking for more trouble that is none of our business.'

'I'm sure you're right,' Kate said with a twinkle in her eye. 'But don't tell me you aren't feeling just a little bit inquisitive.'

'Yes, well, I'll do my best to keep my curiosity under wraps.'

They had reached the house and Mary flung open the door, 'We're so lucky! Everywhere in this house is so lovely and warm.'

Kate didn't answer but a great sense of determination swept through her. 'Can you manage on your own if I pop off into Kingston?'

''Course I can, my love, and I don't need no telling what you're going for.'

Kate gave her a sheepish grin. 'I know we've got several presents for everybody to put round the tree, but I can't stand to see those boys running around in what are little more than rags. I'll be as quick as I can.' With a devilish smile, she added, 'Try not to have a nervous breakdown while I'm gone.'

Mary had gone to the sink to fill the kettle but Kate could hear her chuckling. 'I'll do me best to stop them wrecking the house. By the way, get something pretty and warm for little Peggy and whatever you get for the boys I'll go halves with you. Get yourself ready an' I'll make you a hot drink before you set off.'

'Wanna know something, Mary Kennedy? The older you get the bigger softie you become. Those kids already know you're a pushover and by the time Christmas day arrives they'll have you eating out of their hands.'

★　　★　　★

With her hat pulled well down over her ears, handbag tucked under her arm and clutching a very large shopping bag, Kate set off down the drive at a steady pace. Reaching the towpath she came face to face with the children and was thrilled to see that Joshua was holding little Peggy's hand. He stopped dead in his tracks and pulled his socks up.

'Where are you going, Mum? We're all cold and were coming up to the house for something hot to drink.'

'That's all right,' Kate said, beaming at the funny-looking picture the five children made as they stood shivering in front of her. 'I won't be long, and I'm sure your nan will find you all a big bowl of soup.' Then doing her best to be kind, she smiled at Stanley. 'Found plenty to amuse you this morning, have you? Pity it's so cold. I'll bring you an' your brothers back a long warm scarf to wrap round your necks. That ought to help.'

'No!' Stanley spoke hastily. He was beginning to like this lady but he didn't want to be beholden to her. He hadn't yet worked out what it was she wanted from him and his family or the reason she was having them all to stay in her beautiful house for the whole of Christmas. Nobody did something for others without wanting something in return. He might not be quite grown up but that much he had learnt ages ago. His hand flew to his neck and up the back of his head, apart from his feet, which were freezing, it was the coldest part of his body. 'It's very nice of yer, missus, but me an' me bruvvers don't wear scarves.'

'Well, we'll see.' Kate's voice trembled. The lad had actually been very polite to her and she realised that his tough cockney manner was more likely than not a front he put up to prove how tough he could be. Poor little lad. He couldn't have known many privileges in his short life.

Joshua moved closer to her. 'Don't be too long, will you?'

'No, I promise. Now, go on, all of you. It's far too cold for any of us to stand around here.'

Stanley backed off and gave the order, 'Run!' The laughter echoing down the driveway as the children ran as fast as their legs would carry them did Kate a power of good. She set off on her shopping expedition, facing the prospect of Christmas with a lot more optimism than she had started out with at the beginning of the day.

Chapter Eighteen

ON CHRISTMAS MORNING Kate persuaded Mary to go with her to the early-morning church service.

'It will only be for half an hour. We'll be back before the house is awake and almost everything is prepared for dinner, isn't it?'

'Yes, well, all right. But I'll bet my bottom dollar those boys will be awake, screaming and shouting and most likely wrecking the place by the time we get back.'

'Come on, Mary, you know you don't mean a word of it. It's as I said it would be, those kids have worked their way into your affections and I don't care what you say – it's true.'

'Can't deny that the two little ones have turned out to be really nice kids. Who could resist little Peggy? She's such a shy, sweet little thing, doll-like almost, with her fair colouring and blond curls. And as for that young Tommy, well, you said yourself he'd make any woman feel motherly and I'm beginning to think the little tinker gets away with murder.'

Thick frost crunched under their feet as they made their way along the towpath. The river didn't look at all friendly this morning, but they were both well wrapped up against the cold. Mary wore nothing fussy, her grey hair tucked up under a brown felt hat, her face round and rosy without a trace of face-powder or rouge and her eyes shining. Her long fawn coat, which had a deep fur collar, had been chosen with Kate's help and her high, soft leather boots had been one of Kate's Christmas presents to her.

As they walked, arms linked, she stole a glance at Kate. She looked beautiful. Her dark curls were bobbing on each side of her face though, in the main, her hair was restrained beneath the dark blue, narrow-brimmed hat which suited her so well. Her new coat was a lighter shade of blue, edged only with a narrow strip of fur at the neck and hem. She wore a single string of pearls and her face showed just a light trace of make-up, which was to be expected in this day and age when women were beginning to demand that more notice be taken of them.

The church had that special feel which comes only with Christmas. The altar rail was banked with white Christmas roses intertwined with red-berried holly. Friends of the church had given a great deal of their time to making these floral arrangements. The village children had been involved in setting up the nativity display in the nave and candles burnt brightly at each end of the crib. The rafters rang with the sound of joyful singing and Kate felt she had a lot to thank God for.

On their return, feeling relaxed and uplifted, she put the key in the front door and pushed it open, pausing to stamp her damp boots on the doormat. Sounds of laughter and merriment came to them as they stepped inside.

The door to the drawing room stood open. Mary and Kate smiled at each other, took a deep breath and went in. It felt a bit like walking into one great big happy family. A huge tree had been set up two days ago and decorated by the children with silver bells, tinsel and clip-on candleholders with small red candles. Holly hung everywhere, gathered from their own grounds by Mr White, their gardener and odd-job man. Mary had lit the fire and piled it with logs before they had set out for church. Outside the day was dark and grey, threatening to snow before very long. Inside the pale-coloured walls danced with reflected firelight and the Christmas baubles on the tree glittered. Alice, having been given a lift into Littleton Green by Bob Bateman, landlord of the George and Dragon, and Mrs Flynn, dressed, neatly for a change, in a black skirt, white blouse and grey cardigan, were sitting comfortably, facing each other in armchairs by the fireside, chatting away as if they had known each other all their lives. Mrs Flynn's daughter, Jean, and a smiling Mrs Holt were grouped round them drinking cups of tea.

For an instant there was silence, then the children looked up to see who had come into the room. Joshua laid down the parcel he was opening and was on his feet and by his mother's side. 'Where have you been? All our stockings were filled and you must come and see what we've all got,' he implored, tugging at her arm.

Suddenly, they were surrounded by five children their faces flushed with excitement, their voices shrill with enthusiasm, making such a din that Kate laughingly covered her ears with her hands. 'Please,' she pleaded, 'give us a chance to take our coats off.'

Kate and Mary were acutely aware that four of the children had never before known such warmth and comfort, let alone the joy of waking up to a stocking filled with presents. Mrs Holt set down her cup and saucer and crossed the room to face them. She took Kate's hand in her own and looked up into their faces, 'I don't have the words to say to you . . . what you've done for the children . . .' She looked away, biting her lip. There was something so sad about this young mother. She couldn't bring herself to say more, she didn't have to, the look in her eyes said it all.

With breakfast over, the six women sat with glasses of sherry and gave themselves up to watching the look of sheer enchantment on the children's faces as they were each given a present. Little Peggy had them all on the verge of tears as she held up the new dress Mary and Kate had bought for her.

'Mummy, it's so pretty, can I try it on?'

She didn't wait for an answer, her skirt was round her ankles and her jumper pulled over her head before anyone could stop her. That caused a great deal of laughter as she stood among four boys clad only in her vest and knickers.

'As pretty as a picture,' Mary declared. 'Go on, love, give us a twirl.'

Warm and sensible, but still very attractive the dress

was a mixture of shades of pink, both light and dark. It was long sleeved, with a full skirt and a band of rich velvet at the neck and hem. Kate had had the forethought to buy some extra velvet ribbon in a matching shade to be worn in the child's hair. Peggy needed no second bidding. Using both hands she held the hem of the dress wide as she twirled gaily. Everyone in the room clapped and no one more enthusiastically than young Tommy, which caused more laughter. So Peggy twirled again.

Kate left the room to see how the dinner was doing and was not in the least surprised to find that Alice had followed her.

'You know I nearly never came today,' she said holding her face up for Kate's kiss.

'Oh, Gran, I'm so pleased you have, I can't begin to tell you. The times that Mary an' I have sent you invitations and you never even answered our letters. Not that you need an invite, you know that perfectly well, and I also know it's difficult for you to get out here to us. I'm a lot to blame, I don't visit you half as often as I should.'

'For God's sake, Kate!' Alice yelled in exasperation. 'I'm here now, it's Christmas day, so less of yer chat and let's be seeing to this dinner.' So saying she took down an apron from a hook beside the range and tied it round her ample waist.

'Oh, no you don't, Mary and I have everything under control so just take yourself back into the front room. If you really want to be helpful go and check on the dining-room table, see we haven't missed anything, and then make sure that our visitors' glasses are kept charged.'

Alice pretended to sigh heavily. 'Was a time when it would have been me cooking Christmas dinner.'

'And we don't want any of the self-pity. You've done your share of waiting on me over the years, now please let me have my day.'

'All right. One thing I've got t'say. I didn't go much on this idea of yours, having strangers to stay in the house all over Christmas, but since I've met them I've changed me mind.'

'Glad t'hear it. And you don't have to start on about going home because Mary and I have seen to it that there's a room all ready for you. And before you ask, Gran, yes, the sheets are aired and we've had a fire burning in the room for the last three days.'

'Proper old clever clogs these days, aren't you,' Alice mumbled as she untied the apron and made for the door.

'Gran.'

'What is it now?'

'I'm glad you're here, and before you go back to the others, how about a special kiss for Christmas?'

'Oh, lass, I can't tell you how proud I am of the way you've put the past behind you and tackled the job of looking after Joshua. He's turned out an amazing lad. A credit to you.'

Kate wrapped her arms around her grandmother. 'Praise from the highest,' she whispered, doing her best to turn this serious moment into a lighter mood.

'Nothing more than you deserve,' Alice told her, breaking free. At the door she hesitated and looked back. 'One word of advice, my love. With Josh off to boarding school, it's about time you looked round and started to live a life of your own.'

The door shut quickly, giving Kate no chance to reply.

Still a wise old bird, my gran, she thought as Mary put her head round the door.

'Come and have a drink and then we'll get the vegetables on. Everyone is wondering what you're doing out here.'

'Most of it *is* on now, but there is time for me to have a drink before we dish up.' Kate gave in gracefully.

'Hiding away, were you?'

'You could say that. All right, pour me a sherry an' I'll be there in a minute.'

By half-past one everybody was seated around the big dining table.

'Cor, it does look pretty.' Jean Brown and quiet Mrs Holt spoke in unison.

'You can say that again,' Jean's mother chipped in. 'Must've cost a pretty penny, what with all those crackers an' things.'

'If I know my granddaughter, an' I should do by now,' Alice said, with a smug smile on her face, 'I'll wager her and Mary have spent many an evening making those crackers. They'll have good little presents in them an' all, not like some of the rubbish you buy in the shops, all fancy box and coloured paper they are.'

'Mum, may we pull them now, before we start to eat?'

''Course you can. Help the little ones with theirs first.'

'And each of you can put one of these on your head,' Mary said as she walked round the table letting each child and adult pick a party hat from the big cardboard box she was holding.

The noise was deafening; chattering gave way to squeals

of laughter as whistles were blown, mottos and riddles read, and funny little toys exchanged.

'Now, it's time for the feast to begin. Clear away all the paper and sit up straight,' Alice ordered, in her element, as she helped Kate and Mary to bring in the dishes.

Mary had carved the breast of one side of the turkey out in the kitchen, laying the white slices on the plates, but still the bird was caried in on a huge meat dish and set down in the centre of the table amid yells of surprise and delight. Also on each plate was a sausage rolled and roasted in a rasher of bacon.

'Blimey, that looks good,' Stanley declared, as he grabbed the sausage between his fingers and brought it up to his mouth.

'Ain't you got no manners at all?' his gran yelled, clipping him round the side of his head. 'Put it down. Use ye knife an' fork, you ain't at 'ome now.'

'Leave him be, please, Mrs Flynn, it's Christmas.'

'Come on, ladies,' Mary called out, 'help the children to vegetables and pile up your own plates.'

There were roast potatoes, baby Brussels sprouts, carrots and parsnips, and two jugs filled with thick dark gravy made rich with the juice from the giblets. 'Would you like some cranberry sauce?' Josh asked John who was seated next to him.

John, by far the quietest of Jean's three boys, looked into the bowl that Josh was offering him. 'Naw, we don't 'ave jam with our dinner, it would spoil it.'

Josh replaced the dish near the centre of the table and turned to face his mother who was seated on his other side. They both grinned.

'All right, son?' She winked at him.

'Yes, smashing, Mum.'

Kate reached over and patted his shoulder and in a whisper asked, 'You don't feel neglected?'

He laughed, catching hold of her hand. 'No, I've got you, Nan, and my gran today.'

'Good boy, now eat up before everything goes cold.'

Noisy voices buzzed and little Tommy knelt up on his chair as Mary brought the Christmas pudding to the table. 'It's on fire,' he yelled, his eyes wide with amazement as he stared at the blue flames made by the brandy Mary had poured over the pudding before putting a match to it. Brandy butter for the adults, custard for the children and a silver sixpence slipped into each of their dishes. By the time the plates were cleared from the table, the children were sounding over-excited and Alice was chosen as the best person to read them a story. With five women in the kitchen the mound of washing up was quickly done and finally Mary said that her kitchen was back to being shipshape and Bristol fashion and that they could all relax now. The front-room carpet was strewn with toys and books and Alice said there was only one thing she wanted and that was a cup of tea.

'I'll make it,' Jean Brown offered. 'Anyone else fancy one?'

'Yes, please,' came a chorus of voices.

'And I'll see about organising a few games,' Kate said, as she sorted out a record to put on the gramophone. Mary soon had a ring of chairs set in the centre of the room. 'We're going to play pass the parcel, you've all played this game before, haven't you?'

'Let's start then. Each of you find a chair.' Kate turned

her back to the room, lifted the gramophone needle and asked, 'Is one of you holding the parcel?'

'Yes, I am,' Stanley's firm voice announced.

'Right. Ready, steady, go.'

Some ten minutes later, Kate sank down into a chair alongside Mary and the pair of them gratefully accepted a cup of tea from Jean, who laughingly said, 'You look as if you're in need of that.'

'Never more so,' Mary agreed. 'It's a good job Christmas only comes once a year.'

Later that night, when all their visitors had gone upstairs to bed and Kate had seen that Joshua was sound asleep, Mary made some sandwiches and they, together with Alice unwound with a mug of cocoa.

'You did well – remarkably well – both of you,' Alice told them. 'You made those kids really happy, they've had the time of their lives.'

Kate was touched by her praise, and felt full of love for her. She got up, went across, bent over and kissed her soft cheek. 'It was all worthwhile, wasn't it? But you know, Gran, the best part for me and Josh was having you here. One way an' another I think it's been a smashing day.'

'My sentiments exactly,' Mary interrupted. 'And, Alice, it wouldn't have been the same if you hadn't been here.'

'Well, tomorrow's another day. How do you propose to keep them all amused?' Alice asked, getting to her feet.

'We've boxed clever. We're taking everyone to the pantomine in Kingston.'

'Thank God for that.' Alice made for the door. 'I'm going up. How long will you be?'

'We'll be right behind you, just as soon as we've banked down the fire.'

'Well done, Kate,' Mary said as soon as they were alone. She sounded very emotional.

'Couldn't have done it without you, Mary. I'd say it was a joint effort.'

'Yes, well, turn the light out and let's go up to bed. I think we'll both sleep well tonight.'

Chapter Nineteen

IT HAD BEEN a good Christmas, Kate decided. It was a time for families. Sharing their home this year with three adults and four children had been well worthwhile. The departure of their guests had brought tears, but they had been tears of happiness. When they had arrived their faces had been pinched, their bodies far too thin and their clothes skimpy and faded. How different they had each looked as they climbed aboard the station carrier, calling their thanks and waving their goodbyes. She smiled as she remembered the way Jean's three boys had wound their new, long woollen mufflers tightly around their necks. Scarves that brave little Stanley had vowed they'd never wear.

I hope Charles Collier has found his reward in heaven, Kate sighed to herself. It had been his generosity that had made this Christmas possible.

Now she needed to find calm and an inner strength because in two days' time Joshua was off to boarding school in Guildford and she wouldn't see him again until Easter. Take one thing at a time, Mary had told her, and she had done her best to follow this advice, but there still seemed an awful lot left to do. So, Kate muttered to herself, stop all this daydreaming and start getting some of the jobs done.

'Josh, where are you and what are you doing?' she called from the foot of the stairs.

'Trying on my uniform. Nan told me to, just to check that everything is all right.'

'Well come down and let us see you when you're ready. I hope you're ticking everything off the list as you pack them in your trunk.'

'I will, and I have,' came his cheeky reply.

Kate was torn between laughter and tears. Dear God, she was going to miss having him around the house.

When he came into the kitchen it was as if he had been transformed from a child into a grown lad. What a difference a uniform made!

'Oh, my, my, my,' Mary murmured.

'You think I'll do, Mum?' Josh asked, and, as he spoke, he raised his beautiful blue eyes to meet Kate's. They looked at each other, not needing to say a word, both knew that a very strong bond existed between them.

'Oh, you'll do, an' then some. Now you are ready to go out into the big outside world.'

The station carrier was once again outside the house, this time with a flat open-backed cart drawn by a huge black horse and onto this Joshua's trunk and his case holding his sportswear were loaded. Mary, Kate and Joshua stood in a group and watched as Mr White helped the railway man to rope it all securely. Hardly had the cart disappeared from sight than a car turned into the drive.

'Hallo, young Joshua, all ready for the off? I see your luggage has gone on ahead.'

'Good morning, Mr Weatherford. Yes, everything is safely on the cart.'

Josh watched this big man, who was in charge of his affairs, turn and shake hands first with his mother and then with his nan. A sad thought came to Josh: what a pity my father couldn't have lived to take care of me himself; at least until I was grown up. His mum and nan were wonderful, he loved them both dearly. but he missed his father so much; knowing he wasn't around, would never unexpectedly walk through the door again. It made him want to cry. It was these legal men who had said he had to go away to school. Neither his mum nor his nan really wanted him to go, and he certainly didn't want to leave them or his lovely home.

'Come along, Joshua, say your goodbyes and get into the car,' Mr Weatherford ordered.

Kate had never imagined it would be this bad. It was right that she shouldn't go to Guildford with Josh, but to have to say goodbye like this was terrible.

Mary went forward first, putting both her arms around his strong shoulders. 'Goodbye, Josh, I'll send you parcels.' She couldn't find anything else to say, so she kissed his cheek and pushed him towards his mother.

'Bye, Mum. I'll write.'

'Mind you do. And take care of yourself. The weeks will fly by an' you'll soon be home again.'

Then man and boy got into the car.

'Quick, be brave, let him see us smiling and waving,' Mary implored Kate.

Kate did as she was told, though her heart was breaking. She wanted to run after the car, grab Joshua from it and keep him with her for ever and ever. They could see him waving frantically from the back window, and the pair of them went on waving back until the car was out of sight.

A whole month had slipped by since Joshua had gone away to school and still Kate's emotions were in such turmoil that she couldn't settle to anything for more than ten minutes, and she had walked so many miles that her legs had begun to ache. Once a week, regular as clockwork, Joshua wrote her a letter and from what she could tell life at boarding school hadn't turned out to be half as bad as he had feared.

He liked his form master, Mr Holmes, even though he was very strict. Weekends were the best, Saturdays most of all because they played outdoor games. On Sunday mornings they went to church and every pupil had to write home during the afternoon. There were seven other boys sleeping in the same dormitory as he was. He had made friends with a boy named Nicholas Banks and the two of them had been picked for the rugby team. The last sentence was always the most important: I hope you and Nan are both well and please can you find out from Mr Stuart how far the work on my boat has progressed.

Kate knew the contents of each letter off by heart. Joshua wasn't missing her that much. That's as it should be, she rebuked herself, you'd be much more upset if he wrote that he was utterly miserable and very homesick.

It was the letter that Mary had received by this morning's post that had made Kate's restless feeling so much worse. Mary was going to have to go to Wales.

Kate understood that she had no option. Her sister's husband had died very suddenly leaving Mary's sister Blanche in a terrible situation. Struck down with polio at the age of fourteen she had been left with the lower half of her body paralysed. When she was twenty years old, she had met and married George Edwards, a man whom Mary had never taken to.

'Give him his due,' Mary had said sadly, while they were discussing the letter over breakfast, 'he was fit as a fiddle himself but he took good care of Blanche – though I still think the money our father left my sister had a lot to do with his offer of marriage.'

'Did you voice that opinion at the time?' Kate asked, unable to keep a note of incredulity from her voice.

'Well . . .' Mary looked sheepishly at her. 'When you're young it's difficult to keep a still tongue in your head. It was the day after the wedding an' I overheard George setting up a deal to buy some property. I told him what I thought and he had his say.'

'And you've never seen your sister since?'

'Afraid not. I left Wales, came to Surrey and was fortunate enough to find a job with Mr Collier. Over the years, Blanche and I have exchanged letters and birthday cards, but no, I've never been back home. I've no other relatives left and I didn't see the need. I don't know what will happen to Blanche now; I don't think I can stand by and see her go into a home.'

'Oh, Mary,' Kate was shocked, 'of course you can't,

you have to go and see her, only then will you be able to judge what will be for the best.'

'I'll go tomorrow and I *will* do my best, but that's not to say I'll give up my life here with you. Perhaps the best solution will turn out to be for my sister to remain in her own home and have a nurse live in. We'll have to see.'

'I know what I'm going to do!' Kate's sudden outburst made Mary jump.

'What?'

'I've made up my mind. Today I'm going to get on to the GPO and have them install a telephone.'

Mary laughed. 'What brought that on?'

'Well, if I'm to be stuck here in this big house all on my own – you miles away in Wales and Josh at school – at least it will be some sort of a lifeline.'

'I think it's a great idea. I really do. Don't know why we've never given it a thought before now. I'll be able to keep in touch with you – let you know what's happening – an' I wouldn't be at all surprised if Josh's school doesn't allow boarders to phone home from time to time.'

'Mary! That would be wonderful. That's it. We're definitely having a telephone.'

Kate stood shivering as she watched the taxi bear Mary off to the railway station. During the night the wind had dropped and the temperature had fallen. A mantle of white hoar frost covered everything, gleaming and sparkling on the shrubs and grass and making the pathways very slippery. Kate stamped her feet and blew on her fingers, determined not to go back inside until Mary was out of sight. She wished for the hundredth time that Mary didn't have to go away and leave her. It was the first time that she had been alone in this house since she had come here to take care of Joshua. What am I going to do? she asked herself.

She had so often regretted the fact that she had no brothers or sisters. Because her parents had died in such circumstances, most of her old friends had fought shy of her. She did hear occasionally from her cousin Hilda, but she was married and now had three children and it seemed that life in the East End was far too busy for them to find time to come to sleepy Littleton Green.

Thankful to be back in the warmth of the big kitchen, Kate made herself a fresh pot of tea and set the flat irons out on top of the range. A batch of ironing seemed a very good idea on a cold morning such as this, and when she'd finished she would sit down and write to Josh. That decided, she set a blanket out across the table, covered it with a clean sheet and went out into the scullery to fetch the wicker basket.

What was she going to do? Kate asked herself again as she contemplated the long empty days that lay ahead. The reality was that she had no choice but to live alone and fill her days as best she could. I am twenty-nine years old. Good God! Next year I shall be thirty. The thought depressed her even more. She looked back over the last ten years. Had she been happy? She could truthfully answer yes to that question. Joshua had brought love and joy into her life, Mary had become a dear friend. And she had put the terrible nightmare of what had happened to her father and her mother behind her. A child's love was a wonderful thing, but she wouldn't be human if she didn't sometimes wonder what it would be like to be loved by a man: to feel his hands touching her body, his fingers in her hair, his lips on hers. Had she ever experienced a kiss of passion? Only if you counted Vic Appleton's fumblings when they used to walk together along the towpath and hide beneath Hampton Court Bridge. Dear Jesus, you've suddenly got a good memory. She laughed as she spat on a fresh iron, wiped it clean and began to press a linen tablecloth. She had dragged Vic Appleton up from the past! She'd been little more than a schoolgirl and it was hard for her to remember how she had looked then, some twelve or fourteen years ago. In pretty full-skirted summer dresses, her thick mop of curls blowing in the wind that always seemed to come off the river.

If she were honest she'd fancied the lads who lived and worked on the river. They'd always seemed so lively and carefree, with their tanned skins and dark good looks. A good tug on the boats' steam whistle as they glided past, a cheery wave and a friendly shout had always had her wishing that her own life could be as free and easy. Kate caught sight of herself in the mirror that hung over the fireplace. She shook her head and made a rueful grimace. The few river lads that had paid her any attention had been sent on their way with a flea in the ear by her father; he hadn't intended for his only daughter to associate with those vagabonds! Kate's lips set in a thin, tight line as anger and resentment rose in her. Her father had been a fine one to talk! A pillar of the community only when it suited him. The animosity that had for years existed between her parents had certainly back-washed on to her. Thirty next year and still a virgin!

Come on, she urged herself, at least you're well off. You own this house outright, you still have Bramble

Cottage and the Kearsley Boat Yard which brings you in a very nice income. There's many a woman would give her eye teeth to be in my shoes, so I'd better start counting my blessings and maybe someday, who knows, a Mister Right will come looking for me. It was a brave attitude and one Kate would do her best to believe in. All the same she knew she would lie awake at night now that she was alone in the house and every day would seem long and empty.

Chapter Twenty

'NOW WHAT?' KATE muttered, clicking her tongue in annoyance. Somebody had their finger on her doorbell and wasn't going to go away until she answered it. She was on the top landing sorting out the linen cupboard and putting aside items that needed mending. Getting up off her knees she straightened her skirt and went downstairs. She glanced at the hall clock, saw that it was almost half past ten, tucked a few strands of hair behind her ears, and went to answer the door.

'Jack Dawson? What on earth are you doing here?'

As she asked the question fear gripped her heart. It had to be her gran. Nothing else would have brought Jack all this way out on a weekday. He had his stalls on the go every day except Sunday; it was a hard enough way to earn a living without him taking days off.

'Sorry, Jack,' she mumbled, stepping back and inviting him in.

He removed his cap, wiped his boots on the doormat

and followed her down the hallway and into the kitchen.

'Kate, it's your gran. I'm ever so sorry.'

'I guessed as much, do sit down.'

He drew one of the high-backed wooden chairs out from under the table, sat himself down with his elbows resting on the table. The sad look that passed between them was enough and they remained silent for a minute until Kate asked, 'She's not just ill, is she? Not in hospital or anything?'

'Afraid not, she's gone. Died in her sleep. I found her this morning.'

Kate couldn't speak. She was choked. Crossing the room she filled the kettle, placed it on the gas stove and lit the jet. With her back to Jack, she busied herself setting out two cups and saucers on a tray. When she brought the tea to the table and Jack had a chance to look at her he was utterly dismayed. The expression on her face was enough to make a grown man weep. Such sadness and suffering the like of which he had never seen before.

Kate stirred the tea in the pot and passed him a big breakfast cup, brim-full. 'Help yourself to sugar,' she said.

Still a silence lay between them, and Jack Dawson could think of no suitable words to fill it. Why doesn't she ask me questions? Why doesn't she cry? Blame someone? Me if she likes, but for God's sake say or do something! He couldn't bear to watch her. He had known Kate since she was a mere slip of a girl. Gosh, how she had loved to get to Kingston market with her gran, even in her school holidays. Then life had taken a terrible turn for her. Most youngsters would have gone berserk with what she'd had to deal with. But Kate had weathered it all, including the gossip. Christ, there had been a load more newsmongering when Charles Collier had installed her in this house. But she had shown them all! Kept herself to herself and brought Joshua up to be a credit to her. It couldn't have been much of a life for her though, with only Mary Kennedy for company. Never married. Probably never would now. Such a shame. Jack put his now empty cup on the saucer, and shook his head.

'Are you all right, Kate?'

She nodded.

'Shall I tell you what happened?'

'Please,' she said gruffly.

'Well, yer gran hasn't been out an' about a lot since Christmas. Though she did tell me only a fortnight ago that you'd been in and taken her to Bentalls for tea.'

'Thank God I did,' Kate whispered, raising her head and giving Jack a weak grin. 'I asked her then to move out, come an' live here with me, but you know my gran, Jack, wild horses wouldn't drag her from the place my grandad built for her. "I lived most of me life here and I'll die here," is what she kept telling me.'

'Well, my love, she got her wish. Can't ask for more than that. Funny thing, I knocked on her front door this morning, something I never do. Always go round the back. The door's never locked.

'I knew there was something wrong the minute I set foot in the scullery. In the kitchen her fire had burnt very low during the night, but most telling of all, her big black kettle was to the side of the hob. First thing your gran did every morning was pull the kettle to the centre of the range so's it would come to the boil while she was having a wash.

'I went through to her bedroom. Peaceful as a baby she was. Her eyes were closed. Lovely way for her to go if you ask me. I'm ever so sorry to be the bearer of such sad news. I really liked your gran and so did everyone who knew her.'

'Yes. She was such a special person. So very wise.'

'I know you must feel awful but there are a lot of things to be seen to. Things only you can do, being her next of kin. If you like I can wait for you to get ready, take you into Kingston and run you about all day to the various offices. That's if you want me to.'

'Are you sure, Jack? Can you really spare the time?'

'I wouldn't have offered if I didn't mean it. Go on, get your coat and put something a bit stronger on your feet,' he half laughed, gazing down at her dainty slippers.

'Thanks,' Kate said with feeling. 'I'll be about ten minutes. Help yourself to another cup of tea.'

He rewarded her with a grin and, as she went to get herself ready, she vowed that some way or another she would make sure that he would not be the loser for all the trade he was missing today.

Kate felt she had done her best and that the arrangements she had made for her grandmother's funeral were as right as they could be. Mary wasn't coming home from Wales and Kate fully understood her reasons. What a godsend the telephone being installed in Melbourne Lodge had turned out to be. She and Mary had lengthy conversations, so much easier than trying to find the right words to put down on paper.

After several unsuccessful attempts Mary had at last found a housekeeper cum companion and a part-time nurse who were both in harmony with Blanche's needs and outlook on life. 'None the more for that I am going to stay at least until Whitsun,' Mary had said. Kate's heart had sunk, it was four weeks until Easter. 'By that time, if everything is still going great guns in this household I will feel that I have done my duty and be able to leave Blanche in capable hands and have nothing on my conscience.' With that Kate had to be content.

Joshua was being allowed home from school for the funeral, but only for the day. Kate had been hoping that, as the school holidays were so near, he might have been allowed to stay at home until the new term began after the Easter break. 'No such luck, Mum,' he had moaned down the telephone line. Still, at least she was going to get to see him for a whole day.

The church was sweet with the scent of flowers and there were a lot more people sitting in the pews than Kate had imagined there would be. They had come from all walks of life; poor folk who over the years Alice had given a helping hand to, bargees and boatmen and women of the floating river community who had become her friends, and other kindly friends and neighbours she had lived alongside for a great many years. Joshua looked so grown up, wearing his grey school suit with a black armband that matron had sewn on for him. Reverend Hutchinson was looking old himself. He cleared his throat and looked around at the solemn faces.

'Alice Kearsley once said to me that you take what life dishes out and get on with it or you go under. She was a caring, optimistic lady. Her husband, Jack, died at an early age, leaving her with three small children to bring up. Her two lovely little daughters died before even reaching school age, taken by that dreadful disease scarlet fever. Then in the prime of his life, her only son was also taken from her. Today, I would like you all to know that the endless grief Alice suffered did not make her bitter, rather it gave her endless compassion for others. Anyone who paid her a visit, left feeling merrier, knowing that they had a special friend. She will be remembered with love.'

Kate looked around her. There were a good many people wiping away a tear. It was nice, what the vicar had said. It was true an' all! Her greatest gifts had been her warmth and humanity.

James Hutchinson's voice was deep with emotion as he announced the numbers of the two hymns that the congregation would now sing.

Here comes the worse part, Kate thought as they went out into the spring sunshine and walked the few yards across to the churchyard. Joshua slipped his hand into hers and gripped it tightly. Death was so final, and the lowering of the coffin into the dark gaping hole made him shudder.

'Gran's not really there.' Kate lowered her head and whispered, 'Really she's not, Josh. That's only her tired old body, which she hasn't any more use for now; the best part of her is away free and without pain.'

They had to shake hands with so many people who were offering their sincere condolences. Kate thought about Mary and wished, for Josh's sake, that she could have been here. Though the sun was still shining there was a sharp wind whipping round the tombstones and she was thankful when at last she was able to say to him, 'Come on, let's make our way to the car. Let's go home.'

Most of the afternoon, they spent in front of the drawing-room fire. Kate laughed suddenly, feeling more relaxed than she had done for weeks.

'What's tickled you?' Josh was anxious to know when yet again she let out a peal of laughter.

'You haven't been listening to yourself, young man, or else you wouldn't need to ask that question,' Kate said, wiping the tears from her eyes. 'You've got boats and boat yards on the brain.'

Josh looked at her and he, too, burst out laughing. 'Oh, I see what you mean. I have been going on a bit, haven't I? I just wish there was time for me to go down to the yard and see how far Mr Stuart has got. Do you really believe it won't be finished in time for the Easter holidays?'

'Well, there isn't time for you to go, unfortunately, the car will be here for you at four thirty and, no, I do not think your boat will be finished in time for this coming holiday. In fact, I know it won't be.'

'Aw, Mum . . .'

'There's no way you're getting round me on this one. For a start, Easter is pretty early this year and you can bet your life the weather won't be up to much. And for another thing, good workmen never rush a job. But Mr Stuart did say to me that he might let you and Peter do some varnishing on the woodwork.'

'Cor, that would be great! Can't wait for the hols to start, I don't really want to go back to school today, but I suppose I must.'

'Indeed you must, but guess what? I've packed you a special parcel, stacked with goodies. You can share it with your mates when you get back.'

'You're great. No other mum in the world is better than you are. I'm just going up to my room, I might take a couple of my books back with me.'

Kate listened to him humming as he flew up the stairs. At least she had turned the sadness of Alice's funeral around for him. And if she is looking down on me at this minute, Kate thought, she'd say, 'Well done, Kate. I had a good life and a young lad like Josh shouldn't be upset by my going.'

Kate quickened her pace and, when the road was clear, crossed over to where, not one, but two police constables were standing in the doorway of the paper shop.

'Morning,' Kate said smiling. 'I've walked round and round in circles trying to find the offices of Cooper and Dawes. Can you direct me please?'

The youngest constable's face remained straight, but the older man's lips twitched as he smiled at her. 'Lost are you? An' I would have bet a week's pay that you knew your way around Kingston, Miss Kearsley.'

'I would have backed you an' all, that is until today. Fishguard Lane is the address on their letter heading but I can't for the life of me seem to find the place.'

'Understandable. The old firm of solicitors, Dawes it used to be, in the High Street, moved premises when they joined up with Cooper. Tucked in, well back behind the Griffin where the old warehouses used to be. You have to look up to see their sign and then climb a flight of stairs.' He took hold of Kate's arm and walked her briskly to the corner of the road. 'You probably don't remember me, Miss Kearsley, I was on court duty at the time of your mother's trial. May I say it's good to see you looking so well. I often had a chat with your gran and I was sorry to hear of her death. Nice and peaceful way to go though, wasn't it? Bit different from your mum. I bet, for you, that day still doesn't bear thinking about. Really tragic set to that was!'

'Thanks for your help.' Kate gave him a tight smile before turning off in the direction he had pointed out to her.

The policeman stood rooted to the spot. As he watched Kate half walk, half run across the busy road, he reflected, her mother's trial must have been all of ten years ago, so she must be in her late twenties. He remembered her as a shy, bewildered young girl, but now she had matured into a tall, striking figure. Her face was real pretty and her thick hair still glossy and curly. The dark suit she had on fitted her so well, that it was impossible not to notice what a good figure she had.

Kate's thoughts were very different as she hurried on her way. She had no recollection of having known the policeman and, even if she had, she would have done her best to suppress the memory. She was flustered. Memories swirled round and round in her head. The very mention of her mother, the trial, and the awful events leading up to it were enough to make her break out in a sweat. Even after all this time she felt a chill of horror creeping over her body. Why the hell had he had to bring it up? Visiting her mother in prison had been a nightmare, and she had shoved it to the back of her mind. Now because of his remarks the memory was real again:

the long echoing corridors, the grey clothes her mother had been made to wear, the damp dark walls and the fear. She had felt the fear the minute she stepped through the gate.

And worst of all, that last visit; her mother's sad face as she had turned at the doorway to say her final goodbye. In spite of the passing years and the effort of pushing all the facts to the back of her mind, she knew that was one image she would never, *ever*, forget.

Why, oh why, had she had to meet up with that particular policeman?

She turned into the narrow lane, rested her body against the wall and just stood there, dragging great gulps of air into her lungs. She could feel her heart racing, thumping ridiculously fast and a terrifying sensation of panic seemed to tighten every muscle in her body, making her stomach contract. It was no good, without further warning she was bent double, vomiting all over the ground. After a few agonising seconds she straightened herself up and, in doing so, banged the back of her head against the wall. Still feeling sick and trembling all over, she reached into her handbag for a handkerchief with which to wipe away the bile left in her mouth.

Footsteps sounded nearby and she looked up to see a stranger coming towards her. The gentleman threw Kate a questioning look. 'Can I be of any help?' he asked, looking deeply concerned.

She shrank away, looking most uncomfortable. 'Well . . . I . . .' She eyed him, wondering who he was and where he had come from. He was tall with nice soft grey eyes and his wide mouth smiled at her from under a trilby hat.

'The last thing I want to do is embarrass you, but you do look as if you could use a hand.'

'Don't worry, you haven't,' Kate assured him shakily, instinctively adjusting her skirt, 'but I must look a terrible sight.'

'Where were you planning to go? Perhaps you might let me take you somewhere for a cup of tea, you certainly look as if you're in need of a hot drink.'

'Oh, no, I couldn't. You don't know me nor I you, and I have an appointment with this firm of solicitors,' she said, nodding her head upwards towards a flight of wooden stairs.

'Well, this may be of help,' he said, holding out a large clean white handkerchief.

Kate took it, smiling gratefully as she used it to tidy herself up. The gentleman took a step backwards and said, 'Now might be a good time to introduce myself. My name is Bernard Pinfold.'

'Oh,' she stammered, 'I'm Kate Kearsley, I really must go . . . I'm late as it is, but I'm grateful to you.' She looked at his soiled handkerchief and gave him a bewildered look.

'Please keep it. Any gentleman would help a lady in distress.'

'Well, thank you again.'

He tipped his hat. 'Are you sure you are all right?'

'Yes, I'll be fine now. Thank you again for your concern,' she said with sincerity. 'It was kind of you to stop.'

She watched his upright figure as he walked the length

of the lane and, as she climbed the steps that lead to the offices of Cooper and Dawes, there was a puzzled look on her face.

Mr Dawes, who had looked after Alice's affairs, was a short podgy man with a bald head, and the fact that he had a very bad cold and kept blowing his nose very noisily, into a large handkerchief with a wide red border, did not endear him to Kate. As he leant across his leather-topped deck, she found herself drawing as far back into her chair as possible.

'Well,' Mr Dawes cleared his throat yet again, 'as you are the only relative of the late Alice Kearsley everything is very straightforward. No doubt you are aware that the land on which your grandmother's house stood is entirely freehold as is the field beyond. So that's the first part of her will out of the way.'

'Please,' Kate interrupted, 'am I to understand that the field beyond my grandmother's house also belonged to her?'

'You weren't aware of that fact?' Mr Dawes made no attempt to keep the disbelief from his voice.

'I certainly was not,' Kate assured him firmly. 'What with all the ground at the back of the house, where she kept her animals, I never gave the field beyond so much as a thought.'

'Neither did your grandmother it would seem. It has never been cultivated, but it has certainly increased in value since your grandfather acquired it.'

Kate waited, feeling agitated. Things weren't going at all to order today.

Mr Dawes unscrewed the top of his fountain pen

and drew a folder towards him. 'Yes,' he said, half to himself, 'a very straightforward will, but that is to be expected, Mrs Kearsley was a very straightforward lady.' He took off his spectacles that he seemed to need only when reading, and leant further still across the desk and peered at Kate. 'All her worldly possessions, her entire estate, and that includes a tidy sum of money, she has left to you.'

Kate didn't like his tone, it was . . . smarmy was the best word she could think of. It took a moment before she was able to summon the breath to speak. 'I can't believe all this,' she murmured, 'I truly can't. My gran never had a lot of money.'

'For a working-class lady she certainly did,' said Mr Dawes, this time using a gentle tone.

Kate had a job to stop herself from grinning. I seem to be amassing properties and the funds that go with them like other people collect works of art, she thought as she watched him lay papers out in front of her and indicate where she had to sign.

Mr Dawes took off his spectacles, leant back in his chair and rubbed his eyes. 'You seem overwhelmed by all of this, Miss Kearsley. Have you no idea as to what you will do with the property?'

Kate shook her head.

'There will probably be the need for repairs, in fact it might be much better in the long run if the property were to be demolished and the land sold.'

Hold on, Kate almost shouted at him, this has nothing to do with you! Instead, she said, 'That house holds a great many happy memories for me. There's no hurry for any decision. I shall give a lot of thought to this before I come to any conclusion.' She looked away from him, remembering summer days spent with Alice; the chickens and ducks cluttering the backyard, the smell of the rabbit hutches and how she had hated to have to help to clean them out; the great bread pudding they would eat sitting on the grass beneath the shelter of a tree, the lovely brown eggs she would take home to her mother. It all seemed so long ago now.

The solicitor looked at his watch. Kate took the hint. 'I've kept you too long,' she said, rising to her feet and pulling on her white cotton gloves.

'I think,' said Mr Dawes, also standing up and coming round his desk to stand closer to her than was necessary, 'you will need a lot of professional advice when you have had time to consider just what your grandmother's estate entails. You have my telephone number. Please let me know me if I may be of further assistance.'

'Thank you, you've been very kind,' she murmured, stepping quickly towards the door.

As she left the offices of Cooper and Dawes, her head was still aching and she felt too many recollections had been forced on her. Real decisions must wait until later, but if any help were needed she had made up her mind that it would be to Mr Weatherford she would turn, rather than to the firm of Cooper and Dawes. Mr Weatherford was a gentleman of both good sense and charm; she wasn't sure the same could be said of Mr Dawes.

Chapter Twenty-One

COMING OUT OF the solicitor's office into the fresh air, Kate looked down at the ground before gingerly putting her foot on the top step of the wooden staircase. Her insides were all of a flutter, her mouth as dry as a bone and she didn't feel at all well. First having that policeman remind her of the way her mother had died and then to have to sit and listen to Mr Dawes going on about what she ought to be doing with her gran's home. Needs demolishing indeed! That was his opinion, it certainly wasn't hers.

'Can I give you a hand? You don't look at all steady,' enquired a quiet male voice from the bottom of the steps.

Kate raised her head and found herself looking into the kind face of the man who had come to her rescue earlier.

'Well . . . er . . . thank you,' she muttered, feeling somewhat at a loss, but she took her hand from the wooden rail and held it out to the stranger.

'I hope you don't mind my taking the liberty of waiting for you,' he said gently, as he helped her down the remaining steps, 'only I could see you were rather upset, and as you were on your own I was worried about you.'

'That's very kind of you but I'll be all right now.'

'I'd be pleased to buy you that cup of tea, if you would allow me to,' he volunteered, still keeping hold of her hand.

Kate was taken back, but she recovered quickly and found herself saying, 'There's nothing I'd like more at this moment.'

Kate shifted uneasily on the padded chair, which was set near the bay window of the tea shop. Bernard Pinfold sitting next to her touched her arm.

'Would you like anything to eat?'

She shook her head. 'No, thank you.'

'I think you should eat something, it would help to settle your stomach. How about if we both have a toasted teacake?'

Kate smiled and nodded.

The waitress brought their order, setting the cups and saucers beside the teapot directly in front of her. She knew he was watching her as she poured milk into each cup and then the tea. Her hand trembled slightly as she passed a cup over to him.

'Do you take sugar?'

'No, thank you.'

He took a drink of his tea and swivelled round in his chair to stretch his long legs out to the side.

Kate thought, he must be at least six feet tall, fortyish

or maybe late thirties, good-looking face, and a fine, firm body. He picked up the dish that held their teacakes and held it towards her. Using a knife she slid one onto her plate and in doing so she touched his hand with her fingertips.

'The colour has come back into your cheeks. You really are a very attractive young lady.'

'Oh!' She was flattered but uncertain. It was a boost to her ego being here with such a nice man, and it made her feel good to be told that she was attractive . . . but should she really be here?

They each buttered their teacake and fell into a comfortable silence until Bernard started talking about his reason for being in Kingston. 'My home is in Bristol, you've probably gathered that from my accent.'

Kate thought only how impressive he sounded but she made no comment. Reaching into his inside pocket he took out a business card and handed it to her. 'Bernard Pinfold, Pharmacist.' His address was also printed there and a telephone number.

'I'm here for the next couple of weeks to help set up a pharmacy within the bounds of Kingston Hospital. How about you, what do you do with yourself?'

Kate hadn't been expecting such a direct question. She stammered for a moment. 'Oh, dear. I've never had a job, not as such. My father said there was no need for me to work. Then . . .' What could she tell him? Certainly not her family background; she had never spoken to a soul about it and she wasn't prepared to do so now.

'Then?' he asked.

To cover her embarrassment she took his cup and poured him some more tea.

'My parents both died and I moved into Melbourne Lodge to care for a baby whose mother had died at birth. That was ten years ago. Joshua is away at boarding school now. I look on him as my own son.'

'And you never married?' He looked directly at her, and she felt something jump inside her. She liked his grey eyes, the soft way he spoke and, now that he had taken his hat off, the brown hair that was turning grey at the sides.

'No, I never did,' she answered, picking up her cup and draining the last of her tea. 'Thanks again for your kindness and for the refreshment.' She smiled, bending to pick up her handbag that lay at her feet.

'I don't know where you live,' he said, 'but I have my car parked just down the street, would you allow me to drive you home?'

'That would be nice, if it's not taking you out of your way.'

Why had she accepted his offer? He was a total stranger and already this morning she had let him take her into tearooms and buy her food and drink. She came to the conclusion that Bernard Pinfold was a nice person; there was something about him, something different that made her want to prolong the time she spent with him.

The stretch of river just outside Littleton Green was less commercial than in Kingston, its green and sloping banks glowed with the promise of spring on this early March morning and Kate thought that, with any luck, by the time Palm Sunday came round all the sticky buds would be bursting out on the branches of the trees.

'It must be wonderful to live here,' Bernard Pinfold

said as she directed him where to turn his car into the driveway of Melbourne Lodge.

'Oh, yes. I've always considered myself extremely lucky to live by the river. The waterfront has a kind of peacefulness about it. Would you like to come in and see the house?'

'If it's all right, I certainly would.'

'It's perfectly all right,' she answered, knowing full well she was throwing caution to the wind by inviting this complete stranger into her home. Half of her was saying that she had taken leave of her senses while the other, overriding half, was protesting that Bernard Pinfold was a sensitive gentleman. He's educated, a man of means, it's written all over him, she said to herself as she put her key into the lock of the front door.

He held the door of the sitting room open for her and, as she took off her coat, he was there at her elbow to take it from her and lay it carefully over the back of a chair.

'Would you like a drink? We have some Madeira, or maybe a sherry?'

'If it's all the same to you, I'd rather have coffee.'

'Coffee's fine. I suppose we always offer wine to visitors because it seems the right thing to do.'

'Can I give you a hand?'

'No, and don't stand there twiddling your hat round in your hands, take your coat off and go and sit in one of the armchairs in the bay; you get a glorious view of the garden from there.' He was doing just as Kate bid him when she turned at the doorway to glance back.

In the kitchen she hummed to herself as she set the kettle to boil, then put a handful of coffee beans into the grinder. She laid a tray, choosing one of Mary's best traycloths, opened the top cupboard of the dresser and took out two of the best bone-china cups which they only used on high days and holidays. Not for Bernard Pinfold, a dainty little coffee cup that held only a mouthful, a breakfast cup would be much more in his line! Now how would you know that? she asked herself, then laughed out loud. She just sensed that she was right. When the coffee was ready she added a bowl of brown sugar, a jug of cream and a plate of shortbread to the tray.

He must have heard her footsteps on the hall tiles, and was again holding the door open for her, ready to take the tray, which he placed on a small table near to where he had been sitting.

'Would you like cream?'

'Yes, please, but no sugar.'

Kate let the thick cream dribble over the back of the teaspoon from where it trickled slowly into swirls on top of the black coffee. She placed a cup before him, and set her own cup on the other side of the table. Leaning back in her chair, she crossed one leg over the other, bent over and took off her shoes.

He took a sip of his coffee and watched her. She was small framed, about twenty-five or maybe a little older, he thought, with a beautiful complexion, big dark-brown eyes and arched eyebrows. But her crowning glory was her hair. Thick and heavy, shiny brown in colour with unusual chestnut glints. He'd lay a pound to a penny that when she had set out this morning it had been combed back, restrained by the use of slides or combs. He loved it as it was now – the sides falling free, dangling over her ears. He found himself wondering what that mop of thick hair would look like spread out loosely over a pillow and what it would feel like to run his fingers through those tresses.

'What is it you do, exactly?' Kate broke the silence because she felt uncomfortable knowing he was studying her.

'Well, I'm legally qualified to sell drugs and poisons, and sometimes I get involved in the preparing of medicines. I'm here to help and advise with the setting up of the hospital's pharmacy. I also travel a lot. The company I work for has irons in the fire in many countries. As soon as this project is up and running I am going to South Africa, Cape Town actually, which is South Africa's oldest city.'

Kate felt her heart sink. What difference will that make to you? she sternly scolded herself. You've only just met the man and when he leaves here this morning you're not likely to set eyes on him ever again

'More coffee?' she asked, more to cover her confusion than anything else.

'Thanks, I'll just have a top-up. I'll help myself,' he said, reaching for the coffeepot. 'How about you, what do you do besides taking care of this beautiful old house?'

Kate felt a little piqued. 'I've already told you, I've never had an outside job.'

'Oh.' He sensed he'd touched a raw spot. 'I am so sorry. It was never my intention to pry.'

He looked so crestfallen that Kate reached over and covered his hand with her own.

'It should be me that is apologising, I'm very touchy about my past and I don't want to go into details. But – 'she hesitated, took her hand away, sipped her coffee, looked across the table at him and finally said, 'I've had a great life here. Looking after Joshua has been a privilege and a pleasure. He's a wonderful lad, the best thing that ever happened to me.' Now she had started, she found that words and thoughts that had been at the back of her mind for years were suddenly pouring out. 'Maybe it hasn't been the life that I dreamt of as a young girl. You must know the sort of thing: boyfriend, get engaged, white wedding in church, children, live happily ever after. Every girl has such dreams. They just didn't work out for me.'

'When you offered me a drink, you said "we" always keep wine in the house. I don't think you meant young Joshua, did you?'

'You're fishing. What you're really asking is, do I live with someone? Well the answer is, yes, I do.' She sat back and let the statement sink in, watching a frown crease his forehead. 'Joshua and I share this house with a lady whose name is Mary Kennedy. Mary was housekeeper to Mr Collier, Joshua's father, long before Joshua was born. His mother, Jane Mortimer, died giving birth to him, and Mr Collier asked me to move in here with Mary and take care of the baby. On his death, he named me as Joshua's guardian. From those few details you will have gathered that Joshua's mother and father were not married. Now you have it all in a nutshell, except that Mary is in Wales at the moment, and won't be home until Whitsuntide.'

They sat in silence for a minute until Bernard cleared his throat and said, 'This is going to sound really awful . . . but I'm glad you were taken unwell in Kingston this morning and that I was able to come to your rescue.' He rose from his chair. 'I've really enjoyed meeting you and talking to you. Life can be very lonely when one moves around as much as I do. I'd better be on my way and let you get on with whatever you had planned for today.'

She watched him walk out of the house, get into his car, and drive away.

It took every bit of her will power to stop herself from shouting after him, please, don't go.

It was turned midnight and Kate was lying awake mulling over the events of the morning and coming to the conclusion that it had been fraught with frustration. First off she and that strange, lovely man had seemed to enjoy each other's company; at one point she had felt the electricity sparking between them. Somehow she had done something wrong. Perhaps she had gone into too many details, giving him the pattern of life here in Melbourne Lodge. Well, he must have gathered that this house had, at one time, been a love nest for Mr Collier and Jane Mortimer. Good job he hadn't probed further! She might have been tempted to reveal the gory details as to how and why she had been on her own and only too grateful to have been offered the chance to come and live here and take care of Jane's baby. That would surely have put him off!

He'd said he was here for another two weeks, yet he had made no suggestion that they should meet again. Perhaps he was a married man. That hadn't occurred to her until now. She was suddenly conscious that she was in this large house all on her own. She had no immediate family, no one in the whole world that she could really call her very own. She became aware of a terrible aching loneliness. Much as she loved Joshua and Mary there was still a need in her that had never been fulfilled.

Why, oh why, hadn't Bernard Pinfold suggested that they meet again? She should have called him back. Offered him lunch . . . what would have been the point? He was leaving the country soon, going far away, to South Africa.

Chapter Twenty-Two

KATE FOUND HERSELF in a discontented frame of mind during the days following her encounter with Bernard Pinfold. The house had seemed empty after Joshua went away to school and even worse when Mary went to Wales. Now the place seemed desolate. After such a short time spent with a total stranger he had woken in her feelings that she had never before allowed to surface. They had hardly had a lengthy conversation when she had invited him in to Melbourne Lodge. She'd thought, after he'd gone, that she hadn't even shown him round the house as she had promised and he hadn't pursued the matter. But there was something about him that had intrigued her and, at the time, she'd been sure it was the same for him. She had felt instantly that he was a man to be trusted, a man she wanted to get to know. It hadn't worked out like that, they'd just been ships that passed in the night.

Kate put down the pile of clean linen as she entered her

bedroom and leant against the wall. Heaving a great sigh she let all the tension drain out of her in one long breath. What was she getting herself in such a state for? A man, a good-looking, fit young man, came along and did her a kindness and she wanted to make so much more out of it. Pull yourself together, for goodness' sake, she rebuked herself. Moving towards the bed she began to strip the covers off. No matter how many times she urged herself to be sensible, she couldn't help wishing that she hadn't seen the last of Bernard Pinfold.

After she had remade the bed with the clean linen and dusted the furniture, she stood in front of the full-length mirror set into the door of the wardrobe and studied herself in earnest. Her figure was good, her breasts high and firm. Well they should be! No babies had been suckled at them and, come to that, no man had ever fondled them. Her waist was small, her belly flat and her legs weren't a bad shape. What was she doing this for? There didn't seem much point to it. Not one real man had ever shown any interest in her and at her time of life she was only deluding herself if she still believed that one day a Prince Charming was going to come riding up on a white charger and carry her off to live happily ever after.

I'd settle for an ordinary man, she laughed to herself, one that worked for his living, got his hands dirty and came home expecting me to wash his mucky overalls. She grinned cynically at her reflection. Who are you kidding? You've enough money and properties to keep a whole family for the rest of their lives, but it still hasn't been an attraction where men have been concerned. Her past had been what had put possible suitors off!

Who in their right mind would want to lie in bed with

me, make passionate love, knowing that my mother had killed my father by stabbing him in the back and had met her own death at the end of a hangman's rope? The whole country had read about it in the daily press and avidly followed the court trial. The various books and articles that had been written about the Thames-side murder had been grossly distorting and there would always be someone like the policeman in Kingston popping up, only too willing to remind her of those awful circumstances. I'd have to live a very long time to live it down entirely. Kate shook her head as she accepted that fact.

'My God, you are morbid this morning,' she said out loud. 'And with good reason,' she answered herself.

Just lately she had hungered for a family of her own. Mary was getting on in years and Joshua wouldn't need her in the future as much as he had in the past. What is there left for me? Who will be left for me?

I could do with some company to cheer me up, she thought, as she bundled up the dirty bedlinen, tucked it under her arm and headed for the stairs. Not being able to think of anyone to visit she decided the next best thing would be to get herself out into the garden and dig up a few weeds.

Once out in the open air, with a scarf tied over her head and gardening gloves on her hands, Kate sank to her knees and started to dig in the earth as if her very life depended on it.

Meeting Bernard Pinfold had unsettled her. But soon it would be the Easter holidays and the house would ring with the laughter of Josh and his chums. Then in only a few more weeks, there'd be another bank holiday,

Whitsuntide. Mary would be home and everything would be back to normal.

Resolving not to be so short-tempered, she loosened the earth around a clump of weeds and tugged until they came away in her hand. If I keep this up for a couple of hours, she mumbled to herself, perhaps I shall feel a darn sight better.

Bernard Pinfold was amazed at the effect Kate Kearsley had had on him. He'd thought he could leave it as just a pleasant chance meeting, but she filled his mind. He stared across the dining room, taking note of the starched white tablelinen set out with good china and crystal wine glasses and at the menu which offered a great choice of well-prepared food. Hotel life was good if one experienced it only once in a while. When it was part of your everyday life it became a bore. He counted himself as being fortunate. Anything he wanted, within reason, he could afford. His friends would say he had the best of all worlds. He loved his job and the travelling it entailed. Did he hanker after a settled home? A family? Well, the other man's grass is always greener. He was a professional man and he had achieved what he had set out to do. His father had been a pharmacist and he had wanted to follow in his footsteps since he was ten years old. At this moment he didn't understand his own feelings.

Folding his napkin into a neat square, he placed it on his side plate and rose from the table. He thought it best to use the telephone box situated in the far corner of the hotel's entrance hall. He picked up the ear piece and asked the operator for Directory Enquiries, when connected he asked for the number of Melbourne Lodge,

Littleton Green. Back to the operator, he put two pennies in to the slot, gave her the number and waited.

The light had begun to fade and Kate was in the garden shed. She was cleaning and stowing away the tools she had been using when the phone rang in the house. She dropped everything and ran. It might be Josh, or Mary ringing for a chat. It had rung several times before she grabbed it and breathlessly said, 'Melbourne Lodge.'

'Hallo, Miss Kearsley, this is Bernard Pinfold.'

She felt the colour flare up in her cheeks.

'Hallo.'

'I'd like to ask you something.'

Kate's insides jumped and a happy smile came to her lips.

'Tomorrow being Saturday, I don't have much to do at the hospital. I could get away by eleven o'clock. The weather looks as if it might be pretty good, so I wondered if you'd spend the day with me?'

Spend the whole day with him! Had she heard him right? Oh, yes please, she thought, but said only, 'Thank you, that would be nice.'

'I'd planned to pay a visit to Hampton Court while I'm here, but as it's not far from you perhaps you'd find it a bore.'

'Not at all,' Kate hastened to assure him. 'If you've never seen Hampton Court Palace I shall be able to point out the interesting parts.'

'Good, that's settled then. What time shall I pick you up?'

'You're the worker, whenever it suits you, I'll be ready.'

'About eleven. I'll see you then. All right? Bye.'

For the next hour Kate sat at the kitchen table with a plate of ham salad and fresh fruit for her sweet. Why in the world had he called her? It was what she had longed for; prayed for.

Now it had happened, that old uneasiness was creeping over her again. It's high time you had a day out she told herself. Live for the moment and let the future take care of itself, she decided, as she made preparations to have a bath before going to bed. Coming up to thirty she might be, but there was a spring to her step as she climbed the stairs and thought about what she was going to wear when Bernard Pinfold took her out next day.

Shafts of bright sunlight flashed across the bonnet of the black Austin as Bernard drove along the main road towards Hampton Court.

'It's a lovely day for our outing,' he remarked to Kate, who was looking extremely elegant in a single-breasted beige suit with a saucy brown-velvet cloche hat which dipped to a point over her right eye and had a colourful feather sewn on the left-hand brim.

'Yes.'

'You wouldn't be able to keep your promise and show me all the interesting parts if it had been raining,' he said, making a brave attempt to draw her into a conversation. 'You really do look very smart,' he added, keeping his voice light.

Why, oh why, did she feel so ill at ease?

'There aren't too many occasions in my life that call for me to dress up,' she answered, doing her best to put a smile into her voice.

'Then I'm flattered that you considered being with me

such an occasion.' He concentrated on the road ahead in silence for a while, then said, 'I thought about you a great deal before I gathered the courage to telephone you.'

'Oh!' His frankness pleased her. 'I thought about you too.'

He glanced at her and they both smiled. Kate felt a whole lot more relaxed and, settling more comfortably in her seat, began to enjoy the ride.

Once Bernard had parked the car he suggested they had coffee before starting to walk, and they chose the first café they came too, which overlooked the Thames. As Bernard gave their order to the waitress, Kate hid her mouth behind her hand to cover her amusement – from where she was sitting she had a straight view of the river and there, nestling low down beyond the great bridge, was a broad sign at the entrance to a yard which said, 'Kearsley Boat Yard. Boat Builders & Repairers'.

Kate stole a glance at this good-looking young man. He looked different today than he had at their first meeting. For one thing he wasn't wearing a hat and was dressed in a more casual way. A lovely navy blue jacket – expensive was the thought that came into her mind – grey trousers, white shirt, top button undone and a plain, pale blue vee-necked pullover. The shoes he was wearing were also casual, black, without laces, the slip-on kind. His hair was not smoothed down – more wiry than anything else – and the grey sideboards were really attractive.

He doesn't know much about me, Kate thought as she stared across at her boat yard.

'Lovely setting,' he remarked, as much to himself as to her. 'A good many ducks and swans on the river and plenty of activity. I didn't realise so much industry focused around this part of the Thames.'

'Why should you? Your home is in Bristol. If I were to visit that town I'd be just as unaware of what went on in that part of the world, wouldn't I?' The warmth of the smile Kate gave him matched her mood. She was feeling happy.

'I nearly came here once, on my honeymoon.'

Kate stiffened. So he was married! She should have known right from the start. He hadn't lied to her. It was only natural a man of his standing would have a wife. She felt sad. She didn't want him to be married.

'Only the marriage didn't last very long.'

'What?'

'Sounds daft, doesn't it? I was twenty-two years old, she was twenty-five. Thought she was the most beautiful girl in the world. She was engaged for two years to my best mate. They had an awful row and split up and she married me on the rebound. He came to the wedding. The same evening she told me she was sorry and went off with him.'

'How awful. I'm so sorry.'

Bernard leant across the table and looked directly into her eyes. 'Don't be. It was only my pride that was hurt and I made up for it by sowing a crop of wild oats.'

Kate tried to stifle a giggle but when he began to laugh so did she.

'The pains of growing up,' he said when their laughter became quieter.

If only you knew! My sufferings were a whole lot more severe than yours, Kate thought as she took a sip of her coffee. But she felt good; knowing that his marriage had been a non-starter was a boost, and she fell to wondering what difference that fact made to her. He was being kind to her; sharing his free time with her. Well, she would make the most of it because that's all there would be to it. Very soon his job would be taking him halfway across the world and they would never set eyes on each other again.

He offered her his arm as they walked. It was as if they were two old friends enjoying a day out together. She showed him the great vine, the old clock and the maze. Then they stared at the parts of the palace which were occupied as residences by private persons.

'I suppose you have to have been on a council housing list for a very long time to get one of these,' he teased.

'Could be.' Kate laughed. 'But I think it would be more helpful if one were a friend of the king, or, in your case, perhaps the queen.'

He squeezed her hand and they burst out laughing.

They found a really old-fashioned pub with a restaurant at the back overlooking Bushey Park, with its avenues of limes and magnificent horse chestnut trees.

'Aren't they graceful animals?' Kate remarked, as they sat at a table in the window watching the deer run across the grass and disappear behind the trees.

'Yes. You really are lucky to live in such a beautiful part of the country,' he told her.

Their eyes met and Kate found it hard to look away.

'You've no room for complaint, you travel the world while I stay put in my little corner,' she said jokingly. She was glad when the waiter brought their food because the interruption eased the tension that had sprung up between them.

Bernard did most of the talking, mainly telling her how the new department was coming along in the hospital.

They had settled for the set menu; asparagus tips to start, followed by roast chicken served with a delicious assortment of fresh vegetables, washed down with a glass of white wine, which he had insisted was a must.

'I think it's really nice of you to have invited me out like this,' Kate said when they had reached the coffee stage. 'It was a lovely meal, I enjoyed it.'

'I did too.' He smiled, lying back in his chair. 'But there is one thing that seems all wrong to me.'

'Maybe you'd better tell me what it is,' Kate said, feeling the colour rise in her cheeks.

'Oh, please, I didn't mean to upset you. It's just . . . well, I can't go on calling you Miss Kearsley. I think we've passed that stage and become friends, don't you?'

She let out a deep breath. 'I'd like it if you called me Kate, in fact I'd feel a whole lot more comfortable if you did.'

'Right, and I'm going to ask you to dispense with the Bernard. I have a nickname that most of my friends use. God alone knows how it came about, but over the years it has certainly stuck.'

'Go on then, tell me what it is.'

'Toby.'

'Toby.' She rolled the name round her tongue. 'Do you know, I think it suits you. It has a warm tone to it, not stuffy like Bernard. Yes, I like Toby, I like it very much.'

'I'm pleased that you're pleased,' he teased her. 'And now that we have that out of the way, shall we make plans as to how we shall spend the rest of this week?'

Kate said hastily, 'I thought you were here to work?'

'Only in an advisory capacity, and if I try hard enough I can usually be free by midday. I wish—' He paused for a long moment, looked down, then cleared his throat before saying, 'You know, Kate, I can't tell you when I've enjoyed someone's company as much as I'm enjoying yours. I feel I'd really like to get to know you better. Will you consider spending more time with me?'

'Oh, Toby.'

She put out her hand to him and he gripped it tightly as he outlined the places he would like to take her to. Kate had not meant her impulsive action to be taken quite so seriously and she withdrew her hand as gently as she could. Nagging doubts crowded her mind. Nothing could come of any of this; he wasn't going to be around. Through the restaurant window she could see a pair of graceful swans gliding upstream. Swans mated for life; it wasn't always like that for people.

'How about a walk along the towpath, nothing too strenuous, just a stroll to help our lunch to go down?' he suggested, signalling to the waiter that he would like to settle the bill.

When Kate smilingly agreed, he was on his feet in an instant, helping her on with her jacket. They crossed the bridge and he tucked her hand through the crook of his arm as they walked down the slope and on to the shingle footpath. The Thames flowed as far as the eye could see, its waters smooth and dark. In places trees grew on its banks, their boughs just tipping the surface. Small boats rode at anchor and the sound of hammering from several boat yards hidden from sight by a bend in the river echoed back up to them.

'It's getting cooler now the sun has gone in. Are you warm enough?' he asked

'I think it might be as well if we made our way back to the car.'

'All right,' Toby agreed. Changing direction, his eyes cast downwards, he said, 'You know you haven't given me an answer, Kate. I asked whether you would spend more days like this, with me.'

She stopped and glanced at him. She really didn't want to start something that was doomed from the start. A few days, wonderful memories, and then what? He'd be gone. On the other hand, hours and hours to enjoy his company! It was just too tempting to refuse, even if she would be left feeling more lonely than ever after he had gone away.

'I'd very much like to,' she said.

'Good. How about tomorrow? I'll be free all day.'

'Fine,' Kate agreed, her heart beating nineteen to the dozen.

'I'll pick you up at eleven again.'

Later that night, Kate frowned into the mirror. What had she let herself in for? Did he really enjoy her company or was he just filling in time because he was in a town where he knew no one? A man in his position could go anywhere, dine anywhere. Yes, but as she knew only too well, it wasn't the same doing things by yourself. Company made all the difference. That's all it was to him. Fate had put him in the right place when she had needed a hand: they had met and liked each other, he had spare time on his hands, in a strange neighbourhood and he was simply being polite, seeking companionship. That's all there was to it.

Getting into bed, she had half convinced herself. Nevertheless, as she snuggled her head down into the pillow, there was a radiant smile playing around her lips. She'd had a lovely day. And Toby was coming to fetch her again in the morning.

Chapter Twenty-Three

KATE WAS READY and waiting when she heard the
car turn into her drive and the single blast from the
horn. Toby was leaning against the body of his car
by the time she had locked the front door. He looked
different again today because he was wearing a grey
suit. She had on a dress and a matching long loose
coat. It was an outfit that suited her very well, the
colour being a soft peach with bindings of dark brown,
her shoes were plain high-heeled court shoes of the
same shade of brown, as were her gloves and handbag.
She had decided against wearing a hat and had pulled
her long hair well back and fastened it with a huge
tortoiseshell slide, leaving a few strands to hang free
over her ears.

'Morning, Kate. The weather doesn't look too promising.'

He seemed genuinely pleased to see her, which set her
a little more at ease. Looking up at the sky she said,

'Probably going to rain. I did think about bringing a picnic hamper but—'

'Certainly not,' he interrupted hastily. 'It's no problem, we'll take our time, decide where you would like to go and later on we'll find a hotel in time for lunch.'

'Sunday tradition, eh? Roast beef an' all that.'

'Well, a proper old stick in the mud, that's me. There's nothing I like better than a good old English roast lunch.'

He held open the car door, making sure she was comfortable before closing it. Minutes later he backed the car out of the drive and drove towards the main road away from the village, turned right, and headed towards Brighton. Kate had hardly spoken a word but that didn't matter to Toby. He took his eyes away from the road and glanced at her. She is so lovely, he told himself, aloof, different to any woman I've ever met. All he cared about at this moment was that she was there, sitting beside him and that he would have her company for the whole day.

This is ridiculous, he suddenly thought. I'm a grown man. A man of the world, and not especially unacquainted with women and here I am, very nearly tongue-tied, acting like some love-sick young lad. He felt awkward and he could tell that she felt the same. He took one hand from the steering wheel and covered hers as it lay in her lap, she smiled and shifted to be nearer to him, and the awkwardness vanished.

'I never asked you, but how do you feel about a visit to Brighton?' he asked, bringing his hand back to the wheel.

'Fine, a walk by the sea will blow our cobwebs away.'

He could smell her fresh perfume and felt her hip touching his occasionally. As the scenery changed from quiet country lanes to the great rolling downs with the sea shimmering below, he asked, 'Shall I park the car and we'll walk a while before we decide where to have our lunch?'

She nodded her agreement.

'What say we take a look at the Royal Pavilion?' Toby asked.

'Of course we must, no one comes to Brighton without paying a visit to Prinny's Palace.'

'Are we both having the same thought?'

'Well, that all depends.'

'On what?'

'On whether or not you had the same kind of history teacher as I did.'

They both burst out laughing.

'Go on,' Toby urged. 'You tell me your version of this fairy-tale place.' Kate lifted her head and stared up at the building that was like no other in the whole of England, with its numerous onion-shaped domes and countless fancy towers.

'Difficult to say which is fact and which is fiction. I grew up believing it was a romantic place and that whosoever entered its doors became enchanted. Whereas now I know the reality.'

'Which is?'

Kate was thoroughly enjoying herself, amused to be standing in Brighton discussing events that had taken place a hundred years and more ago. 'The fact is that the Prince Regent, before he became King George IV, had this place built for the true love of his life, Mrs

249

Fitzherbert. Can't you just imagine a royal gathering within those walls?'

Toby stared at Kate, who was lost in daydreams. He felt compelled to say, 'I wish it were possible to build such a palace for you today.'

Her jaw dropped and her eyes opened wide. 'Why, you old romantic, I never thought modern men had such thoughts.'

'I mean it, Kate. If it were possible, I would build you a palace without hesitating.'

She became flustered. This was a strange situation, he sounded deadly serious. They'd only known each other for such a short while. Her face lost its smile as she said, 'Normal people don't get to live in palaces.' Then speaking without thinking, she added, 'Besides I already have three houses.'

Toby's face went blank. What was it she was trying to tell him? He should ask her what that had to do with him, how it altered what he found himself feeling for her, and up to a moment ago would have sworn that she was feeling for him? But he said none of these things.

Instead he let her name come out on a sigh, 'Kate! Oh, Kate!'

Kate couldn't believe how upset he sounded. 'Toby, I'm sorry. What I said came out all wrong. It was that . . . your idea was so charming . . . I couldn't take it in. Nobody has ever said anything remotely like that to me.'

He did his best to laugh it off. 'Oh, don't be silly.' He took her hand and tucked it in through his arm, drawing her close. 'It isn't exactly summer yet, is it? Let's walk and decide about lunch. Have you any suggestions?'

Kate took a deep breath as they turned their footsteps towards the seafront.

'When I was a little girl my father used to bring me, my mother, and his mother here to Brighton and on such days we always had a meal at the Old Ship Hotel.'

'And is that a good memory for you?'

'Yes, it is,' she said, without hesitation.

'Then that is where we shall eat our roast beef today.'

They quickened their pace and she glanced across the road to where the sea was rolling in, cutting up a bit rough, its white rollers crashing down between the iron framework that supported the pier. That had been a stormy few minutes in this new relationship. Well it was to be expected really, wasn't it? She knew very little about him and he even less about her. You're going to have to do something about that if you're thinking of seeing more of him, she said silently and answering herself added, yes, I suppose so.

'Keep your head down against this wind,' Toby ordered with his usual show of care and attention as they headed for the hotel.

He opened the heavy door with his shoulder and stood aside until she had gone through, into the warmth and shelter of the Old Ship Hotel. They went towards the lounge, where a bright, cheery log fire burnt in the grate and several people were sitting around having drinks. Toby led her to a chair, placed in a recess, from where she would have a direct view of the sea.

'Will you be all right on your own for a few moments?' He smiled down at her.

'Of course.'

'I'll get a waiter to bring us drinks, but first I'll go to reception and make sure there's a table free for lunch.'

There was a full-length mirror on the wall to Kate's right and turning sideways she saw her reflection. Her hair was a bit windswept, her cheeks rosy from the sea breeze and her eyes bright and shiny. Happiness shows, she said to herself, thinking how much nicer it was to be here in this lovely old hotel on a Sunday morning, with a nice man for company, rather than spending what would have been a long dreary day on her own.

Toby came back, followed by a very smart waiter bearing two drinks on a tray, which he set down on the small round table in front of Kate.

'I took the liberty of ordering you a glass of dry sherry, is that all right?'

'Perfect,' she told him, raising the glass to her lips.

Thirty minutes later, they were being shown to a table for two in the dining room. Toby was used to dining in hotels but, even so, he was impressed, as indeed was Kate.

'This room had been redecorated since I was last here,' she remarked. 'Mind you, it was a very long time ago. It's very elegant, but still in keeping with its old-worldly atmosphere, don't you think?'

'Yes, I do,' Toby agreed as he studied the menu. 'Good, no problem for our main course, but what shall we have to begin?'

Kate was in two minds, wondering whether to have soup or melon. If she were going to have roast beef she certainly didn't want to fill herself up with a heavy starter.

'Seeing as how we're by the sea, I'd say oysters would be a very good choice. Have you ever had them?'

'No, to me, they always look kind of, well, slimy.'

Toby laughed. 'I'm very partial to them, wouldn't you like to try?'

'I won't if you don't mind. I think I'll go for the melon.'

Toby was still grinning broadly as he gave their order to the waiter, who suggested they leave the choice of pudding till later.

It was a long leisurely lunch and by the time they had left the dining room to have their coffee in the lounge, Kate felt relaxed.

'Do you mind if I smoke a cigar?' Toby asked

Kate had been stirring her coffee, she set her spoon down and shook her head. 'Not at all,' she said at the same time thinking, see, that's something else you didn't know about him; he likes to smoke cigars.

It took a minute or two for him to get it going, then, shaking the match out and setting it neatly in the glass ashtray, he looked at Kate. 'Shall we drive up towards the Downs when we've let our lunch digest?'

Kate nodded. What she could have said was, wherever you want to go is fine by me, just so long as you take me with you. The longer she spent in his company the more she liked him. He struck her as being an extraordinarily capable sort of person, ready to take charge, but nice with it. He's solid. Yes, that was the best way to describe him. Solid and warm and, she'd like to add, dependable, but she didn't know him well enough yet to know if it was true. Time would tell about that one.

★　　★　　★

It didn't take long for Toby to drive out of Brighton and soon they were approaching Kemp Town racecourse where he brought the car to a halt and wound down his window. Kate did the same to hers and stretched her legs out straight. Toby couldn't take his eyes off her. He reached out with his left hand and rested it on her shoulder, in a very casual way. In a matter of a few days – three meetings – he had come to care for Kate Kearsley. She sat quietly beside him. He looked at her thick brown hair with its distinct hints of copper. She had kept it securely held back and once again he felt the longing to free it, to run his fingers through it.

A strange excitement gripped Kate. She didn't want him to remove his hand, in fact she wished he would take her in his arms. It was exactly what Toby had the urge to do, but caution stopped him. Where would be the sense in it all? He could court her, and more than likely before he had to leave Surrey, he would find the opportunity to make love to her. That was exactly what he wanted to do. She was sitting there, looking dreamy, smiling to herself. Let her be, he ordered himself. Take her home before you do something you'll live to regret; Kate Kearsley is not the sort of girl who is looking for an easy affair with a man she has only just got to know. And certainly not a man who is going to love her and leave her, because, be honest with yourself, that is exactly what you will do; not from choice, he argued with himself. It doesn't make a bit of difference that your feelings are strong, something entirely different from what you've ever felt for any other woman, the fact is that you will be heading for South Africa within a matter of weeks. That's what his mind said, his heart was playing a different tune.

'We'd better head for home,' he said, removing his arm and sitting up straight in his seat.

'I could give you tea when we get back to the house, if you like.'

'I have some paperwork I must catch up with this evening, so I'll drop you off, if you don't mind.'

Kate felt herself blush.

He went on hurriedly, 'And I really do have to work tomorrow, but I will ring you and we'll arrange something for Tuesday.'

The journey back was strained. Had he brushed off her invitation or did he really have to catch up on some paperwork? That will teach you to be forward, Kate rebuked herself.

When Toby drove the car up to the house, he got out, walked round to the passenger side and held the door open for her. Taking a firm hold of her arm he walked by her side to the front door and waited until she had put her key in the lock.

'I've had another lovely day and another meal at your expense. I hope I get the chance to repay you,' she spoke quietly, with almost a hint of an apology in her voice.

Toby put his forefinger beneath her chin and raised her face until their eyes met. 'Kate, it is I who am indebted to you. I would have spent two long, lonely days in a strange town if it weren't for you. I really have enjoyed every minute we've been together, and I shall telephone you tomorrow and see you the next day, all right?'

She made no answer, only looked up at him with those big dark eyes which he now saw were glistening with tears. He pulled her close and she nestled into him, and he kissed her, a long, soft gentle kiss, the like of which she had never experienced before. His hand pressed into the middle of her back and she put her arms around his neck. There, on her own doorstep, they kissed each other as if their very lives depended upon it.

It was Kate who finally pulled away. What she wanted, more than anything else in the world at that moment, was to take his hand and lead him inside her house. What she did was let out a huge deep breath, smile at him and say, 'You have work waiting for you, you had better take yourself off.'

He caught her hand as she turned to go inside. 'One more,' he pleaded.

She needed no second urging, she went willingly into his arms and his kiss left her breathless.

Once in the house she took her coat off and draped it over a chair, then sat looking out of the front-room window. In her mind she went over everything he had said and done during this wonderful never-to-be forgotten day. He was going to ring her tomorrow but more importantly he was coming for her the next day. 'I can't wait,' she murmured, hugging herself. Tomorrow she would wash her hair and sort out a very pretty frock to wear. You're mad, like an excited kid thinking about going to someone's birthday party. Only it was better than that! Loads better!

God willing, she was going to spend another whole day with Toby Pinfold.

Every minute of the previous day had dragged. The hands of the clock had, at times, appeared to be stuck. Kate had done her best to focus on one job after another without much success. The only thought that filled her head was that Toby was coming to see her the next day. Well now it was the next day, and a more miserable day it would be very hard to imagine. It was dark, and the rain was simply lashing down.

The noise as it beat on to the corrugated-iron roof of the shed outside the back door was deafening. Already the gutters were overflowing and, apart from the big kitchen where the coal range hardly ever went out, every room in the house felt cold and damp. He won't come, not in weather like this, Kate said to herself but with her next breath she was spitting forth orders; I'll light the fire in the front room, yes, that's the first job; then I'll see what I can prepare for us to eat because he won't want to go traipsing around the countryside in all this rain; I need to get dressed, can't do any of these things while I'm still walking about in my dressing gown and I'll have to have a bath. She stopped still for a moment and looked up at the old-fashioned clock which had stood on the mantlepiece over the black-leaded range for as long as she could remember. It was twenty minutes past seven. I don't suppose he is even up yet! Why don't you fill the kettle, put it on to boil, make yourself a nice pot of tea and sit down and drink it? Yes, that's what I'll do. No, I'll set the fire going in the front room first so there's plenty of time for it to warm up.

When at last Kate did sit down, it was of Mary she was thinking. I wonder what she would say if she knew I was getting myself all worked up because a man I've known for only a short time is coming to spend the day here with me? One thing's for sure, she wouldn't disapprove. Live an' let live, is the code that Mary applies.

When this house was occupied by Jane, and Mr Collier

visited and stayed over whenever he could, Mary was never the one to comment, rather she made all sorts of allowances. It was a happy house then, and it has been ever since. Never mind the weather outside, today is going to be a really lovely day, Kate decided as she rose to her feet. And never mind what would happen when Toby finally had to leave Surrey and go about his business. Today was here and now and she wasn't going to look any further ahead than that.

By ten thirty she had everything ready.

Walking across the bedroom she turned first one way, then the other, looking at herself in the wardrobe mirror. You haven't done badly, she told her reflection. For once not a hair was out of place; she had plaited it into a bun at the nape of her neck leaving several strands free to frame her face. A slight touch of make-up looked perfect and her simple navy blue dress, which had a straight slim skirt, showed her figure off to perfection.

She was at the top of the stairs when she heard him sound his horn. From the landing window, she looked down, saw him get out of the car, turn up the collar of his coat and run through the heavy rain to the shelter of the front porch.

As she flung open the door, he grinned and shook himself, saying, 'God, what a day!' Kate put out a hand, almost dragging him inside. Quickly he undid his coat, unwrapped his scarf from round his neck and, as she took them from him, said, 'That's better, this is a day for the ducks, not for us.'

'That was my thought the minute I got up and looked out of the window, so I've made a few preparations for lunch . . . that is, if you don't mind staying here for the day. Anyway coffee is ready, come on.'

'Sounds fine to me,' Toby told her as she hurried him down the hall towards the kitchen door. When she opened it he gasped in surprise. Cups and saucers, a plate of scones, butter and a dish of jam were set out on the long kitchen table, the iron plate had been removed from the range and the fire was burning brightly, the kettle hummed on the side of the hob and the smell of freshly ground coffee filled the air.

It was all so homely.

'What a lovely welcome!' he exclaimed. 'A sight like this brings home to me what I've been missing all these years.'

'You wouldn't have it any other way, I don't suppose. You must have seen many wonderful things in your travels.

'Come on, sit yourself down. The scones are still warm, though I'm not going to promise that they'll be as good as the ones Mary bakes. It takes me all my time to make decent pastry. This is the first time I've tried my hand at scones.'

'Oh, so I'm to be the guinea pig, am I?'

'I'll nurse you if you become ill.'

Now why had she said that?

'I wish I could believe that was a promise,' he said quietly.

Now who was faking it? What if she said it really was a promise? She could hardly administer loving care if she were here and he was thousands of miles away.

They had their coffee and Toby had said he really liked his scone.

'You sure you wouldn't like another one?'

He laughed, a lovely deep, warm laugh. 'I can see from here that you've already spent time doing a whole host of vegetables for lunch, are you trying to fatten me up?'

'You're only going to get an omelette to go with the vegetables.'

'Fine,' he said, as he crossed one leg over the other and leant back in his chair.

He looked so right sitting there, but there was a strained pause until Kate asked, 'Wouldn't you like to go into the other room? The fire has been alight for ages, so it should be nice and warm.'

'Not unless you're coming with me.' He got to his feet and came round the table and stood looking down at her. Kate felt her heart start to race. 'I have to tell you, I've fallen in love with you,' Toby said, and he meant every word of it.

Every fibre of Kate's being was urging her to tell him she loved him, to grab whatever he was offering. Even half a loaf is better than no bread at all, especially to a starving man. I may not be a man, but I am starving, that's for sure. I've never known love! Never known what it feels like to be the most important human being in any one person's life. I'm tired of being lonely. She said all this to herself as she led the way down the hall, wondering how to manage the rest of the day, and if she had got herself into a whole lot more than she was capable of handling.

They sat side by side on the big sofa and when Toby put his arm around her and pulled her close it seemed the most natural thing in the world. He made her feel very feminine, warm and safe, as if this was how it should be.

She felt wanted. Truly loved. Kate moved into him. She could smell his nice fresh shaving soap, a manly smell. His lips moved over her cheeks, then onto her lips, soft, gentle and warm. She responded until minutes later her kisses were as fierce as his had become.

He raised his head to draw breath and Kate lay curled up in his arms like a well-contented cat. Finally, he slid from his seat, got to his feet and pulled her up. Without saying a word they lay down on the rug in front of the fire and, tucking a cushion beneath her head, he balanced himself on one elbow and stared down into her lovely face. Kate became nervous. She had no idea what to do, how to respond to the flood of strange and wonderful sensations sweeping over her. Would he know that she had no experience with men? Would he mind?

His touch was gentle, pleasing, incredible. She couldn't bring herself to stop him now. She didn't want to. It was as if she was dreaming it all. Her clothes came off, slowly, bit by bit and then both of them were naked. For the very first time in her life she was lying in the arms of a man who was whispering everything she had ever longed to hear. It was the most wonderful sensation she had ever experienced. Toby released her, and held himself just above her and she felt his warm flesh rubbing against hers. As he moved, he first kissed her lips, then her ears, then his tongue licked her bare shoulders moving along down her arm. She was in heaven. Floating.

'Oh, Toby,' she whispered, over and over again.

It was a gentle, tender lovemaking. When it came to an end, Kate could not have described her feelings out loud, not even to save her soul.

More than an hour later they were still lying side by

side, her head on his chest, his hand tangled in her thick hair. Morning had given way to early afternoon. He raised himself slightly and, looking straight into her eyes, said, 'This is what I've been searching for all my life. Someone as sweet and pure as you. After the fiasco of my marriage I became cynical, I trusted no one and I used people. People who had been good friends. I'm not proud of the fact, Kate, I just did not believe that there was any one on this earth like you.' He paused to gently kiss her cheek. 'I was the first! I can't believe that you have gone through life untouched. What of the men in your life? Were they blind? I didn't want to fall in love with you, but I have and I want you to know, whatever happens, it is a deep and lasting love which will stand the test of time.'

'You know so very little about me, there are things perhaps I should tell you.'

'Hush. Hush.' Toby smiled, hugging her tighter. 'Tomorrow we'll talk. I promise. There are things I must say to you and you to me, but they can wait. Today is ours! There is no one else in our world today, just you and me. Does that sound right?'

'Fine,' she agreed, thinking that for once the angels were on her side.

When they were dressed and back in the kitchen the fire had burnt low and the rain was still lashing against the window panes.

'Kate, I have to tell you one thing.' He smiled at her as she fussed with the vegetables and saucepans.

'Yes?' She half turned towards him. Oh, God, I really do love him, she thought. His hair was ruffled, his shirt unbuttoned and he looked so at home here in the kitchen.

'I'm starving.'

'In this household if one works we all work. So, mister, the fire needs to be made up and the table set, for what I fear is a very belated lunch.'

'Yes, ma'am.' He touched his finger to his forehead giving her a mock salute, before striding across the floor to stand at her side.

'Payment in advance please,' he begged.

Smiling, she held up her face to be kissed.

As he held her he was silent, full of thought. God, she is beautiful. She has a freshness about her that I can't explain. It's not only her looks or even her big brown eyes, but somehow the whole of her.

She made to break away, then she hesitated, looked up into his face, and said, 'Thank you, Toby.'

'Oh, my darling, what have you to thank me for?'

Her eyes were bright with unshed tears. 'Because you've made me feel loved, wanted, and so much more.'

'Oh, Kate, Kate.' He pulled her back into his arms, holding her gently, saying, 'I can't believe this, you know, I can't believe it. What if we had never met?'

'But we have, and I, too, am finding it hard to believe.'

'There's only one thing I find wrong with you, Kate Kearsley, you take an awfully long time to feed a starving man!'

Her jaw dropped, then, as she playfully slapped him, they both burst out laughing.

'Move yourself! Make the fire up, and set the table and the food won't be long.'

'Exactly what I was going to do ten minutes ago if

you hadn't distracted me, but I'll get my own back after we've eaten.'

She closed her eyes in anticipation and broke eggs into a basin, all the while sending up a silent prayer of thanks that Toby had been sent to help set up a pharmacy in Kingston Hospital.

Chapter Twenty-Four

TOBY MADE UP his mind to do as little work as possible for the remainder of his stay in Surrey. And except for the necessary jobs around the house, Kate lived only for the moment when he arrived on her doorstep. Wednesday had been spent much as Tuesday had been. The two of them stayed indoors, mostly making love.

On Thursday morning, bright and early they set off in his car to Box Hill, a well-known beauty spot and a favourite with courting couples. Holding hands they stood looking up at the great grassy hill.

'How high do you think it is?' he asked.

'It's about six hundred feet to the top. I've walked this hill so many times with my father. Come on, it's not too steep and the view is fantastic. Besides the climb does have its compensations.'

'Which are?'

'There's a pub right at the top. The Hand-in-Hand.'

'Well, what are we waiting for?'

They took their time, Kate stopped every now and then to pick a long strand of grass which she chewed between her teeth. The ground was too wet for them to sit on, so on reaching the top they made for the pub where Toby fetched her a glass of shandy and a beer for himself. As they were both wearing topcoats and had long scarves around their necks they stayed outside in the fresh air, seating themselves at one of the rustic tables. They could hear voices in the distance but close by there were no other couples.

'Lucky today, aren't we,' Kate said, lifting her face up to let the sun shine on her cheeks.

'Yes, we are. But there's not much warmth in the sun yet. I don't think we'll want to sit still for too long.'

They were silent, yet they knew they needed to talk, although, so far, they had been avoiding it.

'What are we going to do?' Toby asked quietly.

Kate remained silent, torn apart. Then, she spoke in a whisper, 'Before we decide anything you should know about my parents.'

'The first morning we met, didn't you tell me they were both dead and that was the reason you had moved into Melbourne Lodge to take care of Joshua?'

'Yes. What I failed to tell you was the manner in which they died.'

Toby looked concerned. 'You don't have to tell me anything. It won't make a scrap of difference to the love I feel for you.'

'I do have to make all the facts known to you. There is no other way I can deal with it.'

'Kate,' he leant towards her and took one of her hands and held it between his, 'Kate, my darling, there is no longer you and me. There is just us. After what you have given me I would go to the ends of the earth for you. Christ, how can I make you believe that I love you more deeply than I ever imagined it was possible for one person to love another? Whatever you have to tell me, well, it simply cannot alter that fact.'

She believed him, mainly because she so desperately needed to. So, she began to tell him her history. During the telling, there came into her mind distorted and painful pictures of those years. No matter how desperately she tried to put these unbearable memories behind her, there always seemed to come a time when they surfaced.

'I could never have lived with the notoriety that followed if Mr Collier hadn't offered me a haven at Melbourne Lodge,' she ended on a pitiful note.

'My poor Kate,' he murmured, his voice thick with sympathy. 'Sins of the fathers come home to roost on the children, we are taught. Never seems fair to me. My father had been married before he met my mother. He was older than her by fifteen years. When she had me it was his first child and the fact that she had given him a son was something that gave him a new lease of life. He died when I was seventeen years old. My mother never married again. Five years ago I was in Canada when she suffered a stroke and died the same day. I only just made it home for her funeral.'

'A sad story,' Kate said, with feeling. 'But nothing like the horror story my early life turned into. No need for you to wonder now why men have never wanted anything to do with me.'

'Their loss and my gain, my darling. Now I know God

in his heaven has been saving you just for me, and . . .' he stopped talking as he reached out, this time to catch hold of both her hands '. . . If you think what you've told me changes anything then you are wrong. Totally wrong!'

The landlord came out into the grounds at that moment and stood staring up at the sky.

Kate leant into Toby and very quietly said, 'You're a lucky man, because if that gentleman hadn't come out when he did I would have thrown myself at you. And by the way, I would like to make another point clear.'

'I'll keep you to what I think you have just promised me and, as to your point, be my guest, go ahead,' he teased.

'I love you, Toby. I think I'm coming round to believe as you do – we were meant to meet.'

Toby couldn't have cared less if the whole world had been watching at that moment. He got to his feet, almost dragging Kate up and into his arms and placed his lips gently on hers in what she was to think was the sweetest lingering kiss any girl had ever received. Afterwards they held tightly on to each other as they made their way down the sloping path.

He took her for lunch at the inn near Burford Bridge, which stood at the foot of Box Hill, and held her hands across the table. The few other diners on this weekday smiled, there was no disguising the love he felt for her; it was on his face for everyone to see.

Back home, Kate was disappointed when he said he wouldn't come into the house.

'This evening's meeting is a must for me.'

She accepted his explanation but still didn't like it;

she'd had visions of them spending the whole night together. But what could she do?

'Tell you what,' he said, releasing his hold on her, 'why don't I come to breakfast in the morning? I shall be here before you're even up in the morning and after I have told you yet again how much I love you, we have to get down to some serious talking. Agreed?'

Kate stared directly into his eyes. 'Yes,' she replied, smiling thinly.

'Good. It will be easier for both of us when we come to a decision.'

Several seconds ticked by as he kissed her yet again, then as he turned to go, he said, 'You'll never know how reluctant I am to leave you, Kate. And that's the truth.'

He walked to his car. She heard the door click shut, the engine fire, and she was standing alone, staring at an empty driveway.

Kate couldn't sleep. Her thoughts were almost frightening and she wished she could stop thinking about tomorrow and the decisions she was going to have to make. She had suffered before. Gone through hell at times. But this was different. It was a new experience and she was driven mad by the pain of loving Toby, knowing that he was going to have to leave her after such a short time together. It was a hopeless situation.

The damp mists of early morning lay low over the river. She placed the vase of freshly picked spring flowers on the window sill just as Toby turned the car into the drive. He was as good as his word, the time was twenty minutes past six.

They ate a full cooked breakfast, acting just as any married couple might, with Toby getting up to bring the teapot to the table and then returning to kneel in front of the glowing range to make toast, using the long-handled toasting fork to spike the thick slices of bread. Both of them knew they were being overpolite. With the table cleared and the washing up done there was no way of avoiding the inevitable.

It was Toby who spoke first. 'I have just four more days, including today. I have to be back in Bristol next Tuesday, and by the following weekend I leave for Cape Town.'

Kate remained silent, her face a picture of utter despair.

'Kate, you must tell me, what would you like to do?'

'I don't know,' she said softly. Raising her eyes to meet his, she added, 'That's not true, of course I know what I'd like to do, but what I *can* do is something entirely different, isn't it.'

'Look, I do have to go on this assignment, it's a long-term thing which is going to involve a great deal of research, I can't walk away. If you say you'll marry me now I'll set the wheels in motion this morning, get a special licence, see to travel arrangements – and we can leave together. It won't be easy, but I'll move heaven and earth to get it done.'

'Oh, Toby! You've just proposed to me!'

'Well?' He looked dumbstruck. 'Whatever else did you think I had in mind? You will marry me, won't you? Please, Kate.'

'Nothing would give me greater pleasure. But I can't. Joshua has no one but me. He understands that I am not his real mother but he feels and thinks of me as such. If I were to up sticks and leave him now, he wouldn't understand, not in a million years. He'd have no way of dealing with it.'

'Are you telling me that these days have meant nothing to you? You could let me go, just like that?'

'I don't see that I have any option. Josh is only a small boy, his world revolves around me. This is his home and I have to be here when he has his school holidays.'

'Did his father leave this property to him? Do you live here free in return for services to his illegitimate son?'

Kate couldn't believe that she had heard him right! His tone of voice had been so harsh.

'It isn't like that at all,' she declared hotly. 'This house was left to me with no strings attached whatsoever. And Joshua is well taken care of. Charles Collier made me Joshua's guardian, a fact of which I am very proud. As to needing free lodgings, I own a house my parents left me, another house and a plot of ground my grandmother left me and, incidentally, a very prosperous boat yard situated at Hampton Court.'

As Kate brought her outburst to an end, Toby looked at her in amazement. He shook his head, and half smiled. 'My, my! I should have known with all that red in your hair you were bound to have a temper.'

'So you're surprised, are you? You insult me and expect me to take it lying down.'

He started to apologise, but Kate stopped him. 'I'm not finished yet. You coming into my life is probably the most wonderful thing that ever happened to me and I thank God for every minute we've spent together. It seems I've misjudged you, though. I thought you were sensitive, kind, aware of, and caring for my feelings, as well as your own. You live an adventurous life and I shall treasure the fact that you asked me to marry you and share that life until the end of my days. My life must seem lonely to you, boring even, taking care of a little boy who isn't even my own flesh and blood, but I took the job on and Joshua has become my son in every sense of the word. I have a responsibility here. To walk away and leave him is something I could not bring myself to do. It would destroy him. As much as I love you, Toby, and want to be with you wherever you are, I couldn't do it. And you wouldn't respect me if I did.

'Just imagine if we were together in South Africa and I somehow got to hear that Joshua was ill. How do you think that would make me feel?'

Toby was silent. He knew he had overstepped the mark. He understood what she was saying about responsibilities and guilt. He knew she was right. She was good and loyal. It only served to make him love her even more. He got to his feet, walked to the window and, looking out, fought with himself, fought to believe that she was right but wanting to fight to keep her for himself. Never had he expected to find anyone like her. He had loved her from the moment he had set eyes on her. He had to go to South Africa, his job demanded it. How can I leave her? he asked himself over and over again.

Kate had a quiet power that pulled at his heart strings whenever he gazed into her big, dark brown eyes. It sounded daft, even to himself, yet it felt as though she had been secretly waiting for him all her life. She had known great tragedy; it showed in her face at times. She had devoted her life to bringing up a little boy and he was sure she loved the child with all her heart. But what of her own happiness? He would give an awful lot to be able to take her with him into his life, keep hold of her and never let her go.

He turned round to see that her head was lowered and her shoulders shaking. She was crying. In a second he was beside her and they held each other for a long time.

'Kate, I'm sorry, so sorry. I was hateful, I know I was. It's the thought of losing you. It wouldn't be a picnic if you did come with me, I shall have miles of travelling to do, but at least you'd be there. Oh, Kate, Kate, what shall we do? I shall be gone for two years at least, and if the project doesn't prove straightforward, it could be a lot longer. So much can happen in that length of time.'

'I must go and wash my face.' Kate sniffed and took herself off to the bathroom.

He had made a fresh pot of tea and was sitting at the kitchen table when she came back. She went to him and he opened his arms; she buried her face in his neck. They clung to each other for what seemed an endless time.

Kate felt she ought to thank him for taking her to heights she had never known existed, for helping her to discover feelings he had aroused by merely tracing his fingers across her bare flesh, for understanding her ignorance, for being so nice. No, not nice, wonderful. For everything. For being him and for wanting her.

Finally he broke away.

'I think it best if we part now, Kate. I couldn't bear any more days with you, knowing the end was in sight.'

She nodded, beginning to cry again. Although there were tears in his eyes, he kept smiling that lovely endearing smile of his.

'I might even leave for Bristol the day after tomorrow. Tie up all the loose ends and be on my way. Is it all right if I write to you sometimes? Not yet, not until I reach Cape Town and see what lies ahead from there.'

'I'd like that,' Kate said, wiping her eyes on a scrap of handkerchief she pulled from her cardigan pocket. 'Joshua would save the stamps and if you could send him a coloured postcard now and again that would really please him.'

'Kind of keep in with my rival, is that what you mean?'

Kate made no answer and they both smiled.

'I shall be around all tomorrow and maybe the next day – it depends. If you do want to see me or just talk, telephone the hospital.'

She knew she would be tempted a dozen times to ring him while he was still in Surrey but she hoped with all her heart that she would be strong enough to resist.

He wound his scarf around his neck and shrugged himself into his coat.

Don't let him go, her mind raged at her. It's the first chance you've ever had to make a life for yourself. For *you* to be happy. You'll never get another.

Taking her hand, Toby walked through the spacious entrance hall to the front door. He kissed her gently and opening the door, stepped out on to the gravel, then he turned, stepped back inside and held her again for several minutes. Neither of them said a word. Kate couldn't have if she had wanted to. They simply stood there, holding onto each other as if their very lives depended upon it. He released her, holding her at arm's length. Tears were running down his cheeks and Kate's vision of him was blurred because the same thing was happening to her.

He put a foot over the step, and when Kate made to follow him, he whispered, 'Don't come outside, please. Just stay where you are.' Turning, he walked slowly away.

She waited until she could no longer hear the sound of the car, then closed the big oak door.

She had made her decision. But at this moment she wasn't sure it had been the right one.

Chapter Twenty-Five

IT WAS NINE o'clock on Easter Saturday morning and Kate had a smile on her face as she watched Joshua tucking into his porridge.

'What's to follow?' he asked with a grin.

'Grilled bacon and sausages.' Kate's expression was full of love. She felt more relaxed and in a much happier frame of mind than she had for days. Joshua was home and the house had come alive again.

He took his empty bowl and placed it on the draining board, picked up an oven cloth and withdrew his breakfast plate from the oven and took it back to the table. 'Beats a school breakfast any day of the week.'

'Well, to look at you this morning no one would believe you're the same lad who arrived home here three days ago looking so spic an' span. You look positively shaggy.'

'Makes a change,' he replied cheerfully.

He had discarded his school uniform and was wearing

long corduroy trousers and a scruffy, ancient jersey that Mary had knitted for him. His blond hair had grown slightly darker, cut short at the back and sides but kept longer on top, it flopped over his forehead and he pushed the fingers of one hand through it when he realised Kate was watching him. He finished his cooked breakfast and began to spread marmalade onto a slice of toast.

'Would you like a cup of tea, Mum? I'll make a pot if you would.'

'Yes, please, that would be nice. Bring the tray over here by the window, we haven't really had a chance to talk yet. I'm dying to hear what's gone on during term time. Have you made any arrangements to meet your mates?'

'I did invite Nick Banks to drop in if he were over this way, I wrote to you about him. I also phoned Pete Bradley and we've agreed to meet up on Monday.'

'I'd bet a pound to a penny I can guess where that meeting place is going to be. It's all right, Jack Stuart is expecting us on Monday and, yes, the boat yard will be open.'

She turned her chair round to face the window. Joshua drew up a side table and poured tea for each of them, before settling himself down on a low stool. For the next half an hour she listened, as he told her what a smashing form master Mr Holmes was and how pleased he had been with Josh's examination results. Then he got on to the success, or sometimes otherwise, of the school rugby team.

'Heavens! All that energy. You must sleep well at night.'

'I do, an' while I've got your full attention I'd like to ask you a couple of things.'

'Oh, you would, would you? That sounds threatening. But come on, let's hear them.'

'First, before I go back, would you give some thought as to whether I can ask a couple of form mates to stay here during the summer holidays? The lads think it's great that we live so near the river and by then I shall probably have my own boat.'

'That is no problem. It will give me great pleasure to have your friends stay here just so long as they have their parents' permission,' Kate answered. 'Now the other request is?'

'Please may I have two more pairs of long trousers? I know the regulation form stated we required one long pair and two short pairs of trousers for new boys in their first term, but honestly, none of us wear the short grey flannel ones, our knees get cold.'

Laughing, Kate got out of her chair and wrapped her arms around him. Josh wriggled free, a crooked smile on his lips and a mischievous gleam in his eye.

'Can I take it that's a yes as well?'

Still laughing loudly, Kate picked up the tea tray and walked across to the sink. 'Yes, we'll go into Kingston and buy you long trousers but don't give me all that nonsense about cold knees. You just want to make out you're older than you really are.'

Mid-morning, on a bright Easter Bank Holiday Monday, the river was a magic place to be. The early low-lying mist had dispersed, giving way to clear blue skies. Standing beside Jack Stuart, Kate observed the ever-changing scene from the slipway of the Kearsley Boat Yard. She relaxed in the overwhelming holiday atmosphere. She was lucky to have Jack as manager of the yard and, today, she was doubly thankful as she watched Joshua and his friend Peter, together with Bert Lewis, an employee, climb down into the launch, start the engine and set off up the river.

Joshua raised his hand to her, his expression a mixture of suppressed excitement at the prospect of a trip out in a boat and disappointment that his own boat had not yet been finished.

It was great to have Josh at home. She wouldn't want to live through the last few days again, not for a king's ransom. The first day after Toby had left she must have picked up the telephone a dozen times, only to replace it quickly. 'If you only want to talk,' he had said, and she did, so very badly. Tell him she loved him so. Ask him not to leave her. What good would it have done? Somehow she had got through those days until Joshua had come home.

Joshua's Easter holiday break had gone by so quickly. There was no doubt that even one term in the first form of an all-boys school had worked wonders for him. It had changed him from a shy adolescent to a self-assured, interesting young man.

'I can't believe it,' Kate told Mary over the telephone, 'he's grown so much, and you should have seen him working in the boat yard. No half-measures, proper boots, brown overalls, mostly covered in varnish. And I didn't see him at all one day, Jack Stuart took him off to visit two other yacht brokers up river. He came back full of it.'

'Kate, I hope to be coming home the week before

Whitsun. Blanche has made friends with Lily Evans, the lady I hired to be housekeeper. In fact they get on so well together I'm beginning to think that I'm in the way here. Another good point is they both like Nurse Jones so, all in all, it's a load off my shoulders and I feel I shall be leaving my sister in very capable hands.'

'Oh, Mary,' Kate had breathed so sadly down the line that Mary quickly asked, 'Is there something wrong? Has anything happened while I've been away?'

If only I could tell you, Kate thought clutching the telephone receiver so tightly that her knuckles showed white. She wanted to blurt out, I met a man, a man who loved me. A man who taught me what it was like to be a woman. He was kind, someone who didn't think my past made me a freak. Someone I spent only a few days with, just a few days, when what I really wanted was to spend the rest of my life with him. But I had to let him go.

Instead, she said, 'The house is just so big and empty with both you and Joshua away.' Then doing her best to put a smile into her voice, 'You've made my day, Mary. Just telling me it will only be a matter of weeks now before you're home. I can't bring Josh to the phone, he's off round at Peter Bradley's house but I will get him to ring you before he goes back to school.'

It was a horrible day, even for March. Mr Weatherford honked the horn of his car to announce his arrival then tactfully busied himself out of earshot.

In the front porch, away from the drizzling rain, Kate and Joshua faced each other.

'This is it then. Back to the grindstone for you.'

'Yes.' Josh seemed happy enough. 'I know the rules now, I'm not stepping out into the unknown like last term.'

'You would tell me if you had any problems, wouldn't you?'

'Yes.' He was quite adamant. 'And, Mum, I do feel better knowing Nanna will be home soon. I didn't like to think of you here all on your own.'

Oh, he was such a loving little boy. Only she hadn't better air such thoughts to him. Grown up now, he considered he was, and the very thought brought tears to Kate's eyes. Still, I'm allowed to be sentimental today of all days, and I'm not the only mother, I bet. Children returning to school left an empty house and an ache in one's heart.

'Bye, Josh.'

'Goodbye, Mum.'

'I love you.'

'I love you too,' he told her, holding up his face for her kiss.

Then he stood back, staring at her with that funny little grin of his, turned away, and ran towards the car.

Kate wept a little as she went back inside the house, telling herself not to be such a fool. It was right and sensible for Josh to be away at school, enjoying the company of boys of his own age. She was lucky to have had him for as long as she had and come what may she mustn't ever make the mistake of trying to hold onto him. There was a great big world out there and the more his mind was stimulated, the more he would want to get out and discover what was on offer for himself.

Kate made tea, and when it had stood for a few

minutes she poured herself a cup and carried it to the windowseat from where she could look out at the garden sloping down from the back of the house. It was hard for her not to feel empty and bereft. For once she allowed herself to wallow in self-pity. Everybody wins but me, she decided sadly.

Chapter Twenty-Six

KATE HAD SAT up late thinking. She'd had another letter from Cooper and Dawes asking what she intended to do about her inheritance. It appeared that they had a client willing to purchase the ground on which her grandmother's house stood, and the land beyond. Bit of a cheek considering she had never expressed any intentions of disposing of Alice's property. Ideas about what she might do with it had been rattling about in her head for ages now. She would have liked someone, especially Mary, to have sat down with her and let her air her thoughts, get another opinion. She smiled to herself. Would someone else's views have made any difference? She very much doubted it.

She had sat at the kitchen table, her chin resting on her elbows. All round her were sheets of paper covered with scribbled drawings and lists of suggestions. She wasn't going to give up until she had come to some kind of a decision. There were at least three options.

She could sell the old property and the land, invest the money and carry on life as usual. But didn't she have more than enough money already?

She could sell up and invest the money in Joshua's name But again, his father had left him very well provided for.

She rather thought she'd have to take advice on the third option. If it were at all possible this was the one she'd like to go ahead with.

I'll not go back to Cooper and Dawes, she'd decided. That fellow gave me the creeps.

First thing in the morning she'd telephone Mr Weatherford and make an appointment to go and see him. Yes, he'd know what to do, and he could also have the job of notifying the other firm that in future he and his partners would be acting on all matters concerning her gran's estate.

Mr Weatherford listened, without once making a comment, to all that Kate had said. He glanced across his deck to where she sat. He couldn't for the life of him put a finger on it but there was no mistaking the difference in her. She was smartly dressed, in a business-like tailored suit, but then when hadn't she dressed well for the appropriate occasion? No. It was more than that. She had a new air of self-confidence, she held her head up higher. He had always admired her. The way she had coped with the adversity life had thrown at her when she'd been little more than a slip of a girl had earned her a good reputation – at least in the minds of people who mattered.

'Kate, let me run the outline of your proposition by

you one more time. Just to make sure that I have the facts right.'

'Please do, Mr Weatherford. I'd like to hear someone else voice them out loud. These plans have run through my head so many times that even I wouldn't give odds against their survival, always supposing that we do eventually manage to get them off the ground.'

'Your wish is to create something worthwhile from your grandmother's estate. Something that others less fortune than yourself might benefit from.'

'Yes, that's the rough idea.'

Mr Weatherford sorted the sheets of paper on which he had made notes into some kind of order. 'You'd like to set up a mission, to be consolidated and strengthened under a united management of both men and women, the idea being primarily a dwelling place for the handicapped and poor people of Kingston. You would seek other investors and fund raisers for the financing of such a project. Is that correct?'

'Partly,' Kate agreed in a solemn voice. 'It wouldn't only be for residents of Kingston, all deserving cases would be considered. And not all cases would need to be residents. I'd like to see a kind of family place, offering all sorts of services and facilities, to both the young and the old. Not an asylum or an institution, not even an old folk's home.'

Mr Weatherford concealed a smile. She was aiming not only for the moon but the stars and the sky to go with it.

Kate uncrossed her legs and leant forward. 'I thought that if we attracted enough money we could have the main building erected at one end of the field that lies beyond the house, which would be for long-term residents; at the other end, perhaps a small block of dwellings where needy folk or maybe people who had been ill could holiday or convalesce. Then, rather than demolish Gran's house, renovate it and possibly use it to house the matron, because we would need a matron or maybe two, someone on duty at all times, wouldn't you think?'

The stern-faced solicitor, flung down his pen, threw back his head and roared with laughter.

'Kate. Kate!' For a long time now he had dropped the Miss Kearsley and if he weren't so hide-bound by his profession he felt, at that moment, he would be on his feet, round his desk, sweeping this adorable lass up into his arms. She was something else and then some! 'In theory it is a great and worthwhile idea. One that would, without a doubt, persuade many businessmen to contribute. However, the amount of hurdles you would have to overcome and the shackles that would have to be shed . . .' he paused '. . . you don't have any idea!'

'But it is feasible?'

'Oh, it's feasible all right. All we need is several rich benefactors and God on our side.'

They both laughed.

'You've hooked me, young Kate. I'll throw my hat in with you. But the first thing we have to do is convince the council that the idea is so good that they dare not refuse us planning permission.'

'You think they might?' Kate asked in disbelief.

'Nothing's for certain where the council is concerned.' He paused again, smiled knowingly and tapped the side of his nose, 'I've just had a wicked thought. There's more than one way to skin a cat and what we'll do is practise being a little bit devious, how does that sound to you?'

'Just tell me what I have to do.' She was beginning to enjoy herself.

'Well, I have a young friend who is an ambitious reporter on the *Surrey Comet*, and I think you should invite him to visit you one morning. Then, should it so happen that while you were drinking coffee together you were to make known to him what generous plans you have in mind for the property and ground left to you by your grandmother, he might feel he could make use of that item of news, which would be all to the good. And incidentally, it would do no harm for the young reporter to learn that Mrs Kearsley lived the whole of her life in Kingston and was a well-known figure in the market, braving all weathers right up almost until the day that she died. Well ... what do you think?'

'Mr Weatherford! I think I'm going to enjoy being devious. If the whole town is showing approval of a plan for which there is not yet an architect or an application for planning permission ... well!'

'So, shall I ask my friendly young reporter to telephone you?'

Kate's eyes twinkled. 'Please do, I shall forward to his call.'

'By the way, I've been meaning to ask you, how did your Christmas experiment go?'

'It got off on a shaky footing but, as a whole, it went well. Everyone appeared to have a great Christmas. With hindsight it was asking a lot – those children were like fish out of water to begin with.'

'So, you won't be asking more families to stay at Melbourne Lodge?'

Kate looked a bit downcast. 'I'm still thinking about that. Seeing as how it was partly Mr Collier's suggestion I'd feel guilty if I let the whole thing drop, but on the other hand I'm not sure it was fair to Joshua.'

'Did the lad not fit in?'

'Oh, it wasn't that,' Kate hastened to assure him. 'Joshua was fine. He did his best to set the boys at ease and was particularly good with the little girl. No, I just felt that it *is* Joshua's home and, especially at holiday times, he shouldn't be asked to share it with strangers. More so now he is away at school. He has already asked me if he may invite some of his friends to stay with us during the summer holidays.'

'And have you agreed?'

'Of course I have. It will be great. I had thought that maybe I could use Bramble Cottage as a holiday home for needy families. Seems a bit selfish to keep it for myself when I have so much, though Mary and I go there often together. What d'you think?'

Mr Weatherford took off his horn-rimmed glasses, rubbed his eyes and, for a minute or two, sat quietly staring at Kate, wondering if she felt she had a price to pay for what her mother had done?

'Kate,' he said at last, 'if you get this scheme off the ground, I think you will be making a great contribution to the community. Leave it at that for the time being, let's see how things go. In the meantime, I want you to know that I'm here at any time. Any matter, large or small, come and discuss it with me. I would like to feel that you can look upon me not only as a trustee for

Joshua's affairs but as a friend to you both. Will you promise me that?'

'Thank you,' Kate murmured. 'I can't tell you how grateful I am for all you've done for me.'

'I'm delighted that Mr Collier saw fit to leave his affairs in my hands. Have you had news of Mrs Kennedy recently?'

'Yes I have, we speak on the telephone frequently. She will be coming home quite soon now.'

'That is good news. Give her my regards, I'm sure we shall meet up again soon.' There was a twinkle in his eye as he added, 'Mrs Kennedy will want to be involved in the matter of utilising your grandmother's property, don't you think?'

Smiling happily, Kate got to her feet. 'When I outline our plans to Mary it will take an army to keep her out of the front line. Goodbye, Mr Weatherford, and again, thank you.'

'Goodbye Kate. I'll seek out a good architect and get some plans drawn up, and I'll keep you posted. Take care and remember what I've said.'

Mr Weatherford watched as Kate set off down Kingston High Street. What a remarkable young lady, he thought as he went back inside his office.

All the way home Kate felt optimistic. Mr Weatherford had been so encouraging. If all went well she would have plenty to occupy her mind for months to come. If even half her plans got off the ground she wouldn't be bored, and she felt that Alice would approve wholeheartedly. She kept that thought uppermost in her mind as she took off her jacket and carefully hung it inside the wardrobe. Closing the door, she caught a glimpse of the bed reflected in the full-length mirror.

Oh, Toby! In this very bed she had lain in his arms, and had feelings that she still couldn't describe, even to herself. It was five weeks now since they had said goodbye and there wasn't an hour of the day when she didn't think about him. Where was he? What was he doing?

He hadn't called her before he'd left Surrey or written so much as a postcard since. Every time the phone rang she prayed that it might be him. What if it had been? What would he say to her or she to him? She thought he had understood her feelings about Joshua, but had he really? She couldn't have agreed to share his life because of the complications it would cause. She had taken the only possible decision, but it didn't stop her yearning for the one man who had made her feel a woman. God, she loved him so!

She went downstairs and sat at the kitchen table. There was no food on it. Not even a tablecloth. If Mary were here things would be different. At this time in the afternoon, tea would be set out with a plate of scones, warm from the oven, home-made jam and dainty sandwiches. On her own she never bothered; there didn't seem much point cooking and baking just for one's self.

The jangling of the telephone made her jump. What if . . . oh, don't be so daft, get up and go and answer it or whoever it is will hang up.

'Melbourne Lodge,' she said, her heart hammering so hard against her ribs she thought the caller must be able to hear it.

'Kate, it's Mary. I'm ringing to tell you I'm catching

a train first thing in the morning. I shall be in London by twelve thirty. I don't know about connections down to Kingston but I'll ring you from the station.'

'Oh, Mary love, that's wonderful! The best possible news. Don't worry, I'll be at Euston to meet you. It's been so long I can't wait to see you.'

The sound of Mary's laughter came down the line. 'Hang on, Kate, I'm thrilled to hear you're so pleased I'm coming home but there's no need for you to travel up to London to meet the train.'

'Oh, yes, there is. You'll never know. I'll be there. And, Mary, I'm going to buy you the biggest and the best meal that London can provide. See you tomorrow.'

Kate was laughing as she put the phone back on its hook.

What a place, Kate exclaimed to herself as she walked towards the destination board at Euston. The walls were grimed with soot, the very air smelt of smoke and endless pigeons swooped down to gather up any morsel of food they could find and then flew over people's heads to land high up in the metal girders that supported the roof. Everyone was in such a hurry. The clatter and the clanging and loud voices shouting for porters!

Where we live is another world. I'd go so far as to say that there's not a dozen Londoners who have even heard of Littleton Green. Perhaps that's a reason for me to feel grateful. Kate made her way to the platform where Mary's train had already pulled in. She quickened her steps, scanning the passengers, and spotted Mary walking up the platform, lugging her two suitcases. She hurried to meet her.

'Mary! Over here. God, I've missed you,' she said, hugging her friend close. 'I can't tell you how glad I am to see you.' They broke free and Kate held her at arm's length. 'I can't believe it. Wales must have suited you. You look terrific! You've had your hair done – it's all wavy – and a smart new coat!'

'Don't go on so,' Mary said. 'And come to that there's something different about you, young lady. You're turned out as if you were paying a visit to Buckingham Palace.'

'Better than that. I've come to fetch my friend home. The best friend it's possible to have. I mean that. I really have missed you and so did Josh. He sends his love and said you'd better be at home for his next holiday or he'd come down to Wales to fetch you himself. He even told Peter that the reason there weren't any home-made cakes was because his nanna was away.'

'Oh, bless his heart. Was he well? Was he happy?'

'Yes, to both questions and I think it's about time we made a move, we're getting some dirty looks because we're blocking the platform.'

They each picked up a case and started to walk.

'Catch a train straight home or go to a posh restaurant where we can have lunch first?' Kate asked.

'What d'you think?' Mary said. 'I seem to remember you promised me the best lunch in town.'

'Right. You're on. Let's head for the taxi rank.'

Chapter Twenty-Seven

MARY WAS IRONING. Although the April morning was overcast, threatening showers, the big kitchen was cheerful, with the coal fire burning brightly and the table covered with a red chenille cloth, a vase of fresh flowers placed in the centre.

'It's rough out there,' Kate said, coming in the back door. She had been hanging out more washing and Mary smiled at her as strands of her hair blew across her glowing cheeks. 'You sounded happy, Mary. I heard you singing as I was wiping my feet.'

'I am happy. Glad to be home with you,' she replied as she lifted a blouse from the ironing board and hung it carefully on a coat-hanger.

Kate stared at her and lifted her eyebrows. She could have sworn that Mary's mind was far away. She kicked off her garden shoes and watched as Mary took another blouse from the pile in the ironing basket and spread it out. Dipping her fingers into a basin of cold water, she sprinkled little drops up and down the cotton material and began to swish the flat iron gently to and fro. All the time she was humming to herself.

'It's more than you just being glad to be home. You're positively glowing, and I'd like to know why.'

Mary dithered and Kate watched her with growing puzzlement. She was blushing! 'Mary! You're keeping something from me. You've been home two days now and thinking back you've been hinting and smiling knowingly all the time. Are you going to tell me what you're up to?'

'While I was at my sister's I met a man,' Mary blurted the words out, and looked at Kate in alarm. 'Oh, bother! I wasn't going to tell you. Not yet.'

'Why ever not?' Kate cried indignantly.

'Oh, Kate! Dear Kate!' Suddenly Mary looked so sad. 'I shan't blame you if you tell me not to be so ridiculous.'

'Why ever would I do something as cruel as that?' Kate asked impatiently.

'He's sixty-five. Just retired. And I'm sixty-one . . .'

Kate went to her and tenderly kissed her cheek. 'What's that got to do with anything? Put that iron down and tell me how you met.'

'He does voluntary work. He came to the house to repair Blanche's wheelchair. His wife died three years ago, they never had any children and he seemed a bit lonely. I went out with him a few times. I don't think my sister entirely approved.'

'And,' Kate prompted.

'And not much else. We have promised to write to each other and he said he'd like to pay a visit to this part of the world when the weather gets better.'

Kate almost ran from the room, and into the front room. Opening the door to the sideboard she seized a bottle and was back in the kitchen within minutes.

'We must drink a toast,' she declared. 'We can't let this moment pass unrecorded.'

Mary fetched two glasses from the dresser, giggling like a schoolgirl as she watched Kate pour sherry into each glass. 'What's the toast?' she asked.

'We're drinking to friendship. No one should be lonely in this world. Here's to . . . you haven't told me his name.'

'Michael, Michael Kendall. He prefers to be called Mike.'

'Raise your glass then. Here's to you and Mike, may you have a long, lasting, happy time together.'

'Don't rush things. We're not as you put it "together", but it would be nice if later on we could find him a small hotel nearby, just let him visit for a few days, meet you and see what you think of him.'

'Oh, Mary, love, we can do better than that. If you'd rather he didn't stay here in the house we can always let him sleep at Bramble Cottage and have his meals here.'

'Thanks, Kate.'

'You're welcome,' Kate told her, taking in her bright eyes and her new hair style. She looked no more than fifty.

For the rest of the day Kate did her best to smile as she listened to Mary tell her what a wonderful man Mike Kendall was. She felt guilty for feeling so envious when Mary was so happy.

Late that night, when she'd kissed Mary goodnight and they'd each gone to their own bedrooms, Kate marvelled at the change in her. She had known her for so many years and had always presumed she was quite content to be without a man in her life. Today she had seen another side to her character, a side that made her seem so much younger than her years and certainly a great deal happier. What a difference love could make!

Kate wrapped her dressing gown tightly round herself and opened the window wider to let in the cold night air. Why couldn't it have been as easy for her and Toby as it was for Mary and Mike? Why couldn't Toby's job have taken him to somewhere like Wales. Anywhere, just so long as it could have been within the British Isles. As she stared up at the stars, South Africa seemed even further away.

Melbourne Lodge was a hive of activity. It was the Saturday morning of the August Bank Holiday weekend and there were a number of people staying in the house. Three of Joshua's schoolmates, plus Peter Bradley and Mike Kendall, Mary's friend. Even though the windows and the door leading out to the garden were all wide open, the temperature in the kitchen was rising by the minute.

In the dining room, the five boys and Mike Kendall were tucking into a breakfast cooked by Mary. Kate was busy making endless pieces of toast.

Mary now stood at the kitchen table slicing ham from a gammon she had boiled the day before. She was red in the face and perspiring freely.

'Aren't you glad we don't have permanent boarders?' Kate asked.

'I suppose we should have realised that whatever the season, and however hot the weather, men and boys alike enjoy their food. I must say I'm glad it's been agreed that we all spend the day at Hampton Court, at least there should be a breeze coming off the river.'

Kate came back from taking more toast into the dining room and glanced at the wicker backets Mary was putting food into. 'Good God, are you preparing to feed an army?' One basket held savoury rolls and sandwiches, veal and ham pies, Cornish pasties, hard-boiled eggs and enough salad to feed a large family. There had to be a pudding, Mary had declared last night, but Kate wasn't prepared for what she was now looking at: two glass dishes, one containing raspberry trifle, the other fresh fruit, sliced and set into jelly. There was also a Madeira cake and a Victoria jam sponge.

'Just so we don't forget, be a dear and fetch the apple tarts – they're on the slate shelf of the larder. They should be cool enough to pack now. And while you're there bring in the napkins and the cloth that we use for outdoors, will you, please?'

Kate shook her head in disbelief and out loud called over her shoulder, 'What would we have done if Mike hadn't driven up from Wales? As it is, he'll have to make two trips. He can't get us all in his car at once.'

'Don't worry, Josh has already asked Mike to take them first, which I'm grateful for. It will give us time to clear up and get our breath back.'

The kitchen door opened; Mary looked up and immediately smiled her delight as Mike came into the room. Kate also smiled and asked, 'Have the boys driven you mad or just deaf?'

'They're all right, just acting as they should, boys on holiday an' all that. I'm just setting off with them once they've finished stacking all their gear into the boot of the car. I'll be back for you two ladies as soon as I can.'

Mary crossed the floor to stand in front of him. 'Don't hurry on our account, we're glad of the time to freshen ourselves up a bit.'

'All right. I'll leave you to it,' he said, his smile taking in both of them as he went out of the back door to where his car was parked.

Kate looked across at her friend. Mary obviously really liked him. And she was already beginning to think of him as an old friend. He had been remote and stilted when he had come down and stayed at Bramble Cottage for a week at Whitsuntide, but once he had realised that she was not opposed to him and Mary going out together he had mellowed, treating her with as much friendly courtesy as he did Mary. He was a well-turned-out man, fit and lean, about five feet ten inches tall, with dark hair and eyebrows, speckled with grey. Kate had come to believe that he had great feelings for Mary and she wished them both well.

A real holiday feeling was everywhere when they finally arrived at Hampton Court. The water dazzled blindingly in the sun and heat shimmered on the towpath. Only Bushey Park on the opposite side of the road offered shady, cool places. Kate and Mary, with Mike following, picked their way slowly down the steps to the Kearsley Boat Yard. All three were carrying folded deckchairs, the idea being that they would set up their resting place on the hard standing above the slipway rather than struggle for space on the riverbank which, today, was thronged with people.

Jack Stuart and his wife came out to meet them, greeting Kate with the information that their own three children were already on the river in their boat. Jack helped Mike set up the chairs while Mary and Kate stood watching swans back-paddling to catch the bread some small children were throwing to them.

'I love all the seasons on the river, the continual cycle of life,' Mary exclaimed.

'Yes, I know what you mean,' Kate answered. 'We think it's all so familiar and then we find the pattern of it all does change.'

They strolled to the edge of the hard standing where the boats came alongside to tether to the wall. To their right was Joshua's dinghy, newly varnished and resting upside down on two planks of wood. He had been as pleased as punch when he had come home at Whitsuntime to find it ready and waiting for him. This holiday Jack had put a large cabin cruiser into use for a trip downriver with the assurance to Kate that both he and Mike were in charge and the five boys were to go along only as passengers. The river was extra busy, as it always was at holiday time, more so when the weather was as good as it was today. More of the local boats were back in the water and a pleasure steamer was chugging along in mid-stream on its way to Richmond.

Kate became aware of a gentle splashing and looked to see Josh, with Pete Bradley seated behind him, rowing a dinghy peacefully up stream. She watched the water rippling away from the dipping oars, marvelling at how effortlessly the boat moved, and saw Josh hesitate for a second when he glanced over his shoulder and saw her and Mary leaning on the wall. As they came abreast, Peter yelled, 'Lovely day,' and Josh shouted, 'Hope you've brought loads to drink.' Their voices carried easily across the water and it was Mary who answered them.

'Yes, we have. Soft drinks as well as tea and coffee.' Turning to Kate, she said, 'I'm right pleased to see the pair of them are wearing their life jackets.'

'No fear on that score. Jack knows my dread of the river. He wouldn't let anyone go afloat from our slip-way without one.' Kate continued to lean on the wall, regarding the two boys with a mischievous smile, until Mary asked, 'What are you smiling at?'

'I was just thinking how much Josh's standing will have risen by the time he goes back to school, look at his three friends out there.'

Mary looked towards the cruiser at which Kate was pointing. Joshua's three school mates were sitting on the cabin roof, each of them had a mug in their hand. They looked such healthy lads, wearing only shorts and sleeveless cotton vests, their brown legs bare and on their feet rope-soled deck shoes.

'Ahoy!' they shouted in unison, waving frantically at Kate and Mary.

'Are you having a good time?' Kate called.

Nick Banks knelt up, cupped his hands to his mouth and shouted, 'Brilliant, absolutely brilliant. Mr Stuart and Mr Kendall are below. We'll be setting off as soon as Josh an' Peter come aboard.'

Kate and Mary could almost hear the lad sigh with excitement.

'Fancy a coffee?' Mary asked lightly, as she and Kate settled back in their deckchairs.

'Do you want the bother? We could walk up to the shops.'

'Don't talk so daft, the whole place will be teeming with day trippers. Besides I filled two flasks with coffee; we can't let it go to waste. Here you hold the cups while I pour.'

They were sipping the hot coffee when Mary frowned and said, 'It's been some weeks now since I came back from Wales and I feel shaky inside about bringing it up but . . .'

Kate wrapped both her hands round her cup and avoided looking at her friend. 'It might be better if you say what's on your mind.'

'Probably not, but I have to get it off my chest. You know I love you, Kate, I couldn't feel more for you if you were my own daughter. Something happened to you while I was away; I don't know what it was, but it has left its mark on you. Oh, you try hard not to let it show, but in your unguarded moments you look so sad and it breaks my heart to see you. Can't you tell me? Is there nothing I can do to help?' She twisted round in time to see Kate hastily brush a tear from her eye. 'Oh, I just knew there was something!' She leant to the side of her seat, stood her cup on the ground and placed her hand gently on Kate's arm.

For ages Kate had wanted to tell Mary about Toby but hadn't been able to summon up the courage. Mary was her best friend. More than that she was her family, and for years had been her trusted confidante. She didn't want this to change, but it would if she continued to have secrets from her. Mary had given her an opening, so why was she hesitating?

'In some ways it was much the same as happened to you,' she said at last. 'I think I might have got round to telling you if you hadn't come home so happy with the news of how you had met Mike.'

'Oh!' Mary's jaw dropped as she pondered this astonishing piece of news. 'You mean you met a man! Oh, dear Kate, how selfish I've been. I am so sorry.' Without waiting for her to form an answer and, mostly to cover her own embarrassment, Mary gabbled on, 'What a coincidence! I didn't think things like that happened to people like you an' me. I thought they were just romantic stories in women's magazines.'

Kate did her best to smile but wasn't very successful. 'I couldn't believe it either. However, my episode hasn't turned out as happily as yours.'

'Oh, Kate. I feel a bit ashamed—'

'Why? Because you've been so lucky? Don't spoil it for yourself. I like Mike, I really do, and I'm happy for both of you.'

'Couldn't you try and tell me about him? What went wrong? It might make it a little easier.'

'Nothing went wrong. He didn't ill-treat me or anything like that, but I will tell you.' She began, right from the moment she had asked directions from the policeman in Kingston. 'Bernard Pinfold, that's his name, but he prefers his nickname, Toby.'

Sitting with the hot sun beating down on them and the noise and laughter from the folk who were out to make the most of the last bank holiday of the year, Kate relived every second she had spent with Toby. Parts of the story she refrained from telling Mary; they were moments that belonged entirely to her and to him. By the time she got to the telling of his proposal of marriage, the offer to obtain travel documents and whisk her away to South Africa, it was Mary who was crying softly.

'I suppose you did the right thing,' she ventured, dabbing at her eyes with her handkerchief. 'You couldn't have gone off at a moment's notice and left Joshua.'

'No. Knowing that what I did was right hasn't made it any easier though.'

'Have you heard from him since?'

'Not a word. Sometimes I think that's a relief. Anyway I'm too old to start thinking of going halfway round the world.'

'Don't be so silly. Too old indeed! You won't be thirty until January!'

Mary obviously was intent on pursuing the subject. But, even with Mary, Kate did not want to share any more memories. Her stomach was churning madly as she fought for some way of steering the conversation into safer channels and she was saved by the sight of Jack Stuart's wife.

'Would you two like a trip? We could get one of the riverboats; they'll be fun today, music and singing, though we'd probably have to queue for ages before we got on.'

Kate could have hugged and kissed this homely woman whose whole life was wrapped up in her husband and three children. 'Perhaps we ought to wait until Jack brings our boys back – they'll be starving. We've brought a picnic, plenty for everyone . . .'

Mary could see that Kate was upset and hastily stepped into the breach. 'Have a coffee with us now,' she said, rummaging in one of the bags for the flask and another cup. 'Maybe it's not the best day for us to try and get a river trip, far too busy. After lunch I think I'd like a walk in Bushey Park. It will be nice and cool under the trees.'

All the while the three of them sat looking out over the water Mary was saying to herself, if only there was something that could be done to bring Kate and this man together again. But there wasn't. And even if there was, it would just be interfering. She must remember not to flaunt her own happiness; it wasn't fair on Kate. She would do her best to help her friend over this, for Kate had acted in the only way possible. But she realised only too well that being in the right hadn't made her decision any easier.

Chapter Twenty-Eight

KATE RAN A hand through her hair and tried to concentrate on the papers in front of her. Further meetings had to be set up, projects needed so many people's approval, and letters demanded answers. She needed two pairs of hands, she thought irritably, and a lot more hours in the day. The paperwork never seemed to diminish, no matter how long she stuck at it, and she sometimes wondered whether she'd been right to offer her grandmother's house and land for this charity home. For certain she had never envisaged the amount of work that would fall on her shoulders or the number of hurdles the trustees would be confronted with. She had been up since six that morning and working in the dining room by seven thirty, eager to have some suggestions to put forward at the next meeting of the trustees and desperate to clear some of the accumulated papers. She threw down her fountain pen. Her mind was not on her work. The doorbell rang and that, too, irritated her.

Mary put her head round the door, 'It's Paul Richards. Shall I show him in?'

'Might as well, seeing as all the papers are here.'

'Right and I'll bring coffee for you both. You want to ease up, take a breather. You shouldn't take everything to heart so much.'

'Thanks. I could use a cup of coffee. Bring three cups an' come and join us, whatever Paul has to say I'm sure will be of interest to you.'

Kate leant back in her chair, letting her thoughts dwell on Paul Richards. He was the borough surveyor and had been involved with this venture from the beginning, in June 1932. Good God! More than nine months ago. Kate's first impression of him had been of a sharp, slim young man with thinning hair and glasses. Over the months she'd come to know him well. Behind his business-like exterior was a warmth, an impression that he liked his job and this project in particular, which was enough to make her take to him. But not enough for her to agree to go out with him, despite his frequent requests.

Mary pushed the door open with her hip, crossed the room and set the tray down on a side table. Paul came in after her, his arms full of packages and folders, which he dropped onto the end of the table where Kate was sitting.

'Morning, Kate. I've got some good news for a change.' He beamed at her.

'Let's hope your good news will help solve a few of these problems, because I can't for the life of me see how they're all going to get sorted.'

Mary sniffed. 'Take no notice, Paul, she got out of

bed the wrong side this morning.' Paul Richards' eyes gleamed with amusement. 'If you promise to smile, Kate, I'll take you away from it all. This afternoon I promise both of you a tour of the first finished stage of the 'Alice Memorial Homes'.

Kate cleared most of her papers to one side to allow room for Mary to set down two cups of coffee, one for her and one for Paul. Having done this Mary went to the far side of the room, seated herself near the bay window, and poured coffee for herself. She was always pleased to be kept informed about the progress of the building work and she was grateful that Kate always made sure, at least as much as she was able to, that she wasn't left out of things.

Mary was full of admiration for Kate. She had put her heart and soul into getting this scheme off the ground. She looked across to where Kate and Paul were engrossed in conversation. By golly it hadn't been easy! Right from the start there had been many businessmen only too willing to be part and parcel of the venture, but there had been some who were thinking only of the publicity and the limelight that would come their way because of it. Not everyone did charitable work or gave funds simply from the goodness of their hearts.

These men would have excluded Kate if they'd had their way. But she had held her ground like the fighter she was. In the end it had been agreed that a trust would be set up consisting of eight prominent businessmen, Mr Weatherford had been voted the trust manager and, with some deal of reluctance, Kate had been appointed chairman. It seemed to Mary that the title of chairman was a faint disguise for secretary and general dogsbody, but as this was now 1933 and women hadn't had the vote for any length of time she supposed Kate had to put up with what crumbs men sought to throw at her.

Mary's attention was momentarily distracted by Paul, who was perched on the edge of the table, leaning across and holding Kate's hand. Noting the look of devotion on his face, she began to feel rather sorry for him. One didn't have to be a crystal-gazer to know that he had been taken by Kate's good looks from the moment he'd set eyes on her. Kate could do a lot worse; admittedly, he was a bit of a clever clogs and he'd had a good many lady friends in his time, but Mary had made it her business to find out that although he was thirty-two years old he had never been married. But Kate just didn't want to know. There were times when Mary felt she could shake the life out of her. A few days, that's all it could have been, just a few days in which she had known this Toby and yet she was wasting her life hankering after him. He was never going to come back into her life. It had been a year now. Surely if he had any such intentions he would at least have written to her from time to time. Poor Kate! She felt so sorry for her.

Me having Mike hasn't made matters any better, she thought, though Kate, being the generous person she is, always makes him welcome. She and Mike had no intention of getting married but their friendship did mean a lot to both of them and it had become quite expected that he would come to stay with them in Surrey every so often. Mike would take her to London for a few days; they'd visit museums, see a show, go shopping, but although they always brought presents for Joshua and for Kate, it didn't stop Mary feeling guilty that she'd gone away leaving Kate on her own. Whichever way you looked at it, Kate had drawn the rough end of the stick all through her life. It just wasn't fair.

'I'm going now, Mary. Thanks for the coffee. I'll pick you both up about two. Don't forget to wear sensible shoes – there's still a load of rubble to scramble over.'

His long legs took him to the door in three strides.

'I'll just see Paul to the front door, I shan't be a minute,' Kate said.

More's the pity, Mary thought to herself. It would be great if I were to come out into the hall and find that young man had you in his arms and the pair of you were kissing.

'I'll make us a sandwich for lunch, shall I?' she asked, as Kate came back into the room. 'We'll have our main meal tonight. I think it's ever so sweet of Paul to include me in the invitation for this afternoon, I've been dying to see inside the building for ages now.'

'Suits me fine.' Mary's high spirits were infectious and Kate felt her own heart lift. 'I knew the builders were going great guns, but it is nice of Paul to suggest we have a tour. I'll tidy all these papers away. There's just one letter I must reply to, then I'll go upstairs and get ready.'

Left alone in the dining room Kate turned her mind back to business. Taking matters all in all it hadn't been too hard a struggle, not that it was over yet, not by a long chalk – at least another year before the whole site would be completed. However, God had been on their side. Good things as well as setbacks had come about since the first overgrown shrubs and bushes had been cleared from Alice's land and the first army of workmen had moved onto the site. The house, which hadn't had anything done to it for years, had been attacked with vigour and plans drawn up. Restoration and necessary alterations had transformed it to a greater glory and it could now accommodate as many as four staff, each with their own private bed-sitting room. Another set of builders had dug and laid the foundations that enabled them to start on the first of the new buildings only weeks after the trust had been set up.

To make the scheme even more viable, an old derelict property, which adjoined her gran's holdings, together with the surrounding land, had been purchased, and to enable the trustees to pay for this six-bedroom house and the land on which it stood the local newspaper had sponsored an appeal. Socials, sales of work and collections had been organised by Kate and Mary with a band of willing workers. Under Mr Weatherford's leadership, large sums had soon been raised for the financing of each new stage of the work. He had set his sights beyond Kingston to attract funds by letting Kate's wishes be known that the Alice Memorial Homes would be for the benefit of old and young people alike no matter what part of the country they lived in. The Depression made it a daunting period for any campaigner, however, Mr Weatherford was a well-respected businessman who could empty pockets and please at the same time.

Charles Collier had certainly acted wisely in leaving his son's affairs and those of Mary and herself in the safe hands of this kind solicitor, Kate concluded as she dated a sheet of writing paper and settled down to answer an important letter.

*   *   *

Paul Richards was back at the house just as the hall clock struck two. With his usual gallantry he held the door of his car open while Mary settled in the passenger seat, then holding Kate by the elbow, he assisted her into the back of the car. They drove through the small villages with their riverside cottages and homely corner shops, which were open all hours and stocked anything and everything. Soon they were in Kingston and Paul took the turning that led to the site.

Kate gasped. It was only a month since she had been there yet the difference was amazing. She would have been hard put even to recognise the smart house they were approaching as the place where her gran had lived.

As Paul drew the car to a halt the front door was opened by Harriet Tremaine. Kate had wholeheartedly agreed with the trustees' decision to offer the post of house matron to her. Although she was a single lady, aged fifty-two, she could have passed for anyone's grandmother. Homely and jolly was how Kate would have described her, not very tall, dumpy, with short grey hair, set in waves above her forehead. She wore glasses and showed a suspicion of a double chin, but it was her broad smile that had at once endeared her to Kate. Wearing a grey silk dress, which hung loosely from her shoulders, she had adorned the neck with two rows of dark red glass beads, which twinkled every bit as much as her eyes did behind her glasses as she came down the short path to greet them.

After they had greeted Harriet, she led the way inside. Despite all the renovations, Kate still felt it was her gran's house. It was a warm feeling that pleased her enormously.

They were in the second of the bed-sitting rooms when Mary nudged Kate's elbow and nodded to the fireplace, and for the first time she noticed that there were no gas brackets left on the walls.

'Surely electric light hasn't been installed? Not in this old house?' Kate asked, staring at Paul in disbelief.

Grinning broadly he nodded his head. 'This is only one of the many wondrous things you shall see before the afternoon has passed and, in the coming months, we, meaning myself, the builders and craftsmen and, by no means least, your board of trustees, hope to astound you with.'

'Well, if charm has anything to do with it you'll ease your way through without blinking an eyelid,' Mary informed him, and before he had a chance to reply, Harriet Tremaine added, 'I see someone else has cottoned on to you, Mr Richards.'

Paul threw back his head and laughed out loud, but it was to Kate that he said, 'Just so long as you sweet talk the trustees into finding the money, I can easily remove any small obstacles that appear from time to time, thus enabling your dedicated craftsmen to perform what some would describe as miracles.'

'Cut his tongue out an' he'd still have the last word,' Mary said, in a stage whisper.

All three women were giggling as they continued with their tour of the house. There were several pieces of furniture left that had belonged to Alice, old-fashioned, but made by experts of the trade they would last for years. Some furniture had been bought, mainly beds, and some had been donated. Harriet was the first member of staff, so at the moment she was the sole occupier of this fresh, bright, clean house.

Mary, with Kate following, stepped gingerly up the planks of wood placed over a newly laid path leading up to the front entrance of the new main building. It would be completed 'soon', a burly looking workman informed them. This wing was to house twelve adults for short-term stays, each in a single bedroom with a washbasin with running hot and cold water. At each end of the two landings there would be a bathroom, which would also serve as treatment rooms for residents who might need care. On the ground floor there was to be a communal kitchen, a large dining room and a lounge, part of which would serve as a small library.

Back outside, Paul pointed to the other end of the site, where another three-storey building appeared to be in the final stages. This, at the moment, was being referred to as the residents' wing. Plans were for six flatlettes, each to house a single long-term resident and six double units for long-term elderly married couples who would, in the main, be able to cook and care for themselves.

Hearing Kate and Mary discussing the future tenants, Harriet Tremaine stepped forward. 'Residents in this wing,' she nodded her head to the front opening that hadn't as yet any door, 'will be completely independent but with practical help, advice and guidance at hand as and when it is required. I think, at future meetings, it is to be considered whether it will be practical to offer these residents the choice of a prepared main meal delivered to their door or whether they could join those on convalescence in the dining room of the other wing. We shall have to feel our way, some may even prefer to cook all their own meals. It is a tall order for people to settle into a whole new way of life, and we mustn't expect everything to be a great success from the word go.'

'A very sensible lady, that Harriet Tremaine,' Mary remarked as they got back into Paul's car. 'If anyone can promote neighbourliness and thought for others, she's the one to do it.'

Paul settled himself into the driving seat, and twisted his shoulders round until he was able to see Kate. 'Well now, let's hear from you, since you were the one to instigate this scheme. How do you feel about it now?'

Kate felt overwhelmed by the enormity of the project and was asking herself how she could ever have been so reckless as to set out on such a task. Her voice was low as she said, 'Whichever way the Alice Memorial site develops in the future, I have to convince myself that I started it all with the best of intentions.'

Mary was shocked. How sad and despondent she sounded!

Paul got out of the front of the car, opened the back door and slid in beside Kate. Without saying a word, he put his arms round her and pulled her to him. They stayed like that, silent, for a full minute until Kate drew away.

'Too much mess on the site,' he said. 'A bit daunting, wasn't it? Made you wonder if the project will ever be finished. I promise you, Kate, it will be. And a tremendous success it will turn out to be. Honestly, I'm not joking. In a few weeks' time the garden specialists will move in, shrubs and plants, even trees, will appear overnight and, as if by magic, there will be curtains at the windows, residents in both wings and every person from that day forth will bless the names of Alice and Kate Kearsley. Now, wipe your eyes, stop crying, and tell me you're going to invite me into Melbourne Lodge for tea when we get back.'

Kate looked up at him. 'I'm not crying,' she muttered, brushing quickly at her eyes. 'And seeing as how you've given your afternoon up to driving us about, I suppose the least we can do is give you tea.'

'That's my girl.' He playfully punched her shoulder.

Then as he once again settled himself in the driving seat and switched on the engine he winked saucily at Mary.

I wish he were right Mary thought and Kate was 'his girl'. What a pity it wasn't the true state of affairs.

During the lovely months of spring that followed, Kate gave her time to the trustees without complaint, but when Joshua was home on holiday it was a different matter. The house rang with the sound of happy and, more often than not, grubby-looking boys.

Before she knew it it was July and Mr Weatherford drove Mary and herself down to Josh's school for the prize-giving and sports events that signalled the end of term and the beginning of the long summer holidays. Mrs Weatherford had also come with her husband. She had become a great friend to both Kate and to Mary, very much involved with their schemes to raise funds. She was as gentle in her ways as Mr Weatherford was vigorous.

During the summer holidays Kate allowed Joshua and his friends to spend a lot of their time at Bramble Cottage. There were several advantages to this, the main one being that because it was within walking distance of Melbourne Lodge the boys didn't have to keep pleading for lifts down to Hampton Court. The fact that the cottage fronted straight on to the towpath was a source of delight to them. One of the sheds in the garden served as a changing room when they went swimming in the river, the other shed housed their life jackets and other boating equipment, while the front lawn, at times, held as many as three boats. Each day Mary and Kate would walk the short distance, carrying baskets that held hot and cold food and drink. Beneath the big oak tree was the picnic table that her father had built. Over the years she had gone to great lengths to see that this one reminder of happier days had remained in good repair.

Mike Kendall was a frequent visitor, spending almost as much time in Surrey as he did in Wales. He was like an overgrown schoolkid where the boys were concerned. Mary was thrilled that he was definitely part of the family now. It was a wonderful time.

And then, suddenly, it was September. The boys went back to school and Mary foretold gloomily that they were in for a very hard winter because the hedgerows were already covered in red berries and that, she said, was a true sign.

Two-thirds of Kate's project was to be up and running before Christmas. To a man, the trustees agreed that Kate should be asked to perform the opening ceremony, which was to be held on the first Monday in November at eleven o'clock.

It was bitterly cold. The wireless had broadcast that

early snows had reached North Devon and up on Dartmoor everything was white.

Mary was, as always, sensibly dressed. She was wearing a double-breasted camel coat, with a long scarf, gloves and a woollen hat, all of which she had part-knitted and part-crocheted herself. The scarf was wrapped twice around her neck and shoulders as she came out of the house and walked towards Mr Weatherford's car. Her short fur-lined ankle boots gripped the icy surface of the path preventing her from slipping.

Kate, too, was warmly dressed, but what a different picture she made, Mr Weatherford remarked to his wife as they watched the two women approach. His wife, a fashion-conscious lady at all times, readily agreed. Kate was certainly well turned out! Her calf-length coat was the colour of a rich dark plum, fitted at the waist to swirl out into fullness beneath her knees. The two rows of buttons that ran from beneath her chin down to her thighs were criss-crossed with heavy braid. The collar and the turn-back cuffs of the sleeves were made from the same braided material, which was a deeper shade than the actual coat. On her head she wore a black-velvet hat. At first she had paraded before the mirror wearing a cloche hat but had decided it was too tight fitting. The one she now wore had a wide brim which turned back, giving a full view of her creamy complexion and big brown eyes. Most of her hair she had managed to restrain out of sight, only a few strands lying across her forehead and one long coil covering each ear, which she had deliberately arranged so that they would not feel so cold. Her high button-up boots were of soft black leather, as were her gloves.

* * *

What a turn out! So many people! Even Mr Weatherford was surprised.

Three of the trustees had had their say, now it was Kate's turn. She rose from her seat at the back of the platform and walked forward. All she could see was a sea of faces, none of which, at that moment, looked to her to be friendly.

She began by thanking everyone who had helped the cause. 'Without the generosity of so many kind people I would not be standing her today, because my idea would never have got off the ground.' She paused, took several deep breaths and in a much firmer tone, wound up her speech by saying, 'My desire was, and always will be, that the Alice Memorial Homes should be a home in the strictest sense of the word. I hope the trustees and those who work here will never lose sight of this crucial objective. My grandmother lived a long and mostly happy life on this site. I wish the same for all who come here to find rest and shelter.'

Kate cut the royal-blue ribbon tied across the brass plaque to the sound of tremendous applause.

Chapter Twenty-Nine

KATE WAS EATING crusty bread and cheese on the grass just outside the back door. There were so many things she could be doing but, for the moment, they would have to wait. She wasn't in the mood. And, after all, she had no one to please but herself. Mike had taken Mary back with him to Wales for a short holiday. It was a good opportunity for Mary to see something of his home town and to visit her sister Blanche. Mike had promised they would both be back in time for Easter.

Kate pulled a wry face. She couldn't blame Mary. Mike hadn't come up for Christmas and there had just been the three of them on Christmas Day, which had been very enjoyable but not much fun for Joshua. On Boxing Day they had ordered a taxi and dropped him off at Peter Bradley's home. Peter had two elder brothers and a sister so the invitation to Josh to join their family party had been most welcome. Mary and Kate had carried on in the taxi to the Alice Memorial Homes, where they had helped with the Christmas party for all of those who were now in residence.

Why was she feeling so down this morning? Because she was entitled, she told herself. It was two years to the day since she and Toby had parted. She sat, her head tilted slightly forward, staring at the garden. She hadn't so much as one photograph of him yet she only had to close her eyes to see his tall figure, his kind face and soft grey eyes; even the funny grin which she had traced with her fingertips. He might be the only man who had ever made love to her but he'd left her with enough memories to last a lifetime. Through these two long years he hadn't written once. If she'd had an address for him, would she have written to him?

She heard a motor coming up her drive. The postman had already been and she wasn't expecting anybody. Puzzled, she walked through the house and heard the bell ring for a second time just as she was about to open the door.

'My goodness!' she exclaimed, as a smart young man handed her a long white box tied across with a handsome dark green ribbon. Lettered in gold were the words MOYSES STEVENS. What was such a smart London florist doing making a delivery to her?

She signed for the box, asked the young man to wait a moment, laid the package on the hall table and fetched two half-crowns from her purse, which he accepted with a smile.

The box was so beautifully wrapped that she hardly dared to open it but curiosity was killing her. She placed it on the kitchen table and undid it carefully. Inside there lay sprays of red berries, twelve long-stemmed red roses and several sprigs of fern. She bent her head to smell the roses and saw that on the inside of the lid a large white envelope addressed to her was taped.

As she tore the tape away and opened the letter, her hands were shaking. It was a long letter with no return address.

3rd March 1934

Dear Kate,

I hope this finds you well. I am taking a chance that these flowers won't upset your life in any way. I am gambling that you haven't got yourself married, but if you have I shall try to be happy for you. It's asking too much that a lovely girl like you should have remained single.

There is something very important I need to say to you. When I left England I knew I would be away for two years and I came to terms with that. There have been times, many of them, when I just wanted to throw in the towel and come and fetch you. I have never written you a letter or tried in any way to find out what you were doing because, if I had, the temptation would have been too great. Not a single day has gone by when I haven't thought of you, loved you with every fibre of my being. In my imagination I have been there with you; taking you out to dinner, sitting in your lovely garden, walking by the sea at Brighton, even climbing Box Hill. You see, I remember everything. The feel of you, the smell of you. Your unruly hair which would tumble free no matter how much you tried to confine it.

From the moment I met you and you weren't

feeling well, all I wanted was to take care of you and for those few days we had together the wish grew so much that I knew I wanted the commitment to last for the rest of my life. I wanted to share my life with you, to be able to watch you move, to hear you talk – especially to hear you say that you felt the same way about me.

There was a vague sense of tragedy about you, and I wanted to erase all the bad things from your mind. I could not believe that a man had never loved you and claimed you for himself. After we had made love together I was overwhelmed by your emotion and sheer physical beauty. You were a gift from God.

The most wonderful days of my life were those I spent with you. Please believe me, Kate, I came to love you desperately. I love you still and I will until the day I die.

So, why am I writing now after all this time?

I made a pact with myself when I was forced to leave you. I would respect your wishes; that your duty and your love, albeit an entirely different kind of love, lay with Joshua. I had signed an agreement for this South African trip and I would see it through and, as difficult as I knew it would be, I would not contact you in any way during those two years. I would leave you free, maybe to meet another man who could make you happy. But, Kate, my dearest Kate, believe me when I tell you there have been days when I've said, 'I can't wait any longer. I'm going to write and beg her to come and join me.'

But I remembered how strong your feeling of

duty was and how much you loved Joshua. The decision you made was right. I know that. But I also know that leaving you standing in the doorway, getting into my car and driving away was the hardest thing I've ever had to do.

At last my time here was coming to an end and come hell or high water I was going to land on your doorstep.

Then six weeks ago fate stepped in. In the laboratory, where our experiments have been carried out, there was an explosion. One technician, a married man with two children, was killed and several of my colleagues were badly injured. Some of our work, including a lot of our records, went up in smoke. It was heartbreaking, because we were working on a drug that would have been of great help to a lot of suffering people. One day we hope it still will be. For now it is a matter of sorting through what we are left with and getting on with the job. That isn't to say that I am going to stay the course, not this time. However, I cannot desert now and as you, my dear Kate, said to me, you wouldn't respect me if I did.

I am still not going to put an address to this letter. I don't know which would be worse, to receive a letter from you saying that you were no longer free, or to hear that you were longing to be with me as much as I long to have you here. As soon as I am able I shall come home to England. I will first and foremost make it my business to find out how you are and if my returning will not in any way disrupt your life. Being away from you has not kept me from wanting you, loving you, every minute of every day. These two years have been the longest of my life.

Perhaps our having to part, has been some kind of test. If that is true, it has not changed my feelings for you one jot. I love you, Kate. And I always will.

Toby.

P.S. I will be back. I promise.

Kate lowered her head and pushed her face into the box that held the flowers, sniffing hard to inhale the heavy perfume of the roses. Then, holding the pages of the letter close to her chest she went into the front room where she settled herself in an armchair. Wiping away the tears that were blurring her sight, she took a deep breath and began to read the letter through once again.

Toby had not deserted her! He loved her every bit as much as she loved him.

How had he got the letter to England? Had he written direct to Moyses Stevens? How had he paid for the flowers and for the special delivery?

She thought about it for the next half-hour. Finally, she got to her feet, took the telephone number off the box and asked the operator to connect her with the florist. Her heart was thumping against her ribs as the phone began to ring. When she heard the receiver being picked up she almost put hers back on the hook. A young woman's voice said, 'Moyses Stevens.'

Kate swallowed hard before she could explain who she was, thank her for the delivery and ask her questions.

'We are so pleased you like the roses, madam. No, we don't have an address for the sender. If you'd like to wait a moment, I will check in our files as to how and when the order was placed, if that will be of any help to you.'

Kate said gratefully that it would. Her call was transferred and, this time, a gentleman's voice came down the line. 'I am sorry, madam, we have no address or telephone number for the sender. I myself took the order, it was over a week ago and I well remember the elderly man; I dealt with him personally. He was a foreign gentleman and he had instructions written on a sheet of notepaper. The flowers were to be red roses and the date of delivery together with the name Miss Kate Kearsley and the address were all printed in capital letters. Most explicit, I do assure you.'

'Please, would you remember the name and branch of the bank the cheque was drawn on?'

The man coughed discreetly. 'I can understand that you want to thank the sender, madam, but really I can be of no help. The flowers and the delivery charge were paid for in cash.'

Kate thanked him and slowly replaced the receiver, staying exactly where she was for at least five minutes.

Toby really didn't want to have any direct contact with her until he was ready.

She went back into the kitchen, found a tall glass vase and filled it with water. Almost reverentially she lifted the roses out of the box, one by one, grouping them with the branches of berries and the fern until she was satisfied that the whole arrangement looked wonderful. Then, standing back, she blinked several times. 'Oh, Toby . . . Toby . . . Toby,' she said his nickname softly and very sadly, and with that she perched herself on the edge of the table and let herself remember everything that they had said and done in the short time they had had together.

Chapter Thirty

UNLIKE AT MELBOURNE Lodge, meal times at Bramble Cottage were, by necessity, irregular affairs. The last day of the summer term at Josh's school, as always, had been the end of the first week of July. With three lads coming home to stay with Josh for two weeks it had seemed a good idea for the whole family to move to Bramble Cottage for a while.

Breakfast was very much a do-it-yourself meal, with the three boys away to the river long before Kate and Mary were even out of bed.

Now Mary stood at the sink peeling pounds of potatoes in readiness for the evening meal, and Kate whisked eggs in a bowl ready for the cake she was making. The day was far too warm to think of serving soup to the boys at midday so Kate decided that her next job would be to make a batch of salmon and cucumber sandwiches and a few cheese rolls. Independent and bright as buttons Josh and his mates might be, but when it came to feeding time they were only too willing to flop down on the riverbank and allow Mary and herself to wait on them hand, foot and finger.

'A few days time an' we'll be wondering what to do with ourselves,' Mary said to Kate.

'Yes, I suppose we will. You do think I've done right in saying Josh could go off with Nick to France, don't you?'

'Oh, you're not going to start in with all those doubts again, are you? We've been over it enough times already and we agreed we weren't left with much choice. He so obviously wants to go.'

'I know. But it will be the first holiday that he has gone away. And to France! I can't help having my doubts.'

'Well look at it like this, Mr and Mrs Banks have let Nick come and stay with Josh on several occasions, perhaps they think they are repaying our hospitality by inviting Joshua to go with Nick. After all they are not going to strangers. They'll be staying with Nick's aunt an' uncle.'

'You're right, I know you are, and Mrs Weatherford said almost the same thing. Evidently she knows the village where the boys will be staying – it's only a few miles outside Paris.'

'Well, there you are then. All tied up good an' proper. And you'd have to be feeling very brave to turn round and tell Josh that you'd changed your mind and weren't going to let him go.'

'I'm delighted, really, that Joshua is so popular. It's extraordinary, the way he's made friends, right from the first day he went to school. I remember being terrified when Mr Weatherford drove off with him, seeing him kneeling on the back seat of the car, his little face so white and drawn.'

'Me too. I thought my heart would break that day. Suppose I felt a bit guilty. Maybe we had mollycoddled him a bit more than we should have done, but then again he'd never known what it was to have his own mother, and he wasn't very old when his father died. Good job he did have us, all children need to know they are loved and wanted. I've often wondered whether you owning the boat yard had anything to do with Josh being so popular at school. Did that never occur to you?'

'A bit, I suppose. Though not from the money point of view. Most of the friends he's made have rich parents. More likely living so near to the river has been the main attraction and perhaps Josh did boast a bit about having a boat built for him and, as time has gone on, the fact that he has the use of several different motor vessels. Thanks to Jack Stuart we've never had to worry about their safety, he's always found one of his workmen to go out on the river with the boys.'

Mary changed the water in the sink and began to cut the potatoes into small pieces ready for the saucepan. 'Can I ask you something?'

'Sounds pretty daunting, you asking permission.'

'It's not really, but from time to time I have wondered why you've never sold the boat yard. You could have, when you were twenty-one, couldn't you?'

'Yes. Under the terms of my father's will I had to retain it until I became of age but after that I could have sold it.'

'But you never have.'

'What would have been the point? I don't need the

money and it's Jack Stuart's livelihood. He wouldn't have been able to afford to buy the yard and it would have been cruel to sell it over his head. He's a good manager. The staff respect him. He makes money for me as well as for himself.'

'And Josh loves the place,' Mary said, her tone full of merriment.

'Exactly. And he's not the only one, is he? We've had some great times there. Still do. And Mary, to be honest, I did love my parents, each of them in a different way, and when I see the Kearsley Boat Yard sign up over the slipway I think of my dad with a great deal of love. He was a good tradesman and a hard-working man. I've tried to blot out the last months of his life – you know what I mean – tried to remember only the good times. He left me a wonderful legacy, which not only gives me a good income but gives a great deal of pleasure to a number of people.'

'Lovely sentiments, Kate. I have to admit I love going to Hampton Court and I feel pretty special when we use the hard standing outside the yard to set ourselves up for the day. Especially when the riverbanks are crowded. It's like we lord it over ordinary folk by having our own spot.'

'Why, Mary, I didn't know you were a snob!'

'Well, you said yourself it was nice that Josh has rich friends. And even if it is a bit sad for us he's going to France, hopefully the weather will still be good and there'll be some of the summer left when he comes home.'

Kate did mind him going but wild horses wouldn't get her to admit as much. She was looking forward to seeing him come home again. And that wasn't the only person's homecoming she was looking forward to. But she wasn't going to say a word about that. Not yet. Not even to Mary.

That was her secret, to cherish all to herself. Each evening, before she got into bed, she opened her photograph album, filled mainly with pictures of Joshua from his baby days, and gently stroked the two red roses which she had pressed between the pages. She also read the postscript of Toby's letter. 'I will be back. I promise.'

Duty before love. It had turned out to be that way for each of them. There were days when she felt she had secretly been waiting for Toby all her life. In the ten years prior to their meeting she had accustomed herself to living her life through others. But once they had met, it had been magic just being near him. The top of her head barely reached his shoulder yet he made her feel ten feet tall! They had walked and talked, slept together, eaten together, crammed so much into those few days. It had, at the time, seemed so . . . normal.

Now he was coming home. Home to her. She didn't know when, but she did believe it was going to happen. Every night before she drifted off to sleep she would say the words out loud. 'Toby will be back', and then happiness would begin to spread right through her. At times she was so happy it was almost frightening.

Mary came across from the house bearing a tray that held two jugs of lemonade and a bowl full of rosy apples. It was a constant source of wonder to her the way Josh and his friends adapted to life during the holidays. After the strict regime of boarding school it was as if they felt free to do exactly as they liked and especially to dress in any fashion they pleased. Or rather undress, she laughed to herself. About all she ever saw them wear on these warm hazy days were shorts and even they would be discarded at a moment's notice to reveal skimpy swimming trunks before they dived into the river. Not one of them needed any persuasion, they were like river rats, totally at home in the water. These friends of Joshua had all been well raised and indulged by doting parents. But ever since their first visit to Melbourne Lodge, when they were in their first year at boarding school, they, just like Josh, had been entranced by the river folk and the way whole families with many children managed to live on one longboat, some even on working barges. They loved the novelty of going aboard such vessels, being made welcome by the old folk, most of whom had spent their entire life on the river, of diving off the side straight into the water, playing football in the fields beyond with these nomad boys who scarcely ever saw the inside of a classroom. They certainly enjoyed their holidays to the full.

Thank God the weather always seemed to be good, though cool breezes didn't deter the boys. Mary knew full well how much Kate loved having Joshua home and was thrilled to bits when he asked if he might invite his mates once again. Mind you, although the lads teased Kate, she gave as good as she got and she laid down rules. Be it at the big house or Bramble Cottage Kate saw to it that they made their own beds and helped with the washing up after the evening meal was over. The same rules applied to Mike. But then why shouldn't they? Mike was just as big a kid as the boys when the chance presented itself.

Mary was pouring lemonade into several glasses when she heard Josh calling. 'Can you hear what he's saying?' she asked Kate, who was busy clearing away the remnants of the lunchtime picnic.

Kate raised her eyebrows and strained her neck to see what was going on. 'No, but he seems to be pointing to a car parked up there at the corner.'

'Probably someone annoyed that they can't drive along the side of the river. No consideration some of these town folk.'

Josh was now pointing in their direction. They stood still and watched as a woman and a man walked slowly towards them.

'Odd kind of couple,' Mary muttered, 'dressed to kill on a hot day like this, wonder they didn't suffocate in that car.'

As Kate opened her mouth to agree, perhaps laugh at the ridiculous sight this pair made, she was caught by her memory. It was her cousin Hilda and, she supposed, the man was Hilda's husband, Ben Withers.

From ten yards away they could hear Hilda's loud voice, 'Fank God we've found yer. We've bin t'that big 'ouse of yours an' couldn't get any answer. A man with an 'orse an' cart told us you'd be 'ere, an' Christ am I glad he was right. Me feet are burning and me throat's that parched I couldn't spit sixpence.'

Kate forced herself to step forward and submit to being hugged and kissed by her cousin.

'I'll take this tray in and put the kettle on,' Mary said tactfully.

'You sounded just like your mother. Whenever Aunt Dolly arrived here she complained of her bad legs and feet. Here,' Kate pulled two wicker armchairs into the shade of the big tree, 'kick your shoes off and sit yourselves down, there's still a little lemonade left and Mary won't be long with the tea.'

'Don't suppose ye run to a bottle of beer, do yer?' Ben Withers asked.

'No, Ben, sorry, but I'll send for some for you as soon as the off-licence opens,' she said handing him a glass that was half filled with lemonade. 'Have you had a terrible journey? The hot sun couldn't have helped, not while you were driving, and then to find that we weren't at the house, I am sorry . . .'

Kate rambled on to cover her confusion. She only remembered meeting Ben once and he had seemed quite dapper then. A real Jack-the-lad. He certainly looked a lot different today. Kind of flash, and a lot older.

Hilda had gulped her drop of lemonade down and was now rubbing furiously at her feet.

'I knew I never should have bought these basket shoes, the straps are cutting in t'me flesh something chronic.'

'What d'yer expect? Nineteen an' eleven off the market!' Ben groused at his wife. 'I'm always telling yer t'buy one good pair of shoes at a decent shop instead of a dozen pairs of cheap rubbish but will yer listen to me? Oh no, might as well save me breath as talk t'you.'

Kate could feel trouble brewing and was glad that the boys were off out of the way. She didn't know how to calm this pair down, so she didn't try, she just waited.

Mary appeared like the good Samaritan she was and poured tea into a dainty cup with a matching saucer for Hilda and into a large breakfast mug for Ben, then she cut slices of the fruit cake Kate had made that morning and handed a plate to each of them.

'I'm not sure that either of you have ever met Mary Kennedy, she used to be housekeeper to Mr Collier. I know I did talk to you, Hilda, about Mary and Mr Collier, when I stayed with you all in London.'

'Pleased to meet yer,' Hilda said, giving Mary a kindly smile. 'I do know a lot about you, Mary. Me mum gives me Kate's letters to read when I go round there, not that she's written very much lately.'

'Oh that's not fair!' Kate interrupted. 'I never ever got an answer. I don't even know whether Aunt Dolly and Uncle Bert still live at the same address.'

'Didn't mean t'upset yer, Kate. Sorry, luv.' Hilda managed to look contrite. 'You ought t'know better than t'expect any of our lot t'write t'you. Never 'ad the same kind of schooling that you did. But me mum and me dad still live in that grotty end-of-terrace 'ouse which backs on t'the laundry and is a stone's throw from the shipyards. Well, me dad does.' Hilda sniffed and Kate could see that she was having a hard job stopping the tears.

Ben Withers got to his feet, unbuttoned his chalk-striped jacket and threw it over the back of his chair. 'All right, luv,' he said, patting his wife's shoulder. 'There's no need to get yerself all worked up. I'll tell yer cousin why we're 'ere.' He drained the rest of his tea down in one big gulp, placed the empty mug down on the table and faced Kate squarely. 'There's no pretty way of telling yer this so I'll come right t'the point. Yer Aunt Dolly's bin put away. She's gone off her rocker.'

Hilda let out a squeal which had both Mary and Kate

rushing to her side. 'Come on, Hilda, up on your feet,' Mary ordered sensibly. 'Let's get you inside the house. I think you and your husband could do with something a little stronger than tea.' With her arm round Hilda, as if she were an old friend come to visit, Mary led the way and Kate was left to follow on with Ben who was holding her arm so hard it hurt.

He cleared his throat, before gruffly saying, 'It's the truth, Gawd knows it is. Dolly went so bad Bert had no choice. She'd 'ave ended up driving him as batty as she is if they 'adn't taken her away.' He paused in the porch and looking very serious, went on, 'I'd better come to the reason we're down 'ere t'day. Dolly can't 'ardly talk, but when she does make 'erself understood it's 'er sister she wants. An' 'er only sister was your mother, that's right, ain't it? Every minute she's awake, which ain't too often from what I'm told, 'cos they've got her drugged to the eyeballs, she keeps on an' on about 'ilda and we thought at first it were 'er 'ilda she wanted, but it weren't. It were your mum she was on about. So Bert said you was the next best thing an' we ought to ask you t'come an' see yer aunt. Well what else can we do? I'm asking yer, luv, what else is there? We can 'ardly sit round her bed and tell 'er your sister can't come 'cos she killed her 'usband and the law said she 'ad to be hung, now can we? And if not that, what the 'ell do we say? You tell me. 'Cos I've just about 'ad enough of the 'ole tribe of 'opkins. Bert's got the two boys, Stan an' Tom, both doing well, but they and their wives don't wanna know. Well, neither do I fer much longer. I do me best for my 'ilda and our three kids and I don't mind 'elping Bert out now an' agin but I tell you straight, after today I'm washing me 'ands of Dolly. I've tried me best, an' nobody can say I ain't. But now it's going to stop. Did your mate say she'd got a drop of the 'ard stuff? 'Cos if she did, lead me to it fer Christ sake.' And with that he stomped down the passage and into the front room.

Kate was utterly devastated. How dare he talk about her mother like that!

Mary saw that Ben was given a good tot of whisky and Hilda's measure was topped up with ginger wine. Then, with the table quickly set with freshly made tea and hastily prepared sandwiches, together with crusty rolls and great hunks of cheddar cheese and pickles, she motioned silently to Kate that she was going to slip out and wouldn't be long.

Back outside in the sunshine Mary stood still for a minute and caught her breath. Why had that strange pair decided to descend on them now of all times? It wasn't fair on Kate. Coming here when she hadn't seen any of them for years. Raking up the past that poor Kate had tried so hard to live down. Oh well, she sighed heavily, God gave us our relations but it's a jolly good job he allows us to pick our own friends.

She followed the sound of laughter, and there were the boys and with them were several others, lads and, wonder of wonders, three or four girls, all playing with two balls in a kind of criss-cross netball match. She stood still until Josh saw her and he immediately said something to Nick, climbed the bank and was at her side in seconds.

'Is something wrong, Nanna? Who were those people? They asked me if they were in the right place for Bramble Cottage.'

'It's all right,' she hastened to reassure him. 'The lady is your mother's cousin.'

'I've never heard Mum speak of her,' he sounded astonished. 'Are you sure Mum's all right?'

Mary knew he was going to have to be told a lot more about his mother's background but now was not the time. On the other hand she couldn't fob him off with any old story, he was too intelligent for that. 'I promise you your mother is fine. She's more than capable of dealing with the situation. But there is something you could do for her. You and your mates could make yourselves scarce later on. Come into the house, wash and change, and say you all fancy going into Kingston to the pictures or something. That will give your mother time to talk to her relations, we'll give them a meal and they'll be gone by the time you boys get back.'

'Oh, Nanna,' he said, as he punched her shoulder lovingly, 'anything for you, but . . .' he made a face '. . . who's gonna feed us growing lads?'

'If it weren't for the fact that your mates would call you a cissy I'd hug you Joshua Collier. I'll give you some money and you can all have fish and chips, but mind you sit down properly and eat it at a table in the shop, no walking about the streets of Kingston eating out of the paper.'

'As if we would! There are times when you still think I'm a small boy.' He smiled roguishly at her expression of surprise.

'Yes,' she answered quickly, 'and there are times when your mother and I wish we were flies on the wall so that we could see what it is that you really do get up to!'

'Heaven forbid,' he muttered as he turned away.

Mary watched him join his mates and then walked slowly back to the house.

Kate wasn't sure exactly what it was Hilda and her husband expected her to do. She was sorry to hear how poorly Dolly was. Shut away in hospital. It didn't bear thinking about.

When she had needed someone, Dolly had not let her down. She had stuck with her through her mother's trial and the horror of the weeks that followed.

Hilda and Ben had forgotten their troubles for the moment. They had drawn their chairs up to the table and were making short work of the hastily prepared meal Mary had set out for them. Looking at her plump cousin, with her dyed hair and bright red lipstick, Kate found it hard to believe she looked so different. She had always thought of Hilda as pretty, but now her face looked a mess. The fact that she had been crying hadn't helped. The mascara she had plastered her eyelashes with was all smeared. When she had stayed with Aunt Dolly and Uncle Bert she had liked Hilda's good humour and straightforwardness and the fact that she never let anything get her down. She had been kind to her, even offered to get her a job, saying they could work together and go out and about together. Kate couldn't help wondering how her life might have turned out if she had accepted Hilda's offer, settled down and made her home in London with the only relatives she had.

She wanted, quite desperately, to be left alone to live her life in this lovely quiet village and wait and hope, even pray, that Toby would come back to share that life with her. She knew she wasn't going to be let off the hook as easily as that!

It was a relief when, much later, Ben drew a paper from his pocket, leant across the table and gave it to Kate. 'On there is the name of the 'ospital, their telephone number and the special ward that your Aunt Dolly is in . . . I realise that this 'as come as a shock fer you and I'm sorry. Yer need time t'think about what yer gonna do but I wanna get back 'cos tonight there's racing at White City.'

'Oh, Ben! Did yer 'ave t'say that. What will Kate think of us?' Hilda shouted.

The look Ben gave his wife was aggressive, to say the least, and Kate felt a bit alarmed.

'Your mother's been a good woman, I ain't saying she ain't,' Ben continued to glare at Hilda, 'but what's 'appened ain't nobody's fault an' there's nothing more that me, yer dad, or the blinking doctors, for what I can see, can do about it. Life 'as t'go on and whether you like it or not I'm going to see the dogs race t'night, so if yer want a lift 'ome you'd better get yer feet in them ridiculous shoes and come an' get in the car.'

'Hilda, I will come up to London just as soon as I settle things here. Tonight I'll telephone the hospital, ask about visiting times and . . . well, we'll see.'

Hilda rubbed her eyes, came to stand beside Kate and put her arms around her. 'Oh, Kate . . . you're . . . you're . . .' she sighed, cross with herself because she couldn't find the words to express her feelings, 'such a kind, gentle person.'

Kate held her cousin close and said over her shoulder, 'I will come to see Aunt Dolly, I promise.'

'Will yer stay with Ben an' me or with me Dad?' Hilda asked, with a sob in her voice.

Kate was silent, digesting the fact that Hilda didn't expect her to go up just for the day. 'I'll talk it over with Mary, get Josh settled an' I'll let you know.'

'We're on the telephone an' all yer know. Ben did yer put our number on that bit of paper you gave Kate?'

'No, I never give it a thought. Give it 'ere, I'll add it on the bottom.'

It was bright early evening when a solemn foursome walked along the towpath towards the car. The sun was much lower in the sky, there weren't the children about now and most day trippers had packed up and gone in search of something to eat. Kate had persuaded Hilda to go upstairs with her and wash her face and freshen up before setting off on the journey back to London. While they were in Kate's bedroom, Hilda had opened up and told her a lot more details about her mother's illness.

'My Ben means well but he's like me dad,' she began, her voice thick with despair. 'Can't be bothered with women's ailments an' when me mum got real bad they were out of their depth. But they can say what they like she's not mad she's . . . oh, I don't know, Kate, I just don't know, but I do know there's times when I'm there on me own with her an' she talks away almost proper like. Mind you, it is all about what 'appened years ago, but that don't mean she's crazy, does it?

'Old Granny Wallace what lives up the road an' 'as known me mum all 'er life, says she's just going through the change of life. I 'ope t'God she's right.'

Kate had gently hugged her cousin. She felt at a loss what to say and even less confident about being able to help in any way. Now, as she stood beside the car, just looking at Hilda brought tears to her eyes. Even though she had her husband with her, Kate felt she was a lost lonely soul.

'You could have stayed longer, Hilda. It wouldn't have taken Mary and me long to have got you both a proper meal.'

'I know, but I 'ave to go, see t'the kids. It took a lot of arguing to get Ben t'bring me down 'ere t'day. Best not push me luck, eh?' she finished with a remorseful grin as she kissed her goodbye.

Kate held onto Mary's hand as they watched Ben drive off. Mary was quietly telling her that it wouldn't be so bad to have to go and see her aunt in hospital. But it was not Mary who was going to have to make the journey, probably stay a few days in her Uncle Bert's little house and see her aunt in the awful state she was in. She was going to have to do all of that.

Chapter Thirty-One

NICK'S PARENTS, JOYCE and Frank Banks, had collected their son and Josh ready to set off for France the following day. Well into the night and for the next two days Kate had talked and Mary had listened, only giving her advice when asked. They went about their various tasks, the main one being the turning out of Joshua's bedroom and giving the rooms that his friends had used a jolly good cleaning.

Whenever Mary suggested that they stop for a meal or just to have a cup of tea the subject they talked about was always the same: whether or not Kate was going to go to see her Aunt Dolly.

Kate had phoned the hospital and been relieved that the report, while not explicit, was encouraging. 'Mrs Hopkins is under sedation, but if you are a close relative you may visit on Wednesday or Sunday afternoons between two and four. No, I am sorry, I cannot discuss a patient's illness over the telephone except to say that the doctors are very pleased with your aunt's progress. Her condition has certainly improved.' And with that Kate had had to be content.

Although she had not yet come round to admitting it, Kate was well aware that sooner or later she was going to have to go to London. The fear of what she might find when she got there was not the only reason making her waver. What if Toby were to arrive and she wasn't here? If Kate made the decision to visit Aunt Dolly, Mary would have to return to Melbourne Lodge, where Toby would go, if he came at all! Now, don't start in with all your previous misgivings, Kate chided herself, then found herself quickly questioning, why would he turn up now? It had been so long. Half the time their meeting didn't seem real, it was as if she had dreamt the whole affair. But then, if she needed reassurance she had only to open the photograph album and take out his letter and the two roses she had pressed. Did she ought to warn Mary that there was a slight possibility he would be calling at the house? Not necessarily, she answered herself.

She had toyed with the idea of telling Mary about the flowers and letter many a time; now was the right time to do it. Earlier than usual Kate went upstairs, got undressed, put on her nightdress and dressing gown and came back downstairs.

Mary looked up in surprise as she entered the front room with her large book tucked underneath her arm.

'When you were in Wales seeing your sister some flowers were delivered to Melbourne Lodge,' Kate began. 'Perhaps I should have told you before . . . somehow I couldn't bring myself to. A letter was taped inside the box.'

Mary pushed her down into an armchair saying, 'Wait, I'll get us a nightcap.' When they each had a glass she drew her own chair nearer to Kate's and urged, 'If you feel like telling me now, why not start at the beginning?'

She didn't pass the letter to Mary to read for herself. Some parts of it were too personal, so she read most of it aloud. When she had finished, Mary reached over, allowing her fingers to touch the heads of the two dark red roses gently. Her eyes glistened with tears and her voice was filled with emotion as she murmured, 'Oh, Kate! How wonderful! What a kind, considerate man your Toby must be. I shall pray with all my heart that he does return to England and that the two of you find the happiness you deserve.'

The next day they called Jack Dawson, who now owned a small van in addition to his horse and cart, and with his help they transported themselves and all essential articles back to Melbourne Lodge. Then they spent the weekend being thoroughly lazy, enjoying each other's company as only true friends can and finally settled that on Wednesday Kate would make the journey to London.

It was Tuesday evening and Kate was ironing one of her favourite summer dresses, telling herself that it would be muggy going up on the train and it wasn't going to be cool and breezy in London, not if this spell of scorching hot weather continued.

Mary looked up from reading the evening paper, 'Have you decided whether or not you're going to stay up there for a few days?'

'Well, the very thought of having to stay in Uncle Bert's house, just me and him, doesn't feel right, and when he goes to work what am I supposed to do with myself? The only other alternative is to stay with Hilda and Ben.' Mary made a face and Kate shuddered, 'Yes, you know right enough what that means!'

'Well, you did call me to the phone on Sunday morning to listen to the racket that was going on in their house. I thought Ben was trying to kill his children. Job to tell who was making the most noise, the kids screaming or their father shouting.'

'The only thing that is making me feel better about this visit is the good reports we've been getting both from the hospital and from Hilda about Aunt Dolly.'

'May I make a suggestion?' Mary got to her feet, folded the newspaper neatly and came to stand near the table. 'Why not make this a reconnaissance trip – just go up and make a visit, see how the land lies.'

'Don't think I haven't given that idea some thought, but I didn't know how to broach the subject to Hilda. I don't want to hurt her feelings.'

'Why don't I phone her now? I won't tell her a lie, just a half-truth. I'll say you have to attend a meeting on Thursday morning, that you are coming up just the same, but only a flying visit this time. I could suggest she meets you at the hospital, and at four o'clock when visiting time ends you could take her somewhere nice for tea before you catch a train back.'

'Would you? Don't let on that I'm here, then she can't insist that I come to the phone.'

With a resolute step and her eyes glinting, Mary went out into the hall to make her call. In a very short time she was back. 'All settled. Hilda will meet you in the front entrance to St Thomas's Hospital at a quarter to two tomorrow.'

'Thanks, Mary,' Kate said, letting out a great sigh of relief.

The guard walked the length of the train making sure that all the doors were safely closed. He watched admiringly as Kate put her foot on the narrow step and got into the carriage.

Kate's dress was lovely, a pale shade of green with long sleeves, a cross-over bodice that was very flattering to her bust, a trim white belt to encircle her waist and a full skirt that swirled down to reach her calves. The neck and hemline of the dress were trimmed with white daisies. Her thick hair was tied well back off her face and on her head she wore the daintiest of straw hats, the brim of which was trimmed with the same white daisies. White gloves and shoes worn with silk stockings gave the total effect, which at a glance said, cool and fresh.

'Need any help?' the guard enquired, holding onto the door handle of her carriage.

Kate murmured something appropriate and settled down in her seat. The journey took less than forty minutes and as she walked the length of the platform at Waterloo Station and came out into the dusty, hot air, she once again thought how different this world was from the one in which she lived! Great buildings, half hiding the sun, people scurrying past, so many motor cars, creeping along, hooting at pedestrians who endeavoured to cross the road in front of them. A gentleman, seeing her failed attempts to hail a taxi, took pity on her. He stepped out into the roadway, waited until a cab came into view, then raised his silver-topped cane and waved it frantically. The cab driver pulled up right in front of them. The gentleman opened the rear door, helped Kate onto the back seat and asked where she was going.

'St Thomas's Hospital, please, and I am very grateful to you,' Kate replied giving him one of her most charming smiles.

He stepped back, raised his hat and murmured, 'My pleasure, young lady,' before giving the driver instructions.

Kate's first sight of this most famous hospital was a bit daunting. It had steps up to the big main doors and a wide hall that one had to cross to get to the enquiry desk. Kate stood aside watching and listening to the receptionist. She was about fifty years old with brown hair set in rigid waves, and appeared to be as stiff as a board. But as the minutes passed, Kate realised that the poor woman needed to be efficient, and certainly firm, to deal with all the people, many of whom seemed set on demanding that they be attended to right away. Suddenly she felt a hand on her shoulder and jumped almost out of her skin. Relief flooded through her as she turned to see Hilda standing smiling at her. They kissed each other's cheeks and then linked arms. Kate was pleased to see that Hilda was dressed more suitably today: she wore a floral dress, with a cream background and her high-heeled shoes were beige. Still, to Kate's mind, she had far too much make-up on but she sensibly decided that it was none of her business. She even found herself feeling pleased to see her cousin and when she suggested that later on she would like to treat Hilda to a slap-up tea, Hilda squeezed her arm to show her appreciation.

'Cor, that would be smashing. Come on now, it's a long walk through to the annex where Mum's ward is. I told her on Sunday that you would be coming and I think she remembered who you were.'

'That is good news, Hilda. Have the doctors told you any more?'

'Well, yes an' no, yer could say. One doctor told me that Mum had suffered a stroke and that it was because she was having trouble stringing her words together that the conclusion had bin drawn that she was losing her mind.'

'Well, that's not very satisfactory, is it? How terrible Aunt Dolly must have been feeling.'

'Yeah, I thought that an' all. Then another day I gets to see a different doctor, much younger than the other geezer and he tells me that me mum might 'ave 'ad a fall, knocked 'er 'ead, and suffered some loss of memory an' that's why she could recall what 'ad 'appened years ago but wasn't with it at all when it comes to living day by day. So, I suppose yer takes yer choice and 'ope fer the best. I 'onestly don't see what else we can do.'

Kate stopped walking. The smell of the corridors wasn't at all pleasant and looking at Hilda, she knew her cousin was frightened. Despite putting up a brave show Hilda was terrified of what was going to happen to her mother. 'I hope she does recognise me,' Kate said, her voice little more than a whisper. 'I've brought her some biscuits and boiled sweets and in the bottom of my bag is a bowl of fruit that Mary put together for her. Is your mum allowed these things?'

''Course she is, though you'll get a shock when yer see 'er. She's as thin as a rake.'

'I meant to stop and buy her some flowers but I got straight out of the taxi and came into the hospital.'

'Good job too. Waste of money. Flowers don't live five minutes in the wards. Nobody bothers t'change the water an' the nurses ain't got the time. 'Ere we are. Look, the sister's just taking the screens away from the door so that means the visitors can go in.'

They had to walk the whole length of the ward because Dolly's bed was the last of a very long row. Hilda stood at the end of it and, having stared at her mother for a couple of minutes she turned to face Kate and pulled a very odd sort of face, giving her a kind of warning. Why should she warn her? What could she be trying to say?

They moved up to the head of the bed and, as Kate got nearer to her aunt, she knew immediately. Dolly was sitting in an armchair, a tartan rug laid across her legs. She could have been an old woman of about ninety, so thin and wrinkled did she look. Her eyes had a terrified look as if she had no idea where she was or what was happening to her. Kate felt so upset and shocked that she had to force herself to stand still, when all she really wanted to do was turn and run. Hilda put down the bags she had brought and knelt down in front of her mother and very tenderly took hold of both her hands. 'How are you today, Mum? You know I told you me cousin Kate was coming t'see you, remember? Well, she's here. Are yer gonna give her a kiss?'

Kate moved alongside Hilda and she too bent her knees so that her face was on a level with that of her aunt.

'Hallo, Aunt Dolly,' she leant forward and placed her lips gently against Dolly's thin cheek. 'How are you feeling?'

It was as if someone had flicked a switch. A moment ago she had looked as if she couldn't move an inch and was consumed by fear, now she slowly unclenched her fists, lifted her face until she was looking straight at Kate, and appeared to recognise her. As the two women waited, sweat broke out on Dolly's face and she began to shake; from her mouth came small sounds of distress.

'I've brought her a new bedjacket,' Hilda said, getting hastily to her feet and rummaging in one of her bags. It was very pretty, the palest baby blue with a swansdown trimming around the neck and cuffs. She draped it around her mother's shoulders, so gently and with such care that Kate was amazed.

'I'll fetch two chairs,' Hilda said, 'they keep a stack of them over there by the wall.'

By the time the two cousins were seated, Dolly was moving her feet which were encased in cheap scuffed black shoes. Hilda seemed to know what she wanted, because she laughed out loud. 'Mum, you do remember!' she cried. She dived once more into her bags and came out with a neat pair of dark blue velvet slippers. She took the shoes from her mother's feet and replaced them with the new slippers. Straightening up, she looked down at her and said, 'Well?'

Dolly's pale, wrinkled face crumbled and a single tear slid down her cheek, but very slowly a thin smile came to her lips. Hilda could scarcely see, for her own tears were blinding her, and she threw her arms round Dolly's shoulders, this time not stopping to be gentle, and rocked her thin frame back and forth, all the time saying over and over again, 'You *are* with it, Mum. You are. You are. See, Kate, I did get through t'er. It was days ago, but she remembered. She did, she did!'

Hurried footsteps sounded and a nurse appeared at the foot of the bed. 'Whatever's going on? Mrs Hopkins must be kept quiet. Visitors must not be allowed to excite her.'

'Sorry, nurse,' Hilda mumbled.

'Very well. You do have chairs, I see. Sit down and try to be calm.'

'Soppy cow,' Hilda muttered under her breath as she watched the stiff back retreat down the ward. 'Seeing us two is a proper tonic, ain't it, Mum? Better than all the pills they've bin stuffing yer with.'

Kate laughed as she lifted her own bag up onto her knees. The sweets and biscuits she had brought she packed tidily away in the locker. The bowl of fruit Mary had sent she placed where her aunt could see it. Then she held up a banana but got no reaction from Dolly. She tried again with an apple and then grapes; no flicker of desire. Then she tried an orange. Both Kate and Hilda smiled broadly as Dolly's feet started to tap. 'An orange it is then,' Kate declared. She peeled one, broke it in half and then into sections placing them one at a time in her aunt's bony fingers.

'See,' Hilda said quietly to Kate as they watched Dolly suck the juice from each piece of the fruit, 'she can not only feed herself, she can make herself understood if people would only persevere and show a little patience.'

'I agree with you,' Kate assured her cousin. 'I suppose

in a place like this they just don't have the time to give to individuals.'

'That's no reason that they should 'ave said she was . . . well, you know. And it weren't only the staff in 'ere. It were me dad and that dopey 'usband of mine. They're all right when everything's going fine and me mum is running round after everybody like a blue-arsed fly but when she gets sick they can't wait to shove 'er off into some bloody 'ome. Well it ain't gonna 'appen. Tonight I'm gonna go an' see me bruvvers. Perhaps it ain't all their fault. It's more than likely their stuck-up wives that's kept 'em away.'

Kate leant forward, wiped her aunt's mouth with a clean handkerchief, and gave her another section of the orange. Hilda seemed glad to have someone to talk to and the best thing she could do for her cousin at the moment was sit back and be a good listener.

'Funny, you know, Kate, me mum was talking t'me not so long ago about 'er own bruvvers an' 'ow she 'adn't set eyes on 'em fer years. Know what she said? A daughter's a daughter all 'er life, a son's a son till he takes a wife.'

Dolly's feet were tapping like mad.

'What is it, Mum?' Hilda turned to give her her full attention, saying to Kate, 'I bet she's 'eard every word I've said.'

Dolly dropped the piece of orange into her lap, hunched her shoulders, stretched out her hand and touched Hilda's cheek. Her mouth opened and she dribbled a little. 'Mm . . . mm . . . my . . . girl.'

Hilda looked at Kate in amazement, but before they could say anything, Dolly had twisted in her chair to face

Kate. Again her hand came out and her fingers lay across Kate's wrist. Once again she was trying to say something. Kate sat very still, feeling scared, for two bright spots of colour had appeared in her aunt's cheeks. 'Mm . . . mm . . . my . . . sis . . . st . . . er's . . . girl.' The three words were out. Dolly laid her head back against the chair, and there was no mistaking, she was definitely smiling! Both girls were choked.

'Mum! You clever ole gal!' Hilda whispered into her ear, because her face was pressed up against her mother's cheek.

Kate took one of her aunt's hands and held it firmly between both her own; she had to blink several times to keep her tears from falling. It was some time before any of them moved and when they finally did both women laughed as they each brushed a hand over their eyes.

'Daft pair, ain't we?' Hilda said, as she unpacked her bag.

'Look, Mum,' she now spoke quite normally, 'I'm putting a clean towel and face flannel on the middle shelf of your locker and here's a new tin of talcum powder I'm putting in yer wash bag, I got yer lily of the valley this time, I thought yer must be fed up with English lavender. A clean nightdress an' two pairs of drawers are on the bottom shelf and all the goodies that Kate brought yer are on the top, an' that's where I'm putting some coppers an' a two-bob bit just in case you wanna buy anything from the 'ospital trolley what comes round.'

As Hilda straightened up the bell began to ring.

'Does that mean visiting time is over?' Kate asked, glancing at her watch.

''Fraid so. That's yer lot till Sunday.'

Kate gently hugged her aunt and placed her lips first on her cheek and then on her forehead. She moved away a little so that Hilda could say her own goodbyes to her mother. It had been an emotional couple of hours but nowhere near as bad as she had feared. She would come back.

'I expect we'll have a terrible job to get a taxi,' Kate remarked as much to herself as to her cousin as they stood outside the hospital and watched the streams of traffic pour by.

'A taxi?'

'Well, we agreed that I would take you to tea, didn't we? And I think we both deserve it, if only to wash the smell of disinfectant away. I can actually taste it, can't you?'

'Every time I come 'ere it gets worse. So, where we gonna 'ave this tea.'

'The choice is yours.'

'In that case,' Hilda began, simulating Kate's posh voice, 'why don't we try the Ritz?'

'Why not indeed? That is if we ever manage to stop a cab.'

Hilda threw back her head and laughed. 'You mean it, don't you? I was only joking, 'onest. Can yer see me 'aving tea at the Ritz?'

Kate laughed with her. 'You should always mean what you say. I'm dying for a cup of tea and seeing as how I hardly ever see you, or London come to that, today you and I are taking tea at the Ritz. If we ever get there.'

'If that's all that's stopping us, watch this.' Hilda put two fingers in her mouth and whistled loud enough to wake the dead. It worked, though, and as she held open the door and allowed Kate to step in first, it was she who smiled sweetly at the cab driver and said, 'May we go to the Ritz Hotel, please?'

Their tea was a great success and Hilda insisted that she come to Waterloo Station to see Kate safely on to the train.

'I can't begin t'tell yer what this afternoon 'as meant t'me, Kate. Not a soul encouraged me to think that me mum would ever come out of this lot fit an' well. Mind you, I was always determined to fight her corner, but God above knows it was an up 'ill task trying t'do it on me own. You bin marvellous. Can't believe me mum knew who you were, but she did, didn't she? And we never 'ad t'prompt 'er, did we?'

'I'm just so very pleased that I came,' Kate replied, giving Hilda's arm a squeeze. 'I'm certainly going to keep in touch with you from now on. I'll ring you and let you know when I'm able to make the journey again and, meanwhile, I'm going to make some enquiries about Dolly having a holiday when she's fit enough to travel.'

'Aw, Kate! You won't lose by it. I'll see yer right somehow, don't you fret. I'll go on Sunday, an' as soon as I get 'ome I'll be on the telephone t'you. Let yer know 'ow she is by then.

'Now you take care, an' give me love to that Mary Kennedy, a real nice lady I thought she was. Ain't many around like 'er.'

'I mean it, Hilda, about your mum having a change of scene. I'll see what can be done, and when I see you next I hope to have all the details and I'll fill you in on the whys and wherefores.'

'All right, luv. Look, yer better get in 'cos the guard is going to blow his whistle. Goodbye, Kate.' They hugged each other close. 'God bless yer. Fanks for me tea, it was smashing.'

'Goodbye, Hilda.'

When she could no longer see her cousin Kate drew her head back in from the window. She felt utterly exhausted, but she was so glad she had made the effort – as much for her cousin's sake as for her aunt's. Poor Aunt Dolly! And poor Hilda as well! She was right, she had been fighting a battle for her mother's well-being on her own. Everyone else had been ready to give up and what that would have meant for Dolly didn't bear thinking about. Well, now Hilda wouldn't be on her own. I'll do anything I can. Just as Aunt Dolly helped me when no one else wanted to know, I'll do my best to help her.

It would be like repaying a long overdue debt.

Chapter Thirty-Two

THE LONG-AWAITED MOMENT had arrived, Aunt Dolly was very much better and Kate was about to ask permission from the board of trustees that a place be found for her in the Alice Memorial Homes. She had already sounded out Harriet Tremaine, who had turned out to be a thoroughly popular matron, and she had been wholly in favour of Kate's suggestion. Some weeks had slipped by since Kate had paid the home a visit. The whole of her time had been taken up with visiting her aunt and seeing that Josh enjoyed what remained of his summer holidays.

They were a little early so they decided to do a bit of a tour. Kate walked with pride. Every floor she trod and every public room they peeped into was there because of her gran. Alice had loved this spot and, without a doubt, she would be proud that Kate had given it up to be used for such a worthy purpose. So many people had been kind and generous and the finished buildings, now fully operational, were a credit to each and every person who had been involved. The main rooms were beautiful, right down to the smallest detail, well proportioned, bright and sunny. A small rosewood piano, a gift from the local traders, stood in the lounge facing French windows, which led onto what had once been an overgrown field. Now the grass was clipped short and rose bushes lined the borders. This was the largest of all the public rooms. It was used not only by the sick folk who were housed for short stays in the main building, but by the permanent residents who occupied the purpose built flats. Coffee mornings, bring-and-buy sales, afternoon card games and occasional evening entertainment were among the many uses this large lounge was put to. In the main dining room, vases held fresh-cut flowers, the curtains, chair covers and cushions, all hand sewn by willing volunteers, were as pretty as any picture. There were three tables each seating six people, the chairs were wooden ones with wheels, the seats covered with a quilted pad.

Mary looked at her watch. 'Best make our way to the kitchen, if Harriet is about we're sure to be offered coffee.'

'All right,' Kate agreed, giving one last loving look through to the gardens.

The kitchen was unbelievable, so big yet so homely. There was a huge cooking range with the fire-front open and the bars already glowing red at this time of the morning. A dresser took up the whole of one wall. There were rows of white and red banded cups hanging from hooks and piles of matching plates tidily stacked at one end. A rack held pots and pans ranging from enormous to very small, some were copper, some cast iron; all were scrupulously clean.

'Morning, Kate, morning, Mary, come away in.' The beaming, rosy face of Mrs Burton, the resident cook since the home had first opened, peeped out from the open door of the pantry. 'I've trays ready to be sent up to the office but you're welcome to a coffee or a cuppa before the meeting starts. State your preference. I shan't be a moment.'

Kate and Mary looked at each other and quietly giggled. 'Doesn't alter, does she?' Mary whispered.

'Wouldn't want her to, would we? Mrs Burton is about the only person I've ever met who can tackle half a dozen jobs at once, and still talk nineteen to the dozen while she's doing them.'

'True. Turns out the best bread and cakes that I've ever come across.'

'I heard that, Mary Kennedy, and if you're trying t'butter me up there's no need.'

Mrs Burton was quite the opposite to most people's idea of how a cook should look. Tall and lean with a reddish face and an ever-ready smile, she banged her hands against her bony thighs to shift some of the flour that was clinging to them and grinned at Mary and Kate. 'Knowing the pair of you were coming here today I made an extra couple of cakes. They're in that blue tin on the end of the dresser – don't forget to take them when you leave.'

'You sure they're for us?' Kate asked, smiling knowingly.

'Well, you've done more than enough to help this home get under way, generous to a fault I'd say, and it's nice sometimes to be able to show appreciation in return. The date an' walnut one I did do for you and Mary, but I must admit me mind was on master Joshua when I put in the slab of gingerbread.'

'I knew it. Why is it that everyone who comes into contact with Josh wants to spoil him?'

'That's a daft question if ever I heard one.' Mrs Burton sniffed. 'Hark who's talking! Then again a bit of spoiling never hurt no child, an' you have to admit that young boy of yours only has to smile and with those great big blue eyes there ain't a lady worth her salt that wouldn't try to please him. He's a great lad and a credit to you, but then you don't need me to tell you what you already know.'

Mary, having taken down two cups from the dresser and helped herself to coffee from the enamel pot to the side of the hob, was about to hand one to Kate when the kitchen door opened and Mr Weatherford came in. He smiled at the trio of women. 'Ah! Just in time, am I?' he asked, walking towards Mary.

''Course you are. Here, have mine I'll get myself another,' she assured him.

'We'll have to drink up quickly, I saw a couple of the trustees making their way to the office. What made you two girls arrive so early?'

'Oh, I like the girl bit,' Kate cried. 'I haven't been able to give as much attention to this place as I would have liked just lately, so Mary suggested we treat ourselves to a bit of a tour.'

'And what have you found? Everything to your satisfaction?'

'Everything is absolutely splendid,' Mary cut in and

Kate quickly followed with, 'Couldn't be better. The whole place is a credit to all members of the staff.'

Having drunk their coffee and told Mrs Burton that they would pop in and see her again before they left, they followed Mr Weatherford up the short flight of stairs to the first floor where the office was situated. It was a fair-sized room; a pleasant place with comfortable chairs arranged around three walls. Against the far wall stood an oak desk with a swivel office chair set behind it. The floor was covered with a plain brown, hard-wearing carpet. Two windows looked out onto a section of the garden which was hedged in with small-leafed, close-growing shrubs. Kate immediately thought what a lovely quiet place it would be for people to sit and maybe read a book, especially if the person were recovering from a recent illness.

There were four men already in the room when they entered. The only gentleman who Kate felt she had not got to know well in all her dealings with the trust was Mr Belmont, who had taken on the task of treasurer. He was a lively looking man in his fifties, with very brown eyes and thick dark hair. He was the first to cross the room and shake her hand. Mr Weatherford took his seat behind the desk, looked at everyone for a moment and then smiled, his craggy, serious face changed and Kate thought to herself that he ought to smile more often.

'Gentlemen,' he began, 'no introductions are necessary were Mary Kennedy is concerned. You are all aware how tirelessly she has toiled to accrue funds for the Alice Memorial Homes, and she is here today at the invitation of our benefactor, Kate Kearsley. Between them, these two ladies have a request they would like to put forward and I propose that we hear them out and deal with it quite informally, before we get down to today's business. Naturally Miss Kennedy, not being a member of the board, will withdraw before I officially open the meeting.'

This statement brought the men's gaze round to rest on Mary and in unison they nodded their approval.

'Thank you very much,' she stammered.

At a signal from Mr Weatherford, Kate got to her feet and began very timidly to explain what had happened to her aunt. 'My biggest worry is that St Thomas's Hospital feel that everything possible has been done for her as a patient but that she is not, in the opinion of the doctor, fit to be discharged unless there was someone with her at all times. As that is not possible, I would like your permission to have my aunt stay here so that she may recuperate in far better surroundings than any the hospital could provide.'

It was the treasurer who spoke first. 'I take it, then, Miss Kearsley, that your request is not for your relative to be offered permanent accommodation.'

'Oh, no.' Kate answered Mr Belmont quite forcibly. 'It is more a matter of convalescence while she is recovering from having been so poorly.'

'So what's the problem? There obviously is one.'

Kate relaxed a little. 'I didn't want to be seen as taking liberties.'

A couple of the men coughed and nodded, dismissing the fact that any such idea would have entered their heads.

'Have you spoken to matron about vacancies, Miss Kearsley? I do know our list is not overloaded at present,' Mr Belmont spoke kindly.

'Yes, Mr Belmont, I have,' Kate admitted, somewhat shamefaced, 'and she does know that I am making this request to you gentlemen this morning.'

'And you, Mary, have you anything to add?' Mr Weatherford asked.

'Only to say that we would be doing Kate's aunt and her family a great kindness. I know Kate's relatives and they have done their best, but they all have their livings to earn and there is no one person able to be with Kate's aunt at all times. There is another fact to be considered; the family home is in the East End, not exactly a good area in which to find peace and quiet, which we are led to believe would go a long way towards helping her recovery.'

As Mr Belmont stood up, his lips were set in a kind smile and he made a gesture of finality. 'Gentlemen?' There was a rustling of papers as each man got to his feet, all nodding their agreement in the most hearty of ways.

'Kate,' Mr Weatherford beamed, 'perhaps you and Mary might like to go and find matron, ask her to join us and at the same time tell cook we are ready for our refreshments.'

'Willingly,' Kate said, smiling her thanks to each of the trustees as she and Mary made for the door.

She was bursting to get on the telephone to tell Hilda. Aunt Dolly was coming here to Kingston where, God willing, she would soon get her health back and once again be the lovable, lively, reliable lady that she had always been.

367

Chapter Thirty-Three

THESE NEXT FEW days were going to be extremely busy ones, Kate thought as she stood staring out of the window, wishing like hell that she knew where Joshua was. It was almost the first weekend in September and that meant Harvest Festival, before all the children went back to school. As usual, both Mary and herself had been roped in to help with the activities that were taking place. Neither of them minded helping to decorate the church, make cakes, pies, and scrub big potatoes ready to be baked in the bonfires that would be lit up and down the towpath one little bit. But besides all that they would have to eat lunch almost as soon as the morning church service was over because they had promised to be at the Alice Memorial Homes when Ben and Hilda arrived with Aunt Dolly. At the moment though, Kate's mind was on other things. The weekend was the least of her worries.

When she had peeped into Joshua's room at seven

o'clock that morning and found he wasn't there she hadn't been too surprised, but for him not to have put in an appearance when breakfast was on the table was another matter. Josh could smell food a mile off. Now it was three o'clock in the afternoon and she was worried sick. Mary had telephoned the parents of all his friends but Josh wasn't at any of their homes. 'I've walked the length of the village and along the side of the river almost into Kingston, I just don't know where else to look,' she was muttering to herself as Mary pushed the door open and came into the room carrying a tea tray. 'He's never ever gone off without telling us before or at least leaving a scribbled note on the kitchen table,' she mumbled.

'I know,' Mary replied softly, 'and I'm kicking myself because, now I come to think about it, that boy has been very quiet ever since he went out to lunch with Mr Weatherford. I thought perhaps it was because he knows this is to be his last term at prep school. What do you think? It's been some hours now, maybe we ought to call the police.'

Kate looked indecisively at Mary for a moment. 'I know what you mean about Josh being quiet and I feel a bit guilty too. I've been meaning to get him on his own and have a good long talk about so many things. Then Mr Weatherford said he wanted to answer all sorts of questions that Josh had been asking, so I thought I'd better wait until after they talked an' then, what with one thing an' another, I've never got round to it.'

'You mustn't go blaming yourself.'

'I know, but I do. Weeks ago, when Hilda turned up, he remarked about me having relatives that he'd never heard of and when he came home from France he went on and on about Nick's father and uncle all the things they'd done together. I kind of felt at the time that Josh was . . . well, jealous. Once or twice since I've heard him put out the odd remark about his father as if he were his enemy.'

'His enemy? You can't be serious.'

'Well, perhaps enemy is not the right word, but there was something, and I should have made time to sort it out there and then and I didn't.'

'With all the arrangements Mr Collier set up for Joshua, not a soul could dispute that he loved that boy dearly. Let's face it, Kate, he made more than ample provision for his son. Josh will never want for anything. All the same it's understandable, him being envious of other boys with fathers and male relations, when as far as he knows you and I are all he's got. I suppose it is about time that you told him, not only about his early life, but about your own as well. That might help. Sit him down and tell him the truth, Kate. You won't regret it.'

'I'd go down on my bended knees and answer any questions he cared to put to me if only he'd walk in here this minute . . . I wish to God I knew where he was.'

'Mum, Nanna, I'm sorry if you've been worried about me,' Josh whispered, poking his head round the door.

Kate almost fell off her chair. Mary blinked and the cup in her hand rattled as she put it down on the saucer. She crossed the room and put her arms around Josh's shoulders. 'You all right, love?' she asked giving the boy a smile.

'Yes, Nan. I walked much further than I meant to and when I thought I'd make for home and catch a bus,

I remembered I hadn't any money with me, so I had to walk back. Nan, I'm starving.'

'Go and tell your mother you're sorry,' she advised. 'I'll see about getting you something to eat.'

Joshua took a step towards his mother, then a step back. He looked exhausted and he was really grubby. She began to wonder how he had got in such a state.

'Mum? Please? I should have left you a note . . . I just want to tell you I'm sorry.'

'Oh, my love!' The words burst from her and she flew to him, touching his pale face and his thick blond hair which was flattened to his skull with perspiration. 'Why on earth didn't you wake me up if something was bothering you? Or you could have telephoned – reversed the charges – I'd have got a taxi and come to find you. Oh, son, don't you trust me? I know it's more than half my fault – I've had my mind on other things just lately – and you must have felt I'd shut you out. Why, oh why didn't you speak up?'

'Couldn't. I just thought you'd think I was raking up the past. Mr Weatherford told me things. Most of them I kind of half knew about. For a start—' He stiffened and moved out of the circle of her arms. 'I don't know very much at all, do I?'

Kate straightened up. He looked beaten and exhausted. 'Joshua, listen to me. Go up to your room, have a wash and change that shirt and pullover. By then your Nan will have your meal ready, and after you've eaten and had a drink, then we'll talk.'

He bent his head. He made such a sorry sight that Kate's heart ached for him. 'Go on then, upstairs and freshen up, then you'll feel heaps better.'

He nodded and went out meekly as she held the door open for him.

Mary had taken herself off on the pretext that she had to walk into the village to fetch soap flakes and corn plasters from the chemist. Kate smiled to herself. Corn plasters indeed!

'Shall we stay in the kitchen?' Kate asked looking directly at Josh. He shrugged. He had even washed his hair and changed into a short-sleeved white shirt and sleeveless pullover. He looked tons better now that he had eaten, no longer so ill at ease. Kate poured home-made lemonade into two glasses then carried them over to the table. She sat down on one of the pine chairs and, after a moment, Josh took the seat opposite her.

Kate looked steadily at him across the table. 'You'd better begin by telling me what upset you so much that you felt you had to get out of the house.'

'I don't quite know where to begin,' he said guardedly. 'Did you know Mr Weatherford was going to tell me all the arrangements were made for me to go to Eton and that this would be my last term at prep school?'

'Yes, I did. Is that what you wanted to talk to me about?'

He heaved a huge sigh and put both elbows on the table, staring steadily across at her. 'No. I wanted to ask why *you* didn't tell me and – well, that if all my education has been arranged in advance by my father, why aren't you involved more? Only then I started to think some more. I know you aren't my real mother, but I don't want anyone else. Only you – you and me – an' Nanna, only she's not really my nan. I love you . . .

but why is there so much secrecy about me? And about you an' all. One fellow at school said your parents were criminals. I gave him a bloody nose, but then . . . I just started to wonder . . . well . . . what made him say it in the first place?'

Kate reached across the table to catch hold of his hands. He was twelve years old, thirteen come Christmas, but he looked at this moment a sad, lonely little boy. The pain in her heart was almost more than she could bear.

'Joshua, from the moment you were put in my arms, you'd have been about six months old then, I made up my mind that I would always tell you the truth and to the best of my ability I've stuck to that resolution. Your mother was a lovely, kind lady who died the day you were born.'

Josh tugged his hands free from her grasp. 'Maybe, but she wasn't married to my father, was she?' he said stonily.

Kate waited a full minute before she took his shoulders gently between her hands and brought his face close to hers. 'Until this moment, Josh, I never thought what happened between my parents had any bearing on you. Now I see that it does. It was because of them that your wonderful father came to my rescue and I ended up living here at Melbourne Lodge, taking care of you.' She released her hold on him and sat back. 'Come on, we'll go into the front room, get comfortable and I shall start at the beginning, and I think you'll realise that most people have some sort of cross to bear.'

'All right,' Josh agreed sheepishly, 'we do seem to have a lot to talk about.'

'More than you know,' Kate said, as she led him

towards the two comfortable chairs that were set in the bay window.

Before starting, she kissed him. 'Just to let you know you mean the world to me, son.'

He didn't answer, just flung his arms around her waist and buried his face in her chest, and she held him tight for what seemed ages. At last they settled in the armchairs.

'A lot of the trouble started when I was only about two years old and my little brother was drowned in the river. My mother blamed my father and things were never the same between them after that, although they were marvellous, loving parents to me.' Kate paused, lost in thought. This was going to be very hard for her. Very hard indeed.

'Is that why you always insist that I wear a life jacket?' Kate nodded. Then slowly and painfully she recalled every minute of what had, at the time, been a ghastly nightmare. There were times when her voice was little more than a whisper, other times when she protested, 'You're too young to have to listen to all of this.'

Eventually she got to the time of the trial.

'My mother was found guilty of the murder of my father and the law decided that she had to pay for that act with her life. That was when I found out how dearly we need good friends in this life.'

Josh was crying quietly, yet Kate felt that she could not comfort him at this point, for if she were to stop now she would never have the courage to continue again.

'My cousin Hilda, who you met a few weeks ago, and her parents were as good as gold to me throughout the whole time. Hilda's mum was my mum's only sister.

Now you know why I had to go to London recently to find out what I could do for her now that she so badly needs a friend.'

Josh sniffed and rubbed his knuckles across his eyes but made no comment.

'After I lost my parents, my aunt and uncle persuaded me to go to London to live with them and I accepted, but it wasn't the kind of life I was used to and I came home. It was one morning soon after, when I was at my very lowest, that your father paid me a visit. The rest you know.

'I have thanked God every day of my life for the kindness and generosity of Charles Collier for allowing me to take care of his only son, Joshua Collier, whom he loved so dearly. And that is a fact that you, young man, would do well to remember throughout the whole of your life.'

Kate let out a deep breath and sat back. That was the first part of it over.

'Be a good boy and take those glasses to the kitchen and refill them, my throat is parched. Then you can tell me what you think is so wrong about having to change schools and anything else that is worrying you.'

Josh went around the end of the table and perched rather uncomfortably on Kate's knee. 'Poor mum, I didn't know . . . I always thought you were ever so happy.'

Kate did her best to stop herself from crying, picked up his hand and held it against her cheek. 'I am happy as long as I know that you are. Now, fetch us our drinks and then it's your turn to talk.'

When they were both once again sitting opposite each

other, Josh blurted out, 'Mum, you still haven't said why my father never married my mother. There must be a reason, or didn't he love her?'

'If only I had the words to tell you, Josh. He adored your mother. The pity of it was that they met late in his life. As a young man he married a lady who was always in poor health and they never had any children. When he met Jane, your mother, they fell in love. His wife never suffered because of their association, she was well provided for and both your father and Jane were very discreet. Jane lived here, in Melbourne Lodge, for years before you were born. Your nan took care of her and your father visited almost every day and stayed whenever he could, just the same as he did after you were born and right up to the time he died. You were the apple of his eye. More so because he had given up the hope of ever becoming a father; both he and your mother thought their prayers had been answered when they learnt that they were to have a baby. He was so proud of you, Joshua, but devastated by your mother's death.'

Josh touched her hand solemnly. 'Thank you for telling me.'

Kate could hear the tears in his voice. It was all too much for such a young boy, and it was a long time before he spoke again.

'Mum,' he began quietly, 'do you think I shall like it at Eton?'

That simple question broke the ice. They sniffed back their tears and grinned at each other. 'Oh, Josh, is it any wonder that I love you so much! You are going to sail through life. You and those big blue eyes of yours will melt the hearts of all the ladies, you know that, don't you?'

'I don't want any ladies, only you and Nan. Mr Weatherford said I had to grow up now, because Eton is a big boys boarding school, but that doesn't mean that I can't get a cuddle from you two now an' again, does it?'

'I'll kill anyone that tells you different. No matter where you go, how tall you grow or how old you are, to me you will always be my baby, and the day you don't want to kiss me or cuddle up to me will be the day that I'd want to die.'

'Eton sounds so grand and so far away.'

'Don't be so daft. It's neither of those things. First off, you want to remember that it was your father who chose which schools you would go to, not Mr Weatherford or his partner. They look after your affairs very well and they care about you, but they are carrying out your father's orders. In his will he set out what he wanted for you in explicit terms. As you grow older you will begin to realise just how much you meant to him and the full extent of the legacy he left you.' Kate paused and took several deep breaths. Joshua was looking puzzled so she gave him a moment to let everything she had told him sink in. 'Your father went to Eton. I'm sure Mr Weatherford told you that, and then he went on to Cambridge University, just as you will in time.'

'Yes, he did tell me, but he said I will have to take the common entrance exam.'

'Is that all that is worrying you? Your housemaster told me at the end of term that you'd sail through. There is one thing you may not be aware of; you were registered to go to Eton almost on the day you were born. All you have to tell yourself is that you are there because your father wanted it. No one else. You will be walking in his footsteps and, though he couldn't make your mother his legal wife, he has done everything within his power to announce to the world that you are his son and heir. He has made sure that his own social background will secure a place for you at a school that takes pride in its historic role of educating the sons of gentry.'

'Do you have any idea what the uniform looks like?' Josh wailed.

Now Kate really did laugh. 'Not really,' she teased him, 'do you?'

'Mr Weatherford showed me a photograph. Black tail-coat, a waistcoat, pin-striped trousers, and you should see the daft winged collars that you have to wear with white bow ties.'

At the sight of Joshua's woeful face the tears trickled down Kate's, but they were happy tears now. 'Pity you have two more terms after Christmas to serve at Guildford. I can't wait to see you all dressed up. Still, as I was about to tell you before you started moaning about the uniform, Eton College is situated on the north bank of the Thames. Opposite Windsor. The castle stands just above the town. I shall be able to visit often. Besides seeing you I shall treat myself to a tour of the castle as I've never been inside it. That's another thing I'll have to do; inform Jack Stuart that I shall need a launch at my disposal so that I may cruise up the river to see how my son is faring at one of the best-known schools in all the world.'

'You're tormenting that poor boy!' Mary cried, as she came into the room.

'You're dead right, Nan, you've arrived back just in time to stop her.' Josh giggled and got to his feet to relieve her of some of the parcels she was carrying.

'I thought you were only going to the chemist,' Kate said, looking at the bags that were now spread out on the hearthrug.

'I called in at the farm to buy some tomatoes. They taste so different when they're picked straight off the vines, and guess what? They were just putting out a few punnets of strawberries, they'll more than likely be the last we shall see this year, lucky to find them so late. I thought they'd make a nice treat for tea and I got a lovely tub of thick cream while I was there.'

'Cor, great, Nan. What else is there for tea? I've only had one meal today,' Josh said, seeking sympathy.

'That's one more than you deserve, my boy,' Mary told him, pulling him close and giving him a hug. Over his shoulder Mary looked across the room at Kate and raised her eyebrows. Kate gave her the thumbs-up sign and a winning smile to go with it. If there was one thing that these two women, of very different ages, had in common it was the love and well-being of this young lad. They would go to the ends of the earth to ensure his good welfare and woe betide anyone who ever tried to hurt him.

Chapter Thirty-Four

JOSHUA'S HIGH SPIRITS were infectious and Kate felt her own heart lift as she watched him and Peter Bradley sort through the box of fireworks they were taking to the harvest celebrations. The frankness with which she had dealt with all his questions seemed to have worked. His anxieties and anguish appeared to have receded, and all at once Kate was filled with happiness, suddenly sure that the future was going to be right.

The evening was all that anyone could have hoped for: dry and quite warm with very little wind.

'It's the hustle and bustle of these occasions that I like, takes years off me,' Mary said as she helped several women to spread thick paper cloths over the trestle-tables the men had set up.

'They're going to light the first bonfire!' a young lad shouted and the cry was taken up all along the bank.

'Keep an eye on our fireworks, Mum,' Josh called

over his shoulder as he and Peter ran as fast as their legs would carry them.

Soon the air was filled with laughter and noisy singing as the scout master organised the children into groups. The smell of burning wood and the appetising aroma coming from various braziers helped to get folk into a party mood. Sausages by the dozen, rissoles, faggots and thick rashers of bacon were all sizzling away. Shrieks from excited kiddies sounded every now and then as great showers of sparks shot up through the air lighting up the dark sky. Farmers and farm labourers had all turned out with village residents to celebrate the bringing in of yet another harvest.

'Here, have a glass of cider,' Mike's voice cut into Kate's daydreaming.

She smiled her thanks as she took hold of the glass he was offering.

'Great turn out.' He beamed. 'We have a great many dos like this in Wales but there's something special about the whole affair when it's held right beside the river.'

As if in agreement with his comments, several tugs, barges and longboats that were anchored along the whole stretch of the towpath sounded their steam whistles and hooters at the same time and were greeted by loud cheers from the crowds. Kate smiled across at Mary. 'It's fun, isn't it?'

'Yes. Worth all the hard work that has gone into it. Yes, it's great fun.'

After a very late night everyone in the household, with the exception of Mike, was loathe to get out of their bed.

It was only after Mike had knocked on bedroom doors offering cups of tea and urging them to hurry otherwise they'd all be late for the special church service that Mary and Kate finally crawled downstairs.

'I shall never, as long as I live, touch another drop of cider,' Mary declared, holding her hand to her throbbing forehead. 'I hope I don't look as bad as I feel,' she continued, looking for sympathy that was unlikely to be forthcoming. 'Mike, did you wait to make sure that Josh was out of his bed?'

'No need, Mary, love. He was up and out as soon as he heard me about and he's eaten quite a good breakfast.'

'Thank the Lord for small mercies,' Mary declared, not feeling at all like cooking. 'Will toast be all right for you two?'

'One slice will be enough for me,' Kate replied.

'How about you, Mike?'

'Don't fret yourself, Mary, you'd probably pass out if I said I felt the need of bacon an' eggs. No, no, don't get flustered, I'm only teasing. I had all I wanted when Josh had his.'

Mary heaved a great sigh of relief.

Josh came in through the back door, all smiles as he said, 'It's a lovely morning, Peter's been round to say that his parents are having people round today and don't want him about, so is it all right if we clear off after we've been to church?'

'And where were you thinking of going?' his mother asked.

'Hampton Court,' Josh said eagerly. 'We can buy something to eat at midday – save us trailing back here

– 'cos if we wait until after lunch there won't be any of the day left to enjoy. You don't really mind, do you, Mum?'

Kate was sensible and understanding as always. 'You're doing the right thing, Josh, making the most of the weather before it breaks. I'll give you enough money to buy something decent to eat. Now, fifteen minutes and we must set off for church.'

'While you ladies sort out which hat you're going to wear I'll bring the car round to the front of the house. Come on, Josh, you come with me and then they won't be able to complain that it was us men who made them late,' Mike said, laughing loudly as, with his arm round Josh's shoulders, the pair of them went out through the back door.

The church looked beautiful. A credit to all the women who had worked so hard to achieve this final result. Each station of the cross was decorated with ears of corn while the steps to the altar glowed with floral arrangements, consisting mainly of Michaelmas daisies and sunflowers. Tables set to each side were laden with gifts of food which the children had brought and which, after the service, would be distributed among the poor. Three local bakers had each baked a huge loaf of bread, the top layer of dough having been intricately woven to form a sheaf of wheat. The service, taken by the Reverend Hutchinson, was one of thanks for the bountiful harvest which had been safely gathered in.

The last hymn of the morning was chiefly for the children and as the first chords of the organ rose up to the high rafters the congregation hastened to its feet.

*We plough the fields and scatter the good seed on the
  ground,
But it is fed and watered by God's almighty hand.*

No hymn books were needed the words were so familiar.
Then, a few minutes of silent prayer, each person alone
with their thoughts, and on out into the autumn sunshine.

'This lamb is very tender,' Kate remarked looking across
the table to where Mary sat.

'Yes, it was a good job I put the joint in the oven
before we set off for church.'

'Don't I get any praise for having done all the vegetables before either of you were out of bed?' Mike asked,
feigning hurt.

'Oh, you big baby,' Mary teased. 'You seem to be
eating your fair share of them, only right that you should
have done some of the work.'

He laid his knife and fork down on his plate and put
his hands up in the air. 'All right, I can see I shall get
nowhere by starting an argument with you two. Instead,
I shall offer to drive you out into the countryside this
afternoon and, to show my appreciation of your kind
hospitality, I shall buy you both the best cream tea we
can find. How does that sound?'

They looked at each other in dismay, but it was left
to Kate to answer. 'Have you forgotten, Mike? My
cousin and her husband are bringing my aunt down this
afternoon. I promised I'd be there when they arrived.
Somewhere about two o'clock is what Ben told me on
the telephone.'

Mike looked apologetic, thinking to himself that there wasn't much difference between hospitals or convalescent homes and he couldn't bear the thought of spending this lovely Sunday afternoon sitting around talking to an invalid.

Mary read his thoughts and Kate was quick to see disappointment show on her friend's face.

'Mary there isn't any need for you to be there.' And as she started to protest, waving her hand in the air to emphasise her intentions, Kate went on, 'Now don't be silly, Aunt Dolly will be here for a few weeks and you'll have ample opportunity to visit her, and if we think about it, it's probably much better that there's only me there when she arrives. She's sure to be tired after the journey and won't want a lot of company. No, you do as Mike says. Let him take you for a nice drive. I'll see you back here tonight.'

'I'll drop you off at the home, Kate, and we could come back for you later, if you're sure you don't mind.'

'I'm quite sure. And I will accept your offer of a lift into Kingston but, please, don't even think about coming back for me. I've no idea what time I shall leave. It all depends on how quickly Aunt Dolly settles in.'

Mary got up from the table.

'I'll fetch the tarts. I made two yesterday, one gooseberry and one apple,' she said, signalling to Kate with a nod of her head to follow her out. Once inside the kitchen Mary kicked the door closed and turned to face Kate. 'I know you're being considerate. Are you sure you can manage to settle your aunt in on your own?'

'I'm positive. Besides I won't be on my own. There's plenty of staff on duty and I don't suppose I shall stay that long myself. Aunt Dolly will need all the rest she can get. So, please, Mary, go off with Mike and have a nice afternoon. You deserve it. Both of you do.'

'Thanks, Kate,' she said, gently planting a kiss on her cheek.

Kate was getting worried, Mike had dropped her at the home at a quarter to two, almost an hour ago and still there was no sign of Aunt Dolly. Just as she was about to go to the front of the house the lounge door opened and Harriet Tremaine poked her head round the door.

'They're here.'

'Thank goodness for that,' Kate answered with relief.

The car was drawn right up to the entrance and Kate watched with mixed feelings as Hilda and Ben climbed out of the two front seats. Kate sighed to herself. Neither of them looked pleased and both were more than a little dishevelled. Bending her knees Kate peered into the back of the car and saw her aunt lying full length on the back seat, her head resting on a pillow. Her eyes were closed and she looked very hot. Kate introduced Harriet to Hilda and Ben, telling them she was the matron of the home.

'How do you do, Mrs Withers, Mr Withers? Pleased to meet you both,' Harriet said. 'I will be helping to take care of your mother. Hopefully a nice rest will have her feeling much better.'

Hilda cleared her throat and in what she thought was a posh voice said, 'I'm ever so grateful. It's really very good of you t'ave me mum like this.'

'Do we 'ave to stand 'ere on the blinking doorstep?' Ben asked, his voice sounding really rough.

Kate took a good look at him and came to the conclusion he was in a filthy mood and hoped to goodness he wasn't going to be rude to all the staff.

Harriet stepped back. 'I think the first thing is for me to get two nurses to help Mrs Hopkins up to her room.' Turning to face a well-built man who had been hovering in the doorway, she asked, 'Bob, will you take Mrs Hopkins things up to her room, while I show her relatives through to the lounge.'

'Certainly, matron,' he said, looking down at the small tattered case and brown paper parcel that Ben was taking from the boot of the car. 'Is that all there is, sir?'

Ben nodded as he stared at the two nurses in their smart white uniforms who were already gently assisting Dolly from the car and settling her comfortably in a wheelchair.

'You're very sleepy, aren't you, pet?' the taller of the two nurses remarked. 'Never mind, we'll soon have you tucked up in bed. Rest is what you need today, time enough tomorrow for you to get your bearings.'

'The doctor gave us a couple of pills to give 'er,' Hilda whispered to the nurse, 'she's been out like a light ever since we left 'ome.'

Good job too, Kate thought wryly to herself, as she watched the nurses wheel her aunt inside the building. With Dolly gone they stood around looking as if they weren't quite sure what to do next.

'Off you go, all of you,' Harriet said. 'I'll have some tea sent in to you and you can go up and see your mother once the nurses have made sure she is comfortable.'

Kate pulled her chair up close to the one that Hilda had plonked herself down on. Ben was standing with his back to them, staring out of the window.

'Now we're alone,' Kate said, 'you can tell me what's upset Ben, and why you have got dirty marks all down the front of your dress.'

'You wanna ask 'im,' Hilda loudly retorted, pointing a finger in the direction of her husband. 'We 'ad t'push the bloody car 'cos he was too mean t'put enough petrol in the tank.'

'Hilda, love, please don't shout and don't swear. You don't want to give the wrong impression on your first visit, do you?' she chided her cousin, but only half-heartedly for, to tell the truth, she felt really sorry for her.

'You 'aven't told 'er why I didn't put petrol in the motor,' Ben shouted angrily. 'Oh, no, you're the goodie an' I'm the baddie. I didn't 'ear you offering to pay for any an' after all it is your old lady, not mine, that I've given up me Sunday for, and what thanks do I get? Nothing but an ear bashing from you all the way down 'ere. Nag, nag, nag. Just you going on an' on about money.' Red in the face, Ben stuffed his fists into his trouser pockets and if looks could kill his wife would have fallen down stone dead. 'I can't 'elp it if I'm skint,' he mumbled.

'Hmm, I'd like to know whose fault you think it is then.'

Ben mumbled something else.

'I didn't hear that,' Hilda snapped.

'I said I had a good tip, risked a bundle, an' it didn't come off,' he retorted.

'How much is a bundle?' she snapped at him, her voice louder than before.

'None of your business. I never 'ear you complaining when I come 'ome with me pockets bulging, then it's let's buy this or the kids need that. I thought I could win last night,' he shouted back.

'Stop it, the pair of you. This is neither the time nor the place for you to air your differences.'

Hilda muttered, 'Sorry.' She sounded bitter.

Kate looked directly at Ben, but he steadfastly refused to meet her gaze. She leant across and squeezed Hilda's hand. Speaking softly so that Ben would be unable to hear from where he stood, she said, 'Before you leave I'll slip you some money. You needn't say anything about it to Ben.' Then seeing Hilda start to cry, Kate had the urge to leave the two of them alone. It wasn't any of her business. She excused herself hurriedly saying, 'I'm going to see what's happened to our tea.'

The next half-hour dragged by. They had drunk their tea, eaten the dainty sandwiches and fancy cakes that Harriet Tremaine had so thoughtfully provided with hardly a word passing between them.

'Right,' Kate said eventually, with a lot more determination than she was feeling, 'I'm sure it will be all right for us to go up and see Dolly now.' Looking directly at Hilda, she added, 'There's a bathroom at the end of the corridor, I'm sure you'd like a wash and brush up before you set off home.'

'Well, don't take all day about it,' Ben muttered sullenly. 'I wanna get on the road soon as I can.'

Neither Hilda nor Kate answered him, nor did they look in his direction as they made for the door, they took it for granted that he didn't want to come up to Dolly's room to say goodbye.

A nurse was just coming out of a front bedroom as they reached the top of the stairs. She smiled and held open the door. 'Mrs Hopkins is very comfortable but I'm afraid we haven't been able to rouse her properly. She's still very groggy, but she has had a long drink and drifted off back to sleep. Probably the best thing,' she added brightly.

'Thank you, nurse,' Kate answered.

'Sorry, but I've got to go t'the lav,' Hilda exclaimed and as soon as Kate raised a finger and pointed, she was off at a run heading for the bathroom at the far end of the landing.

Kate was so pleased that Dolly had been given one of the nicest rooms in the home. It had a beautiful view. The round bay window looked out across a well-kept lawn and further onto the quiet leafy area that Kate had come to know so well. For a moment she laughed to herself, for the image that was uppermost in her mind was that of Alice in her old coat, floppy felt hat and lace-up boots, her workworn hands scattering corn for her hens where now there was such smooth green grass. She turned from the window and sat down in the wicker armchair that had been placed beside the bed. Oh dear, she sighed softly, how small Aunt Dolly seemed lying in the high wide bed, but at least she looked comfortable, her shoulders and head were resting on a mound of snow-white pillows which were, in turn, supported by a metal bedrest. Her arms lay on top of the bedclothes and Kate took one of her hands between both of her own. She was still sitting whispering soft words of comfort when the door was pushed open and a much cleaner, tidier looking Hilda came into the room.

'Cor, ain't this nice,' Hilda breathed almost reverently. 'If being 'ere don't make me mum get better I don't know what will.' She looked across at Kate, then at her sleeping mum and more to herself than to her cousin she mumbled, 'I wish t'God I could stay 'ere with 'er for a while. Do me a power of good t'get away from my lot.'

'She does look comfortable, doesn't she? There's not much point in either of us staying here much longer today. I'll come back in the morning. In fact, I shall visit her most days and I'll ring you each evening and let you know what progress she's making.'

'Aw, Kate,' Hilda cried, quickly crossing to her side, 'I'll never be able to thank yer for all you're doing. You're a brick, you really are.'

'You're not so bad yourself,' she told her cousin, slipping a five-pound note into her pocket.

They stood each side of the bed and quietly said their goodbyes to Dolly.

'Poor ole Mum, 'asn't she suffered enough?'

'Being here will make all the difference, you'll see. She'll soon be her old self.'

'I 'ope you're right,' Hilda said as the two of them linked arms and went back down the stairs.

Ben was standing only a few feet away from the front door. 'I thought you said you weren't going to be long,' he snapped, facing Hilda angrily across the wide hall.

'I wasn't. Anyway, you should be glad that Kate has got my mum in such a lovely place as this, rather than keep on complaining all the time.'

'Yeah, yeah, just get in the car, will you? And for heaven's sake, let's be on our way. I've stood more than enough for one day.'

Kate said goodbye and watched until the car was out of sight. Listening to them bickering had made her realise what a comfortable, quiet life she led. Sometimes a bit too quiet, she thought as she went back inside to have a chat with Harriet Tremaine.

But if Hilda and Ben's life was anything to go by she wasn't going to complain too much. Instead she would count her blessings.

Chapter Thirty-Five

THE AFTERNOON WAS still lovely. Kate had left behind the hat she had worn to church that morning and now the breeze coming off the river blew her hair across her face. She had decided to walk home, but then asked herself, Why? There's nobody there.

Presently she realised she had turned away from the towpath and was heading for the town centre. Across the road, standing outside Kingston bus depot she saw a green double-decker bus. The conductor was just changing the destination blind and out of curiosity she stopped to see where it was heading. DORKING came up, and this surprised her; it being a Sunday she hadn't known that the buses ran on that route.

She hesitated, then shaking herself, she said out loud, 'Why not?' and with that, she ran across the road and boarded the bus. Her foot was half on the lower deck when she changed her mind, turned about and swung herself up the stairs. There were few folk on the top deck and those who were had chosen seats at the back. She walked the length of the gangway and settled herself in the very front seat which would give her a splendid, clear view throughout the journey.

Having paid for a return ticket she settled back to enjoy the late afternoon sunshine wishing that the driver was allowed to slow down whenever a particularly beautiful place came into view. Couples joined and got off the bus at various stops. She envied them each other's company and fell to wondering if they were going to visit parents or friends or perhaps have tea together. Be nice to have someone to talk to. Then she grinned, scolding herself at the same time. You were glad enough to see the back of Ben and Hilda, now you're feeling sorry for yourself because you're on your own. You can't have it both ways.

Now the area seemed familiar and Kate knew they were nearing the end of the journey, but suddenly she had no intention of going as far as Dorking. She pulled on her white gloves, picked up her handbag and made for the top of the stairs.

The conductor looked upwards, 'Not there yet, love.'

'I realise that, but aren't we nearing Box Hill?'

'We are indeed. Next stop. D'you want to get off there?'

'Please,' she said, descending the last few steps to stand on the platform, making sure she held on tightly to the handrail.

She stood at the foot of the hill. It looks a long way up she mused to herself, oh well, never mind, I'm here now and I've nothing better to do. She walked and, as the footpath became steeper, she paused, breathing heavily, thinking, it's beautiful. Further up still, she gasped, oh, the air is like wine. She rested three times before she finally reached the top where the footpath petered out. A track continued under leafy trees that had mossy, gnarled trunks, the grass was sweet and green, and there was a bank covered in cow-parsley and buttercups. 'Mmm,' Kate said drowsily, 'I'm going to sit myself down under this tree and have forty winks.'

The last time she had been here was with Toby. Just for a moment his face came clear to her mind, the soft grey eyes, the wide smiling mouth, the way his hair was flattened down when he took his hat off and he would run his fingers through it. She let herself recall every detail of that rainy day when he had first made love to her. The day he had taught her what it felt like to be loved. To be a real woman. She looked across to where, in the distance, the pub lay where they had sat outside and enjoyed their drinks, and he had never stopped telling her how much he loved her. Two years ago. Two hard, long years with never a word or a sign that he had meant a word that had been said. But had she ever doubted him? Not really! An odd moment when she had felt utterly alone, longing to feel his arms around her, with his body close to hers, but only momentarily. Toby was a good man. It was unfortunate that the time hadn't been right when they met. But they had met! Coming together in just a few days to experience such a deep love that many couples never encountered in a whole lifetime together. Of that much she was absolutely sure.

And two years to the day her faith had been justified. Red roses, a letter and a firm promise had come. I will be back.

She had believed it at Easter when the package had arrived and although it was now September she still believed it.

Could she bear to go to the pub and buy herself a drink? No, that would be too painful. The sun was going down, already it was much cooler, but she would stay for a few minutes more. Presently she got to her feet, brushed the leaves and grass from the skirt of her dress and began to descend the great hill.

One day she would come back here again with Toby. He would take her hand to make sure she didn't slip. He would again tell her how they had been destined to meet; that he had loved her from the moment he had come to her rescue that day in Kingston and that he would go on loving her for the rest of his life. She would feel whole again. Just as a woman in love with a man who adored her should and would feel. She stood still for a long moment. Kate closed her eyes and prayed with every fibre of her being, 'Please God, let it be soon. Bring Toby back to England and grant that we may never be parted again.'

She was still silently saying that prayer as she boarded the bus that would take her back to Kingston.

Chapter Thirty-Six

KATE DECIDED THAT she had to live for today. She longed for the time when Toby would be back in England, but the months were stretching out. It couldn't possibly be another two years before she was able to set eyes on him again.

She did her various tasks: mended Joshua's sport kit, sewing name tags inside all the new items, took him to London twice to select books for his last term at Guildford. She helped Mary pick the Bramley apples, which had grown in such abundance this year, and then they'd bottled them, stored them and also made lots of pies. She took bags of these lovely cooking apples with her when she went to visit Aunt Dolly, which was at least three times a week. It was a wonder to the patients and the staff just how many various tasty puddings cook managed to turn out from them.

It was also a wonder to Kate the remarkable change in her aunt. In the few weeks that Dolly had been staying at the Alice Memorial Homes, she had put on weight, her cheeks had filled out, her hair looked thicker and certainly had more shine to it. Best of all, her eyes were brighter and her speech much improved. Hilda, in that typical cockney way she had of putting her finger right on the heart of the matter, had summed her mother up by saying, 'She's more with it now than she's been for ages.'

Since that unforgettable day when Ben had driven his wife and mother-in-law down to Kingston he had never put in another appearance. But Hilda had never missed a Sunday, coming only once by train. Her twin brothers, Stan and Tom, both now car owners had taken turns to drive her down to visit their mother, even bringing their father with them, though he had vowed he would never visit her while she was in a home. Seeing Bert and her boys had been as good as any tonic for Dolly.

This morning Kate walked along beside the high stone wall until she reached the black, wrought-iron gates which were always open during daytime. Her feet made a crunching sound as she walked down the clean, weed-free gravel driveway and up towards the main entrance of the convalescent block.

A big ginger cat came slowly across the lawn and stood looking at her out of large, green eyes. It brushed against her legs and stayed close until she reached the front door, then it miaowed loudly.

'So you want to come inside, do you, cat?' she asked. 'I don't blame you, the weather is not so nice this morning, is it? In you go then.' She held the door open, allowing the cat to go by.

She popped her head round the door of the lounge and

was greeted by several ladies calling, 'Good morning, Kate.' She answered them, smiling at each in turn. Although it was still quite early, some were reading the morning papers, others were knitting or sewing. Two men, both seated in wheelchairs, whizzed across the room and came to a stop in front of her.

'Come in, come in,' Joe said pleasantly.

Edward, Joe's companion, grinned. 'I'll give you two guesses where your aunt is at this moment.'

Kate leant forward and in a conspiratorial manner whispered in Edward's ear, 'Then I had better get upstairs quickly before she drowns herself.'

Both men laughingly agreed.

She climbed the stairs to the first floor and was met by Molly Symonds, who had been working as a daily cleaner from the first day the home had opened. Kate felt they had become good friends.

'Morning, Kate,' Molly greeted her, nodding her head towards the end of the corridor.

'Morning, Molly. I guessed as much. My aunt will never get used to the luxury of running hot water.'

'Can't say as I blame her, wish we had it in our house. Anyway Nurse Davison saw Mrs Hopkins safely into the bath and there is a bell in there if she needs help, though she's come on like a house on fire since she's been here. Proper under the weather when she arrived, wasn't she?'

'Yes, she certainly is better,' she agreed, before walking down the corridor to the bathroom.

'It's only me,' Kate called, pushing open the bathroom door. Dolly stood leaning against the white tiled wall with a bath towel wrapped round her body, enveloped in a cloud of steam.

'Are you all right?' she asked cautiously.

'Never better in the whole of me blooming life,' Dolly answered as she began to rub her hair vigorously. 'D'yer want t'know something, Kate, luv, I was scared witless the first time those lovely nurses lowered me down into this bath full of water. Thought I was about to drown and that was no joke, I'm telling yer!'

Kate laughed loudly and, taking a small towel from the rail she helped finish drying her aunt's hair.

'Where's your talcum powder? I'll do your back for you. Sit down on the stool. The way you're weaving about you're going to fall over.'

'Well, I'm trying t'get me knickers on before that lass comes back.'

'Oh, Aunt Dolly, you are a one, and no mistake.'

'That's as may be,' Dolly retorted, wriggling her long bloomers up over her ankles. 'It's all right for those that are used to all these newfangled luxuries but when, like me, you ain't never 'ad the whole of yer body dunked into 'ot water before, it comes as a bit of a shock t'yer system.'

'Now you're stretching it a bit. I know for a fact you have regular baths at home. Don't forget I lived with you for a while.'

'And you think our tin bath in front of the fire amounts to the same thing, d'yer? Well, young lady, let me tell yer this. Four or five kettles of water, yer knees propped up under yer chin and yer bum stuck to the ridges of a tin bath don't exactly compare to what I'm fast becoming used to 'ere. And . . .' Dolly paused and grinned wickedly . . . 'more's the pity that my Bert ain't 'ere wiv me, Gawd knows what capers we could 'ave got up to in that tub there. More than enough room for him.'

'Aunt Dolly! Behave yourself!' Kate had a hard job to keep a straight face and was quite relieved when Nurse Davison put in an appearance and took charge.

'Don't suppose you've got a spare pair of stockings in yer bag, ave yer, Kate?' Dolly asked.

'No, but I'll slip out to the shops presently and buy you some,' she called back.

At the foot of the stairs, Harriet Tremaine was waiting. 'Been experiencing your aunt's bath session first hand?'

'You can say that again. I'd say she is almost back to normal, which rather poses a problem, don't you think? We can never be sure what Dolly will say or do next and I dread the day when I have to tell her the time has come for her to go home.'

'Come and have a coffee with me,' Harriet suggested, 'and don't let it worry you. Nobody, staff and patients alike, wants to see the back of Mrs Hopkins. She's liked by everyone and that includes the doctors. And as to going home, you'll see. This peace and quiet and sitting around with no chores to do has suited her just fine while she hasn't been feeling so well, but come the day when she has her full strength back, that's when family, friends and familiar surroundings will begin to call. What do they say about East Enders? Never happy for long away from the sound of Bowbells. Your aunt will let us know when she's had enough of us.'

Kate put out a hand to rest on Harriet's arm, 'You've been a saint. I can't begin to thank you. I mean it. You've done a lot for my aunt.'

'Ever thought that without your generosity these premises would never have come into being?' Then without waiting for Kate to reply Harriet hastily added, 'Come through to the kitchen, Cook will no doubt find us a morsel to have with our coffee.'

Kate did as she was bid. Following Harriet down the corridor she thought that what goes round comes round. It wasn't only the patients who had gained. The homes had provided jobs not only for professional people but for lots of ordinary workers such as cleaners, maids and gardeners. They have meant a lot to me too, she prompted herself. They have given me and Mary a new interest in life. Something useful with which to occupy our time, and we both really do enjoy the fund raising. When it came to boiling it all down, the main people responsible for all of this had to be her grandparents. None of this could have come about if her grandfather hadn't been prudent as a young man. To have bought the first plot of land and built his own house had shown foresight but the purchase of the field beyond had increased his investment no end. Add all that to the fact that Alice, although widowed early in life, had never felt the urge to sell up and live on the proceeds. She had worked, out and about in all weathers, and finally left the house and all the land to her only granddaughter. I hope you can see what has been done with your home, Gran, she murmured to herself and, most important, I hope you approve. She smiled. I wonder what Dolly would say to my gran if she were to appear now. Gawd bless yer, more than likely!

Kate stayed the day with Dolly, taking the opportunity to pop to the shops while the patients were being given their lunch. And about four o'clock, when she took her leave, Dolly was busy helping three other ladies to set up the card table for a game of whist.

By the time Kate got into bed that night it was raining hard and a fierce wind was blowing the rain against the window panes, causing then to rattle in their wooden frames. She huddled down in bed and pulled the sheet high up over her head, thankful she wasn't out on a night like this.

Suddenly something made her stir and she immediately felt that someone was there, in her room. She sat up, stretched . . . and saw him.

Was she dreaming? Charles Collier was dead! But he looked real enough as he stood staring at her from the foot of the bed. He looked well. A fine gentleman, dressed as she remembered in the height of fashion. Lovely jacket, corded breeches and knee-high boots.

She tried to slide back down, her hands flying to cover her mouth; she didn't want to scream, but she was having a hard job stopping herself. He smiled at her.

In little more than a trembling whisper, she asked, 'Why . . . what . . . ?'

'I don't mean to scare you.' His voice also was just as she remembered. 'First I have to thank you. Your efforts on my son's behalf have been extraordinary. He is a credit to you and to my name. I chose well.'

Kate couldn't find words to answer him. This wasn't happening! It couldn't be. She felt apprehensive but not scared, well, not very.

'Please, go up into the attic. Find my small leather

attaché case. It has my initials on it.' His tone of voice turned the request into a plea.

She said nothing, but drew in a deep breath. Suddenly the room felt awfully cold.

'I have used up my allotted time,' he said sadly. 'Thank you so much, Kate.'

And before she could say any of the things that were racing around in her head his outline became misty, he dropped his arms to his sides and slowly vanished from her sight.

To go back to sleep was impossible, she tossed and turned, got out of bed and stood staring out of the window. The wind seemed to have died down; the garden looked peaceful. Everything was in order except for her thoughts. Had she imagined it? She knew full well she hadn't. Would she tell Mary about the visit? No! And certainly not Josh! She got back into bed, longing for daylight to break. She made up her mind that as soon as a favourable time presented itself she would be up in the attic. If I have to move every piece of old junk up there then I will, she vowed. If a case with the initials C. C. C. was there then, by golly, she was going to find it and see for herself what the significance of Charles's ghostly appearance would turn out to be.

When, at breakfast next morning, Mary said she thought she really must go into Kingston and get her hair cut Kate felt like getting up from her chair and throwing her arms around her.

'Why don't you call a taxi, go in early, look round the shops, treat yourself to lunch – make a day of it,' she gabbled, trying to use her powers of persuasion.

'If I didn't know you better, I'd say you were trying

to get rid of me,' Mary said, giving Kate a funny look. 'Why don't you come with me?'

'I don't feel like it. Not today. I've several jobs I've been meaning to do for ages and with the place to myself I think today will be the day to sort them out.'

Mary stood up, not totally convinced. But thinking that Kate really did want some time on her own, she nodded. 'Well, if you're sure, I'll get dressed and then I will phone for a taxi.'

Oh, thank you, God, Kate breathed softly, wondering just how she was going to get herself up into the attic with no one else in the house to assist her.

She stood at the door, waving to Mary as the cab driver closed the passenger door, climbed into the driver's seat and drove away.

She felt guilty. She knew that Mary was aware that her excuses for not going with her had been only half-truths. But what else could she have done? Told her that a man who had been dead for more than three years had come to see her last night and asked her to fetch down a case he had left up in the attic? Mary would think she had gone mad. And who could blame her? She wasn't sure herself that it hadn't all been in her imagination. Now was the time for her to prove that Mr Collier had appeared in her bedroom last night, and the quicker she got herself up in the attic the better she'd be able to do just that.

First things first. From the cupboard under the stairs she fished out a wraparound overall with long sleeves and once she had it on, with the tapes tied securely around her waist, she rummaged for a mop-cap, pushing her thick tresses well in under the brim because there would be layers of dust for her to contend with. She climbed to the top floor of the house, thankful that a pair of stepladders was kept up there.

She set them up immediately below the trapdoor. Climbing to the top of the steps wasn't too bad, but balancing herself and at the same time reaching up and using both hands to force the square door upwards and inwards was a job and a half, and she was quivering from head to toe by the time she had managed to do it. She reached in, laid the torch down and switched it on.

'Good gracious me,' her cry was one of exasperation when she finally stood up straight between the rafters and looked around, 'half this stuff must have been here from the day the house was built.'

Instinct told her that a small case would probably be on a shelf and seeing a number of them set between the supporting beams to her left she turned and went in that direction, moving several tea chests and a couple of old trunks out of her path as best she could. There were three cases of sorts and she felt someone must be guiding her to have found them this quickly. With a great deal of trepidation, she reached up, pulling the top one towards her, which was a mistake. 'Good God,' she muttered, dropping the soft leather case and bowing her head as low as it would go. A thick cloud of dust encircled her. She sneezed and waved her arms trying to disperse it. She had expected dust, but this was beyond anything she had imagined. It was choking her. She wished she had thought to bring some wet cloths up with her. She felt in the pocket of the apron. A duster, that would do to tie around her nose and mouth. Having done just that she grinned, what a sight I must look and what a good job Mary isn't here to see me. She drew in a deep breath, causing the duster to suck in between her lips. It tasted awful.

The case she had lifted down was not an attaché case, more like a music case, soft with a bar that slipped over the handle. She didn't bother to pick it up from where it had fallen, just moved it aside with her foot.

Learning from her first mistake, Kate gently wiped some of the dust away from the second case, using the sleeve of her apron. It was a cheap papier mâché case with a tin handle.

'Third time lucky? I hope so,' she said out loud.

She wasn't enjoying being up here, not one little bit. All she managed to do with the aid of her other sleeve was smear the dust enough for her to realise that this third case was one of good quality. Somehow she had to get it down from that shelf. Closing her eyes tightly and lowering her head she reached up, groped for the handle, and grabbed it, at the same time taking a step backwards, thus avoiding the worst of the swirling dust. Still grasping the leather handle she banged the case once on the floor, loosening some of the still clinging dust. When she brought it up to eye level she could not believe what she was seeing. Faint, yes, but they were there.

She pulled the duster from her face, wrapped a corner of it around her forefinger and spat on it. With the case flat on the floor she rubbed furiously at the embedded dirt and grime, and got her reward. C. C. C. The initials were there, just as Charles Collier had said they would be.

Two hours had sped by but still Kate was being cautious. With great difficulty she got herself safely down from the attic, the only casualty being the big torch she'd taken up with her. Having dropped it as she climbed through the hatchway back onto the stepladder the glass had broken and she'd hidden it away in the cupboard under the stairs. She didn't want Mary asking awkward questions. Not yet anyway.

Are you by any chance being a coward? Kate asked herself. She had cleared away all traces of a disturbance from the top landing, had a bath and washed her hair but still she had not looked inside. Well, she couldn't put it off any longer. With newspapers spread all over the kitchen table she sat herself down with the case in front of her and her heart in her mouth. She slid back the locks and opened the lid.

Some fifty minutes later she sat back and rubbed away a tear from her eyes.

'Joshua,' she breathed, 'your father was indeed a true, kind gentleman. If I were offered a pot of gold I could never explain how, when or why he came to me last night. But I am totally convinced he did! He must be watching over you, Josh. He somehow knew the fears you had about going to Eton and the unanswered questions that lingered in your mind about your parents. In here is the history of your father's life; at least all his early years until his coming of age and starting out into the world, just as you are about to do.'

Kate rose from her seat, filled the kettle and placed it on the hob to boil. She badly needed a cup of tea. She felt now that she would be able to tell Mary what had taken place. After all, she had been with Mr Collier for years and she would probably be familiar with a lot of the events that the documents in the case referred to. She wouldn't write to Josh about her find. Neither would she tell him over the telephone. She'd wait until he came home at half-term and then he could take his time, going carefully through each and every document, tracking his father's younger days. There wasn't an item missing as far as she could tell. Right from his baptism at the age of one month, until the day he had left Cambridge University. It was all there: school reports, awards for swimming and diving, dozens of certificates for all manner of sporting events. Even school photographs, which over the years had turned brown with age but from which she and Mary would have no difficulty in pointing out his father from among his colleagues.

There was one photograph in particular that she felt would thrill Josh more than the ones taken as a group. It was of his father and a friend walking beneath the portals of Eton, each wearing wing collars, the kind Josh professed to hate so much, their arms full of books. It was a great gift that Mr Collier had somehow seen fit to give to his son. One that she was sure Joshua would really appreciate.

Chapter Thirty-Seven

SEPTEMBER HAD COME and gone and more than half of October with it. In the early mornings the air was sharp and filled with the smell of burning wood as folk lit their fires and the smoke curled upwards out of the tall chimney stacks. The trees had shed most of their leaves, making a carpet on the earth of reds and golds. Why was it that sometimes time sped by so quickly but whenever Kate thought of Toby days seemed like weeks and the weeks like months?

It was half-term and Josh was home again. Before she had settled down to sleep the night before Kate had made up her mind that in the morning she was going to collar Josh before he went out. It was difficult. For the short time he would be home he had so much he wanted to do, so many friends to see and, of course, he never came home without paying a visit to his beloved boat yard. Come what may, she had to tell him about the case, get him to sit down and go through it for himself. Despite her determination it hadn't worked out that way. She was still in the bathroom when she heard Peter Bradley arrive at the house and minutes later Josh called up the stairs that they were going to Hampton Court to see Jack Stuart.

Kate had told Mary of everything that had happened, resulting in her finding the attaché case. Mary had been wonderful, never once did she ridicule any part of what Kate had said. Only when she described Charles Collier standing at the foot of her bed, did Mary risk an interruption.

'I have always believed that there is more goes on not only in heaven but on this earth than we mere mortals will ever fathom.'

Kate nodded her head at this comment, for she now knew it to be true.

'Come on,' Mary eventually said, 'let's clear the table. I'll wash up and you can wipe.'

A little later she spoke again, 'Kate, you've wiped that saucer so many times it's a wonder there's any pattern left on it. I'm not daft, I know what's bothering you; it's that you haven't got round to telling Josh yet.'

'It isn't that easy,' Kate said indignantly. 'How can I possibly say to a young boy that his dead father paid me a visit?'

'Nobody's asking you to do that.'

'So you tell me, what do I say to him?'

'Keep calm. Tell him the truth, that you were up in the attic, sorting things out and you discovered the case with his father's initials on it. There's no need to go into any more details than that.'

'I suppose you're right.'

'I know I am. Now get yourself ready, go to Hampton Court, get Josh on his own and tell him what can only be good news. This find will be worth a lot to him. I for one can't wait to see his face when he gets a look at some of those photographs.'

'I wish I could be as sure as you are that he will be pleased, and most of all I hope he won't start asking awkward questions.'

'There you go again, meeting trouble before it troubles you.' Mary gave her a little push. 'Go on, get yourself ready. And while you're doing that I'll pack you some food, luckily I made some pasties first thing. If you show up with some food and drink you're sure to get a welcome from Josh.'

The river was not all that busy but as Kate walked down the slipway she paused at the entrance to the Kearsley Boat Yard and stood staring upriver. What she saw brought a smile to her face and revived good memories. A brightly painted longboat, its sides covered with intricate pictures, was being loaded with timber. Two great carthorses were tethered out on the grass.

''Ow yer doing, Kate?' Mickey Wilson yelled from where he was precariously perched on top of the load.

'I'm fine, Mickey. Good to see you,' Kate responded. 'We missed you and your family at the harvest festival party this year. Where's Bert? Don't often see one of you without the other.'

'I'm 'ere.' A tousled mop of dark hair appeared over the side and within seconds Bert had jumped down onto the bank and was coming towards her. 'Luverly t'see yer, gal.' He threw his arm round Kate's shoulders and held her close. 'Seen that lad of yours this morning, my he can 'andle a craft, you'd think he'd been born on the river.'

Kate laughed. 'He practically was. And how's all your brood? Is your mum with you this trip?'

'No, she's the reason we didn't turn up for the end-of-the-season do. One of me sister's had another baby. Me mother's twenty-third grandchild. She wasn't going t'miss that. Anyway, must get cracking else Mickey will be saying I'm skiving. See you, Kate,' he shouted, waving like mad as he walked several paces backwards before turning and breaking into a run.

Kate had more than an hour to wait before she heard Josh hailing her. She turned to look upriver, my God those two boys had some energy. Josh and Peter were rowing with a steady rhythm. Knees up under their chins one minute, then legs outstretched, shoulders hunched forward then straightened, elbows bent, arms out full-length. Their actions never altered; perfectly in time with each other, their oars skimmed the water as they steered into the bank. Both lads were wearing thick white polo-necked jerseys, which accentuated the tan they had acquired during the summer months. With the boat securely moored, Josh grinned at his mother, and asked, 'And what's brought you out here so early in the morning?'

'I just thought I'd like to see what the two of you were getting up to.'

He looked unconvinced. 'I was going to see if there was anything I could do in the yard, Peter has to go home, his grandparents are coming for lunch.'

'See you. Bye,' Peter called, as he trotted off down the towpath.

'Come on now, Mum, tell me why you're really here. Do you have something important to tell me?'

'Why is it you always seem able to keep one jump ahead of me?'

'It's because you have such an open face, it's easy to tell when you have something on your mind.'

'Well, we had better find somewhere out of the wind where we can have a picnic, and I think I can safely say that you'll be pleased to hear my news.'

'You've brought food with you?'

'Now, would I come without? Or, more to the point, would your nan let me leave the house without a basket filled with good things for her favourite boy to eat? I've left the basket back in the office. I didn't see Jack Stuart about anywhere.'

'No, he was leaving just as Pete and I got here. He's taken the biggest launch up to the Port of London Authorities. I think he said they wanted a demonstration of some kind. Most of the other men are working in the yard. Did you want Jack for something particular?'

'No, I knew he couldn't be about or he would have come out to see me the minute I arrived. So, where are we going to have this picnic?'

'Let's fetch the basket first and I'll bring a chair out for you to sit on,' he said, running on ahead.

As always it's first things first with Josh, she thought as she sat eating a sandwich while he munched away on pasties and sausages, still warm thanks to the way Mary had wrapped them. When he had finished with the savouries and was winding up with an apple, he suddenly said, 'All right, let's hear it.'

'A few days ago,' Kate began, 'I made a rather interesting discovery.' She hesitated and Josh gave her a puzzled look. Sure now that she had his full attention, Kate told her story and then patiently answered several questions he carefully put to her. Satisfied that his mother had said all she was going to on this strange matter, Josh leant back on the rug, resting on his elbows, and stared up into her face.

'This case you've found must have been up in the attic even when my father was alive,' he murmured thoughtfully. 'Directly after dinner tonight, if it's all right by you, I'll take the case up to my room and go through it.'

'Good,' she said, knowing that his head was still full of unasked questions.

'Can I ask you a personal question?' Josh broke into Kate's thoughts, catching her unawares.

'Of course.'

'A little while ago you told me all about your parents and your relations in London, but you never said whether there had ever been a special man in your life. Didn't you ever wish there was?'

Kate held her breath and hesitated.

'Come on, Mum, no lady as pretty as you can have gone all this time without at least a few men showing interest.'

'Flattery won't get me to tell you all my secrets! I suppose there have been a few. When I was a young girl I had a boyfriend and when we first started the scheme that resulted in the Alice Memorial Homes being built, the borough surveyor took me out a couple of times.'

'And?'

'And nothing. I liked him but it went no further than that.'

'So you're telling me there's never been anyone else. Was it because you had me to look after that you hadn't time for a life of your own?'

'Oh, Josh! You mustn't think that. I've had a wonderful life, there's not a moment from the day I set eyes on you that I would have changed.'

'I know how much you love me. But you still haven't answered my question. Was there ever anyone?'

Kate sighed, thinking that this adopted son of hers was wise beyond his years. 'All right,' she said softly, 'there was and, hopefully, is someone.'

Josh let out a whoop of delight. 'Tell me. Come on, tell me.'

Kate began to tell Josh the bare outline of her meeting Toby just before Easter in 1932. He was still staring at her spellbound when she wound up her story by giving him an account of the day the roses and the letter had arrived, two years from the day that he had left her to go to South Africa. When Joshua remained silent Kate found herself praying desperately that he wouldn't read more into the story than she had seen fit to tell him, and also that he wouldn't blame himself for the fact that Toby had gone and she had stayed.

Quite suddenly he raised his head and, looking wistful, said, 'I hope he does come back to you, and I hope he likes me.'

Kate looked at him feeling totally bewildered, asking herself if she had heard him right. 'Josh, you just said you hoped he would like you. How about whether or not you would like him?'

Josh gave her one of his special boyish grins. 'I shall like him. If you like him so much that you've waited all this time, I'd say he has to be a really special kind of chap.'

'Oh, Josh! You're a very special lad yourself,' she told him in a voice trembling with emotion.

During dinner that evening Joshua appeared happy, not in any way upset or anxious because of the attaché case.

It was just eight o'clock when Kate went out into the hall and came back with the case, holding it out to Josh and smiling at him. He stood still for a moment, staring at his father's initials and Kate knew that he was feeling more apprehensive about the contents than he was letting on.

'Goodnight, Nan,' he said in a strangely quiet voice. Then turning to his mother he took the case from her, kissed her cheek and said, 'I'll see you in the morning.'

'You can come down and ask me questions if there is anything you don't understand,' she said, finding it hard to refrain from offering to go upstairs with him.

'Yes, perhaps I will,' he agreed cautiously.

Kate and Mary sat reading. The evening seemed endless and as soon as the hall clock struck ten, Mary closed her book and got to her feet. 'Well then, I'll leave you to it, Kate. I'm away to my bed.'

Kate rose and they kissed each other goodnight. She watched while Mary crossed the main hall before closing the door behind her. Then she stood with her hand pressed against her mouth, listening to Mary's footsteps as she climbed the stairs. She so badly wanted to call out to Josh to come down and talk to her and it took great willpower to stop herself from doing so. She waited another two hours before she decided that he wasn't going to put in an appearance that night.

A little after six o'clock next morning Josh opened the door and stood regarding his mother. She was curled up in the armchair, her head on one side, her eyes closed and her hair uncombed and tangled. As if she felt his presence she wriggled her body until she was sitting up straight and only then opened her eyes.

'You've been there all night,' Josh said, sympathetically. 'I'm going to make you a pot of tea. It's my fault you didn't go to bed, isn't it?'

Kate struggled to her feet, glanced at him anxiously, and said as briskly as she could, 'Of course it's not. I just fell asleep. We'll go to the kitchen and make some tea together.'

It was Josh who took the poker and rattled it between the bars of the grate, letting the grey ash fall though to the cinder box. When a red glow appeared he opened up the top and threw on some dry wood and a shovelful of coal.

'Come and sit over here by the fire and get yourself warm.'

Kate was so completely unnerved by the way he was taking charge that she meekly did what he asked. When they were both seated with a large mug of hot tea, Kate tried to gather her thoughts. First she had to know what Josh's reaction to the contents of the case was. With two hands round her mug, she took a sip, cleared her throat nervously, and then said in a voice that quivered, 'Josh, did you . . .' She stopped again and then blurted out quickly, 'Tell me what you're thinking.'

He looked across at his mother and smiled his own special smile which lit up his face. 'Will you stop worrying? I can't believe it all. I am just so glad that you went up to the attic and found the case, I wouldn't have missed it for the world.' He looked beyond her and spoke as if to himself. 'When I started reading I felt my father was nearby and as I picked up each sheet of paper and each certificate the feeling grew stronger.'

Kate stared at him. Afraid to say what she was thinking. Something had changed in Joshua. He was sitting up straight in the chair, tranquillity showed in his face and his eyes were clear and comprehending.

'You learnt a lot about your father?'

'Didn't I just!' He made a funny face and laughed. 'It won't seem half so bad going to Eton, not now that I've taken the grand tour mapped out by him. Wasn't it great that he made a kind of catalogue, listing books, pictures, university courses with detailed descriptions and, best of all, those photographs. They're fabulous! Wasn't it lucky that you chanced on that case?'

Kate swallowed hard; her heart felt as if it were turning a somersault. In her mind's eye she could picture Charles Collier smiling at her as he mouthed, 'A job well done, wouldn't you say?' There was no luck connected with that find, she said to herself.

'Josh, I'm so glad you are pleased, you don't know what a relief it is to hear you say so. Shall I cook you some breakfast now?'

'You worry too much. Please could you make it an extra big breakfast, I'm starving.'

As Kate laid rashers of bacon into the frying pan and broke an egg into a bowl she said a passionate thank you to Charles Collier. She was certain he was keeping a watchful eye on his only son, and with that kind of care being lavished on Joshua, Kate felt that she would have no qualms about sending him off to his big boys boarding school.

Chapter Thirty-Eight

'IT'S NO GOOD arguing with her,' Harriet Tremaine said when she telephoned Kate. 'Your aunt has made up her mind. Ever since her husband came down and stayed two days with us she's let it be known that she intends to be back in London with her family in time for Christmas. What do you want me to do?'

'What can we do if, as you say, she's made up her mind?'

'Help her to pack her bags and wish her well. At least she's a lot healthier than when she arrived. The problem now is she's restless and bored.'

'I know what you mean, when I was there three days ago she was hinting that she could rest just as well at home. Anyway, thanks for calling, I'll be in this afternoon and have a talk with her.'

Harriet waived aside Kate's thanks and said to be sure to pop in and have tea and rang off. Kate replaced the receiver and stood still, a thoughtful look on her face.

It was only natural, she supposed, now that Aunt Dolly was back to her usual jolly form that she would want to have her children and her grandchildren round her. Especially with Christmas coming up and half the fun were the weeks before the festivities actually began. Buying presents, stocking the larder with food. Making mince pies and Christmas puddings. She pondered for a few more minutes, telling herself that she seemed to be pretty good at straightening out everyone else's lives, but what of her own?

Mary was well settled with Mike; Kate felt a little envious. There was talk of his coming to stay at Melbourne Lodge over the whole of this coming Christmas and she sincerely hoped he would, because a man in the house made all the difference and he was great with Josh.

Thinking of Joshua had Kate smiling a satisfied smile. He was all right, she was convinced of that. Come next July his prep school days would be over. Then in September he'd be off to Eton. There were no more fears or doubts where he was concerned. Two other boys from Guildford had also been granted places at Eton and one of them was Nick Banks, which had thoroughly pleased Josh, even causing him to show off and produce the photograph of his own father taken with a friend at Eton College.

'Are you going to stand out in the hall all day?' Mary called from the kitchen. 'You said you'd make the pastry while I made a start on the ironing, but we can swop if you prefer.'

Kate stared guiltily at her, having been miles away and being close to self-pity, because everyone, with the exception of herself, seemed to have tidied up their lives very nicely. And where does that leave me? she asked herself. The only answer she could come up with was either playing gooseberry or being around to make the numbers up. Not a very encouraging thought!

She still had no idea when Toby was going to return to England or if he ever would. There were times when she imagined herself ending up a dry old spinster clinging to the memory of a long-lost love. That would be awful, but it could possibly happen. I shall just have to wait and see, I suppose. Keep on hoping that the work Toby is occupied with in South Africa will come to an end and that he will come knocking on my door like a knight in shining armour and we'll be able to spend the rest of our lives together. She sucked in a deep breath. For goodness' sake stop being such a romantic old fool, she chided herself. If he does return, all well and good, and if he doesn't . . . well, I'll just have to get on with my life and stop dreaming about things that happened in the past.

When Kate arrived to visit Dolly she found her waiting in the entrance hall and the minute she saw Kate walk down the hall her expression changed.

''Allo, Kate, luv, what d'yer think? I'm going 'ome,' she said excitedly.

'Well, that is good news,' Kate responded. 'If you're sure that's what you want.'

''Course it is, luv, got all me kids' presents to get for Christmas, ain't I? Been sitting around 'ere long enough. Not that I ain't grateful t'everyone of these luverly people what's looked after me so well.' She stood looking thoughtful for a minute then hastily added, 'And I ain't ever gonna forget that it was you what set about bringing me down 'ere and seeing I was looked after. We won't say too much on the matter, 'tis water under the bridge now, but it'll be a long time before I forget that some members of my family, and I'm sorry t'say that includes my Bert, would 'ave give up on me, 'ad me locked away like I was some bloody geriatric. It's only 'cos my 'ilda and you persisted that I got better.'

'Oh, Aunt Dolly! I don't think there's a person in this world who could manage to keep you down for long. And you mustn't blame Uncle Bert, he was frightened, out of his depth; he's so used to you taking charge and seeing to everyone's needs that he couldn't cope with you so ill.'

'What you're telling me, luv, is me 'usband thinks of me as a right loudmouth bossy boots.'

'I never said any such thing and you know it,' Kate laughingly rebuked her. 'By the way you haven't said when you're thinking of going home.'

'Termorrer night. Sam is gonna come and fetch me when he knocks off work.'

'Don't you feel nervous?'

'A bit, I suppose. Be noisy, won't it, after this place? But I'm excited an' all. Me neighbours will be in an' out of the 'ouse before I've 'ad time to take me 'at off. They'll all be wanting to know the insides out of a donkey's hind leg.'

'And you'll be just the person to tell them. I almost wish I were coming to London with you. Be an experience, your homecoming, I bet.'

'Kate, luv, I don't 'ave t'tell you, do I? There's no one on this earth that I'd love more to see walk through my front door, day or night, an' I mean that. You want a change or just a cuppa and a chat, you can always count on my 'ouse as your 'ome. And, gal, down or up, don't you ever forget it. I think of you as being as much my daughter as my 'ilda is and I thank God everyday for the pair of yer.' Leaning forwards, she gave Kate a resounding kiss on the cheek. 'Thanks, luv. 'Ow about taking me into Kingston now? I've been cooped up 'ere far too long.'

'That's a lovely idea, and you know what? I'm taking you to Bentalls. You can have a look round, choose something nice, because I'm going to treat you.'

Dolly threw back her head and laughed loudly before saying, 'An' I'm gonna let yer, gal, 'cos I ain't never bin one to look a gift 'orse in the mouth, but I can't 'elp wondering if you ain't palming me off with a present 'cos you're glad to see the back of me.'

They both started talking at once.

'Come on, let's fetch your hat and coat,' Kate said, reaching out to grasp her aunt's hand, holding it tightly in hers, all the while thinking to herself just how much she was going to miss this splendid lady who had such an indomitable spirit.

There were just four weeks to go now to Christmas.

Kate lay in bed, in the quiet darkness, staring at the ceiling, and decided that, in a strange way, finding Charles Collier's attaché case had marked a new era. Not only had the contents of the case helped to give Joshua more confidence with which to face the future, it signified that he would no longer need her as much in the future as he had done in the past. Also, now that her aunt had decided to return to London, she was left with more free days, which she sometimes found hard to fill.

Her thoughts returned to Toby. She had been experiencing an uncanny feeling for days now; it was as
if she felt him near her. She only had to close her eyes
to imagine the way he had kissed her, she could clearly
remember his arms round her, his hand fondling her
breast, the weight of his body on hers when they had
made love. The pain they had each suffered when it had
come to their parting.

She was suddenly consumed with the pain of wanting
him. She turned on her side, tugging the bedclothes up
tightly around her body, telling herself not to be so silly.
Just because Charles Collier had made himself visible to
her didn't mean that because she now felt Toby to be
close he also was unexpectedly going to appear at the
foot of her bed. Wishing didn't make it so!

Alone in the darkness, Kate cried as she hadn't done
for years. She not only felt lonely she felt rejected.

The hall clock was striking nine when she walked slowly
down the stairs. Her thick hair was damp and curly
after her bath, quite uncontrollable. She had dressed
casually, pulling on a loose skirt, a high-necked blouse
and a v-necked jumper over the top. She had dallied
with the idea of tying a multi-coloured scarf around her
neck but had then discarded it. She sighed. When the
Christmas holiday is over and Josh is settled back for
his last two terms at Guildford, she promised herself, I
shall go away. Leave Mary to have some time alone with
Mike. I will, I mean it. I'll have a holiday. It's something
to think about. Something to look forward to. They say
the journeying is always better than the arriving; well I'll
see. Cheered by the prospect, she opened the kitchen

door to find Mary sitting in the big chair by the fire, reading the morning newspaper and enjoying what was probably her second or even third cup of tea.

'Morning, Kate, you've slept late,' she said, putting the paper down and getting to her feet. 'That is a fresh pot of tea, pour yourself a cup and I'll cook you some breakfast. What do you fancy?'

'Please don't get up. I don't want anything to eat, not yet. I lay awake for ages and then when it was getting light I fell asleep. Sorry.'

'Nothing to be sorry for, time's our own. I was wondering what you'd like to do today. Anyway let me get you that tea.'

Mary bustled about, not sitting down again until Kate was seated at the table. A brimming cup, a tray which held milk jug and sugar basin, with the small silver teapot being kept warm with the aid of one of Mary's hand-knitted tea cosies. Hardly had her bottom touched the seat of her chair than the doorbell rang. 'I'll get it,' Mary offered. 'You sit still and drink your tea.'

Some minutes ticked by before she returned and when she did her face was so blank that Kate could read nothing from her expression. Without saying a word, she stood beside Kate and held out a small, flat parcel.

Kate took it, saw it was addressed to her, turned it over in her hands twice, then stared up at Mary, her eyebrows raised in question.

'Why don't you try opening it?' was all that Mary said, which bewildered Kate even more because she thought she detected a chuckle in her voice.

Mary took her seat by the fire and sat back, contentedly watching while Kate removed the brown paper from the small package. Inside she found an oblong white leather box measuring approximately three inches by two inches, which she laid on the table and just sat there staring at it.

'Open it. Go on,' Mary urged.

Kate undid the gold clasp, and raised the lid. Her eyes almost popped out of her head. The leather box was lined with cream satin; cradled between a slot that ran through the middle lay two rings. One, a single diamond, set with intricate gold shoulders, dazzled her with a twinkling of sparkling rainbow colours. Beside it lay a plain gold wedding ring.

Tears blurred her vision, but not completely. She didn't allow them to stream down her cheeks until she had removed the small card that lay inside the lid of the case. Six short words that would remain vivid in her mind for the rest of her life. Six short words that would erase the long wait. The lonely days and the nights that had seemed even more lonely. Six short words that could mean only happiness.

Please, will you be my wife?

She sat silent, for a full two minutes before she sniffed and rubbed at her eyes with her handkerchief. Then she frantically grabbed up the brown paper the box had been wrapped in. There were no stamps, no postmark. She turned round to face Mary.

'Who brought it? Did you get the name of the delivery firm? Oh, why the hell didn't I answer the door?' she yelled, her voice filled with desperation.

Mary rose slowly to her feet and said gently, 'Kate, it

was delivered by hand. The gentleman is outside waiting for an answer.'

'What? Are you sure?'

'Yes, I'm sure. Your Toby is in the garden. I did ask him to come in, but he said he preferred to wait outside.'

'Oh, Mary,' Kate's voice was little more than a sob, 'what shall I do? I look an absolute mess. My hair is all over the place. I can't let him see me looking like this.'

Mary smiled her understanding. 'You've both waited this long – you think he'll care that you aren't neat and tidy? You're wasting time. If I were you I'd have been out there by now. My feet wouldn't have touched the ground.'

Kate released the leather box, which she had been holding in a tight grip, and laid it down on the table. She ran her fingers through her hair, got to her feet and walked slowly to where Mary stood. 'Mary, oh Mary,' was all she could manage, her voice sounding as if she were once again a small child.

'Just go, Kate,' Mary urged, pushing her towards the door. 'He really is out there waiting for you.'

Kate fumbled with the front door and paused a moment before stepping out into the sharp fresh air. After all the years of waiting she couldn't believe this was happening.

There he was!

Taller than she remembered, the same good figure, hair with more strands of grey, his complexion fresh but certainly not pale. Just a glance and one could tell that he had recently lived in a hot climate.

He strode towards her. She was rooted to the spot.

Stop being so daft, she muttered, move, let him know you're pleased to see him. Still she couldn't lift a foot. He was within yards of her, she staggered forward and his arms wrapped round her, holding her body close to his, so tightly she could scarcely breathe. Minutes passed before he loosened his hold and, when eventually he did, they looked into each other's eyes before he lowered his head and covered her lips with his. Their first kiss was long and tender, and when it was over he still held her close to him, as he murmured, 'God I've waited so long for this. Kate, my own dear Kate, say that you still feel the same about me, say it quickly, tell me you will marry me. You haven't changed your mind, have you?'

He raised her face and then his lips were on hers again and she knew she was not dreaming. Toby had come back. Just as he had promised he would. He was here. We shan't have to be parted again, she promised herself.

When he finally released his grip he kept one arm around her waist. 'You came back,' was all she could think of to say.

'Did you doubt that I would?' he asked and, without waiting for an answer, added, 'I came back as soon as I could. I still feel exactly the same about you as I did on the day we parted. I want you to be my wife.'

She badly wanted to fling herself at this man who had meant so much to her from the moment they had first met, yet something held her back. She was afraid. Supposing she didn't come up to his expectations? He was a man of the world. She had lived such a quiet life, could she be a suitable companion for him? More to the point, would she be a good wife?

Kate said anxiously, 'Toby, it's been more than two years.'

'Two years and eight months to be exact. Thirty-two wasted months. We've got a lot of catching up to do.' He drew her into the shelter of the porch and proceeded to try to show her just how much he had missed her.

It was a long time before Kate had enough breath to say, 'You don't know anything about me now.'

He leant his tall body back against the glass wall and laughed, 'I know a great deal more about you than you imagine and I'm afraid there I have the advantage over you, but I'm willing to spend the rest of my life making sure you find out everything there is to know about me and everything we do in future we shall do together. That's a promise, and I think you know now that I keep my promises.'

Kate loved the sound of that. Her heart sang with happiness.

'How do you know such a lot about me? How did that come about?'

He grinned sheepishly, in fact Kate was sure he had a guilty look about him.

'Shall we go inside the house? I don't want you catching cold before I have time to get you to the church.'

'Toby Pinfold, is there something you're not telling me? I asked you a question and you're shilly-shallying about giving me an answer.'

'All right. I've been back in England for two weeks. There were a lot of matters that I had to settle. But the main reason for my not contacting you earlier was in your interests. I am absolutely sure of my own feelings, I bought the two rings while I was in South Africa I was that certain. But, as I said in my letter, I had to be sure that I wasn't coming back and treading on any toes. It was a lot to ask of you to wait so long, Kate, and I couldn't have blamed you if you had found another man. If you had and you were leading a happy life I would never have let you know that I was back in this country. I would have gone away and left you in peace. I had to find out how you were and how life had dealt with you, in all fairness to you. Do you understand?'

'Yes,' she agreed half-heartedly, 'but how . . . ?'

'With the help of your lovely friend, Mary Kennedy.'

'What? You've met Mary? She's met you?'

'One could hardly have happened without the other.'

'Oh, you know what I mean.' She punched his shoulder playfully.

'Yes, my darling, and I'm sorry, I shouldn't tease you. I was outside the house one day, just sitting in my car wondering what to do, when Mary came out and I took my courage in both hands and introduced myself and since that first time we have met regularly. She has been an absolute gem.'

'I bet she has! You'll be telling me next that you've met Joshua as well.'

'No. But I have learnt a lot about him and I sincerely hope it won't be long before I have the pleasure.'

Kate didn't have an answer to that. Things were bowling along and she was feeling utterly bewildered.

'Come along then,' she said shyly. 'Welcome home. Let's go inside and see if your friend Mary will feed us both because I haven't had any breakfast yet. And besides, there're a few questions I think I need to ask her.'

'Not so fast, young lady,' he exclaimed holding on tight to her arm. 'There's something I haven't had yet and neither of us is moving out of this porch until I get it.'

'And what might that be?'

Toby turned her round until she was square with his own body. He cleared his throat, looked straight into her eyes and said, 'My question is, Kate, will you marry me? Please? I've waited so long.'

'Yes,' she answered holding up her lips for him to kiss.

Chapter Thirty-Nine

ON THE LAST Saturday of March 1935 Kate Kearsley woke up at five o'clock feeling full of the joys of spring. Today was her wedding day.

By the time Joshua helped her out of the car and up the steps of Kingston church she felt sure no one in the whole world felt happier than she did on this beautiful afternoon. She linked her hand through her son's arm, then proceeded slowly down the aisle to the sound of the organ playing the 'Wedding March.' She paused for a moment before taking her place beside Toby at the foot of the altar steps, to smile first at her Aunt Dolly and Uncle Bert, her three cousins, Hilda, Tom and Stan, who were all there with their families, seated in the front pew; then, at Mary and Mike, Mr and Mrs Weatherford, Harriet Tremaine and most of the staff from the Alice Memorial Homes, who sat together in the second row.

After all those months of waiting, three years almost to the day, the service seemed to be over very quickly.

'You may kiss the bride,' Reverend Hutchinson said, smiling broadly, for he was thinking to himself that performing this ceremony had been one of the highlights of his career within the church, and that no bride had ever looked happier or, indeed, deserved happiness more than today's bride.

Kate and Toby left the church to a thunderous peal of bells and a shower of colourful confetti. Their hands clasped tightly as they sat in the back of the chauffeur-driven car, quietly smiling. Arriving at Hampton Court where a large marquee had been set up at the back entrance to the Kearsley Boat Yard, they were surrounded by their guests. Trying to welcome every one of them was proving to be a hard job and Kate found herself separated from Toby.

'You're looking very thoughtful for a new bride,' Jack Stuart touched her arm.

'Yes,' she agreed, looking up at the sign over the wide double doors of the boat yard that had been in her family for four generations.

'Are you thinking of changing the name now?'

'Oh, Jack! No. Never in a million years. My father deserves better than that. When it came to this boat building business he was held in great respect, as were his forefathers. Wouldn't you agree?'

'Yes, indeed,' he hastily assured her.

'The name Kearsley still carries a lot of weight up and down the Thames and I take this opportunity to say thanks, Jack. The yard couldn't have carried on without you and, seeing as how we're having this chat, I also want to add my thanks for all you've done for Joshua. It's down to you that he is safe on the river and so well versed in the art of handling so many different boats.' Seeing that Jack was looking slightly embarrassed Kate continued hurriedly, 'I mean it Jack, you've been a godsend to me in the bringing up of Josh.'

Before he had a chance to reply, Toby's arms came round her neck and in a teasing voice he muttered, 'Trying to swop me for another already, are you?'

Jack Stuart laughed. 'She wouldn't want an old crock like me.'

'That's not exactly true, I still need you badly, Jack, but . . .' she paused and twisted her body round '. . . you, Toby Pinfold are stuck with me for the rest of your life.'

'That is what I've been waiting to hear from the day we met.'

'Well, you'll have to wait a while longer before you can have me all to yourself. We must see that our guests are fed and watered.'

'And you'd better think about getting on with your speech,' Jack told Toby, adding, 'Good luck to you both. And I'd like to say on behalf of my wife and children and all those that are employed here at the Kearsley Yard that we think you two make a smashing pair.'

Toby, having shaken Jack's hand, was about to move off with Kate beside him when they saw Josh, Peter Bradley and Nick Banks, still in their wedding attire, standing gazing longingly inside the main shed to where a new motor launch was perched up on blocks.

'Josh,' Kate shouted. Her son turned and waved. 'Don't even think about it. Not even a rowboat! Not today.'

All three lads laughed, and gave her the thumbs-up sign before trotting off in the direction of the food tent.

* * *

Later that night, the length of the towpath was lit by dozens of coloured lanterns. Owners of vessels that had been specifically made to order from the Kearsley Boat Yard, jostled with barges and longboats for a position on the river. Steam whistles blew, barrel organs, concertinas and accordions bellowed out melodious tunes. Free ice creams and drinks were available for old and young alike.

Folk, having heard that Kate Kearsley was to be married, had come from far and wide. Most had known the suffering and notoriety that Kingston Kate had endured without complaint when tragedy had struck. But that was all in the past. She had survived the long ordeal and over the years had earned respect. Those close to her knew she had proved herself to be a wonderful substitute mother to young Joshua Collier.

Today, however, was Kate's day! She had found herself a man she loved and who in return loved her and, against all the odds, they had been married.

'Happy, Mrs Pinfold?' Toby asked Kate, as Joshua urged their guests to raise their glasses and drink to the happiness of 'Kate and Toby'.

'Happy, beyond my wildest dreams,' she whispered. Then, clutching his hand and squeezing it tight, she said, 'Nothing can hurt me now, because I have you.'

He lowered his head until his lips were close to her ear. Gently he moved aside the soft white veil that shrouded her shoulders and in a voice full of tenderness he said, 'Oh, Kate. My own dear darling, it is even better than that. Every day for the rest of our lives we have each other.'

COCKNEY COURAGE

I have to say thank you to:

My husband, Bob, for putting up with me writing almost every day. For his love over so many years, and for so often suggesting a story line.
My son, Robert, for all the love he gives me and encouragement when I need it most.
Darley Anderson, as much a wonderful friend as my agent.
Darley's girls for the way they take care of me. A telephone chat with Kerith always brightens my day.
To everyone at Little, Brown who gave me the chance to write.

Chapter One

ANNIE BATEMAN LAUGHED TO HERSELF. Her father had gone off to work in very high spirits, making her wonder just what he was up to now. Her dad was lovely, the best-looking man in the whole of the East End of London. He was far more handsome than her grandfather, and that was saying something.

Grandfather had been Irish through and through; a good devout Catholic till the day he died. The same couldn't be said for his son James. Known to friends and neighbours as Jim, her father was tall and dark with clear velvet brown eyes that had a piercing quality to them. It was as if they could see right through you, looking into your mind, knowing exactly what you were thinking. With all that, he had a smile that could charm the birds from the trees. He was forty-five years old but looked years younger, boyish, carefree, always laughing.

'God 'elps them that 'elps themselves,' he was fond of saying. Never taking heed of her gran's reply, which always was, 'And yes, my son, you want to remember it

1

can be a case of Christ 'elp them that get caught 'elping themselves.'

Every lady her father came into contact with was soon half in love with him, though many a one declared he had actually kissed the Blarney Stone. If the truth be known, he had never set foot in Ireland. 'Lucky Jim Bateman' folk called him, and so he was and had been for years.

All the more so during the years of the war. He hadn't been called up, because of his reserved occupation in the dockyards. Though, to be fair, he'd done his bit as part-time air raid warden from the very start, and when the bombs began to fall over London he and every other available man had acted as auxiliary firemen, tackling fires the like of which they could never have imagined. Nevertheless he'd done all right, seen that his family never went short. And it hadn't stopped with family. If anyone needed something, Jim could almost always lay his hands on it. At a price.

Annie got up out of her chair and dragged the coal-scuttle to the centre of the hearth, at the same time shaking stray strands of her dark hair back off her face. She was of average height for a girl, but thin, too thin. Her fine-boned face was dominated by huge dark eyes that marked her as her father's daughter. It was however her hair that was her greatest glory, a mass of luxuriant curls which fell down at the back of her neck forming ringlets over her shoulders. This morning her tresses were knotted back tightly at the nape of her neck with a dark ribbon.

Not bothering to use the tongs, she put several knobs of coal in the centre of the glowing embers, then, tilting the scuttle, she shovelled up as much coal dust as she could manage and tossed it to the back of the grate. 'I hope to God the outside toilet doesn't freeze up this winter,' she muttered to herself. They were only one week into January and already it seemed as though the winter was going to last for ever. 1948 was forecast as going to be a good year. Three years after the peace treaty had been signed, things should have settled down and life returned to normal. What was normal? Did anyone know any more?

Grieving for the dead was supposed to be over. But you can't wipe out memories of your loved ones just like that, Annie thought bitterly. High explosives and incendiary bombs had all taken their toll of London. Many of the streets of terraced houses still had not received adequate repairs. Broken windows, old wood and crumbling bricks, not to mention the grime, did nothing to lift the spirits of the people who had suffered so much. Most goods were still in very short supply and nearly all food was still on ration. Coupons were needed to buy clothes; as to furniture, bed-linen, towels, linoleum and rugs for the floor, permits and dockets had to be granted by the Town Hall. Nothing could be bought without one or the other.

Except from men like Lucky Jim!

So much cash her father handled, it worried Annie a great deal. She knew well enough about the tin trunk he kept under his bed, but nothing stayed there for long. Where did her father salt it all away? Best she didn't ask. What she didn't know, she couldn't tell.

Her mother had worshipped the ground her father walked on. Such a pity she had died right at the beginning of the war. In one of London's first air raids she had been hit by flying shrapnel and killed instantly.

Dad had been marvellous to her and David, her only brother. Not a day passed that he hadn't shown his two children love and understanding. Between their dad and their gran, they'd wanted for nothing. Now look at the mess they were in!

All those years without a wife, and then out of the blue their dad had brought home a quiet woman with two young children, six-year-old Mary and nine-year-old Ronnie, and declared they were to live in their house and become part of the family. Still waters run deep, they say, and that certainly turned out to be the case where Dorothy Wilson was concerned. An attractive woman with blond hair, aged about thirty-six, for one whole month Dot, as she'd asked Annie to call her, washed, cooked and kept her father happy. Then she'd upped and disappeared, taking a large wad of notes from her father's tin box but leaving her kids behind. It wasn't the children's fault, Jim had declared, and never for one moment had he considered turning them over to the authorities. It was up to him; they were his responsibility, he argued with his mother.

Gran voiced her opinion loud and strong. The woman was a chancer, she'd warned him the moment she'd set eyes on her. Tarted up to the nines herself while her kids were dressed in little better than rags, with Ronnie not owning a pair of trousers that didn't have the backside out of them. It wasn't as if he'd got round to marrying the woman, was Gran's constant grumble. Gran could bandy words till the cows came home; nothing shifted Jim Bateman from the idea that it was his bounden duty to care for the pair of them.

That's as maybe, Annie often thought to herself, especially when the two of them played up rotten, but why am I the one who mainly has to take care of them? It just doesn't seem fair, more so when you take into account that they aren't even blood relations. And it was because of them and their mother that her brother David

4

had upped sticks and left home. It was six months now, and not a word had they heard of him or from him. Annie smiled to herself – David could take care of himself. A lovely-looking lad with dark hair and big brown eyes; in fact many folk took her and David to be twins. Annie frowned. She missed David, missed him more as the days went by and still there was no word from him. Then suddenly the thought of her ridiculous situation brought a broad smile to her face, and soon she had to grip the arms of the chair to stop herself from falling, for now she was laughing helplessly.

Just eighteen years old, living in this terraced house that had no hot water or electricity. The kitchen had a sandstone sink, just one cold water tap, and an outside lavatory. The black fire range built into one wall of the living room and open grates in the front-room and the two main bedrooms were the only means of heating for the whole house. The small box bedroom had no fireplace. As if that wasn't enough to cope with, she had to try to keep tabs on her father and at the same time have full responsibility for two rebellious children that were not related to her in any way. Shaking her head hard, Annie got to her feet, saying to herself: If you didn't laugh, you'd cry, and what good would that do? You've coped so far and you'll go on coping, because what other choice do you have? Then, on a brighter note, she added: Things will turn out all right, they always do. Dad will see to the children, he'll find out where David is and what he's doing. He'll see to everything, eventually.

Bending over the stove to stir the porridge that was simmering in the double saucepan, Annie was softly hoping to God that she was right.

Chapter Two

ANNIE STOOD AT THE foot of the stairs glaring up to where young Mary sat clinging to the banister. 'Where's Ronnie?' she asked, her voice indicating her impatience.

'He can only find one sock,' came Mary's muffled reply.

'Well, take your thumb out of your mouth and go an' tell him to come downstairs right now. You 'aven't had any breakfast yet an' the way you're going on you're going to be late for school.'

'All right,' Mary answered sulkily, then quickly added, 'Ronnie said 'e ain't going t'school terday 'cos 'e ain't done his homework, an' I wish I didn't 'ave ter go.'

Annie tilted her head and stared up at the forlorn-looking little figure, and her heart felt heavy. Poor little mite, what she needed was her mother, and God above only knew if she'd ever seen her real father. No mention of him had ever been made – not to her knowledge, anyway.

'Well, you both do have to go, so it's no good wishing,' Annie told her softly. 'Now run along and tell Ronnie that breakfast is all ready and if he isn't down here in two minutes I'll come up after him, an' then he'll be sorry.'

Mary took her thumb from her mouth and struggled to stand up straight. 'I'll tell 'im,' she mumbled.

'I might as well talk to a brick wall,' Annie said to herself as she poured tea into two big blue mugs and set each one beside a bowl of steaming porridge. Then she heard footsteps on the stairs and heaved a sigh of relief. Maybe just for once she might manage to get the pair of them into school on time.

Breakfast was eaten in silence until Ronnie declared that his shoes hurt and he thought Annie should meet them after school and buy him a pair of boots like all the other boys wore. Cheeky little devil! was Annie's first reaction, when I think of the few rags they had when they first came here to live. Still, better not to start an argument at this time in the morning, as the way things were going she herself was going to be late for her job in the Market Café.

'I can't 'elp it if me feet won't stop growing.' Ronnie spoke sharply, sensing that Annie was none too pleased. He was going to give her a bit more cheek, then he remembered the last time he'd played up and shouted the odds and he regretted the way it had upset her. He'd heard her crying when he passed her bedroom. She wasn't so bad. In fact she was very good to his sister, showing a lot of patience and being kind when of course she didn't have to be. She no more wanted him and Mary living in this house with her than they wanted to be there. But then again they were better off here than they'd been for many a long day, sort of settled like, not shoved from pillar to post as they used to be. It couldn't be easy for her trying to look after them all. Ronnie did his best to black out an angry thought, but it wouldn't go away. No matter what happened, he was never going to forgive his mum for going off and leaving him and Mary behind. It wasn't fair the way she'd just dumped them on almost strangers and, to top that, she'd stolen a lot of Jim's money. That was a dirty trick to pull! Jim was a good bloke. He'd been good to their mother, bought her no end of things, not to mention what he'd bought for him and his sister. Not many blokes would have bothered with two kids that weren't his. Some way to repay him, wasn't it? Couldn't have blamed him if he'd called the council and asked them to take him and Mary into care. It wouldn't be the first time. They had been fostered out once before, and that had been a bad nightmare. The woman hadn't wanted them, but only the money the council paid her to take them in. For days, Mary hadn't stopped crying. That was another thing that he'd never forgive his mother for.

Annie poured boiling water from the big black kettle into the tin washing-up bowl and piled the dirty breakfast dishes and mugs to soak. Turning, she saw Mary struggling to get her arm into the sleeve of her navy blue coat. 'Here, I'll help you,' she offered, bending her knees so that she was on a level with the child's face.

'I can do me own buttons up,' Mary said with a small grin.

Annie picked up the long scarf that Gran had knitted for her – despite the fact that she didn't approve of her son holding on to these children, she was good to them in more ways than one – and wound it round Mary's neck and shoulders. As she tucked a strand of loose hair under the brim of her woollen hat, Mary looked straight into her eyes and asked, 'Will my mummy come back one day?'

A lump came up in Annie's throat that was big enough

to choke her. How could any mother be so callous as to walk off and leave a dear little mite like this? For all she knew, Jim Bateman had turfed her and her brother out into the street. Six months – and never a word, not even a postcard to her own kiddies.

Annie took a deep breath. 'Course she will. Now, let's be off,' she replied quietly, leaning forward to plant a kiss on the little girl's soft cheek. 'I've packed your dinners and I've put in an apple and a chocolate biscuit.'

Ronnie grinned and had the grace to say, 'Thank you.'

Ronnie took his sister's hand as they stood a moment while Annie went back indoors to fetch an umbrella, because she was sure it was either going to rain or to snow before the day was out. Most of the neighbours had their front doors wide open and called cheery greetings to Annie and her two small charges. Annie knew what most of them were thinking: Jim Bateman was mad to keep Mary and young Ron, especially when the brunt of it all fell on Annie's shoulders.

Annie allowed herself a small grin. Most would also declare that she was well able to take care of herself. She knew full well how they saw her: confident, absolutely in charge of any situation. Always in a hurry to get things done. Brooking no argument, allowing nothing or no one to stand in her way. A fitting daughter for Jim Bateman! I only wish it were always true, Annie sighed softly. Today she felt like following her brother's example and running off. But where would she go?

She had always lived in Bermondsey, but it wasn't much of a place these days. Streets and streets of what could only be called hovels. A sprawling mass of factories overlooked by dirty blocks of flats and ninety per cent of all the homes were still lit by gas. Annie's thoughts were grim as she watched the two children still holding hands as they walked in front of her until they reached the iron railings that surrounded the school they now attended. 'I'll be here at a quarter to four to meet you,' she said, planting another kiss on Mary's cheek and giving her a quick hug.

No such familiarities were allowed where Ronnie was concerned. 'Bye!' he yelled as he ran across the playground, dragging his little sister by the hand.

Annie thought as she watched them go that her dad had acted big where those kiddies were concerned. He'd rigged them out in brand new clothes from top to toe. No second-hand clothes for his family, and she hadn't dared ask where the clothing coupons had come from. They were nice enough kids. Ronnie could be a bit obstinate at times, but who in their right mind could blame him? If he had a chip as large as a house-brick on his shoulder, it was no more than could be expected. He'd as good as told her one day that he couldn't fathom out why his mum had left them this time when Jim had been so good and he thought they'd landed on their feet. Now he seemed to have assumed that because he was big and his sister was small he had to see she came to no harm.

Annie turned away, puzzled. It was a right old carry-on and no mistake, and it would take a wiser person than her to predict the outcome. It was ten minutes to nine, so with luck she still had time to call into her gran's before she started work at the café. The thought of her workplace had her hoping that she wouldn't be burdened with too many sad stories today. Christmas hadn't been so bad; somehow folk had found the extra money to put decent food on the table and still buy small gifts for their children's stockings. Now, many long cold weeks of winter still stretched ahead and what little money there was had to be spent on coal as well as on food. With so many men out of work and all the disabled soldiers returning home without a hope in hell of ever obtaining a job, life was proving to be totally different from what they had been promised when peace had been declared. That's not to say that life is all that bleak, Annie rebuked herself, and as she quickened her footsteps some of her fears receded.

There was another side, though, to this East End of London. An incredible strength of determination, a love of family and kinship beyond the ties of blood. A friend was a friend for life. And despite the horrors and deaths there still existed a gaiety and zest for the future which was quite common among Cockneys. The East End of London could never be described as pretty or even attractive but in some peculiar way it had charm. And that is not down to the place but to the people who live here, Annie told herself brusquely.

Working in the café from the day she'd left school, Annie had heard endless tales of the riots of the nineteen-thirties. Then as a young girl she had lived through month upon month of bombing, nightly destruction of homes and small businesses. Now she was experiencing first hand the plight of the homeless and the hardship of those unable to find work. Yet she felt, and for once her gran agreed, all this had contributed to the character of the folk that lived in the East End of London. Cockney humour was known world wide. And, during the years of the war, Cockney courage had certainly been put to the test.

Now on this cold, raw January day, Annie stood in front of a terraced house which looked as smart as a house could look when set in such bleak surroundings. She slipped her hand through the shiny letterbox. Hardly a day that

Gran didn't give it a good rub with a cloth smeared with Brasso or fail to clean her doorstep and buff it up with red Cardinal polish. She withdrew the length of string from which dangled the key to the front door. As Annie slowly turned it in the well-oiled lock, she paused to look at her gran's neat little patch of front garden and smiled at the two green-painted tubs that held bushy-leafed shrubs. Looking up at the front window, she smiled even more at the stiff white lace curtains hung behind panes of glass that sparkled even on this dreary winter morning.

As the door swung open, Annie entered the small passage and wiped her feet on the thick rag rug, one of several that Gran had made for herself. Facing her was an inner door that served to keep out the wind, its upper section consisting of two stained glass panels. Before Annie could reach out and open this door, it swung inwards to reveal the large figure of her gran.

'Allo, luv! I was 'oping you'd call in on yer way t'work. I've been watching out for yer.'

Annie stepped forward to be enveloped in her gran's big brawny arms, and she sighed happily as she was hugged close. As her gran released her hold, Annie turned her head and looked into the face of Jack Higgins, her gran's lodger. She smiled at him as much as she felt able, for she didn't like this young man. Well, it wasn't so much dislike she felt for him, more bewilderment. Having served in the Navy during the war, he had come home to no family and nowhere to live. The street where his whole family and relations had lived for years had been wiped out by a land-mine. Gran had let him her back bedroom and he now worked on the Thames as a lighterman. The arrangement well suited Gran, who felt nothing but admiration for Jack Higgins, a most kind and helpful young man, in her opinion. Annie's thoughts were different. He was different! Very handsome in a rugged sort of way with a mop of thick dark hair and bright blue eyes. But formal and haughty as if he's always trying to keep me at a distance, she grumbled to herself.

'See you later, Mrs Bateman,' he said with a smile, yet, as he squeezed past Annie, he merely muttered, 'Bye, Annie,' and even those two words were said very coolly.

Rhoda Bateman looked steadily at her grand-daughter, aware of the discomfort she seemed to feel whenever Jack was around. It puzzled her a lot. He was about nine years older than Annie, and the two of them should be friends. They've a lot in common, both losing their mothers so tragically, she was thinking as she ushered Annie through into the warmth of the kitchen. Rhoda was a big woman, all of five foot eight, with broad shoulders and muscles that would have been more suited on a man, yet not an ounce of fat on her bones. Today she was dressed in a grey corded dress with rows of buttons down the front. Her grey hair was scraped back into a bun at the nape of her neck showing clearly how weather-beaten her face was.

Annie gave a contented sigh, feeling as she always did when she came into her gran's living-room. Not so far from the Old Kent Road or from the docks, this terraced house was like a little palace. A proper home, full of old furniture and heavily curtained, it was warm and snug. A safe haven. A rich heavy chenille draught-excluder smothered the door, and stretched along the mantelpiece a fancy cover of the same material was made extra posh by its hem of rich tassels. The grate below it shone like a dollar, as did the saucepans that hung to the side. A big well-scrubbed table took centre pride of place. Along the back wall a sideboard displayed so many lovely pieces of china and figurines and framed photographs that it always set Annie wondering how ever her gran managed to dust it all.

'Come on,' Rhoda urged, pointing to two well-worn chintz-covered armchairs that stood one on each side of the fireplace. 'Sit yerself down. You've got time for a mug of broth, surely.' Without waiting for Annie to reply, she went over to the fireplace that had an iron oven at one side and a glowing hob on the other. Before opening the oven door, she took down a rough towel from a string line which ran beneath the mantelshelf and, unhooking the steel latch of the oven, she took out a deep stew-pot. This she set on the table and removed the lid before hanging the towel back on the line.

'Umm!' Annie sniffed the appetizing steam. 'Cor, Gran, that smells gorgeous.'

Rhoda picked up one of two thick mugs which were lying on top of the broad brass fender and took a spoon from the table drawer, setting a place at one end of the table before saying, 'Well, do you want some of the broth or not?'

Annie needed no second bidding. Within seconds she had dipped her mug into the huge pot, straining off some of the rich liquid, and was soon sitting back noisily supping away.

'By the time you meet the kids from school, the meat in there will be right tender, and I'll add a load more vegetables, but I won't drop the dumplings in until you get here,' Rhoda told her, replacing the lid on the pan before plonking herself down at the other end of the table and resting her elbows on the edge.

The affection between these two was obvious, and the

arrangement they had sorted out worked well. Well, most days it did. The more so since the School Board man had had a word with young Ronnie about hopping the wag and taking his little sister with him. Monday to Wednesday, Annie worked from ten until three, giving her plenty of time to meet the two children from school. Some days they went straight home, other times Gran had a hot meal ready for them. On Thursdays, Fridays and Saturdays, Annie put in a long day starting at eight in the morning and not finishing until six-thirty at night. On two of these days Ronnie was responsible for seeing Mary to school, and Gran was round at their house by the time they got home and stayed with them until either Annie or Jim got home to take over. Annie thought it was a cheek to involve their gran. She was after all well past her three-score years and ten, not that anyone was allowed to mention that in her hearing.

In actual fact, two years before the last century had ended, Rhoda had been the owner of the working men's café where Annie was now an assistant. As a bonny, quite well-off young lass of twenty she had been serving huge dinners and mighty mugs of tea to the Irish lads who were working on the roads as well as the market porters and the stall-holders. Amid the boisterous noise of the café she had heard this throaty, warm voice laced with an Irish brogue, and several times her eye had caught big Paddy Bateman watching her. Even today she still groaned when his name was mentioned, and his photo was in every room of this house where he had brought her as his bride three months after their first meeting. Silver-tongued as he was, he had never managed to convert her to his religion. That, and the fact that she had only ever borne him one child made her an enemy rather than a friend of their local priest, but that hadn't made the slightest bit of difference to their marriage. A pair of love-birds till the day he died. A marriage made in heaven, so it t'was, had been her Paddy's favourite saying. If only her son's marriage could have lasted as long. Bloody war, she muttered to herself whenever she let her mind dwell on the ruddy awful mess his life was in. Bad enough to lose his lovely wife, but to have struggled on and seen to it that his own two children wanted for nought, and now to be saddled with two more that he knew absolutely nothing about.

Course it wasn't the kids' fault that their bitch of a mother had left them, but where the hell had they come from? They must have a father or at least some living relative somewhere. And what broke her heart even more was knowing that, because of that hard-hearted woman, her own lovely grandson had been driven from his home and God alone knew where he was now or how he was coping.

Then there was Annie. She glanced at this lovely young lass drinking her broth before setting off to do a hard day's work. This evening, her Annie should be togging herself up, going to the pictures with a nice lad, not staying in looking after someone else's children. She was going to have to have another showdown with that son of hers! This time she'd make him see sense, and do something to right this awful situation.

Annie caught Rhoda glaring at her, and knew by that look what was going through her mind, but now was not the time or the place to go over it all again. As always, it would get the pair of them nowhere.

'I have t'be going, Gran,' Annie said, rising to her feet and taking her mug over to the wooden draining board.

'Leave that, luv. I've all the day before me to wash a few pots.'

'All right then.' Annie knew better than to argue, and instead smiled at Rhoda, saying, 'If that broth is anything to go by, tonight's stew will be exceptional! If I get sight of me dad I'll tell him you're doing the dinner tonight an' that it's neck of lamb and dumplings. That'll have 'im sitting up to the table on time, I bet.'

'Get on with yer,' Rhoda said. 'I've already got yer father thinking he only has to smile at me an' I'll do whatever it is he's asking, without you starting. You might 'ave some Irish blood in yer veins from yer grandfather, but don't you go forgetting I was born 'ere in London within the sound of Bow Bells, which makes me a true Cockney, and I can tell when you're soft-soaping me before you've finished getting the words out of yer mouth.'

Annie grinned. She knew Gran loved to be complimented on her cooking. 'As if I would give you any flannel! You're a sweet old dear. Anyway, must dash now. See you later, don't let the kids play you up.'

'Just let 'em try,' Rhoda muttered as she followed Annie to the front door.

Head tucked down well into her coat collar, Annie strode along laughing to herself. Dear Gran tries to make out she's got such a ferocious bite. If the truth be told, she doesn't mind having Ronnie and Mary to see to one bit. Half the children in the street knew where to come when they wanted a treat, and as for the older folk they had a lot to thank Gran for. Whenever she was baking, it was never for herself alone. Later that day she could be seen delivering small cakes and pies, neatly wrapped in a clean cloth, to several dwellings where folk were not too well-off or lived on their own or were not easily able to fend for themselves.

Probably enjoys it, Annie said to herself, but getting her to admit that, well, t'would be easier drawing teeth!

Chapter Three

THE STEAM HIT ANNIE as she pushed open the door of the café, yet she was pleased to see so many customers and, looking around, she gave everyone a friendly smile.

Sid Owen, the café owner, was filling a line of large mugs with strong tea from a huge metal teapot. 'Morning, Annie,' he called as she went behind the counter. 'Fings 'ave bin a bit 'ectic 'ere ever since I opened the doors. Too perishing cold for most of 'em t'ang about out there in the 'ope of a day's graft.'

'I'll be with you in a tick, Sid. Just let me get me coat off an' me apron on.'

'No, luv, I'm managing, It's the missus that could do wiv an' 'and.'

The kitchen was worse. It was like walking into an oven. Smoke was pouring from the grill, and in two strides Annie was across the room and had removed the pan that held six slices of bread which were well toasted, the edges quite black. Taking the pan to the draining-board, she found a knife and gave each slice a good scrape before covering it with a generous amount of pork dripping, making sure that each slice had a fair share of the rich jelly sediment at the bottom of the basin. Slicing each piece in half, she laid all six slices on a dinner place and put it at the bottom of the grill to keep warm, but only after she had turned the gas right down.

'That's what I love about you, girl. You don't 'ave t'be told what t'do all the time. You get stuck straight in.' Flossie Owen grinned at Annie as she expertly lifted rashers of bacon out of a huge frying-pan with the end of a wicked-looking carving knife. 'Get yer coat off, and then would yer take that toast through to Sid? Get yerself a cuppa at the same time. Yer look frozen, me darling. Bit nippy walking this morning, wasn't it? Proper murky an' all, I bet. We pay a price in the winter, living so close to the River Thames, don't we?'

By now Annie not only had her coat off but a clean white apron with a bib was firmly tied round her waist. Flossie meanwhile had laid the rashers on thickly buttered slices of bread, flipped another slice on top, and cut each one in half.

'Three bacon sandwiches, an, yer can tell me ole man that he's lucky he's getting service wiv a smile now you've arrived.'

With plates in each hand and two lying up her arm, Annie made for the swing door, 'Flossie, d'yer want me to bring you a tea or coffee?' she called back over her shoulder.

'Please, luv. I could murder a mug of tea. I might even get time t'drink it now an' all.'

Sid drained his own mug and set it down with a wry smile.

Annie was weaving between the tables, sorting out who

had ordered what, and suddenly stopped at a table where four dockers were sitting. Seeing one of them had two angry-looking scratches down the side of his face, she leant across and grinned. 'Ave you been up to your old tricks again, Bill?' she asked.

Bill Whatley was a tall, solidly built young man, so good-looking that Annie thought he could well be a film-star. Thick wavy dark hair, nice brown eyes and always a healthy-looking colour from working out in the open. He also had the relaxed manner of a man who knew the effect he had on women and enjoyed it to the full. Trouble was, he already had a wife. And a good one at that, was most people's opinion.

Annie was of the same mind. She knew Peggy Whatley well and her two nice kiddies, because the family lived in the same street as her gran. For all that, Annie could well understand why women did fall for Bill.

'Terrible the treatment I get at 'ome, it is, Annie! Don't suppose you'd consider running off with me like, would yer?' he asked, flashing Annie one of his broad smiles which showed off his perfect white teeth.

'She's got more bloody sense,' his mates chorused, then, laughing impatiently, the men banged on the table with their knives and forks. 'When we gonna get our breakfast?' one asked and another said, 'Yeah, me stomach thinks me throat's bin cut.'

'Carry on like yer going, an' I'll make sure Flossie doesn't give you any fried bread,' Annie retorted.

Watching from behind the counter, Sid was thinking to himself that the lass had got some spunk. Still, being born an' bred around here, it's no wonder she can take care of herself. True, most of his customers liked to have a laugh and a joke with Annie, but they knew just how far they could go. She would soon let them know if they overstepped the mark, and if she didn't, her father soon would. Lucky Jim Bateman might appear easy-going, but upset him, and he could certainly become a different animal together.

It was nigh on two o'clock before Annie was able to take a breather. The market outside was still busy, and even though it was bitterly cold, the crowd of shoppers wore a cheerful air. Despite the shortage of money, trade in the café had hardly let up. With Sid charging only threepence for large bowl of thick pea soup and a crusty roll, a tanner for egg, bacon, sausage and a slice and a shilling for meat pie or pudding plus as many vegetables as Flossie could pile on the plate, most days folk must have thought it was fair value and too good a chance to miss out on.

Sid, taking a short break to recover his breath, was sitting at one of the tables talking to the market policeman about a young lad that had been in the café that morning. 'Make yer 'eart bleed to look at 'im, wobbling along looking as if he ain't 'ad a decent meal in ages and, when he talks, which ain't very often, I don't think he knows what time of day it is,' Sid was saying loudly. 'Ain't got a chance in 'ell of getting a decent job, yet all the bloody government is going to give 'im is a bit of a disabled pension. In the First World War they'd 'ave said he was shell-shocked. Gawd knows what they're going do with lads like 'im that 'ave spent years in prisoner-of-war camps. Seem's t'me to 'ave lost his wits, that one at least, an' there ain't much anyone can do about that, is there?'

'Don't ask me, Sid,' the bobby answered. 'I can't begin to tell you all the hard luck stories we 'ave to cope with. Some as would make yer hair stand on end, and it don't seem right. Was supposed t'be the war to end all wars. To my reckoning, now the lads are home, the trouble is just starting.'

Annie had cleared up behind the counter and decided she'd leave them to it. Bit depressing, listening to them two.

Flossie looked worn out. 'I've made a fresh brew,' Annie told her as she set two steaming mugs on the table. 'Why don't you knock off for a bit, come an' sit down and we'll both drink our tea while it's hot.'

'I've only got one pair of hands,' Flossie complained as the two of them sat supping their tea. 'My Sid seems t'think I've got two pairs, shouting out the orders thick and fast. Oh, it's lovely that we do get so much trade an' I'd be the first t'say that this place gives us a jolly good living, but the way we're going on I'm beginning t'think I'll end up with a load of flowers that I won't be able to smell, lying in the best grave in the churchyard. I wish t'God that he'd listen to me and get someone in to at least wash a few pots and pans. Must be some poor old man that would be glad to earn a few bob.'

Annie covered her mouth with her hands so that Flossie wouldn't see she was laughing. It wasn't that she didn't agree with every word she said. She could certainly do with a bit of help out here in this kitchen; it was just the funny things she came out with. Flowers she wouldn't be able to smell! 'I'll get stuck into the washing up,' she said, rising to her feet. 'I don't mind, and it's pretty quiet out there at the moment.'

'Ta,' Flossie said gratefully. 'You're a love.'

With only a half-hour to go, Annie was busy wiping down the table-tops with a thick cloth that she frequently wrung out in the bucket of hot soapy suds at her feet. The blast of cold air as the door opened made her turn her head quickly. Doris Simmonds, who had attended the same school, swept in with her bleached blond hair and painted fingernails, teetering in heels so high that Annie didn't know how she managed to walk in them.

Doris was a war widow. She was very young still, only four or five years older than Annie, but her youth and natural resilience were working to heal the heartbreak that her husband's death had caused. Childhood sweethearts they'd been. But Doris wasn't the type to put on widow's weeds and spend the rest of her life mourning for what might have been. She was one of life's corks, destined always to bob back up to the surface no matter how far fate knocked her down. She had started going out again, filling the evenings with the distraction of company. She could be found drinking in pubs, dancing the hours away in the local palais de dance, or in the various cinemas drooling over the screen lovers. Like everywhere else, things had changed in London because of the war, and it wasn't unusual to see groups of young women out together for the evening, bent on enjoying themselves. She wasn't the type to be left out of anything. Bold as brass, fond of a drink and a joke, and always ready for a good time. For all that, Annie liked her. She was always telling her she was wasting her life looking after two children that weren't even her relations. 'Come on,' she'd say, 'I've got a couple of bob t'spare. Let's go down the King's Arms and 'ave a bit of a laugh. There's nearly always someone down there that gets on the old Joanna an' knocks out all the old tunes.'

'Annie, you still 'ere? You wanna be thinking about getting yerself 'ome before the snow really starts t'fall,' Doris half shouted as she struggled to shut the door.

'Allo, Doris! I thought you'd got a job as I 'aven't seen you around for a few days.'

'Blimey, no, I ain't worked since I left Sadie's dress shop. She was all right – well, most of the time she was, it were 'er old man, 'ee liked t'finger more than the gold sovereign he wore on the end of 'is watch chain.'

Annie threw back her head and laughed loudly. 'Doris, you're enough t'make a saint laugh. What are yer doing 'ere anyway?'

Doris grinned, untying the chiffon scarf round her head and loosing the fur collar of her heavy coat. 'I've got a message for you from yer dad.'

Annie's face lit up. 'Well, spit it out.'

'Your dad's doing a bit of business down at the Surrey Quays but said t'tell you he'll be at yer gran's about 'alf past five.'

'What kind of business?' Annie asked, glancing up quickly.

'Nothing for you t'worry yer 'ead about,' Doris answered with spirit, 'but I'll tell yer this. I 'ad a right good laugh listening to Jim delivering his spiel, better than going t'the music hall any day. Curtains he's got 'is 'ands on this time, an' none of yer old utility rubbish.' She took a deep breath, and then it was her turn to laugh. 'Remember, Annie, when yer dad 'ad a few of us working in that lock-up of his?'

Annie's face flushed. 'Only too well,' she said softly. 'I only wish he wouldn't get mixed up with all these different carryings on at his age.'

'What d'yer want him t'do? Sit back an' take it easy? That ain't Jim's style. He likes a bit of a risk an' he ain't really 'urting nobody. In fact, he 'elps a lot of folk one way an' another.'

27

Annie didn't answer for a moment. She was thinking how she and three more girls, Doris included, had unrolled yards and yards of net curtain, removing the utility labels so that her father could sell it. Utility goods were set at a fair price by the authorities, but sold only to holders of vouchers or permits. People who were in need and newly married couples qualified, as did folk who had lost their homes and all their worldly goods because of the air raids.

'Give over, fer Christ's sake,' her dad had bawled when she'd questioned his right to be handling such goods. 'As much right as Sammy Harris and a few others I could mention,' he quickly retorted. 'They got the gelt to buy up whole warehouses that were supposedly ruined by bombs or by flood water when the firemen were called. Then they pay daft buggers like me to clear the places out. Pretty grim some of the muck we find, I can tell yer. Some 'ave lain stinking for years.'

'But how come you're able to sell some of the stock?' Annie had asked in a voice that she tried hard to keep from sounding impatient.

'Sam, or whoever, is going to put in an insurance claim, no doubt about that, they aren't bothered enough to sort through soggy bales of cloth or racks of mucky clothing to see if anything can be salvaged. If the warehouse or building came with a good insurance policy, it's far easier for them to put in a claim, cop the lot an' turn a blind eye to anyone with the will to get their 'ands dirty and make a bob or two for theirselves. Sometimes it pays off for me, other times I've hired a van or tramped the streets trying to flog the gear and ended up well out of pocket. Now I've got good contracts and the matter of vehicles all sorted, they're there whenever I need them. With all the shortages there still are and people longing for something new to brighten up their homes, not to mention the youngsters that have money to spend but no clothing coupons, it's beginning to pay off nicely. You, young lady, have benefited from it to a very great degree, so don't you go turning all saintly an' toffy-nosed at this late hour.'

Annie had been unable to sleep that night. Some of what her father had said made sense, and most of it was true. But then he always could turn a tale to suit himself. As regards her benefiting from things he got on the black market, she couldn't deny it. She, more than most, had gloated over the very first pair of silk stockings he had given her. And she had never refused the extra clothing coupons when her dad offered them, nor the cash he was always so generous with.

There had been a long silence while Annie finished wiping the tables and Sid had passed a mug of tea over to Doris, which she was slowly drinking, at the same time staring at Annie, a thoughtful look on her well-made-up face. She knew Annie was troubled by what her father got up to and also the thought of those two little kiddies who somehow seemed to have become her responsibility. It wasn't fair. Annie was too young. 'Yer don't want t'be worrying yerself about what yer dad gets up to. He can well take care of himself,' Doris said, breaking the awkward silence. 'By the way,' she added, grinning broadly, 'I bet when yer see these curtains yer dad's got you'll be wanting one pair at least to put up at yer front windows. All in their own boxes, lined an' all, an' colours like of which we ain't set eyes on since the beginning of the war. Make a ruddy good change from the 'orrible blackout stuff we've 'ad t'put up with all these years.'

Annie looked across to where Sid was standing behind

the counter and saw he was winking saucily at Doris. Suddenly both she and Doris were laughing fit to bust and Sid came out from behind the counter and patted Annie's back. 'Yer got a good un there in your dad,' he said to Annie, 'an' he ain't called Lucky Jim Bateman for nothing. Besides, whatever he does he does well, just as you do 'ere in this café. We wouldn't 'ave 'alf the customers in an' out if it weren't for you an' the nice way you treat 'em all. Now enough's enough for one day, so go on, get yer coat and make tracks.'

Annie smiled happily. It was not often that Sid said anything complimentary to her and she held her head high as she went in to the kitchen to fetch her coat and say good-bye to Flossie.

'I'll walk part of the way with yer,' Doris said, tying her scarf back over her blond hair and knotting it under her chin.

Once outside, the girls linked arms and did their best to walk in a dignified manner between the empty boxes that littered the pavement as the stall-holders set about closing up for the day.

'Yer ain't kissed me goodnight, Annie,' one man called out.

'An', Doris, I wouldn't mind taking yer out tonight if you're at a loose end,' another chimed in.

'Go 'ome to yer wives and children,' Doris shouted back, chuckling as they both quickened their steps.

'Doris Simmonds, you ain't half as bad as you try to make out! Get yerself home,' Annie said, taking her by the arm and almost pushing her round the corner.

'I suppose you're off t'meet Mary an' Ronnie,' Doris sighed as she allowed Annie to withdraw her arm. 'Oh well, take care. I'll try an' see yer tomorrow.'

It wouldn't be long and it would be really dark, Annie was thinking to herself as she walked into the playground and joined what few mothers were there to meet their children.

'I've bin waiting in the cloakroom for ages,' Mary complained, tugging her hat down over her ears as she drew level with Annie. 'Ronnie grumbles if I don't look sharp, but he wasn't there today.'

'Never mind,' Annie said, smoothing strands of hair off Mary's face and squeezing her little hand tight. 'He won't be long, an' then we're going to Gran's for our dinner. You like going to Gran's, don't you? It's nice and warm and she's always got a treat ready for you and for your brother, hasn't she?'

'Yes, an' I do like Gran, she's nice.' Mary added a few more words but they were spoken so softly that Annie couldn't hear.

So she lowered herself to Mary's level. 'What did you say, pet?'

'Ronnie says . . . well . . . he says she's not our gran an' we shouldn't like her too much 'cos we won't be able t'stay with you for much longer.'

Just the sight of that little pinched face and those sad eyes that now shone with tears made Annie want to cry herself, but she put on a bold face and lifted Mary up into her arms. 'D'you believe everything Ronnie tells you?'

'Yes,' Mary answered defensively, her body shaking as if she were very cold.

'Well, Ronnie may be bigger than you, but he doesn't know everything.' Annie felt vaguely uneasy. She didn't want to make any promises that she couldn't keep, but on the other hand she just had to find a way to reassure this little mite. God knows she's confused enough what with

31

her mother disappearing, and all. 'Gran loves you, truly she does, and as soon as we get home we'll make sure she tells you so. You'll believe what Gran tells you, won't you?' She saved herself from having to answer further awkward questions from Mary by uttering, 'Oh lor! Here comes Ronnie.'

Looking back over her shoulder, Mary put her hand to her mouth in alarm. Running with her brother were three or four other boys all with squat scowling faces. Skidding to a halt a few yards from where Annie stood, they began shouting to each other at the tops of their voices. They each seemed undersized for their age, but what they lacked in inches they more than made up for in aggression.

'Well, Ronnie,' Annie called, 'why didn't you go looking for Mary?'

'I started to, then I remembered I 'adn't got me satchel an' I'd feel a right twerp in the morning if I ain't done another lot of 'omework, so I went back in t'get it.'

'You don't never do yer 'omework,' said the tallest of the boys.

'No, yer try an' copy Tommy Reid's, 'cos yer know he always gets his right,' said another lad.

'I don't! You're a blooming liar an' I'll get you for that. You see if I don't.'

'Ronnie!' Annie cried, then seeing the resigned anger in the eyes of this lonely lad she spoke softly, 'Say good-bye to your mates. We'd better get going. It's too cold to stand around here.'

Ronnie sulked for a minute, unwilling to let the boy get away with calling him a cheat, but contented himself for the moment by clenching his fists and glaring at him. All the same he was going to have the last word. Stepping

forward and braving the boy face to face, he muttered, 'I'll
be in the playground early termorrow an' yer can repeat
what yer just said then.' Then, very churlishly, he turned
to Annie and said, 'Well, what are we waiting for?'

O help me, God, Annie prayed silently, not at all sure as
to how she should be handling this situation. Mary saved
the day.

'I'm ever so hungry,' she pleaded. 'Have you anything
in your pocket for us to eat?'

Her face was raised and Annie saw the pitiful look of
concern. She was frightened for her brother, and Annie
reached out and took hold of her hand. Only last week
some of the bigger girls at this school had caught hold
of her in the playground and pulled her hair. One had
stolen her hair-ribbon, and Annie had had an awful job
trying to persuade her that it didn't matter because they
had plenty more ribbons.

'No, I haven't, but how about a pennyworth of chips
to eat as we walk home?'

'Cor!' Ronnie saw this as a get-out. He could save face
now and walk away 'cos there wasn't one of his mates that
would refuse the offer of a bag of hot chips. 'Can we put
our own salt and vinegar on them?' he asked Annie, his
face now wreathed in smiles.

'On one condition.'

'Oh, I knew there 'ad t'be a catch.' He sighed heavily.

'All I want you to do is promise me you won't let on
t'Gran that I've bought chips for the pair of you, 'cos she
goes to a lot of trouble to cook you a great big dinner.
And you won't go leaving half of it, will you?'

'Course not,' they chorused. Ronnie added, 'I'll even
wipe me plate up with a piece of me bread.'

The tuppence had been well spent, Annie decided as

she walked behind the two children. 'Good, ain't they,' she'd heard Ron whisper conspiratorially to his sister as they each dug their fingers into the newspaper holding their chips, by now soggy with vinegar. Fancy, a penny-worth of chips, and you'd think she had given them the earth. She supposed it was because they hadn't had a great number of treats in their lives. How lucky I've been, she said to herself. I've never wanted for much, but most important of all I've always had at least one parent who cared for me, and at their age I still had two. That is something that all the money in the world wouldn't be able to compensate for.

'Wait a minute,' Annie implored as they crumpled the now empty papers and prepared to break into a run to see who could reach Gran's front door first.

'For goodness sake, let me wipe your fingers and mouths before we go in. Gran will kill me if she finds I've been buying yer chips before you've had your dinner!'

They both laughed. 'I can see t'meself,' Ronnie said, spitting on his fingers and rubbing the sleeve of his coat across his lips.

Mary obediently stood still, holding out her hands for Annie to wipe with her handkerchief. When her lips had been given a good rubbing, Mary grinned, 'The chips were lovely, thank you, Annie.'

Annie gathered her up into her arms, holding her close.

Gran, who had quietly been watching all three of them from behind the lace curtain in the front room, was smiling. Yet she couldn't help thinking, once again, that Annie should never be burdened with the responsibility of those two youngsters. But at the same time she felt that she'd make someone a fine wife one day and be a jolly good mother, too. She heaved a sigh. That's if she's ever given the chance to have children of her own.

Chapter Four

RHODA BATEMAN WIPED HER hands on her pinafore before opening the inner door. 'Allo, me darling,' she said, scooping Mary up into her strong arms. Ronnie's eyes were quickly appraising, taking in everything that was going on. As they entered the warm kitchen, his eyes slid sideways to where a number of saucepans were bubbling away on the hot range. He sniffed appreciatively, a fact not lost on Annie.

'I don't suppose you're ready for your dinner yet, are you?' Rhoda said, turning from helping Mary off with her coat to look at Ronnie. Then, straightening herself up, 'I'll get you all a nice hot drink,' she stated, giving Annie a conspiratorial wink. 'I've heated up some of my elderberry wine and added a bit of ginger. It's good, really it is.'

'I'll have some,' Ronnie piped up before Annie had a chance to accept. 'And me, please,' Mary added.

Annie hid a smile as she watched Rhoda busy herself with the green quart bottle that held some of the homemade wine.

37

'Dinner don't 'alf smell good,' Ronnie stated, between sips of his hot drink and smacking his lips.

'Well, you won't have long t'wait,' said Rhoda, looking at him over the top of her own brimming glass. 'I've made the dumplings, only have to drop them in. I'll do that in a minute while you two can 'elp Annie t'lay the table.'

'I'd rather help you, Gran,' Mary stated. 'Once before, you let me roll the dumplings round and round in the basin of flour before you cooked them.'

'So I did, my luv, an' so you shall t'day.'

Mary, who was sitting on the rug in front of the fire, wriggled her bottom nearer to the brass fender, and rubbed her hands together. 'Have I t'wash me 'ands first?'

Rhoda laughed. 'Course you 'ave. When you've drunk all yer wine you an' me will go out into the scullery an' we'll both wash our hands.'

Mary tossed back her hair. 'See, Ronnie? Gran lets me help her wiv the cooking. Well, she don't let you, does she?' Mary asked, as he said nothing.

'Boys don't 'ave t'know about cooking,' he replied slowly, 'but I'm glad she lets you do things.'

A moment later, they heard the front door bang, and then the latch to the kitchen door was lifted and the door flew open to reveal Jim Bateman and a young man who was tall and red-cheeked and known to the family as Freddie the Fox. The two men came lumbering across the room, their arms loaded high with cardboard boxes. Rhoda's sense of relief almost overwhelmed her. She laughed. 'Blimey, son, d'yer 'ave t'make quite so much noise when yer come in? I thought 'alf the street was busting in, an' if it's not too much trouble, I'd like to know what the hell you think you're doing bringing a load of stuff in t'my house. You know I don't hold with 'alf your dodgy trading.'

Freddie the Fox, his greasy black hair hanging untidily over the collar of his overcoat, looked sheepishly at her, and murmured, 'Evening, Mrs Bateman.' He was one of the men who drove a van for Jim when he needed them. At one time he'd shown a lot of interest in Annie, but Rhoda had soon sent him on his way with a flea in his ear.

Jim hadn't bothered to reply to his mother, as he was too busy stacking the boxes into two piles against the far wall. 'Thanks, Fred,' he said, laying his hand on his mate's shoulder. 'I'll come t'the door with you an' we'll meet later to settle up.'

You could have heard a pin drop in the kitchen. The silence was heavy as the two women and two children waited until Jim came back from seeing Freddie the Fox off the premises.

Jim Bateman stood in the doorway, his cheeks glowing from the cold air, his eyes twinkling brightly as he pretended to glance around the room. 'Somebody told me the prettiest little girl in the whole world was here in my mother's house. I wonder where she is? I know her name is Mary.'

'I'm here,' Mary said, her voice little more than a whisper.

'Well, so you are, me darlin', an' there's me banking on getting me first kiss today.' Jim got down on his knees, flung his arms wide open and waited.

Mary's face reddened, and all she managed to utter was, 'Oh,' but she got to her feet and practically ran round the table to be swept up into Jim's arms and held for a long moment in a massive bear-hug. 'Did you miss me today?'

Jim asked as she stayed still, her little arms wound tightly round his neck.

'Yes,' she murmured, nodding her head at the same time.

'An' have yer had yer dinner yet?' he enquired, setting her down but still keeping hold of her hand.

'No, but we've had real wine, an' you can't 'ave any dinner until Gran and me wash our 'ands and pop the dumplings into the gravy.' That was a long statement coming from Mary, who rarely uttered more than five or six words at a time.

'Well, I'm blowed,' said Jim. 'D'you mean t'tell me that yer gran is making you work before she'll let you eat?'

'She likes 'elping Gran,' Ronnie piped up.

Everyone laughed as Rhoda took Mary by the hand and the went into the scullery.

'Here,' said Annie, handing her father a glass of the hot wine. 'That will warm yer insides while you're waiting for yer dinner.'

'Thanks. Have a good day, did you?' he asked Annie, stooping to ruffle the top of Ronnie's head before taking the glass from his daughter.

'Much the same as usual, except Doris came into the café to tell me what you was up to down at Surrey Quays.'

'No, she did not,' said Jim with a faint smile. 'Doris came to you with a message to tell you I would have me dinner here with all of you tonight. As t'what I was doing, no need t'make a song an' dance about it. Best deal I've had me 'ands on for many a long day.'

'Every deal is heaven sent, according to you, Dad,' Annie, told him.

Ronnie was feeling left out of things, so, plucking up his

courage, he looked over to where Jim was
butter-wouldn't-melt-in-his-mouth kind of
'Uncle Jim, seeing as 'ow Mary gets to 'elp Gr
Annie lets her do things when she's in a good i
can't I help you down on the docks some of th

Ronnie had any amount of common sense, was Jim's
sincere opinion, and the lad had had a rough time of it one
way and another, so he took his time before answering.
'Ronnie, you're a bit young t'be coming on the docks.
'Sides, you need a card. It's more a case of who you know
than what you know that gets yer a job in the first place,
but, once yer name comes up, through the family-like,
well, you're made fer life. I'll tell yer what, lad, I'll 'ave
a word in the right ear, see if I can't get permission t'show
you round, perhaps one Saturday, an' then, if you do think
it could be the life for you, I'll get yer name listed. Can't
get in too early. Not if you really want to be a docker.'

'Cor, Uncle Jim.' An impish smile was showing on
Ronnie's face. 'I'm nearly ten, but it would be a long
time before I get a real job. I was thinking more of giving
you a hand with some of yer sidelines.'

Annie looked quickly at her father. Neither of them
could suppress their laughter.

'You're a cheeky bounder, so you are,' Jim was saying
as Rhoda and Mary made a great entrance.

'Jim, you and Ronnie sit back over there by the dresser.
Annie, you cut some bread and finish laying the table,'
Rhoda instructed. Then, making a great show of the
importance of what they were doing, she lifted the huge
black stew-pot from the oven, set it to the side of the hob
and removed the lid. Helping Mary to stand up on a
wooden footstool, they waited until the appetising steam
had dispersed a little. One at a time Mary gently took the

ell-floured suet balls from the basin and passed them to Rhoda, who dropped them into the rich gravy. As each one fell with a slight plop, Mary giggled.

Watching and listening, Ronnie looked up at Annie and then transferred his gaze to the man he had come to call his Uncle Jim. Not a word did he say. Though each of them knew, as they gazed into the little lad's big brown eyes which were bright with unshed tears, that he was doing his best to show them that he was grateful for the care and kindness they and Gran were showing to his little sister.

Big Jim Bateman was moved more than words could tell. Scrawny Ronald Wilson did his utmost to be known as a tough nut who could take care of himself and his sister, but beneath the surface he was only a bewildered little boy whose mother had abandoned him. And on top of that, the lad had no idea as to who, or where, his father was. 'Jesus Holy Mary,' Jim was muttering to himself, 'how the hell did I ever let that bitch of a woman take me in so?' And, more to the point, how could she have ever walked away from these two dear little children not knowing, and apparently not caring, whether or not he would continue to care for them or toss them off to some home or another and forget all about them? Be Jesus, how Dot Wilson could live with her conscience was beyond him!

'Sit up to the table all of you,' Rhoda told them, putting a wooden board on the table and bringing the stew-pot from the oven again. With a pile of deep plates at her elbow, she began ladling big lumps of meat out of the thick gravy. While she was doing this, Annie was draining the cauliflower and cabbage. When four plates were piled high with meat, dumplings, carrots, turnips and onions, Rhoda took the fifth plate and carefully took the bones out of two pieces of lamb, cut them into small pieces and added a few of the vegetables that had been cooked in the stew. 'Pass that to Mary,' she said to Ronnie.

As her brother went to take the plate, Mary sat up straight and said, 'But, Gran, you haven't given me a dumpling!'

Rhoda pretended she had forgotten. 'Now how could I be so silly when it was yourself that helped cook them!' she beamed, laying two of the well-risen suet treats on the side of Mary's plate.

'Hmm,' muttered Ronnie in appreciation as he held a knuckle-bone between his fingers and bit into the meat.

'There's treacle pudding for afters,' Rhoda informed him.

Ronnie wiped his mouth with the back of his hand. 'I'll make sure I leave room for some of that,' he assured her, which set them all off laughing.

The news that Lucky Jim Bateman had quality curtains for sale with no coupons or permit required must have zipped around the streets of Bermondsey like a forest fire, Annie was thinking as her father rose from the table for the third time in answer to a female voice calling from the front door, 'Cooee, are yer there, Jim?'

'Whatever's going on?' Rhoda muttered for the umpteenth time.

'Don't worry, Gran,' Annie told her with a smile. 'Me dad's in his glory, got some real nice curtains, according to what Doris told me when she came into the café. Pity we can't hear what he's saying. Bet he's in his element with all the ladies clamouring for his attention!'

'I'll creep up the passage and 'ave a listen, if yer like,' Ronnie gallantly offered.

Annie nearly choked on her food, and Rhoda banged the table with the handle of her knife.

'You'll do no such thing, young Ronnie. Just get on with yer dinner.' But even she couldn't hide a smile. Seeing Annie and Gran both amused at what her brother had suggested, Mary gave a loud titter and was rewarded with a sly wink from Annie.

Suddenly Rhoda stopped eating, looked across at her grand-daughter and solemnly stated, 'Colourful new curtains and covers would work wonders in my front room, don't you think? It's years since I've been able t'have anything new.'

'You wouldn't, Gran,' Annie said, laying her knife and fork together on her empty plate.

'You've always said you wouldn't touch anything dad got hold of on the black market.'

Rhoda sighed heavily. 'I know I have. But the war's over now, and it's becoming a bit 'ard watching everyone else benefit from me son's gains while I remain righteous. It ain't getting me anywhere. Daisy Turner from the corner shop showed me a lovely thick new rug the other day. Said she'd *acquired* it for her front sitting-room. She didn't fool me, not for a minute! Dying for me to ask where she got it from – I could see it on her face. Never gave her the satisfaction, did I? Knowing full well she'd got it from yer dad!'

'So,' Annie grinned broadly, 'you gonna ask Dad what's in them boxes?'

Rhoda stared at her and then smiled at both Mary and Ronnie in turn. 'We'll do better than that,' she stated, using a mock whisper. 'We'll wait until the great man takes himself off to the pub to settle up with his mates and we'll 'ave a look an' see for ourselves just what all the women are so anxious t'get their 'ands on. We won't 'ave long, mind. Jim won't let you lot walk 'ome on yer own, so we'll 'ave t'be quick. You're going to help us, aren't you, Ronnie?'

Ronnie stuck his chest out with pride, just as Rhoda had known he would. For him to be treated as a man in order to help the women did a great deal for his ego. 'Course I will, Gran. Just tell me what you want me to do.'

'Can I help you look?' Mary pleaded.

'You, my precious, can choose the colour.' This promise had Mary really smiling.

Hearing Jim's footsteps coming back down the passage, Rhoda put her forefinger to her lips and said, 'Ssh, it's our secret.'

'Gran,' Ronnie whispered back, 'you ain't forgot we 'aven't 'ad our pudding yet, 'ave you?'

Before she could form an answer, Mary butted in. 'Are we going to 'ave custard with the treacle pudding?'

Rhoda couldn't help herself, and let out a snort of laughter.

At that minute her son came back into the kitchen, and looking first at his mother and at the children who were both grinning from ear to ear, he raised his eyebrows in a question. 'Is there something I should know about?'

'Just family life. I wouldn't swap it for all the tea in China,' his mother said, leaning across the table and lifting up his plate.

'Hey! I 'aven't finished yet,' he protested.

'I know. I'm going to refill your plate and hot yer dinner up a bit. After all, there ain't many women blessed with such a hard-working son as you are.'

Jim sat down, giving his mother a quizzical look. She didn't often hand out praise. She was up to something –

but what? Looking round the table at the smiling faces, he was equally sure that his own daughter and the two children were all plotting something.

Later, when everyone, children included, declared they couldn't eat another morsel, Jim offered to do the washing up. His offer was firmly refused. In fact Rhoda urged him to get along to the pub and have a drink.

'But don't be too long,' she called after him as he went towards the front door. 'We don't want these kiddies out too late in the cold night air.'

He was sure he heard them all laughing as he quietly closed the door behind him. Whistling to himself, he turned up his coat collar, pulled on his gloves and set off up the road deep in thought. His mother was forever going on about Annie and himself taking on Dot Wilson's two children, but just look at her tonight. She was in her element, mothering the pair of them. In future he'd say to her: You're the one to talk! Mind you, it had been a really happy meal time, so good to see Mary come out of her shell. He'd despaired for her when her mother went off like that. Really thought the child was going to be very ill. Then how would they have coped? All in all, God had been good. Seeing the lights of the pub only yards ahead, his thoughts went back to the deal he'd pulled off that morning. He still had another van packed tight with boxes of curtains stashed away on the other side of the river. Going by today's events, it didn't look as if he was going to have any trouble in selling the lot. Pushing the door of the saloon bar with his shoulder, he thought to himself that pulling this bit of business off would add nicely to his savings. Oh yes, God was good. Then he smiled broadly. Maybe he should consider it was more a case of the Devil looks after his own?

Chapter Five

A FEW WEEKS LATER Annie was walking to work and thinking how good it was to be out in the fresh air. January and most of February had been bitterly cold, but in comparison today was quite mild. She decided as she was early she'd make a detour and take a stroll through what was known as the children's park, which although only a small neat lawn was sheltered by a line of trees at one end. It also boasted two swings and three see-saws set off in a play area near the gate.

Thick clumps of snowdrops and colourful crocuses were showing beneath the leafless trees, and here and there the first green spears of daffodils were shooting up from the cold earth. She drew level with the one and only park bench and sat down. She tucked her legs beneath the seat and watched a flurry of sparrows fighting over a worm that they had managed to draw up out of the grass. She loved to sit like this, quiet and alone, almost believing that she was in the heart of the countryside and that the world of the East End was far away. Drifting away from

47

the world of warehouses along the sides of the wharves and the men who were always identically dressed in stained jackets and trousers, shirts without collars, merely a white muffler wound around their necks and tucked into the top of their shirts. And their caps – mustn't forget their flat caps, it seemed to be a badge of honour to the casual labourers who had no regular work but hoped against hope every day that they would get taken on. Given the opportunity, Annie loved to dream of living in a house with many rooms, especially a bedroom all of her own. It must have big windows looking out over a large garden that was tended by paid gardeners. Oh, and it must have running hot water and a bathroom. A bathroom inside one's own house! Now that would be sheer joy.

If she spoke of anything like this to her gran, she always got the same reply: 'You 'ave yer nose stuck in a book far too often for yer own good, my girl. Going off into a place of fantasy like you do won't never get you anywhere.'

That's as maybe, but it doesn't cost anything to dream, Annie said to herself, reluctantly getting to her feet and setting off to do another long day's work in the Market Café. Thinking of her father now, and the way he was acting, spending money as if it were going out of fashion, she wondered whether he had given any thought to making long-lasting arrangements for Mary and Ronnie. She gave a deep, unconscious sigh, remembering another thing Rhoda was fond of saying: 'If things don't alter, they'll stay as they are.'

That was all very well, but how could she allow things to stay as they were? Gran helped out. Of course she did. However, she could go home to her own neat and tidy house, sit down, enjoy a bit of peace and quiet, go to bed when she liked and get up when she liked. Bit different for me! Annie sadly reflected. My life is not my own. Certainly everything I have to do these days is not always of my choice. She felt mean, just thinking such thoughts; while she loved Mary and Ronnie, there was their future to think of, and on a day-to-day basis she worried herself sick about Mary. Such a frail beautiful little girl, with her blond hair tumbling down her back, but so withdrawn. There are times when I really don't know what to do for the best. She sighed. As for young Ronnie, he'd try the patience of a saint! When he was in a bad mood she had no idea how to handle him. It shouldn't be my problem, she told herself, indulging in a rare bout of self-pity. So far, she had resisted the temptation to accept Doris Simmonds' invitation to go out with a party of girls of a night-time. To be honest, I envy them their freedom, she muttered to herself as she pushed open the door of the café.

Very quickly she was brought back to the matters of today as a deep voice shouted out, 'Cor, are we pleased to see you, Annie! We thought we were gonna 'ave t'wait all morning for our dripping toast.'

'I'll see you all get served right away,' Annie told them, smiling sweetly as she went through to the kitchen to give Flossie a much-needed hand.

Jim Bateman woke up to feel an icy draught blowing in through the ill-fitting window. Outside might be showing signs of spring, but the house felt cold this morning. For weeks he had been meaning to put new sash-cords into all the windows at the front of the house, but like a good many more jobs that needed doing, there never seemed to be the time.

He turned over on his side, looked at the bedside clock and saw it was turned ten. Tugging the bedclothes higher up round his neck, he snuggled down again. He felt guilty. He had first woken up at six, and all he had done was just lie there, listening to the muted sounds of Annie making preparations for the day. First the ashes being riddled in the grate, the chink of crockery as she laid the table for the children's breakfast. Annie calling the children, and after what had sounded like a lot of heated arguments the three of them finally leaving the house and setting off for school. He hadn't come home until half-past two that morning, and it was more than likely that she had heard him come upstairs. He smiled to himself; it was just like his daughter to let him lie in bed knowing he was on late turn at the docks this week. But it hadn't been legitimate business he'd been about – not in the early hours, it hadn't.

Jim sat up, and shuddered. God, that had been a close shave! Too close for comfort! It was the first time he had sailed so close to the wind and he never wanted to repeat the experience. He should have followed his own instinct, worked on his own as he'd always done and not listened to what Arthur Kent had been going on about for weeks. Leather flying jackets, worth a bomb, he'd said, which of course was very true. Any ex-RAF gear was bound to have a good street value, but that sort of thing had never been his line. There were men up to their elbows in the black market, men who had real money to lay out, men who had formed a close syndicate and by the look of things they felt that he and his mates were stepping on their toes by branching out into the big time. Have I got greedy? I suppose the answer to that has to be yes, he admitted grudgingly to himself. He was letting what had started out as a mere dabble take over his life. He had never meant to get so involved. Well, not at the beginning he hadn't. He groaned inwardly when he thought just how deeply he was implicated. And then another matter forced its way into his mind – his daughter Annie. He should be giving a lot more thought to her. My God! What kind of a father have I become?

He swung his legs over the side of the bed, sat still and closed his eyes, knowing he should never be letting Annie shoulder all the responsibility for Dot Wilson's two children. She was a lovely young girl who should be out and about. Meeting boyfriends. He kept promising himself that he would get all their lives sorted. He had the means. His schemes had paid off well. Very well indeed! What he had done, was still doing, was in the eyes of the law wrong, but it had become his way of life. And I'm not hurting anyone, he argued with himself. Things hadn't eased with the ending of the war. Folk were fed up to the back teeth with austerity and the opportunities were there if only people were willing to take a chance.

He pulled on his trousers, tugged a thick seaman's jersey over his head and shoved his feet into a pair of slippers. Downstairs all was neat and tidy, just as he had known it would be. The kettle was filled and sitting to the rear of the hob. He dragged it to the centre, took a poker and rattled it up and down between the bars of the grate and within minutes steam was spouting and he was able to pour boiling water on the three spoonfuls of tea in the large brown earthenware teapot. With a steaming mug in his hand, he settled into his well-worn armchair.

Even when he had drunk the last drop of the strong hot tea he stayed still, staring into the fire, watching the leaping flames without really seeing the cheerful glow behind the black-leaded bars. Suppose the police had caught up with me last night? Or, even worse, some of the big boys' own heavy mob, employed to deal with men they thought might be encroaching on their patch. Men like Sam Sullivan would only have to get an inkling that good gear was going into the wrong hands, and they'd be on to it like a shot.

Everyone knew about Sam Sullivan, who was into more dodgy business deals than you could count on two hands. And not just small fry which sold quick and easy on the black market. Oh no! Word on the street was that he was in with the big boys, pulling off deals that included war surplus such as Jeeps and even tanks. Lot of money to be made in what was being passed off as scrap metal these days.

If Sam had got wind that leather jackets were up for grabs, it was ten to one that he'd have put his oar in. Jim shuddered at the thought. What on earth possessed me to get involved with a bloke like Arthur Kent? It was a miracle they hadn't got caught. Would I have been able to wriggle my way out of it? There was no longer the cover of the blackout. Streets lamps were now lit. Was I recognized? Thank God I'd had the energy to make a run for it. But what if I hadn't got away? There would have been an awful lot of sorting out to do. Could Annie have coped? And what of my mother? Questions were running riot through his head.

He put the empty cup down on the fender and got to his feet with a sudden sense of purpose. The first thing he'd do today was pay a visit to Mr Ferguson. Until the day he'd met him he had always been very wary of solicitors and lawyers, but Mr Ferguson had turned out to be all right. His thoughts flew back to the first appointment he'd had with this older man.

Climbing the stairs to an office that overlooked Wandsworth Common, Jim had felt he was taking a very big chance. After all, if he engaged this solicitor to see to the legal side of things for him he would have to take the man into his confidence, trust him to a very great degree. Up until then that hadn't been Jim's style. He preferred to play things close to his chest. But – and at the recollection he now sighed heavily – matters had got beyond his control, more so than he would ever have believed when he'd paid out his first amount of cash to clinch a somewhat shady deal. There must have been a guardian angel watching over him somewhere along the line, because deals had gone from good to blooming marvellous. Manna from heaven, you could say! And at that thought he found himself grinning.

An hour later, a smart-looking Jim Bateman emerged from the terrace house where he had come to live three days after he had married his lovely Lily. Only the good die young, he thought sadly as he stepped out on to the pavement. His Lily had been, and still was, the best thing that had ever happened to him. Annie, nor yet David come to that, didn't look a bit like her, but both had her kind and generous nature. We all make mistakes, he sighed, as he walked towards the waterfront, wondering just where David might be and for the umpteenth time asking himself why he had allowed things to get to such a pitch with Dot Simmonds living in the house that David had felt he had to leave. The truth was, he'd been besotted with the woman.

The tightly packed rows of houses were soon left behind as he made for the warehouse area. With the ending of the war, most firms had invested in motorized vehicles, yet the older type of firm that resisted change still existed.

Turning a corner, he saw an example of this very fact. Over the cobbles, huge horses pulled drays loaded with bales, barrels, boxes and sacks of coal. Hard-working horses still played a part, proving that London was a great industrial city. The horses' big hooves splashed through puddles left by the early morning cleaners when spraying the carts, spattering the passers-by. Others stood patiently by the kerbside while being loaded or unloaded and men wearing steel-capped boots and leather aprons shouted up to others peering down at them from behind the blocks and tackle used for hoisting goods to the upper floors of the warehouses. Without warning, a huge bale swung dangerously near to Jim's head. He dodged quickly to the side.

'You should know better, Jim,' a huge brawny man shouted urgently.

'Mind yerself, man!' another said, coming up behind and pushing Jim roughly aside. A second sacking-covered bale was lowered swiftly on to a stationary dray cart at the kerb.

'Sorry, mate, and thanks,' Jim muttered, knowing he had come uncomfortably close to being hit. 'Me mind was on other things. Miles away I was.' He smiled at the loader and thanked him again.

The first man who had called a warning knew Jim Bateman well and was amazed that a man of his standing, who earned his own living on the docks, could be so careless. 'You all right, Jim?' he called, stepping from the road to stand by Jim. 'Got time for a drink, mate? You look as if you could use one.'

Jim could well have used a stiff whisky; last night's escapade had affected him more than he would admit. But no, he was on his way to see Mr Ferguson and, having made up his mind to set matters in better order than he felt they were at the moment, he didn't want any distractions. So he said, 'Bit off colour today, Tom. Another time, eh? But thanks. Could have got meself a nasty whack there.' He smiled again and turned away.

Forty minutes later he was being ushered into a spacious office and as he shook the hand of Mr Ferguson, he was reminded again that this clean-shaven older man had about him an air of great self-confidence and dignity. Jim also noted that he was immaculately dressed in a dark grey suit that hadn't come from the fifty bob tailors.

'Please take a seat, Mr Bateman,' the lawyer said, seating himself behind his desk and placing his spectacles on the bridge of his nose. Unbeknown to Jim, he was carefully noting the reaction of his somewhat different client. He had been aware that Mr Bateman had seemed very hesitant at their first meeting and he had found this likable young man hard to fathom. However, after watching for years the reactions of the many clients who passed through his office, he had learned to observe the slightest sign of tension. Several encounters later, he knew Mr James Bateman to be a confident, capable person, but of one thing he was absolutely certain: Mr Bateman told him only precisely enough of his affairs to enable him to deal with the legalities of the matter in hand at that particular moment. There was a lot this client held back. Indeed, yes, Mr Ferguson was saying to himself. A whole lot more! His eyes blinked behind his steel-rimmed spectacles, and then he said, 'And how may I be of service to you today, Mr Bateman?'

Jim withdrew a hefty bundle of papers from the inside

pocket of his overcoat and handed them across the desk without saying a word.

The only sound to be heard in the wood-panelled office was the ticking of the tall clock against the far wall. Mr Ferguson had his head lowered and his eyes glued to the typewritten sheets. When finally he laid the tenth one down on top of the other nine pages, he drew himself up to his full height and settled back in his chair. 'I see,' he said noncommittally, then remained silent for a full two minutes.

He was fairly sure that James Bateman had made it his business to find out just where he stood with regard to the law, and therefore he also presumed that Mr Bateman knew exactly what he was asking him to do. It was possible, of course, that he had also confided in someone other than himself, although he thought not. With a wry smile, he said to Jim, 'Most of your instructions are pretty straightforward, but there is one point I would like to raise.'

There was an awkward moment between them before he spoke again, during which he glanced out of the window and then began. 'Mr Bateman I . . .' He seemed to be groping for words, which was most unusual for him. He sat up straight and stared at his client and as though he had come to a sudden decision, in a very firm voice he began again. 'I take it you do not anticipate dying within the near future? However, I agree, you should make a will, and without delay. I'll attend to it. We can take the first draft while you're here this morning. As to these papers and your list of written instructions, I presume you wish me to proceed straight away? There are no questions you wish to ask? You have given enough thought to these matters?' Mr Ferguson still felt James Bateman was a bit of a puzzle and he couldn't help feeling curious as to his private life.

The questions he had put to James were loaded ones, and he watched carefully for his reaction. His client was not to be drawn, however, and answered 'Yes' to the first one, 'No' to the second, and 'Yes' to the third.

Mr Ferguson nodded, picked up his pen and began to write. All the time he was thinking that there must be two halves to this young man: one half had him acting with complete honesty and courage, the other half he kept completely to himself.

Meanwhile, Jim wanted to go round the desk and explain everything in detail to this man who could so easily, given different circumstances, be a jolly good friend. But he felt Mr Ferguson had to be on the side of the law. He must at all costs keep him at a distance. Thoughts such as he was having now made him feel very lonely.

Chapter Six

ARTHUR KENT AND TWO of the men who worked for Jim were picked up by the police as they attempted to drive away the two vans they had abandoned during the early hours of that morning. They were taken to the police station and Arthur, terrified, tried to save his own skin by telling them everything they wanted to know. What frightened him most was that he might be set on by Sam Sullivan and his boys. He told the police he was only working for Jim Bateman and that the whole job had been planned by, and was down to, Jim.

Jim was arrested as he set foot back on his own side of the river. He had chosen a solicitor's office in south London to do his business so as to keep away from prying eyes. Somebody had certainly shopped him to the police, and he only hoped that they hadn't followed him. Not that it would matter too much if they were on to his dealings with Mr Ferguson. All in that area was well above board and there wasn't anything bad that Mr Ferguson could tell them because he'd made sure he was unaware of any business that wasn't strictly honest. One officer read him his rights, and then his arms were pinned to his sides by two officers who were attempting to throw him into the back of a Black Maria.

Oh no! was his immediate thought. Lucky Jim Bateman was the handle he'd lived with, and he wasn't going to let that luck desert him now. Quick as lightening he kicked one policeman in the shins so hard that he curled up with a howl of pain. With the other officer taken off guard for a moment, Jim raised his knee, slamming it hard into the man's groin, and then he was gone.

His heart was thumping nineteen to the dozen and he could feel the sweat trickling down from his armpits, yet his mouth felt as dry as a bone. A lorry hooted, and Jim dodged to the side. Ducking and diving between the heavy traffic, he had almost reached the other side of the road where he felt sure he could run fast enough to gain the darkness and cover of the Underground. He was half grinning to himself when his luck ran out. His foot was raised, one more stride and he would clear the curb and hit the pavement running. At that moment a bus hit him, lifting him off his feet, knocking him sideways.

Jack Higgins walked up the litter-strewn market street that led to Sid Owen's café. Good job the dinner-time rush was over. Sid's customers were a rough lot, from street traders and dockers to lightermen, labourers and building workers. It also catered for a number of villains, men who had ready cash and were using the aftermath of the war to buy and sell anything they could lay their hands on. Sid's grub was good. Terms strictly cash, eat up, mind your own business and make way for the next lot of customers was

Sid's philosophy. Jack took a deep drag on his cigarette and threw the stub into the gutter before opening the door. Sid was behind the counter, holding a huge enamel teapot beneath the tap of a brass urn: boiling water plus any amount of steam was hissing away like mad, making the whole operation look extremely dangerous. There were only about half a dozen customers, and they were seated at the tables at the far end of the café. Jack watched Sid smile across at him, and he relaxed a little.

'Well, well, Jack Higgins! Nice t'see yer, lad. Yer don't often work this part of the Thames, do yer?'

'Annie hasn't left yet, has she?' Jack enquired, not bothering to answer Sid's question.

Sid grinned. 'No, her an' Flossie will be gossiping while they clear up. Bin right busy, we 'ave. I'm just making a fresh brew – will you 'ave a cuppa while you're waiting for her?'

Thinking he'd better make matters clear straight off, Jack walked towards the counter. 'This ain't a social call, Sid. When I got home, the police were at the house. Mrs Bateman were in a right state – her son Jim has been knocked down by a bus an' he's in the London Hospital – you know, the big one in Whitechapel. She asked me to come and fetch Annie.'

'I can't tell you any more than I've told you already, Annie. I wasn't there when the police arrived. I walked in on them questioning your gran, and I did my best to calm everyone down. I think you'd better come home first before you go to the hospital.' Jack's voice was quiet but indignant and Annie closed her eyes before answering him.

'I'm sorry, Jack, I didn't mean to have a go at you.'

Elizabeth Waite

She drew in a deep breath, trying hard not to panic. Her heart was beating erratically and she had no idea what she ought to do first.

Sid Owen felt for Annie; her life was hard enough as it was without this! He looked at his wife, who had come out and was standing beside him. 'Go get her things, luv, I'll 'ave a quick word with her,' he whispered to Flossie as he came out from behind the counter. Twisting Annie round to face him, Sid pulled her into his brawny arms and held her close. 'Annie, for God's sake calm down! You're shaking like a leaf.' He stared down into the lovely face of this young girl, noting how sad her huge brown eyes looked. He touched the top of her head, and he let his fingers run down the length of her long dark hair. Even though she had worked in the steaming café all day and her hair was tightly tied back with just a piece of cotton tape, it still felt like glossy silk.

Flossie bit on her lip and watched her great hunk of a man tenderly holding Annie and wished there was more they could do for the lass who had become very dear to both of them over the years. 'Come on, luv, put yer arms in here,' she said, holding up Annie's coat. 'At least yer got Jack t'see yer 'ome, an' I'm sure he won't let you go to Whitechapel on yer own, will yer, Jack?'

Suddenly Flossie was stunned. She had been looking at Jack Higgins and seen the different expressions flitting across his face. One minute the anger had been plain to see, now she wasn't at all sure what she was watching. Jack Higgins's family had been well known to her. It had rocked the East End that such a large and well-respected family had been wiped out, leaving only the one son alive. To come back from having served in the Navy to find you had no home and no family would have been enough to

62

send many a man off his rocker. Jim had settled in as Mrs Bateman's lodger, keeping himself very much to himself. Some would say he was a dark horse. Her Sid was of the opinion that working on the river all the hours that God sent had been the salvation of Jack Higgins.

Meanwhile Jack was telling himself, Annie won't buckle, she'll handle this just the same as every other problem her father seems to heap on to her: she's a fighter. I just wish she wasn't . . . he couldn't decide just what it was he was wishing, then the word he was searching for came into his head. She's difficult! Yes, that was it, difficult and independent, never willingly asking anyone for help.

He looked down at his feet, knowing that Flossie had been staring at him, waiting for him to say something. Taking a deep breath, he raised his head and quietly declared, 'Best get a move on, Annie. Your gran will be worried sick, and as soon as you've seen her, we should make for the hospital.'

'All right, and thanks for coming to fetch me, Jack.' Annie's voice was serious, her whole demeanour crushed. The fact that her father had met with an accident and was in hospital was bad enough, but why were the police so heavily involved? Suddenly she felt very frightened that there were new problems to contend with before the old ones had begun to sort themselves out.

Jack held the door open while Flossie kissed Annie on the cheek and Sid said, 'Now you're not t'worry about coming in t'work termorrow. If we ain't 'eard anything from yer by the time the lunch rush is over, we'll get a couple of the men t'mind the café and we'll come over t'yer gran's t'find out 'ow things are.'

Flossie shook her head. 'We ain't waiting that long!' Turning again to Jack, she declared, 'As soon as yer get news from the 'ospital, you get on the blower. I can always get in a cab and be with yer in no time.'

Annie smiled sadly. 'You're both so good t'me. I'll make sure we phone as soon as we find out what's happened to me dad.'

Flossie and Sid stood in the doorway of the café and watched as Jack Higgins took Annie's arm. Flossie was wondering for the second time just what Jack's feelings were towards Annie. He certainly was her friend, and at a time like this friends were sorely needed. She had a feeling that Annie was about to find that out.

Chapter Seven

ANNIE, RUSHING IN THROUGH the front door, was
surprised to see Mrs Dawson coming down the stairs.
'It's all right, Annie. I've just put an 'ot water bottle
in yer gran's bed. Proper turn she's 'ad what with one
thing an' another. Thought the damn policemen were
never gonna go. Later on, maybe, I can get 'er to go up
and have a lie down.'

Gladys Dawson was a neighbour of long standing.
Through the hard times of the thirties and the lean and
horrifying years of the war it was women like her and
Rhoda Bateman who had found the true meaning of being
neighbourly. Short and fat with a mop of straggly grey
hair, she was still a woman to be reckoned with and she
had a tremendous reputation for helping those in need.
Annie was relieved to find that she was in the house and
doing her best to take care of her gran.

As Gladys reached the bottom stair, Annie smiled at
her. 'Oh, thanks, Mrs Dawson. It is good of you to come
in like this.'

'Rubbish!' Gladys grinned, showing a remarkable fine set of teeth. 'Yer know, Annie, I'm not one t'interfere, but when I saw the police arrive – three of them there were at first but one went off – I was in 'ere like a shot. Right sorry I am about yer dad; let's 'ope he'll be all right. Keep our fingers crossed, eh, luv?'

'Are yer all gonna stand out in the passage much longer?' Rhoda's voice sounded strained, and Annie quickly covered the distance between them.

'Oh, Gran,' breathed Annie, putting her arms around Rhoda's neck, and now beginning to cry.

'Come on now, pet, there's nothing that can't be sorted. Here, blow yer nose,' she ordered, passing her a handkerchief. Annie dabbed at her eyes and blew her nose. 'Gladys 'ere has said she'll go t'the school t'meet young Mary and Ronnie, so that's one weight off our minds. D'yer think I ought to come to the hospital with yer?'

It was Jack Higgins who now took complete charge of the situation. 'Better if you stay here, Mrs Bateman, and give the kids their tea. I'll get a cab, go along with Annie, and as soon as we know how Jim is, I'll leave Annie with him, come back, give you the news and when I've had a wash and change I'll go back to fetch Annie home. Best if you wait and come with me then.' His voice held a note of authority and not one of the three women in the room felt like arguing with him.

'Of course, Jack. I wasn't thinking,' Rhoda said softly. 'You came straight in from work to find this mess, never even offered you a cup of tea. Just asked you t'go and fetch Annie. Sorry, lad. Didn't mean t'be so thoughtless.'

'That's all right, Mrs Bateman. Sid Owen gave me a cuppa the minute I set foot in his place.'

'Oh, he would,' Rhoda agreed. 'I never did object to

our Annie going t'work for him and Flossie. Right nice pair they are.'

'Couldn't agree more.' Gladys threw her two penny-worth in. 'Done a great deal for the folk around here when we were getting them Jerries over 'ere every flipping night. Live over the café they do now. Time was they 'ad a lovely 'ouse, but like a good many more it took a hit when the city was bombed. Sid was buried alive; took more than a day to dig him out.'

You could have heard a pin drop in Rhoda's kitchen, and it was only when a cinder from the fire dropped through into the ashpan that anyone moved.

Gladys realized what she had said, and her hand flew to cover her mouth. Seconds later, and the poor soul was looking at Jack Higgins, her eyes pleading with him not to be angry with her. 'Oh, Jack! What can I say, lad? Except that I've got a mouth that's far too big for me face. I wasn't meaning to be detrimental t'yer parents, God rest their souls.'

'I know, I know,' he said, patting Gladys's arm. 'They were bad years for us all.' He turned to Annie. 'Everything is sorted here, then. Yer gran will see to the tea, and Mrs Dawson will fetch the kids from school, so shall we go?'

Looking absently around her, Annie asked, 'Will you be all right, Gran?'

'Course we shall,' both women hastened to assure her. 'Just make sure you wrap yerself up warm and tell yer dad I'll come along later to see him. And don't go getting yerself all upset.' Rhoda wagged a cautioning finger at her. 'He's in the right place. The hospital will take good care of him.'

In the taxi, Annie nudged Jack's arm. At every turn she

could see elderly men that looked so ill dressed they could be taken for tramps. It got even worse at the Bishopsgate end of Middlesex Street, with many men of all ages resting anywhere they could find shelter from the cold. Why were there so many men that couldn't find work? They looked so aimless. Some seemed to be drunk, even at this hour of the day. Annie shuddered to think how their families were coping. She was glad when she realized they were in the Whitechapel Road going towards the London Hospital, though thinking about what they might find when they arrived made her shudder even more.

It had been raining all night. With morning it had got worse, coming down in torrents, beating against the ward windows as the nurses went round switching on the lights ready to start another day's shift.

Seated at the side of her father's bed, Annie turned for a moment to listen. From somewhere along the corridor beyond the screens covering the double doors of the long ward came, faintly but persistently, the cry of a newborn baby. What a day to choose to come into this world! A grey old world. At that moment there was a heavy clap of thunder, which didn't help. She turned to her father. Dear God, he looked so ill!

On their arrival, Jack had stayed with her for half an hour. Then he had left, returning at seven o'clock in the evening with her gran. Poor Gran, she had gazed at Jim lying so still in the narrow white bed and must have found it hard to believe that the sunken, waxen face was that of her son. For the first time in her life Annie had sat helpless watching the tears stream down her grandmother's face. Not even when her grand-dad had died had she seen her gran cry.

At ten o'clock the staff nurse had called them into her side office, saying the doctor wanted to have a word. Rhoda had insisted that Jack accompany them. Annie couldn't fail to notice that a uniformed policeman still sat on a chair in the corridor outside the ward. A tall, white-coated, serious-looking doctor had spoken quietly, directing most of his words towards Rhoda. 'Your son has internal injuries, Mrs Bateman. We have done all we can and now we must hope for the best. One good sign is that although Mr Bateman is very seriously ill, he is from time to time quite conscious. If one of you wishes to remain in the hospital during the night, we can offer you a bed quite close to the ward. A nurse will be on hand to call you if needed and you would be able to phone should you wish to ring any member of your family.'

Jack had been the one to shake hands with the doctor and to offer their thanks. Annie wondered how she and her grandmother would have coped if Jack Higgins hadn't accepted responsibility for them. After a quiet but quick conversation, it had been decided that Jack should take the old lady home and that Annie should spend the night with her father.

'And don't worry about Mary an' Ronnie. I'll see they get to school on time,' were Jack's parting words.

Annie had refused the offer of a bed. She stayed in the ward throughout the night, except for a brief visit to the toilet and fifteen minutes when a kindly nurse had urged her to join the night staff in the ward kitchen where a welcome mug of Horlicks had been offered her. Jim had moved from time to time and seemed to know that she was there. Now one arm lay outside the bedclothes and she took his hand between both of her own. Using her thumb, she gently massaged the back of his hand and the motion seemed to soothe him, for a soft sigh came from between his pale lips. As she watched, his eyelids fluttered and half-opened, and he moved his head a little on the pillow, saying faintly, 'Mum—?'

'No, it's me, Dad. Annie.' She let go of his hand and leaned over the bed. 'Gran's gone home but she will be back soon. Do you want something?'

'No . . .' He was silent again for a while, and then, 'What time is it?'

Annie glanced at the clock high up on the opposite wall. 'Ten minutes to eight.'

At that moment a nurse came to the bedside, her starched apron rustling as she moved to take her patient's pulse. Taking a chart down from its hook, she looked solemnly at Annie before writing her notes. Then, using what seemed to be a forced cheerful tone, she said to Jim, 'You've had a good long sleep. Is there anything you'd like? How about a drink?'

He made a slight sound like a sigh, turning his eyes towards the windows. Even in his helpless, weakened state he still tried to make a joke. 'I'll skip the beer – just a drop of water, please.'

'Come now, Mr Bateman, we can do better than that. How about some warm milk?'

He moved his head slightly to get his daughter into focus. 'See, Annie, the women still want t'mother me.'

The nurse turned away, giving Annie a very sad smile. Soon she was back, and Annie got up from her chair and went to stand at the foot of the bed. Her eyes were blurred by tears as she watched the nurse easing her arm gently behind her father's head, raising him enough to hold the spout of the feeding-cup to his mouth for him to take a few small sips. 'There, now, isn't that better than ale?' the efficient nurse teased him.

When he'd had all he wanted, she propped him carefully back against the mound of pillows and wiped the corners of his lips with a paper towel. Even that slight exertion seemed to have drained him.

'I'll bring you a cup of tea, Miss Bateman, and when the day nurses come to wash your father and see to his bed, perhaps you'd like to come to our canteen and have some breakfast. You must be famished?'

Annie shook her head. 'No, I'm not the least bit hungry, but a cup of tea I wouldn't say no to, thank you.'

However, she wasn't given the choice. Two nurses arrived pushing a large trolley holding clean towels, linen, enamel bowls and jugs of steaming hot water. Pulling the curtains around the bed, they shooed Annie away. 'You haven't lived till you've sampled our staff breakfast,' the youngest of the two nurses assured her. 'Go on. We'll spruce your dad up and you'll both feel better to face the day.'

Left with no alternative, Annie did as she was told. By nine-thirty she was again seated at Jim's bedside, feeling so tired that she almost dropped off to sleep. He looked peaceful. He had lain with his eyes closed ever since she had returned to the ward. Just as she began to think that he was drifting off into a deep sleep, he said suddenly, 'Annie, I have to talk to you. It's important.'

She looked at him, wondering. 'Not now, Dad. You need to rest.'

He moved his head, to look at his daughter's face there beside him. Her huge brown eyes reflected the sadness he knew she must be feeling. That thick glossy hair she got from his side of the family made him want to reach out

71

and stroke the length of it, but his arms felt too heavy to be raised that high. 'Now,' he insisted. 'There's things I want t'get off me chest, and things you need t'know.'

'All right, Dad, take it easy.'

Slowly, and with long laborious pauses, Jim Bateman began to tell her how he had begun to get into black market deals in the first place. 'Things just snowballed – suppose I got greedy. My black tin box holds all the details you'll need t'know.' It was a simple truthful statement. His strength was running out, but after a lengthy pause he began to speak again, telling her the plain unvarnished facts. 'I've made more money than I dreamed possible, but you're to keep it, Annie. D'you 'ear me? I hurt no one, and that's the truth. I've wronged you, Annie – more than anyone, it's you I've hurt. Maybe the money will make up for it in some small way.'

He seemed to sense there was no time for niceties, but his mind didn't keep to the subject. He wandered, telling her how much he had loved her mother. For that reason he'd not married again. 'I adored my Lily. She was irreplaceable.' Then, after all those empty years he had met Dot Wilson. 'It wasn't love. Pure lust.' That last comment had been said with conviction. He had liked her kiddies. They'd reminded him of his own two. They were in need of a proper father. Their mother had gone off and left them. That was wrong. Very wrong.

Now there was such a long pause that Annie became frightened. He'd really tired himself out. With a great effort, his voice very low, he began again. 'Great man me! I decided to keep them. But I've put all the responsibility for them on to you. I made you take them on. Left you no choice. I know that now. Feel terribly guilty about it. Annie, you should 'ave the love and security of a good man. Instead, you've no life of yer own. All my fault, selfish . . .' He started to cough, a harsh racking cough, and blood appeared on his lips.

Annie watched in stunned silence as two nurses ushered her away and went one each side of his bed.

What was it he really wanted to tell her? Most of what he had said she knew already. She didn't understand the urgency. Did he have something else on his conscience? It had taken a quarter of an hour, no more, for him to say what he felt had to be said. Was there more? If there was, it would have to wait because he had drained himself to the point of exhaustion by talking so much.

Annie walked from the ward to get a breath of fresh air. No matter what her father had done, she had no complaints. He'd always been the best of parents to her and to David, the kindest and most loving and, even more important, fun-loving man. She even found herself smiling as she went towards the door; fun had always played a great part in their upbringing. When Jim Bateman was around, children and adults alike were happy. If they weren't, Jim would want to know the reason why and if at all possible he would put right whatever was worrying them. Laughter came freely to Lucky Jim Bateman. Well, it had up until now.

Mid-day, and Jack Higgins arrived, bringing Rhoda with him again.

'Aw, Annie, you looked washed out,' was the first comment her grandmother made as she took a seat on the other side of the bed from Annie. Then, leaning over the bed, she gazed long and hard at her son, who appeared to be sleeping peacefully. 'At least he's holding his own,' she declared, 'and he's got a much better colour.'

'He has indeed,' a voice of authority agreed, and she

looked up into the smiling face of a middle-aged doctor. The man standing beside her was tall with thinning blond hair and piercing blue eyes.

'I wish to examine the patient. Sister, will you please ask a nurse to accompany these relatives to the rest-room?'

'Certainly, Doctor,' the ward sister replied, indicating that they should follow her down the ward.

'But I've only just got 'ere.' Rhoda began to grumble, but was stopped in her tracks by a young ward orderly who was waiting outside the rest-room.

'I thought you might like a cup of coffee,' she said, using her hip to push open the door, then laying the tray she was carrying on a table before placing a steaming mug in front of Rhoda the minute she sat down. 'It's not bottled coffee. It's real, and freshly made!'

'Thanks, luv,' Rhoda said graciously. 'Ain't 'ad real coffee since before the war. Never did take to that bottled muck.'

The young woman tucked a stray piece of her hair back into the side of her green uniform cap, and smiled. 'Awful, isn't it? But I bet you'll enjoy this.'

'Really dreadful,' Rhoda agreed. She sipped the fresh coffee and murmured in appreciation.

Jack picked up a mug and handed it to Annie and, as he did so, he winked.

Leaning over, Annie whispered to him, 'The lass has done us a good turn. Gran's already in a happier frame of mind.'

He touched her lightly on the shoulder. 'I'm sorry I couldn't get here earlier this morning. I had an unloading job booked. Had t'be done. Can't clog up the Thames, or I'm in trouble. The police have been to see your gran again this morning. I am sorry I wasn't there.' He sighed.

'What a business! The police are acting like a dog with a bone, yet they won't say exactly what they're charging your father with.'

What a business indeed, she thought bitterly. At that moment Annie wondered why she had never taken to this man. Well, it wasn't so much that she hadn't taken to him, but she had never felt she could understand him. Surrounded by kind of a barrier, he was. Hard to get through to. He'd never given her any encouragement, so she'd never bothered to strike up a conversation, just treated him as Gran's lodger. Today he seemed different. More approachable. And he'd certainly gone out of his way to be helpful.

The silence in the rest-room was growing heavy. They had finished their coffee and were deep within their own thoughts. Annie had stared at blank walls long enough and now faced her gran. Smart today she was. Her best navy blue coat with the narrow trim of fur around the collar, her large-brimmed felt hat under which all her grey hair had been tucked out of sight, and the hat secured by two pearl-ended hat-pins. Sitting upright, her back as straight as a ramrod, she looked every inch a formidable lady. Though, as Annie knew well, she could be soft as butter, especially where little kiddies were concerned.

Annie now turned her attention to Jack Higgins. He was slumped in his chair, head resting back, his eyes closed. Poor Jack. He'd done all the running about yesterday, and had to have been up at the crack of dawn this morning. No wonder he looked dead beat. His long legs were stuck out in front of him and for the first time she wondered just how tall he was. Over six foot, for sure. He'd had his hair cut recently, she noticed. Dark like her father's, only it was short, brushed back at the sides. He had a clean-cut look about him. Annie was thinking that must come from being in the Navy.

Her day-dreaming was cut short as the door to the rest-room was thrust open and the doctor and the ward sister came in, both smiling. 'Good news, Mrs Bateman. Your son is holding his own. We are having him taken down to X-ray, and then there are a couple more tests we need to do. See just what is going on inside that chest of his. The fact that he has come this far is very rewarding.'

'Thank God!' Rhoda Bateman sounded as if she were praying. Then, remembering where she was, she got to her feet, hand extended, and was generous in her thanks and full of praise for all the staff who were caring for her son.

'So,' the Sister said sternly, 'you may have just ten minutes with him now and then no more visiting until tomorrow.'

It was Annie who murmured their thanks this time, and the three of them trooped out and back down to the ward. All the way trying to walk quietly, glancing around nervously, knowing the Sister was watching their every move.

'Bye, Dad, I . . .' Annie stammered, desperately trying to think of something good to say. 'I'll see you first thing in the morning.'

'Move over,' Rhoda ordered. 'We 'aven't got long.' She busied herself unpacking her shopping bag, putting clean pyjamas and toilet things into the locker at the side of Jim's bed. She said her good-byes, but Jim was drifting half-way into sleep and didn't respond. With a lump in her throat she allowed Jack to take her arm and lead her out of the ward.

*   *   *

Back home at last! Annie shivered as Jack pulled the front door key through the letterbox. All three of them were soaked to the skin. There hadn't been a taxi to be had and they'd come home on the bus.

'I've settled it all with Jack,' Rhoda announced, once they were in the kitchen. 'He's gonna stay on at my place, look after himself for a bit and I'll stay 'ere with you and the children. Is that all right with you, Annie?'

Annie heaved a sigh of relief. She'd been worried sick, seeing herself all on her own and the responsibility of Dot Wilson's two kiddies getting heavier by the day. 'Aw, thanks, Gran. That is good of you.'

'Yeah well, you get yourself upstairs and into yer bed. You've bin up all night, an' no one can keep going without sleep. No,' Rhoda almost shouted as Annie made to protest, 'no arguments. Upstairs and get yer clothes off. I'll bring you up a bit of dinner on a tray when it's ready.'

All Annie could do was smile her thanks, both at Rhoda and at Jack Higgins. She was too tired to find any words.

She had to drag her feet up the narrow stairs but, as she turned the handle of her bedroom door, tears began to sting sharply at the back of her eyelids. 'Oh, how lovely, how kind,' she murmured out loud. Gladys Dawson had lit a fire in the small grate. With the curtains drawn against the foul weather, she looked at the glowing coals and the reflections the flames were making on the darkened walls. It all looked so cosy. She stripped off every article of clothing she'd been wearing, letting it lie in a heap at her feet. Taking her nightdress from beneath the pillow, she pulled it over her head and crawled in between the blankets.

What was going to happen now? Would her dad be carted off to prison the moment he was well enough? Would she have to take full charge of Mary and Ronnie? And, if so, how would she manage? She snuggled her head into the pillow and closed her eyes. All that would have to wait. She was too sad and too weary even for tears.

Chapter Eight

ANNIE ARRIVED HOME FROM work carrying a Fuller's coffee and walnut cake and a bag of fruit. Flossie had been out specially to buy the cake, and the fruit was from the stall-holders in the market. Flossie had handed both over with the instructions that Annie and her gran were to be sure and have a piece each with a nice cup of tea before they set off for the hospital. 'Oh, and you can take your dad in a nice big slice, 'cos if he isn't able to eat it, you can bet your bottom dollar the nurses soon will!' Annie had thanked her and asked her to tell all the stall-holders how grateful she was.

Flossie and Sid were a lovely couple, and Sid's café was a good place to work. Old and tatty from the outside and in need of a lick of paint, it was cheerful and warm inside, and known as a good meeting-place. Flossie certainly had a big heart, and over the past three days since Annie had returned to work, she had been kindness itself. It was more than a week since Jim had been knocked down, and not a day that Sid Owen hadn't either run her to the hospital in his own car or paid for a taxi to take her there. The good news was that the doctors had pronounced Jim out of danger, though it would be some time yet before he could leave the hospital. Perhaps that was just as well. He was far better off where he was for the time being. The bad news was that the police hadn't given up. Their presence was always apparent outside Jim's ward, and there hadn't been a day that one or more constables hadn't called at the house.

One night on the way home from the hospital Jack Higgins had urged Annie not to worry so much. 'How can I help it, Jack?' she had quickly retorted. 'I know me dad was always doing deals, but surely none of it was that bad for him to have to go to prison? An' another thing that I can't get out of my mind is that when he was very bad, you know the first day or two after the accident, all he kept telling me was to keep the money. Said I deserved it and he hadn't hurt anyone to get it. What money is he talking about, and how much? I've looked in his tin box an' there's about fifty pounds – a goodly sum, I know, but I've a feeling he's talking big money. Though where it is and how much I haven't a clue.'

At that point Jack had lit a cigarette and thought carefully before he formed an answer. 'Look, Annie, me an' yer dad, well, we've always got on. Respected each other in many ways. When I first came home he would sit up half the night talking to me about my family, and it helped. Believe you me it did. I had no one else, and if yer gran hadn't let me a room God knows where I would have ended up. Since then, we've often talked about all sorts of things, and well . . . I know some of his dealings haven't always been kosher – you must know what I'm talking about? There's another thing; yer know he liked a bet, and the gee-gees were good to him. Lucky Jim Bateman, eh?'

After Jack had seen her safely indoors, Annie thought about what he'd said. Over the years she hadn't had a lot to do with Jim's business; neither had she ever queried where the extra money came from. She wasn't fool enough to believe he earned that much on the docks. Not from just his weekly wage packet, anyway! Oh well, as soon as he was up and about again there would be a whole lot of questions she'd have to put to her father; meanwhile she'd do as Jack had urged and try not to worry so much.

Annie slipped the key string through the letterbox and let herself in. Oh no! Loud male voices penetrated the passage. Sighing, she hung her coat on the hall rack and walked forward, forcing a smile on to her face as she entered the warmth of the kitchen.

Rhoda stood up painfully, as her legs had been playing her up for days. 'Hello, pet. Tired out, are you? With a bit of luck these officers are just going.'

'I'll make a pot of tea,' Gladys Dawson said, getting to her feet and heading for the scullery.

Annie turned to see one policeman in uniform and another older man dressed in a dark suit, whom she automatically took to be a plain-clothes officer, leaning against the dresser.

'Miss Bateman, I'm sorry about your father,' the older officer said quietly. 'We need to know if you can shed any light on what happened immediately before the accident.'

Annie shook her head.

'Why don't you tell her the truth?' Rhoda challenged with a steely note in her voice. 'You've already admitted you can't wait to get my son inside. You've been after him for a long while and now you think you've got him at last, you're determined to make him pay.'

The officer shook his head. 'Your son has had a good run, Mrs Bateman. Playing a hand close to his chest. Now he's overstepped the mark and, if you want my opinion, it was bound to happen. He's become too cocky for his own good.'

Annie was amazed at her grandmother's outburst. At the same time, she was shocked at the officer's comments and the truth of them. Smiling sadly, she realized there was no way they could go on pretending her father was innocent.

'Whatever he is, whatever he's done,' Rhoda said vehemently, 'he is still my son. There's a lot more good in him than you're giving him credit for. I swear to God I don't know what he's got himself involved in this time, but whatever it is it can't be that bad. Armed robbery and gangland fights are not in his league. No, I'm sorry, but you're chasing small fry, keeping coming here to pester us with questions. I've told you all we know and it's about time you accepted that fact, 'cos as God's my judge, it's the truth.'

Annie stared at Rhoda and felt her temper rising. This shouldn't be happening. Getting all worked up like this wasn't good for Gran. She was an old lady, and this last week was beginning to tell on her. 'I'm not standing for any more of this, officer. My grandmother has had enough to contend with over these past few days and she doesn't need you to keep calling here. Will you please leave now, and don't come back unless you have a very good reason to do so.'

The plain-clothes policeman looked straight at Annie.

'I can't promise this will be our last visit, but we will leave now. You're obviously tired and in need of your tea.'

Annie led the way to the front door without saying a word. She even walked out to the pavement, her body bristling with indignation and upset. She watched until the two men were out of sight and then she could no longer blink back the tears. They weren't tears of sadness, though, she admitted to herself. They were tears of anger. She loved her father. Even more, she adored him. And he adored her. She would do anything she possibly could to help him. Anything. So too would his mother. All the same, she said to herself, he should never have landed us in a fix as bad as this. She so badly wanted him to get better, yet what would happen when the time came for him to be discharged from the hospital?

All she could think of as she went back into the house was, please God the police wouldn't have enough evidence of his wrongdoing to send her father to prison. He would sort everything out if only he were allowed to come home. Back to her, Ronnie and little Mary. We all miss him. We all need him. Perhaps her brother David might even come home soon and then they really could start to be a complete and happy family again, just as they used to be. She badly needed to believe in the possibility that all that would come about.

'Come on down, you two,' Rhoda was calling from the foot of the stairs. 'The policemen have gone an' I'm just about ready to dish up yer tea.'

As the children came running into the kitchen, Mary, looking at Gran, said, 'I'm ever so hungry.'

'Course ye are, pet. Sit up at the table, chips won't be long, you can start on some beans with a slice of bread and butter. How does that sound?'

'That'll be nice. I like baked beans.'

'So do I,' Ronnie piped up.

'Tell us something you don't like, young man!' Gladys Dawson pushed playfully at Ronnie's shoulder, and chuckling, added, 'I'd rather keep you a week than a fortnight – you'd eat me out of house an' home.' She picked up her coat. 'I'll 'ave t'be going, but I'll look in in the morning t'see if these two 'ave got off t'school all right.'

'Won't you stay for a bit of tea and have a chat with Annie here?'

'I can't, Rhoda . . . You see . . .' She glanced towards the scullery where Annie was keeping an eye on the chip pan, then muttered under her breath, 'I've got to be in the pub by seven. Bill Weaver is gonna sell me some clothing coupons. I badly need underwear and winter shoes,' she stated, sounding a little uneasy. 'He said t'be in the snug before it got too busy.'

'Aw, I see, Gladys, I understand, I do, course I do.' Rhoda flapped her hand. 'We've all got t'get by as best we can.'

'It's me shoes, mainly. I'm sick of all this rain, always getting me feet wet an' the cobbler said these boots ain't worth repairing.'

'Get on with yer.' Rhoda smiled, giving her a push towards the passage. 'You're being wise. I've never known weather like this, an' let's face it, the few clothing coupons the government are still dishing out don't go nowhere. We all dabble in the black market from time to time.'

She looked at the children who were tucking into their beans, and nodded her head, indicating that they should say good-bye. They each put down their knife and fork and Gladys laughed loudly amid cries of, 'Bye, Auntie Gladys,' from Ronnie and a shy, 'Thank you for coming to meet me from school,' from Mary. She pushed her way past Annie as she came bustling back into the living-room bearing a huge dish of golden chips.

Rhoda came back from seeing Gladys off the premises and both she and Annie sat down to have their tea with the children. 'Chips are Uncle Jim's favourite,' Mary said, shaking vinegar over her plateful. 'Is he going to get better an' come home to us?'

She had such a sad look on her face that Annie wanted to sweep her into her arms. 'Course he is,' she whispered.

Ronnie was in fine fettle. 'What did the police want t'see you again this time for, Gran?' he asked quickly.

'Nothing that you have to worry yer head about.' Rhoda was still finding it hard not to smile at his inquisitive questions.

'I was only asking, 'cos some big-mouth at school made it his business t'tell me that Lucky Jim Bateman was gonna go inside this time.' Ronnie sounded quite matter of fact as he reached for another slice of bread. 'I didn't wanna argue wiv him, so I let it go.'

'You were a good boy not to argue the toss,' Rhoda told him, and this time she did smile. 'Next time the lad comes out with a statement like that you can tell him, from me, not to bank on it. You just eat up and remember that ever since my son brought you an' your sister here to live with Annie, he's watched out for both of you in more ways than one. Same goes for me and Annie. We never want and we never starve! Not while my son is around. He might sail a bit near the wind now an' again, but that's his business.'

Hardly had Rhoda spoken when there came a knock on the front door. 'Not again! Not at this time of night.'

Rhoda slanted her eyes towards Annie, who hurriedly got to her feet, saying, 'I'll go.'

'Now if it's more police, act natural like,' Rhoda shouted after her. She was getting to her feet when Annie's voice from the hall checked her.

'Oh, it's you, Mr Hart. Come in, come in, you're soaked to the skin. Here, take yer coat off – let me have it.' Taking the heavy overcoat, Annie shook it gently before hanging it on one of the pegs in the hall.

'Go through. Me gran will be pleased to see you.' Annie was thinking to herself that Tommy Hart was a kind jolly man with eyes that always seemed to twinkle at you. He was their butcher, the one they were registered with, and although they had four ration books, including those of Ronnie and Mary, what they were officially allowed to buy wasn't very much each week. About one-and-tenpence-worth per person. Less than two shillings, and not all could be taken in fresh meat; part had to be corned beef.

Rhoda was standing with her back to the fire, a broad smile lighting up her face. 'Good of you t'call round, Tom, especially on a night like this. And what 'ave yer got there?' she queried as he laid a large parcel, well wrapped in newspaper, on the corner of the table.

'I really came to get first-hand news of how Jim is doing. Couldn't come empty-handed, could I? It's some nice shin of beef, a few pork chops an' a couple of pounds of me best sausages. Ought to see yer through a few days, eh?' He dusted the front of his jacket down, smiled at Annie, and asked, 'Could you bring a meat dish? I don't want yer gran telling me off 'cos the blood 'as stained her tablecloth.'

As Annie passed him, he turned to the two children still

seated at the table. 'You're quiet tonight, the pair of you. Not even a peep out of you, Ronnie? That's unusual.'

Ronnie wasn't daft. He knew what the parcel would mean. Gran was a great cook at all times, but with what the butcher had bought, his mouth was watering at the very thought. So in an attempt at jocularity, he said, 'We're always being told, kids should be seen but not 'eard, an' it's difficult t'get a word in when you adults get going.' There was loud laughter at this statement.

'You sure you can spare us all this?' Rhoda asked as Annie unwrapped the parcel and set the meat out on a dish.

'Course I can. Swings and roundabouts, don't you know. Jim's helped me out on more than one occasion. Must say I was glad to hear that he's been taken off the danger list.'

'I'm very grateful,' Rhoda murmured, reaching up for her purse which she always kept behind the photograph of her dead husband on the corner of the mantelshelf. 'How much do I owe you, Tom?'

'Put it away.' Tommy Hart's head was up, his lower lip thrust out. 'I'm not going to argue with you, Rhoda. If I can't do you a favour at a time when your Jim is laid low, it's a pretty poor deal. Did you ever see me an' me missus go short of a bit of sugar an' tea?'

'The circumstances were a bit different then, Tom. We were in a war, and that made fiddling almost a virtue every day of the week. It was the only way most of us managed to survive.'

'Aw, get along with you! England being at war kind of made fiddling legal, eh?' He threw back his head and let out a great belly laugh. 'I've a few more calls to make, so I best get going. Don't forget t'tell Jim I was asking after him. Indeed, make that *we*, for there ain't a customer comes into me shop that doesn't want t'know how Jim Bateman is. And that's how it should be.' Tommy paused, and turned his gaze to Annie. 'Never mind what the cops have t'say, lass, your dad's a good 'un and there's half the East End and more will testify to that. Chin up, Annie, yer dad will be home before long, you'll see.'

'I'll get yer coat for you, Mr Hart,' Ronnie declared, slipping from his chair and diving out into the passage. Cor, the lad was thinking to himself, I'm ever so glad Mr Hart came here tonight. All those bangers! Him and Mary loved the way Gran did bangers and mash. Pity was that Jim had been knocked down by a bus. Everyone was being ever so kind, but that didn't really help matters. Flipping police worrying Gran, and Annie always looking so sad. I wish someone could turn the clock back, he thought to himself as he watched Mr Hart give him a cheery wave. All the gifts and concern couldn't make up for Jim not being around. Ain't many good blokes like Jim. Well, if there are, me and me sister never came across one before. Ronnie wiped a hand over his face. 'Jim's gotta get well, God. There ain't anyone else to look after me an' Mary,' he whispered, raising his eyes to the ceiling. 'I know I don't often say me prayers but . . . well . . . I'm asking for me sister as well as me. Jim's our only hope, that's what bovvers me.' Ronnie was still pondering as to whether he'd done right to pray when he came slowly back into the kitchen.

'Mug of tea and a hunk of bread pudding there for you, Ronnie, if you can find room for it,' Rhoda told him.

Ronnie had to blink once or twice. Not that he was going to cry. Big boys never cried. As far back as he could remember, no one had ever treated him and his sister so kindly or looked after them so well. The Batemans treat us as if we really are part of their family, he said to himself as he climbed back up to sit at the table. As Annie pushed a plate of steaming hot fruity pudding towards him, he made a wish. With all his heart he wished that he and his sister could be part of Gran's family for the rest of their lives.

Chapter Nine

IT WAS A PARTICULARLY lovely spring-like day. After a brief shower the sky had cleared and patches of clear blue were showing and the only clouds to be seen were puffy white cotton-wool ones. Annie got off the bus only a few yards from the Royal London Hospital and, as she walked, the sunshine, weak though it was, did a great deal to lift her spirits. Her father was well on the road to recovery, now able to sit out in an armchair whenever they came to visit him. She had taken a great deal of trouble with her appearance today. Her hair was freshly washed, brushed until it shone and coiled up into a neat bunch of curls at the nape of her neck with only a few inches left to hang down over her shoulders. She was wearing a tan jumper under a cream wool suit that, set against the darkness of her hair, emphasized her complexion and those big brown eyes. She knew that looking so well-turned-out would please her father.

The staff nurse came down the corridor to meet Annie,

and in a hushed voice, said, 'I'm so glad you've managed to get here. Your father's been asking for you.'

'What's up?' she asked quickly as she tried to read the nurse's face, but wasn't able to. She was holding open the door to a side ward, her young features carefully held in check, revealing only concern.

'Your father's had a heart attack,' the nurse explained.

An orderly came out from the kitchen wheeling a laden trolley. The cups and saucers rattled as the maid did her best to steer it straight. Seeing Annie and the look of terror on her face, she paused, about to offer her a cup of tea, but the staff nurse waved her on and guided Annie into the single-bedded side ward.

Annie was having trouble breathing as she approached the bed, afraid of what she was going to see and what was going to happen now. The very thought that her father had taken a turn for the worse and might die made her throat ache and her eyes sting with tears. The idea of losing the one person who had always taken care of her, who had loved her without any reservations, was more than she could bear. 'How is he now?' she asked as she stood looking down at her father.

'I'll ring for Dr Winter. He'll be able to explain, but it may be a while before he gets here as he's on duty at the moment. So, take this chair. I'll pull it up to the bed and you can sit with your father,' the nurse said briskly but sympathetically.

Annie did as she was bid. The nearer she bent to look into her father's face, the worse she felt. He had been doing so well. He'd been well on the road to recovery, or so they had been led to believe. The sight of his sunken cheeks and lips that had a blue tinge was too much, and a tear spilled over and ran down her cheek. She angrily brushed it away, and feeling for her father's hand, she gently began to massage the back of it with her thumbs.

If only she could put new life back into him, bring colour to his cheeks! He was too young to be so ill and certainly too young to die. She didn't want to believe that he might die. She wouldn't believe it! She wouldn't let such a dreadful thing happen. It was too awful to even think about. 'Dad, it's me, Annie. I'm here now, and I'm going to stay here until you feel better.'

As if drawn from somewhere distant by the sound of Annie's voice, her father's eyes opened. She forced herself to smile at him. His eyes remained vague, unfocused for a minute or two, then they fixed on her, and he too smiled. Finding a burst of energy, he clutched at her hands that still had hold of his.

'Oh, Dad!' Annie's voice sounded strained but her smile became less forced. 'Whatever have you been up to?' Without waiting for an answer, she pressed on. 'You're gonna be fine, Dad. You always do go at things like a bull in a china shop. You've just got to realize that you've been very ill and take things easy for a bit. Not be so stubborn.'

'Annie, listen . . . you must listen an' take in what I'm telling you.'

She leant over the bed and smoothed his thick dark hair back from his forehead. The wide brown eyes that were always laughing, especially when he was doing deals, now looked deep into her own and she felt the sadness flow from him. 'If only,' he began, his voice so weak he didn't sound a bit like her jovial father. 'Annie, are you listening?'

'Yes, Dad, but you should save your strength, not talk, not now.'

'I want to make sure you understand. Remember what I said to you the other day about money?'

'Yes, of course I remember, but it doesn't matter.'

'That's just the point.' He paused and drew in a gulp of air. 'It does matter. It means that you'll have no worries. Wherever I am I'll know that I've done me best for you. Me will's at the solicitors; he's been in to see me and it's all signed and sealed. His address is in me tin box.'

'I wish I knew what you're talking about. You could sort all these matters out when you come home. Please, Dad, you must rest.'

'You'll find out,' her father said, gasping again for air. 'Just remember I love you. What you do about David and about Dot's two children will be up to you, but I like to think . . .'

'Dad, we're doing our best to find David, and as far as Mary and Ronnie are concerned, well, you know me better than to think I wouldn't look after them. And those kids are the apple of Gran's eye, though she wouldn't come out straight and admit as much.'

There was to be no more talking. Dr Winter stepped into the doorway, paused, then beckoned Annie to follow him. Outside in the corridor, he told her, 'I'm very sorry. We weren't expecting this to happen, but your father has had a massive heart attack.' Annie couldn't speak. Couldn't find any suitable words. 'I don't think he'll last the day, so, if you'd like to stay with him . . . I'll send the nurse in now.'

In the few minutes that Annie had been out of the room it seemed as though her father had deteriorated rapidly. It was as if, having seen Annie and said what he had to say, he had given up. She sat with her hand on her father's arm for the rest of the afternoon. Jack Higgins came, bringing

Rhoda with him, and although her gran said her tearful good-byes, she got no response. Jim never spoke again, but at a quarter to six he breathed what sounded like a contented sigh, and all at once Annie was afraid and pulled back her hand. She forced herself to look at what she now knew was his lifeless face.

Dr Winter, the staff nurse and two other nurses came crowding round the bed. The youngest of the nurses gripped Annie's arm and propelled her from the room. In no time at all the doctor was saying to her, 'Please accept my condolences.'

Annie didn't need to be told that her father was dead. She walked away, very slowly. At the end of the corridor Jack Higgins was waiting, hands jammed into his pockets, head downcast. 'Thank you, Jack, for being here. I'd like to go home now,' she told him, barely able to stand up, but doing her best to keep a lid on her emotions. Time enough to cry and to think about her dad when she was alone in her own bedroom.

'Come on, then, let's go. I'll ask them at the desk to phone for a taxi. You have to get some rest, because tomorrow there'll be arrangements to make ... You know, the funeral, and so forth. I'll help you with that, if you like,' he offered.

'That is very kind of you. I wouldn't know where to begin, and we can't ask gran to bear all that burden, can we?'

'We'll get it sorted. And, Annie, I'm really sorry about yer dad.'

His sympathy was too much. She burst into tears. He put out his arms, and Annie gave a deep groan as she thankfully let him hold on to her.

Jack stared grim-faced over her shoulder at the busy

reception desk, caught the eye of one young lady and quietly asked her to phone for a taxi. He felt he knew a little of the sadness Annie was feeling at this moment. Nearly eight years ago his own family had been wiped out by a German bomb, and still he had no one to call his own, no proper home and no roots. He said, 'Annie, you've got your gran, and David will turn up soon, you'll see. You must try and be strong. There's still Mary and Ronnie to think about.'

'I know. I know. That's what makes it worse,' Annie sobbed. 'All that responsibility. What will I do, Jack?'

Jack took a deep breath. 'You'll manage, Annie. Take things a day at a time. Let the dust settle before you make any decisions.'

Annie pulled away from him, searched in her handbag for a handkerchief, wiped her eyes and blew her nose.

All the time, Jack was watching her. He was, he knew it, half in love with her. She had the dark good looks of the Bateman family combined with her grandmother's strength of character. He had no doubt she would, with a little help, be able to cope with her father's death and all the responsibilities he had left behind. He would dearly love to offer to take care of her for the rest of her life, but what had he to offer her? He had a good job on the river. The life suited him, and he loved the Thames. But again his mind turned to reality. He had no home, no roots, no family. Absolutely nothing! No family photographs, no family bible that would have recorded the dates of his family's lives – the day they were born, the day they were wed and when and how they had all died. Everything had been destroyed. Everything. All he had was pictures in his head. That was what the war had done to him. Others had fared just as badly, and some much worse, he chided himself.

He had been serving in one of the ships that had brought the prisoners of war home from Singapore. He shuddered at the memory of the dreadful time those men had endured in the prison camps. They had looked ghastly – just skin and bone because of the rotten, inadequate food. Many of the men had infected sores, and the stench of gangrene was something he would never forget. He never talked about that time, not willingly. He swallowed hard. Annie had a great deal still going for her, and though at times he thought her very young for her age, there had been times when she had surprised him. Certainly she had been doted on by her father and would be bound to miss him. He hoped against hope that now she would be able to deal with whatever the future was likely to hold. He could only watch and wait, and hope it would include a lot of happiness.

Annie broke into his thoughts, murmuring more to herself than to him. 'It's just not fair! My dad was getting better. Why did he have to die? It's not right.'

'I know, I know.' Jack hugged her close, rubbing her back. 'Come on,' he said for the second time, 'let's get you home.'

Annie's jacket was slung round her shoulders, and Jack imagined she had probably worn her school blazer in exactly the same way. Her mop of unruly hair was now really untidy, her eyes sad and lost. He put an arm round her shoulders and led her to the front entrance of the hospital, all the while quietly assuring her that everything would be all right. He handed her into the back of the waiting taxi, and in return she gave him a small smile and a murmured 'Thank you'.

As he settled on the seat beside her, his emotions were getting the better of him. He would have loved to take her in his arms and kiss her. Not just on the cheek, but properly. He heard his own voice saying, 'We'll soon be home.' The eternal comforter, that's me, he told himself ruefully. Then another thought hit him. If you want this lovely lass, you had better develop the ability to wait, because a lot of water will flow beneath the bridge before Annie comes to think of you in those terms. That's if she ever does!

Annie gave a deep sigh and reached out to take hold of his hand, saying, 'I'm so glad you were there, Jack.'

Jack smiled sadly. 'I'll always be around. Anything I can do you only have to ask. You know that.' He managed to look away from her tear-stained face. The amazing thing was that he'd managed to keep his voice sounding completely normal when his heart was beating so fast.

Chapter Ten

'DID YOU GET ANY sleep, Annie?' Rhoda asked as she came into the bedroom carrying a mug of tea.

'A few hours, Gran. How about you?'

'Much the same, I guess.' Keeping her voice low, she handed Annie an official-looking letter that was franked on the outside with the name and address of a firm of solicitors. 'This came for you.'

Annie glanced at the letter, then at her gran. 'I suppose this is to do with what me dad kept trying to tell me about?'

'Maybe, but you won't know until you read it.'

Annie slit the envelope with her thumbnail, then withdrew the one folded sheet. She read the letter once, then once more. She passed it over to Rhoda, saying, 'I don't know what we're going to do. According to this, I have to get in touch with this firm as soon as the funeral arrangements have been taken care of.'

'Leave it for now,' said Rhoda as she folded the letter carefully back into the envelope and returned it to Annie.

'Hell of a mess! Don't know why yer father had to have dealings with lawyers an' suchlike. Never had no truck with them before. Well, not to my knowledge he didn't.'

Annie drained the rest of her tea, put the mug down on her bedside table and clenched her fists. Then, leaning back against her pillows, she looked hard at her grandmother and chewed on her bottom lip. Finally she took hold of Rhoda's hand and began muttering more to herself than to her gran. 'I can't believe the stuff we've found in that damn tin box, not to mention the cash,' she fumed, both hands clenched tightly around Rhoda's wrist. 'To top it all, I've still got to keep that appointment with that police officer. Wonder what he wants now. He'll fire dozens of questions at me, I know he will. How will I be able to answer them all?'

'Take it one day at a time, pet. What you don't know you can't tell the police, and they can't shoot you for holding yer tongue!'

'I know, but I just wish it wasn't left to me to sort it all out.'

'Yeah, it don't seem fair. It's a pity yer dad didn't open up a bit more to yer – then we might have some idea as to what we're heading into.' Rhoda drew her back up straight and gave Annie a wry grin. 'Your father certainly had his fingers in a number of pies, and I wouldn't mind betting that the deeper we delve the more trouble we're gonna find. Still, as I've said, we've the funeral to get through first. Time enough to unravel all of this when we've laid him to rest.' With a heavy sigh, she got up off the bed before saying, 'I'll start seeing to the breakfast. We've all got to eat, and then there's Ronnie and Mary,' she reminded Annie. 'Someone has t'see that they get to school on time.' She gave Annie's shoulder a reassuring squeeze. 'Come on now! Get yerself washed and dressed an' come an' have a good breakfast. You're going to need all your strength.'

At the doorway she stopped and looked back, and stared silently for some moments at her grand-daughter's white face and those sad eyes. My poor Annie! It doesn't seem any time since she was at school. She's only just coming up to nineteen. So much she's had to bear, and there's no telling where it's all leading to. Rhoda had to turn away, overcome with emotion.

If it weren't that the air was filled with sadness, it was a beautiful day. A strong sun did its best to brighten the morning and add colour to the mass of floral wreaths decorating the pavement outside the Batemans' terraced house. Annie watched from the upstairs bedroom window as the hearse drew up. This had been her parents' bedroom. She had been born in this room. Her mother had been dead a long time and now her father was also dead too. She had lain awake half the night feeling utterly lost. She would give anything to have her parents back, but death was so final, so irreversible. She took a brief glance at her reflection in the mirror, then said aloud, 'All the wishing in the world won't alter the facts.'

Neighbours' blinds were drawn, women stood in clusters, heads bowed. Men doffed their caps. 'Time to go,' Rhoda called from the foot of the stairs.

Annie ran her hands down over the simple long-sleeved black dress that Doris Simmonds had helped her buy. Checking in the mirror, she placed the small straw hat on her head and pulled the veil down over her face, glad that it helped to cover the fiery hues of her long thick hair.

Her shoes looked right. Plain low-heeled court shoes. Not at all what Doris had wanted her to buy.

'How you doing?' Rhoda asked from the doorway. 'They're waiting for us.'

For one awful moment, Annie felt she was going to burst into tears, but swallowed hard. 'Gran, you've been wonderful! I just couldn't have managed without you. Thanks.'

Rhoda gave her a brief glance, wishing there was a whole lot more she could have done. 'We'd better go down. Come on, pet.'

The church was packed. Street traders, dockers, riverboat men and women of all ages had come to take their last farewell of a man who was well liked and respected. The deals he did had been regarded as fair, and it was generally agreed that Lucky Jim Bateman had been a man to be trusted.

'God bless him. He was a real good bloke, one of the best,' seemed to be the general verdict.

Annie sat at the front of the church, willing herself to remember only the good times and that her dad had always tried to do his best for everyone. She didn't pay much attention to the service because she was fighting to keep herself from crying like a child. A child that didn't want to lose her dad.

Afterwards in the churchyard, when the final prayers had been said and the coffin lowered into the ground, there were no words to describe her sadness. The undertaker's men were bringing out the wreaths, and as she looked across in their direction Annie noticed a lone figure standing by the porch. The man looked very familiar.

At that moment, Rhoda touched her arm. People were beginning to approach now for a word or two of murmured sympathy, and she gave them her attention: thanked them for coming to her father's funeral, shook hands, accepted their commiserations, all the while doing her best to hold back the tears. It was some time before she managed to look again at the figure by the porch. Yes, he was still there, hanging back in the shadows, a young man with thick dark curly hair and broad shoulders that were noticeable even though he wore a long dark overcoat.

Annie's heart leapt. She recognized him now. It was David! Her brother.

Nodding at Gladys Dawson to keep an eye on Rhoda, Annie left the graveside to go down the path, excusing herself to those nearby. Throwing back her veil, she quickened her footsteps until she drew within a foot of this tall elder brother of hers. Her heart pounded. For a moment her head spun. Some seconds passed before she was able to say, 'Hello, David.'

He said simply, 'Hello, Annie.'

She tilted her head back to look at him. He had not changed, only grown even taller. His hair was as black and curly as ever, his eyes as dark. He smiled lopsidedly and held out his arms. Without a word, Annie went into them and as she felt them round her, she laid her head on his chest and began to cry very quietly, very gently. For several minutes they stood still, he holding her close, hugging her tightly. When at last he released her, she sniffed, took the large white handkerchief he offered and rubbed at her eyes. 'Oh, David, David!' she wailed. 'Where have you been?'

David had concocted his cover story and stuck to it doggedly. He had made a life for himself. A good life. More than that he wasn't able to tell her at present.

'Why ever not?' Annie demanded to know. 'Aren't you

coming back to the house? Gran will be so upset if she finds out you've been here and she hasn't set eyes on you. Are you in trouble? Do you need money?'

'That's enough, Annie,' David told her, cool as could be. 'I can't tell you about myself, not at the moment. Sufficient for you to know that I am happy and quite prosperous. I do keep tabs on you, as how else would I be here today? I know you won't want for anything – Dad has seen to that – but remember, Annie, I love you. I always will.'

'Oh, David!' Annie's words came out on a sob.

'I know, luv! I know.' Again he put his arms round her.

She buried her face in his shoulder. 'The two children are still with us,' she told him. 'What shall I do?'

'You've got Gran. You'll manage, love,' he said. 'You'll manage.' He knew these words were inadequate, but what words wouldn't be?

'There's something else, David.'

'What is it, luv?'

'Dad's affairs are in such a mess! You wouldn't believe what he had stuffed away in his tin box and, to make matters worse, I've had a letter telling me to make an appointment with his solicitor.'

David wasn't sure how to reply. They looked at each other, each searching for a way to express emotions too bewildering and too deep to put into words.

'Did you know he was in trouble with the police?' Annie blurted out.

'You mustn't hold that against him,' David said gently. 'Even if things do seem a bit of a puzzle at the moment, you mustn't ever do that. Go to the solicitors and to the bank. Ask to see the manager.'

'I have to report to the police station again,' Annie said wearily. 'I dread all their questions because I honestly don't have the answers.'

'You will have,' David assured her. 'You'll get it all sorted. Just remember that Dad was into some shady deals, but a villain he was not. Anyway, the police can't touch him now and there's nothing they can hold you responsible for. Just don't let on about any papers or cash that you find and you'll be all right, I promise. Look out for yourself and the kids if you can. You're a fighter, like I am, like our dad was. All the Batemans have been fighters, you ask Gran! So, come on, give us a smile because I have to be on my way. But, before I go, will you promise to go and see that firm of solicitors and pay a visit to the bank?'

'Yes, I will,' Annie said, after a pause.

Her only brother, and he was leaving again. Was there never to be a lasting relationship in her life? Once more he held her to him, kissed her on both cheeks, then heaving a heavy sigh he let her go.

Annie rubbed her eyes and watched him walk away along the path towards the lich-gate. The sight almost broke her heart. He was a young sprightly version of their father, and he'd promised to keep in touch. Would he? As long as she lived she would think of David with regret. Where was he going? Why had he not been back before? David was by now out of sight. There was no one to give her any answers.

On the morning of the funeral, Annie had let Ronnie and Mary stay in bed until the coffin had left the house. Doris Simmonds had volunteered to stay behind to see to the children and with the help of two more neighbours have food and hot drinks ready for the mourners when they returned from the cemetery. Rhoda had agreed that Ron and Mary needn't go to school today. When they were up and eating their porridge, Ronnie asked Doris if she knew what would happen to him and his sister now that there wasn't any Uncle Jim to take care of them.

Doris let out a deep breath. Poor little mites! The things that must have been going through their little minds. When she was slow in forming an answer, Ronnie said to his sad little sister, 'See, even Mrs Simmonds doesn't know. I betcher we won't be able to stay 'ere. Annie will more than likely go an' live with 'er gran. Mind, it ain't her fault. She 'as to go to work and can't stay 'ome just t'look after us.'

Tears welled up in Mary's eyes. 'A girl at school said I would be put in an orphanage, but I told 'er I ain't no orphan 'cos I got a mum.'

'Don't cry, Sis,' said Ronnie, laying his spoon down and putting an arm round her. 'We just got t'wait an' see before we decide what we're gonna do.'

A little dry cough from Mary became a sob, and it tore at Doris's heart the way the child stared at her brother. 'I don't care much what 'appens, as long as they don't send me somewhere different from you.'

Doris could feel the tears prick at the back of her eyes. She couldn't stand any more. Clearing a place at the table, she sat down between the two children. 'First things first,' she said. 'Eat your porridge up, Mary, then I'm going to help you to have a good wash. I'll comb your hair, tie a nice ribbon in it and by the time Gran and Annie get back I want to see the pair of you not only shining like dollars but with a smile on your faces as well. All right?'

'I s'pose so,' answered Ronnie.

'How about you, Mary?'

Mary got down from the table, tugged at her frock and darted an uncertain glance at Doris. 'I just want someone t'tell me that I won't 'ave t'go to another foster family without me brother.'

'Oh, come on, yer daft ha'porth,' said Ronnie sternly. 'I've told yer we must wait an' see.'

'Mary, love,' said Doris kindly, 'I don't for one moment think Annie or yer gran will be sending you away, but I promise you this, as soon as I can get Annie on her own, I'll ask her. Get her to tell you the truth. Let you both know where you stand. How does that sound?'

'Thank you,' muttered Mary. 'That's just it, though. She ain't our gran. I wish she were.' Then, after pondering for a moment, she blurted out, 'If they can't keep me an' Ronnie, could we come an' live with you, please, Mrs Simmonds? We wouldn't be no trouble.'

In spite of the lump in her throat, a smile flickered across Doris's face as she leapt to her feet, almost sending the kitchen chair flying. 'That's a promise, me darling,' she yelled, scooping Mary up into her arms. 'Before I see any social workers or even council officials try and split up the pair of you, I'll go t'court an' claim yer both for me own! It won't come to that; I know it won't. But from this very minute I am going to make sure you know I'll always do me best to help take care of you.' She tickled Mary under one arm and was rewarded by a slight grin. Turning to Ronnie, she asked, 'Is that OK by you? Because, if it is, from now on will the pair of you please do me a favour and start calling me Auntie Doris.'

Ronnie smiled. 'Fanks, Auntie Doris. You're a swell!'

'And you, Mary?'

'All right then, but how do we know you won't go away?' Mary's eyes looked very doubtful.

''Cos I promise to give you a lot of notice if that should ever happen,' Doris told them, fingers crossed behind her back. 'Will that do?'

'Yeah, all right then,' Mary said for the second time.

Doris gave a sigh of relief, set Mary back on her chair, told her to finish her breakfast and went to the scullery to help put the finishing touches to the food. Her mind was in a whirl. Unusually for her, she sent up a silent prayer: Please, God, don't ever let me fail those two kids.

Ronald Wilson was coming up to ten years old. It could be said that he had a wise old head on his young shoulders. He watched as Doris Simmonds went out to the scullery, closing the door behind her. He was grateful to her. Very grateful. Any person that could pacify his little sister, stop her from crying and help her through these awful days when every adult they came into contact with wore a sad and worried expression, he felt beholden to. Having admitted that much, he wasn't daft. Their new-found Auntie Doris was a lovely lady. Good with kids, he had to give her that. He hoped with all his heart that Mary had believed her. For the moment the poor kid had to have someone she could believe in. Mary was only six. Not for the first time the bottom had once again fallen out of her world when Jim Bateman had failed to come home.

I'm different, he said firmly to himself. Old enough to know that Doris wasn't deliberately telling lies, but neither was she telling Mary the truth. 'I promise to give you a lot of notice if ever I have to go away and leave you.' That's what she'd said. And God bless her for it. But what if, like their Uncle Jim, she didn't get any warning?

His heart sank as he watched his sister scrape up the

remains of her porridge from the bowl. Let's hope we never find out the answer to that one. If only he were older. But he wasn't. Both he and Mary needed the protection of at least one grown-up, but he still wasn't sure they would get it.

The house was quiet at last. The neighbours had all gone home, Rhoda had gone upstairs to have a lie down and Doris and Annie were in the scullery washing the plates and glasses. Doris had seized her opportunity and related, almost word for word, the conversation she had earlier had with the children.

'Honest, Annie, it would make yer heart bleed, the way that little mite kept looking at me.'

'Strewth!' Annie cried. 'I never gave it a thought! I took it for granted that they would know we wouldn't turn them out. How could I have been so bloody thoughtless?'

'For Christ's sake don't start blaming yerself,' Doris protested. 'You've had enough on your plate these past few weeks. Just take the kids on one side and reassure them. Ronnie's not so bad, yet even he has the idea that they'll be back with foster parents. It's Mary that troubles me. Kids can be so cruel. Some kid at school told her she would likely be carted off to an orphanage. Can you believe it?'

'I'll be up at that school tomorrow,' Annie said sharply. 'If I start to take her and fetch her on a regular basis, maybe the other children will realize that both the kiddies are part an' parcel of our family.'

'Does that include me?' Doris asked, giving Annie a cheeky grin.

'I reckon you've well established yourself; if I haven't

told you before, I'm telling you now, I'm grateful. Really I am, you've been a brick.'

'Just as well then, 'cos I've turned meself into a relation. From now on the kids are calling me "Auntie Doris", and I've told them, whenever you can't be around, I'll make a good stand-in. If that's all right by you? I will do what I can, 'cos I like those kiddies and that's the honest truth.'

'You set a lot of store on being honest, don't you?' Annie said.

'I suppose I do,' Doris agreed. 'Anyway, I know what it feels like to be left on your own, and it seems to me that Ronnie and Mary, in their short life, have been pushed from pillar to post. If in some small way I can help to put a bit of stability there for them, so be it. I'll do me best.'

'I'm sure you will,' said Annie quietly. Today she was seeing a different side to Doris. Outwardly she was a bit flashy, often boisterous, seemingly bent on having a good time. Now, each of them having let their hair down and exchanged confidences, it would appear that what she had always suspected was true: beneath that showy front Doris had a big heart.

Ronnie and Mary both sat up straight and eyed Annie in disbelief. The boy was the first to grasp what he had been told. 'Cor, Annie, do yer mean it? Honestly mean it? It'll be 'ard for you, won't it? Trying to go to work, keep this house going and look after us two.'

'Oh, we're all of us luckier than you think,' said Annie. 'We've got Gran, and Auntie Doris, not to mention Mrs Dawson and a good many more very helpful neighbours. There is always Mr Higgins we can rely on to do any heavy jobs for us. I think we'll manage very well.'

'I like Auntie Doris,' said Mary with a surprisingly happy smile.

'Are you really going to see people down at the Town 'All and get it registered that we live 'ere?' It was a searching question from Ronnie – one that Annie knew she had to reply to with the truth.

'I most certainly am. For better or for worse, you and Mary are completely part of this family for as long as you decide that is what you want. Do you understand, and, more to the point, do you believe me?'

Ronnie breathed out and visibly relaxed. 'I guess I always knew you wouldn't chuck us out, but it's nice to 'ear you say so straight out. Fanks, Annie.'

'My pleasure.' Annie beamed at him.

'I like living 'ere and I like you, Annie, even more than I do Auntie Doris, and I love Gran, but . . .' There was silence while Mary put her thumb into her mouth and sucked noisily.

After a suitable time, Annie enquired, 'But what, Mary?'

She took time to answer. 'What about when me mum comes back?' Her little head drooped and her eyes were suddenly full of tears.

Annie knew instinctively that she had to be very careful how she answered this one. Taking a deep breath, she began, 'The day your mum knocks on our front door, we'll have a party. I'll make the tea and a jug of lemonade and we'll send Ronnie up to the bakers to buy a whole box full of cream cakes. We'll give her such a welcome she will know how much we've all missed her.'

Mary turned to Annie, 'Will you give Ronnie the money for the cakes?'

Annie couldn't help herself, and laughed. 'You bet I

will! And if he doesn't run all the way there and all the way back, we'll box his ears, shall we?'

Mary considered, but only for a moment before touching her brother's arm and saying, 'But you would run, wouldn't you, Ronnie?'

'Oh, don't be so daft! Yer know I would, and I bet I'd be back before our mum 'ad taken her coat off!'

'That's all right then,' said Mary grudgingly.

'So,' said Annie, 'now we've sorted everything to everyone's satisfaction, we had better start to get the evening meal ready.'

'Who's we?' Ronnie asked.

'All of us,' said Annie. 'In this family everyone is equal and everyone helps.'

As they made their way downstairs, Annie and Mary were grinning while Ronnie was muttering to himself, 'I knew there had to be a catch in it somewhere.'

Chapter Eleven

THE WEEKS FOLLOWING HER father's funeral were for
Annie the worst of her life, and it seemed as if the weather
set out to match her feelings. Having taken the children
to school, she breathed a sigh of relief as she stepped
indoors, took her raincoat off and gave it a good shake
before hanging it on the clothes-peg. All weekend it had
been raining, and still it was chucking it down. It was the
kind of Monday morning when nobody wanted to get
out of their bed. It was the third week in June. What
had happened to flaming June? It was days since the sun
had shone. Summer was very late making up its mind
this year. After she had busied herself with tidying the
kitchen, washing up the breakfast things and had finally
made the beds, she returned to the kitchen and was just
about to make herself a cup of coffee when the front door
opened and Rhoda called, 'It's only me, luv.'

'Aw, Gran, you shouldn't have come out in this weather,
but I have to say I've missed you. Come on, come by
the fire, and I'll make us a hot drink.' Annie dropped

to her knees, pushed the poker between the bars of the range, wriggled it about until the embers burnt more brightly, then pulling an armchair up close to the hearth she half pushed her grandmother down into the well-padded seat.

'Don't fuss so, Annie! Anyone would think you hadn't seen me for ages. I only went 'ome for the weekend 'cos you insisted I should. Did the kids play you up?'

'No, honest, Gran, they were as good as gold, considering they were cooped up indoors all the time. Mary helped me make some cakes and Ron chopped me up a whole load of sticks to light the fire with. I read to them Saturday night and last night we played all sorts of board games.'

'Well, that's all right then. I still think we should think about giving up one of the 'ouses. Either mine or this one, an' all live together. Be much cheaper all round.'

'Gran!' Annie sighed in exasperation. 'We've been all through that, and you know we decided we'd let the dust settle before we made any big decisions. If we were to all settle in one house there wouldn't be room for Jack Higgins, and it doesn't seem fair to tell him to find somewhere else to live, not when he's been so good an' all.'

'I'm well aware of that,' Rhoda said huffily, 'but what about the expense, especially since you're only doing part-time at the café now?'

'That's another thing I keep trying to drum into you, Gran. Money is no problem – not at the moment, it isn't. You know there was more than five hundred pounds in Dad's box, and his insurance well covered the funeral and quite a bit to spare, so stop worrying, please.'

'You're taking too much on yerself my girl,' Rhoda

114

grumbled warningly as she took a cup of coffee from Annie. 'I don't know why you won't let me do more for you.'

'Sorry, Gran, I don't mean to brush you off as you do more than enough for us already.' Then, as if she realized they'd got off on the wrong foot this morning, she smiled, bent over and placed a kiss on Rhoda's cheek and said, 'Tell you what, when we've drunk our coffee, I'll get Dad's box down again and we'll go through it together. Perhaps you'll be able to make more sense of some of the items than I've been able to.'

'All right,' Rhoda answered quickly, feeling glad to be of some use again. 'Can't believe that son of mine was such a dark horse.'

Annie just smiled. You don't know the half of it, she was thinking. Thank God Gran hadn't been around when she'd first opened up that tin box. Or anyone else for that matter! She'd told her there had been a little over a hundred pounds in cash. In truth she had found five hundred and forty pounds. The amount had scared the living daylights out of her! And having to keep the money hidden away, even the fact that it existed, and she couldn't tell a soul about it was driving her round the bend. Imagine what it would do to poor old Gran! No doubt she would have thrown a blue fit and lain awake half the night wondering how all that money came to be here in the house. Another thing had made Annie keep the find secret: Gran wouldn't have been able to keep it to herself. She'd be sure to let it slip to Gladys Dawson, and God alone knows whom she would tell. Before you knew it, this place would be swarming with police, and this time they really would want some answers. No, my girl, she chided herself, you have to keep a still tongue in your head until you really do get to the bottom of what your dad was involved in. Annie shuddered. It was hard! Not being able to discuss it with anyone, she felt like a criminal herself.

Rhoda Bateman wasn't daft. She had observed the different expressions that were crossing her grand-daughter's face, and not only today. True, Annie had a lot to cope with, much more than a young girl of her age should be asked to take on, but there was more to this than appeared on the surface. Oh yes! She'd lay money that whatever it was that her son had been entangled in, Annie knew a lot more about it than she was letting on. It's all very well for her to keep telling me not to worry. How can I help it when I can see by the look on her face that she doesn't know which way to turn? I hope to God that she chooses the right way, and if she doesn't, let's hope I'm still here to help her pick up the pieces.

With the coffee cups cleared and a cloth spread over the scrubbed table, Annie sat opposite her grandmother with the tin box that had belonged to her father in the centre of the table. Its lid was open and a heap of papers were piled up nearby.

'This box brings back memories,' Rhoda said softly. 'I can see your grand-dad now, Big Paddy Bateman, walking over the threshold of the house that I still live in. This very trunk, as he called it, was perched on his shoulder. His Irish brogue was so thick you could have cut it with a knife in those days, his face so ruddy and his hair that jet black that I used to imagine I could smell the Irish peat oozing from him as he held me in his arms!'

Annie looked at her gran in sheer amazement. Sentimentality had never been one of her weaknesses. 'Wow!' she said. 'You are sure it is the same tin box?'

Moving some papers aside, Rhoda studied the brass fittings for a minute, then lifted out the side section with its small partitions, set it aside and began removing the items from the bottom, which were mainly exercise books. She tipped the box on its side and turned it this way and that while Annie watched. 'I can't remember what it is I'm looking for.' She felt around the inside and examined underneath. 'All I do know is that Paddy would keep anything that was important to him in here – union papers and insurance papers, you know, all that sort of thing went in from the top but there's something else and I just can't bring it to mind.'

'Maybe the bottom lifts out. Would that be it, Gran?' Rhoda tried. 'No.'

'Let me try.' Annie leaned across the table and Rhoda pushed the box over to her.

Time ticked by. Rhoda got up and filled the kettle, dragging it to the centre of the hot range. Annie was intrigued by what her gran seemed unable to remember. This was the umpteenth time that she herself had gone through the contents of this box. Some of the papers she had deemed it wise to remove and conceal at the back of her wardrobe. There would come a time when she would have to deal with them, but not now. For hours she had sat on her own poring over pages and pages of figures, surprised at how detailed some of her father's transactions had been. No names were mentioned – only initials were pencilled in – but some of the figures had her gasping. Never had she realized he had made this kind of money.

But where was it all? If these figures were to be believed, the cash she had found was peanuts. Several exercise books showed different items he had bought and from where, but never the actual person. Most had been bought and sold straight on at a great profit. So again she'd asked herself what had happened to these sums of money? There was no way her father could have spent these amounts. She'd found no material goods that would justify that claim.

Some goods were recorded as having been 'acquired'! Did that mean they had been stolen? Her father had said there was enough cash to keep her safe for life. He'd talked of making it all legal with a solicitor. Well, she'd had the letter, but so far had not made an appointment to visit their offices. There's a hell of a lot more I need to find out before I start talking to strangers. She had found a cheque book, but it was unused. At least it gave her the name and address of the bank where her father must have had an account. Was it a large account? Would the manager of the branch know how her father had come by so much money?

Annie straightened up, her back and her head aching. 'Gran, I think I'll shove all these papers and the books back into the box. We can finish going through them another time. I've had just about all I can take for now.'

'All right, pet,' Rhoda called over her shoulder. 'I'm making a pot of tea, and I've had a thought, so don't close the lid down yet. There's something I want to show you.'

Rhoda returned to the table and continued fiddling with the box. 'I've got it!' she said suddenly. 'There's a little bit that clicks open, but it's in the lid; nothing to do with the inside of the box.' Grabbing the box, she up-ended it so that the outside of the lid rested against the table, got a heavy-handled knife out of the cutlery drawer and using its handle began to tap gently over the inside surface of the lid. In the right-hand corner a flap, about three inches square, dropped open, revealing a small dark hollow space that went back into the domed lid.

'Crikey, I was right! I hadn't dreamt it,' Rhoda exclaimed. 'It's all coming back t'me now. Your grand-dad used to keep a sovereign in there, well, most of the time it was more like half a sovereign. It's there for a rainy day, is what he used t'say.' She shook her head, and Annie could tell that her thoughts were miles away. 'Well, I'll be blowed! Who'd 'ave thought that Jim would still be using his dad's trunk after all these years? Somewhere along the line I seem to have lost touch with my son. I've no more idea what he was up to than the man in the moon. All I do know is that, whatever it was, it got the police on his back, an' if they hadn't been chasing him he would still be with us today, instead of lying buried up in the churchyard.'

Rhoda was muttering more to herself, and Annie didn't want her to get all sad and despondent. She had enough to cope with without that. 'Well, seeing as how you've managed to open it, Gran, let's see what's in it,' Annie cried, getting up and rushing round to stand beside her.

Rhoda's face showed only disappointment as she withdrew an old yellowing envelope, small enough to have been a wage packet, and passed it to Annie.

'Well, Gran, what did you expect? There's hardly room in there for the crown jewels, is there? But there is something – feels like a key.'

'Well, for God's sake open it up and let's make sure.'

'Safe deposit box number 1478,' Annie read from the label attached to the small key.

'Well, I'll be blowed!' Rhoda exclaimed again. 'Now all you've got to do is fathom out where the ruddy safe deposit box is. Then perhaps we might begin to find some answers.'

'You are a clever old thing, Gran, to remember about the box after all these years,' Annie said, making her voice sound as cheerful as she could, because truth to tell she felt like bawling. She already guessed that the safe deposit box would be held in the bank where presumably her father had an account. Would it be a relief to open it up and perhaps find out more of what he had been mixed up in? Or would she feel more anger and resentment? Of one thing she was certain, when she did go to the bank, she'd go on her own. Gran was the last person she'd want to be there if this box revealed more secrets. She put her arms round Rhoda and kissed her.

She looked at her doubtfully. 'I do wish you didn't have all these matters to deal with, Annie, it's too much for you. It's not something you can brush under the carpet, or chuck all the papers in the dustbin. Sooner or later someone is going to start asking questions. Oh dear, you're so young. Whatever are you going to do? Are you sure your dad didn't tell you more than you're letting on when he was lying so ill in the hospital?'

Annie shrugged. 'Gran, we've been over it a dozen times and more. Dad told me this crazy story about how rich he was. Said there was enough money to last me all my life. Said I wasn't to feel guilty about any of it. He'd hurt no one in the gaining of it, but that it was me he'd hurt the most by leaving Ronnie and Mary for me to cope with.'

'Well, he got the last bit right, that's damned sure.'

'There was even one time when Dad seemed to be raving – said he owned some property.'

'No! I don't think I want to hear any more. Let's pour

that tea I made down the sink, it'll be thoroughly stewed by now. Move yerself, Annie, and fill the kettle again.' Annie laughed, and her laugh had a hysterical edge to it. 'Maybe the doctors had pumped a whole lot of drugs into him,' Rhoda said thoughtfully.

'Of course, that could be it,' Annie agreed, mainly to pacify her.

By the time she had made fresh tea and poured it out, Rhoda had her nose in another sheaf of papers. 'I think you should hang on to all these exercise books,' she said without looking up. 'Maybe we could ask Arthur Kent about some of these deals? It's pretty obvious that he is this A. K. and we do know that yer father did many a deal with him. Though anything on this scale wants some believing, if you ask me.'

'Maybe,' Annie agreed, without the slightest intention of doing anything of the kind. What her father had been up to was gone and done with. The less she had now to do with his old comrades, the better off she would be. That feeling was firmly fixed in her mind. So much so that she almost choked when Rhoda suddenly looked up, saying, 'Freddie the Fox seems to have come in for a great many payments, or hadn't you noticed?'

'Yes,' Annie said, almost afraid of what she was going to come out with next. 'But that's no surprise, is it? Freddie was always driving the van for me dad, and he didn't do it for nothing, did he?'

'Yeah, I suppose that's true.'

Annie was feeling utterly drained. 'Gran, let's clear all this away and start thinking what we're going to have for dinner tonight. You can make the pudding – Ronnie and Mary always say your puddings are far better than mine.'

'If you're trying to humour me, my girl, it won't work. But you're right – enough is enough for one day. But you aren't going to be able to put off your visit to the solicitors, nor yet to the police station, for much longer, so you'd better make up your mind and get it sorted.'

'All right, Gran,' Annie said, smiling gently. 'Anything for a quiet life.' But as she packed the exercise books back into the bottom of the tin box and shuffled the papers into some kind of order, she was well aware that a quiet life for her in the near future was something that she could only dream of.

Chapter Twelve

SERGEANT LOVERING, A JOVIAL, middle-aged man whom Annie had known for most of her life, held open the office door and nodded for her to step inside. As she passed him, his eyelid dropped in a wink and in a stage whisper he said, 'His bark is worse than his bite, I promise.'

Detective Inspector Schofield was sitting at his desk as Annie was ushered in. 'Miss Ann Bateman, sir.'

The inspector looked up, removed his glasses and pointed to a chair beside his desk. Annie wasn't so sure that what the sergeant had said was true. Inspector Schofield was a giant of a man in a charcoal grey suit and a white shirt, but that didn't alter the fact that he was a policeman through and through. He waited until Annie had sat down before he carefully laid his glasses on the desk and gave her a smile. Then he cleared his throat. 'Miss Bateman, I really am very sorry about your father.' Annie said nothing, but stared at the inspector as if she hadn't heard. 'We know your father wasn't a hardened criminal, yet he had become involved with the big-time boys, which would have eventually led to his downfall. You are aware of that much, aren't you?'

Annie nodded. 'I suppose so.'

Inspector Schofield sighed. 'You don't sound too sure, but take it from me, he had gone beyond the odd bit of black market dealing.'

Annie sat up straight and said seriously, 'I don't know any more than I've told your officers over and over again. I thought I knew my dad. He worked hard, and we never wanted for anything. I felt safe. Now, I have a brother who doesn't want to know, two children that are not even related to me but somehow seem to have become my responsibility, a grandmother who is worried out of her life, and as if all that isn't enough, I have you lot asking endless questions. I'm beginning to wonder exactly what crime you think my father might have committed.'

The inspector was thinking of his own daughter, almost the same age as this Annie Bateman. Comparison between the two girls didn't bear thinking about. His daughter Joan was pampered. Over-indulged by two sets of grand-parents. Good education, all set to go to university. Her life was all mapped out for her. Bit different for the lass who now sat beside him.

He had heard the loneliness and the hurt in her voice, and realized that Jim Bateman had never let on to his family half of what he'd got up to. This girl was out of her depth, way out of her depth. She was frightened, felt intimidated and worried. And not without good cause. 'Would you like a cup of tea or coffee?' he asked kindly.

Annie snapped at him, 'I don't want anything to drink. I don't need you to be kind to me. I just want you to tell me that from now on you will be leaving me and my gran alone. We really have told you all we know.'

'All right, all right.' The policeman grinned, thinking to himself: this one has spunk, she'll get by. 'Annie, listen to me,' he said, leaning across his desk. 'In so far as I am able, I will call off the inquiry into your father's affairs. I don't think the serious crime squad were ever sure that they could tie Jim Bateman in with what they've got on hand.'

Annie held her head up high, more relieved than she cared to admit. 'Thank you, Inspector,' she murmured.

He rose to his feet. 'If anyone does contact you – and I'm sure you know I'm not talking about the police force – please, Miss Bateman, come in and see me. We can always sort something out. You can trust me, do you believe that?'

Annie only nodded, doubtful as to whether she should take his outstretched hand. Stammering, having difficulty in finding the right words, she managed to say, 'I'll remember. Thank you.'

She left the police station and walked slowly towards the bus stop, noticing the litter-strewn pavements, the thick red brick-dust from where bomb-damaged buildings were being demolished, the noisy bustling traffic. So few horse-drawn vans were on the road now. Gran was right. The East End of London was changing, and she wasn't sure whether it was for the good. But now she had to pay a visit to the south side of London. A long overdue visit to the firm that had acted as solicitors when dealing with her father's affairs.

Annie felt she must be nearing her destination. The bus had stopped outside a public house named on the swinging signpost. 'The Surrey Tavern'. What a difference from the pubs around where she'd been born! This one lay back from the road with at least three entrances. Neat, short, heavily starched, lace curtains on gleaming brass rods showed at each tall window. Tubs of flowering plants were set out on the pavement. The surrounding streets were lined with trees. The bus was on its way once more, passing very elegant terraced houses, four storeys high, well proportioned with tall sash windows and wide front doors with colourful fanlights above. The deep-cream-coloured stone of these properties had somehow escaped the soot-carrying winds from the East End factories on the other side of the Thames. On the right lay Wandsworth Common, and to Annie it looked as if she were travelling into the heart of the country; everywhere was so clean, hardly like London at all. The trees were leafy, the grass green, flower beds were neat and orderly.

Then suddenly it felt as if someone had walked over her grave. The conductor was helping a young woman with two children off the bus, handing down to her a pushchair that had been folded and tucked away under the stairs of the bus. Annie twisted in her seat, watching as the young mother smiled her thanks.

'Poor cow!' A middle-aged woman sitting in front of Annie turned her head and nodded backwards. 'She's probably going to visit her husband in there. Not much of a life for her and them little kiddies, is it?'

Annie didn't need to be told what the sturdy well-built place was that lay back on the opposite side of the road – it was Wandsworth prison. She had seen it often enough on the newsreels at the local cinema, never thinking that she would be as close to it as she was now. If things had turned out differently, it could have been herself visiting her father inside that prison. The very thought was so awful that for a moment she thought she was going to be sick.

After a short while, 'Come on, love,' the conductor called impatiently, eager to be off with his driver for a cup of tea. 'This is the stop you asked for and where we change crews.'

'Oh, sorry . . .' Annie mumbled, snatching up her bag and making her way off the bus.

It was a very ordinary building that housed the law office that Annie was looking for. One of the four brass plates on the wall told her that she needed the third floor. A middle-aged secretary, very smart with short blond hair and a friendly smile, told her that Mr Ferguson would be with her shortly, and asked if she would like a cup of tea. Annie thanked her, thinking that everyone was being extra nice to her today. She refused the tea, and sat down to wait.

Less than ten minutes later the door to another office opened and a well-built clean-shaven man came out. He was wearing a navy blue three-piece suit, and as he approached her with his hand extended, Annie was relieved to see he was smiling broadly.

'I am so pleased to meet you, Miss Bateman. I'm Robert Ferguson.' He looked for a moment admiringly at Annie, before saying, 'Come on in and sit down.'

Annie felt she might panic. Her father had been here, sat in this office, discussed his affairs with this man. Now she was about to tread in his footsteps. The big wood-panelled office had an unexpected soothing effect on her the minute she set foot inside it.

Ferguson held a chair for Annie and saw her seated before settling himself behind the wide desk. 'Well, now.' He swivelled his chair until he was facing her. 'I was sorry to hear about your father's death, and equally sorry that we have to meet under such sad circumstances.' He gazed out of the window for a moment, smoothing his grey hair with his hand. Annie didn't think his comments needed any answer. Finally he said, 'I think we should get down to business straight away. Your father's will is pretty straightforward. You are the only one it concerns.'

Annie wanted to yell, What about my brother? but decided silence was the best policy until this man had laid all the facts before her. Then would be the time to fire questions at him. There was one thing, however, she couldn't help asking. 'Did my father leave any deeds to property with you? For safe-keeping, like.'

Ferguson looked puzzled. 'No. I'm afraid not. Aside from his will, there is nothing else. Is there something you expected to be here?'

Annie felt the colour rise in her cheeks. 'Not really. I'm sorry.'

'Don't be sorry. This must have put an awful strain on you. If I can help in any way . . . Have you tried your father's bank manager?'

'Not yet,' she said apologetically. 'My grandmother and I did find a key to a safe deposit box. Maybe the deeds my father spoke of will be in there. I have an appointment at the bank tomorrow, so I'll find out then.'

'Oh, I don't think it will be as easy as all that,' Ferguson informed her quietly.

'Why? Do you think there'll be a problem?'

'I'm afraid the bank won't let you open the box,' he said sympathetically.

'Why ever not?'

Annie's disappointment was so obvious that for a moment Ferguson wanted to laugh. Instead, he leant across his desk and patted her hand, saying, 'I think it's best if I explain matters a bit more thoroughly, don't you, Miss Bateman?'

She was lost for words, embarrassed. He must think I'm a right simpleton, she was thinking. His next words went a long way towards easing her feelings.

'There is no way you could have known, as not one in ten people would be familiar with the proceedings that have to take place when a person dies. First off, let me say that your father wished my firm to be executors of his will, which means that I have a legal duty to see that his estate is wound up properly and that all outstanding debts are discharged and that a tax return is submitted to the Inland Revenue. Now, as to this safe deposit box that you have reason to believe may be at the bank – the manager would agree to the box being opened were I to accompany you. He would be present, and one other bank official would also be required to be on hand. You would unlock the box, and the entire contents would be removed, listed in detail and sent for probate. After that, you will have to wait. Until you can go to the bank with a court-validated certificate of probate, the contents cannot be removed.'

Annie couldn't take it all in. There was I deciding that no one else, not even me gran, should be present when the box was opened, and now it seemed that three strangers had the right to be there. What will I say if they find a load of cash? Or even deeds to a property? Probably one or the other of these businessmen will send for the police there and then! And what was all that about the Inland

Revenue? Surely I haven't got to get myself tangled up with that lot? Oh, I wish t'God that I'd never let on that me an' me gran had found that flipping key!

Annie was sitting with her head bent low, staring at the carpet, when she felt Ferguson give her hand an encouraging squeeze. 'It's nowhere near as bad as you are imagining, Miss Bateman. You and I are the sole executors, and since no one else benefits, that does simplify matters. It will just be a normal procedure. Once we have a final accounting of your father's assets, we shall petition the court to admit his will for probate and, depending on how busy the courts are, we could get certification in a matter of weeks.'

Annie sat back and said nothing. Everything wasn't simple to her, even after all he had said. She didn't trust herself to speak – she was thinking about her dad. It wasn't his fault everything was in such a muddle. He hadn't expected to die. He should have had a long and happy life stretching before him. It wasn't fair! But why were the dealings he'd had so much more complicated than any of them could have imagined? Gran had been right – he'd bitten off more than he could chew.

Now her mood changed. Of course it was all his fault and nobody else's! It looks like he didn't let his own left hand know what his right hand was up to. Devious, that's what he'd been, and that was putting it mildly.

Annie raised her eyes and saw that Ferguson was looking at her with sympathy. 'Would you like me to telephone the bank to make an appointment that will give us access to that safe deposit box? It is worrying you, isn't it?' he asked, sounding very concerned.

'Yes, that would be kind,' Annie murmured. What other choice did she have?

'All right, good. I'll get moving on that and I'll be in touch as soon as the arrangements have been made. D'you have any other questions? Is there anything you don't understand?'

Plenty, Annie nearly came out with, but stopped herself just in time. 'No, not really,' she managed to say.

Robert Ferguson got to his feet, came round his desk and, smiling broadly, said, 'I'm here to help in any way I can. Please don't look so sad. I know all legal matters must seem bewildering at the moment, but I'll deal with them. You really don't have any need to worry.'

Don't I? was the question rolling round inside Annie's head. You don't know the half of it, mate! She shook his hand and thanked him

Standing at the top of the stairs, she took a deep breath, saying to herself: Christ, am I glad that's over! If anyone deserves a cup of tea, I damn well do, and with that she started down, heading for the first café she could find.

'I can't believe we can't just go to the bank on our own and get into that damned deposit box,' Annie fumed at Rhoda, clenching her hands round a cup of tea.

'Good job we didn't try,' Rhoda argued. 'We'd 'ave looked right fools turning up there with a key and demanding the rights to it.'

'I can't stop thinking about what we might find. We, or rather I suppose it would only be I, might find we're in a load of trouble.'

'Just leave it all to this Mr Ferguson, luv; he seems t'have given you some good advice. And, from what you've told me, he was very nice t'you,' Rhoda reminded her, trying to calm Annie down. 'By the way, a man from the assurance company called while you were out. He wants a copy of the death certificate, and is coming back this afternoon. Should be 'ere any time,' she added, glancing up at the clock.

'But I've already given them one certificate, and they've paid me. You know they have. Mr Haines from the London and Manchester brought the cheque – you were here when he came.'

'Not that one,' Rhoda informed her. 'This was a different man from some other company.'

'You mean Dad had another policy? When did he take it out?'

'How the hell should I know? The more I hear about what's been going on, the more I realize that I hardly knew me own son. And as for this bank business, the sooner that lot's sorted the better. And you don't want to lie awake at night worrying about it, neither. Won't do no good, and I can't for the life of me see how the law, the tax people or anyone else, come t'that, can 'old you responsible for whatever it was yer father was up to.' Rhoda had hardly time to draw more breath when there was a loud knocking on the front door. 'That'll be him. I'll go,' she said, easing herself up out of the chair.

Annie heard her let the visitor in, and then she was talking quietly. A minute later she was back, ushering in a man a good few inches shorter than herself. 'This is Mr Gibbs,' Rhoda smiled. 'He gave me this. It states who he is and what company he represents.' She grinned again as she handed Annie a business card.

The short man had iron-grey hair and a severe, lined face, but when he smiled the severity suddenly disappeared and a warm friendliness took its place. He said politely to Annie, 'As you can see from my card, I represent the Prudential Assurance Company. Harold Gibbs, at your service, miss.' He took the seat that Annie indicated and beamed at her, and for the first time in weeks she felt that here was somebody who might possibly give her some straight answers.

'I'll make a fresh pot of tea,' Rhoda suggested, and Annie was grateful that for once she was being tactful and leaving her to get down to business with this unexpected caller.

Mr Gibbs spoke first. 'Did your grandmother explain that my company needs a copy of your father's death certificate?'

'Yes, she did,' Annie said, staring at him in some surprise. 'But I really don't understand why.'

He told her, 'Your grandmother has informed me that you were not aware that your father had taken out a life policy with our company. You may not know it, my dear, but Mr Bateman was a prudent man, heedful of the future. A very wise man, as it turns out. This was a full life policy for the sum of five thousand pounds on the life of James Bateman, naming you as the sole beneficiary.'

This was unbelievable! Annie just could not take in what this man was telling her! Oh, Dad, she sighed to herself. Oh, Dad! Then such a strong feeling of loneliness swept over her that her eyes filled with tears. Had he had a premonition that his life would be cut short? Had this been what he was trying to tell her as he lay dying? Had he only wanted to make sure that she would have enough to live on, to keep her safe when he was no longer around? At that moment she felt only a forlorn and desperate abandonment. It was like losing him all over again. She had been calling him devious. She half smiled through her tears. Well, he'd been that, all right. In more ways than one. Yet the fact that he'd had the forethought to make provision for her surely went a long way to proving just how much he had loved her.

They sat in silence, but it was a comfortable silence, until Mr Gibbs suddenly said, 'Was the coroner notified of your father's death?'

'Yes, the hospital saw to all that. There had to be an inquest.'

Mr Gibbs frowned. 'Do you remember what was stated as the cause of death?'

Annie's head jerked up; she was wondering why all the questions. 'Not exactly. All I know is it was a long-drawn-out process. Maybe me gran could tell you more, as she dealt with the undertakers.'

'But you did obtain death certificates? She told me Mr Bateman had a small life policy with the London and Manchester Assurance Company.'

'Yes, that's right. Does that matter? Wasn't he supposed to have more than one policy?' Annie was getting very agitated by all these questions. She had thought that, her father having been buried, all this kind of thing was behind her.

'No, it's perfectly all right. I didn't mean to upset you,' he said, feeling very sorry for Annie. 'More than likely the death certificate was sent direct to the registrar of deaths, and I'm sure your grandmother will be able to get another copy. Then if you would pop it in the post to our head office, the address is on my card.'

'Yes, I'll ask Gran to do that,' said Annie, feeling relieved that he had come to the end of his questions.

'Is there anything you would like to ask me?' Mr Gibbs had seen a thoughtful look come to Annie's face.

She was still going over in her mind everything that Mr

Gibbs had said. She felt stunned. 'Five thousand pounds,' she said solemnly. 'It's a lot of money.'

'Yes, it is,' Mr Gibbs confirmed. 'I will bring the cheque to you, or you may prefer the company to pay it directly into your bank account.'

'I don't have a bank account,' Annie blurted out truthfully. 'But my father did, and I have an appointment to see the manager.'

'That's good,' Mr Gibbs said, nodding his head. 'You may want to think about investing some of the money. He'll be the best person to talk to about your father's estate.'

Annie looked guilty suddenly, and said, 'I don't feel this money should be coming to me. Can you tell me when my father took out this policy?'

'Just six months ago, and I do assure you, Miss Bateman, you have full entitlement to the final payout.'

'Ready for your tea, are you?' Rhoda called from the scullery.

'Yes, please,' Annie answered thankfully.

Rhoda came in with a loaded tray. 'I made a few scones this morning, so I've buttered some of them. Help t'keep yer strength up if you eat something. All this legal jargon is wearing me granddaughter down.'

'Thank you, Mrs Bateman. They look delicious! Don't often get offered home-made fare,' Mr Gibbs answered, helping himself to two halves of buttered scone and placing them on a small plate. 'I think when your granddaughter chooses to tell you of our little talk you will understand that it was good news I brought. Not happy circumstances, very sad, but an ill wind, an' all that.'

Annie had been about to start on her hot tea when a thought hit her so hard that she slopped it, making Rhoda get quickly to her feet and hand her a paper serviette, saying, 'Watch it, Annie, you could have scalded yerself. What's wrong anyway?'

Annie wiped her chin, set her cup down on its saucer and looked directly at Mr Gibbs. 'This great amount of money – do I have to notify the tax people? Mr Ferguson said the whole of my father's estate had to be calculated and a return made to the Inland Revenue.'

Mr Gibbs had to wait a moment before replying because his mouth was full of sultana scone. When he had swallowed, he excused himself, and his whole face lit up as he smiled broadly. 'My dear Miss Bateman, I am happy to tell you that the money will be paid direct to you, and no, you don't have to pay any tax on it.'

'My God!' Annie said softly. 'Five thousand pounds, tax free!'

'HOW MUCH?' Rhoda cried in disbelief.

'Five thousand pounds, Gran,' Annie confirmed.

'Gawd above! Whatever next? I think I'm gonna 'ave a drop of something a bit stronger in me tea. Me nerves won't stand much more.' By this time Rhoda was on her knees in front of the dresser. Her arm went straight to the back of the shelf and came out holding a bottle of whisky. Clutching it to her chest, she came back to the table. 'If there's one thing I was sure I could still rely on my son for it was that he'd have at least one bottle of Scotch tucked away for just such an occasion as this!' Having unscrewed the cap, Rhoda proceeded to pour a good measure into each of the three cups, saying, 'No arguments! Let's drink t'me son's wellbeing, wherever he is.'

Twenty minutes later, after thanking Rhoda profusely for the scones and declaring that she made the best cup of tea he had ever drunk, Mr Gibbs followed Annie to the front door. 'I will be in touch,' he promised. 'Good luck when you visit your father's bank manager.'

Annie couldn't wait to see him off. She wanted to get back to her gran and talk about this latest development. Talk about a windfall! Her dad had certainly been a dark horse.

Chapter Thirteen

ANNIE HAD SLEPT BADLY, waking up several times, and finally just after six she gave up altogether. She crept downstairs, boiled the kettle, had a good wash and dressed herself in a tweed skirt and jumper that she mainly wore about the house.

While the kettle was boiling for the second time, she sat at the kitchen table and read through the exercise books that held Ron's and Mary's homework. Ronnie seemed to be doing very well, especially at arithmetic: seven out of ten was the lowest mark the teacher had awarded him, and on two pages he'd been given nine out of ten. Dear little Mary was a different kettle of fish. The only lesson she seemed to take an interest in was drawing. Dear God, if only I knew what to do about these children, Annie was saying to herself when the kitchen door opened and they came in.

Mary nudged her brother. 'Go on. Ask Annie – you said you would.'

'Ask me what, Mary?'

Mary took a step nearer. 'I asked Ronnie about our dad, Annie. He said he thinks he must be dead. Did you know 'im?'

Annie turned her chair round and stared down into the frail little face framed by lovely blond hair. She wanted to tell her the truth. It wasn't right to keep fobbing her off with make-believe stories and promises. She had a right to know. Yet she couldn't tell her what she didn't know herself. 'I'm sorry, Mary. I didn't know your dad. Maybe Ronnie is right and he died when you were a baby.'

'When me mum lived here, didn't she ever bring 'im round to see you and Uncle Jim?' she asked, her bright blue eyes glistening with tears.

'No, luv, she never did,' Annie said truthfully.

'I wonder 'ow did he die.'

'I honestly don't know, Mary. Your mum never talked about him.'

Mary turned her gaze to her brother. 'What did 'e look like?'

'I dunno.'

'But you said he used to live with us when I was little.'

'Yeah, well, he did. But I don't remember,' Ronnie said, thrusting his hands deep into his trouser pockets.

'S'pose we got t'get used to not 'aving no dad,' Mary stated sadly.

Annie had had enough of this conversation; she just couldn't cope with it. If only she had some answers, but she didn't. At the moment she had no more idea than the man in the moon as to what the future held for herself, never mind these two dear little children. Of one thing she was certain, she'd do her best. Hold on to both of them. See that they were well fed and clothed, went to school regularly and had a few treats now and again. Could she see to it that they were happy? She doubted it. Life for them had been so insecure. What could she possibly do to alter that fact? She couldn't promise them that she'd never let them go. Their mother might turn up any day and take them off. Even the local authorities might decide that two young children should not be living with a girl of nineteen. Poor kids, she sighed heavily, poor me, caught in the middle. I hope I never have to break the news to them that they can't stay with me. Take one day at a time, she decided; not much else she could do.

The fire wasn't burning too brightly, so Annie used it as an excuse. Getting to her feet, she shovelled more coal on to the embers, saying, 'I've got the porridge all ready. How about one of you taking the long fork out of the drawer and start making some toast? I've cut the bread, so we can all have breakfast together.'

With Mary fully occupied, Annie turned her attention to Ronnie. 'How old were you when you last saw your dad?'

She saw a strange look come to the boy's face. 'Me real dad or me other dad?'

'Tell me about your real dad,' she prompted, hoping that since she had got him started, he would go on to tell her more.

'Was he Mary's father as well? Tell me what you remember about him,' she repeated.

Ronnie didn't answer. He was silent for so long that she thought any minute he would say, 'It's got nuffin t'do with you.'

Finally he sighed. 'S'pose I'd better tell you,' he began. And then he told her as much as he could draw back from his early years. Yes, Bob Wilson had been father to both him and his sister. They lived in a flat in Camberwell and he had been a long-distance lorry-driver, often being away for what had seemed ages to him. Late one night he had come home without warning and found his mum in bed with a man named Charlie Bradford. His dad had nearly killed Charlie, and he'd given his mum a jolly good hiding as well. He didn't think they'd ever seen his dad since that night. Soon after that, Charlie had come to live with them all the time and his mum had said Charlie was their new dad. 'But it didn't last. The police came and took him away. Don't know what for,' he added thoughtfully. 'That's when we got put in a 'ome for a little while and then later fostered out. Not t'gether like. Mary was still ever so little, and me, I went to some people that already had two boys. My place wasn't so bad. Mary's was 'orrible.'

As Annie listened, afraid to interrupt in case Ronnie came to a halt, her heart ached for the love-starved, forlorn little mites they must have been. She thought of her own life, her lovely gran and grand-dad, her own mum and dad who had adored each other and had done everything within their power to see that she and her brother were not only safe and well but happy. True, there had been the horror of the war years, and the fact that her mother had died had made this a sad period of her life, yet she had always felt wanted and loved. The same couldn't be said for these two children. Was it any wonder that Ronnie wanted to fight the world and that Mary clung to anyone who showed her the slightest affection? She winced as she imagined the two small children being woken up in the middle of the night by their father fighting a man he found in their mother's bed. She imagined the hurt Ronnie must have felt. His dad had been away for weeks, and he should have been swinging his son up into his arms, hugging him close, saying, Look, son, I've brought you home a present. Mary had probably been too young to realize what was going on, but Ronnie! He must have been devastated. And never to have seen or heard from his father from that day to this. It said a lot for the boy's character that he had turned out as well as he had. The way he always protected his little sister had to be seen to be believed. Christ! she thought, feeling a lump rise in her throat. How the hell could a man have walked away from his own two children?

Then Ronnie was talking again, this time with a small smile on his face, telling Annie how her dad had become their Uncle Jim. She was learning so much this morning. About how his mum had brought Jim to visit him at the house of his foster parents and how the people wouldn't let him in. How the same thing had happened when they tried to see Mary. She listened with admiration as Ronnie told how he had bunked out of the house, climbed over the back wall and run after them.

'From that first minute I knew your dad was a good bloke. He told me I had guts, and that he'd move 'eaven an' earth to get us both out and take us t'live with him. He did, an' all, didn't he? About the only grown-up person up t'then what kept a promise.'

Then as Ronnie began reminding her how good her father had been to them and how for him and his sister it was the best time of their lives when they'd all lived together, a sudden thought came to Annie. It's not a good idea to have these two children solely dependent on me. Nothing in this life is guaranteed. Her father had taken them on in good faith and look what had happened to him! What if they come to rely on me and I suddenly pop off?

143

Ronnie was clenching and unclenching his fists. 'Don't you think it was a rotten thing for me mum t'do? Going off like that and stealing that money from Uncle Jim?'

'Do you think about her much?' Annie asked, side-stepping his question with one of her own.

'I try not to, 'cos I think she's with Charlie. She must love him more than us.'

'What makes you think that, Ronnie?' Annie quietly asked, her insides twisting with pain for him.

The lad hung his head. 'Well . . . one day when we were coming out of school I saw me mum talking to Charlie down by the gates.'

'And you're sure it was him?'

'Yeah, I am, 'cos me mum never waited for us. She went off with 'im, and me and Mary came 'ome on our own that day.'

'Best not to think about it,' advised Annie.

'That's what I tells meself,' replied Ronnie in a hard voice, 'but it ain't all that easy.' His face wrinkled into a sneer. 'One of these days I'll get that swine,' he muttered.

'Come an' sit up to the table, love,' said Annie, giving his shoulders a reassuring pat. 'Nothing will be gained by losing your temper.'

Mary tossed her hair back, her cheeks red from sitting so close to the fire. 'I've made six bits of toast; is that enough?'

'Cor, you are clever,' Annie told her, taking the plate of toast. 'You and Ronnie eat your porridge while I butter all of this.'

Mary grasped Annie's hand. 'Are you going to take me t'school today?'

'Yes, I am, my luv, and I'll be there when you come out

144

this afternoon. An' because you've been so good helping me with the breakfast, I'll take you round Woolworth's and you can choose a little present. How does that sound?'

Mary grinned. 'D'yer really mean it?'

Annie nodded. 'But only if you hurry up and eat your breakfast and get ready quickly, 'cos I mustn't be late for work.'

'All right.' Mary happily agreed.

It took such little things to please Mary, Annie was thinking as she watched Ronnie sprinkle sugar over his sister's porridge, and she came to a decision. As soon as I get my dad's affairs sorted out, I'm going to see what I can find out about their parents. Not that I want to be rid of them – in fact I need to put this arrangement on a much more permanent footing. It shouldn't be too difficult to trace their father, not now that I know what he does for a living. As for Dot Wilson, she wasn't bright enough to have covered her tracks that much. As she sipped her own tea, Annie was daydreaming. What would be good, and a solution to everything, was if she met a real nice young man. They could fall in love, he could become very fond of the two children, then they could get married and start a new life with a ready-made family. That's not going to happen, she told herself firmly. Wishes don't come true. Well, hardly ever.

The whole morning had been busy in the café. The weather was real summer, and the stall-holders had their shirt-sleeves rolled up, showing their brawny arms which were well tattooed. The young ladies wore sleeveless pretty dresses, while even the older women had forsaken their shawls. Their felt hats had been exchanged for straw ones which were adorned with artificial flowers and in some cases bunches of bright red cherries. From the back kitchen window Flossie and Annie had a good view of the Thames.

'Busy down there today,' said Flossie, as the two of them took a break. 'Watching them lightermen move all that wood you get the impression that they're walking on water.'

'Yeah, me gran told me that Jack Higgins would be working all hours this week. Imported timber, she said it was. Funny, ain't it? Dockers aren't allowed to move the baulks, only licensed lightermen and the special highly skilled workers they call rafters. Jack was telling young Ronnie that these men are among the fittest and most skilled of dock-workers. He also said that mostly their jobs were handed down from father to son.'

'Well, that's the tradition of the docks for you,' remarked Flossie, 'and today they've certainly got the weather for it. Even the Thames looks good when it's got the sun rippling on it. Pour us another mug of tea, Annie, I'm fair parched. It's been that hot in here t'day.'

Annie moved away from the window and went to the stove. As she poured milk into Flossie's mug, her thoughts were on Jack Higgins. He was a funny one and no mistake. No matter what she did, she could never fathom that man. He never seemed to be the same two days running. At first, when Rhoda had stayed at her house to help with the children, Jack had joined them for his evening meal. He had been so helpful, running about here, there and everywhere, dealing with the authorities, taking her gran back and forth to the undertakers. Then all of a sudden it was as if he didn't want to know them any more.

Rhoda didn't seem to notice, but put it down to the fact that Jack had always been an independent man.

Annie felt there was more to it than that. He was still perfectly polite towards her. Still went out of his way to do things that would make life easier, but, and it was a big but, somehow she couldn't put her finger on it. The easy comradeship they'd had when her dad was in the hospital, and even during the trying days of the inquest and the funeral, had gone by the board. She tried not to let it worry her, but somehow it did.

'Flossie,' Annie began as she held out the steaming mug, 'd'yer think Sid would let me slip off a bit early today, as I've got to meet that solicitor I told you about. He's made arrangements with the bank for me to open me dad's safe deposit box.'

'Aw, my Gawd! Bet you ain't looking forward to that?'

'No, I'm not. But, Flossie, it will be a weight off me mind, to find out one way or another what me dad was up to.'

Flossie heaved up her large bosom, threw back her head and let out a roar of a laugh. 'You know, Annie, me an' Sid 'ave 'ad many a laugh over yer dad, bless 'is 'eart. Talk about playing yer cards close t'yer chest! From what you've told us, he did that all right an' he seems t'have got away with it. Lucky Jim Bateman while he was alive, but it's not fair the way his luck ran out all of a sudden. Not fair on you, either. Still, I'll come an' visit yer if they cart yer off to Holloway. They tell me they let the prisoners use make-up while they're inside now, so you'll be all right.'

Annie flicked the teacloth she was holding, aiming at Flossie's head. But Flossie ducked. 'Don't joke about it,' she pleaded. 'I'm already having nightmares just thinking about it.'

'Couldn't resist, my luv. And I can't 'elp laughing.

What I wouldn't give to be a fly on the wall this afternoon. Bundles of money, bags of gold sovereigns and Gawd knows what else you might find – you'll be in clover. I couldn't agree with yer gran more, can't for the life of me see how the hell they can touch you for something you knew nothing about.' Seeing the unhappy look on Annie's face, Flossie relented. 'Go on, pet, I'm only teasing. Go upstairs to me bathroom, wash and tidy yerself up and get off to meet this solicitor. I'll make it all right with Sid.'

Annie had only a few minutes to wait outside the bank before Mr Ferguson put in an appearance. 'Good afternoon, Miss Bateman,' he said, raising his hat. 'Beautiful day, isn't it?' Annie nodded her agreement. Mr Mathews, the branch manager, greeted her cordially. He was a stout middle-aged man in a dark suit, grey tie and the merest tip of a white linen handkerchief showing in his top pocket. He introduced a younger, slimmer man as 'Mr Nicholls, my chief clerk'.

Mr Mathews escorted Annie and Mr Ferguson into the vault, where he located the box and used both her key and the bank's to remove it from its locked chamber in the wall. Directing them into a small room which had a table and two chairs, he told them, 'I'm afraid I must be the one to remove each item from the box, while Mr Nicholls will make a detailed record that will enable the probate court to decide if any article should be construed as part of your father's assets,' he explained. 'You take the chair this side, Miss Bateman,' he suggested, indicating that Ferguson should take the other seat. 'I and my clerk will stand.'

Perspiring, feeling she might be about to faint, Annie

watched as Mr Mathews lifted the lid. The small box was packed tight. On the top was a brown envelope filled with cash. Without saying a word, Mr Mathews passed it to his clerk. Another envelope held a few war-time savings certificates. There was a silver frame that held a photograph of her parents, taken on their wedding day. Another ornate heavy silver frame held a photograph of a very young Rhoda and big Paddy Bateman on what appeared to have been their wedding day.

As Annie watched this stranger handle what to her were her father's precious memories, a huge lump came into her throat. Underneath there lay several exercise books, and as they too were removed and placed with the other items in the centre of the table, Annie was thinking, surely to God they're not going to stand here and read through that lot. Though if they did, and they could make sense out of what her father had recorded, then they'd be a darn sight cleverer than she had been.

Keeping his expression calm, Mr Mathews said, 'There doesn't seem to be anything more.' He looked towards Ferguson before pushing the tin box across the table so that Annie could see for herself. Then he exchanged a meaningful look with Mr Nicholls and asked, 'Have you counted the sum of money?'

'Yes, sir. The exact amount of cash is six hundred pounds.'

'Not exactly a fortune.' Mr Mathews smiled at Annie.

Maybe not to you, mate! Annie had to stop herself from retorting.

'That would appear to be everything.' The manager addressed this remark to Ferguson. 'You'll be aware that the cash will have to be held along with all the contents of

Mr Bateman's box until the estate has cleared probate.'
Ferguson nodded his agreement.

After Annie and her solicitor had signed their names
at the bottom of the clerk's recorded list as executors for
the estate of James Bateman, Mr Mathews shook hands
with her. She thanked him for his help. He wished her
well. Then she and Ferguson walked out into the early
afternoon sunshine.

Once they were well away from the bank, Annie whispered, 'I'm glad that's over. I'm still shaking!'

'Would you like me to take you somewhere for a sandwich and some coffee?'

'Oh no, thank you. I've taken up enough of your
time. Besides, I promised to meet two little children
from school.'

'Well, if you're sure. There wasn't anything to worry
about, was there? Not even the deeds you were expecting.'

Annie shook her head. What was that look he was giving
her now? Inviting her to tell him more about papers or
deeds that she had enquired about when visiting his
office? Well, he's going to be unlucky, 'cos I know no
more about them now than I did then. Perhaps Dad had
been wandering, talking aimlessly, maybe because of the
drugs they'd given him.

'It shouldn't take long to clear matters,' Ferguson was
saying, his tone telling her that he was anxious to be off.

Annie thanked him for coming. He turned away, and
then quickly added, 'I'm sure we shall be able to take
care of everything. Please don't hesitate to contact me at
any time.'

'Thank you, Mr Ferguson. I appreciate that.'

She watched as he walked away. Well! That had been

a right let-down! No dark secrets had been revealed. One relief, though: it didn't seem as though she was going to be in trouble with the law. So far, there was no evidence to prove that her father had been the out-and-out villain she had begun to picture. What her father had said had to be put down as the ramblings of a dying man. There was the cash she'd found in grand-dad's old box and now six hundred at the bank, plus that wonderful assurance policy he'd had the forethought to take out. Hardly enough for him to say it would keep us for the rest of our lives, but a very nice windfall for all that. All the palaver of the safe deposit box was over and done with. Now she could meet the children, see their faces light up when she gave them sixpence each to spend in Woolworth's. From now on she would forget all about deeds to property and the like, get on with her life and, for the sake of the children, make it her business to find out as much as she could about Bob and Dorothy Wilson.

So that was that, she decided, striding out, purpose in every step. Tomorrow was another day. A new beginning, and she intended to make the most of it.

Chapter Fourteen

ANNIE WAS WOKEN BY sounds coming from downstairs. She sat up and listened. It can't be the kids, she said to herself. They never get out of bed on a Sunday morning until I've called them at least twice. Now, she eased herself from her bed, reached for her dressing-gown and slippers and crept downstairs, where she was amazed to see Doris Simmonds sitting at the kitchen table, cradling a cup of tea and looking as if she'd lost a shilling and found a penny.

'Hello,' Annie said. 'What on earth are you doing here at this time in the morning?'

'Yer don't mind, d'you, Annie? I know I've got the devil of a cheek. I used the key on the string to let meself in.'

'Course I don't mind,' Annie answered quickly, but still very curious. 'But whatever has happened? You look awful.'

'Oh, thanks a bunch. You wouldn't look so good either if you heard that the council were going to pull yer home down round yer ears.'

'Oh,' Annie muttered, grasping the situation at once. 'You've had a letter saying that your block of flats is going to be demolished.'

'Got it in one. Unsafe for habitation due to bomb damage, is what they say, an' don't tell me it's 'appening all over London 'cos I already know that, an' it ain't any consolation.'

'Oh, Doris, I am sorry,' Annie said, pulling out a chair and sitting down opposite her friend. 'Have they said anything about rehousing you?'

'Yes, they have. Too much, if you ask me. I got the letter on Thursday and went straight down the Town Hall. Never got t'see anyone that had an ounce of sense in their noddle, so I went back again on Friday. After being shoved from pillar to post, some dozy old geezer informs me that because I am one person living on my own, no temporary accommodation will be offered. I can put my name down on the list for new housing, and when and if it becomes available, my application will be considered sympathetically.'

'And what are you supposed to do in the meantime?'

'That was my question exactly,' Doris announced, picking up her cup and draining it. 'And you're never gonna believe what the answer was.' Annie hadn't the heart to reply, so she reached for the milk jug and then the teapot and refilled Doris's cup. 'I can be offered a place in a hostel! Can yer believe it? Me a married woman! Or maybe I should use the title the council gave me, "a widow". Honestly, Annie, if I could have got over that counter I would have throttled that housing manager! A war widow, I reminded him. Didn't make the slightest bit of difference.'

Annie pushed back her chair and threw her arms round

Doris's shoulders. 'Never mind, luv. It's like Gran is always saying: what you deserve and what you get in this life are two different things. You ain't going t'live in no hostel, that's for sure. You can come and live here, if you don't mind the kids.'

Doris brushed her hair away from her face, stared up at Annie, and burst into tears. Several minutes passed, during which Annie held her and let her cry it all out. Then, having wiped her face, Doris took a deep breath before saying, 'Thanks, Annie love. I thought it was bad enough when I got the telegram to say my John had been killed, but even then I didn't feel quite so alone. Getting the news by something as chilling as a telegram was awful, but I still had familiar things around me, things I could touch that brought back good memories. Now what am I supposed to do? Honestly, Annie, these past few days I just haven't known where t'turn.'

Annie wasn't given a chance to answer. The door opened and Ronnie and Mary, still clad in their nightclothes, peered round the door.

'Don't cry, Auntie Doris,' pleaded Mary.

'No, yer don't 'ave to,' Ronnie said, sounding quite masterful. ''Cos we 'eard Annie say yer can come an' live 'ere, an' we'd like that. Wouldn't we, Mary?'

Mary nodded her head.

'You've been listening outside the door,' Annie accused them.

'Only 'cos we didn't like t'come in when Auntie Doris was telling you fings.' Accepting that they were forgiven without question, the pair of them came into the room.

'You staying for breakfast, then?' Mary enquired hopefully. 'It's Sunday, innit? We always 'ave bacon an' eggs.'

'Not unless you're washed and dressed and back down

here within fifteen minutes,' Annie told them, unable to stop herself laughing.

Ronnie caught hold of his sister's hand and they were out of the door before Doris could find any words.

Right on time, the children came down just as eggs were being cracked into the frying-pan. 'Doris has cooked breakfast for all of us,' Annie informed them. 'I've made the tea and I've done some fried bread.'

They climbed up to the table without saying a word, their anticipation showing. 'Oohh . . . lovely,' murmured Mary as Doris put a plate down in front of her.

'Fanks! A sausage as well!' said Ronnie, beaming at the two women whom he now saw as being a very special addition to his and his sister's lives.

While the children were busy eating Doris turned to Annie and said, 'Thank you. Just looking round this table makes me feel wanted. Their happiness is catching, isn't it?'

'Yes, it is. But there's no need for thanks. Fetch your things and move in whenever you're ready.'

'You're wonderful, Annie. I shan't forget yer kindness.'

Annie shrugged, passing her cup to Doris for a refill. 'It works both ways, you know. You've helped me out with the kiddies many a time, and if they and you weren't here, I'd be the one that was feeling lonely.'

They heard the front door open, and Rhoda calling out, 'It's only me.'

The first thing she did when she came into the kitchen was to kiss Mary. 'You must 'ave been a good girl by the look of the breakfast you've got there?'

'Yeah. Auntie Doris cooked it today, an' Annie said she can come an' live with us 'cos the council is gonna pull her 'ouse down an' she ain't got nowhere t'go.'

'Did she now? Well, that's very nice,' Rhoda said, nodding first at Annie and then at Doris, showing her approval.

Annie squashed up nearer to Ronnie, while Doris pulled an extra chair forward. Rhoda sat down at the table and instantly asked whether there was any tea in the pot and whether, as it was Sunday, anyone was going to feed her. Annie, smiling broadly, got to her feet.

Rhoda turned to sympathize with Doris. 'Have you 'eard what the council are going to do when they've knocked yer old building down?'

'Rumour 'as it that they're gonna build another massive new tower block.' Doris shuddered. 'Hideous!'

'Yeah, well,' Rhoda agreed. 'They're doing some daft bloody things in the name of progress. Still, you'll be all right here with Annie. Tell you the truth, gal, it will be a weight off my mind. You'll be 'ere to give a hand with the kiddies. I don't want t'have to give up my own little house. Lived in it since the day I was wed, an' hope I can stay there till they carry me out in a box. Thing is, I'm set in me ways. Me living here all the time wouldn't work. I don't mind 'aving Jack Higgins as a lodger, he's as good as gold, no trouble at all, but it's best all round if Annie and I carry on as we are.'

Annie was about to set a cooked breakfast down in front of Rhoda when she caught the tail-end of their conversation and she laughed. 'Gran, you look thoroughly at home, but may I remind you that you're still wearing your hat and coat? Are you staying for the day, or do you intend to eat this breakfast and then go back 'ome?'

Rhoda sniffed. 'Seeing as 'ow me bag is full of fresh vegetables and on top of them is a pie I made last night for our afters, I 'ave every intention of spending the whole day here.' The determination in her voice had not only Doris and Annie laughing but the two children as well.

'I hope we're gonna get custard with the pie,' Mary whispered to her brother, which set them all off again on another merry burst of laughter.

Even Doris looked much happier since the children and Gran had joined them, Annie was thinking as she looked around at the smiling faces, and it dawned on her that for the first time since her dad had died, the house seemed to be alive. A real home again. All of us seated in this kitchen have lost someone, she reminded herself. We need each other. This isn't a posh house, but what it lacks in luxuries it makes up for in comfort.

Chapter Fifteen

IT WAS JUST ON nine o'clock when Annie got home from taking the children to school. She was just about to shut the front door when she heard her name being called. Turning, she saw Harold Gibbs from the Prudential walking up the path.

'You've been out and about early on a Monday morning, Miss Bateman,' he said as he came towards her. 'May I come in for a moment?'

'Of course.' She stood back and allowed him to pass. 'Though I haven't a great deal of time. I have to leave for work by half-past nine. Is there something wrong?'

'Quite the opposite,' he replied. 'I merely wish to give you the cheque due to you from your father's policy.' He set his small attaché-case down on the kitchen table, clicked the two locks, opened the lid and withdrew a long official-looking envelope. 'Open it, my dear, I'm sure you'll find it all in order.'

Annie thought he was giving her a funny look. She looked straight into his eyes, but although he half smiled, he gave no indication of what he was thinking. The envelope was not sealed, and she quickly untucked the flap and warily drew out the cheque. She registered the amount the cheque was made out for, and gasped. She was stunned, and said the first words that came into her head. 'This can't be right! There has to be some mistake.' Shaking her head in disbelief, she moved back slowly and sat down in the nearest chair, having a job to catch her breath. Unable to find words that would cover her confusion, she stared at Mr Gibbs.

He nodded at her and then he smiled, saying, 'It really is absolutely correct.'

'Ten thousand pounds!' Annie said in awe. 'How come? You told me the policy was for five thousand pounds.'

'I do apologise for not having given you the full details. There were several factors that had to be clarified before the policy could be paid out. The main point was that a full inquest was held, and the coroner sent a cause of death certificate direct to the registrar of deaths. Until we had a copy of that certificate stating the cause of death, we were unable to settle your claim. The coroner's verdict was that the severity of your father's injuries was the cause of his death. Those said injuries were sustained in a road accident, and his death was recorded as accidental.'

Annie still stared at the amount for which the cheque was made out. Then she turned to look at Mr Gibbs. 'I still don't understand why the amount is twice what you told me previously,' she stammered.

This time Gibbs allowed himself to smile broadly. 'Miss Bateman, when your father took out this policy he had a double indemnity clause added, which in plain terms meant that should his death be the result of an accident,

160

our company would pay out, to the policy-holder, double the amount of the sum insured.'

Annie didn't answer. She couldn't believe what she was hearing or what she was seeing as she continued to gaze at the slip of paper in her hand, it was supposedly worth TEN THOUSAND POUNDS!

Once again her father had astounded her. There flashed across her mind the thought of his making provision for her. Had he had any premonition that he would die so young, or had he merely acted very cautiously? Was he still watching over her? She let the picture slide away. She had enough to think about for the time being. Mr Gibbs was relocking his case, getting ready to leave. Annie felt compelled to say, 'I haven't been very hospitable, Mr Gibbs. May I offer you a cup of tea, or would you prefer coffee?'

'You've had a shock, or perhaps I should say a surprise,' he answered, smiling. 'Thanks, but I'm all right, really I am, and you have to get off to your work. I would like to give you one little piece of advice before I go; that's if you don't mind.'

Annie stood up, feeling less ruffled, her expression unreadable now. 'I don't mind at all, and whatever you tell me, I'm sure I shall take heed of it.'

He turned to face her and said, 'Well, young lady, there will be plenty of folk only too ready to help you spend that large amount of money. You should take the cheque to the bank. Do it today, and should you decide you need advice, talk to the bank manager. He'll be the one for you to turn to, and he'll have no axe to grind.'

'Thanks,' Annie said sincerely, 'I will do as you say. You have been very kind.'

She led the way out into the hall, then with her hand on

the front-door latch, she turned to him and said slowly, 'I'm very grateful. Truly I am.'

'There's no hurry, you know, lass. No hurry at all to decide what you're going to do. Just get the cheque safely deposited in the bank.'

'I will,' Annie promised, her voice trembling. She gave him a last smile, then quickly shut the door and leant against it. Whatever was she going to do with all this money?

Well, first, I'm going to be late for work, she decided. Flossie won't mind for once. I just can't leave the house till I've had a cup of tea and a darn good think. She stood still for a moment; she clasped the cheque in both hands and stretched it wide. Ten thousand pounds, it said in writing, and £10,000 was written in figures. There was no mistake. Then with a brief thoughtful smile she folded the cheque in half and went through to the kitchen to put the kettle on.

I'll take my time thinking about this, she decided, feeling a great deal more confident than she had half an hour earlier. But for the moment I don't think I'll tell anyone. Gran hasn't got over the fact that I'd got five thousand pounds coming to me. If I tell her the amount is double, she'll have forty fits! Still completely in a daze, she went through the motions of making a pot of tea and within minutes was seated at the table with her hands wrapped round a steaming mug.

So now, she said to herself, I have to figure out what's the best thing to do with this money. Oh, Dad, she sighed, and then remembering his face and those dark eyes that were always full of merriment, she suddenly saw the funny side of all this. What with the cash found in his old tin trunk and the six hundred pounds at the bank, not to mention the cheque that was now in her possession, she had to admit her father had played a blinder and he'd be the first to admit it. The opening of the deposit box had been a let-down. All that worrying, having to have the bank manager and the solicitor present, afraid of what she would find. Then what! Apart from the six hundred pounds in cash, the box had produced nothing such as deeds of which her dad had spoken. Had he meant the assurance policy? It had certainly come out of the blue.

Suddenly she found she was laughing, and she gave way to this new feeling. Once she'd let the dust settle, sorted out what she could about Ronnie and Mary's parents, she could decide then how to spend at least some of the money. That part of it could turn out to be fun, and on that thought she threw her head back and laughed out loud.

consult the librarian that was pacing for pleasure she had a gift for father too provide a stroke and he'd be the first to admit it. The realities of the moment don't all have a balcony. All that derelict leaning, to leaning back manager, and the rotator system, afraid of what she would like. There must figure from the air, let them go out in under my way as I produced nothing such as dead whisper his that out spoke'n. Had its power, the laboratory policy. It had saving a good state of the blue. Buildest the troubled and toughest, and the only way is the new ceiling. Gone the eye the that spe'ck. Sorted out what she could about Ethanis and Mars' motoris, she could figure that flew to see that kept some of the moons. They just at it, oder and next to tonight, and an arm through the throadhat ared took and stepped can long.

Chapter Sixteen

ANNIE WAS UPSTAIRS IN the bedroom she now shared with Mary, once again brooding over the exercise books she had found in her father's tin box, when at five o'clock Doris tapped on the door and came in.

'Not again!' she exclaimed in disbelief. 'How many times 'ave you said that you can't make head nor tail of those books? All this brooding over them ain't gonna alter things. Why don't you just put them back in the box and shove the box under the bed an' forget all about it? What you need is cheering up, and it's for that very reason I'm 'ome early. You an' me are going to a party tonight, an' don't say yer can't come 'cos of the kids, 'cos I already called in at yer gran's and she said she's only too pleased to stay with them. About seven she said she'll be 'ere.'

'Whose party is it?'

'Beryl Robinson's, one of the girls on the same shift as me. You know I got this job at the lampshade factory day after I moved in 'ere? Well, Beryl started two days later and I showed 'er the ropes. She's a good mate; you'll like her.'

'I don't really like parties, and I'm not in the mood. Anyway, how can you say she's a good mate? You've only been at that factory two weeks.'

'Oh, for goodness sake!' Doris cried in exasperation. 'Don't you ever feel like living it up a little? Trouble with you, Annie, is you've always been molly-coddled. What with yer mum and dad, not t'mention yer gran an' grand-dad, you've been spoilt rotten. You've led such a sheltered life it's a wonder you even know what time of day it is.'

Annie looked so shocked that Doris immediately felt sorry, and to cover her embarrassment she laughed too boisterously. Then came a long silence, eventually broken by Annie. 'Do you really think I've been wrapped in cotton wool?' she asked, her voice quiet and serious.

Doris shook her head. 'I didn't mean it like that. It's just that you never seem to have any fun. You're always too busy looking after everyone else. 'Ave you never 'ad a boy-friend?'

Annie's cheeks coloured. 'Yes, of course I have.' Then, feeling as though she owed Doris some kind of explanation, she opened up. 'At the beginning of the war, Rose, one of the girls who was in the same class as me at school, well . . . we met these two soldiers. We never told them we were still at school. We used to dress ourselves up and as soon as we left the house we use to make our faces up so that we looked a lot older. We kind of went steady with them for quite a while. Then they got shifted. But the night they told us they were leaving London we all got a bit tipsy. They were buying us gin and orange. First time me and Rose had ever really tasted alcohol. The long and short of it was, when the pub shut, we went into the park. It was ever so dark and well . . . lots of things happened. I ran off, but Rose wouldn't come. Not long after that, Rose's family moved away. Me gran said at the time it was a wicked shame that a girl so young had ruined her life by getting pregnant.'

'But that was ages ago, and you were only a kid! You're older and wiser now,' Doris protested.

Annie smiled knowingly. 'Could so easily have been me.'

Doris's common sense came to the fore. Jumping up, she took hold of Annie's hand and pulled her up from the bed. Sitting here glooming over the past, trying to unravel her father's affairs, afraid of what might happen in the future was no way for a young girl as lovely as Annie to be spending her days. She already had the door of the big heavy wardrobe open and was sorting through Annie's clothes. 'No more arguments! Me and you are going to this party, and I promise you we will both have a really nice time. Now, let's see what you've got.'

Skirts and tops were pushed to one side. Jackets followed. Then came the dresses – there were only three, and Doris did not hesitate. The one she selected was a deep orange, a straight short-sleeved shift with a round neckline and a double row of brass buttons down the front.

'I've ever only worn that once. It never suited me,' protested Annie.

'Well, I think it's dead smart. The colour will bring out the glints in your dark hair a treat.

'Ere, try it on . . . let me see 'ow it looks,' Doris commanded. 'It fits perfectly.' She sounded a little surprised. 'All of a sudden you look so different. I told yer how well that colour would go with yer hair, but we'll 'ave t'do something different with it.' She lifted up several tresses of Annie's thick hair and let it run through her fingers. She muttered, 'Most women would kill to 'ave hair like this. What do you do with it? Tie it back with bits of tape most of the time. Tell yer what, when we're washed and dressed, I could try putting it up . . . Sit down, let's 'ave a bit of a practice.' Doris brushed Annie's hair so hard she was ready to scream, then she piled it on top of her head, twisting its coils to lie in different ways, using every hair-clip she could lay her hands on, but the result was worth it. Even Annie agreed enthusiastically as she stared at her reflection in the mirror and grinned at it. 'There you are, see. I'll do it proper-like later on and you can use a bit more make-up than you usually do. I'll lend yer some of mine.'

As Rhoda entered the kitchen at a quarter to seven, her jaw dropped and her mouth gaped open in astonishment.

Ronnie nudged his sister. 'See! I told yer Gran would have a fit when she saw our Annie.'

'Well, I think she looks luverly,' Mary answered, still not able to take her eyes off Annie.

'My word!' Rhoda exclaimed, 'talk about a transformation!'

'Don't you think I look all right?' asked Annie, not feeling at all confident.

'My luv, you look marvellous,' Rhoda was quick to reassure her. 'It's just that when I saw you standing there I was thunderstruck.' And she had every right to be.

What she was looking at now was a very different Annie. Her dark hair was piled on top of her head in a profusion of curls. She was wearing make-up that had been applied so professionally that it worked wonders. Her eyebrows had been plucked and shaped. Face powder and rouge, pale green eyeshadow, all finished off with bronze-coloured lipstick. As for the dress! It was showing a bust that Rhoda had never been aware of where her granddaughter was concerned. The length bothered her a bit. It was very short, barely covering her knees.

Annie saw Rhoda staring at her legs, and felt she had to say something. 'Make my legs look great, don't they, Gran? They're not ordinary stockings, they're nylons. Doris gave them to me. First pair of nylons I've ever had, though I have seen Flossie wearing them sometimes when Sid's been taking her out.'

Rhoda couldn't take her eyes away from the tan-coloured shiny hose emphasized by a fancy heel and a straight seam going up Annie's legs. With a pair of plain black court shoes, the overall effect had changed Annie from a pretty girl into a beautiful sophisticated young lady.

Doris, on the other hand, was into the more revealing look. She wore a tight black dress that had a gold belt. Rhoda thought the neckline was too low cut and showed too much of her bosom. She wore black nylons and shoes with very high heels. She had set her own blond hair into soft waves, the ends flicking upwards.

''Ope you 'ave a great time,' said Ronnie, grinning broadly.

'I do an' all,' Mary told them, her eyes still wide with wonderment, as they had been ever since Annie came downstairs.

'Enjoy yourselves! I'm glad you're going out,' Rhoda said approvingly to Annie, 'but watch what you're doing.'

'She had to add the last bit,' giggled Doris as she opened the front door.

*　　*　　*

The party was only two streets away, in a flat over an ironmongers shop, and when Annie and Doris arrived it was in full swing. Music was blaring out and the big room seem packed with couples who were supposedly dancing. As it was a warm July night, all the windows were wide open. Even so, the smoke from many cigarettes hung heavy on the air. Everyone was greeting Doris as if she were a lifelong friend, the men taking pleasure in lingering kisses.

'This is my friend Annie,' Doris repeated over and over again.

Someone thrust a glass at her, saying, 'Have a drink, loosen up, we don't bite.' Annie took this to mean that her bewildered nervousness was showing, so she took a big sip. It looked like orange juice but she knew that the tang to it came from one of the several green bottles of gin lined up on the table. As she had no intention of getting tipsy, she would make her drink last a long time. She had lost sight of Doris. The big room was too full of people and more seemed to keep arriving all the time. When somebody grabbed her, she made no protest, though she had no idea who the young man was, only that he was a good dancer and she had no problem in following his steps when ever he could find enough space on the floor to manoeuvre. The record finished and the young man left her abruptly. A few minutes later she was surprised when he reappeared with a plate of sandwiches and two glasses both held in one hand. She took a sandwich from the plate he offered, but looked suspiciously at the drink.

He grinned, 'It is only orange juice, I promise. I poured it out myself, but you can have my beer if you prefer. By the way, I'm Mike, and you're?'

Annie took a sip of her drink. This did taste different,

it was fresh and sweet with no gin added. She smiled, 'Thanks, my name's Annie.' From then on she enjoyed every minute of the evening.

His name was Mike Maland. Twenty-nine years old, he had just got his first job since being demobbed from the army, as a porter at Covent Garden. A lanky young man with an infectious smile, enthusiastic about everything and everybody that interested him. During the weeks that followed the party it seemed as if Annie were at the top of his list. He very soon found out where she lived, called round uninvited to introduce himself to Gran and to Jack Higgins, who happened to be there at the time. Rhoda liked him a lot, and teased Annie unmercifully whenever Mike came to take her out for the evening. Jack Higgins clammed up. He made no comment on the subject of Mike Maland. Startled by the fact that Annie was going out such a lot, he admitted that he was jealous. Remember, though, he chided himself, she's picked a man who acts a great deal younger than he probably is, someone who is showing her a good time, and she isn't ready to settle down to a serious relationship. Yet he couldn't help worrying. Annie was so vulnerable it would break his heart were she to get hurt. He wanted to protect her against the world.

Annie herself began to think that things were moving too fast. She enjoyed going out with Mike. He was good company and he made her laugh. But she didn't feel that he was the kind of person she wanted to spend the rest of her life with. For one thing, he hadn't much time for Ronnie or Mary. He openly showed this one evening when Annie said she hadn't got anyone to stay with the children and would he like to spend the evening indoors with them.

'No, thanks,' had been his definite answer as he turned on his heels and walked away.

Then one Sunday morning when she was preparing dinner, she heard Rhoda arrive and stop on the doorstep to talk to Gladys Dawson. She couldn't help hearing their conversation.

'I see that Mike's taken a shine to young Annie,' Gladys said in a loud voice. 'I 'eard he danced with 'er all night up at the palais. My Eddie reckons he's a bit old for 'er. An' when yer think about it, our Annie's always bin a quiet sort o' girl while I'd lay me bottom dollar he's bin around more than a bit. If she marries him she'll 'ave her work cut out keeping tabs on him.'

'Well, it ain't got t'that stage yet,' Rhoda said sharply.

Annie was thankful that when Rhoda came into the kitchen she kissed her warmly and never mentioned the fact that she'd been talking to Gladys Dawson. Nevertheless, as the day wore on and Jack Higgins joined them for Sunday lunch, the conversation that Annie had overheard bothered her.

'Would you like to come for a walk? We could take Ronnie and Mary with us if you like?' Annie's head shot up. She was on her knees in front of the cupboard putting the washed dinner plates away. Rhoda was in the scullery making a pot of tea, the children were in the back yard and Doris had gone out for the whole day. Annie turned round, got to her feet, and looked at Jack.

'Well, would you? Yes or No?'

'Do you mean it?' Annie asked, seeing how serious he looked and noting how weather-beaten his face was.

'I wouldn't have asked if I hadn't wanted you to say yes,' he told her truthfully.

'I'd love to come out. It's a lovely afternoon and the kids are always thrilled when you take them anywhere. I am grateful the way you're always there for them. You know, every child should have a man in their lives – more so, little boys. It's some comfort to know that Ronnie has you to turn to when he gets fed up with all us women.'

Jack was thinking that he wished she would turn to him a bit more. I could do with a lot more of your company, he was saying to himself as he went to the back door to call the children.

In the hours that followed, Annie found she was rediscovering haunts of her childhood. Rides on a tram, walking beside the Thames, staring up at the magnificent Tower Bridge, seeing the two sections of the footbridge being raised to allow vessels to pass through, a function that had the children thoroughly enthralled. Jack looked at his watch, declared that it was already half-past three and that he knew just the place to take them to now. Stepping out into the road, he hailed a taxi. The cab drew into the curb, Jack opened the passenger door and helped Annie and Mary inside. 'Regent's Park, please,' he told the driver.

'Righto, mate, taking the kids t'the Zoo, are you?' the grinning cabby enquired.

'Yeah,' Jack answered, settling Ronnie on the pull-down seat and seating himself so that Mary was between himself and Annie. 'We ain't decided yet whether we're going to feed them to the lions or the tigers.'

'Ere, come off it!' Ronnie said. 'We're too young t'die.'

The driver moved off into the stream of traffic with a broad grin on his face.

Mary clutched Annie's hand and said, 'Jack don't mean it, does he?'

Jack looked at Annie, she looked at Ronnie, and they all three burst out laughing.

'Oh, Ronnie,' Mary wailed, 'making out you believed what Jack said. I'm gonna get you for that!'

As the day wore on, Annie got great pleasure from watching the children's faces as they walked from one cage to another seeing all the different animals. Several times when Mary couldn't see over the barrier or was a little bit frightened, Jack swung her up to sit astride his shoulders. Came the time when they were all dragging their feet, Jack took them off and bought them tea, which included an ice cream for each of the children.

Time to head for home, and Annie had a quiet word with Ronnie, which resulted in him saying, 'Jack, me an' me sister 'ave 'ad a smashing time an' we want t'fank you ever so much. Don't we, Mary?'

'Yeah, I ain't never been to a Zoo before.'

Jack patted Mary's head affectionately, then, turning to Ronnie, he asked, 'How about another day we all go to Whipsnade Zoo? It isn't very far and there you can see the animals in a very different setting. They live in wide spaces out in the open air.'

'What, no cages?' Ronnie asked, not at all convinced that Jack was telling the truth.

'No cages, Scout's honour,' Jack assured him.

'That'll be nice, won't it, Mary?' Annie asked.

'I ain't sure, but I'll come if Jack will 'old on t'me.'

'Pet, that's an absolute promise,' Jack told her as he lifted her up and carried her to the bus-stop.

As soon as they set foot inside the house, Rhoda was bustling back and forth from the scullery to the living-room, loading the table with good things to eat that she had got ready while they were out. Ronnie was soon tucking in. Between mouthfuls he talked nineteen to the dozen, telling Gran of everything they'd done and seen.

Mary's head drooped, and Annie whispered, 'She's whacked. I'll take her up to bed.'

As she took off the little girl's clothes and wiped her hands and face with a warm soapy face-flannel, Annie was asking herself what other man would have given his Sunday afternoon up to take out a couple of children that were no relation to him. It was a thought-provoking question. One thing she was sure of: in Jack Higgins she had a good friend.

Chapter Seventeen

ANNIE HAD A PROBLEM. A problem that was making her feel very guilty. The children were due to break up from school this coming Friday, and what she was going to do with them for the next six weeks she had no idea. By rights, she supposed, she should give up her job at the café, stay home and take the children out during the long hot days of August. She didn't relish that idea. She didn't want to be tied down to housework, cooking, washing and ironing. There had to be a bit more to life than drying little Mary's tears when she fell over, soothing Ronnie one minute and scolding him the next. No matter what happened or what either of them wanted, it was always her that they came running to. That was nice, as it should be, the way things had turned out. Truth to tell, she loved it. But twenty-four hours a day? What about me? Who am I supposed to turn to? Besides, it was good to work with Flossie and Sid; most of the customers were jolly and their conversations were on interesting everyday topics, not only about children and what she would give them for their next meal.

She knew she was taking a very selfish attitude – on the whole, the kids were great and she loved having them around. Wouldn't it be nice, though, she was thinking, if they could just be my little brother and sister instead of my having to act as a lone parent. Sometimes the responsibility was too much. The alternative, such as getting in touch with the social people, didn't bear thinking about. She had only to imagine the look on Ronnie's face if she were to tell him that he and his sister were being taken into care. She *would* give up her job and stay at home before she'd let that happen.

'I've been waiting all afternoon for the chance to talk to you,' said Rhoda, the minute Annie put her head round the door. 'Yeah?' Annie grinned. 'An' what am I supposed to have done now?'

'Oh, lass, it's nothing like that. I'd have 'ad t'be blind these last couple of weeks not t'see that you've been worrying yerself sick as to what you're gonna do with the kids while they're on holiday.'

'You think I should stay at home and look after them, don't you, Gran?'

'Now 'old on a minute; don't start putting words in my mouth that I've never uttered. The truth is, no, I don't think you should give up yer job. It gets you out of the house, you meet people and you like working for Flossie an' Sid. Being cooped up with two children all day and every day is no life for a girl of your age. Besides, we think we've come up with a solution.'

'We? Who's we?'

'Well, Doris for one. Since she's living 'ere now, she's said she's more than willing to do her share. It's better when she's on the early shift, but Gladys will fit in with whatever we work out and several of your neighbours along this street 'ave said you only have to ask an' they'll give an eye to both the children.'

'Oh, Gran, people are good. And it's funny you bringing this up now, 'cos today Flossie did an' all. She's got two women who between them will do all day Saturday and another young woman who's offered to do Mondays. Her and Sid said if I can manage just four days, Tuesday to Friday during the school holidays, that will be all right by them.'

'Well, there you are then, luv. It's like I'm always telling you, a problem shared is a problem halved. The kids will be all right, you'll see.'

First things first, Annie decided as she walked up the steps of the Town Hall. Twenty minutes later, having explained her business to no less than three different clerks, she was being shown into a small office on the first floor.

Mr Clemence was a well-built man, late forties, about five foot ten tall, with his shirt-sleeves rolled up and looking decidedly busy. Nevertheless he stood up, greeted her warmly, and said, 'Pull that chair up nearer to my desk, sit down, and if you'll just give me one minute I'll be with you.'

Annie watched him flick papers from one pile to another. Occasionally he jotted notes on a writing pad. Smiling to herself, she was thinking that he radiated energy. Settling his desk into some kind of order, he lifted his head, smiled, and said, 'Right, now we can talk. I got the message that you are trying to trace the parents of two young children who have been in your care for some time, but I wasn't given much in the way of details. If you tell me your problem, we'll see if I can be of some help.'

Annie had already formed the opinion that he was a caring person and she found this surprising, seeing that most Town Hall clerks were too busy to give you the time of day. Whatever the reason, she was grateful. It made telling her story far easier, especially since he listened carefully. When she came to the part where her father had died and she and her grandmother had taken on the responsibility for the children, he never once looked away, rather the reverse. His concentration intensified.

When she had finished, she handed him an envelope. 'I've jotted down every detail that I can think of that might be of some help. Not much, I'm afraid, and some dates and places that I've earmarked are only hearsay that I've picked up from the children from time to time. Well, from Ronnie mostly. His little sister Mary doesn't have much to say. I'm sorry that I've left it so long. To be honest, I've been afraid to make contact with the authorities in case they decided to take the children back into care.'

'And that is the last thing you want to happen, is it?' Mr Clemence asked with feeling.

'Oh, yes!' The words shot out. 'The kids deserve a better deal than that. That was not my reason for coming here.'

'I appreciate that. Now let me tell you what I am able to do. First, I shall pass these details you've given me to the Electoral Registration Officer for the area who will confirm if someone by the name of Robert Wilson or Dorothy Wilson was ever included in the Register of Electors for the constituency of Camberwell, and I will write to you when I have the information. As to the present whereabouts of the children's parents, that's another matter entirely. Pity you know only the Christian name of the gentleman involved in the triangle.'

180

'Yes,' Annie agreed solemnly. 'I don't like to ask Ronnie questions, but just listen when he's in the mood to talk.'

'Shame, really. It's not easy to trace people if they firmly make up their minds to disappear. My advice is, go back to where they used to live, where the boy went to school and so forth. You'd be surprised what one can learn from neighbours.'

Annie laughed. 'I didn't think of that, and I'm sure you're right. Thank you for your help.'

Mr Clemence rose to his feet and came round to the front of his desk. Annie smiled at him, paused, then offered her hand. He returned the smile, shook her hand, and said approvingly, 'You're a plucky young lady. I hope things work out for you and for the two children. Good luck.'

Annie murmured. 'Thank you,' suddenly feeling very shy.

Mr Clemence stood rooted to the spot, watching Annie walk across the room. So young, he thought, so fresh and beautiful, so slender and so unaware of the effect she had on him. A pity, he sighed. She shouldn't be carrying the burden of two young children. She really is lovely. Her crowning glory was her long, thickly waving, rich dark brown hair which she had caught up at the sides with two tortoiseshell combs. Any man in his right senses would go overboard for her.

'Well, that was a turn-up for the books! Never thought anyone would be that helpful. What made him so interested?' Annie wondered aloud as she came out of the Town Hall into the bright sunshine.

Suddenly she had the feeling that this search wasn't going to be anywhere near as hard as she had thought. Why had it never dawned on her to go in search of Dot

Wilson's old neighbours? Like Gran was always saying, you don't need to buy a local paper if you've got nosy neighbours. Maybe I'll get Doris to come with me to Camberwell one day. With that thought in mind, Annie grinned. If anyone could get the local women to gossip it would be Doris. Oh, yes, she'd rush in where angels would fear to tread, and that was exactly what would be needed if she were ever to get to the truth about where Dot and this Charlie went off to.

Don't get your hopes up too high, Annie told herself quietly. You've done well today. At least you've made a start, but not everyone you come up against is going to be as helpful as that nice Mr Clemence. I think the best idea is that this whole thing is going to be one step forward at a time and not to get too upset when we come up against a brick wall. If Dot doesn't want to be found, who knows how long this could take? Anyway, that's enough for today. My first Monday off, and I've left the children with Doris. Still, I'll make up for it this afternoon. It's only just after eleven, so I'll stop on the way home, buy some food and fruit for a picnic and we'll all go to Hyde Park. We'll rub shoulders with the nobs for a change. The kids will love it if I take them boating on the Serpentine. 'It'll be great,' Annie said out loud, as she ran towards the bus-stop.

Meeting Mr Clemence was her first piece of luck, Annie decided as she reread the letter that had arrived only three days after her visit to the Town Hall. Headed Camberwell District Council, Civic Centre, it stated, 'I confirm that I have someone by the name of Robert James Wilson and also Dorothy May Wilson included in the Register of Electors for the above constituency. I regret, however, that I am unable, because of restrictions placed upon me, to disclose their address to you.'

Annie re-folded the letter and asked Rhoda, 'What did you think of it?'

'Well, I can't see what 'elp it is gonna be t'you,' Rhoda sniffed disapprovingly. 'Running round, asking questions all the time.'

'Somebody has to,' Annie defended herself stubbornly. 'How much longer do you imagine we can go on caring for Mary and Ronnie before we have some do-gooder knocking on our door wanting to know the ins an' outs of a donkey's hind leg?'

'Well, since you ask,' Rhoda began, pulling herself up straight and looking righteous, 'I'd leave all the official bodies alone; what they don't know can't worry them. I do understand though, luv, that yer do need to delve a bit into what 'appened to their parents. Poor little mites, beats me how any father or mother could go off into the blue like they 'ave and not give a damn as to whether their kids are being looked after or not. Best bit of advice I can give you is: do what that man at the town hall told yer to. Find some of Dot Wilson's old neighbours, get chatting t'them. You'll get a lot more details from women who lived in the same street than you ever would searching through old records.'

Annie went through to the scullery to refill the teapot, laughing softly to herself because of the thought that had just come to her. If anyone was suited for the job, her gran was, and no mistake. Seated again at the table, she took her time pouring milk into Rhoda's cup and refilling it with fresh tea before quietly asking, 'What are you going to do with yourself today, Gran?'

'Well, as soon as I've seen you off t'work, I thought I'd

give your bedroom a good turn out, and Ronnie's as well, if I've got the time. It's nice that Doris does her own.'

'It's such a nice day, Gran. Do you have t'stay indoors? Besides, Doris did Ronnie's box-room when she did her own on Saturday morning, and mine can stay for another couple of days.'

'What d'you mean, it's such a nice day? Where were you suggesting I go?'

'How about Camberwell?' Annie said, grinning wickedly.

'Oh, I get you! You want me to go an' do some snooping for yer. Is that it?'

Annie avoided a direct answer. 'Do you know anything about Camberwell, Gran?'

'Well, it's many a long day since I set foot there, but that's where I was born. We didn't move to Bermondsey till . . . sorry, I can't remember what year it was but I wasn't very old.'

'So, who better? You might not remember much about the place, but you could ask a few questions. From what Ronnie told me, they lived in a council flat and he went to Peckham Rye school. As least I think that's what he said.'

'Suppose it wouldn't hurt . . . Though I ain't promising nothing, mind.'

Annie laughed. 'What used me dad t'say: you're a diamond? Well, I think you're a double diamond,' she told her, leaning over and planting a kiss on her lined cheek.

'Get on with you! The sooner you take yerself off t'work the sooner I can get meself ready. If I'm gonna go, I may as well make a day of it.'

'Me feet are killing me,' Rhoda moaned out loud. 'Why

in 'eaven's name did I let that daft granddaughter of mine talk me into this?' I must have walked round Camberwell Green twice, she was thinking, nothing is as I remember it, it was such a long time ago when I lived here. She had cut down several side turnings, seen evidence of what damage the bombs had caused. Like everywhere else, demolition was being carried out and supposedly new buildings would rise from all this débris, but it would take a very long time. Can't imagine the time will ever come when there are no scars to remind us of what Hitler and the madness of war had done. Oh, well, she sighed, I've had enough.

'Excuse me.' Rhoda put out a hand towards a passer-by.

The woman stopped. 'Can I help you?'

Rhoda looked around. 'Sorry t'trouble you, but I'm dead beat. Could you tell me if there's a café near 'ere where I could get a cup of tea and a sit down?'

The woman looked hard at Rhoda, suddenly smiled, and said, 'You're in luck. There's a place just up the street. Nothing posh-like, but I pop in there sometimes. It is very clean and the food is extremely good, all home-made. If you turn round and go back the way you've come, after about fifty yards you'll see a lane off to your right. The café is just down there.'

'Thanks ever so much,' said Rhoda. 'You've just about saved my life.'

The woman nodded, moved off, still smiling and Rhoda did a quick turn-about. The café was busy, filled with all sorts of people. Rhoda spied two men just leaving and made her way to what was now an empty table in the corner of the shop. She laid her shopping-bag down on the spare chair, unbuttoned her short coat and carefully hung it on the back of her chair. She would have liked to kick her shoes off, but thought better of it. A blackboard hung on the wall with the day's menu chalked on it in full detail. Having studied it with intense interest for three or four minutes, she sought a waitress.

'You 'ave t'go to the counter t'give yer order.' The woman on the next table was leaning towards Rhoda. 'You fetch yer own tea or coffee, but then they bring yer food over to you when it's ready.'

'Oh, I see. Thank you,' said Rhoda, getting to her feet.

Very nice, clean, homely place, Rhoda decided as she took her mug of tea to the table and settled down. She sat silently for about ten minutes gratefully sipping her tea until a woman, not much younger than herself, wearing a long dazzling white tie-round apron, came with her food. She had ordered home-cooked gammon ham with a poached egg and a roll and butter.

The woman regarded her with sympathy. 'I've been watching you drink yer tea. You must 'ave been gasping.'

'I was,' Rhoda agreed. 'I've been walking round in circles all morning an' I never did find the place I was looking for.'

'Well, eat yer food, luv. It will empty out here in a bit, and I'll come back an' 'ave a chat wiv yer.'

Having drained her mug, Rhoda set about eating her meal and very quickly told herself, this is a treat. The ham was delicious, the egg poached to perfection, while the hot roll was the best bit of bread she'd tasted in many a long day.

'Ready for another cuppa, are yer?' the woman in

the spotless apron asked as Rhoda set down her knife and fork.

'Yes, please. I was just coming to get myself one,' Rhoda replied.

'Stay still. I'll fetch us both one. It's all right for me to take me break now.'

Very soon the two of them were sitting facing each other, drinking tea as if they were old buddies. 'By the way, my name's Daisy. I got this job 'ere soon after the war ended. Should be retired really but who wants t'sit at 'ome all day doing nothing? Be different if my Harry had still bin alive. You a widow an' all? You don't mind me asking, do yer?'

Somewhat taken back, Rhoda said, 'Course I don't,' and concentrated on putting some sugar in her tea.

'You said you'd been walking round looking for some place. Can I 'elp at all?'

Rhoda shook her head. 'Be great if you could, but I doubt it.' Then, throwing caution to the wind, she gave Daisy the outline of the story of just why she was here in Camberwell.

'What did yer say the kiddies' surname was?' Daisy asked.

'Wilson. Their mother was Dorothy and their father was Robert.'

'Sorry, luv,' Daisy said, shaking her head. 'Don't ring no bells with me, but when I've drank me tea I'll ask the missus t'come an' 'ave a word with you. She talks a bit posh like, but got an 'eart of gold. Lived in Camberwell all her life. Had this café for donkeys' years, and if this Mr an' Mrs Wilson lived anywhere near 'ere, it's ten t'one she'll know of them.'

Rhoda was trying to sort things out in her mind. Was

she mad coming here? What the hell had it got to do with her where Dot Wilson had taken herself off to. And who with, come to that! It was no business of hers.

'How d'you do?'

Rhoda came back to the present with a bump, and looked up into the smiling face of a tiny, neat little woman whose grey hair was scraped back into a bun at the nape of her neck.

'I'll sit down, if you don't mind. Daisy tells me I may be able to assist you. My name is Mrs Marjory Sinclair.'

Rhoda had to struggle not to laugh. Daisy was right. She did speak posh. It was so out of keeping, the fact that this elegant lady was the proprietor of this establishment. Clean it certainly was, the food, from what Rhoda had seen, was excellent, yet it could hardly be classed as little more than a working men's café. Oh well, she made an instant decision: in for a penny in for a pound. And with that she once more related the bare details of why she was there.

'Fate,' Mrs Sinclair stated, when Rhoda had finished speaking. 'If it is the same Dorothy Wilson as the one I am aware of, then it has to be fate that has brought you here to my café.'

'Are you really telling me you know her?' Rhoda sounded as astonished as she felt.

'Take me through the details again,' Mrs Sinclair requested calmly.

'Robert and Dorothy Wilson had two children, Ronald, coming up eleven and his sister is now seven years old. The father was, as far as we know, a long-distance lorry-driver.' Rhoda looked doubtful, still wondering if she was doing the right thing. 'What about the children's father?' Mrs Sinclair asked.

'I don't understand. I've told you all we know of him, and we only got that from the little boy. I don't think, in fact I'm quite sure, that no member of my family has ever met him and certainly he's never been to see the children since my son took charge of them.'

'That's probably because Dorothy Wilson went off with a man whose name was Charles Bradford.'

'But that's incredible!' Rhoda stammered. 'You do know them? What was this Charlie like? Where did the pair of them take off to?'

Marjory Sinclair raised her eyebrows and shook her head. 'First answer, yes, my dear, I knew Charles Bradford very well. Second answer, a good-looking bugger, and I mean that. He was a bugger in *every* sense of the word. As to where they went and why and the eventual outcome, you should pay a visit to the offices of the local paper. They didn't print all the details but on two occasions there was a small paragraph.'

Rhoda looked her full in the face, not believing what she was saying. 'Paragraph? About Dot Wilson and this Charlie Bradford, you mean? In the local paper? Whatever did they get themselves mixed up in?'

'With the best will in the world, I don't think it is up to me to relate all the details. Just do as I say and, I assure you, you will have all the answers you need.' Mrs Sinclair was now speaking as if she were humouring Rhoda. 'I am glad I have been able to help. But, as I say, it was fate that brought you here today. It was meant to be.'

Rhoda felt as if she had been dismissed. Deep in thought, she got to her feet, put her jacket on and made her way to the front of the shop. She stopped to pay her bill at the counter. Turning round, she gave Daisy a two-shilling piece as a tip, thinking after all it was Daisy who had suggested she talk to the missus.

'Thanks ever so much,' Daisy said. 'Hope you find what you came looking for, and even if yer don't, come an' see us again sometime. We can always have a cuppa an' a natter.'

Rhoda promised that she would. Of Mrs Sinclair there was not a sign. She walked down the lane, back into the busy thoroughfare of Camberwell Green. She couldn't go home. She had come this far and her next stop had to be the offices of the local paper. Whether she would be sorry afterwards was a chance she had to take. Having this time asked a kindly policeman for directions, and discovered that she had only yards to walk, she set one foot in front of the other, very slowly. Was she about to open a can of worms?

Why, she asked herself, did she have to believe that it was bad news she was about to discover? Why couldn't Dot Wilson and her fancy man have won the Irish Sweepstake and gone on a world cruise? Perhaps they had! Well, she breathed heavily as she pushed open the heavy glass doors of the newspaper offices, there's only one way to find out.

For a few moments Rhoda was floundering. Everyone seemed so busy, until she found an older man who was willing to listen to her request. He had grey hair, steel-rimmed spectacles perched on the bridge of his nose and his whole attitude was reassuring. 'You don't happen to know the date of the issues we're searching for, do you?'

Rhoda confessed that she had no details, only the names of the two people who had supposedly been written about at some time, as near as she could say, within the last eighteen months.

'Not to worry. I was about to go down to the den, as we call it, an' have a smoke. You grab yourself a seat over there by the door where you won't be in anybody's way an' I'll see what I can rake up for you.' So saying, he pulled a pencil from behind his ear and a notepad from the inside pocket of his tweed jacket. 'Now give me the full names of the folk concerned.' Rhoda spelt them out. 'And you say they were local people, and the period you want to know about is within the last two years?'

'Yes, that's right,' Rhoda confirmed.

'Well, that shouldn't be too difficult. Downstairs in the print room we have a memory man. He's as old as Methuselah and there isn't much that goes on in Camberwell or involves any local inhabitant that he doesn't get to know about. Once he has that information, he never forgets it.'

Rhoda fidgeted in her seat. It seemed she had been sitting there for ages. For a time she had watched a young lady behind the counter work a stamping machine. The number of letters and packages that she handled were endless. Although the work appeared to be repetitive, she seemed happy enough. The telephone fixed to the wall rang several times, but not once did the girl attempt to answer it. Each time, a young lad appeared as if from nowhere, shirt-sleeves rolled up above his elbows, speaking to each caller with the same amount of enthusiasm.

Just when Rhoda began to lose interest in her surroundings and had decided that her bottom had gone to sleep and she couldn't sit still another minute, the grey-haired man, whose name she hadn't found out, came striding back across the floor.

'Here you are,' he practically bellowed. 'Methuselah

pulled out the two copies you wanted just like a magician would pull a rabbit out of a hat.'

Rhoda struggled to her feet and fiddled with her bag, endeavouring to find her purse. 'Thank you so much,' she said, at the same time wondering if she would still be grateful when she read whatever it was she would find in these two back copies of a local paper. 'How much do I owe you?'

He tucked his hand into the crook of Rhoda's arm and walked her towards the double doors. 'Oh, I don't think the paper will go bankrupt simply because we've given a charming lady two back numbers. I only hope they will divulge the right kind of information for you.'

So do I! Rhoda was thinking to herself as she shook the newspaper man's hand. So do I!

Chapter Eighteen

AT LAST THE HOUSE was quiet. Annie came down the stairs after having seen the children into bed. Doris was on a late shift, and now there was nothing to stop her and Rhoda from searching through the two newspapers. The children had just arrived home when Rhoda had returned from Camberwell, and after a hurried conversation, carried out in the scullery so that they wouldn't be disturbed, Annie and Rhoda had decided they'd have to wait until the coast was clear.

How she'd got through these past few hours, she didn't know. Her head was whirling. So many unanswered questions. She had cooked the tea and listened to Ronnie's excited chatter about the holidays, but her mind had been elsewhere.

'Come on, sit yerself down, girl. The quicker we get this over, the better,' Rhoda said, laying out the newspapers on the table. 'I've had a quick look-see while you were upstairs but I ain't come across anything yet. Trouble is, I don't even know what it is we're supposed t'be looking for.'

Annie simply stared at the papers, trying to come to terms with what they were doing, terrified of what they might find. It couldn't possibly be good news, otherwise the owner of the café would have come straight out with it and Rhoda would have returned bursting to tell everyone. Eyes down, Annie was perusing the front pages quickly, one at a time. Rhoda made to turn one page, when Annie caught hold of her hand. 'Wait a minute, Gran. Look at the top of each sheet.'

'Well, I'm blessed! All the way home on the bus I was dying to search through these papers and felt I couldn't open them up, not with someone sitting next t'me, 'specially since I didn't know what page I was looking for. All the time, the pages I needed were marked.'

'I'm thinking the same as you,' murmured Annie, noticing the number written in green ink on each top right-hand corner. 'Let's see if we're both right. You take one an' I'll take the other.'

There was a painful silence, only the rustling of the newspapers as they turned the pages, then absolute quiet as they each found the appropriate paragraph and began to read. Rhoda was the first to exclaim, 'Oh my God!' and shook her head so hard that her hairpins became dislodged and fell with a ping on the table. Her hands then flew to cover her mouth as she once again did her best to read the short passage that nevertheless gave so much information.

Annie wasn't watching her gran. Her heart had contracted painfully as she felt the colour drain from her own face. She bravely swallowed, then took a very deep breath. Had she not been able to do so, she would have been sick there and then. This was awful. Absolutely horrifying! Minutes passed. They both continued to stare at the printed words. At last Annie, in a voice that was little more than a whisper, said, 'Dot Wilson is dead. Choked on her own vomit.'

Rhoda didn't answer, and Annie was suddenly afraid. Jumping to her feet, she was at her gran's side. 'Are you all right?' When she felt Rhoda's wrist, her pulse was very rapid, and although her hands were freezing cold, by the look of her face and forehead she was sweating; her colour was decidedly grey. 'Whatever was I thinking about to drag you into all this? Oh, Gran, I am so sorry.'

Pushing aside the newspapers, she half dragged Rhoda to her feet and led her to an armchair. 'Sit down, stay there, I'll get you a nip of whisky.' Oh, why the hell did I send her to Camberwell? I'll never forgive myself if I've made her ill. Seconds later Annie came back, squatted in front of her and placed a glass to Rhoda's lips.

After a couple of sips Rhoda said, 'God, me pore 'ead's spinning! For a moment I didn't know whether I was on me 'ead or me 'eels. I'm all right now. I can hold the glass, anyway, you're making me spill good whisky.'

Annie burst into tears, then laughed. 'I am so sorry. I haven't read your bit yet but I suppose it was dreadful. It certainly hasn't done you any good. I know my blood ran cold when I read Dot Wilson was dead . . . and the way she died!'

Rhoda drained the last of the whisky. 'Hey,' she said gently, doing her best to smile, 'it's not your fault. I knew it wasn't going to be good news. I shouldn't have got so worked up, but it was worse than I ever imagined. When I read it . . . if you want t'know the truth, I thought I was gonna have a heart attack.'

Annie gave a sigh of relief. 'Are you sure you're OK?

We'll leave it for tonight. I'll get us both a hot toddy and we'll forget it.'

'We'll do no such thing!' It was more an order than a request. 'I've told you, girl, I'm fine. Now you make those hot toddies an' don't be mean with the whisky, and then we'll read both reports thoroughly. Together, this time. And then we'll decide what we're gonna do.'

In the course of the next few hours, the two of them went over and over every one of the few words that the reporter had written.

'You're tired to death, Annie, an' so am I,' Rhoda stated.

Annie nodded dumbly. 'My eyes keep wanting to close. I'll put the kettle on and make a cuppa. You're staying here tonight – you can have my bed an' I'll sleep on the sofa.'

'That's a point I'm not going to argue about; me legs wouldn't carry me home tonight. But before you see about the tea, let's get the facts into some kind of order. You go first.' 'For the last time, then,' Annie said, giving her a smile, 'and neither of us is going to get upset.'

So, putting the facts together and in order, it appeared that Dorothy Wilson and Charlie Bradford were involved in a pub brawl. They were both so drunk that the landlord had felt he had to evict them. 'That much we know for sure,' Annie said patiently. 'The next part is supposition. Dot got angry, too drunk to walk, she fell down. Charlie cleared off and left her there.'

'Poor lass,' Rhoda muttered softly, her mood abruptly changing. 'Bad as she was, she didn't deserve that.'

Annie pulled a face. 'Doesn't bear thinking about, does it? She wasn't found until the next morning and by then she had choked on her own vomit. Isn't it awful . . .' Words failed her. She got up and hugged her gran, whispering tearfully, 'How are we gonna tell the children?'

'We'll deal with that later,' Rhoda said, hugging her back, then holding her at arm's length. 'Let's get on with what's happened to their father.'

Annie reached again for one of the papers and re-read the paragraph for the umpteenth time, saying, 'Whichever way you read it, it comes out the same.'

Short and to the point, the reporter had written only the bare facts. Robert Wilson had flatly refused to attend the inquest on his wife or even pay for her body to be buried. He told the police she had left him for another man, and that, in his book, relieved him of all responsibilities. The police had other ideas. They'd issued a subpoena.

At the hearing, Robert's temper got the better of him. He tore into Charlie Bradford like a madman. As if that wasn't bad enough, he threw a punch at the policeman who tried to restrain him. The result was that he was charged with breach of the peace and also with obstructing a police officer in the execution of his duty. Remanded on bail, he again went after Charlie, convinced he was responsible for his wife's death. This time there was no one on hand to stop him.

With Charlie seriously ill in hospital, the police apprehended Robert for the second time, and he was charged with grievous bodily harm. Bail was refused. At the court hearing he was convicted and sentenced to two years in jail. He was in Wormwood Scrubbs prison.

'Complicated, isn't it?' Rhoda sighed.

'Yes,' Annie agreed, 'but at least we're on the right track. What we have to do now is find out if the children's

197

father is still in prison or whether he has served his time and been released.'

'Meanwhile, we say nothing to the kids. You agree on that, don't you? 'Cos the way I look at it is, if they have a father knocking around somewhere then it's up to him to break it to them that their mother is dead.'

'Yeah, as usual you're right. But now can we have that cuppa and get ourselves to bed? I feel so drained, and as for you, God knows what you'll feel like in the morning. Tell you what, Gran, I'll help you up the stairs, get you undressed and into bed and then I'll bring tea and a couple of custard cream biscuits up to you. How does that sound?'

'Tea an' biscuits in bed sounds fine, but I ain't exactly decrepit yet. The day I can't take me own clothes off an'get into bed is the day I'll give up.'

Annie yielded, saying, 'Off you go then, wonder woman. I'll be up to tuck you in as soon as I've made the tea.'

Rhoda laughed and threw her arms round her granddaughter. 'You'll do! Too cheeky for yer own good, but with time we'll knock the rough edges off you and some nice young man will come along and carry you off.'

Much later Annie lay awake thinking about what her grandmother had said. With every day that passed, the responsibility for Mary and Ronnie seemed to grow heavier. Someone would eventually have to tell them about their mother, and in the meantime she would now have the unenviable task of tracking their father down. What had happened to her own daydreams? Obviously her gran still thought there was a lovely young man out there somewhere just waiting to marry her and take care of her for the rest of her life. Although she still went out with Mike Maland, she was well aware that he would never fulfil her dreams. The very fact that Gran, having listened to so much gossip about him, had come to dislike him heartily made him a non-runner.

What a day! If only she could go to sleep and dream about all the nice things that might one day happen to her. After all, she was still young. Ridiculous! she chided herself. There was a whole web of complications concerning two little children that had to be thoroughly unravelled before she could give any thought as to what she wanted out of life. At present Ronnie and Mary had no one to turn to except herself. Hopefully their father might be able and willing to alter that fact. If only they could find him.

She pondered again on the dreadful way their mother had died and the fact that their father hadn't been around because he'd been sent to prison. Suddenly it was all too much, and at that moment all the pent-up emotion drained away and, out of sheer exhaustion, she fell asleep to dream her own dreams.

Chapter Nineteen

THE PREVIOUS DAY'S EVENTS had left Annie feeling as if she were carrying the troubles of half the world on her shoulders, and her legs ached as she waited on the customers in the café. Being Friday, naturally there was fish on the menu, which made the kitchen very hot with all the frying, and trade had been brisk. She'd heaved a sigh of relief when at about two o'clock Sid told her to take her own dinner break.

Sitting at a corner table she enjoyed her meal of pie and chips, thinking that Flossie went to a lot of trouble slowly cooking braising steak for hours and making her own pies. The mass-produced Ticky-Snack pies that most cafés served weren't a patch on them, and the customers knew it.

Sid came across, set a large mug of tea beside her, picked up her empty plate and asked, 'What d'you want for yer pudding, Annie luv?'

'Nothing, thanks, Sid. I'm full up. But I will sit a bit longer an' drink me tea, if that's all right?'

'Course it is, pet. You take yer time.'

Annie watched him pick up a few more dirty plates and mugs, thinking that for such a big man he moved swiftly on his feet. Both he and Flossie were not only good employers but downright good friends. She still hadn't decided whether she would tell Flossie straight away about the way Dot Wilson had died and that Robert, the children's father, had been sent to prison, or whether she'd leave it until after the weekend. By that time she might have worked out how she was going to set about tracing Robert's whereabouts.

When the door opened, Annie didn't look up and was somewhat startled to hear a voice filled with laughter say, 'An' how is my darling Annie today?'

Coming over, Mike Maland put his arm round her shoulder and, his face near to hers, said, 'I've missed you.'

'Have you now?' said Annie. 'Well, you've a funny way of showing it.'

'And what's that supposed to mean?' he asked, pulling himself up to his full height.

'Only that it's nearly three weeks since I've set eyes on you.' Annie was thinking it was no wonder he was such a favourite with the girls. He really was good-looking, sun-tanned and healthy, wearing thin navy blue trousers and a short-sleeved white shirt, wide open at the neck.

'I told you I was going away . . .' Annie cut him off short. Rising to her feet and tilting her head back, she stared straight into his eyes. 'Don't come the old soldier with me, Mike, 'cos it won't work.'

'Aw, Annie luv, don't be like that. I thought we were good mates. You haven't given me half a chance to tell you why I'm here now.' His tone was coaxing.

'Mates? Is that what we are?' His face became wreathed in smiles, and although she knew him to be nearing thirty, she realized his boyish manner made him look years younger. She also recognized that she *had* missed him. She turned her own scowl into a smile, saying, 'You know, Mike, when you're nice, there's no one better, but at times you really are a right bastard.'

'Now that is not fair, Annie! You have no cause to say that.'

'No? How come if you've been working away that you were seen in the Empire Theatre with Rosie, the barmaid from the Two Pheasants? And two nights later you took her to the pictures?'

Mike had the grace to look sheepish. 'You seemed to be spending so much time with those two kids that live with you that I thought you had no need of me.'

'So why not come straight out an' tell me, not spin me a load of lies?' Annie tossed off the remains of her tea. 'I've got t'get back to work. I don't finish till five today.'

'Hang on,' Mike protested, 'give me one minute. Look, what if I say I'm sorry? Will you come to the club with me tomorrow night? I've heard they've got a new manager, an' you wouldn't know the place now he's done it up. What about it?' He squeezed Annie's hand, adding, 'I really have missed you. We can have a bit of a dance, or a quiet drink, just as you like.'

Annie didn't answer, but she was remembering that party that Doris had taken her to and how good a dancer Mike had been even in that crowded room.

'Please, Annie,' he pleaded softly. 'It's a long time since we had a dance together.'

What could she say without appearing crabby? Besides, she badly wanted to go. A night out would make a nice change. So she said, 'All right, Mike. Yes, I'd like to go.'

He moved his tall angular frame to make room for her to pass, smiling like a cat that had got the cream. 'That's settled then. Good, we'll make a great night of it. It's about time you let that beautiful hair of yours down and started to enjoy life. You've been acting like a mother to those two kids for long enough. I'll pick you up about half seven. Will that suit?'

Annie just nodded. Why did he always have to have a dig at Ronnie and Mary? You'd think he could spare a little compassion for two abandoned children.

As she went behind the counter to get through to the kitchen, Mike called after her, 'By the way, make sure you wear something snazzy. I want to show you off.'

Flossie, who had heard Mike's last instructions, was laughing. Sid, however, wasn't so pleased. 'Cheeky sod! Wanting to show 'er off. Bit too much of a fly-by-night for my liking, that one is.' He was grumbling as he followed Annie into the kitchen. 'Still, I gotta agree that a night out will do you a power of good, Annie, luv. Just make sure that slippery eel keeps his 'ands where you can see them!'

Annie and Flossie exchanged glances, and both burst out laughing. 'Slippery eel or not,' Flossie whispered, 'at your age I wouldn't 'ave needed much persuasion t'go out with a good-looking bloke like Mike. You make the most of it, luv. They say that what you've never 'ad you never miss, but don't you believe it! Make hay while you can, is what I say, and when you get old, at least you can look back on yer memories.'

'Oh get on with you, Flossie! I've seen the way you and Sid carry on, an' I'd say you don't have a bad love life.'

'And how would you know?' Flossie retorted, pretending outrage.

For answer, Annie gave a knowing smile and for the rest of the day she appeared a lot more relaxed and certainly in good humour.

At twenty past seven when Annie came downstairs with her coat on, Doris, Rhoda and the children were gathered in the living-room. She had washed her hair and Doris had kindly set it for her, only this time she hadn't put it up. Only the front was piled high and soft tendrils left to trail down over her ears and on to her cheeks. The remainder had been curled into ringlets, then bunched together and secured back with a large black velvet bow. She was wearing a long linen coat of the palest shade of blue.

'Honest t'God, you look regal!' Doris declared, her voice sounding excited. 'I almost wish I was coming with you.'

'Then why don't you?' asked Annie. 'I'm sure Mike won't mind waiting while you get ready.'

Doris roared out laughing. 'And play gooseberry? Not a chance! Besides, I need a night in. I'm whacked after the week I've just had. We're gonna play some great games, we four, an' I've got some really smashing prizes for the winners.'

'Cor, I 'ope I win a prize,' Mary piped up, not taking her eyes off Annie.

'Course you will,' Annie was quick to assure her. This little girl was growing into an extraordinarily pretty child, with golden hair that seemed to float around her head in little wisps. Her big blue eyes were sort of knowing, and although she never had much to say, there was always a hint of childlike curiosity. Annie smothered a sigh, desperately hoping that she wouldn't have to be the one to break it to Mary and Ronnie that their mother was dead.

Rhoda had kept quiet too long. 'Well, come on, let's 'ave a look at you. Open yer coat,' she ordered.

'But you've seen me dress before, Gran. It's what they call the "New Look".'

'Yes, I know, but I want to see it again.'

When Annie undid the buttons and opened her coat, Rhoda, looking at her from head to foot as if she were trying to find fault, remarked, 'You look very nice. At least the dress is calf length and the skirt is nice and full, not like those other two you wear that make you look so thin. That pale blue certainly suits yer. Let's 'ope that Mike Maland knows a bit of class when he sees it!'

There was no need for Annie to reply, as everyone heard the sharp rap of the door-knocker.

'I'll go,' Ronnie volunteered, shooting out of the room before anyone could stop him. 'It's Mike,' he shouted, 'and he's got a taxi waiting.'

Annie bent to kiss Mary, whispering, 'Night, night. Be a good girl and we'll all go out somewhere tomorrow.' The child threw her arms round Annie's neck and hugged her tight.

Doris took hold of Annie's arm, pushing her towards the door. 'For goodness sake get going.'

Walking up the passage, she couldn't fail to hear her grandmother's comments. 'Taxi? He's laying it on a bit thick. Club's not ten minutes walk!'

Ronnie was holding the door open and he winked at Annie. 'She don't mean 'alf of it.'

She tousled his unruly hair. 'You and I know that, Ronnie, but don't you dare let on to Gran that we know.'

'What d'yer take me for? She'd 'ave me guts for garters!'

Annie went down the front path to meet Mike, feeling a darn sight happier than she had for a long time.

The working men's club was very popular, more so on a Saturday night. As Mike and Annie came through the swing doors they could smell fresh paint. The hall was well over fifty feet long with a secluded L-shape addition that boasted well-padded seats. Small tables and gilt chairs were set around the edge of the dance floor that dominated the main area of the hall. At the far end there was a long bar, and adjacent to that a raised platform on which tonight a four-piece band was set up.

The club was already packed, and Mike eventually found two seats in a corner against the wall. Annie sat down while he stood for a moment making signs with his hands and nodding his head to acknowledge greetings from his mates at other tables.

When the band stopped playing, amid great applause, Mike made his way to the bar counter while Annie, with wide smiles, acknowledged the greetings from the girls and women that she knew. To their 'Hello, Annie, how yer doing, girl?' she made suitable replies and when Gladys Dawson's daughter-in-law, Phoebe, came towards her, saying, 'Don't tell me you've been let off the lease, Annie? How come you're not stuck indoors minding young Ronnie an' his little sister?', Annie laughed. 'Even I get a break now an' again, Phoebe.'

'I must say you deserve it. Though honest t'God

I 'ardly recognized yer. You look smashing, you really do, especially yer hair.'

'Thanks, Phoebe,' Annie murmured, feeling herself blushing.

'I see you came with Mike Maland,' Phoebe said solemnly, feeling she'd like to warn Annie off that one. Perhaps it was something in Annie's face that deterred her; she looked so happy and she must have spent a long time getting herself ready because she really did look different. 'Well, luv, have a good time,' was what she did say. 'I'll see yer later.'

Mike came back with the drinks, a gin with a slice of lemon in it and a bottle of tonic water for Annie and a pint of bitter with a whisky chaser for himself. As they drank and talked, Annie got the feeling that Mike had been drinking before he picked her up, but pushed that idea to the back of her mind. The atmosphere in the club was one of jollity and good fellowship. When the master of ceremonies announced that before they continued with the dancing they were going to have community singing, this was greeted with loud laughter and much hand-clapping. And when everyone around her was singing all the old songs, she too sang, and wondered why she didn't come to this happy place more often. These people were her friends and neighbours. She had been brought up among them. They'd all lived through the terrible long years of the war and in the main had proved they were good solid people, working hard and playing hard, like now. She had the sense to realize that the club was nothing like a smart restaurant or a night club that you'd find in the West End; none the less, this way of life suited these folk.

The band was trooping back on to the stage, and Mike

was saying, 'That's over. Now we can get on that dance floor. Come on.' He pulled at her arm.

'But they haven't started playing yet.' She was reluctant to be the first on the floor.

'They will in a minute. Do come on.' Mike, being a show-off, did not want to appear as one of the crowd, but as one of the best dancers in the club. This would be achieved only if he and Annie were first on the floor.

The first tune was a quick-step and Mike was in his element; so was Annie. He really was a superb dancer and she had no difficulty in following his varied and complicated steps. As the tune ended, the clapping was long and loud and Annie was aware that a great deal of the applause was for Mike and herself. Back at her seat, Annie looked around. Everyone was enjoying themselves and the ladies, young and old alike, had taken pains with their dresses. After the necessary utility clothes of the war years, the colourful fabrics and the wide full skirts were a joy to behold, while the low necklines were very feminine.

After a waltz and a slow fox-trot, in both of which Mike would have said they were the star performers, then came the entertainers. Singers, dancers, comic turns and stand-up comedians, each following hard on the other. Excellent entertainment, but it did not hold Mike's attention. During a short time he had consumed two double whiskies and two pints of beer, and now he was becoming hard to handle. He kept trying to kiss her, and she thrashed her head from side to side doing her best to stop him until he took her chin in a grasp so tight that it hurt.

'Listen, Annie, I want to tell you something.' Knowing he now had her full attention, he let go his grip on her

209

face and pulled out a flashy cigarette case, offering it first to her.

'Mike, you know I don't smoke,' she said, looking at him closely, and suddenly she came to the conclusion that, despite his strong sexual attraction, his mouth looked cruel and his eyes were cold.

'Is something wrong?'

'No, nothing,' she replied, laughing a little falsely.

'What I'm trying to tell you is, my mother and father are going to Southend this weekend.' He leaned enthusiastically across the table. 'You can come and spend the weekend with me. We'll have the whole house to ourselves.' He put his face close to hers and grinned, leaving Annie in no doubt as to what he was thinking.

Very quickly Annie shot back, 'I couldn't do that, Mike.'

He raised his head and his eyes flashed. 'Don't you dare use those kids as an excuse! Get yer gran or someone to mind them for a change. I've got the whole weekend mapped out for us and I'm buggered if I'm gonna let two kids spoil my plans.'

'I can't.' Annie's voice suddenly faltered and her cheeks reddened.

'There's no such word as can't. We'll have a great time,' he told her, his voice thick and his words slightly slurred.

Suddenly he leaned across her and placed his hand tightly over her breast. Annie gasped. His face was only inches from hers. His other hand was travelling slowly all over her body until he brought it to rest on her thigh. He was trying to kiss her again, and when she wouldn't open her mouth to his probing tongue, he bit her lip. He was insistently pulling at the front of her dress. There was nothing tender about his actions, no love nor yet kindness.

Making a supreme effort, she pushed hard at his shoulders. 'Mike . . .' she gasped in a voice that was hoarse and pleading. 'Please . . . stop it . . . please.' By now she was feeling utterly wretched.

'What's the matter with you?' His voice, tight, ruthless, made her give him another shove, enabling her to sit up straight. 'You're nothing more than a bloody tease,' he hissed. Then suddenly he became aware that a good many people were looking at him curiously. He could see the contempt in their eyes. He took his hand off Annie's thigh and raised his glass to his lips in an act of defiance.

Annie straightened her skirt, took a deep breath and felt the swift beat of her heart slow down. She felt terrible. How could Mike act like this? And in a crowded place where more than half the people sitting near them knew her so well. Whatever would they be thinking of her? 'I'm going to the ladies,' she murmured, looking down to search for her handbag on the floor. It was as she straightened up that her eyes locked on to those of Jack Higgins.

At that moment she wished with all her heart that the floor would open up and swallow her. He was only yards away, standing with a group of men, all of whom had a pint glass in their hand. How long had he been watching her and Mike? Feeling utterly embarrassed at the way Jack was staring at her, she stood still a moment with her bag clasped under her arm, before turning and walking the long way round the hall to get to the ladies rather than passing near Jack Higgins.

'Annie, don't you like me even a little?' Mike whispered in a pleading voice, the minute she returned to her seat.

By now she was aware that he was more than half drunk. She sat still, staring at him, too angry to answer. There was no sign of Jack. Her face flamed up as she again remembered the look in his eyes. Had it been shock or, even worse, loathing?

'Annie say something, anything,' Mike wheedled. 'It was mostly your fault anyway, you've always led me on.'

'I have not!' she cried indignantly. 'You should know by now that I like you, when you're sober that is, and I truly like dancing with you. But as for the rest, well . . . that's just not me. And to be carrying on like that with all these friends and neighbours looking on, I'd say that was taking things too far, wouldn't you?'

Mike glared at her. 'Aw, go to hell,' he said, getting to his feet and roughly pushing past her. He made for the bar, and there he stayed.

Annie was undecided as to what to do. She just wanted to get out of there, to go home, but it would be daft to start walking off on her own as it was already turned midnight. Then Phoebe was looking down at her. She took a packet of cigarettes from her bag and lit one before sitting down next to Annie. 'Well, that was a right performance! I knew I should have warned you off him, but me mum said you'd been out often enough with him to know what he's like, so I kept me mouth shut.' Annie looked down at the polished table. She picked up a beer-mat and bent it back and forward between her hands, and as she did so, Phoebe leant forward quickly and said under her breath, 'Come on, Annie, you don't have to feel uncomfortable in front of me. At least you should know that.'

Annie closed her eyes and swallowed, then asked, 'What

did you mean when you said you knew you should have warned me?'

'You sure you want me to tell you?'

'Yes, I do. It was terrible the way Mike began mauling me, but I'm trying to make allowances for him because he was drunk. But if you know something that I don't, I'd like to hear it.'

Phoebe smiled at her through the smoke of her cigarette. 'You mean to sit there an' tell me you don't know about Mike an' all his lady friends?'

Annie hesitated. 'I know he's lied to me sometimes, but . . . let's hear what you were going to say.'

'All right, straight answer to a straight question without going into the intimate details. I know for a fact that Mike Maland is a womanizer, a liar and an' all-round rotter.' Annie slumped against the back of her seat. Phoebe remained still for a time as she looked into Annie's face, then said quietly, 'You know, luv, you can do a darn sight better for yourself than that toe-rag. You're young, you're good-looking and you dress well. If only you'd put yourself about a bit more you'd have quite a few decent men knocking on yer door. That's no baloney, it's the truth. One more thing, an' then I'll shut up. You're well rid of Mike Maland, believe me, Annie, you are. Well rid!'

The force with which Phoebe said it was something else, and Annie couldn't keep a straight face. As Phoebe started to laugh, Annie felt compelled to join her. Some minutes passed before their chuckling ceased and even then Annie had to wipe her eyes before she was able to say, 'Thanks, Phoebe. You've been great. I'm ever so glad you were here tonight. But I think I'll go home now; I'm feeling a bit tired.'

'Go home, on your own? Like as hell you will.' She looked warningly at Annie. 'Come on over to our table. If you don't want any more to drink, me old man will get us both a coffee. We'll all be going home shortly. You come along of us, we'll see you safely to yer door.'

Annie was glad to do as she was told. She enjoyed the women's company and was grateful for the hot coffee. It was when the band was playing the last waltz that Annie saw Mike and a heavily made-up redhead standing at the bar. The young woman had one elbow on the counter and was looking at Mike, but Mike, with his broad back tight against the counter, was looking directly at Annie.

Phoebe had seen him too, and leaning towards Annie, whispered, 'Don't let him bother you. I'll come with you to get our coats and then he'll know we're taking you home, all right?'

'Yes, thanks. Thanks for everything, Phoebe, you've been a brick.'

'Just so long as you don't let that tike put you off coming to the club again. It's a great place, an' the way you dance you ain't never going to be short of a partner. Besides, you can always come with me an' the family, no problem. We all of us believe the more the merrier.'

They were both smiling as they made their way to the cloakroom and Annie was telling herself that all in all it hadn't been such a bad night. She would have admitted to having had a great time if only Mike hadn't got so drunk. But he had got drunk, and now the effect of the drinks she'd had were wearing off, the worst outcome didn't bear thinking about.

She knew well enough that many a long day would pass before she'd be able to wipe out the memory of the way Jack Higgins had looked at her. She was furious with herself and with him. Why had he had to be in the club at that particular moment? Oh, the humiliation! What will I say to him when I meet him face to face? What if he tells Gran? What am I going to do? How can I explain that I sat there and let it happen?

Even when she was safely home and in her own bed, she was still asking, How could Mike cheapen her so in front of all those people? Some might even think she was a tart. Dear God, what am I going to do? She didn't know. She really didn't know.

breakfast and with him? Why had he had to be in the club the same night... that morning? Oh, the humiliation! What will I say to him when I meet him face to face? What if I talk. Or am I... What am I and I going to do? How can I explain that I am alone and let it happen?

Alice... there was being shown that if... her own back she was still waiting... How simply then... damper but... then all those foolish... Sure that to... why must anyone... tomorrow... then come or the best... together... her vision in part... that one might still be funny.

Chapter Twenty

'DO PLENTY OF POTATOES, Jack's coming for his dinner,' Rhoda called through to the scullery where Annie and Doris were doing the vegetables. 'By the way,' she said, appearing in the doorway, 'better make it a good Sunday dinner, 'cos it's the last Jack will be 'aving with us for some time.'

Annie turned to stare at her gran. Jack hadn't come for his dinner last Sunday, which was the day after she'd had that to-do with Mike in the club. During the past week she had dreaded the moment when he would put in an appearance and wondered constantly what she would say to him when they met face to face. Her heart raced as she asked, 'Why will it be the last dinner he'll have with us for some time?'

Rhoda was bending over the oven, lifting the joint of beef out in order to baste it, and didn't answer straight away. Annie had said nothing to Doris about that Saturday night, but on the following Monday evening Doris had taken her aside and very quietly told her, 'I heard at work today what a good dancer you were. I also got several versions of how Mike Maland behaved. Four words, Annie luv, and then we'll never refer to him again.'

'Well, go on,' Annie had urged her.

'He's not worth it.'

At that they had both laughed, and Doris had clasped her arms round Annie and held her close for a moment. The fact that Jack Higgins had been in the club and had seen it all was never mentioned.

'That's a lovely bit of beef. Can't beat cooking it on the bone,' Rhoda said, patting her stomach as she dropped into a chair.

'Gran, what was that about Jack?' Annie asked impatiently.

'Oh, he came in on Wednesday evening and said that in about a week he was taking his boat up to Grimsby and that he'd be away quite a while.'

'But Grimsby's a fishing port. What would Jack be doing with fish? He's a lighterman,' Doris wondered.

'I was just about to ask that question,' said Annie.

'Well, I asked him that very same thing an' as it turns out we're all wrong. Jack told me, at great length I might add, that yes, Grimsby docks do deal with an enormous quantity of fish but there is also a good trade in coal and timber. Said it's the timber he's interested in. Don't ask me anything more, 'cos I don't know.'

'That's all he told you?' Doris still sounded surprised.

'Yes. Except that he still wanted to keep his room an' gave me a month's rent – t'be going on with, is what he said.'

At that moment they heard the front door open and Jack walked in carrying a cardboard box from the off-licence which he placed on the kitchen table. 'Why are you all out in the scullery?' he called, adding, 'Bring some glasses with you. I've bought a few bottles.'

Annie came through to the living-room first and for a couple of minutes they stood looking at each other without speaking, until the silence became unbearable and she said, 'Hallo, Jack.'

'Hallo, Annie. How are you feeling?'

'I'm all right, thank you,' she said, reaching up to take glasses down from the dresser.

Jack poured a Guinness for Rhoda and a milk stout for Doris and Annie. They had hardly raised their glasses to their lips when the children came bursting in, shouting that they'd seen swans on the river and if Annie had any bread to spare, could they go back after dinner and feed them?

'Don't we get a drink?' Ronnie asked cheekily, his eyes shining and his cheeks flushed.

'*Ronnie!*' Annie cried. 'You wait to be asked, and if you're that thirsty there's plenty of water in the tap. Now say you're sorry to Jack for being so rude.'

'Sorry, Jack,' said Ronnie, doing his best to look sheepish.

'That's all right, lad. Now ask your gran if I may make a shandy for Mary and one for you.'

Rhoda was smiling to herself. It was good to see the kids so happy and looking carefree. Being out in the sunshine was doing them good, and although she daren't mention the fact to young Ronnie, his forehead and across his nose was covered in freckles. He'd be bound to take some teasing from his mates at school about that.

'Go on, then,' she grinned at Jack. 'Give them both a

drink, but then see to it that while we're finishing off in the scullery they set to and lay the table in 'ere.'

'Always 'as t'be a catch,' Ronnie muttered.

'I 'eard that, young man,' Rhoda called over her shoulder. 'Any more of yer cheek, an' you'll get no dinner.'

Jack winked at the lad, and like two grown men they touched glasses and said, 'Cheers', before taking a big swig of their drinks.

'Hey, what about me?' Mary wailed, her hands wrapped tightly round her glass.

Jack bent down, touched his glass against the edge of hers and said, 'Cheers, Mary.'

'Cheers,' she answered, her face wreathed in smiles. 'I'm ever so glad you've come t'dinner today, Jack. You didn't come last week.'

Jack felt his throat tighten. She was such a sweet little girl. In fact if he were honest, he thought that the pair of them were great kids.

Their long-drawn-out Sunday dinner was a happy one, mainly because Ronnie kept up a constant stream of chatter. He was a good mimic, and putting his school teachers to the test, he had them all smiling. Annie did her best to avoid looking at Jack and, apart from politely asking him if he would like more meat and again at the pudding stage whether he would like more custard with the steamed treacle pudding, they never said a word to each other.

With dinner over and the children out in the back yard, Rhoda asked Annie, 'Would you mind if I went upstairs an' 'ad a lay down on your bed? Rest me legs a bit. I'll get up in time t'get the tea.'

'You go ahead, Gran. Would you like a cup of tea or coffee now? I'll bring it up.'

'Cup of tea would be nice,' Rhoda said as she moved towards the stairs.

'I'll make it,' Doris offered, diving towards the scullery. 'Annie, you stay there and talk to Jack.'

When again the silence became unbearable, Annie told him, 'The children are going to miss you when you've gone.'

Jack laid his head back against the top of his chair and stared up at the low ceiling as he said, 'I have to get away. I could cheerfully have murdered Mike Maland last Saturday.'

'Oh, Jack.' She lowered her head.

'I suppose it was nothing to do with me. You must have agreed to go out with him. It was him you came to the club with, but how I kept my hands off him I'll never know. I had to walk out of the place or I would have done him over good an' proper.'

'Oh, don't say that.' Fear showed in her eyes. 'It sounds awful . . . You never would have really hurt him.'

'How do you know, Annie, what I would have done?'

Their eyes locked, and it was some seconds before he went on, 'Mike's always had a reputation where the ladies are concerned, and it never worried me one jot. That was his business. But not you, Annie. No, I couldn't stand by and watch that happen. You always appeared like a child to me. You must have been about nine years old when I went into the Navy and even then you were a lovely girl. At the time I thought . . . Well, it doesn't matter what I thought then.'

Annie was taken aback by the warm, tender expression on his face. She couldn't bear it. He'd told her what he used to think of her, but what about now? She felt dirty. Soiled. He'd said he could have murdered Mike. What about her? Did he think she'd carried on like a tart? The last thing she wanted was for him to think she had encouraged Mike.

Very abruptly he got to his feet. 'Annie,' he paused and cleared his throat. 'I'd better be going. Lot to do before Wednesday. Your gran told you I'm going to Grimsby?' She stood up and looked into his face, close to hers now. Jack was a nice kind man. Look how he always had time for Ronnie and Mary. Suddenly he straightened up and grasped her hand tightly, then looking at her very solemnly, said, 'Take care, Annie. Watch what you're doing.' He let go her hand and she stood rooted to the spot, listening to him stride away up the passage. The front door opened and closed.

She felt overwhelmed by a feeling of emptiness, as if she had lost someone or something very dear to her. But she had never truly got on with Jack, never felt at ease with him, not until the children had suddenly become her responsibility. Then she remembered the time her father had lain so ill in hospital, and especially the night he had died. Jack Higgins had been her mainstay at that time. He had certainly been there for her, every day. She could never have coped without him. Now, she didn't think that his opinion of her could be very great, and she felt sorry for that. Very sorry.

The hot weather continued, and the children were as brown as berries. They let it be known how much they missed Jack. Especially young Ronnie because, as he said, Jack had taken him to a couple of football matches and even played ball with him and his mates in the park. Once Annie had heard Mary say to him that she wished they had a daddy like everyone else.

Annie, too, found it very difficult to accustom herself to the fact that Jack Higgins was no longer around. She had done her best to keep them happy and occupied during the long summer holidays, taking them to see Buckingham Palace and the changing of the Guard. A whole day they had spent in Kew Gardens, another morning they'd fed the pigeons in Trafalgar Square. The most interesting, as far as Ronnie was concerned, was their visit to the Tower of London.

Young Mary had been terrified of the beefeaters and even more so of the yeomen.

'There's an awful lot of ghosts in 'ere,' Ronnie teased her. 'My mate at school said he saw two walk right through the walls.'

'Well, I ain't going any further,' Mary said, scowling at him.

At this point Ronnie had run off on his own, but not before he'd called his sister a scaredy-cat. Annie had been quick to defend her and given her a bar of chocolate, telling her to eat it up quickly before Ronnie came back. Left on her own with Annie, Mary was soon pacified and grinned broadly as she ate the last square of chocolate, and Annie spat on her handkerchief and used it to wipe all traces of the treat from her mouth.

Now there was only one week left of the school holidays. Annie decided that the time had come to spend some of the cash her father had left. The five hundred and forty pounds she had found in his tin box she had been using to pay the rent and household bills, because the money she earned at the café was enough only to buy food for the three of them. There was still quite a bit left, but not enough to rig out the children and herself in new clothes ready for the coming winter. However, there was the cash, six hundred pounds, that had been discovered when her father's safe deposit box had been opened. Mr Mathews, the bank manager, had assured her that she could draw on that at any time. As to the vast amount from the insurance company, she had deposited that cheque with the bank and so far had no idea whatever of what she was going to do with it. Somehow it still didn't seem right, all that money!

Time and time again she had puzzled over why her father had taken out such a policy, and furthermore why he had made her the beneficiary. Surely her brother David was entitled to at least half of the amount, if not the whole sum, seeing as he was the elder? She would give a lot to be able to talk to David about this, to share the money with him. But apart from that short glimpse of him at their father's funeral, she hadn't seen or heard from him since the day he left home. And that was all because of Dot Wilson and the way she carried on. Annie sighed deeply. The poor woman was dead now and had died in the most horrible of ways, but she still had an awful lot to answer for.

Breakfast was over and everything tidied up. Annie looked hard at young Ronnie, trying to decide how to tell him that he was about to get a new school uniform. He'd probably moan like hell at the idea of a day going round the shops. The lad was all energy and go from the moment he got up to the time he fell exhausted into bed. He'd much rather spend the day down near the docks or kicking a football about in the park.

'I was going to take you to the Elephant and Castle this morning but I've changed my mind,' Annie told them with a smile. 'Thought we might go to Brixton instead. There's the Bon Marché, that's a super shop, and there's also a great street market. We should all be able to get decent new outfits, but if we can't find what we're looking for today, there's always tomorrow to try somewhere else.'

'Crikey, Annie, what you on about?' asked Ronnie.

'School uniform mostly,' she answered seriously.

'Oh no,' Ronnie moaned. 'I might 'ave guessed it was something like that.'

'Well,' Annie pleaded, 'not only you. Mary needs new clothes and so do I, come to that. There's only a week before you go back to school and I'm sure that what you wore last term won't fit you now. I have to get you both rigged out.' At last, since March, clothes were no longer rationed, thank goodness. They would never have had enough coupons to get everything they needed, after all the years of making do.

Poor Ronnie! He looked so . . . Annie couldn't find the right word, but she knew what was coming and she felt for him. He was too young to be so embarrassed.

Ronnie said, 'You're probably right about our clothes not fitting us, but new outfits will cost a packet, though.'

'We don't have to worry about that, thanks to your Uncle Jim,' Annie solemnly said. 'I know it was sad when my dad died, but he left enough money to see us all right, and he left a special letter with the money – it's called a will – saying that we should use it and be happy.'

'I think that's ever so nice. I loved Uncle Jim,' said Mary dreamily.

'That sounds like 'im,' said Ronnie. 'But 'ow could he 'ave known that he was gonna get knocked down by a bus an' killed?'

'I can't tell you the whys and wherefores of why people

225

make out wills before they die,' warned Annie, casting an eye in Ronnie's direction, 'only that parents mostly do so in order that their children will be taken care of should anything happen.'

'But he wasn't our dad.' Ronnie muttered so low that Annie barely caught the words.

'Yes, but wasn't it a good day for me when he brought you and Mary to live here? Just you think about it. I would be all on my own if it weren't for you two,' she coaxed, knowing full well what was still going through Ronnie's mind.

'Am I gonna get new shoes? 'Cos my old ones I wore to school last time hurt my toes,' Mary complained.

'The best in the shop,' Annie told her. 'Then you'll be leaping about all over the place.'

'What yer mean – I might be a ballet dancer?'

Ronnie roared with laughter at the sight of the serious look on his sister's face. 'Ain't she the best tonic there is, Annie?' he said when he quieted down.

'Yes, she is. Just having her around does me a power of good. And you, an' all,' she hastily added.

'Why, thank you, mam,' Ronnie mimicked. 'I shall do me best t'behave while you're dragging us round the shops. Just don't take too long choosing dresses, and don't try too many fancy hats on, will you?'

Annie was suddenly filled with happiness, feeling as though it wasn't going to be such a bad day after all. It was true what she had told Ronnie. She would be all on her own were it not for these two smashing youngsters.

She was still feeling good as she shut the front door, took hold of Mary's hand and set off down the street. Ronnie was well ahead, and Annie laughed to herself. His curly hair had been smarmed down with Brylcreem from an old jar that her father had been known to use. Ronnie turned to look back at them. He must be happy, she was thinking, just look at his wide grin and those laughing, cheeky big brown eyes. 'Come on,' he yelled, walking back towards them with what seemed today to be a swagger in every step.

'I suppose we'd better concentrate on Mary first,' Annie suggested as they got off the bus at Lambeth Town Hall.

'We'd better get in the shops pretty quick,' said Ronnie, looking up at the sky which was gradually darkening. 'It's gonna chuck it down in a minute.' Annie and Mary trudged after him as he darted between the traffic.

She breathed a sigh of relief as they pushed open the swing doors of the big department store and made for the children's section. With great composure, Annie explained their needs.

The young lady shop assistant had the patience of Job. Mary was being awkward, not liking any of the clothes the girl offered. Annie was annoyed as she once more pushed aside a navy blue drill slip, refusing to go into a cubicle and try it on. 'Mary, you cannot have any of those pretty dresses you're looking at. School uniform is what you need today. She's usually such a good little girl,' Annie murmured to no one in particular.

'You, Mary, try behaving yourself,' said Ronnie. 'Annie's doing 'er best for you.'

Mary sounded indignant as she answered back. 'I never asked for no uniform, did I? An' you didn't ought to take 'er part.'

'Well, I'm flabbergasted,' Ronnie sighed. 'It's a long time since she showed off an' 'ad one of her tantrums.

227

I'm gonna go if she don't pack it in, or maybe you'd better give 'er a slap,' he added, staring hard at Annie.

'Eh?' For a moment Annie gaped at him, a puzzled frown on her forehead. 'I've never raised a finger to either of you, and I'm not about to start now.'

'A slap is all she understands when she gets in a mood,' Ronnie said with his usual candid honesty. 'It would be better coming from an old 'un like you, Annie, 'cos if I slap 'er she'll scream the place down.'

'You cheeky beggar!' Annie scolded him. 'I'm fast losing my own temper, and we've hardly started on what we came out for. Never mind,' she smiled apologetically at the assistant, 'we'll leave the uniform for next time,' thinking, there won't be a next time if I have anything to do with it! I'll let Gran bring Mary, and see how she gets on with what she wants an' what she doesn't.

They gathered their belongings and Annie helped Mary on with her coat, then saw that Ronnie was grinning. 'And what is it that's amused you?' she angrily enquired. And without waiting for a reply, she said, 'How come you said a slap would come better from an old 'un like me? Is that how you see me? A really old one?'

Ronnie's grin broadened. 'Not me, Annie! A slip of me tongue, but I knew straight off I shouldn't 'ave said it. Caught you on the raw, didn't it?'

'Answer me,' Annie demanded. 'Is that what you always call me? An old one?'

'Not me, Annie, I wouldn't dare! Come on, I'll race you to the boys' department.' Darting her a cheeky grin, he strode off, leaving his peevish sister for Annie to coax into a better frame of mind.

By the end of the morning, Annie was completely exhausted, but Ronnie didn't seem to be flagging at all.

'Let's go to the shoe department next,' he suggested, then asked, 'Annie, will your money run to football boots? I've never 'ad a real proper pair.'

'We'll see,' Annie told him, taking the neatly packed blazer from the gentleman assistant and putting it in her shopping bag.

'I wouldn't mind trying on some shoes.'

Annie and Ronnie turned to look at Mary. It was the first time she had spoken since they'd left the girls' department.

Annie cleared her throat and said firmly, 'It's about time we had a drink and something to eat. Besides, if I don't sit down for a little while I think I shall fall down. Wouldn't you like a cool drink, Mary?'

'Please,' she murmured, her voice a little unsteady.

It was the 'please' that brought tears suddenly to Annie's eyes, and she was tempted to sweep the little girl up into her arms. Who knows what had brought on her fit of resentment? Maybe she was thinking that her mother should have been here to buy her school uniform. Whatever, Annie now had a lump in her throat.

They made their way up to the next floor and into the restaurant with Annie leading the way to a table near the window. The children looked around before seating themselves. Their mouths dropped open, and Ronnie gasped, 'Crikey, ain't it posh?'

Mary clapped her hands, saying, 'Are we gonna 'ave our dinner 'ere?'

Annie told her, 'We most certainly are. I'll read you the menu and you can choose whatever takes your fancy.'

Annie remarked later, as they emerged at last from the store, 'It was much more fun buying shoes, wasn't it?'

'It sure was. I got lace-up shoes an' me football boots. Mary got shoes for school and a pair for best, and even you bought two pairs for yerself.' Ronnie had insisted that they did want the shoe-boxes, so he was struggling with three bulky carrier bags each containing two pairs of shoes neatly wrapped in tissue paper and packed in their boxes.

It was late by the time they got on the bus; all the workers were going home. 'On top only,' the conductor called, swinging round the pole to ring the bell before they'd hardly got on board.

Ronnie got a double seat to himself and sat surrounded by their parcels; in the seat behind, Mary sat cuddling up to Annie. 'I never got my stuff for school,' she said softly.

'Never mind. Tell you what, another day we'll let Ronnie go off with his mates an' you and I will come shopping on our own. Or we could ask Gran to come with us, if you like.'

Mary didn't answer straight away. She was curled up against her, holding her hand, feeling warm and safe. 'I do love you, Annie,' she said drowsily, her voice so low that Annie had to strain to hear the words.

Oh, Mary, whatever am I going to do with you? Annie wrapped her arms even more tightly round the child. There was no denying it, even her teachers at school complained that she was often disobedient and wilful, but when it came to the crunch how could anyone be hard on such a child?

Very late that night, Annie sat up in bed, hugging her knees and staring into the darkness, thinking about Dorothy and Robert Wilson. One of them was dead and God alone knew where the other one was. It was no good – the children had to be told, but who was going to do the telling? She was quite sure that it couldn't be herself. Annie loved them both, of course she did, but it was such a big responsibility. How she wished their father would turn up and tell her it was all right for the children to stay with her, but that at least he would be on hand to make decisions regarding their welfare.

Her own father had been a good man. When he had brought Dot Wilson home, he hadn't balked at the thought of her having two children. Even when she played such dirty tricks on him, he still never took it out on them. His every thought had been for them, doing his best to help in so many thoughtful ways to ease the pain of their mother going off like that.

It had been bad enough for David and herself when their mother had died, but at least they had had family. Gran had been marvellous and their dad had never let them down. Why wasn't he here now? Why had he had to die? Silly questions, she told herself. Questions that had no answers. For nothing and no one could bring back her own beloved father.

Chapter Twenty-one

FOR A FEW MINUTES Annie was flustered. It was the fifth of September, the start of a new school term. Having seen the children safely into the school gates, she had stood watching until they disappeared from sight. They both looked entirely different: Ronnie with his long grey trousers and navy blue blazer with smart shiny silver buttons, Mary in a pleated drill-slip, underneath it a white long-sleeved blouse, the whole finished with a pure wool cardigan. Turning away, she had braced herself and made for the housing department offices.

In the course of the next hour and a half she had repeated her story at least three times. One middle-aged housing officer had listened solemnly, written down the names of Dorothy and Robert Wilson, shuffled off and twenty minutes later had told her, 'Yes, there was a time when Mr and Mrs Robert Wilson had been housed by the council in this area, but the tenement building has long since been demolished.' She told part of her story again, answered questions about how old the children were and what school they had attended, and lost track of the number of suggestions she was given as to how she should go about tracing their parents.

In the end she had given up and made for the ladies' toilet, feeling incredibly tired although it was not yet midday. As she was making to leave the premises, she heard someone calling her. Going back to the front desk, she was met by a very smart woman whom Annie judged to be in her late thirties. She wore a wedding ring and her blond hair was permed and set in the latest fashion.

'How d'you, Miss Bateman, I'm Ivy Thornton,' she said, holding out her hand across the counter.

Annie shook her hand, raising her eyebrows in a question.

Mrs Thornton smiled. 'I understand you are enquiring about a family by the name of Wilson.'

Annie said, 'Yes, I am – a Mr Robert Wilson and his wife was Dorothy Wilson. They had two children, Ronald and Mary.'

'I've just been reminded by a colleague that I did have dealings with a Mr Robert Wilson. Mind you, it was some time ago, but if I can help . . .'

'I doubt it,' Annie sighed. 'It seems streets and streets of houses have been razed and there's no record of where the Wilsons ended up. I did discover they were on the voting list in Peckham, but that too was a long time ago.' Annie looked into Ivy Thornton's eyes, decided she was sympathetic, and lowered her voice before saying, 'Unfortunately, all I've been able to find out is that Mr Wilson has been in prison.'

'Wait a minute. I'll get some one to cover for me and we'll go somewhere where we can talk. Would you like a coffee? We have a canteen, very small, but quite good.'

'That would be nice.' Annie did not believe for one moment that Mrs Thornton would be able to shed more light on the whereabouts of Robert Wilson than other members of staff had been able to.

However, she was entirely wrong. Seated opposite this remarkably kind woman, Annie didn't know what to think or how to thank her.

'It's true,' Ivy Thornton was speaking again. 'I felt nothing but compassion for Robert Wilson when he came in here. He'd been out of prison only a few days. I wasn't the only one, either. His firm thought so highly of him that they had offered him his old job back. Seems they felt that he had drawn a rough deal.'

Bewildered, Annie said, 'Can you tell me where he lives now?'

'No, sorry,' came the answer, 'but I can tell you the name of the firm that employed him. It's local, and surely they'll be able to help you, especially when you tell them that you have been taking care of his children.'

'Oh, thank you,' Annie managed to stammer.

'Just stay there, finish your coffee, and I'll get you the details. Probably I have their phone number as well. I won't be many minutes.'

Ivy Thornton was back in ten minutes. Holding out a folded sheet of paper to Annie, she said, 'Will you ring me sometime, if you have any luck, and let me know how you got on?'

'I will,' Annie promised, longing now to be on her way. All this time, and maybe, just maybe, the children's father had been out of prison and working locally.

It had taken Annie only twenty-five minutes to locate the premises at the address she had been given. She stood on the pavement outside the yard and slowly read the signboard over the iron gates: WILLIAM WEBB AND SONS LTD. A member of the Road Haulage Association. National and International Carriers for Industry.

It looked to be a very prosperous business: several heavy lorries were parked, two near a loading bay, around which several men were working. To the side of the yard was a well-proportioned office, on the plate glass window of which the firm's name was embossed in gold lettering. The ringing of the telephone startled Annie as she opened the office door. 'Sorry,' she mumbled to a young man who had a shock of ginger hair. 'I'll come back later.'

'No, it's all right,' he said, quickly motioning her to take a seat. 'Yes, OK, that'll be fine. Yes, yes, I'll see to it.' He spoke quickly into the phone, hung up, and looked at the clock. 'Well, young lady, what can I do for you?'

'Here we go again,' Annie was thinking, wondering if she had the energy to go through the whole story yet again, and decided she'd cut it short. 'I am Miss Bateman, and for quite a while, since my father died, I have been taking care of two small children. I recently found out that their mother died in tragic circumstances. Today I have been lucky enough to trace their father to this firm, and I hope you will be able to put me in touch with him.'

'Well, you put that nice and clearly,' he told her, taking a pencil from behind his ear and grabbing a note-pad.

'By the way, I'm Max, one of the sons in Webb and Sons. Now, if you'll just give me the man's full name we can soon find out if he is one of our employees.' Annie did so, and he left the office.

'Yeah,' Max said with a sad shake of his head as he came back. 'Bob Wilson did work for us and does again at

236

present. He's a good bloke, and my father said he deserved a break. He's had a hard time, what with one thing and another.'

'Thank God for that,' Annie breathed out.

'You said you've been caring for his kids?' Annie nodded her head. 'Good for you. I'm impressed. Not many young ladies would have taken them on.'

'So, when can I talk to him?' Annie enquired.

'Ah, there's the snag. Bob works away most of the time. His choice. He's in Scotland at the moment – been there quite some time. When he first returned to work for us he was mainly in Germany.' Annie's heart sank. She knew it had been too easy. 'Don't pull a face like that,' Max grinned at Annie. 'Bob phones into base every so often, and he's due to ring up tomorrow morning. Can we relay a message for you?'

'If you would be so kind,' Annie spoke softly, not at all convinced that this was what she wanted.

Seeing how bewildered Annie looked, Max felt sorry for her. 'Come on,' he urged. 'Let's figure out what you want to say to him. I personally will see that he understands.' For the time being, Annie felt she had no option. Reluctantly she took the pencil and pad from Max and busied herself trying to compose a message that was short but at the same time to the point. Twice she wrote several sentences and twice she scratched it all out. 'Not doing very well, are you?' Max asked, with what appeared to be real concern.

'I don't know where to start, or how to put it,' she answered truthfully. 'The hardest part is telling him that my own dad has died and it's just me and my gran who are taking care of his children. I don't want him to think that we don't want them. Besides that . . .' Annie shook her head. She couldn't go on. Her worries were nothing to do with this young man, and yet . . .

Max stared at her for several seconds, then said, 'You might as well tell me the rest, or I could get my father to come through and talk to you. I'm sure he'd want to help.'

'Oh no. He must be busy and you've done enough already.'

'Nonsense! You said "besides", and it sounded serious, so tell me.'

Annie took a deep breath. 'The children don't know that their mother is dead. I just can't bring myself to tell them.'

'Good God! No wonder you're so upset. I wouldn't envy anyone who had that task.' He looked hard at Annie. 'I think it's time you were given a bit of help. I'll only be a moment.'

It seemed to her that Max was gone for ages and she was beginning to think she ought to leave. She hated to think that she was being a bother. He came through the door with an older man that she knew at once was his father. They had the same reddish hair, and Max was totally a younger version of him.

'William Webb,' he said, stamping his boots on a mat before coming over to Annie.

'I've got the gist of why you're here, Miss Bateman, and let me say right off, I'll help you all I can. This is what we've decided.' He spoke in a stern, schoolmasterish tone. 'When Bob Wilson phones in tomorrow, I'll speak to him and suggest he talks to you direct. No messages or such-like. Straight talking.'

'How do you know that he'll speak to me?' Annie gave him a rueful smile.

Mr Webb came a step nearer. He was not a tall man, and Annie's eyes were almost level with his steady gaze. He put both his hands on her shoulders, resting them there. He didn't answer her question immediately, but instead asked, 'Could you be here tomorrow afternoon? Say about half-past two?' When Annie nodded, he seemed to take a deep breath as if coming to a decision and said solemnly, 'He'll speak to you all right, lass. I'll see to that.'

It took a few seconds for his words to sink in. Then she said simply, 'Mr Webb, I don't know how to thank you.'

'No thanks necessary,' he answered, grimly determined. 'Just be here.'

All the way home, she shuddered to think what was going to happen come tomorrow.

Annie had been waiting about ten minutes, but it seemed like hours. Nothing in her life had equipped her to deal with this situation. Max had offered her tea or coffee; she had refused. He'd smiled at her and twice had urged her to relax. The shrill ring of a telephone made her jump, though it wasn't in the front office where she was sitting. Max came out from behind the counter and in a kindly way said, 'That will be Bob Wilson. My father's taking the call in his own office. Come through.' He held the door open and closed it behind her.

Mr Webb was saying, 'That's right, she's here now.' A pause while he listened. Then, with a smile, he said, 'I'm passing the phone to her now.' Another pause. 'Yes, all right. I'll make sure of that.' He held the receiver out to Annie.

Her heart was thumping, her hands were damp. She took the receiver, wet her lips, and said, 'Hallo.'

The man on the other end had a loud gruff voice. 'I'm glad you've contacted me. I honestly didn't know my kids were with you. I thought they were in care or maybe fostered out. There's so much I need to tell you, but at the moment I can't think rationally. I don't know anything about you.'

'I understand. It's bewildering for me, too.' Annie said, her hand slippery on the receiver. 'It was different when my dad was alive. He wouldn't let anyone take the children away, but I'm not sure how I stand.'

'I am sorry. This is the first that I've heard of your father.' He stopped talking and caught his breath.

'You mean to say you didn't know my dad brought your wife, Ronnie and Mary to live with us?'

'No, I didn't. Sounds incredible, doesn't it? But we're never going to get it sorted over the phone. I'll come to London over the weekend. Could you meet me somewhere?'

'You could come straight to our house – see the children.'

'I'd rather not,' he cut in sharply. 'Not until I've explained a few things to you. Could you meet me at the office on Saturday? I'm sure Mr Webb won't mind.'

'Yes, if that's what you want. Although it will have to be the afternoon because I work in the morning.'

'That's all right. I'm going to hang up now. I've got a lot to sort out. I'll see you on Saturday.' He said what sounded like a strangled good-bye, and hung up.

Annie fumbled the receiver back into place, hastily brushed a tear from her eye, and said to Mr Webb, 'He didn't want to see his kids. Never even asked if they were fit an' well.'

Mr Webb was embarrassed and also angry, but he

managed to keep a lid on his reactions. He gave Annie a minute or two to recover, then from the door he said, 'I'll get my son to get us some tea. I have a few things to get under way, but I'll be back. You take my chair, the one behind my deck, and make yourself comfortable.'

Annie felt so drained that she barely had the energy to sort out her thoughts. She couldn't make head or tail of Robert Wilson. Fancy not wanting to see his son and daughter! 'Thank you, Mr Webb. I appreciate this,' Annie said as she sipped her tea. She had already decided that this portly man not only looked a typical father, but was indeed kindly and caring. The trouble he was going to on her behalf was much more than she had expected, especially as she was a total stranger and he owed her nothing.

'There are a few things you should know, Miss Bateman, before you condemn Bob Wilson entirely,' Mr Webb quietly told her. She nodded, thrown by the fact that in her mind she was calling Bob Wilson every bad name she could think of. 'First off, he had a rough time in prison and all that came about only because of his wife and the way she carried on. I could give you a whole lot more information, but I think it's best if I leave it all to Bob to tell you when you meet. Sufficient to say that Mrs Wilson gave Bob a hard time throughout the whole time they were together.'

Well, she didn't exactly do our family any favours! was what Annie was thinking. 'Neither of them seem to have been very good parents,' she said unhappily, getting to her feet. He walked with her to the door. 'Thanks again, Mr Webb, for everything.'

They shook hands. 'I'll be here when you come on Saturday.' He smiled kindly as he held open the door.

Annie walked slowly towards the bus-stop, feeling utterly exhausted. Had she done the right thing in making contact with the children's father? She thought over their telephone conversation yet again. He didn't seem over-concerned as to their welfare. Thought they were in care or even with foster parents, he'd said. Why the devil had he never exerted himself enough to find out?

She joined the queue of people waiting for the bus. Her head ached. Her feet were burning. What the hell was she doing trying to sort out everybody else's life when she should be enjoying her own? All she longed for now was to be at home, to tell her gran everything that had happened, see what she had to say about it all. I'm tired, she sighed. It's been a funny old couple of days. Next Saturday when she met Robert Wilson face to face was probably going to be even worse, and definitely more difficult.

The bus arrived. There was standing room only. She clung to the leather strap as the bus swayed its way through London, praying she'd be able to get through this week without dwelling too much on what might happen on the following Saturday.

Chapter Twenty-two

IN THE YARD AT Webb's haulage firm, Annie stood waiting, unaware that she was being watched from the office by Mr Webb and Robert Wilson.

Now the man coming towards her, carrying a sheaf of papers, gawped at her. 'Miss Bateman?' He looked at her hard before saying, 'By heck, you're very young. I had no idea.'

'And you are Mr Wilson?'

'Yes, sorry. It's just that you've taken the wind out of my sails. I expected someone much older.'

Annie didn't know what to say. Before her stood a man about six foot tall, on the stocky side, with thinning dark hair cut short and brushed straight back behind his ears. He had dark eyes, and Annie could at once see the likeness with Ronnie. His manner seemed stern though apologetic, but whatever it was, she didn't take to him. Yet she was determined to get answers to several questions that worried her more as each day passed.

'It's difficult to know where we start, isn't it?' he said,

not moving an inch. The only sounds in the yard were coming from the far side where heavy machinery was being loaded on to an enormous trailer. Firmly he said, 'I'd better take you somewhere where we can talk. Would you like to go to a café or would you prefer Mr Webb's office?'

Annie didn't hesitate. 'If he doesn't mind, Mr Webb's office will be fine.' She didn't fancy going off with this man of whom she knew little or nothing, and if he didn't start doing some straight talking soon she felt there was a danger that she might lose her temper and tell him a few home truths. Far better to talk to him in an office than in a tea-shop where other people would be able to hear every word.

Robert Wilson said nothing, just nodded. He led the way across the yard and through the outer office until he reached Mr Webb's private office. It was empty, and Annie felt her pulse quicken as he shut the door and they sat down facing each other. Half expecting him to have a go at her, she undid the buttons of her jacket and laid her handbag down near her feet.

'I still can't get over the fact that you are so young,' he muttered, shaking his head. 'How the dickens did you come to take on the responsibility for two children that were no relation to you at all?'

'Do you want me to start with my side of the story, then?' Annie asked.

'I think that might be best. At least it would help me, or is that too selfish?'

Annie considered for a moment. 'Well, I think that will be all right. I'll make it as short as possible. My father met Dorothy Wilson when her two children were fostered out separately. Both kiddies were very unhappy.

He brought Dot, as we were told to call her, home to live with us. Having applied to the authorities for permission, he brought the children to live with us as well. Everything was fine for a while. Then my elder brother left home, as he couldn't get on with Dot. Not so very long after that, Dot herself left. Ronnie and Mary were, by this time, well settled and happy attending the local school. My grandmother helped out with the caring of them and we seemed to be a nice happy family.' Annie had to use her handkerchief to wiped her forehead, which felt very hot.

'Would you like a drink or something?' Bob enquired.

'No. I know I'm being long-winded but I don't see any other way of relating all of this.'

'You're doing fine. Take your time.'

'Then came the bad bit. My dad died.'

'Oh, I'm sorry.'

'Well, that's about it. We've carried on as best we could. The kids love Gran and she adores them. I've kept on renting the family house, and a friend, Doris, lives with us, so there's always plenty of people around to give a hand to seeing to the children.'

'But you blame me. They're my kids, and you are accusing me of being neglectful and uncaring. And you want rid of them.'

'That's not true!' Annie's voice had risen. 'I wouldn't care if they stayed with me for ever. In fact, I'd like that very much. But they ask questions and I don't have the answers. Only last week Mary said, "I wish we had a daddy like everyone else." What would you have me say to that?'

He regarded her shrewdly. 'Mary is not my daughter, and I don't care if I never see her again.'

'What?' Annie covered her mouth with her hands, afraid of what she might come out with.

'Sorry to be so painfully frank, but it's about time the truth was told. D'you mind if I smoke?'

'Of course not,' she replied in a voice that was little more than a squeak. He took a tobacco tin from his pocket and proceeded to roll himself a thin cigarette. When he had it lit and had taken a draw deep down into his lungs, he replaced the tin in his pocket, and looked hard at her again. 'Right to the last minute when I was getting dressed to go the register office, my dad kept saying, "You're mad, son. It's not too late to call it off. Dorothy Wilson is a tramp," he insisted. But when did any of us ever listen to our parents? We got married mainly because she was pregnant and I know Ronnie is my son. But that's it. It wasn't that Dorothy was a bad woman, because she wasn't, not really. Self-centred, oh yes. Sex mad, definitely, and my work took me away too often and too long. She wasn't fitted for waiting. I tried my best, but I had a living to earn. Dot wasn't going to alter; she was always going to remain precisely what she'd been since about the age of fourteen. We'd never have lasted together. There came a time when I finally knew it.'

'That's sad,' Annie said softly.

'It was,' Bob agreed. 'I gave in so many times. I even went along with the pretence that I was Mary's father when I knew darn well it wasn't true. I came home, the baby was born, the birth registered, and me named as the father. Looking back, I stood for the five-card trick. Dot rubbed my nose in it and no mistake.'

'D'you mind if I ask you something?' Annie queried.

'No, go ahead.'

'Why did you disappear? Have you no feelings for your children?'

Bob looked shamefaced. 'Suppose you are entitled to

ask that. Truly I knew nothing about you, or your father, come to that. I thought Dot had been with Charlie Bradford all the time. Mary's his kid, if you must know.'

'Oh, I see!' Annie snapped scornfully. 'So you wrote Ronnie off at the same time?'

'Now look here, young lady! I don't have to be answerable to you, but in a nutshell the bloody answer is yes.' Annie stared wretchedly. Now she had put the cat among the pigeons! 'Perhaps you've a right,' he said by way of an apology. 'Had you not known about Charlie Bradford?'

'Not until very recently. My dad may have known, but I didn't. Then Ronnie let slip that his mum had met Charlie outside the school gates one day. And that was when she was still living with my dad! Recently my grandmother got hold of some old newspapers and we read all about what happened. Perhaps this is where I should tell you that the children don't know that their mother is dead.'

'Oh, Christ,' Bob groaned. 'Even now I can't get away from that damn woman! Because of her, I've been to prison, got a record to me name now, all because I bashed that bastard a couple of times. Any decent man would have done the same. Whatever Dot was, she didn't deserve what he did to her. Mind you,' he gave Annie a wry smile, 'I suppose I ought to be grateful to her. At least she made me a survivor. I've met another woman and I have a great life now.'

Annie gazed at him steadily, took a deep breath, and though her voice wobbled a little bit, she said, 'So you're all right and your children can fend for themselves?'

He made no answer but got to his feet and stretched his arms above his head. Then suddenly he swung round to face her, and in a voice that sounded desperate, he said, 'I was very bitter against everyone and everything when I got sent to prison, and inside was no picnic, believe me. I was in for GBH, and that, to the inmates, made me a hard man, a man that had to prove himself to every nutter that thought he was even tougher. When I came out, I was amazed when Mr Webb not only offered me my old job back but fell over backwards to help me. I suppose I wanted to believe that my son was being well cared for. To be honest, I couldn't have cared less what became of the girl, and I'm bound to admit, where that child is concerned, I still wouldn't lift a finger.'

Annie sensed that he meant every word he was saying.

He sighed. 'Life moves on. In Germany I made good money, but I was terribly lonely. Then Webb's got a contract with the forestry commission up in Scotland, and for me . . . well, it turned me round. I met Pauline . . .' He smiled to himself. 'She's a widow. Husband was killed in the war. She has twin boys, ten years old. I lodged with her at first, then one day she told me that she loved me and I found I could love her too. She's a good woman, lives for her boys and her home. She's a great cook. I told her about Ronnie but not about the girl. There's no need, as I said, she's nought to do with me. In meeting Pauline I've been lucky,' he murmured. 'She knows everything, even about me going to prison. She understands.' He stopped speaking, then added defiantly, 'So now you know it all.'

That's not the end. Not by a long chalk, you selfish beast, Annie mused, but she kept that thought to herself. She took a deep breath. He took out his tobacco tin again rolled another thin cigarette, lit it and took a deep drag. 'So, what happens now?' she ventured at last.

'I don't know about you, lass, but I'm away back to Scotland first thing in the morning.'

She stared at him in dismay. 'You're not even going to see your son? Tell him about his mother?'

'I'll see the authorities and get the pair of them taken into care, if that's what you want. I can't understand why your father took them on in the first place. If as you say they were both being fostered, why the hell didn't he leave well alone?'

'Because everything wasn't well. They were separated and neither of them was happy,' Annie told him with a sob in her voice.

'So! It was nothing to do with him. And what beats me even more is when Dot decided she had enough and cleared off – and I'll lay you ten to one she went straight to Charlie Bradford – why in heaven's name did he hang on to kids that were nothing more than a liability to him?'

'Because my father had taken them into our home, shown them that someone cared what happened to them, and he wasn't the kind of man to turf them out just because their mother had done the dirty on him.'

'Well, all I can say is that men like him are few and far between.' He hesitated, and when he spoke again his tone was lower, even a mite softer. 'I am sorry that your father died, and grateful for what you've done. I know you've acted as you saw best, but to be truthful I still think the kids would be better off taken into care. I'll set the wheels in motion as soon as I get back to Scotland.'

Annie knew without a doubt that he was calling her bluff. Well, two could play at that game! 'You will be held responsible for both children, seeing as they have birth certificates which state you are their father.'

'Even though I—'

She cut him short. 'I'll go the welfare people, just as my father did. Get the case heard here in a local court. You'll be tied up here in red tape for quite a while. I'll make sure of that.'

'Why, you little madam!' he muttered, clenching his fists but keeping them close to his sides. 'What sensible option is there? I don't mind sending money if you really want them both to stay with you . . . I've never tried to avoid that.'

'Blimey, you take the biscuit, and then some,' Annie retorted, her Cockney courage coming to the fore. 'How much have you ever sent? Go on, tell me that. How much? You've been so hard done by, so busy taking care of number one. When you came out of prison, did you bother to make enquiries as to where the children were and how they were? Don't you think they have a right to know that their mother has died?'

Annie could see that he was clenching and unclenching his fists and his face showed that his anger was almost at boiling point, but she wasn't going to stop now. For too long this man had lived his life with total disregard for two little children who had never done him any harm. Mainly because of the chip he had on his shoulder, both Ronnie and Mary had known no stable home life, no permanent loving kindness, not even to whom they really belonged.

Drawing a deep breath, she went on, 'Then you discovered this other woman and her boys who are suddenly the light of your life. Nothing will be too good for them. Is that the idea? All right, let's leave Mary out of it for the moment. Let's consider your son. He's about the same age as these new boys you've acquired. When you buy their clothes and put food in their mouths, will you daily or even weekly send the same amount to your own flesh and blood? No. More than likely you'll just say, Sod him!'

Annie knew she was being coarse and vulgar. It was the only way she could give vent to her feelings. When she thought about Ronnie and Mary and what had already happened to them in their short lives, how this brute of a man was talking about getting them taken back into care. It was as if they were total strangers that he didn't give a damn about. He was paying them back for what their mother had done to him.

He went bright red. 'Of course I won't.'

'Well?' What will you do?' Annie prompted.

'I'm not sure.'

'Well, I am. You will at least see Ronnie, tell him in a kindly way about his mother, but you won't tell him that you're not Mary's father. Spin him whatever story you think best as to why they can't live with you. Just don't, I beg, destroy all his illusions.' He shrugged, but made no comment. 'Of course it would be much kinder and avoid so many awkward questions from your son if you were to see both children together. Couldn't you pretend, just for a couple of hours? Take them to the zoo or somewhere?'

He stubbed out his cigarette and went to the door to ask if someone could bring some coffee. When he turned back, he wagged a finger at her. 'You might look young, but the way you go on you could be fifty years old.' He stared at her for a moment, a quizzical look in his eyes, then turned away, muttering, 'All right, I'll do me best, but I won't feel comfortable. I'll tell you that.'

'I wonder why?' Annie said, tongue firmly in cheek.

He sighed, and flopped down again on a chair. 'Does Ronnie believe I'm Mary's father?'

'Funnily enough, I asked him that very question, and he

was dead sure you were. He loves that little mite. Watches out for her come wind or high water. Sometimes I get the feeling that Ronnie is insecure, and God knows he has every reason. He is still gawky and awkward, sometimes touchingly young for his age, yet in other ways, such as his concern for Mary, quite mature.'

Bob had the grace to look ashamed. 'So he wouldn't want to leave her and come and live with me, if Pauline were to agree to it?'

'You surely wouldn't have the heart to put that proposition to him, would you?' Annie couldn't keep the revulsion from coming through in her voice.

'I suppose not,' he agreed sheepishly, 'seeing as how they've been together since the day she was born.'

'That's not exactly true. When my father came on the scene, the children were in separate foster homes. I've already told you that. No one seemed to give a thought to them.'

Bob made a fist and smashed it into the palm of his other hand. 'The daft things we do when we're young! I wish to God I'd never set eyes on Dorothy.'

'But you did, and as my gran says, you should think before you act, 'cos all chickens come home to roost.'

'There you go again.' He half smiled. 'Looking like a teenager and talking like an experienced woman. If all this wasn't so pathetic, it would be laughable.'

'I don't see it like that,' Annie said, letting her temper show again.

'If I do take both children out and do as you suggest, what then?'

'What you're asking is, Will I then let you off the hook? Let you go back to the nice Pauline and play happy families?'

Now he really did clench his fists, and for a second time Annie knew she had gone too far. 'You don't know the half of it,' he hissed through clenched teeth.

She was saved by the opening of the door and Max putting his head in, saying, 'Coffee for two.' Then, as if sensing it was an awkward moment, he swiftly arranged the cups, poured out the hot coffee and said, 'You have to admit the service around here is pretty good! I'll leave you to add your own hot milk and sugar.'

Phew! Annie let out a deep breath. She was thoroughly shaken by the fact that she'd been so rude. 'I'm sorry,' she muttered, pouring milk into his cup and asking if he took sugar.

'Yes. Two, please.'

She added the sugar and stirred it well before giving it to him.

'Am I right?' he ventured, having taken a sip of coffee. 'You'd like both the children to stay with you?' Annie looked him straight in the eye. 'Yes, I would. They've become like my young brother and sister. I would miss them terribly. I may not be able to stop you doing what you threatened, but I bet my gran would move heaven and earth before she let either of them be taken into care again.'

'What a mess!' Bob Wilson moaned. 'I'd willingly send you a sum of money, say once a month.'

Annie shook her head. She had a job to control her features, so that the disgust she was feeling didn't show. 'That really isn't necessary; we manage quite well.' Then, almost as an afterthought, she added, 'What you could do is open a post office savings account in the children's names. Just a few shillings each week would mount up and be there when they need to be a bit independent.'

Just let him say he'll do it only for Ronnie, and I swear to God I'll bash him! Annie's temper was still simmering and she felt if she didn't soon get away from this man she would do and say something that later she might be very sorry for.

To her great relief, he said, 'I'll see to it. Would tomorrow be too soon to pick the children up?'

'No. I'll talk to them tonight, and I'll have then ready, say, about ten o'clock.'

'I'll be there, if you'll write your address down before you go.'

Annie drained the remains of her coffee and sighed, momentarily lost for words. This whole meeting had been dreadful. Of course he was a selfish man, but on the other hand she couldn't help feeling a little sorry for him. She toyed with the idea of offering to spend the day with him and the children. Then, hastily getting to her feet, she thought better of it. She picked up her handbag, saying, 'Well, I'll see you tomorrow. I'll leave the address at the main desk.'

'Thanks, I'll be there,' Bob mumbled.

Glad to be out in the fresh air, Annie decided to walk part of the way home. Boy, oh boy, she had taken a chance! She, a young woman, had forced, even threatened, Robert Wilson, a tough man who had been in prison! As good as told him if he didn't take the kiddies out, both of them, and tell them that their mother was dead, she'd make sure he'd be sorry. She had also suggested that he think up a jolly good story as to why they couldn't go and live with him. God alone knew how he'd manage that.

It was a big risk she'd taken, and it would be up to her to deal with Ronnie and Mary once Robert Wilson had taken himself back to Scotland. She weakened. Perhaps it had been a hazardous thing to do. Ah well, she sighed, it was all arranged now, and if things did go wrong it would be she who had to face the consequences, whatever they turned out to be.

Chapter Twenty-three

DORIS STUDIED ANNIE, WHO was standing staring out of the front room window. Her feelings were mixed, but she felt Annie had done the right thing in contacting Robert Wilson. It was about time the children were told of their mother's death, and it was only right that he should be the one to break the news to them. 'A penny for them!' she called out.

Annie turned and sighed, 'It would have to rain today, of all days, wouldn't it?'

'The man's not daft. He'll have taken the children somewhere in the dry. Maybe to the pictures. Stop worrying about them.'

'He's had them out since ten this morning, when it was quite nice. This downpour only came on about midday and it's turned very cold. I hope he's fed them.'

Doris burst out laughing. 'Really, Annie, you are like hen with her chicks – they'll be all right. Come in the kitchen an' we'll have a cup of tea. It's not all that warm in here, and you staring up the street all the time isn't going to bring them back any quicker.'

'All right, You make the tea and I'll put plenty of water on to boil. Those kids will be frozen as well as wet.' She pushed up her sleeves and used the poker to raise one of the iron lids on the range. She then shovelled in more coal, filled two iron pots from the cold water tap in the scullery and put them at the centre of the hob where the heat was fiercest. Hardly had she done this than she heard the front door opening and flew down the passage. The children were soaked to the skin, both shaking with the cold. Poor Ronnie had only a thin jacket on over his shirt. Mary's hair hung down like wet rat's tails over the shoulders of her Sunday best coat.

'Sorry,' Robert muttered, as Annie stared at him in disgust. 'We were down by the river when it started to pour. There wasn't much shelter and the wind tore through us like knives.'

'Go through, Ronnie, and you, Mary, and get those wet things off. Yer Auntie Doris is in the kitchen. She'll give you both a hot drink. I won't be a moment and I'll see to you.'

The children did as they were told, slipping past Annie without so much as a glance at their father.

'Sorry,' Robert said again.

'Well, I suppose it's not your fault; you couldn't help the weather.' Then Annie asked, 'Did you tell them about their mother?'

'Yes, I did that first off.'

They were still standing in the passage, though Robert had had the good sense to shut the front door. 'Would you like to come through and have a hot drink?' Annie felt bound to make the offer.

'No, I won't, thanks all the same. I'm catching a train at a quarter to five so I'd best be going.'

'Tell me, how did the children take it?'

He shrugged. 'Few tears from Mary. Ronnie . . .' He shrugged his shoulders again. 'Who can tell? Hasn't had much to say for himself at all.'

'They know you're going back to Scotland today?'

'Yes. I told them it was important work. The kind of work I wouldn't be able to get if I stayed in London.'

'At least they know where they stand now,' Annie sighed.

Robert shifted his weight from one foot to the other, and looking extremely uncomfortable, said, 'I'd better get going. I'll do as you asked. You know, two savings accounts in the post office.' At least that was something, Annie said to herself, and he had said he would do it for both children. He had his hand on the door-latch when he hesitated, turned, and said, 'If Ronnie needs anything else at any time, please will you let me know?'

Well, I'll be blowed! He had to go and spoil it! If he had said 'If *the children* need anything' she would have felt kindly towards him, but to say only Ronnie and again ignore Mary was too much. He's lucky he was half-way through the door, or I might just have done him an injury, she was thinking as she watched him turn up the collar of his jacket against the wind and rain. I hope he catches a rotten cold and his beloved Pauline refuses to feel sorry for him, was her angry thought as she shut her front door.

When Annie came back into the kitchen, Doris had already dragged in the big tin bath from the yard and put it in front of the fire. Ronnie was stripped to the waist, and Mary had all her clothes off, and was wrapped in a big bath towel, sitting on Doris's knee. Annie removed the guard from the fireplace and knelt down to poke the fire, which she'd previously banked up in readiness for the children's return, into a blaze.

'Have yer cup of tea,' Doris pleaded. 'By then the water will be boiling and I'll help you bath the children.'

'Nobody's gonna bath me,' Ronnie stated with some force.

Doris and Annie laughed and even Mary tittered. 'Of course not, lad,' Annie quickly assured him. 'We'll see to yer sister first, then we'll go into the front room while you get into the hot water. Meanwhile you'd better get those trousers and those socks off – we don't want you coughing and choking all day tomorrow.'

'I ain't got nothing else to put on,' he quietly answered.

'Oh, I know. Hanging behind my bedroom door is a short dressing-gown. Go up an' get that, it will cover you.'

Doris set Mary down on the hearth-rug and reached for a fancy glass jar that stood on the second shelf of the dresser. Winking at Mary, she said, 'We'll put a handful of my crystal bath salts in the bath before Ronnie comes back, 'cos if he's sees us doing it, he won't want to get in the water in case we say he smells like a sissy.'

'Get up, luv, and move over there for a minute while I pour the water into the bath,' Annie said to Mary, who was grinning broadly.

Doris came back and forth twice with bowl of cold water that she added to the hot that Annie had poured in. Then, one each side of her, they removed the towel and lifted Mary in to the warm scented water.

'Cor, that's lovely,' she whispered, wriggling around and dabbling her hands through the water.

Ronnie came back downstairs, Annie's pale blue fluffy dressing-gown tied tightly around his body, looking first

260

at Doris and then at Annie, daring either of them to say a word.

Annie poured shampoo on Mary's wet head and gently began to rub it on her scalp. A couple of minutes later, she said, 'Bend forward, Mary, and shut your eyes tight.' She then poured a jug of warm water over the child's head to rinse the soap out of her hair. Mary squeaked and gurgled, then gasped.

Doris came over with a big dry towel, and said, 'Stand up, Mary.' Wrapping the towel round her small body, she scooped her up, carrying her to Annie's empty armchair, where she sat down with the little girl in her lap.

'You are a right water-baby, aren't you?' she said as Mary wriggled her head clear from the folds of the towel.

'I'm not a baby,' Mary said indignantly. 'I'm six and soon I'll be seven. Won't I, Annie?'

'You will that, pet. And we'll give you a proper birthday party.'

'Never mind about all that,' Ronnie said in protest. 'I'm supposed to be having a bath and the water's getting cold.'

'I'm just about to add more hot water if you'll hold your horses,' said Annie.

'And I've lit the gas oven out in the scullery, and left the door open to warm the room, so we can all go out there while Sir has his bath,' Doris said, trying not to laugh.

In the first week of October, the mornings had a sharp chill to them. Another two weeks and the children would be on half-term holiday from school. Life seemed to have settled into a good routine. Annie felt she was lucky to have her job at the café. Both Flossie and Sid were great to work for. Although the greatest number of their customers were rough and ready men there was never any awkwardness as she weaved in and out amongst the crowded tables. They all liked a laugh and a joke but none went beyond the pale and she knew full well should she ever be in need of help of any kind she would only have to say the word.

There was always plenty to do in her free time. She went round to her gran's almost daily and Rhoda came to her house every weekend. Doris still lived with her, and Annie was grateful, because when Doris was around there was never a dull moment. Every Saturday she gave the two children a few coppers for pocket money and, even more important, she had time for them. Ronnie and Mary looked upon Doris as a happy and fun-loving aunt, but the children were a problem. There was no getting away from the fact that since the day that their father had taken them out and given them the news that their mother was dead, they were not the same.

Ronnie was a lot quieter, but it was Mary that was worrying Annie the most. She had never had much to say, but she had scampered about the house always willing to join in the board games they played each evening after their meal had been cleared away. As for a cuddle or a hug, she'd climbed up on to either Doris's lap or her gran's – mostly mine, I like to think – Annie mused, but not any more. Mary now sat silently in a corner, watching and listening. All the coaxing hadn't helped. Twice she'd woke screaming from a nightmare and Rhoda had suggested they put a waterproof sheet over the mattress, because on those two occasions she'd wet the bed.

'It's as if her insides are tied up in knots,' Doris said one evening as she and Annie left the house together. 'Several times when I've fetched her from school, she's just been waiting in a corner of the playground on her own, while all the other children are racing around like mad, screaming at the top of their voices.'

'It's the same when I fetch her,' Annie agreed, 'and when she's home she follows me around like a shadow. She's got me really concerned. She wasn't ever too talkative, but never like she is now.'

'I know,' Doris sympathized. 'That's half the reason I suggested that Gran come over tonight so that you and I could go to the pictures. You've got to get out now and again, Annie. Besides, I've got something I want to tell you. I've met a fellow.' The sheer happiness with which she made that statement stopped Annie in her tracks. Doris giggled, then went on enthusiastically, 'His name is Frank. Frank Smith, would you believe? He's a bit older than me, never been married, has his own place, and if I do decide to marry him, I wouldn't have to bother about the council rehousing me – I'd step into a ready-made home.'

'Doris, you take my breath away! You've just met him, an' you're talking about marrying him and so forth!'

Doris really laughed now. 'I met him ages ago. Just never told anyone. It's not a case of love's young dream. It couldn't be. First time around was that . . .' Those last five words had been spoken so sadly that Annie caught hold of her arm and squeezed it. Very quietly, Doris went on, 'Not everyone gets a second chance. God knows the country is full of war widows. I'm one of the lucky ones. Frank is steady, has a good job. He never married because his mother was an invalid and he looked after her when his father died.'

Annie stood still, 'Come here,' she said, arms outstretched. The two young women stood on the pavement with their arms locked around each other. The damp dark evening that threatened a winter which would bring fogs, frost and ice was forgotten.

'I really am happy for you,' Annie smiled, 'though I never thought anyone as dizzy as you are, most of the time, would end up telling me they were going to marry a good steady bloke.'

'Well, there you go, then! Got to think of the years ahead. When me hair has turned to silver an' all that. Now come on, the film will have started if we don't get a move on.'

Very much later that night as Annie settled herself down on the sofa in the front room because Rhoda was staying the night and sleeping in her bed, she went over every detail that Doris had told her about Frank Smith. She was truly glad that Doris had accepted the fact that while she would never forget her first love, she was content to look forward and find a different kind of happiness with a good man.

Then her thoughts turned to her own future, and, more to the point, the present. What on earth was she going to do about Ronnie and Mary? Although she was doing her very best for them, it didn't seem to be anywhere near enough. Ronnie was growing up knowing that his father had deserted him without so much as a backward glance, and handed him over to someone else to care for.

As for Mary, God forbid that she should ever come within a mile of learning the truth!

Her mother had walked away. Was Charlie Bradford her father? One day the child would be bound to ask that same question. Time enough to worry about when the moment came. That's how it had to be. But the fact that Robert Wilson had not only strenuously denied that he had fathered her, but had also declared that he would never lift a finger to help where she was concerned, was a matter that must never be brought to light. Annie knew she could never let that happen.

She had no idea how, but somehow she was going to keep the children with her. They had this house, it was their haven. Thanks to her own father they had money for the bills that needed to be paid. They could face the world owing nothing to any one. They'd stay together and would make their own happiness. She would get Ronnie and Mary on their own and talk to them straight. Tell them just what they needed to know and no more. See if she couldn't get them to feel that she truly loved them both. Make them see that, with her, they were secure. Point out that she not only wanted but needed them, and that she would be here for them at all times, doing her best to give them a happy life. At least until they were old enough to make up their own minds about their own futures.

She sat up straight, plumped her pillow hard, tucked the covers in more securely around her legs before turning over and settling down to go to sleep. As she felt her eyelids grow heavy she knew she would sleep. There was a new sense of purpose about her now.

Chapter Twenty-four

ANNIE HEARD VOICES THE minute she opened Rhoda's front door. It wasn't a familiar voice, none of the neighbours, and certainly not that of gran's best friend Gladys Dawson. She walked down the passage, turned the doorknob and put her head round the door.

Rhoda was sitting in her easy chair, legs stretched out in front of a blazing fire. She filled the chair, and she had a job to turn to face Annie. 'Ah, there you are, pet!' Her weatherbeaten face broke into a broad smile as she greeted her granddaughter. 'As you can see, I've got a visitor. You won't remember her I don't suppose, but come on in and say hallo. And for God's sake shut the door! The wind is whipping through every crack today.'

Gran's visitor got to her feet and came towards Annie. She was a middle-aged woman with a pale complexion and short dark curly hair. 'Hallo, Annie,' she said in a very formal sort of way. 'My, but you've grown into a lovely young lady. You used to call me Auntie Vera . . .' She trailed off, giving a friendly smile.

267

All this time Annie had been standing in front of the fire, but the heat soon became too much against her face and she moved over to lean against the sideboard. She didn't know what to make of this unexpected visitor.

'I think too much time has gone by for you to remember me.' Vera shook her head ruefully.

Rhoda explained at last. 'Vera and her husband Peter used to be great friends with your mum an' dad when they were all young. She's come here today with a story that takes some believing, but I'll leave 'er t'tell you all about it while I shift meself and put the kettle on.' She struggled to her feet, gave Annie a reassuring nod, and went out into the kitchen.

'Vera James,' she spoke quietly, introducing herself. 'You really are very lovely, Annie, tall like your father but that brown hair with all the reddish glints in it you get from your mother's family.'

Soon Annie, sitting in a chair near the window, was listening in amazement to what Vera was saying. 'It's true. I promise you it is. Your father bought this house when it had been badly damaged by bombs in the terrible air raids. He got it ever so cheap because of that. His idea was to do the whole place up and let it out in three flats.' She paused. 'I didn't know, until your gran just told me, that Jim was dead. I did know about your mum, and then after that, well, Peter was so ill and we all lost touch. When I met your dad again, an' he found out how things were with my Peter, he offered me the bottom flat. It was in a bad state, mind, but we managed. Jim promised me the flat would be ours even after the house was all done up. Said we could act as caretakers, collect the rents from the other tenants and so forth. It's been months since we heard from Jim, so I think I knew something terrible must have happened. I'm really dreadfully sorry.' She took hold of Annie's hand. 'I wouldn't be here now if these letters hadn't started to pile up and I took the liberty of opening one.' Vera leant across to where her handbag lay on the table, reached inside it and withdrew a bundle of letters held together by an elastic band. 'I've shown them to your gran, but she seems to think you had better deal with it.'

'Are they all from the same person?' Annie queried.

'No. Some are not important. It's the ones from the Co-op that need sorting.'

'Co-op? I don't understand.'

'Sorry, luv. It's the mortgage repayments on the house. Your father paid a lump sum in advance every so often; the last one covered six months, but now apparently instalments are well overdue and the company is threatening foreclosure.'

'Hang on a minute,' Annie pleaded. 'I'm having a job to take all of this in. You say my father owns the house you live in?'

'Well, I don't know about now, but he was the one that bought it.'

'I still don't see where the Co-op comes in to all of this.'

Still holding Annie's hand, Vera asked, 'Did your father never tell you?'

Annie's mind flashed back to her father's last days in the hospital. The conversations about property Annie had long since dismissed from her mind as just being her dad's ramblings. This lady she was talking to was neat and tidily dressed, spoke nicely, and, it would seem, had been a good friend of her parents. However, she wasn't about to open up her heart to her. She'd have to get to know her a darn sight better before they started to swap confidences.

'No. No one told me about a house and a mortgage. And I still don't see the connection with the Co-op.'

'It's the Royal Arsenal Co-operative Society, to give it its full name, and the mortgage was granted to your father by the manager at their Tooting branch. Upper Tooting, to be exact. There is a very large store there as well as a bank.' Vera's expression as she looked at Annie was full of anxiety. 'I suppose your dad not being with us any longer means that Peter and I will have to get out of the house?'

'Oh *no*!' Annie cried impulsively. 'I'm sure it won't come to that.' Then, after a pause, she asked, 'How did my dad know your husband? Did they work together?'

'For a time they did. Every lad round here went to work on the docks if they were lucky enough to have relatives employed there. But we all go back much further than that. We lived in the same street, went to the same school and now Peter would still be in Roehampton Hospital if it weren't for your dad giving us this ground-floor flat.'

'Roehampton? That's an ex-servicemen's hospital, isn't it?'

'Yes. Peter went into the army as soon as war was declared. He was wounded in North Africa . . .' Suddenly Vera lowered her head and was crying uncontrollably.

For a moment Annie didn't know what to do. She thought of calling for her gran, then slowly she started gently to stroke Vera's hair. Giving Vera time to compose herself, Annie looked round the room. It was a cosy little living-room where her father had grown up. Her glance took in the pictures on the wall, the ornaments on the mantelpiece, the heavy furniture that had served a lifetime. Framed photographs were standing on the sideboard on a white lace-edged runner. Most of them were of her father, and she smiled to herself thinking how everyone called him 'Lucky Jim Bateman'. The centre one was of a family group, probably taken on Hampstead Heath at bank holiday time. There was Gran and her lovely grand-dad in the middle, with her mum and dad to each side. Sitting on the grass in front the two children, she and David looked as if they were eating something on a stick. I know, she remembered, recalling the happy day quite vividly. We were licking toffee apples that Dad had just bought. When that picture had been taken they had been such a lovely happy family. She frowned thoughtfully. We should all of us learn to live for the day, for who knew how many tomorrows there were going to be. My parents never knew that they wouldn't live to see David and me grow up, she thought bitterly. There was also a very faded photo of a bridal pair on their wedding day. It was of her grandparents. The young man was very tall and broad and, though it was difficult to tell from the faded picture, she knew his hair to be jet black and curly, just as David's was and her father's had also been. Grand-dad had been dead a long time. Poor Gran! She must wonder sometimes what fate had been about to take her husband, her only son and a daughter-in-law that she had loved just as much as if she'd been born to her, and yet leave her here.

Annie was brought back to the present with a jerk as the door opened and Rhoda came in with a tray. 'Here we are. I've brought you both a cup of tea and a buttered scone. I made them only this morning, so I did.' Setting the tray on a small table, she moved towards Vera, and touched her shoulder. 'Come on, luv. I told you my granddaughter wouldn't turn you and Peter out of house and home. You'll feel a lot better when you've had a cuppa.'

As Vera lifted her head and wiped her face, Annie thought, I suppose my own mother would be about the same age as you if she had lived. What had they been like when they'd been young girls? That would have been before the war, so perhaps they had been quite carefree. She hoped that was true.

'I can't stay much longer, else Peter will start to worry,' Vera said, accepting a cup of tea from Rhoda. She said to Annie, 'I think it best if I leave all these letters with you. The address of the house is on all of them so, as soon as you get a chance, perhaps you could come over and see what you think of the property. Then you'll be in a better position to decide whether you feel able to keep it or . . .' Her voice faltered.

'For a start, it depends on whether the mortgage could be transferred into my name,' Annie answered cautiously.

'But you will come and look?'

'Yes. Yes, of course I will.'

The anxiety on Vera's face immediately cleared. 'Oh, I can't tell you what a relief it is to be able to talk about this!' There was now a smile on her face and the look of fear had gone from her eyes. 'I've been worried sick ever since I opened that letter and found that the mortgage on the house wasn't getting paid. It wasn't like Jim to let something like that slip. Besides, he called in every now and again – cheered Peter up no end it did, just talking to your father. I knew something must be wrong, but I never thought for one moment that he was dead.'

Annie picked up a cup and saucer and held it out. 'Drink your tea, Vera, and you'll upset Gran if you don't eat at least one of her scones.'

Vera said, 'It was my Peter that suggested I come and see your gran. He said he'd bet anything that she would still be living in the same house that we used to come to when we were kids. I was ever so pleased when she opened the front door to me.'

Now there was a friendly silence as the two of them ate and drank. Rhoda had very tactfully retreated back to her kitchen.

Having finished her scone, Vera wiped the crumbs from her mouth, placed the plate back on the table and once more faced Annie. 'It wouldn't matter so much if there was just me to consider, but there's Peter. At first it was all a great effort, him leaving Roehampton. But now, on a good day – and just lately he seems to have more good days than he used to – he gets around really well. The part of the house in which we live is what the agent would call a garden flat, but you and I would call a basement flat. We've got it nice, and Peter can get in and out mainly on the level. He does try, makes a big effort.' She stood up, hesitated, then said, 'I don't know what else I can say. We've lived rent free all this time, but I do work and I could manage to pay. I don't want you to think that we're sponging off you.'

'Oh, please!' Annie was really embarrassed. 'Let's leave all that until I come over.' She gave a little laugh. 'You haven't even told me where the house is. It could be in Timbuktoo, for all I know.'

At that they both grinned, and Vera said, 'It's in a lovely district, right near Wandsworth Common. Like I said, the full address is on all these letters.' She passed the tight bundle across to Annie.

Thoughts were whirling in Annie's head. She couldn't

wait to be on her own to sort it all out. Wandsworth Common! That was where she'd gone to visit Mr Ferguson, her dad's solicitor. Perhaps a lot of the loose ends that hadn't made sense when her father died would now get tied up.

When Vera had her hat and coat on and had kissed Rhoda good-bye, Annie walked to the front door with her.

'Good-bye, Annie,' Vera said, holding out a gloved hand. 'I'll look forward to seeing you. Wednesday, we agreed, but if you should find that's not convenient, drop me a postcard, will you?'

This was not the time for further questions, although Annie had several big questions that she wanted answers to, but they could wait. It would take her all day and probably all night to sort out what she had learnt in this short time. From inside the house she heard her grandmother call, 'For Pete's sake come in and close that front door before my legs start to freeze!' It was in a very thoughtful frame of mind that Annie made her way back into the warmth of Rhoda's cosy living-room.

'Kettle's not gone off the boil if you want to make a fresh brew,' said Rhoda as Annie sank down on to the hearthrug in front of the fire. 'Some surprise that was, eh? Coming in to find someone from the past sitting here talking to me large as life.'

'It wasn't just finding her here, Gran, it was what she'd come to tell us. Talk about surprised! I'm beginning to think that whoever said life was full of surprises was telling the truth.'

'Eh, lass, you've 'ad yer fair share just lately, an' no mistake. What with what we found out about Robert Wilson and then him coming down from Scotland, letting on to you that he wasn't Mary's father, not to mention that although Ronnie was his son he could walk away from him just like that.' Rhoda put out a hand and tousled Annie's hair, then grinning, she said, 'Makes you wonder what you're gonna hear next!'

Annie laughed wryly. 'Sometimes I wonder how I'm supposed to get by. Each day seems to bring me more burdens.'

She was probably right, Rhoda was thinking. A young lass like her shouldn't have to be listening to everyone eles's troubles. Her tone of voice sobered and there was a trace of bitterness as she answered, 'God gives a broad back to those who need it.'

Annie stared at her, but Rhoda's understanding smile took away the bitterness. She nodded firmly. 'I'll manage, but right now I think I will make another cup of tea.'

Rhoda smiled and her voice was husky as she said, 'That's a good idea, luv.'

Chapter Twenty-five

DOING AS VERA HAD suggested, Annie took the tube from the Elephant and Castle to Tooting Bec Underground station. Coming out into the weak sunshine she was once again struck by the difference in this area from where she lived. Outside the station she waited at the stop until a number 19 bus came along showing Highbury Barn on its destination board. When she stated she wanted to go only as far as Wandsworth Common, the conductor clipped her a ticket, gave her a wicked grin, and said, 'That's tuppence, please, luv.' She laughed to herself. Obviously Tooting wasn't that far from the East End, as bus conductors, and more than likely the barrow boys, still called all the ladies 'darlin' or 'luv'. It was a happy start to her day, and she got off the bus cheerfully. Memories of her visits to Mr Ferguson, in this same district, came to her mind. She was on the edge of the common, and she looked around, taking her time. It was lovely out here, south of the Thames. Green grass and trees, hardly any smoke-blackened old warehouses or factories.

Having asked an errand boy directions to Tremaine Road, she found it without any difficulty. Number forty-eight was the last in a terrace of double-fronted tall houses, each with a tiny front garden and six deep steps leading up to their front doors. Annie viewed the whole front of the house she had come to see, and wasn't over-impressed. In fact her heart sank into her boots. There wasn't a pane of glass to be seen, every window had been boarded over, the paint was peeling and the whole house had an air of despair about it. Not that others in the row looked any better, but at least the occupiers had tried. It would seem that most of the properties were let as flats. Name-plates listed individual names against consecutive numbers. Clean lace curtains hung at several of the windows, door-knockers and letterboxes had all been polished, while the front steps were painted white. It made number forty-eight look like the forgotten poor relation.

Annie was half-way up the front steps when someone called her name. She stopped and looked over the wall, so that she could see down into the basement area. Looking up at her was Vera. She was standing in a doorway holding a long-handled broom and wearing a wrap-round floral apron. For a moment Annie stood gazing down at the small, grey-haired woman with the plump, young look-ing face.

'I've been looking out for you,' Vera explained. 'Come back to the pavement, walk back a couple of yards and you'll see the steps which lead down here.'

When Annie was finally down in the paved area, her first thought was how nice it looked, even pretty. There were brightly painted tubs holding green shrubs and round earthenware pots filled with bright flowers still struggling to believe that autumn was not quite here yet. The window that faced the front wall was sparkling clean, and it too had crisp white lace curtains hanging in full folds.

Vera spontaneously stretched out her arms and Annie, coming forward, kissed her awkwardly on the cheek, wondering suddenly what she was letting herself in for. Sensing that Annie was fearful Vera put an encouraging arm round her shoulders and drew her into a very pleasant square hall. There was a half-moon-shaped table set back against the wall on which stood a bronze bowl filled with chrysanthemums. A gilt-edged mirror hung above the table reflected the light from the open front door. Having been told that the Jameses lived in the basement, Annie had expected the place to be dark and dreary, but it was quite the opposite. Warm, cheerful and welcoming was how she would describe it.

Vera quickly stood the broom against the wall, undid the strings of her apron, and said, 'I've done enough cleaning for one day. Come on through.' She opened a door which led directly into the main room of the flat, which was large and pleasantly furnished, mainly with old-fashioned pieces: a large sideboard with a mirrored overmantel, a round polished table on which stood a bowl filled with dried flowers, leaves, twigs and fir-cones. This floral arrangement reminded Annie of harvest festival when she used to go to Sunday school. There was a big sofa with plump cushions, two armchairs and two footstools, all covered in a beautiful matching chintz. Colourful tiles surrounded the open fireplace, in which a cheerful fire was burning. In the hearth lay a poker and a long pair of tongs, the whole being surrounded by a shiny brass fender. The floor was covered with worn-looking linoleum on which there were two small but good-looking rugs. The room as a whole looked slightly shabby, yet homely; it gave out a feeling of warmth and friendliness and Annie felt herself begin to relax.

'This is very nice,' she said. 'You've done wonders. It really is a comfortable room.'

'We think so,' Vera said, looking pleased, 'though all the furniture was second-hand. I did make the covers for the sofa and chairs.'

'Really? I think they look smart, and I like the material very much. You must be very clever and you must have a special sewing machine. You couldn't sew heavy cloth like that, not by hand.'

Vera laughed. 'Well, it is my trade. It's what I do. I told you I work.'

'Oh, I see,' said Annie, but it was clear that she did not understand.

'Sit down, Annie, take your coat off, and I'll start at the beginning. First, I'd better tell you that today is not one of Peter's good days so he's staying in bed. Maybe he'll get up later. We'll see.'

Annie mumbled, 'I'm sorry,' looked round, and then went to sit in the armchair nearest to the window.

'Right from when I left school,' Vera began, seating herself on the end of the sofa, 'I went to work for Dickens & Brown, an old, well-established firm of furniture-makers. I was taught to make loose covers and sometimes to strip and recover small items such as a bedroom chair. I suppose you could say I'm still on their payroll. They send me plenty of orders, though I work mainly on my own, and in my own time, so I don't have to answer to anyone. It's a great help on the days that Peter is bad, as I don't have to leave him on his own. I have managed to get hold of an industrial machine and most of the tools that I need.'

'But where do you work from? Surely you need a lot of space to cut out cloth to make loose covers for such large furniture,' Annie asked, when Vera stopped talking.

'In that respect I've been very lucky. I rent a shed. Well, more like a big hut, it's only round the corner from here. I'll show you later if you're interested.'

'I'd like that,' Annie told her truthfully.

'Would you like to see the rest of this flat? There is only one bedroom, but we do have a bathroom with a toilet. Then there's the kitchen, and from there the back door leads out to a very long garden. I'm very lucky in that someone put me on to a couple of men who have allotments of their own, and they come and cultivate the bottom part for me. They grow all sorts of vegetables, we go halves with the cost and we share the produce. The surplus from here and from their own plots they sell, and that money goes toward expenses.'

'That must be very handy,' Annie said. Then she continued, 'I'd love to see the garden, but we won't disturb your husband, not today. I can see the rest of the flat another time.'

'What about the house? Don't you want to see over that? I've got the keys, so it wouldn't be a problem.'

Annie raised an eyebrow. 'I noticed all the windows were boarded up. How many floors are there?'

'There's the ground floor above this and then two more floors, plus the top rooms which are more or less attics but quite roomy. We can get through from down here.'

Annie looked a bit wary.

'I know what you're thinking – the look of the house from outside has put you off. Sorry, luv, it's worse inside. Ever so dark. As you say, what with the windows being

281

boarded up, it's in a right state and there's quite a bit of rubble still lying about.'

'I don't think we need bother today. Why don't we go out into the garden and you can give me the general outline.' Annie got to her feet and put her jacket back on, then sounding thoughtful she said to Vera, 'You do realize that unless we can take over the mortgage there is no way I could buy this house outright.' She added, 'It's gonna cost a fortune to get this house fit to let out in flats. But that is what has got to happen if we should manage to hold on to it. We'd need the rents from tenants to meet the repayments. Where would we start? How would we go about it? Whatever must my dad have been thinking of when he took this on?'

'I know what you mean. I've thought of nothing else for weeks, an' I can't see any way round it.'

'Well, at least we can talk about it and maybe get some advice. Come on and show me the garden.'

They went through to the kitchen, which was almost as large as the main room. The long closed-in range had an oven to each side of the fire and the hooks on the walls held saucepans and other cooking implements. In the middle centre of the floor was a farmhouse type of table, around which were four ladderback chairs. Annie sniffed appreciatively at the appetizing aroma coming from the stove and decided it was making her feel hungry.

Vera noticed her expression, and laughed. 'Early this morning I made a big stew. It's been simmering in the oven. You will stay and eat with me, won't you?'

'I can't put you to all that trouble,' Annie protested. 'Besides, you have enough to do seeing to your husband.'

'You'd be doing me a favour,' Vera told her. 'I don't

282

get much female company. You won't mind eating in the kitchen, will you?'

'Course not,' Annie grinned, as Vera opened the back door. They had five steps to go up and at the top Annie stopped, staring down the garden in amazement. It was long. Very long indeed. And, in contrast to the outside of the house, it was well tended and utterly beautiful. Near the house was a lawn with ziz-zag stepping-stones that led to a pond. Ferns and greenery of different heights and hues surrounded the edges. A tall tree stood close to the side brick wall, beneath which was a stone bird-bath. Neat and tidy flower-beds were set each side the whole length of a long winding path. Beyond lay another lawn surrounded by clumps of flowering shrubs. To one side was a bower of trees interwoven with climbing plants which formed a shaded place to sit, with a long high-backed bench. Then came the vegetable garden, and even from this distance Annie could see that it was not tended by amateurs. Tall stately trees formed the boundary.

'Oh, Vera!' Annie looked at her in wonder. 'This is all *so* lovely.'

'Yes, I think so. It has been a life-saver for Peter. Are you cold?' she suddenly asked.

'No, not a bit. There's not much heat in the sun now but it's still a bonus, and this high stone wall all round must provide shelter.'

'Well, if you're sure, let's walk down a bit; there's a bench we can sit on.' Then, as if on an impulse, she said, 'You go on. I won't be a minute.' Vera disappeared back inside the kitchen, emerging almost as soon as Annie had sat down. She carried a jug of lemonade and two glasses on a tray. 'Don't know what you must think of me! All this time, an' I've not offered

you a drink.' She proceeded to pour out the lemonade.

Annie took several sips; it tasted really good. It wasn't
fizzy shop-bought stuff but nice and sharp, made with
real lemons. 'You know, you are a great surprise,' she
remarked, smiling at Vera over the top of the glass.

'In what way?'

'In ever so many ways. You keep your home beautiful,
you work, you have your own business and to top the
lot, there's this garden.' Annie paused, still trying to take
in the beauty of it all. 'This garden would do justice to
a stately home, and I'm not kidding. However do you
manage to look after it?' Before Vera had a chance to
answer, Annie was smiling with delight as she watched a
couple of sparrows and a starling all fluttering their wings
in the water of the bird-bath. 'It's as if they're giving one
another a shower! I can't believe we are sitting in London.
Do you get many birds?'

'Yes. Quite a variety, too. Peter hangs things like half a
coconut from the branches of the trees during the winter
months. He likes to sit out here and watch them.'

'I can imagine,' Annie said with conviction. 'No wonder
you said the garden had been a life-saver for him.'

'You know, Annie, you're doing me a power of good
just by being here today. It's what I needed, to be taken
out of myself and reminded that I have a lot to be grateful
for. I suppose we all have a cross to bear. When your gran
told me about Ronnie and Mary, I wasn't surprised. It was
just like your father to do something like that. He always
had time for lame dogs. Look what he's done for me and
Peter. But, there again, it must be hard for you. You're
very young to be taking on such a big responsibility.'

'I don't have to manage on my own. I get a great deal

of help,' Annie hastened to assure her. Then she picked up her glass and drank before saying, 'Do you want to tell me about Peter?'

'Well,' Vera let out a deep breath, 'I'll give you the bare details. The lorry he was travelling in went over a mine and some of his mates were killed. Peter's injuries were such that he will never make a complete recovery. He's had one leg amputated. Really his entire system has been affected: all his limbs are weak and there are days when it's impossible for him to walk. He gets frequent headaches, blacks out sometimes, and, worst of all to my way of thinking, is when he gets periods of depression. I, or anyone else, can't help him then. He won't ever be able to hold down a job that requires any degree of concentration.' Vera broke off.

The quietness was such that it made Annie jump when Vera suddenly said, 'I remember one terrible day when Peter looked me straight in the eyes and told me to get on with my own life because he was useless and I should write him off.' She sat gazing into space as if unaware of Annie's presence.

'Vera?' Annie prompted, worried about the sadness that seemed to surround her.

'Sorry,' Vera mumbled, 'I shouldn't be unloading all this on to you.' She drained the remains of her lemonade and said, 'I didn't mean to be so morbid. I'll go in first and take Peter a tray if he's awake, but more than likely he won't fancy his dinner until tonight. That won't matter. A stew won't spoil. We'll have ours, then I'll take you round to my shed, let you see my thriving industry.'

Annie sat on in the garden, still wondering how Vera, with all her troubles, had managed to create such a beautiful, peaceful haven. Some time later Vera called her from the house, and very reluctantly she made her way to the back door. Coming here had certainly given her much to think about. What wonders her father might have worked on this house had he lived. She could only use her imagination, and that wouldn't do her much good. She was the one who had to see if it were at all possible to hold on to this property. Even if she could, look what it would entail! Council permits, builders, plumbers and carpenters. Of course she had money, but even if she were willing to sink it all in this project, would it be enough? And if it were all to go wrong, how then would she manage to keep herself and Ronnie and Mary? No, one thing she had to be sure about. She'd not put in every penny – the money in the bank was her safeguard. It had to be there for her to fall back on if ever she or the children should need it. She sighed heavily. Didn't I have enough on my plate before I came here without adding more to it? But could she walk away, now that she had met Vera? It would be so simple to say that the Jameses were not her problem, but could she do that? She went back into the house with a heavy heart.

Even so the midday meal managed to be a happy occasion. Vera kept Annie enthralled with tales of things she, Peter and Annie's mum and dad had got up to when they were youngsters. 'We were hardly ever short of a penny between us, and shared out, that gave us a farthing each. And you mark my words, Annie, you could buy several things in the sweetshop for a farthing,' she told her with laughter in her voice.

It did Annie good to hear her and she encouraged her to tell more. 'Where did the penny come from?'

'Mostly from the cart-horses. It depended on the time of the year, mostly.' Seeing Annie's look of bewilderment,

Vera laughed. 'Jim and my Pete would walk slowly along the pavement carrying a bucket and shovel, following the brewery drays drawn by four huge horses or the laden carts from the dockyards. They always had at least two horses, and as soon as a horse did its business, those two boys would be out there in the middle of the road, shovelling it up while it was still steaming.'

Annie wrinkled her nose. 'You're making it up!'

'I swear I'm not! Then the lads would race off up to the allotments, and any one of a dozen men would gladly give them a penny for what they'd collected in their bucket.'

Annie smothered her giggles as she helped Vera to take the plates over to the sink. She wiped up as Vera washed.

'It's coming up to November soon,' Vera suddenly stated. 'Now that's a time the boys, an' us girls to tell you the truth, really loved, the fifth of November, gunpowder, treason and plot. That's how the rhyme went – can't remember the rest of the words. For weeks we'd all be on the look-out for old clothes. Some we got off the totters' barrows and of course we had to have a titfer, the bigger the better. Couldn't 'ave a Guy Fawkes without a big hat. And we 'ad to 'ave a barrow an' a set of old pram wheels. Hours we'd sit on the doorstep stuffing the guy, then dressing him. Had to have a 'alfpenny to buy a gruesome mask from up the corner paper-shop. When all was finished we'd set off with our guy sitting in splendour in our push-cart, and while the boys pushed, us girls did the begging. "Spare a penny for the guy, mister," we'd yell, standing outside the pubs, specially on Friday evenings when the men had just got paid. Saturday morning we'd be at the gates of the docks. We did all right as kids, one way and another.' Then, she shook her head, her mood changed quickly. 'Pity we ever 'ad to grow up, an' an even bigger pity that the country 'ad to go to war.'

Annie, who had been constantly smiling as she tried to picture the happenings that Vera was going on about, suddenly felt so sorry for this kind brave woman who was battling along against a great many odds. She gave the teacloth she had been using a good shake and hung it up to dry.

'Would you like a cup of tea now, or when we come back?' Vera asked.

'Oh, later I think, if there's time. Best get going as I have to leave in time to meet the children from school,' Annie reminded her.

'Right then, I'll pop in on Peter again, leave a glass of milk by his bed, and then we'll be off. Shouldn't be gone long, there's not that much to see.'

They turned sharp right as soon as they came up the basement steps, and within minutes Annie caught sight of a lovely old church, the sun glinting on its stained glass windows, the stout stone walls softened in the autumn sunshine.

'Catholic church,' Vera said. 'Must say the priests have been very good to me. We go through the churchyard, and the place they rent to me is round the back. There is another way to get to it, by the road, but it's a long way round and I do have their permission to come this way.'

Most of the graves they were passing were well kept, a few seemed sad, their headstones dirty, stained and sunken with age. Maybe there were no relatives left alive to tend them, Annie was thinking, when Vera said, 'Here we are.'

Set well back off the path, they saw what was little more

than a large brick hut. 'It was used at one time for Scout meetings,' Vera told her as she fished in her bag to find the key. 'They've got a brand-new building now, much bigger than this.'

The door opened outwards and Vera stepped aside and allowed Annie to go in first. Once again, it was not what she had been expecting. The shed was much lighter, for a start, on account of the windows on both sides, plus another long narrow pane of glass set into the far wall. A trestle table almost the length of the hut was cluttered with pattern-books, swatches of material, boxes of small and large pins, several large pairs of scissors, tape-measures and yardsticks. Running along the far wall was what had to be a specially made heavy bench. It had to be stout and durable because on it, arranged in a line, were two small hand-operated sewing-machines and a large industrial one that was worked by a foot treadle. She could at once see the reason for the long glass window which had been put in directly above the machines to throw light on the work that would be carried on below.

'I bought those three machines with a bank loan,' Vera told her. 'So far, I've managed to keep up with the payments.'

Annie shook her head in wonder. 'It all looks very business-like. It certainly does you credit.'

'There is a chair over there in the corner if you want to sit down, and there's a lavatory through there, an' all.'

'How about if you want to eat or drink here?' asked Annie.

'The management doesn't run to luxuries, and we don't have a union. Or perhaps I should say *I* don't have a union, seeing as how this is a one-man band.'

Annie thought for a moment. 'But you do well?'

'More successfully than I imagined. I often turn work away.'

'Have you ever thought of getting bigger premises? Perhaps you could employ a few people.'

'Annie, luv, you're just voicing my own thoughts. I often consider giving up this place. It's lovely in the summer, when I can work with the door propped open. Come winter an' I'm almost crying with the cold, my fingers go numb sometimes, and I have to pack it in for the rest of the day.'

'So . . .' Annie didn't know what to say.

'I know,' Vera sounded weary. 'Maybe I'm afraid my luck would change. Or maybe I wouldn't be able to afford a high rent. It's difficult to know what to do for the best. But if I'm honest with myself, the thought of a big workshop and that I would have to employ other people and would need to have an office, all of that frightens the wits out of me. If things are running smoothly and Peter is not doing too badly, I employ a male nurse to take care of him four days a week, two days I try to work from home, and the other day is my day off and I devote every hour solely to Peter. You'd be surprised what we pack into that day sometimes.'

'Vera,' Annie asked with great caution, 'would you be offended if I asked you a personal question?'

'You go ahead and ask, luv.'

'Do you need to work to make ends meet?'

'You mean, don't the government give Peter a pension? And the answer to that is yes, they do, but truly it's a pittance. Roehampton Hospital have been marvellous, they really have, and it was our choice that Peter lives at home, they didn't turf him out. The artificial leg they fitted is great, but some days he's just too weak to strap it on and that's one thing he won't let me do for him. He lets the nurse, as they've become kind of mates, which is nice. I need this business for more reasons than one, I can tell you.' Strewth! Annie was thinking. How much can any one woman take? 'If you've seen enough, shall we walk back? Then you'll still have time for a cuppa before you get your bus.'

Annie reluctantly agreed. She watched as Vera locked the door, and then they linked arms as if they were old friends, or even, Annie was thinking to herself, mother and daughter. 'I think you're doing marvellously,' Annie assured her as they walked along.

Vera let out a deep breath. 'That's what I tell myself on a good day, and I suppose I am. But the truth is, Annie, I get so lonely. I was ever so grateful when your dad suggested Peter leave the hospital and we live in his house, but it ain't the East End is it?'

'I know what you mean,' Annie said convincingly. 'No neighbours popping in an' out, that sort of thing.'

'That's it exactly, luv. There's days when I'd give me back teeth to be in Bermondsey again. The days when Peter is half-way to being his old self an' I catch a glimpse of how life could have been for both of us. It's those times that I have to tell meself not to be bitter. Sometimes I sense that Peter is watching my every move, and I realize it's a hundred per cent worse for him than it is for me.'

While Vera checked on Peter, Annie put the kettle on and made the tea. When the time came for her to leave, and they stood at the top of the basement steps, there was a lump in her throat that was almost choking her. She threw her arms round Vera's plump shoulders and felt the sharp stinging of tears behind her lids. Vera hugged her, then patted her back, just as if she were a small child.

'Thanks for coming, Annie. In a way I'm glad those letters came. At least I got to see yer gran again after all this time.'

'An' you found me,' Annie half sobbed.

'Oh, luv, don't cry. Please don't cry! Even if we can't keep the house, the hospital will find us somewhere to live. Just promise me one thing.'

'Anything,' Annie was sniffling into her handkerchief.

'That you'll keep in touch with me whatever happens.'

'Oh, Vera, I will. I promise I will.'

'Go on then. Get yer bus an' make sure I 'ear from you again soon.'

As Vera watched Annie's back retreat down the road she stood still, saying to herself, 'God works in a mysterious way, and no mistake. There's her mum and dad both dead and buried, leaving two lovely children. Then there's me and my Peter, never had no kids, ain't hardly got a relative left alive, at least not any that give a damn for us, the state we're in. No one would be worse off if we were taken, yet we're still here. It don't make sense, taking those that are needed and leaving the useless ones behind.' Shaking her head, she went slowly down the steps to the basement, hoping that Peter would wake up feeling well enough to put on his dressing-down and come to have his dinner in the kitchen by the fire. She didn't fancy her own company. Not tonight.

Chapter Twenty-six

By ten o'clock on Sunday morning, Annie was as jumpy as a cat on a hot tin roof. She had spent the last few days in an absolute panic as to what she ought to do about the house in Tremaine Road, Wandsworth Common. Undecided, she had phoned Mr Ferguson's office from a call-box, only to be told he was away and wouldn't be back in the office until next Wednesday. Then she had made an appointment to see Mr Mathews, the bank manager, but within the hour she had cancelled that.

Rhoda had laughed her socks off when Annie had related the details of her visit to Vera James. 'Set up a business, 'as she? Well good luck to 'er, is what I say. Just goes to show how much bottle women born in the East End have got when it comes to the push! Her poor husband, sent home not 'alf the man he was when he signed up to fight for king an' country, and what 'appens? They shove him off with a few shillings a week an' forget all about him. Like a good many other wounded men, our members of parliament hope they'll all die off quietly. When men of the services were killed in action they became heroes. Blown 'alf to pieces and sent home, they become an embarrassment.'

'All what you're saying, Gran, is probably true,' Annie had agreed, 'but that doesn't tell me how I can get help and allow the Jameses to go on living in that flat, does it?'

Once more Gran had just laughed. 'Trust my Jim! Buys a great big house on four floors and not a word to anyone. If he's up there and knows what's going on, he'll 'ave a word. You'll see.'

'And what the hell is that supposed to mean?' Annie had screamed in desperation.

'Just bide yer time. Something will turn up.'

Yes, but . . . Nothing was being paid on the house. The mortgage people were threatening to evict Peter and Vera, and her gran sat there saying something will turn up. She'd half decided to ask Mr Mathews to arrange for her to withdraw enough money to cover the outstanding debts. That would tide things over. Until when? Then, what? She knew it was pointless to keep asking herself the same questions over and over again, but her mind was like a mouse on a treadmill trapped in a cage. Something more permanent had to be sorted out, otherwise it would be like pouring water into a bucket that had a hole in it.

It was on Friday that she had decided to do nothing until she had spoken to Mr Ferguson. Her appointment with him was for two o'clock on Wednesday afternoon. Annie's recollection was that he was a very confident, dignified gentleman who would certainly advise her as to the best course of action. Having come to that conclusion she had settled in her mind that worrying further was useless; she'd let the matter rest until Wednesday.

Then, yesterday, Saturday, just as she was about to set off with the children to do the week-end shopping down the market, Rhoda had arrived and dropped her bombshell. Jack Higgins was back home and she'd told him to come round to Annie's for his Sunday dinner!

'Cor, that's great,' Ronnie yelled, his smile splitting from ear to ear. 'Is Jack indoors now, Gran? D'yer think he'll take me to football this afternoon?'

'He is, lad. He'd only just got up when I came out, as he got in very late last night. I expect he'll be going down t'the docks later on; perhaps he'll take you with him if you ask nicely enough.'

'Can I go round to Gran's house now, Annie? Please, can I?'

'What about me?' Mary wailed.

Annie stood her ground, looked at Rhoda, and said, 'See, now you've put the cat among the pigeons!'

'Oh, go on. Let the boy go. He must get sick an' tired of always trailing about with us women,' Rhoda coaxed Annie, at the same time giving Ronnie the nod to slope off.

Annie smiled at the recollection. Ronnie had been out of that door like a shot. It had taken Annie and Doris, who had just come downstairs, all their time to pacify poor Mary. 'Don't cry,' they had both urged. 'We'll all go down the market together and when we've done all the shopping we'll go in the market café and you can have anything you choose.'

Before the shopping expedition had finally taken place, it had been Doris's turn to spring a surprise on both Annie and Rhoda.

'Seeing as how it's going to be a real family Sunday lunch tomorrow, will it be all right if I invite Frank

Smith to join us?' she had asked, using a very soft tone of voice.

'The more the merrier, I say,' Rhoda had chipped in before Annie had a chance.

Doris looked at Annie and raised her eyebrows in a question. Annie nodded her head, saying, 'Doris, I'm only too pleased. You know I've offered long before this.'

'Thanks, Annie.' Swallowing hard, Doris looked at each of them. 'I'm really grateful to you both. You, Annie, for having taken me in, and your gran, for looking after all of us. Especially cooking such lovely meals an' all. We love Gran's cooking, don't we, Mary?' Doris had bent and picked up the little girl, settling her firmly on her left hip, making sure she didn't feel left out of it.

'Is your Frank as nice as Uncle Jack?' Mary wanted to know, snuggling her small face into Doris's shoulder as she assured her that he most certainly was. Doris had made toast while Annie had brewed a pot of tea, and then they had set off for the market.

Now it was Sunday, and Annie was feeling self-conscious about meeting Jack Higgins again. Up since six o'clock, she'd done all the vegetables, laid the table for seven in the front room, instead of in the kitchen as usual, telling herself how lucky the number seven was supposed to be and maybe this dinner would go off very well. She kept peering into the oven where the loin of pork was slowly roasting.

Ronnie had taken Mary round to Rhoda's, for which Annie was very grateful. When he was in the mood, that lad could talk the hind leg off a donkey. Last night, from the time he came home until the minute he went to bed, he had never stopped talking about what a great guy Jack Higgins was. Of course Jack was popular, and would be for ever in young Ronnie's eyes. He'd taken the lad to see

Queen's Park Rangers play a home match and that was something Ronnie wouldn't forget in a very long time. Ronnie was a great little lad really. Trouble was, he could have her near to tears one minute and helpless with laughter the next. He could mimic his school teachers with a wicked accuracy and she often wondered if he did the same of Gran and herself when they weren't listening.

Doris had gone to fetch Frank Smith, just in case he got cold feet and didn't turn up. Annie looked at the clock. It wouldn't be long before they'd all be coming back together. Time to go upstairs and make herself presentable.

Half an hour later, staring at herself in the mirror, Annie acknowledged she had indeed done her best. She had drawn her hair up on to the crown of her head as Doris had shown her, threading a narrow velvet ribbon through her curls, pulling only little tendrils down over her forehead and a few to fall over her ears. The tiny crystal stud ear-rings made her face look thinner, and she'd spent time on her make-up, using a slightly tinted powder. The two-piece Doris had persuaded her to buy yesterday had come not from a market stall but an expensive shop. They'd left Rhoda and Mary happy in the café and gone off on their own. Annie felt pleased with her appearance. It was a good buy. Palest of blue in colour, the skirt had narrow pleats that fell in gentle fullness from the waist to below her knees. The jacket was straight and boxy with buttons of the same soft woollen material as the suit. There was also what the very posh assistant had told her was known as a modesty slip to be worn beneath the jacket. Pale cream silk, sleeveless and round-necked, it shimmered like gold and felt gorgeous against her bare skin.

She had barely reached the living-room when the front

door burst open and the kids came tearing down the passage, followed by four adults. She couldn't resist a smile when Jack Higgings stopped dead in his tracks, and he certainly boosted her confidence when he said, 'Annie, whatever you've done to yourself, keep doing it! You've blossomed out and then some.'

It was unusual for her to have spontaneous compliments, and she wanted to bash Doris when she saw her grin and then wink at her.

'You look all right yourself,' she said to Jack.

He seemed even taller in his Sunday best than in his seagoing jersey which she was more used to. His dark hair, lively blue eyes and tanned complexion made him look almost foreign and somehow younger.

Frank Smith stepped forward and shook Annie's hand. 'It was good of you to invite me to Sunday dinner.'

'I've been wanting Doris to bring you round for ages,' Annie told him.

Both men had brought a bottle with them, and while Doris was taking everyone's outdoor coats upstairs to lay them on a bed, Jack was making sure that everyone had something to drink. Rhoda was talking to the children, or rather Ronnie was still going on about the wonderful football match he'd seen yesterday and how *their* team had won.

Annie was finding Frank Smith pleasant and very easy to talk to. Not over tall, about five eight, Annie judged, clean and smartly dressed, he had sandy hair and a ruddy complexion, though clearly he had little idea of family life. Doris had said he had never been married, always a bit of a loner.

'You and Doris are very good friends,' he smiled, it was a statement, not a question.

'Yes, we are.' Annie returned his smile.

'She's a lovely young lady.' His voice was soft with love and Annie wondered what it must be like to have a man feel that way about you. Doris came back into the room, and Frank rose to his feet and asked her what she would like to drink. Annie couldn't but notice how his face lit up. As far as I can see he idolizes the ground she walks on. She looked away. A lonely man, besotted with you. He wants you badly and I do so hope he can make you happy. And you him, come to that. Doris had such high spirits. What Annie had almost said to herself was, would he be able to tame her? There had been a time when she would have answered a definite No, but just lately, well, Doris did seemed to have quietened down. She dressed less flamboyantly for a start, and she didn't wear such high-heeled shoes any more. Still very smart, her blond hair always perfectly groomed. Nobody would miss Doris, even in a crowd.

Jack Higgins had been standing with his back to the window, watching Annie's every move. He raised his glass to her in salute, and smiled. 'Table looks nice,' he observed. 'Reminds me of long-ago Christmases.'

'Oh Gawd!' Gran butted in, pushing a hand through her hair. 'Don't you go all morbid on us, lad, not today!'

'It was only a remark.' Annie looked pleadingly at Rhoda; after all, at a time like this with everyone gathered together to eat their main Sunday meal, it would be only natural for Jack Higgins to think back to the time when he had a family of his own. Now that she thought about it, she realized she hadn't shown him much warmth, hadn't said welcome home, or thank you for being so kind to Ronnie yesterday. She made a promise to herself that once she'd got the dinner over she would make time to talk to Jack. Ask him how he had got in Grimsby, let him know that she was interested in what plans he might have for the future.

'And how have you been, Annie?' Jack looked up at her suddenly.

'Oh, all right.' She flushed, conscious of his gaze, terrified in case he guessed what she had been thinking. It made her feel uncomfortable that he could be remembering that last time at the club when Mike Maland had behaved like a pig.

She banished the thought, got up quickly, and smiled at Doris. 'I'll leave you to entertain everyone while I finish off in the kitchen. Dinner won't be very long.'

'Sure you don't want me to give you a hand?' Doris asked, half-heartedly.

'No, you stay where you are,' Rhoda was insisting as she lumbered to her feet. 'Ronnie can take care of Jack, and I'll 'elp Annie in the kitchen.'

Mary set her glass of lemonade down on the sideboard, darted a defiant glance at Gran, and said to nobody in particular, 'Ronnie was out with Jack all day yesterday. It's my turn terday.'

Quick off the mark, Jack responded, 'It certainly is, my poppet.' Two strides, and he was across the room and had the child up in his arms.

At the doorway Annie stepped back to let her gran go first. She glanced back into the room and felt the sharp sting of threatening tears. The look on Mary's face as Jack held her was a joy to see. In fact, she'd go so far as to admit it was the happiest she'd seen the child look since Robert Wilson had taken her and her brother out for the day, only to bring them back to her and abandon them without so much as a postcard since.

It was a good half-hour later when a hot and flushed Rhoda put her head round the door of the front room and ordered everyone to sit up at the table.

Annie was putting dishes piled with vegetables on the table while Rhoda was setting a plate in front of each person and finally a jug of steaming hot gravy at each end of the table. Again Rhoda ordered, 'Come on and help yourselves while it's all still hot. There's plenty of serving spoons.'

Annie slid into a seat next to Frank and, as she did so, he exclaimed, 'Good gracious me! Roast pork, apple sauce *and* sage an' onion stuffing!' Everyone seemed to like what Annie had cooked; good humour was the byword throughout the whole meal. When the time came to carry the plates and dishes back to the kitchen and see to the puddings, Doris did help. The three women were scraping and stacking the plates on the draining-board when she suddenly said, 'Frank's over the moon, he really is over the moon. He can't believe that you've made him so welcome.'

Annie looked at her, and touched her face in an endearing gesture, whispering, 'It's great to see the pair of you so happy.'

Rhoda had taken the rice pudding and an apple pie out of the oven and put them on a tray. 'Will the pair of yer stop being so mushy an' get these on to the table before the men in there fall asleep.' The girls looked at each other and burst out laughing. 'Get on with yer! I'll bring the jug of custard,' Rhoda said, but her voice was soft because Annie had just bent her head and brushed her gran's cheek with her lips.

'I think we all ought to go for a walk, and leave yer gran

to have forty winks in peace,' Jack stated, plunging in where angels would have feared to tread. Dinner was over, everyone had mucked in with the washing up and tidying away. All the adults had had enough to drink and had refused Annie's offer of tea or coffee. 'Should soon be full tide. We could take the children either to London Bridge or Tower Bridge,' he added, getting to his feet.

'Yes, yes, yes!' Mary was jumping up and down with excitement.

'All right,' Annie just had to agree. 'Go upstairs and get your things. You can wear your best coat.' As Mary looked up at her silently, she smiled. 'It's going to be a nice afternoon, and we'll all be together. You'll like that, won't you?'

Mary didn't answer, but whispered, 'I'm glad Jack's come home. You are coming as well?' she asked Jack.

'I am, and I'll be walking along with the prettiest little girl in the whole of London.' Jack was bending down, looking into her face.

Mary looked thoughtful, then smiled before saying, 'Well, I'd better go an' get ready.'

Annie watched the child go, then raised her eyes to Jack. He wore a deadpan expression and said, 'She's quieter than usual.'

'It's been hard for her. We found her father, and he took them both out. Haven't heard a word from him since. At least she now knows her mother is dead.' They could hear both the children laughing as they came back down the stairs, and Annie gave Jack a warning glance. Now was not the time to tell him that Robert Wilson had denied he was Mary's father.

'We must talk,' said Jack. 'Seems I have a lot to catch up on. What about tomorrow?'

'We'll be seeing more of you now, Jack?'

'Yes, I suppose so.'

'That will be nice. The kids are ever so pleased you're back.'

'Only the kids?'

Annie was saved from having to answer because the children came running into the room again. 'We're ready! We're ready,' they chorused.

Annie seemed to be trailing along all by herself. Doris and her faithful Frank had Ronnie walking between them. They seemed every inch contented, lost in a world of their own. Mary was holding Jack's hand. Every few yards he would stoop, lift her into his brawny arms and swing her round. Giggles of delight were something you didn't get to hear coming from her very often, and Annie was so pleased to see the child happy and the centre of attraction for once in her life. Funny, Annie was thinking, here we all are out for a walk on a nice autumn Sunday afternoon, just as if we were one big happy family. Whereas nothing could be further from the truth! We're like a lot of lonely waifs and strays, clinging to each other for comfort.

Doris was a war widow turfed out of her home because of bomb damage. She'd had no children and no close relations. Frank Smith seemed financially well off. During the course of conversation after dinner he had told them he was a van driver for Fortnum & Mason in Piccadilly, one of the most prestigious stores in the whole of London. He owned his house somewhere in Clapham, by all accounts, yet he lived alone, had no immediate family. It showed in his every action and word how happy he was to have met Doris. Then there was Jack. Fate had served him badly. Coming home from the Navy only to find that his home had been obliterated and his entire family wiped out. He ended up as Gran's lodger. Gran did her best for him and she knew that Jack appreciated her efforts, but there had to be times when he felt very lonely.

Suddenly Annie found she was comparing the two men. Frank was of medium height and square set, had fair hair bleached by the sun, grey eyes and a sprinkling of freckles on his forehead. Jack's eyes were as blue as the sky, he was tall and muscular, quietly spoken but very assertive. The love of Jack's life was the river. His knowledge of all the vessels that came to the docks was vast.

Since she was sorting everyone else out in her mind, she let her thoughts dwell on herself. She wasn't exactly in the best of family situations. David, her only brother, was God knows where. Suddenly she gave herself a mental shake. So, she had a few problems. But why not try counting her blessings for a change? She had a decent house to live in with only a small rent to pay. Money in the bank and, the greatest blessing of all, she had her grandmother. And Ronnie and Mary! Some would say they were a burden; she knew differently. If only she could be sure that she'd be able to put the upbringing of those two small children on a firm legal footing, she would feel a darn sight happier. Most days everything went well. They loved her and she loved them, but there was always the threat at the back of her mind that one day some do-gooder would come knocking on the door saying she was not a fit person to be in charge of two under-aged children. Without Ronnie and Mary, who did she have? We really are a funny bunch when you work it out. Searching for answers hurt too much, and Annie felt quite relieved when they turned on to the towpath and she was forced to pay attention to a very excited little girl.

It had been unanimously decided that they would make for London Bridge. As usual, Jack was right. It was nigh on high tide and the river was teeming with activity. Sunday was no different from any other day, as he reminded them. Time and tide wait for no man, and certainly no ship.

Frank stood with his arm round Doris's waist. Jack had Mary up in his arms so that she could see better, and Ronnie was chattering away to anyone who would give him half an ear. Staring down river looking east from London Bridge they all had a good view of a tall-funnelled ship passing under the raised arms of Tower Bridge. Other big ships, which had been moored or anchored, moved off. Pilots were taken on board, men were busy throwing lines to tugs. The large ships were slowly towed upstream towards the dock entrances. Barges and launches crossed from one side of the river to the other. They were steered and powered towards their destination. But it was the high tide that did most of the work. Quite a few coastal vessels and short-sea traders were coming right up to the wharves just by London Bridge. Inside the holds of the ships, dockers hurried back and forth. Cranes on the jetties lifted out the boxes, crates and barrels from the holds.

'What kind of vessel do you operate?' Frank asked Jack as he stared fascinated by all that was going on down on the river.

'Let me tell him, Jack? Go on, please. An' if I get it wrong you can butt in.' Ronnie's eyes were pleading and Jack knew there would be no peace unless he let him. The boy was interested in everything that was in the docks or on the river. He asked a great many questions but he listened attentively and soaked up any information he received.

'All right, then.' Jack gave in with a smile.

Ronnie grinned, and leaned so far over the edge of the bridge that Annie's heart came up into her mouth. Then making sure that he had Frank's full attention, he pointed a finger. 'Can you see that fleet of boats tied up on the other side of the ships?'

Frank released his hold on Doris and came to stand by young Ronnie. 'Yes, I see them.'

'Well, they're Thames lighters. Small cargo is being loaded on to them by means of the ship's rig. And . . .' Ronnie paused to let the importance of what he was telling Frank sink in, 'that's what Jack owns. A lighter, don't you, Jack?'

Jack told him, 'You're dead right, son. You stated the facts well. We'll have you on the docks or the river the minute you leave school.'

If Jack had told Ronnie he had won the football pools he couldn't have beamed more broadly. 'Cor! I wish you meant it.' The lad's voice was choked with emotion.

'Have I ever lied to you?' Jack asked.

'No . . . But a job on the docks. No one gets that, not right off, they don't.'

'Ronnie, lad, you just carry on doing yer best at school. You need certificates – don't forget that. The rest you can leave to me. You've about five or six years to go yet, just see you make the most of them.'

'I will, Jack. 'Onest I will. And can I come to work with you sometimes now you're back 'ome?'

'Let's say I'll stow you away on board whenever I get the chance. Which, mind you, won't be that often.'

Ronnie was punching the air, saying, 'Yes. Yes!'

'You don't need a promotion manager with Ronnie around, do you,' Frank asked, laughing, then quickly added, 'D'you know, Jack, I've driven round these streets

306

of London for more years than I care to remember and yet I've never bothered to find time to stand and stare as we have today. I had no idea that so much went on, right here on the Thames. It's certainly been an eye-opener for me.'

Suddenly the men, with Ronnie between them, had their heads close together and were swapping tales and pointing down at the ships as if they'd known each other for years.

'How far down river is Gravesend?' Frank asked. 'That's where I was born.'

'About twenty-six miles,' came Jack's ready answer.

Not to be outdone and feeling really grown up this afternoon, Ronnie piped up, 'If you look downstream, past all the wharves, you can see Billingsgate Market, and Jack said a lot of the fish in there comes from the North Sea.'

Annie looked over to where Doris was holding on to Mary, and she raised her eyebrows and nodded towards the men. 'Once started, we're never gonna get them to come away! What say we three creep off and find a real old London teashop where they do nice toasted crumpets and teacakes?'

'I was just beginning to think that a cold wind was blowing up,' Doris replied, bending down and doing up the top button of Mary's coat. 'Would you like some tea, pet? Or would you rather stay here a bit longer?'

'I would like to come with you an' Annie.' Mary, standing between them, slipped her hands into one of theirs.

'You'll find us in the nearest teashop,' Annie called over her shoulder as they half ran and skipped along the bridge, lifting Mary's feet off the ground every so often and giving her a swing.

It really was an old world teashop. Set beside the Thames, its oak panelling could have told a great many tales. A bright wood fire crackled in the open fireplace, and as an elderly gentleman threw another couple of logs into the basket it shot flames up the chimney. A motherly type of waitress dressed as only a London waitress should be, black dress and stiff white apron, asked, 'Table for three, is it, my loves?'

'No,' Annie smiled. 'Could you make it for six? I don't think it will be long before our menfolk come to find us.'

Annie was right. The smell of fresh baking had led the men to the same spot and it was indeed a happy group that tucked into homemade fare and hot tea, with the exception of Mary, who was battling with the tallest glass of milk she'd ever seen.

Much later, as Frank went to pay the bill, Annie glanced at Doris. 'Nice day, as it turned out, don't you think?'

'Super,' Doris agreed. Then in a very conspiratorial whisper she said, 'Frank has asked me to marry him.'

Oblivious to all the other customers, Annie threw her arms round her friend's shoulders and hugged her close. 'That's wonderful! Oh, I am so happy for you, Doris.'

Mary, who never had a great deal to say but seemingly did not miss much, tugged at both of their skirts. They broke apart and stared down at her. 'Please, Auntie Doris, can I be your bridesmaid?'

'Well I never!' Doris exclaimed in disbelief. 'You're quick off the mark, young lady!'

'Well?' Mary's face demanded an answer.

Doris looked at Annie, and she returned the look. Then they both burst out laughing, bent their knees and scooped the little girl up until she was sitting between them, held tightly by two pairs of arms. They each planted a kiss on her cheek, and Doris whispered in her ear. 'I won't get married unless you are.'

'Promise?' Mary wanted to be absolutely sure.

'Cross my heart an' hope to die. You can help choose your own dress and we'll have the prettiest posy of rose-buds made up for you to carry. Will that do?'

The smile on that child's face had to be seen to be believed, and Doris and Annie went to bed that night knowing that for once something really good had happened for Mary.

again by the hardness of himself' said, placed a kiss on
her cheek, and Josie, whether or not, fell once more
forward and straight up.

'Cheated, Nicky wanted to be absolutely sure . . . . . .
when has been an agony of life. You can both choose
. . . . me over their present part, the moment peace of love
. . . . she maddens the past another,' you then . . . .

. . . . to his spirit,' they replied, 'be sure so as
'supercall, Curtis and Christie were of both that could
annoyed . . . . . the her once something really good between
. . . . paralysed alone.

Chapter Twenty-seven

MR FERGUSON WAS BOTH delighted and intrigued. Having listened to Annie's tale of how Vera James had appeared out of the blue with enough troubles for a grown man to deal with, never mind a slip of a lass like Miss Bateman, he had nothing but admiration for her. He sighed and carefully took off his spectacles and laid them down on his desk. Then he smoothed his hair, pushing back a strand that had dangled over his forehead. He leaned back in his chair and allowed a slight smile to come to his lips. 'Well, well, young lady, with hindsight, one has to admit that your father was a dark horse. It seems to me you have a decision to make. Are you going to take responsibility for Mr and Mrs James or not?'

Annie was facing a dilemma. 'It isn't as straightforward as that,' she said lamely. 'How do I know if the Co-op will allow me to take over the existing mortgage? And even if they were to agree, I would need to let out the rest of the property in order to have an income. And I certainly couldn't begin to think about that until extensive repairs have been done to the house.' She shook her head in despair. 'I haven't been over the whole house, but even from the outside you can see the property needs a fortune spent on it.'

Her worst fear was that she would be taking on too much. Mr Ferguson had used the word responsibility with regard to Vera and Peter. Did she want that? After all, she had her hands full looking after Ronnie and Mary. With Peter being disabled, would the authorities become involved?

Mr Ferguson drew his chair nearer and leaned across his desk. 'As I said, you have a decision to make. It might be as well for you to make an appointment with Mr Mathews at the bank and most certainly, without delay, you must visit the Co-operative Society and bring them up to date as regards your father's death. You say your father last made a payment that covered a period of six months?' Annie nodded. 'That's the reason all this hasn't come to light before. Whatever you decide, I will phone the Tooting branch before you leave here today, speak to the manager, make an appointment for you. That way at least you will know where you stand and you can take it from there.'

Annie sat still for a whole minute thinking over what she had just been told. Realizing there was only one way to tackle this problem, and that was head on, she took a deep breath before saying, 'I would dearly love to help Mr and Mrs James. I don't think I could tell them face to face that they would have to pack up and leave the place that they have made their home.' She shuddered. 'It would probably mean that Mr James would have to go back into Roehampton Hospital, and that wouldn't be fair.'

'And that makes you feel guilty?' Ferguson was sitting upright now.

'Yes . . . I suppose it does.'

Ferguson regarded her curiously. 'I might be jumping the gun, but I think I can shed a ray of light on this matter, albeit a very small one.'

Annie knew she could trust this man, so she said, 'I will willingly accept any advice. Mrs James has so many troubles, you see,' Annie explained. 'I kind of feel we could become good friends, and if I can help to keep a roof over her and her husband's head, well . . .'

'I imagine you've had more than enough troubles of your own, Miss Bateman. You can't put the whole world to rights.'

'What you say is true, but I've always had people on hand to help me. Vera James has no one. Besides, my father must have thought the world of the pair of them to go to such lengths to help. If at all possible, I would dearly love to carry on what he started.'

Ferguson was torn two ways. On the one hand he could sympathize with this kind young lady and with this Mr and Mrs James who had experienced such bad luck. On the other hand he had to be very careful about any advice he put forward. It was his duty to protect this girl from getting in too deep . . . protect her from herself if need be.

Annie saw the doubt registered on his face. 'Please, Mr Ferguson,' she pleaded. 'You said you might have thought of something.'

There was a pause while Ferguson pondered the matter, then in a voice that held authority, he said, 'The main repairs to the building may not be such a problem as you imagine. I would have to know the exact date on which your father signed contracts for this house, so perhaps you'd have a good search and bring me all the relevant papers, including those appertaining to the granting of the mortgage, and I'll see what I can do.'

Annie didn't know whether she was supposed to feel pleased or not. 'I don't really understand,' she whispered.

Fearing he might have given the wrong impression, and knowing how decisions could go either way in matters like these, Ferguson spoke with caution. 'The government have set up a commission to deal with bomb damage. At first, money was available only for repairs to public buildings. Now, however, ministers have toured the country from one end to the other and have made it known that there is hardly a town, village or hamlet that hasn't been scarred by the effects of the bombing raids. Praise where praise is due, they have moved fast on this one. All boarded windows are being repaired and glass fitted without delay. There will be no quibble about that. And grants are to be made where structural damage has occurred. These grants won't come in the form of a loan. They will be outright payments to make homes and businesses completely habitable again.' As he finished speaking, he saw the determination in Annie's expression. Suspecting the reason for it, he argued, 'Don't go getting your hopes up too high. I've promised to do all I can. I hope by now you know me well enough to realize I won't go back on my word.'

Annie's smile lit up her face, and Ferguson gave a sigh of relief before getting to his feet and saying, 'Now you just sit there. I am going to make a couple of phone calls. I won't be long.'

Half an hour later Annie left, clutching a piece of paper on which was written the time she had to be at the bank on Friday afternoon and another appointment made for tomorrow. Two-thirty at the Tooting branch of the Co-operative Society to see the manager, a Mr Selwyn.

When the door had closed on Annie, Ferguson sat deep in thought. He decided he was going to break all the rules and personally pay a visit to Mr and Mrs James in Tremaine Road. He had to find out for himself whether the couple were worthy of all that Annie was hoping to do for them. He also had a compelling urge to see for himself just what kind of a state this large house was in, and what on earth had driven James Bateman to buy it in the first place.

By ten o'clock the next morning it was a very surprised Vera James who stepped back and allowed Mr Ferguson to enter the basement flat that Jim Bateman had provided for her and her husband to live in.

When he left at noon, he was already, in his head, writing a report, a copy of which he would be sending to both Mr Mathews and Mr Selwyn. Providence had been kind. Peter James, with the aid of his male nurse, had been up, washed and dressed and ready to receive visitors when his wife brought this solicitor into their living-room and made the necessary introductions. Some time during the next hour Ferguson had made a decision. It was his opinion that two more worthy people, deserving of all the help that could be given to them, would be hard to find. After having shared a pot of coffee with them, he had gone with Vera to her work-shed and been utterly amazed. One as talented as she was should be able to make her way in the world. The fact that she had so many other demands on both her time and her energy was not her fault.

When the time had come to discuss Annie, and he had reluctantly admitted he had not told her, or anyone else for that matter, that he was coming to Tremaine Road, he had sat not knowing what to say as he saw tears slowly trickle down Vera's face.

'I don't believe I've ever met anyone so strong-minded as young Annie! Nor as kind-hearted,' she exclaimed.

Later, after he had had a long talk with Peter and it was time for him to leave, Ferguson shook hands with both of them and wished them well. He meant it. Every word.

He had certainly underestimated Miss Bateman! He had been on every floor of that house, and renovating it was not a task that he would willingly tackle. It was a well-built sturdy house in a very good area of south London. It might turn out to be an absolute gold-mine; on the other hand it could be a long-term liability! That young lady had the kind of courage that would move mountains, and henceforth, as far as he was concerned, he would go out of his way to offer her all the help he possibly could.

Annie walked out of Tooting Broadway tube station. Suddenly her troubles didn't seem half so bad. 'Morning, luv!' A rosy-faced flower-seller gave her a friendly smile. Returning her warm greeting and making a decision to buy some flowers for her gran on the way back, Annie crossed the Broadway, turned right and made for the high street. She rummaged in her bag to check the directions Ferguson had given her. Walk up past the Castle pub, Selkirk Road and Broadwater Road, she read, '. . . and on the same side you will see the Co-op, which is well spread out. Ask directions for the bank, as it's easily missed.'

He was right. It wasn't one big store. Annie had passed

a shoe-shop which had RACS above the doorway; two doors up was the gentlemen's outfitters; then she came to the main grocery department, which had more than one entrance, and even further along was a furniture store and an enormous haberdashery departmental store which looked extremely posh. So many shops, selling almost everything, and all belonging to the Royal Arsenal Co-operative Society. Nowhere could she see any sign of a bank. A van was drawn up at the kerb, its two back doors wide open, and a man in a fawn linen coat was loading trays of bread.

'Could you tell me if the Co-op Bank is anywhere round here, please?' Annie asked, giving him her sweetest smile.

''Alf a mo, luv, I won't be a tick,' he told her. Giving the tray he was holding a hefty shove to make it slide on runners into the van, the driver closed the doors. Stepping back, he pointed a finger. 'See the end of the grocery shop, or the beginning, whichever way you're looking? Well, right beside it is a door. Easy to miss, I grant. Push 'ard, 'cos it's 'eavy, and you'll see a flight of stairs. Three flights t'be exact, about thirty or forty steps in all. Bank's at the top.'

'Are you 'aving me on?' Annie asked without hesitation.

'No. Gawd's truth. Though there ain't many that use the bank except on divi days, cos the blooming steps is enough to kill yer.' He looked Annie over from the top of her head to the tips of her toes and, liking what he saw, added, 'You'll be all right. Fit as a fiddle, I'd say. If I didn't 'ave a delivery t'make I'd sling yer over me shoulder and carry yer up there meself!'

'I'll come back another day then, shall I?' It was Annie's turn to grin.

He laughed at that. 'So long as yer don't let on ter me

missus that I've got that much stamina. She keeps me awake 'alf the night, as it is. Better get going. So long, luv.' As he climbed into his van he was thinking that the lass was young and friendly, and very lovely with that gorgeous head of hair. Still, there was something else; even behind the banter there was a certain sadness. She obviously didn't come from round here, and whatever had brought her to Tooting, he hoped her journey would be worth while.

Annie's heart was thumping, her legs ached and she was short of breath by the time she reached the top of the three flights of stone steps.

Only one half-glazed door led off the landing. On the other side was what looked more like a long office than a bank. A counter ran the full length of the room, dark mahogany, very highly polished and unusually high. It was fronted by a brass-coloured mesh grill, behind which three girls worked.

From the far end, a voice asked, 'Can I help you?'

Annie smiled nervously at the young lady. 'I have an appointment with Mr Selwyn.'

'Miss Bateman, is it? He's expecting you. You'd better come through.' She beckoned to Annie.

Annie walked the length of the room, thinking that the clerk didn't look very old. The girl bent down, a bolt was shot, and then the counter-top was raised, allowing just enough room for Annie to slip in.

Another door opened and before her stood a tall, angular gentleman who looked to be about fifty. He held out a hand in welcome. As Annie shook it, she noted that behind his horn-rimmed glasses there was a twinkle in his grey eyes. 'You're a bit early, Miss Bateman,' he said, 'but you might as well come in.'

Annie braced herself and went forward. Mr Selwyn closed the door, then took a seat behind his desk. It struck her that this was a funny-shaped office. It had only one window, and that was set high in the wall. There was no view to be seen, and the centre ceiling electric light was on. What little furniture there was, seemed old-fashioned. The floor was covered by a well-worn red carpet.

Mr Selwyn broke the silence, and his deep voice made Annie jump. 'Now,' he began, 'I had a telephone call from your family solicitor, Mr Ferguson. Very enlightening . . .' He paused and shook his head. 'I do offer my condolences on your father's untimely death. I understand you knew nothing of his dealings with this company as regards being granted a loan on the property in Tremaine Road?'

Mr Selwyn looked up and smiled briefly, and Annie tried to do the same, but wasn't sure she had succeeded. She felt so nervous that her face had gone numb.

'Did you bring papers with you?'

'Yes. And several letters from you to my father that I only recently came to know about.' She passed over the large envelope containing all the documents that dealt with the purchase of the property, several letters that Vera had given her, and also the account book which held a record of all the payments her father had made on the mortgage, saying, 'Are these papers all proper and legal? I have to find out.'

'If you'll give me a minute,' Mr Selwyn said, as he bent over the pile of papers, studying everything, spending several moments on each sheet.

Annie began to feel frightened, feeling worse as the minutes ticked by. Would he want to know how her father had come by so much money? Why he had several times paid the mortgage well in advance rather than regular small monthly repayments?

Mr Selwyn took a deep breath. He would freely admit that he had an endless curiosity about people and what they got up to, especially when they happened to be his customers. This young lady seated in front of him was no exception. He forced himself to look calm and composed. There was no way round it. He was going to have to lay out the bare facts and simply tell her the truth. 'Miss Bateman,' he began, looking at her with sympathy, 'there is no way of wrapping this up. I'm sorry. Truly I am . . . Despite all the extenuating circumstances that Mr Ferguson has acquainted me with, there's nothing that I can do. Head Office would never allow the transfer of this existing mortgage from your father's name to yours.'

It wasn't unexpected. Annie merely sighed and was about to get to her feet when Mr Selwyn spoke again. 'For one thing, you are a single young lady. I take it you don't have a regular weekly income that would cover the amount due as one month's repayment on the said property?'

'No. I do have a regular job,' Annie answered defiantly, 'but I don't earn much. I was hoping that the company would allow me to rent out the house in three flats and that the income from the tenants would more than cover the repayments.'

'Ah! I gathered that much from Mr Ferguson. That fact alone would go against you at Head Office.'

'What? I don't understand.'

Mr Selwyn allowed himself a slight smile. This young lady had guts. 'The strictest of the rules laid down by the RACS is that any property on mortgage to the company shall at no time be sub-let.'

What Annie wanted to yell was: In that case, I've been wasting your time and my own, but instead she answered, 'I'm sorry I've troubled you. Can you tell me what will happen now, and how quickly . . .' She couldn't put into words the thoughts that were troubling her.

'Don't be too hasty.' Mr Selwyn had risen to his feet. 'Mr Ferguson has told me all about the arrangement your father had with Mr and Mrs James, and I think we both knew from the off that your visit here today could only end with Head Office foreclosing.'

Annie smiled ruefully. 'So why did he suggest this meeting?'

'I've been made aware that you are the sole heir named in your father's will, and that all ends must be tied up legally. I feel sure that your case will be viewed with sympathy and you will be allowed time to make other arrangements.' Mr Selwyn was struggling; he did his best to joke his way out of what he now saw as a sad situation. 'I'm sure you won't find bailiffs knocking at the door.' Then he saw Annie's shocked expression and quickly added, 'No, of course not. It won't come to that. I'll do my best to see you get ample time to make other arrangements. Try to be patient.'

Again Annie would have loved to reply, I just want to be able to tell the Jameses that no one is going to take their home away from them. Instead, she kept her own council. Quietly rising to her feet she held out her hand. 'Thank you, Mr Selwyn. You've been very kind and at least I now know where I stand.'

By the time she had got to the bottom of those terrible stone stairs, she was fuming. Damned red tape! Can't borrow money 'cos I'm a single woman. Won't look at what could be a very viable business proposition 'cos it's not company policy. My dad had the right idea!

Now she leant against the wall and laughed until the laughter turned to frustration and she began to cry. 'Oh, Dad.' The words came out loud like a cry of pain. You would have gone ahead and just done it. You settled the Jameses in, warm and comfortable. Without letting on to a soul you would have had the builders in, three flats all let and rent coming in regularly. The mortgage payments would have been met. No one would have been any the wiser as to what you were doing. The Co-op wouldn't have been a penny out of pocket. Rather, there would have been tenants that would be properly housed and eternally grateful to you. Ducking and diving, some would call it, but you got things done. She heaved a great sigh. God, how I wish you were still here! She wiped her eyes, buttoned her coat and stepped out into the fresh air.

When Annie had walked the length of Tooting High Street she was glad enough of the excuse to stop. The Broadway was an exciting place: the hustle and bustle of both trolley-buses and trams, the newspaper-vendors crying 'Star, News or Standard', all the early evening papers on the streets for just a penny each, the policeman on point duty, white gloves on his hands, waving frantically at the traffic and woe betide any driver, of a motor, a horse-drawn cart or a cyclist, who didn't obey his commands.

Slowly and carefully she crossed the busy main road. Ah, that's good, she thought when she saw that the flower-seller was still outside the tube station, though it didn't look as if she had much left in her basket.

'Allo, luv, on yer way 'ome now, are yer?'

'Just about. Can you make me up a nice bunch of flowers for me gran, please?'

'Course I will, me luv.'

To Annie's astonishment, the stout little woman added, 'Shan't be a tick.' And with that she trotted off towards the kerb, where a long-handled barrow was standing half loaded with wide flat cardboard boxes. Fascinated, Annie watched as she raised the lid of three of them and removed a few blooms from each. The old lady replaced the lids before bringing the flowers back to Annie.

'Me old man's been up to Covent Garden.' She flashed a toothy grin at Annie. 'He's just gone fer a pint, then the pair of us were off 'ome. I've got an order for two crosses and two wreaths for termorrow; that's 'ow come I've got the extra boxes. At least yer know they're fresh. Shall I put a pennyworth of gyp and a few nice bits of fern in with the bunch?'

'Oh, yes please. That would be lovely,' Annie replied, watching again as the roses, carnations and colourful daisies were laid against the white of the gypsophila and the green of the fern.

'That d'yer, darling?' The woman held the bunch up for Annie's inspection. Annie nodded her head in delight as she took out her purse.

'Half a crown t'you, luv.' Knees bent, the flower-seller laid a sheet of white paper across her legs and expertly wrapped the flowers into a remarkably shapely cone.

'They're absolutely lovely,' Annie told her as she handed over the money. 'My gran will be thrilled to bits. Thanks ever so much.'

'You're more than welcome, me darling. I know you ain't one of me regulars, but now you know where I am, come an' see me again.'

'I will,' Annie promised.

'Gawd bless yer. Take care.' The Cockney voice had

Annie smiling as she went inside the station to get the tube home. Standing on the escalator, she put her nose to the colourful blooms. The perfume was really nice. Gran will love these, she told herself. When she finally reached home, she withdrew the key from the letter-box and opened the front door. Then she leaned against the frame for a moment, wanting to gather her wits, to sort out exactly what she was going to say to Gran. And, worse still, how she was going to deal with Peter and Vera James. When there came down the passage the sound of Ronnie and Mary's voices and their lovely hearty laughter, answered by her gran's deep chuckling, she was glad she was home. She straightened up, felt in her pocket for the two bars of Nestlés chocolate she had just bought for the children at the corner shop, and laid the flowers across her arm so that Gran would see them the minute she walked in.

Head high, shoulders back, sure of a welcome, she called out, 'I'm home.'

Chapter Twenty-eight

ONCE AGAIN ANNIE DID not know how she got through the next couple of days without exploding, for things seemed to be closing in on her from all sides. She loved working with Sid and Flossie in their café and, in a way, she looked upon it as an escape from the house and the children. Was that wicked? There were times when she knew it to be the truth. The darker evenings didn't help. The children couldn't go out to the park or play in the street. It was straight home from school, and some form of amusement had to be found each night to keep them occupied. Strange as it seemed, Ronnie was not the problem. Since Jack Higgins had come back into their lives the lad had buckled down and started to study. She no longer had to coax him to do his homework, and come the weekend, Ronnie would proudly show Jack his exercise books, gloating over the number of marks his teacher had given him and on certain subjects even a gold star.

No, it was Mary who was making her heart ache. If

she didn't know differently, she'd swear the child had found out that Bob Wilson had denied being her father. What other reason could there be for the way the little girl was acting? It wasn't sulking – it was more serious than that, almost as if she wasn't with them half the time. Withdrawn, her gran had said. But why? And just what did 'withdrawn' mean? On leaving work Annie had a splitting headache and now she was home, she'd decided to have a lie down before going to meet the children from school. It's no good, she said to herself, she couldn't rest, her mind was so full.

About ten minutes later the front door opened and Jack Higgins called from downstairs, 'Are you home, Annie?'

Good God! Jack hardly ever came round during the week, and never during daytime. She rolled off the bed and pulled her skirt straight, grabbed a comb from the dressing-table and smoothed her hair back from her forehead, swept the rest of it from her shoulders, then quickly tied a dark ribbon to hold it all together at the back. As she opened her bedroom door she called, 'Yes, Jack. I'll be down in just a minute.'

'You all right?' he asked.

'Yes, I was only resting me legs.' She looked down to where he stood waiting in the passage and smiled at him.

He returned her smile. Then he watched her coming down the stairs, her skirt swaying her shoulders well back, her head held high. 'I'm sorry. Did I disturb you?'

'No, it's all right. But I'm dying to know what brings you round here at this time of day?'

Jack laughed. 'You'll never guess, not in a million years!'

Annie shivered. 'Oh, Jack, you've left the front door

wide open!' She pushed by him and went to shut it. It was a miserable afternoon, sleet had begun to fall and the sky was very dark. 'It's a good job you've come, as I didn't realize it was so late. I have to get ready to meet the children from school.'

'There's no need to hurry. I'll take you.'

Annie turned quickly because she'd heard the laughter in his voice. 'What d'you mean, you'll take me?'

'I left the door open on purpose. Open it again and look outside.'

Jack's tone was such that Annie put her head out, then quickly withdrew back into the warmth of the house. 'There's no one out there.'

'I never said there was. But there is something standing at the kerb right by your front gate.'

Annie turned her head and looked again. 'Oh . . . It's a car!'

'My car. It's a Ford – I bought it this morning. Couldn't wait to come and show it off to you. I thought we'd go together and meet the kids. They probably won't mind riding home instead of walking, especially as the weather has turned so rotten.'

'Jack, you are an angel! You really are.'

He looked down at his corded trousers, thick fishermen's jersey his heavy boots. 'Angel? I don't think so! But if you put the kettle on and make us both a cuppa, I don't mind in the least being classified as your chauffeur for the rest of the day.'

'Oh, Jack! I think it's great. Your own car! The kids will be thrilled to see you turn up in it outside the school. You'll probably end up having Ronnie's mates climbing all over it.'

'I was hoping you'd be pleased. My first thought was:

327

I'll fetch Annie, and together we can go and meet Ronnie and Mary.'

'Well, if you really mean it, I suppose I do have time for a cup of tea now.'

Jack grinned. 'Tell you what: you put the kettle on and I'll set the cups out.'

When they were in the living-room, Jack took a poker to the fire, raking the packed embers, encouraging the flames to burn more brightly, while Annie lifted the kettle from the hob and took it out to the scullery. She lit the gas and in only a few minutes the water was boiling, as it was already hot from standing on the range.

Soon they were seated one each side of the fire, the tea-tray on a low table between them, and as Annie held out a plate of shortbread biscuits to Jack, he murmured, 'You're looking a bit pale, Annie. I felt at the weekend that something was troubling you. Do you want to tell me about it?'

She shook her head and, her voice breaking, said, 'It's not fair to burden you with all my problems.'

Jack took her hand and held it tightly. 'Our lives have somehow become entwined, and I for one am more than grateful. You know that I have no family of my own, and if it weren't for your gran, I'd have nowhere to live. Anything, anything at all, that I can ever do for you, you only have to say the word.' He paused, took a deep breath, then added, 'If you've got that straight in your head, how about starting at the beginning, because we're not moving from here until I know what is troubling you so much.' She turned from staring into the fire and looked at him. 'Come on,' he urged. 'A trouble shared is a trouble halved.'

Oh dear! Annie sighed heavily, Jack was nice, a kind man. Yes, that was what it was about Jack, his kindness to others. 'Jack, it would take so long. I've more than one problem, and it just doesn't seem fair to involve you.'

'Look, I know we have to leave soon. The children come out at half-past three, don't they?' Annie nodded, got up from her chair and began to walk around the room. 'Just tell me the bare facts for now, and maybe we can meet this evening and see what's to be done.'

Making a quick decision, Annie started talking first about Robert Wilson. It took a full ten minutes to describe their meeting in the offices of Webb & Son, and by the time she had got to the fact that Robert refused to have anything to do with Mary because he was not her father, Jack was livid.

'You confronted him *on your own*?' he yelled at her. 'It's bad enough that you've taken on two children, let alone trying to sort his problems out.'

'Who else is there?' Annie asked sensibly. 'It has worked fairly well so far, but . . . Well, just lately I'm worried sick about Mary. She looks so sad, and I can't reason out why.'

Jack became overwhelmed by a feeling of uselessness. He had valued Annie since she was little more than a baby. He wanted to take care of her and never let her be troubled. But how could he tell her that he loved her? He was nine years older than her. He had been through hell during the war and what had he come home to? Nothing and no one. He had convinced himself that Annie should get out and about – find herself a young man. She was beautiful, and she was so young. He couldn't ask her to tie herself down with an old stick-in-the-mud like himself. 'Annie.' He cleared his throat. 'You said that more than one thing was troubling you. Tell me about that.'

Annie smiled, 'You are a glutton for punishment today, aren't you?'

He got to his feet and looked about him as if not sure what to do. Then he saw that Annie was twisting her hands in her lap. 'Oh, Annie, for God's sake get it off your chest! Just tell me. Whatever it is it has to be a case of two heads being better than one.'

So she gave him the outline of her visit to the house in Tremaine Road, the fact that her father had bought the house with a mortgage and now the bank was going to foreclose, and that would mean that Vera and Peter James had to be turfed out of their home, unless . . .

'Good grief! Do you really believe that you can shoulder everybody else's troubles all by yourself?' he asked her gently. She made no effort to answer, just gave a slight shake of her head. His hand was tender as he touched her cheek, and his voice was low as he said, 'Annie, I'm almost sure that I'll be able to help out on this one.'

She raised her eyes to meet his and now she really smiled. 'Oh, Jack, you don't know what a relief it is to hear you say that!'

'Now, hang on a minute, don't go getting your hopes too high.' Having said that, Jack added quickly, 'The trouble with you, my girl, is you don't stop to think. Just because the Co-op Bank won't allow you to continue paying the mortgage, the matter doesn't have to stop there. There are other banks, and even private individuals are sometimes willing to invest in small ventures.'

'You mean there might be a chance? I have an appointment tomorrow to see Mr Mathews – he's the bank manager that dealt with dad's affairs – and now I have an account at his branch.'

'Well, there you are!' Jack practically jumped to his feet.

'Will you let me take you for a drink tonight? Somewhere quiet where we can sit and talk?'

Annie nodded. 'Yes, I'd like that.'

'Good. That's settled, then. Now move, get your coat and let's be on our way. I can't wait to show my little beauty off to Ronnie.'

'Aw, but . . .' Annie put her hand on Jack's arm in a kind of protest signal.

'No aw buts! Go on, get yourself ready.'

'Please, Jack, just listen. When the kiddies come out from school, don't leave Mary out of it.' She paused, half undecided as to whether she ought to say more. She was really thrilled at the way Jack and Ronnie had taken to each other. She could well understand why Jack liked taking the boy out and about – he was good company. She herself really loved the lad, with his sprinkling of freckles, his laughing eyes and his saucy chatter. 'But . . . What I'm trying to say is, don't make a big thing out of showing the car to Ronnie and just leave Mary standing looking on, will you?'

After a moment the penny dropped, and he said, 'I see what you're getting at. Maybe that is half the trouble where the poor little mite is concerned. I can be such a blasted fool at times. I'm sorry.'

'No, I never meant it like that.'

They looked at each other, and when Jack said, 'Oh yes, you did,' they both burst out laughing.

It was well over an hour later when Jack drove the car right up outside Annie's front door again and switched the engine off. The door was wide open, and on the doorstep stood Rhoda Bateman and Gladys Dawson.

'Oh, oh, news travels fast in our street!' Annie leant

over the back seat of the car and whispered in Jack's ear.

'Hallo, Gran!' Mary was first out of the car and racing up the front path.

'Hallo yourself,' said Rhoda. 'Travelled home in style today, I see.

Annie sat still for a minute regarding what was going on. Her grandmother now had Mary up in her arms and the child was chattering away as though somebody had just wound her up. Annie had to smile. Rhoda had such patience with children.

'I got to sit in the front seat next to Jack,' Mary was happily telling Rhoda and Mrs Dawson. 'He said ladies had to have a gentleman sitting beside them, and Ronnie should sit in the back seat with Annie. He did say Ronnie could sit in the front seat when he takes him to football on Saturday, 'cos there won't be no ladies with them then.'

'We didn't come straight 'ome.' Ronnie threw his comment into the conversation. 'Jack took us fer a drive round. Gran, you'll 'ave t'get him to take you out sometime. It's a spiffing motor-car.'

'Did he give you yer tea while he had you out?' Rhoda asked, a mischievous grin on her lips.

Ronnie stood stock still. 'No, we ain't 'ad nothing t'eat since our packed lunch at dinner time. I'm starving, an' I bet our Mary is an' all.'

'Oh, so I've still got me uses, have I?' Rhoda said, still grinning. 'I arrive here to have the whole street tell me that me granddaughter has gone off with Jack Higgins in a new motor-car, and all I find is an empty house.'

'But we're back now, Gran,' Ronnie protested, 'and truly I'm famished.'

'Then me sausages, mash and baked beans won't be

wasted after all? Silly old me. I was thinking I'd have to be scraping them all into the bin.'

'Aw, come off it, Gran! You're tormenting me stomach,' Ronnie said as he pushed his way past and ran down the passage.

Rhoda set Mary on her feet, patted her head, and said, 'Go on, pet, get yerself ready for yer tea.' Then she yelled, 'And you, me lad, don't think you're sitting up at that table until you've washed yer hands!' Both Annie and Jack were grinning broadly. 'Jack, are you coming in for a bite?' Rhoda said, and without waiting for an answer she turned Gladys. 'There's more than enough to feed an army, so if you've no one indoors, come in and eat with us. You're more than welcome. Ain't she, Annie?'

Annie linked her arm into that of Gladys, and said, 'Of course you are. Come on in. I hope Gran's kept the fire well made up. It's really chilly out here.'

'Annie,' she turned as she heard Jack call her, 'I won't come in now. I've a few things I need to see to, but I'll pick you up about half-past seven. Will that be all right?'

'Fine,' she answered, 'I'll be ready.'

While Annie was helping Rhoda to dish up the meal and Gladys was busy laying the table, Annie suddenly said, 'Look, Gran, I know I'm always asking you to do me favours, but can you do one more? Would you stay the night here? Jack's asked me to go for a drink with him and I'm not sure what time Doris will be home. I can't leave the children in the house on their own.'

Rhoda kept her face straight, yet inwardly she was smiling to herself, and thinking, Pity he doesn't ask you more often. Out loud she said, 'No trouble at all. Anytime, you know you've only got to ask. That's another thing; you don't get out often enough.' She scolded Annie in a loving way. She worried about her granddaughter.

'I'm all right, Gran, honest. I'll have plenty of time to go out and about when Ronnie and Mary are a little more settled.'

Rhoda wasn't so sure. She shook her head at her, and wagged a finger. 'Time passes a whole lot quicker than you think. I married very young, and I never regretted it, not for one moment. When your grandfather died I thought I'd never get over it. But at least we had some good years together.'

She sounded so sad that Annie immediately threw her arms around her neck, saying, 'Oh, Gran, I do love you.'

Rhoda hugged her close, and when they broke apart, she had to have the last word. 'You'll regret it one day, Annie, if you don't get married and have children of your own.'

'I'll think about what you've said, Gran.'

'You do too much thinking about it! Let's see a bit of action for a change.'

'Yes, ma'am,' Annie said good-naturedly. 'Now, if we don't take this food into the living-room we shall have a riot on our hands.'

With that, Rhoda laughed at her, leaned down and kissed her cheek, saying, 'You're too sharp for your own good, but you'll do. Yes, you'll do.'

Chapter Twenty-nine

BY THE TIME ANNIE had finished telling Jack all the details of how Vera James had turned up, and her own subsequent visit to Tremaine Road, plus giving him a much fuller account of her meeting with Bob Wilson, the landlord of the pub was calling 'Time' and Jack was staring at her very seriously.

'Your dad obviously thought buying that house was a good business proposition.' Then he added, 'I'll come to the bank with you in the morning, if you like.'

'Would you, Jack? Do you really mean it?'

'I would have offered earlier, but I thought you might think I was interfering. Listening to all you've had to say, I think it would be a crying shame if the Jameses were turfed out of that flat.'

'Oh, Jack, you don't know how relieved I am to hear you say that. Wait till you see what they've done with their part of the house and the garden. I couldn't believe my eyes! It must have been really hard work.'

'Finish your drink. If we don't soon make a move, we're gonna get thrown out of this pub!'

Annie raised the glass to her lips and drained it. Jack was helping her on with her coat. He patted her shoulder as she did up the buttons. 'I'll pick you up in the car. I can always wait outside if the bank manager objects.'

'No!' Annie protested angrily. 'I want you there. Just to be able to talk to someone about all this is such a relief.'

Jack held the door open and then firmly took hold of her arm, pressing her close to his side as they walked the short distance back to her house.

'How about your gran?' he ventured. 'What does she have to say about all this?'

'Well, taking first things first, she was absolutely livid when Bob Wilson came and took the children out. Wasn't his fault, but he brought them back like a couple of drowned rats. It's ever since then that Mary has been . . . different, that's the only word that I can think of. Somehow, in deeds if not in words, Bob Wilson must have made it plain that he wanted nothing whatsoever to do with her. I can't think of any other reason for her to have become so sullen and withdrawn. More than likely he gave all his attention to Ronnie, ignoring Mary, and she would have sensed that something wasn't right. Gran says she'd like to murder the bugger!'

'She's not the only one!' Jack laughed, but his laugh had a hollow ring to it, and beneath his breath he muttered, 'I'll see my day with him! No one should be allowed to treat children the way he has.'

'As for Vera and Peter, all Gran keeps on about is what a dark horse my dad was and that we've only to wait an' see and everything will be fine. If you ask me, she believes that her son is up there looking down on us, and that he can still wheel an' deal with the help of the angels!'

Annie had drunk two gin and tonics and Jack had had two pints of beer and a double whisky. They stopped and looked at each other, and Jack solemnly said, 'Let's hope she's right.' Then raising his eyes to the dark sky he called out, 'We could certainly do with a bit of help down here, Jim, me old mate!'

'Yeah, wish us luck, Dad,' Annie muttered.

With that, they both burst out laughing.

The next day the weather didn't let up. It was bitterly cold. Only two more days and they would be into November. Annie felt grateful that Jack was picking her up in his car. As soon as she arrived at the café she had asked Sid if she could make a phone call to check with Mr Mathews that it was all right to bring a friend when she kept her appointment.

At two p.m. sharp she presented herself, together with a very differently dressed Jack Higgins. He was wearing a navy blue overcoat over a dark suit, which Annie thought made him look very businesslike.

Mr Mathews, attired exactly as she remembered, stood smiling in the doorway of his office. Annie hesitated, her nervousness obvious. 'Nice to see you again, Miss Bateman,' he said reassuringly, holding out his hand.

They shook hands, and Annie introduced Jack as a friend of her family. When they were all seated, she loosened her heavy coat, and decided that Mr Mathews was not as stout as she remembered, but that his fair hair had started to recede. She was telling herself: What the hell is it to do with me whether he's been on a diet, when he spoke.

'Now, Miss Bateman, I've had a couple of lengthy phone calls from Mr Ferguson so I am somewhat in the picture. How can I help you?' His voice was not only soft, but kind as well.

Annie looked first at Jack, who gave her an encouraging nod. In a barely audible whisper, she said, 'You know about the house my father bought, and about Mr and Mrs James who are living in the basement flat?' She paused and waited until he nodded to confirm that much was true. 'My father was granted the mortgage by the Co-op Bank, but they don't approve of sub-letting. In fact, they will not transfer the loan into my name. Mr Selwyn, the manager, says there is no alternative. I have to sell the property or they will do it for me. I was wondering if you would advance the money to repay the Co-op? Would the bank consider taking over the mortgage?'

If Mr Mathews had burst out laughing, Annie wouldn't have held it against him. Her request, spoken out loud, sounded ludicrous even to her. But he didn't laugh, leant towards her and courteously said, 'We'll do our best. There are ways and means by which you could hold on to the property. At least for the time being, I think the arrears payments should be brought up to date. That will at least give you breathing space. I would appreciate knowing exactly what you have in mind for the property before we go any further. Could you give me a bare outline?' Annie sighed, wondering where to start. 'Take your time, Miss Bateman,' he encouraged her.

Slowly to begin with, Annie told Mr Mathews that there was a slight hope of a government grant to pay for badly needed repairs to the house which in the main had been caused during the bombing. Then her hesitation gave way to resolution. No longer was she searching for words, and they poured out. How Mr James had been wounded. How remarkable he was in dealing with his disabilities. How

Mrs James had set up her own business in what was little more than a shed. What a comfortable home they had made out of the basement flat. How unbelievably lovely the garden was. If and when the house was made safe and sound, she felt she would have no difficulty in finding tenants for what would be three self-contained flats. The rents should hopefully cover the outgoings. Suddenly Annie realized that she had been talking non-stop for a very long time. Not once had Mr Mathews interrupted her, though from time to time she had glanced at Jack, who had been ready with a smile and a nod of his head to buoy her up. 'That's about it,' she wound up. 'I haven't the foggiest idea of where to start, or whom I have to contact about this grant.'

Mr Mathews sat up in his chair. From the first, the day he had been present when the safe deposit box belonging to this young lady's father had been opened, he had begun to respect her. Having listened to her now, he was certain she had a great deal of common sense. He wondered how Jack fitted into things, but still felt his handshake had been firm and that had to count for something. He could prove to be a useful ally to Miss Bateman. 'You've no need to do anything about the grant,' he said, and his eyes twinkled at her. 'Mr Ferguson has all that in hand. He has the necessary forms and will make the application on your behalf.'

'Really? Well, that is good of him,' Annie replied, only half believing what she'd been told.

He turned to Jack. 'May I take it you are here because you are prepared to help Miss Bateman?'

'Most certainly,' Jack answered quickly. 'In any way I can.'

Cautiously he asked, 'Do you have regular employment, Mr Higgins?'

'Yes, I am a lighterman, as my father was before me. I own my own lighter, which, by and large, I work with on all the major docks up and down the Thames. And . . . I may be jumping the gun here, but if you are considering asking me if I would be willing to stand as a guarantor for Miss Bateman against any loan, my answer would be Yes.' Jack looked into the bank manager's eyes, and, unable to judge what he was thinking, he pressed on.

'When I was demobbed from the Royal Navy, my own bank financed me, thus enabling me to work for myself ever since I have been back in civvy street. The loan was for a period of five years, and I repaid it within twelve months. I can give you the branch at which I bank, and the manager's name. I feel quite sure he will vouch for me.'

Annie's thoughts were in a whirl. First Mr Ferguson was supposedly doing his best to secure a grant so that the repair work could be started on the Tremaine Road house, and now here was Jack sitting up straight, sticking his chest out and as good as telling Mr Mathews to give her the money she needed, and if she couldn't keep up the repayments, he would be responsible for them. At least, she thought that was what his words amounted to. Without thinking where she was and who was present, she swivelled round to face Jack and burst out, 'Do you mean if I was lucky enough to get a loan and at some time I found I couldn't pay up, you would? You'd meet the repayments?'

'Yes, that's exactly what I mean,' he answered seriously.

'Bloody hell! I knew you were a good friend, but to take a risk like that. Well . . .'

The tension was gone. The two men looked at each other and burst out laughing. Annie's cheeks flamed up and she covered her face. Then she did her best to apologize.

'Not at all, Miss Bateman. There must be something about you – all these men falling over themselves to help you! I'm sure the bank will consider your application favourably. I need to get a few details, and I would like your permission to send surveyors round to the house. In fact for several reasons, I'd very much like to go there myself.' For the next few minutes Mr Mathews fired questions at her and Annie answered to the best of her ability. He wrote notes on a pad in front of him. Finally he got to his feet, came round, and held out his hand to Jack, saying, 'I'm sure we shall meet again.'

'Thanks, I shall look forward to it,' Jack said, his voice still deep with sincerity.

He held out his hand to Annie, who solemnly shook it. Then this bank manager did surprise her. He put his arm over her shoulders and looked into her face. 'Now, I don't want you to worry. Especially not about Mr and Mrs James. Mr Ferguson has promised to keep in touch with me and I shall be sending my report off to Head Office straight away. Do you have a telephone?'

'Not at home I don't, but you could ring me at the café where I work. My employers are good friends, they won't mind in the least.'

'Would you write their number down on this pad,' he said to Annie, handing her his fountain pen. 'I shall do that just as soon as I have any news for you.' Mr Mathews sat back. Watching Annie's face, he felt he could read her thoughts. He saw doubts turn to hope, and he chuckled to himself. 'You'll be surprised how quickly things will get moving now. I meant what I said: you have no need to worry any further about Mr and Mrs James being turned out of their flat. From now on you should start looking upon 48 Tremaine Road as being a good property that is owned by you. Just remember that there are a lot of people who believe in you and are more than ready to help. True, there are a lot of loose ends to tie up, but you may safely leave all that to Mr Ferguson and myself.'

'Thank you,' was all Annie managed to mutter.

Mr Mathews had been right. Annie was more than a little surprised. The bank had agreed to grant her a loan on the Tremaine Road property and Mr Mathews had successfully dealt with the authorities regarding a grant for the repairs to all bomb damage. Within a week she had signed all the necessary papers and within three weeks the builders had started work.

On Saturday at breakfast, Annie said to the children, 'Like to come over to Wandsworth with me? I can show you the house I've been telling you about.'

'All right,' said Ronnie, 'but I really want to be back in time t'go to football with Jack this afternoon.'

'Never mind about him, Annie,' Mary protested. 'I'd love t'come.'

Annie and the children had spent the entire morning with Vera and Peter, and Annie was worried about leaving her friends because of all the noise the workmen were making upstairs. Peter was sitting in his deep armchair, busily discussing the merits of different football teams with Ronnie. In spite of his injuries, Annie had never once heard him moan. His legs, or rather one leg and a stump, were bad at times and Vera told her he still suffered a great deal of pain which made it difficult for him to get around. He and Ronnie seemed to be getting

342

on like a house on fire. If she had her way, she would make life a lot more secure for both him and Vera. In the short time she'd known this kind couple Annie had come to know that they would never accept what they would regard as charity. They'd be independent to the last. About forty, Annie judged Peter's age to be, yet his hair was pure white and his face lined, but he and Vera were jolly, looking on the bright side of everything. Annie had come to love them both.

'I'll make another cup of tea before you go,' Vera suggested. 'I'll also cut a few sandwiches while I'm waiting for the kettle to boil. Suppose I ought to take some more tea up to the workmen. I couldn't believe it when they told me yesterday that they were coming to work here today. Don't get many firms working on Saturdays.'

Annie didn't get a chance to answer. The front door bell was ringing. 'I'll go,' she offered. Walking through the hall, she felt sad. Although the connecting door was firmly closed, the noise was deafening and the dust had settled everywhere. It didn't seem fair that Vera and Peter had to put up with so much hassle. Tugging hard at the heavy front door that sealed off the basement, she was hoping the ends would justify all the inconvenience.

She stared in utter surprise. 'Why, it's you!' she exclaimed as Jack Higgins grinned at her.

'Your gran told me where you were, and I thought I'd kill two birds with one stone. Take Ronnie off your hands for the rest of the day, and at the same time see over this property I've heard so much about.' All Annie's misery came out in a shuddering sigh. 'Is something wrong? Aren't you going to ask me in?' Jack sounded really worried.

'I'm sorry.' Annie allowed him to step inside. 'I couldn't

be more pleased that you've turned up. It's just that I feel so guilty making Vera and Peter put up with all the noise and the mess. It doesn't seem fair,' she told him ruefully.

For a moment, Jack was lost for words. He had never before seen her look so woebegone. He stretched out his arms, drew her to him and quickly hugged her.

'I'm being daft,' she muttered, her head pressed tightly against his chest.

'No, of course you're not. You're just a bit down in the dumps, that's all. It's a wonder you haven't cracked up before this, what with the worry of one thing after another. All this noise and mess will be well worth it in the end, you'll see.' He stayed still, cradling her in his big brawny arms, until at last he said, 'Hadn't you better shut the door?'

'Of course! Vera will be wondering what's going on out here.' At last a smile came to Annie's lips as she thought how pleased young Ronnie would be that Jack had turned up. 'Come on through and let me introduce you, and then I'll take you on a grand tour upstairs.'

It was just as Annie had pictured. A whoop of joy from Ronnie, now he knew he'd be going to see a football match with Jack. Mary was made a fuss of, and she beamed when he told her that she and Annie would stay here all day with Auntie Vera and he'd come back later and take them home in his car. Vera clucked round him like a mother hen, offering tea and asking what would he like to eat. Man to man, Peter and Jack's eyes met. There was no pity on Jack's part, just admiration as they gripped each other's hand.

'Go on, then, the pair of you. Go take a look upstairs,' Vera urged. 'I'll get you a cup of tea and a bite to eat while you're gone.'

Treading gingerly, Annie said, 'At least it's light everywhere now. What a difference since the workmen pulled all the boarding down and fitted new panes of glass.'

Jack was amazed. 'It's a wonderful house. They don't build them like this any more. Just look at those marvellous high ceilings and all the woodwork.'

The very top floor was the worst. Every bit of floor space was covered in thick dust. One broken window-frame was still hanging dangerously by its sash-cords. A workman who had followed them up quickly cut it down and began to knock out the jagged shards of glass that were sticking out from the sides of the frame. The man was humming. Suddenly he turned his head to Annie, saying, 'Many of the old houses are having to be knocked down, too badly damaged to do anything with. Not the case here. Solid as a rock. Another week or ten days, an' you won't know this place.'

'Yes,' she answered meekly, ashamed that she'd been upset about the noise and the mess.

'We're very lucky,' she said, smiling at Jack. 'My dad really did seem to know what he was doing.' When they were about to start back down the stairs, Annie paused and called back over her shoulder, 'I'll be back in a few minutes with a tray of tea for all of you.'

'Thanks, luv,' came one reply, while another voice rang out, 'Thank Gawd for that! Me throat's so dry I couldn't spit sixpence.'

'I won't be long,' Annie called out, before saying to Jack, 'I think they've all earned it, don't you?'

'Yes, I do,' he answered enthusiastically. 'Before long you'll have this place looking like a palace. They'll be queuing up to rent your flats.'

Annie told him, 'Vera and I still can't believe how

quickly this work has got started. You know what I'm beginning to think – that it's a case of not what you know but who you know that works wonders.'

'You may well be right, Annie. I think you put forward a good case when you let it be known that the Jameses were in danger of losing their home. They really are a deserving couple and there are still people who care and are willing to help.'

'Well, whatever. All I know is that I could never have got things moving so fast if it had been left to me.'

'I agree,' Jack told her shrewdly. 'I think from now on I shall have to mind my manners 'cos it seems that you have friends in high places.'

'Oh, Jack! Now you're taking the mickey.'

'No, I'm not. But if you don't move yourself and get the workmen the tea you promised, you are going to have a strike on your hands.'

'And that will never do.' She laughed as she ran down the stairs, feeling that at last things might just be starting to improve not only for herself but for Peter and Vera.

Chapter Thirty

THERE WAS SO MUCH to be done before the year was out.
Annie rested her arms on the dressing-table and stared into
the mirror. She looked a mess. Her face was drawn, her hair
needed washing. For Christ's sake pull yourself together, she
sternly told herself as she went downstairs to put the kettle
on. She made a pot of tea, drank one cup and stood staring
out at the back yard, reflecting that the children had to go
back to school two evenings this week because they were
rehearsing for the Christmas nativity play, and on Saturday
Doris and Frank were getting married.

Now that Doris had agreed to be his wife, Frank was in
a hurry. Why wait, when neither of them had any doubts?
Doris had told Annie that he been very nervous when he
made the suggestion. He wasn't giving her a chance to
change her mind, and Doris was happy to go along with
whatever he wanted. Anyway, she had confided to Annie,
she wouldn't have wanted a church wedding. Too public,
too fancy. A quick ceremony down at the registrar's office
would suit her very well.

'Just so long as you haven't forgotten you promised young Mary she could be bridesmaid,' Annie reminded her.

'As if I would!' Doris had protested.

They had gone together with Mary up to the West End, where they had bought her the loveliest dress they'd ever seen. Palest shade of peach and made from the softest of silks; a hoop fixed into the hem made the long dress stand out like a crinoline. With white satin pumps peeking out from beneath the dress, and soft white flowers woven into her long fair hair, the little girl was going to look as pretty as a picture.

Annie was happy for Doris, of course she was. Nevertheless she'd be glad when this week was over. What with this wedding, the school play and Christmas barely weeks away, she certainly hadn't had much time to herself. Ah well, she sighed, what doesn't get done will have to be left undone. Then glancing up at the clock she chided herself: If you don't get a move on and make yourself look a bit decent you're going to be late for work.

The days this week had flown by. Today, Friday, had been long and hard, but as she was having the next day off to go to Doris's wedding, Annie had worked late. It was seven o'clock when she left the café and it wasn't until she turned towards the river that she realized how foggy it had become. She might have taken a taxi, but there wasn't much traffic about and she thought that while she was searching for one she'd do just as well to keep walking. The thick fog soon had her eyes running and her throat feeling quite sore, and already she had bumped into a lamp-post. She stood still, took out a handkerchief and tied it so that it covered her nose and mouth.

The yellow fog was swirling in places and thick as pea-soup in others. A man carrying a lantern was walking in the road and it took a full minute for her to realize that he was walking in front of a bus, enabling, in a small way, the driver to see where he was going. The bus was travelling at a snail's pace and Annie would have hopped aboard, except that it was going in the wrong direction.

She still hadn't gone very far when she heard a muffled sound and a flickering glimmer of a light coming towards her. All her insides went tight. At first she thought it must be a small car that had mounted the pavement, or had she somehow wandered out into the main road? No, it was a bicycle. Then, wham! it slammed into her. She was tossed off her feet, and then falling, her hand caught in the spokes of a wheel. Someone was shouting at her. Her head hit a wall, hard, or maybe it was the ground. She struggled, but couldn't free her hand. Then everything went blurry. She wanted to call out but couldn't, because she was choking. 'Oh my head,' she murmured, and then she passed out.

The cyclist knelt down next to her and shone his bicycle lamp on to her face. 'Oh, God!' he cried, when he saw how badly hurt she was. Blood was oozing through her hair and trickling down her cheek. She must have bashed her head pretty badly, and her arm was lying oddly with her hand still caught up in the twisted tangle that had been his front wheel.

He wasn't sure if he should try and sit her up. She seemed to be unconscious, yet gasping for air. Better leave her to lie still and go and see if he could find someone to help. Even as he straightened up he heard footsteps, and seconds later two men were standing beside him.

'What's the matter, son? Bashed into the wall and smashed yer bike up, 'ave yer?' one burly man asked while the other hunched down and peered into the murky darkness.

'Oh, my Lord! Shine that bloody lamp down 'ere. There's a young lass, and it looks as if she's in a pretty bad state.' Then he put his hand beneath Annie's head, and found her hair soaked with blood. 'Get an ambulance, quick!' he called out to his mate.

The young lad was shaking like a leaf. 'It wasn't my fault, honest it wasn't. I didn't see her till I was on her.'

'Course it wasn't.' The man did his best to reassure him. 'Can't see yer 'and in front of yer t'night. Damn ambulance is a long time coming.'

When the ambulance did arrive, the driver and his mate worked quickly. 'It looks pretty bad,' the ambulance man said honestly. 'She's got a nasty gash to the back of her head and it looks as if her wrist is broken.'

The driver was going through her handbag to find her identity card. 'Come on, Annie, open your eyes for us . . . You're going to be all right . . . We're going to take you to hospital. Annie, can you hear me?'

Rhoda was supposed to be staying with the children only until Annie got home. When it was eight o'clock and there was no sign of her granddaughter, she began to worry. She'd been to the front door at least three times, but peering out into the thick smoky yellow fog did nothing to ease her fears. At nine o'clock when Doris came home, she asked her to go to the phone box at the corner of the road.

'I shouldn't think Sid and Flossie would have let her leave the café, not in this pea-souper,' Doris wisely suggested.

'That's as maybe, but we have to know. If she did leave,

it would have been a couple of hours ago, and from inside the café maybe they weren't aware of just how bad it was outside. If Sid does tell you she left work on time, you'd better ring the police and find out if they've heard of any accidents.'

'Right, just give me a minute to go to the lavatory,' Doris said, shrugging her coat back on. Having done her best to reassure Rhoda and the children that Annie would be home soon, she quickly made her way down the passage. What a night to have to go out in again, she was thinking when, with her hand still on the front door, the figures of two policemen loomed up. Doris felt her blood run cold. She now knew for certain she had been wrong, and that something terrible had happened to Annie.

'Does an Annie Bateman live here?' the larger of the two officers asked.

'Yes, she does. You'd better come into the house.'

Doris led the way into the living-room. After moment of silence, Rhoda said, 'It's my granddaughter, isn't it? Is she all right?'

The officer told her, 'I'm afraid not. She was knocked down by a bicycle. Sounds silly, I know, but in this thick fog . . .'

'We don't have all the details yet,' the other policeman took up the story.

'Where is she?' Rhoda's hand shook as she reached out to hold on to Doris.

'She's in the London Hospital.'

'How bad is she?' Fear was making Rhoda raise her voice. That's where her son, Jim, Annie's father, had died. Surely history wasn't about to be repeated. It couldn't be. It wouldn't be fair. Annie's so young, and so full of life, and so lovely.

'We really don't have the details. We have been told she has a head injury. That seemed to be the main concern. If you'd like to telephone the hospital, maybe they can tell you more.'

The colour had drained from Rhoda's face, and Doris, fearing she might fall, grabbed her arm and propelled her into an armchair. 'Thank you both,' Doris said to the officers. 'I'll come to the door with you.'

'No need for that, lass. You see to the old lady and things here. Drop of the hard stuff if you've got it wouldn't go amiss. We'll see ourselves out.'

The moment the police left, everyone started talking at once. Mary was crying – she didn't want Annie to be in hospital. Doris was trying to calm Rhoda and at the same time work out the best and quickest way they could get in touch with the hospital.

Ronnie came up with the best suggestion. 'Shall I take the big torch that Annie keeps in the coal-shed an' run round t'your 'ouse, Gran? D'yer think Jack will be indoors?'

Rhoda hesitated. The lad could run fast, but should she send him out in this thick fog? It wasn't very far, and the boy knew the way like the back of his own hand. Ronnie sensed her hesitation and went out into the passage, took his coat off its peg and was shrugging himself into it when Rhoda said, 'You will be careful, lad, won't you? And if Jack's not in, don't you dare go looking for him. You come straight back here.' She wound his long football scarf twice round his neck and stood back as he dived out of the front door. 'Stay close to the wall and feel your way,' she shouted up the street. The fog really was a pea-souper and she doubted if a taxi would venture out tonight.

'Why, oh why, 'as one of us never thought t'ave the

telephone put in the 'ouse?' she grumbled to Doris who had her arm around Mary's shoulders and was leading her back into the warmth of the living-room.

At least Ronnie had a bit of luck. Having pounded with his fists on Gran's front door, he was rewarded by light faintly penetrating the fog and the reassuring figure of Jack pulling him inside and demanding to know what was wrong.

Words tumbled from Ronnie's mouth. 'We don't know much, only that Annie's in the London 'ospital. Seems daft, don't it? Being knocked down by a bike, I mean.'

Jack couldn't stand still a moment longer. 'Come on, I'll take you back home. You did well, lad, coming to fetch me.'

'Jack,' Ronnie ventured as they stepped out into the horrible night, 'are you going to the 'ospital to see Annie?'

'Just as soon as I see you safely indoors, have a word with yer gran, and then I'll be off.'

'Won't be no buses on the road ternight, will there? Going to take yer car, are you?'

'No, I don't think I'll risk getting me car out, but I'll get there, lad, never you fear, even if I have to walk every inch of the way.'

Luck was on Jack's side. A cab slowed down and the driver said to him, 'I'm on me way 'ome, mate. Where you 'eading for?'

'The London Hospital.'

'Op in, mate. Don't know 'ow long it will take us, but with a bit of luck I'll be able to drop you near by, so you won't 'ave far t'walk.'

'Thank Gawd fer that, an' thanks a lot,' Jack told him as he gratefully sank on the back seat of the cab.

*   *   *

There were two nurses with Annie when he finally got to her bedside. They told him the doctors had been and nothing more could be done for the time being, but if he wanted to, he could sit with her as long as he liked.

'Will she know I'm here?'

'I doubt it. She hasn't yet regained consciousness,' the nurse told him.

Jack leant over the bed, and the very sight of Annie lying there, her face a mass of bruises, her head and one arm swathed in bandages, tugged at his heart-strings. He sat by her side, unable to believe how badly bruised her face was. He held her hand and gently stroked it. 'Hallo, Annie, it's me. You're going to be all right.' He spoke very quietly, so he wouldn't disturb anyone, but he wanted to let her know that he was there right beside her. Also, he was hoping against hope that she could hear him.

A hand gently came to rest on Jack's shoulder and he nearly jumped out of his skin. Shaking his head, he looked up into the kindly face of an elderly, white-coated gentleman. 'Oh, I'm sorry. I must have nodded off,' Jack said, struggling to stand up.

'Please,' the doctor pressed him back on the chair. 'I just popped in to check on Miss Bateman.'

'Is she going to be all right?'

'She could be fine,' the doctor answered. 'It's hard to say yet. The injuries to her ribs, hand and arm should heal pretty well. It is her head that worries us at the moment. All we can do is wait and see. It all depends if she comes round in the next few hours. Is she a relation of yours?'

'I've known her all her life. I'm a family friend.'

'Such a pity. She's a lovely girl. We just have to be patient.' Jack felt sick as he listened to the doctor's footsteps going down the ward.

★   ★   ★

It was daylight. New nurses were coming on duty. Curtains were flicked open, the rattle of a tea-trolley could be heard, and Jack was still there with Annie. He couldn't bring himself to leave her. I really ought to go home and let Gran and Doris know what is happening, he was thinking. They'll be worried sick if they don't get some news soon. He looked again at her poor bruised face. He remembered telling Gran how tired Annie was looking and that he felt she was doing far too much. Going out to work and having the two children to take care of, rushing here there and everywhere with Doris, making plans for the wedding. It was all too much, and now look what had happened.

An orderly gave him a cup of tea, which he drank gratefully. Getting to his feet, he put the cup and saucer on the bedside locker, then stretched his arms above his head, doing his best to loosen up.

Again he took her hand and began to talk to her. 'Annie, I'm going home now, but I'll be back just as soon as I can. You are going to be fine, you do know that . . . We've so many places we promised to take Ronnie and Mary, and we will, if you hurry up and get well.' He leaned back and heaved a great sigh. How could he tell whether she had heard him or not? 'Bye for now, Annie. I promise I won't be long. You know what would be nice? If I could tell the kids that you opened your eyes. Maybe tomorrow, if you're feeling better, the doctor will let them come and see you.'

He had been talking soothingly to her, and just as he was about to kiss her forehead, her eyelids fluttered. 'Oh, thank God! Nurse, Nurse!' His heart was pounding. She wasn't going to die. He wouldn't let her. But neither did he want her head injury to be serious, leading to brain damage. Even as the thought entered his head, he was saying, No! No, she had to be all right! There were so many things he had to tell her. Things that he'd made up his mind he would keep to himself because she was so much younger than him and had her own life to lead. Now he just wanted to ask if she would let him take care of her, not only for now but for all their days to come . . . Perhaps, if he could summon up enough courage, he might get round to letting her know that he loved her. Not as a friend. Not just as a helpful man that lodged with her grandmother. But as a man should love a woman that he wanted to spend his whole life with.

'Are you all right, Mr Higgins?' The nurse's voice brought him back to earth.

'Yes, I'm fine. Did you see? Annie tried to open her eyes.'

'It's probably just a reflex,' the nurse said with a sympathetic smile, placing her thumb and finger on Annie's unharmed wrist in order to take her pulse.

Then she did it again; this time both the nurse and Jack stood and watched her. Jack had to get rid of the lump in his throat before he could say a word. A whole minute passed. 'Blink again, Annie,' he said quietly. 'Please? Come on, I know you can do it. Do it so that I can tell Ronnie and Mary.' She did. She opened both eyes briefly, moaned, and closed them again. 'Thank God!' he wanted to shout, to tell everybody that Annie was going to be all right. 'It does mean she's not as bad as the doctors thought, doesn't it?' he asked the nurse.

'It tells us that she is regaining consciousness.' She smiled at him. 'I'll fetch the doctor.'

'Well done, Annie,' he praised her, stroking the arm that wasn't bandaged. 'Doris will get married today, feeling much better now that I can tell her that you're back with us. Don't worry about missing the wedding – you'll be the most important person at another wedding soon, if I have my way. And I'll make young Mary's day, because I'll tell her she can be bridesmaid on that day, an' all.' He was saying anything and everything that came into his head and then he almost burst into tears when her forehead puckered in a deep frown, her eyes opened and she stared at him blankly.

'Wha' . . . wedding?' she mumbled through her bruised swollen lips. Then her eyelids dropped again, and this time he couldn't help himself. He let the tears overflow and run down his cheeks. She *had* heard him!

Then the doctor was there. Annie tried to turn her head away as he did his best to raise an eyelid and shine a light in her eyes, and she cried and moaned when he touched her forehead. Then even more as he lifted her wrist.

'She is in pain, and letting us know it, and that's a great sign,' the doctor told Jack. 'Today we shall do several tests on her but she won't know anything at all. We shall sedate her. During the next few days she will be feeling very miserable but hopefully she will soon improve.' Just as the doctor was about to leave the beside he turned, held out his hand to Jack, saying, 'No visitors today.' They heard Annie moan again and the doctor gave instructions to the nurse regarding an injection to ease her pain. 'It's all right,' he assured Jack. 'She's in agony – bound to be from all her bruises – and when we get the results of the X-rays I'm pretty certain that her left wrist is broken. Now you get off home; you've been here all night.'

'I'll be back tomorrow with her grandmother, if that's all right, and is it OK if I ring tonight to see how she is?'

'By all means.' The men shook hands and went their different ways, Jack wishing that he could have stayed with Annie but knowing that she was in the best of hands. Now he had to face Rhoda, and for Doris's sake put up a brave front and do his best to see that her wedding to Frank went off as smoothly and as happily as possible.

The day had been nice. Even happy, if not exciting. When Jack had got back from the hospital, it seemed as if half the street and a good many more besides were gathered in Annie's living-room eager for news, though terrified as to what he might have to tell them.

'I can't possibly get married today,' Doris had pleaded. 'Not with Annie lying in hospital!'

To everyone's surprise it was Rhoda who had taken charge, issuing orders left, right and centre, stating that Annie would be so upset if she learned that the wedding had been called off because of her. Then she had lifted Mary on her knee and quietly and calmly explained to her that what Jack had told them meant that Annie was badly hurt but, with the help of the doctors and nurses and the love of everyone that knew her, she was going to get well and would be coming home soon.

'I'll tell you what,' Rhoda had exclaimed so suddenly that Mary had almost fallen off her lap. 'We'll get you dressed up, we'll all go and see Frank and Doris married, and then we'll have the man that is taking all the pictures take a *very* special photograph just of you. All by yourself. We'll ask him to develop it very quickly so that we can take it into the hospital and stand it right beside Annie on her locker, so that she'll be able to see it whenever she wakes.'

Mary started to cry.

'Oh, don't! Don't do that, pet,' Rhoda had begged her. 'You could also send Annie your posy after the wedding, if you'd like to.'

'Jack said Annie can't have any visitors,' Mary sobbed.

Jack took over. 'That's only for today. In any case, yer gran and I are going to go up to the hospital tonight. Even though they won't let us see Annie, at least the nurses will be able to tell us how much better she is by then and we'll ask them to give her your flowers.'

'As soon as we get the all clear, your Auntie Doris and I will take you up to see Annie,' Frank had promised.

And so, just after two o'clock on a murky November day, Doris Simmonds had become Mrs Frank Smith.

It had taken Jack a good few minutes to persuade Ronnie that it was a manly thing to do. He stood beside Rhoda and watched Ronnie, in his first long trousers, his hair slicked down with a dab of Jack's Brylcreem, go to the front of the gathering of well-wishers and shyly present Doris with a silver horseshoe and a big sprig of white heather.

Frank had patted his shoulder, saying, 'Well done, Ronnie.' To say that the boy was embarrassed as Doris pulled him to her and kissed him on both cheeks would have been an understatement, but the moment had been captured on film, and young Ronnie was going to have to live with that.

Jack was as good as his word. When the wedding breakfast was over and the evening was drawing in, he brought his car round to the front of the house and gingerly helped Rhoda into the passenger seat. Frank had insisted that he and Doris forgo their honeymoon, at least until they heard that Annie was on the road to recovery. 'We were only going down to Brighton, and we can easily go later. Besides, what kind of a break would it be if we went now?' Frank had asked Jack. 'Doris would drive me mad, wanting to telephone the hospital every hour on the hour. No, you get yerself off. We're happy enough to stay here with the children till you get back.'

On their arrival at the hospital, the night nurse took one look at poor Rhoda's face, then took in the bridal bouquet she was carrying and the small posy that Jack had in his big hand. 'Missed a family wedding, has she?' the nurse asked with concern.

'Afraid so,' Rhoda answered. 'Would it be asking too much for you to put these in water and put them where she can see them when she wakes up?'

'I'm not as hard-hearted as all that,' came the reply, and it was said with a smile. 'Come on. I know you'd like to see her – only for five minutes, mind.' The nurse led the way, pulled the screens around the bed and tiptoed away.

Jack settled Rhoda on a chair beside the bed and stood a little apart, sensing that her gran would appreciate a few moments on her own. Annie was fast asleep, but Jack comforted himself with the thought that she didn't look as though she were in as much pain as she had been the day before. 'I'll go an' see if I can rustle up something to put the flowers in,' he said, aware that Rhoda was too choked to answer. Annie was her granddaughter, and she had every right to be upset. All the same, he was very grateful that the nurse had let them in. At least he felt sure Rhoda would sleep better for having seen with her own eyes that Annie was not as bad as she had been imagining.

'We'll come back tomorrow,' Jack whispered as he led Rhoda away.

They drove home in silence. Jack sat in the car while Rhoda went to tell Doris and Frank that he was outside waiting to drive them home. Having dropped the newly-weds at Frank's own house in Clapham, he drove slowly back to Rhoda's house, where he would spend the night in the room he rented there. Rhoda would obviously stay with the children in Annie's house until she was better and able to come home.

The house seemed unbearably quiet, and never had he felt more lonely. What a day! He hadn't slept the night before, only dozed, sitting at Annie's bedside and now he felt whacked. Though I'd still be at the hospital now if I had my way, he decided, as he pulled on the bottom half of his pyjamas and climbed into bed. There was so much he wanted to say to Annie. Why the hell hadn't he bucked up courage and told her how he felt about her, long before this? I'll make sure I do tell her just as soon as she gets home, but I don't think that's on the cards for a while. With that last mournful thought, he at last fell asleep.

Chapter Thirty-one

FOR THE NEXT FEW days Rhoda went every afternoon to visit Annie, and Jack went every evening. On Friday evening Jack brought Frank and Doris to the hospital with him. Doris burst into tears when she saw Annie and had to wipe her eyes before gently kissing her forehead.

Jack assured them that she looked a lot better now. The swelling on her face had gone down, but she was still in a lot of pain. The doctor had said she was doing remarkably well. The thing that upset Doris the most was that when Annie moved her head, a big bald patch was visible where they had had to cut away her beautiful hair. As she lay still, with her head on the pillow, her tresses still looked great. The nurses had given a lot of time to arranging her hair. It was bunched each side of her face and tied in place by two blue ribbons, and from the front, no one would know the difference.

There wasn't any colour to her face, but she was smiling broadly as she whispered, 'So, it's Mrs Smith now! Gran told me you looked lovely. Thank you for sending me your flowers. I am so sorry to have missed your wedding.'

'Don't, pet,' Doris was still struggling to keep the tears away. 'We'll have a proper party the minute you're up on your pins again.'

Frank had some magazines for her, and bought chocolates, poshly wrapped, from Fortnum & Mason.

'Don't worry, Annie! He gets a staff discount,' Doris teased as she saw Annie mentally counting the cost of such a large box of the finest chocolates.

On Wednesday, twelve days after the accident, the doctors had told the nurses to get her out of bed and help her to walk to the bathroom. As Annie put a foot to the floor, she almost fainted. She hadn't realized just how weak she had become. They lifted her into the bath, and the warm water felt gorgeous. She had just got thankfully back into bed when Flossie and Sid arrived with a cake and a bottle of fruit juice.

'What are you two doing here? Who's looking after the café?'

'Well, that's some greeting,' Sid scolded her. 'There's us an' more than 'alf our customers pining away 'cos we ain't got your company, and when we arrange for somebody else to take over so that we can come an' see yer, what d'we get?'

'Oh, Sid, I'm sorry. I didn't mean it like that. I just felt worried about your business.' Having said that, Annie was breathless. Her fading bruises were all the colours of the rainbow, and she looked as if she'd lost a great deal of weight.

Flossie elbowed Sid out of the way because he was in danger of hurting her in his efforts to give her a loving hug. 'Sit down an' behave yerself,' she told him. Then, taking packages from her shopping bag, she undid the wrappings and laid out on the bed a pale blue bed-jacket, made of such fine wool that it felt almost like silk. Next there came slippers in exactly the same shade of blue, some toilet water, scented soap and lastly a very pretty hairbrush.

'Flossie, you shouldn't spoil me like this!' Seeing all these gifts had brought a little colour to Annie's cheeks, yet a sob could be heard in her voice.

'That special hairbrush ain't from me an' Sid, it's from the customers. They had a whip-round for you,' Flossie confessed proudly.

'I don't know how I'm ever going to be able to thank everybody,' Annie said tearfully. 'Me gran brought me a really nice dressing-gown. Phoebe, Mrs Dawson's daughter-in-law, had collected money from the neighbours and bought it for me.'

'No less than you deserve, Annie, gal,' Sid told her, and then as his wife nudged him, his face flushed and he looked embarrassed. 'I reckon it's more than 'alf my fault that you landed up in 'ere. Sorry, gal. I should 'ave known about the fog. Shouldn't 'ave let yer put a foot outside. No, I mean it,' he hastened on as Annie tried to protest. 'We'd been that busy that Friday, all nice an' warm in the shop, an' what with all the lights on an' all . . .'

'Don't try trotting out all those excuses, Sid,' his wife cut in. 'You were tired, I'll give yer that, but both you and I were at fault. The customers had been saying all day that it was foggy. Did we let it bother us? Oh no. Off we sent Annie, never giving a thought as t'how she was going t'get 'ome. So, go on, tell 'er what we've decided as a way of making it up to her.'

'We're paying your wages to yer gran, for all the time

you'll be off work, an' when you feel fit enough, we'll pay for you to have the 'oliday of a lifetime. Just say where you'd like to go, and we'll do the rest.'

Annie laughed at the very idea. 'Where would I go? And who with? Besides, all I really want is to get home.' Then turning to Flossie, she murmured, 'I do miss the children. Jack said they wouldn't let them come to see me, but Mary has sent me a card that she made herself, even drew the picture inside.' She paused, took a deep breath and smilingly said, 'Ronnie sent me a bag of toffees. Don't tell him I can't eat them, will you?'

'How about the photographs of the wedding? Did you like them?'

'Flossie, I think they are wonderful. It was so good of Doris to send them in for me to see. Mary looks so sweet and as for Ronnie, well, ask the nurses. They've taken that one of him giving Doris the horseshoe half-way round the hospital. Hope to God he doesn't find out!' Annie was surprised as to how quickly she got tired, and it showed.

'Come on, Sid, she needs 'er rest,' Flossie said, getting to her feet and gathering up her bag and gloves. She bent low and gently kissed Annie, then moved back so that Sid could say his good-byes.

For such a big man he could be surprisingly gentle. He put his arm across the top of the pillow, careful not to touch Annie's head, and told her, 'We do miss you, Annie, and that's Gawd's truth. It'll be a long time before I forgive meself for sending you out in the fog like that. Get well quick, we all love you.'

Jack hung back and quietly said his own good-byes.

It would have been hard to tell which one was the most choked: Annie, as she watched these dear kind friends walk down the ward, or Sid and Flossie Owen, a pair of rough and ready EastEnders, who would do almost anything to protect her but at that moment were feeling pretty helpless.

Jack hadn't been to see Annie for two days. He had told her that he had a job at the docks that would take a good forty-eight hours. She hadn't minded – in fact she was touched that he had spent so much time with her. On Sunday afternoon Rhoda had arrived with enough home-made cakes to feed the whole ward.

Now it was five o'clock. They'd been round with the patients' teas and Annie was just settling down to have a nap when Jack came striding down the ward. 'I've made it! Bit late – didn't think they'd let me in,' he said, looking happy to see her.

Annie beamed at him. She had actually missed him a lot, but she kept telling herself that he wasn't related to her, even if she had known him for most of her life. She had no right to expect him to come to the hospital day after day. 'Did you get the ship unloaded all right?'

'No,' he said honestly, 'we ran into a few snags. Besides, my mind wasn't really on the job. I was thinking of you.'

Annie didn't know how to answer that, so she kept quiet. He drew his chair up close by the bed and told her funny stories about the goings-on in the dockyards, and when he rose and said he thought she should get some sleep, she was disappointed. Little did she guess that he didn't want to leave her.

But that night, as he lay in bed and thought about Annie, Jack started to panic. Why the hell couldn't he get the words out and tell her how he felt? He wondered whether Ronnie and Mary were a stumbling-block to each of them. She was devoted to them, although it didn't seem right that she should spend her whole life taking care of two children who weren't in all honesty anything to do with her. She hadn't even started to live a life of her own.

How did *he* feel about the children? He forced himself to face that question. He liked them both. A lot. Ronnie and he had become great mates, and who in their right mind could look at Mary and not care for her? She was a sweet child just longing to believe that she belonged to someone.

Well, who knew that feeling better than he did? To come home from a life in the Navy where you lived hand to mouth, day in day out in close quarters, men absolutely relying on one another twenty-four hours a day, only to find that you were suddenly on your own. No mates, no relations and no family. It had taken him some time to come to terms with that.

So how much worse must it be for two small children? Ronnie might put on a brave face and play the tough kid, but what did he feel inside? He had been told his mother was dead and that his father had walked off to begin a new life. The lad had so far coped well. Whether Bob Wilson would ever turn up again was a matter that could be dealt with in the future.

He didn't have to decide anything now, yet in his heart he knew that if Annie wanted to go on caring for those two children, it was all right by him. He worried about her, and now he lay there wishing she were by his side, wanting to put his arms round her and protect her. If having Annie for his wife meant the added responsibility of the children, then so be it. There could be many worse things in life than taking on a ready-made family. Then, oddly enough, he was smiling. The very idea of being a father figure was a sensation he'd never felt before.

Oh, Annie, he breathed. All our lives could be so different if only . . .

On the following evening Rhoda made a statement that startled Jack. It was a bold statement, about a matter that had never been discussed between them. 'You're in love with Annie, aren't you?' she said.

The question really came as a surprise. Jack got up out of his chair and stood looking down at Rhoda while his lips were moving, some seconds before he got any words out. 'What makes you think that?'

'Look, you don't 'ave to pretend with me, lad. I've lived a long time, an' I've watched you. I've known how you felt about her for ages.'

Jack shook his head, turned his back on Rhoda and walked to the window, parted the curtains and looked out into the dark wintry night.

Rhoda sighed. 'I feel sure I'm right . . . The very way you look at her sometimes. Anyway, if I'm wrong, well, I'm sorry.'

Jack took a deep breath. 'No, you're right. But you knowing, well what difference does it make? Why had you to bring it up, Mrs Bateman? It's no good. Annie doesn't care for me, at least not in the way that I care for her.'

'Sit down, Jack. The trouble with you, my lad, is that you don't know your own worth. You never have.' She wriggled forward in her chair and leant towards him, saying earnestly, 'Tell her 'ow you feel. She won't bite you. And, while you're about it, ain't it time you started calling me Rhoda?'

Jack giggled, 'All right. Rhoda it is from now on, but talk sense. Do you think for a moment she'd take me on?'

'Yes, I do, and so does Doris. Women have a way of sensing these things quicker than men. Doris feels you won't have much persuading to do.'

'How many other people think they know how Annie feels?' he asked in a tight voice. 'Hasn't she got enough t'do with Ronnie and Mary?'

'Do you see the kids as a stumbling-block?'

'I've been asking myself that very question, and the answer is No. I'd really like to help where they are concerned.'

'Well, that's something.' Rhoda clasped her hands together. 'But don't make the mistake of asking her to marry you for the sake of them. Let her know the true feelings you 'ave for her. D'you understand me? It's you and her. If, when you've sorted that out, you both feel you'd still like to take care of Ronnie and Mary, that's another matter. An' I 'ave t'say it, there ain't many that would take the pair of them on. Not youngsters starting out. No, they wouldn't.'

Jack got to his feet again. 'I have to tell you that I went away to work in Grimsby only because I couldn't stand the sight of Annie going out with other blokes, especially a rotter like that Mike Maland. But I had to let her live her own life.'

'You think I didn't know that, Jack? Wasn't my place to interfere but even then I felt like giving you a shove.'

'Wasn't a day that I didn't think about her, wondering what she'd say if I spoke up.'

'You make me mad, Jack, you really do! I think it would be a good thing for both of you.' Rhoda tilted her head to look at him. 'You could make her 'appy,

I know you could. And she could make a different man out of you. Not that I'd want you to be any different, but you know what I mean.' She put out her hand and touched him. 'You can be a bit gloomy at times, all work an' no play, if you get what I mean. When you're around Annie and especially the kids, you come out of yer shell as if you're feeling different, self-assured.'

'I hear what you're saying, but I'm still pretty certain she wouldn't want an old stick-in-the-mud like me.'

'You won't know until you ask her, will you? And you won't be any worse off if she refuses you, will you? It you truly feel so strongly, surely it 'as t'be worth a try. Think about it, there's plenty of time.'

'Do you think so? I mean about there being plenty of time. I don't think she can carry on as she is, and I'm afraid she'll get married to someone else for all the wrong reasons.'

'Well, there you are, then. My advice is jump in with both feet.'

'Aw, but . . .' Jack put his hand out in protest.

'No aw, buts! As we decided, you've nothing t'lose. Just tell her, man, and get it over an' done with and, who knows, Annie might just grab you with both 'ands.'

Jack was thoughtful for a moment, then he sighed heavily. 'As you say, nothing ventured, nothing gained. I might just give it a try.' Then he stooped, and gently put his lips against her wrinkled cheek. Straightening up, he said, 'Thanks, Rhoda. Thanks for everything, and that includes taking me into your home and treating me as if I were one of your family.'

She stared at him for a moment before throwing back her head and letting out a roar of laughter. 'If you shift yerself, Jack, act kinda bold-like, you just might end up with me as your grandmother-in-law.'

Now the pair of them were really laughing. He was still laughing as he picked up the coal-scuttle and went out to fetch more coal so that he could bank up the fire for the night.

Chapter Thirty-two

A FEW DAYS LATER when Annie was discharged from the London Hospital it was Jack who came to take her home. She felt much easier by then, but still didn't have as much stamina as she would have liked. The doctor told her to wait some time before she went back to work. Sid and Flossie told her not to worry because she couldn't come back to the café until after Christmas. They would manage.

Jack continued to spend a good many evenings with her. They talked, and they laughed, and played cards with Ronnie and Mary. They had gone to the school together, taking Rhoda, to see the children in the Christmas play. Doris had turned up, looking absolutely radiant. Three small girls, one of whom was Mary, acted the part of angels, and just looking at them had caused most of the audience to have to dab at their eyes. Annie had felt as proud of Ronnie, who had been one of the three wise men, and Mary as any other mother in the audience.

Jack had brought her a selection of Christmas cards

and a catalogue from which she could choose presents rather than having to traipse round the shops. He also got a Christmas cake from Warren Brothers, a well-known local bakery. It was all frosty icing, with Father Christmas on a sleigh siding down a heap of snow. Mary stared at it wide-eyed, and asked if, when the cake was cut at Christmas, she could have the big red ribbon round it.

'How can you do all this for me?' Annie asked. She felt shy with him suddenly, but ever so pleased. He had done nothing but spoil her since the accident. Spoil her and be kind to her, and spend time with her. And with the children.

'Yeah, you're kind to us as well, Jack,' Mary piped up. 'You're always bringing us sweets an' things an' you take us out in your car.'

Not to be outdone, Ronnie cut in, 'It's 'cos of you that I can go to football matches.'

'I like doing things for you, all of you,' Jack answered. 'I don't have any children, so maybe I should adopt you?' He turned to Annie, saying, 'Now, there's a thought!'

She smiled at the suggestion. It would certainly make things easier for her. Rhoda had gone back to live in her own house, though never a day went by that she didn't call in, and in both houses the telephone had been installed. Weekends were still going to be the same: Sunday midday dinner at Annie's house with Rhoda doing some of the cooking, and Doris and Frank frequent visitors. The plan was that they would all spend Christmas together. Annie felt that her relationship with Jack had changed since she'd come home. It was somehow more intimate, closer, even though the children were quite often around.

It had been snowing on and off for two days, and the bookies were taking bets on whether it would be a white

Christmas. Annie had not yet been out to go shopping. This evening Jack had bought four parcels of fish and chips in with him. She could hear the laughter coming from the scullery as Mary helped him to put the portions on the plates and butter the bread he had cut, while Ronnie laid the table in the living-room. She had tried to help, but he had made her sit in a chair and watch. 'I'm not helpless, you know,' she protested, 'even if I do still have one arm in plaster.'

'We're doing fine without any interference from you, aren't we, kids?' he overruled her.

It felt right him being here. The kids were happy, the atmosphere was comfortable. Much later, when the children were in bed, they sat side by side on the sofa in front of the fire and talked. He told her stories of what had gone on in the East End when he was growing up, and about his parents and the rest of his family, all killed while he was at sea. How much he had loved them and what nice kind people they had been. His father had always been a docker, earning good money, and had provided well for his family. He'd had a good upbringing, and he knew it.

Annie told him funny things about herself and David and how she was absolutely sure that at some time he would be in touch with her. It was an odd assortment of memories that seemed to be good for each of them. Jack was aware, more so since he'd had that talk with Rhoda, that before he became friendly with Annie he had been intense, very self-involved, even indulging in self-pity, and also had the feeling that she had been a little afraid of him. Now it was different. She made him feel young, she was intelligent, giving, caring. She'd had a lot to cope with, and yet she was still kind and so gentle with the children even when they weren't in the best of moods.

As always, he wanted to take her in his arms, tell her what his feelings were, but was desperately afraid because she seemed even younger since she hadn't been well. Without even thinking, he put his arm round her shoulders and her head just naturally came to rest against his chest. What with the peace and quiet and the heat from the fire, it wasn't long before they were both fast asleep.

It was almost midnight when Jack moved sleepily and whispered to her, 'Annie, would you consider marrying me?'

She struggled to sit up straight. Had she heard him aright? She looked puzzled. 'What?' She almost shouted the word and he opened an eye in shocked surprise. 'What do you mean?'

'You heard me,' he said cheerfully. 'At last I've found the courage to ask you. But please don't look so worried. I'll understand if you say No, but first I must tell you that I've been in love with you from the day you came into your gran's house and she had just agreed to rent me a room.' He was sitting bolt upright, wide awake now.

She looked at him in disbelief, trembling when she answered, 'But that was a long time ago.'

'Yes, I know. Three days after I had been demobbed.'

'You're not serious?'

'I am very serious. All I ask is that you think about it. Will you?'

She still couldn't believe it as she sat looking at him and he laughed at her. 'I don't have to think about it. I love you too, Jack.'

'What? Really?'

'Yes, really. I didn't realize how much until I had plenty of time to think while I was in hospital.'

He didn't wait to hear any more. He gently pulled her into his arms and kissed her as she had never before been kissed.

When he released her, he whispered, 'Say it again, please.'

'Say what again?' she teased, giving him a mischievous grin.

'Stop kidding,' he pleaded. 'Just tell me again.'

'I do love you, Jack, and yes, I would really love to be married to you.' And with that she put her good arm around his neck and *she* kissed him.

Christmas was unbelievable. To the kids, the tree with its glistening decorations, their presents, all the wonderful food and adults who had time to play games with them left both Mary and Ronnie in no doubt that they were both loved and wanted. To Rhoda, it meant that she had a big family all around her and half the time she was waited on hand, foot and finger . . . To Frank and Doris, being their first Christmas together, it couldn't have been happier, with Frank declaring that if anything, Boxing Day had been even more brilliant. Doris told him that was only because he had bought tickets for them all to go to the pantomime, and he and Jack had behaved like a couple of kids throughout the whole show.

As for Jack and Annie, they wouldn't have cared if they'd opened the front door to six feet of snow. They had heat, light, food, friends and family, but most of all they had each other.

Annie never went back to work for Sid and Flossie

although she was a frequent visitor to the café. Then on the second Saturday in February she and Jack were married in the same registrar's office as Doris and Frank had been. It was Sid Owen who gave Annie away. Frank was Jack's best man. Mary was bridesmaid, Doris matron of honour. Ronnie heatedly refused the teasing offer to be a pageboy.

Posing outside for the photographs, Annie had looked across at her grandmother. Rhoda was smartly turned out in a heavy camel coat with a fur-trimmed hat to match, wearing a smile that wouldn't have looked wrong on the Cheshire cat. Annie sighed happily to herself, knowing that this day was the answer to her gran's prayers. What would she have done without this good woman? Most likely had a nervous breakdown, for there was a time after her father's death when she felt so desolate that she didn't know which way to turn.

During all that time her gran had been there for her, and for Ronnie and Mary. Cooking, washing and ironing, wiping away tears, giving little Mary cuddles to reassure her that she was wanted and loved and, most of all, she had spoken words of comfort and wisdom. She herself was a married woman now with a husband to take care of her, but yes, of one thing she was certain: the love she had for her grandmother would last until the day she died.

They went to Blackpool for one week's honeymoon, leaving the children in Rhoda's care. Everyone said they were mad to go to Blackpool in February. They were all wrong. True, the town was not crowded but there was still plenty going on.

As for the hotel, the management guessed they were honeymooners and did everything within their power to make their stay really happy. They were given a first-floor front room with bay windows that looked straight across the golden sand and out over the sea. The furniture was large and Victorian with two enormous armchairs covered in a pretty chintz, and the cover on the huge double bed was of the same material. There was even a bottle of champagne, compliments of the management.

'They've thought of everything,' Annie said as Jack shut the door to their room and took her in his arms. She watched him happily as he opened the bottle, poured the champagne and handed her a glass, but she took only a sip, too excited to drink it all. They had eaten a lovely evening meal, gone for a brisk walk along the seafront, and now it was time for bed.

Annie wasn't scared, but she was apprehensive. Jack was older, he'd travelled, seen the world and she didn't for one moment expect she was the first woman he'd been with. But for her it was very much a first.

'Don't be scared,' he whispered as they slid into bed. She was wearing a beautiful peach-coloured nightgown which had been a present from Flossie; he had only short pants on. 'Come here,' he said and she nuzzled her face into his bare neck while he held her close. 'Do you want to go to sleep yet?' he asked a few minutes later.

Annie raised herself into a sitting position, looking startled. She might not have been the whole way with a man before, but she was certainly not ignorant of the facts of life. What was the matter? Didn't he fancy her? Was there something awfully wrong?

At the look on her face, he laughed. 'I didn't mean it.' He kissed her then, very much wanting to make love to her, but not daring to yet. He began to fondle her very gently, he didn't want to hurt her. He loved her very much and he'd waited so long for this moment, and now it was turning out to be more difficult than he had imagined. But as they kissed, he forgot about hurting her, and the misgivings of the past few weeks slipped slowly away from her.

There was no one else in the whole wide world who mattered. There was only Jack who was treating her with incredible gentleness, letting her know that his passion was a sign of his love. They became closer and closer, until suddenly it was as if they had melted into each other and become one. Yes, she felt pain, but also the joy of knowing the full extent of what she had given to this man who was now truly her husband.

Much later as she lay still in his arms, he said, 'I waited a long time for you, Annie, but it was well worth the wait and now we have our whole lives to spend together. Are you happy?'

She placed her lips on his, and after a sweet long lingering kiss she asked, 'Will that do for an answer?'

'Every time,' he replied holding her close.

They still had six more days. They spent some of the time in their room, discovering each other, and the rest warmly wrapped up, walking in the pale sunshine because even the weather was being kind to them, and taking bus rides. One evening they spent in the famous Blackpool Tower, where they danced the night away to the music of a big band. That was something else Annie discovered. Jack Higgins was a fantastic dancer and when she remarked on this, he told her, 'All sailors are. They learn to roll with the ship, and that gives them the ease with which to keep in time and step with the music.'

When they got back to London on Sunday night, they lay in what had been Annie's bed and made love. 'Just to make sure that it's as good down here in the South as it was up in the North,' he teased her.

'And was it?' Annie asked later.

'Even better!' he assured her.

Jack moved his belongings into Annie's house and they settled down to married life with a ready-made family of two children. They'd been home for exactly a month when they had their first row.

At long last they had received a letter from David. He had written to his grandmother, not to Annie. It was a sad letter. A story of silly mistakes made by a young man who had paid dearly for his experiences.

David had been almost twenty when his father had brought Dot Wilson home to live with them. From the very start she had, for some unknown reason, resented David. She had taunted him practically every day that he wasn't half the man his father was. He had tried so hard to live up to his father's reputation of Lucky Jim Bateman. He'd even got himself into a couple of scrapes that had landed him in trouble with the bookmakers. After a really bad show-down he'd left home and got lodgings with a large family. Besides the parents there had been four sons and three daughters. Three of the sons and two daughters were married, with children of their own. All lived in the vicinity, close to their parents. Lorna, the unmarried daughter, lived at home. She was big: fifteen stone, if she was an ounce, David had written, and that was the only part of the letter that had made Annie smile because her brother hadn't exactly been a puny lad but he certainly didn't weigh anything like as much as that.

'She came into my bedroom one night and almost ate me alive!' That phrase had stood out from the notepaper, and both Rhoda and Annie had read it over and over again. The next morning David had come downstairs to face a gathering of her brothers. Lorna's version was that David had forced himself on her. No one had believed that it was Lorna who had come into David's room. Her parents had demanded that David marry their daughter, and her brothers had promised that, if he didn't, they would break both his legs. They even threatened to seek out his relations and make them wish they'd never been born. My poor brother, Annie sighed to herself, every time she read that paragraph. From the day their mother had died, it would seem that nothing had gone right for David. How she wished Dot Wilson had never driven him away from home.

She read on:

'I couldn't stay. I never even liked Lorna, let alone loved her. I hadn't the gumption to stand up for myself. I wanted to contact you long before this, but I told myself that if her brothers found out where my folk lived and came asking where I was, you couldn't tell them if you didn't know.'

It was such a sad letter, until you came to the fourth and last page. 'In a roundabout fashion I ended up in Plymouth. Got a job in the shipyards. Met a girl. Her name is Marion – you will like her, I know you will. Her parents seem to have taken to me. We were married a week before Christmas and I can't wait for Annie to come and visit us. Please, Gran, make sure she understands that Marion wants her to come as much as I do.'

The closing paragraph of David's letter had made Rhoda and Annie shed many a tear. 'Well, now, I think have told you everything you needed to know, except that I've missed you both so much. It was as if I no longer had a family, no one that actually belonged to me. Especially after Dad died.'

There was a postscript: 'What did Annie do about young Ronnie and Mary? I've thought about them such a lot.'

Annie wanted to be on the next train to Plymouth, and she couldn't believe that Jack wanted to stop her.

'Are you crazy? You don't know how much room they have. Are they living with her parents or in a couple of rooms? You write first, and get to know a whole lot more than what is in that letter. Tell them about us and about the children.'

'But if I go and visit, I could tell them all of that,' she kept insisting, but Jack was even more stubborn than she was.

'Absolutely not!' He wasn't going to budge.

'Well, when will I get to see him?' she asked, near to tears.

'When you've exchanged a couple of letters, found out how the land lies, we'll all go. We'll take the children and your gran, make a holiday of it.'

'Is that a promise?'

'Yes, it is,' he grinned. 'By then the weather will be much warmer, and a week in Plymouth will be great.'

'I'll write today. Gran said she answered David's letter the same day it arrived. By the way, Jack, I thought I might go back to work with Sid and Flossie, part-time like. What d'you think?'

'I don't want you to. There's no need. You have quite enough to do as it is.'

'No, I don't. The children are at school all day. Gran still does a lot of the cooking and she insists on doing all the ironing. What am I supposed to do with myself?' Their words were becoming heated again. Both felt very strongly on this point.

'Cooee! Is it all right if I come in?'

Neither of them had heard the front door open, and now Annie opened the door into the passage and gave a cry of delight. 'Oh, Vera, it's you! Come on in. Jack's home today. He will be so pleased to see you.' Then as an afterthought she spoke over her shoulder, 'Is everything all right? Is Peter well?'

Jack was on his feet. 'Give the woman time to get in and take her hat an' coat off before you start bombarding her with questions!' He leaned over short dumpy Vera, giving her a resounding kiss on her cheek. 'You feel so cold! These March winds are awful. Come and sit near the fire an' talk to Annie while I put the kettle on.'

'No, just a minute, Jack. I want you t'hear what I 'ave to say. The nurse is with Peter today so I got up early and was ready to leave the house as soon as he arrived. I couldn't wait to get over here an' give yer all the news.'

Jack and Annie looked at her. She was panting like a horse that had just run a race, but her eyes were shining and her ruddy, round face was all smiles.

'You're never gonna believe it!' Vera told them.

It was said in such a way that Jack laughed, a deep laugh, a man's laugh. 'How can you know if you don't tell us?'

'Yes, come on, Vera,' Annie pleaded. 'For God's sake spit it out. Is it the flats? Are you 'aving trouble?'

'No, course it ain't the flats. Though t'be 'onest I am worried. Only that top one's been let. Nice couple, good tenants, no trouble whatsoever. Not a soul's been round even t'look at the other big one.'

'Never mind all that,' Annie almost yelled at her, her impatience showing.

By this time Vera had removed her hat and Jack was taking her coat from her. She was well aware that they were both watching her every move and suddenly she burst out laughing, saying, 'Oh all right. Some time ago I had a visit from Mr Mathews and Mr Ferguson. They came together and what they said was, they 'ad a proposition t'put to me. The long an' short of it was they were suggesting that I take a lease on some premises which, in their opinion, was ideal for me to set up shop. In other words, they wanted me to move out of the Scout hut, still do me upholstery and recovering work, but in more roomy and pleasant surroundings, was 'ow they put it.'

'Vera, that's wonderful.' Annie was on her feet and throwing her arms round Vera's shoulders.

'Get off, you great baby,' Vera said, smiling and at the same time giving her a little shove. 'I ain't finished yet. Not by a long chalk, I ain't. They said I ought to employ people and, what's more t'the point, Dickens & Brown are gonna let me buy all the materials I need through them at cost price. And, Annie, your bank manager is setting me up with an account at 'is branch an' I'm t'ave a working overdraft. That means that I can use money what ain't really mine. I can't believe that so many people are going out of their way to 'elp me and Peter.'

Jack was having a hard job to keep his laughter under control. 'Use money what ain't really mine! She's a card, is Vera, and no mistake!'

'Where are these premises? When are you going to move and how are you going about getting staff?' Annie was so pleased and excited for Vera that she was firing question after question at her without even waiting for an answer.

'It's no more than you both deserve,' Jack managed to cut in. 'Now I think we'll get a bottle out, not bother with tea. Has t'be some kind of celebration,' he stated, getting down on his knees to open the sideboard. 'Don't you agree, Annie?'

When no answer was forthcoming, Jack raised his head, only to see that both women were standing, their arms tightly entwined, and each was crying softly. He got to his feet, set three glasses on a side table, then a bottle of ginger ale and lastly a bottle of whisky. All the while he was doing this he was muttering to himself, 'Women! I'll never understand them, not if I live t'be a hundred years old!'

Chapter Thirty-three

YOU ONLY HAD TO look at Annie, to know that she was happy. She was constantly busy with the children, taking them to and from school, to parks and down by the river, making sure that they were involved in doing everything with her and Jack. At first she had worried about Jack. Had she saddled him with the responsibility of two children against his better judgment?

Not at all, he assured her, time and again. He loved their new life. 'I have a young, beautiful wife, a young family and a nice home. What more could any man ask for?' It was words like these that made Annie think how lucky she was to be married to such a remarkable man.

Towards the end of March the mornings became brighter, making it seem as though spring might be on its way. Then almost suddenly the trees were full of blossom, the grass was greener and the barrow-boys were selling spring flowers for tuppence a bunch. Then it was May. From the first day of the month there followed a very busy time.

The old saying: It's not what you know but who you know, certainly applied to Vera and Peter James when it came to their signing a five-year lease on the premises that Mr Mathews and Mr Ferguson had found for them. Almost daily Vera was on the telephone keeping Annie and Rhoda up to date with what was happening.

It was unfortunate that on the day when Annie was about to see the actual building, Jack was tied up on the river. Some trouble had arisen among the crew of a large ship, which had delayed the unloading of her cargo. Now with the matter settled it was all stations go, and the port authorities decided that Jack Higgins was capable of handling such an affair.

'There'll be plenty of other opportunities for me to come with you,' Jack said as he kissed Annie good-bye and left the house at a quarter past five in the morning in order to catch the tide. 'Anyway,' he added as she leant over the gate to plant a final kiss on his rough cheek, 'you'll do ten times better without me around. Sort things out between you, make all the right decisions. As soon as this job is finished, I'll bring Peter in the car and we'll let you know if we both approve.'

'You saucy swine!' Annie gave him a playful swipe. Dawn was just breaking and Annie stood still listening to her husband's deep laugh as he strode away down the street.

'I'll meet you at Tooting Bec tube station at half-past ten,' were Vera's instructions. I don't feel like going back to bed, Annie said to herself as she poured another cup of tea. I'll use the time to catch up on a bit of house-work, cook the kids a decent breakfast, even though it is a weekday, and then I'll walk to school with them. That was something she didn't do every day now. Both

Ronnie and Mary appeared to be much more settled and independent since she and Jack were married and the fact that Jack now lived in the house seemed to please both of them.

So, at twenty past ten, Annie came up the escalator at Tooting Bec and walked through the crowded station out into the spring sunshine just in time to see Vera waiting on the other side to cross the road. Annie smiled and waved at her jolly-faced and neatly dressed friend. During the time that Annie had known Vera she had come to admire her very much. Not only was she proving to be a kind and loving friend but also a very competent woman.

'Well, we've got a great day for it, 'Vera said as they hugged in greeting.

'Do we have to take a bus?' Annie asked.

'No, it's not far to walk.'

They linked arms and set off at a steady pace. Annie remembered that she was now in Trinity Road and they were walking in the direction of Wandsworth Common and she recalled the first time she had come this way by bus to 48 Tremaine Road. What a day of surprises that had turned out to be. Look at the outcome of that first meeting with Vera! It wasn't so long ago, and yet the turn of events had ripped along and here was Vera, marching her off to see her new business premises, which hopefully would turn out to be very beneficial.

They hadn't gone very far when Vera tugged at Annie's arm. 'We turn off left down here into Wandle Road.' Annie was quite startled when Vera stopped at the entrance to what looked like a long passage. At the end was a very tall building, but she seemed to be seeing it through a mist, for the alley was not exactly dark but dusky.

After climbing a steep flight of stairs, Vera took out

a key, unlocked the stout door and pushed it open. Immediately Annie saw that the inside of the building was much lighter than the outside would have one believe. There were several long windows on each side of the room interspersed with panels which looked as if they were made of heavy dark wood. After having had a good look around, Annie murmured, 'It's more like a hall than a room.'

'Yes, it is,' Vera agreed. 'But come to the far end and you'll get a surprise.'

Annie walked down the room and at the far end she gasped in delight. 'How lovely,' she cried. Through the tall window she was looking down on a peaceful country lane sheltered by high trees and flanked by untidy hedgerows.

Annie would always remember the next hour that she spent in what were to become very businesslike premises for not only Vera and Peter James but for everyone who became involved, herself included. If she had been amazed at the first big room they had set foot in, she was utterly dumbfounded by the adjoining rooms and the amount of equipment that was already installed. There were two more rooms followed by what could only be described as a café, with a gigantic kitchen equipped with everything needed to cook for and feed a small workforce. Vera opened the doors to a cupboard and stood aside. The shelves were loaded, with everything from china and crockery to dishcloths, towels and tablecloths.

'Look at them!' Annie lifted the corner of a pile of white linen. 'They must have lain here for ages; the edges are turning a yellowish brown.'

'It will all come clean, given a good wash,' Vera replied.

'Where did all this china come from?' Annie asked as she handled a thick white china cup.

'It's all been treated carefully. There don't seem to be any cracks or chips.'

Vera eyed her, then said, 'I can't quite believe it even yet, and this is the fifth time I've been here. Mr Ferguson knew of this place and he asked Mr Mathews if he could trace the owners of the property. It couldn't have worked out better if we'd planned it. The owner happened to be one of Mr Mathews's clients at the bank. Can't you even make a guess at what this place was once used for?'

'No, I can't.'

'Well, you ain't really old enough to cotton on to it, I suppose, but it didn't take me long to work it out. These are premises that were used in the war. We're standing now in what was the works canteen.'

'Well, I'm blowed!' As Annie stifled a laugh she heard a man's voice calling out, 'Is that you, Mrs James?'

'Yes, it's me, Mr O'Halloran,' Vera called back.

Coming into the big kitchen area, Mike O'Halloran studied the young girl, and he summed her up as having had a much easier life than poor Mrs James. He'd known her only for a short time and met her husband only once, but he knew darn well that those dear people deserved all the help that they could get.

'This is Mrs Higgins,' Vera introduced Annie. 'A great friend of mine.'

The man, who was well into his fifties, removed his cap to reveal a shiny bald head. Then, smiling broadly, he took Annie's hand and held it for longer than was necessary, saying in a thick Irish accent, 'You can't be a married woman – you're far too young. It don't give a man such as meself half a chance.'

Vera burst out laughing. 'Oh, Mike, you take the biscuit, you really do.' Then turning to Annie, she told her, 'Mike is the watchman-cum-handyman.'

'Yes, 'tis true,' Mike nodded his head vigorously. 'You take on this building, an' you get me thrown in, so you do, as Mrs James has already found out. I saved this 'ere lot from being burnt to the ground when the incendiaries were falling, and Mr Mason, he's the rich toff that owns the place, says I have a job for life. Anything I can do today t'elp you ladies?'

'Yes, there is, Mike, if you'd be so kind.' Vera faced him squarely. 'When I've finished showing Annie around up here I'd like to take her to the basement, but there isn't much light down there.'

'Oh, missus, you've only got t'ask. Electric will be back on all over the place, so I'm told, as soon as you're up an' running, but that ain't terday, is it? Never mind, I've got plenty of torches. Batteries ain't bad in them, but I tell you what, while you finish off up 'ere, I'll take meself off and get the sacking down from some of those basement windows. Mind 'ow yer tread, the two of you – we don't want no accidents before we're even open for business.'

'That's very good of you, Mike. We'll be down soon.'

'As you say, missus. You're the boss, but I'll come back and see you safely down those stairs, so I will.'

They went back the way they had come, and when they were again in the main room, Annie pointed to several trestle tables against one wall. 'What are all those tables for?' she asked. There were also two long sturdy benches, although, set side by side, there was sufficient room between each one to enable a person to walk the entire perimeter.

'I wondered when you were going to ask, but I'm not going to answer until we 'ave been downstairs.'

'Goodness me,' Annie exclaimed. 'I had no idea of what I was letting myself in for by coming here this morning, and now you are acting very mysterious-like. Come on, Vera, don't stand there grinning at me like the cat that stole the cream! Tell me whatever it is that you've got up your sleeve.'

'All right, I'll give you one more clue.' She walked across the wide floor and without saying another word opened the doors to a cupboard and stood aside.

Once again, Annie's eyes nearly popped out of her head.

The shelves weren't stacked like the store cupboard in the canteen, but a couple of them were full of material. Some were bales of lightweight stuff, lining maybe, while the weighty material was mostly of plain dark colours. These shelves were tidily stacked; each bolt of cloth had a label showing quantity and quality. The lower shelves held reels of thread and cones of cotton, graded neatly by colour. Weighty open boxes displayed scissors of enormous proportions, tape measures and wooden yardsticks, also numerous gadgets that Annie vaguely recognized as being bobbins and suchlike implements that were used on sewing machines.

'Saints alive! Where did it all come from?'

Vera watched Annie's reaction, and as she turned, she murmured, 'I know what you're thinking. It was the same for me. How could anyone give up these premises and yet leave so much behind? And it's all good stuff. Come on now, you'll understand a whole lot more after we've been downstairs.'

Mike O'Halloran was as good as his word. He led the

way down to the basement, then ushered them along a narrow passage, opened another heavy door, stood aside and let them enter a large room similar in shape and size to the big main hall upstairs.

Vera couldn't take her eyes off Annie as she looked about her in utter amazement. 'I still know exactly what you're thinking, and I'll say it again. It was the same with me the first time I came through those doors.' She looked away to stare out over the room. Silently she was still thanking God for what she looked upon as nothing short of a miracle. 'It is as if it were all lying 'ere, just waiting for me to come and set up a workshop. It was a struggle for Peter to get down 'ere, but you know what he said?' Annie shook her head, still not quite able to take it all in. 'He said, "There 'as to be a God somewhere up there. Nobody falls into this kind of good luck without someone somewhere steering the course."'

'I agree. I really do,' Annie murmured more to herself than to Vera, which was just as well because Vera wasn't listening.

She was clearly remembering the day Peter had visited these premises with her. He had walked about humming to himself and she knew that he was feeling more at peace than he had in a long time. It was amazing how fate or God had directed them to this place which, given time, could provide them with steady work and a reasonable income. Vera had known without a moment's doubt that this place was just what he needed. Somewhere where he could be his own master. Work at his own pace without anyone looking over his shoulder, and if some days he didn't feel up to it, well, nobody was going to take him to task. She also felt with total certainty that she would be able to get enough work to make a go of it. The room wasn't exactly furnished. There was a lot of empty floor-space.

However, the reason for Annie's fixed attention was the five sewing-machines that remained, well spaced out, all arranged as if ready for a worker. All it needed was a chair to be placed by each machine. Each one looked gleaming bright, newish, as if they been well cared for, and certainly well oiled.

Annie walked slowly, touching each machine almost reverentially. Gleaming black, each one slightly different, the maker's name embossed in gold, '*Singer*'. They were heavy industrial machines with electric motors underneath and a foot-controlled treadle.

The women stood side by side until Vera said, 'Well?'

Annie said, 'God in heaven! Your Peter has to be right. It's all there ready for you to set machinists on.'

'Well, nearly.'

'And are you ready now to tell me how all this equipment and suchlike came to be just lying here as if waiting for you to come along and discover it?'

Vera was bubbling over with happiness. She turned to Mike and with a laugh in her voice asked, 'Shall you tell 'er, or will I?'

'Oh, missus, let me do the honours. The telling will come easy, 'cos the lass is right, all this was waiting for just such a couple as you an' yer dear man to come along. It 'as t'be the work of Our Blessed Lady. It surely has t'be. T'would be herself that used a guiding hand. How else would you have found all this good stuff which, if left to the government, would have lain here going to rot.'

'Oh, Mike!' Vera cut in on his flow. 'Cut out the sermon on politics and get to the telling, else we'll be here all day.'

'As you say, missus. As you say.' Then briskly now, he began. 'Even before the war, military uniforms were made here on these premises. Mind you, officers' uniforms only in those days, so they were. Then in the summer of thirty-eight, when everyone, except our Mr Chamberlain, knew that war was inevitable, work here was speeded up. Cutting-rooms were upstairs. Men did the cutting, women were taken on for the finishing work. Down here was where the stitching was all done. There was a time when only men were employed on these machines, but the war put paid to all that and lassies were shown the ropes.' With a wave of his hand he led the way back up to the first floor, saying, 'Tis cold and damp down there, but everything will be sorted soon, all in good time. Yes, it will all get sorted.'

'Has this place been left like this ever since the war ended?' Annie ventured the question.

'Even before that, miss.' Mike thought this lass was far too young to be referred to as missus. 'When the raids were so bad over London, the powers that be had this whole place evacuated down to Leigh-on-Sea, which is just outside Southend.' He paused, took a deep breath. 'There was no saying you didn't want to go. Oh, no! It was civilian conscription, an' no mistake. Billets were found in houses and hotels according to where yer face fitted in the company's rank an' file. You got yer orders and you went.'

'Wicked shame, all these machines plus everything else just left lying idle,' Vera remarked sadly.

'They took the bulk of it with them when they evacuated, an' I've done me best, missus, with what they left behind . . . Machines are all in working order, or they will be given the once-over. That's more than can be said for a whole lot more equipment that the government abandoned. How d'you think the scrap-merchants 'ave suddenly become rich fellows? A great many of them jumped on the band-wagon – all they had t'do was follow the trail.' He looked at their faces. 'You think I'm 'aving yer on, don't you? Well let me tell you there's many a back-street scrap-merchant who 'as reason to be grateful to the authorities, 'cos they've ended up buying loads of surplus war material for little more than a song. 'Tis said that God helps those what helps themselves, an' that ain't such a bad philosophy as long as yer remember that it's Christ help those that get caught helping themselves!'

Annie couldn't bear to look at Vera, for she knew they would both start laughing. At that moment a shrill ringing of a bell could be heard coming from the lower regions of the building.

'I'll see t'whoever that is,' Mike volunteered.

A couple of minutes later Mike was calling, 'Mrs James, someone wants t'see you.'

Vera put her head round the door. 'Who is it?'

'Two women, say they've come about a job that's advertised in the paper.'

'Oh? Ask them to come in.'

Mike ushered them in. They could easily have been two sisters or even mother and daughter. The elder looked to be about forty, neatly dressed in a navy blue coat and a felt hat of the same shade. She wore a thin wedding ring and clutched a shabby handbag under her arm. The younger one could have been anything from late teens to early twenties, dressed in a stylish dark green skirt with bolero to match and white blouse. She wasn't wearing a hat, but her long brown hair was scraped back into a bun at the nape of her neck. Annie's reaction to this was that it made the girl look much older than she probably was.

'Good morning, mum,' said the woman so timidly that Vera regarded her kindly. 'I'm Maudie Williams, Mrs, an' this is me daughter, Maureen. We'd like t'ask about the jobs you're advertising in the *Wandsworth Borough News*. You know, for experienced machine workers.'

Vera was instinctively on the alert. 'You say you read the advert in the *Wandsworth Borough News*? It doesn't come out until Friday, and today is only Wednesday.'

Maudie Williams hung her head. 'I didn't say I read it, mum.' Vera waited. 'Me 'usband works on the paper and he tipped us off . . . about you starting up 'ere an' looking for operators.'

'Oh, I see. Have either of you 'ad any experience?'

'Well yes, mum. Both of us 'ave. Not on the sort of work that we've been given to understand went on 'ere previous-like. But if what yer say in the ad is right, curtain-making and upholstery, then that's what we both used to do before we were bombed out.' She paused. 'I worked for Bronnerley's in Whitechapel for twelve years, and me daughter ever since she left school. We lost our 'ome and our jobs in the air raids. Since we moved south, I've only done cleaning jobs; couldn't get nothing else. But Alf, me 'usband, he struck it lucky, got a good job on the Wandsworth local paper.'

Vera could feel for the woman and wanted to spare her any more distress. 'Tell me exactly what kind of work you were used to.'

'Meself, I was always on the upholstery. Loose covers an' all. You know the kind of thing, piping, frilling, box pleating. Maureen 'ere 'as only ever done curtains.'

Vera now turned to the young woman, hoping that she

would speak up for herself, which she suddenly did. 'I can show yer me references, missus. I brought them with me. One is from Bronnerley's 'an another is from a lady in a big 'ouse.' Maureen's voice was quiet, very respectful.

'What work did you do in big houses?' Vera enquired.

'Oh no, mum, I never worked there. Only went with one of the foremen to hang the finished curtains, and especially to make sure that the swags and tails were draped right. Very fussy the owners are about all that palaver. Looks all right t'begin with, but what with all the coal fires and the master of the 'ouse always puffing away at fat cigars, I reckon the pelmets they choose are bad enough but the swags an' tails are nothing more than dust-traps.'

'Maureen!' Mrs Williams had raised her arm and Vera felt sure she was about to clout her daughter around the head.

'Please, it's all right,' Vera cut in quickly. 'I know exactly what Maureen means. I've done a stint or two of hanging curtains meself. Some of the places I've been sent to were more like mausoleums than family homes.' This broke the tension, and Vera swiftly made up her mind. 'It will be another couple of weeks before we can be up and running, but if you'd like to leave me your full names and addresses I would be more than happy for both of you to come and work here. Shall we say on a fortnight's trial, just to be on the safe side?'

Annie thought the girl and her mother were going to do a little dance. She and Vera felt like joining them. They checked the impulse.

'Oh, thank you, missus. Thanks ever so much. I'll do me best t'see that my Maureen keeps a check on her lip.'

'You're more than welcome, Mrs Williams,' Vera told her, smothering a laugh. 'I haven't had the wages worked out yet. You've rather jumped the gun, but when I confirm all this in writing, the terms will be set out in that letter. All right?'

'Oh, yes. Thanks again.'

'Very well. Mike will see you out and I look forward to seeing you soon.'

Mrs Williams did a funny little bob before she left.

Annie, holding in her laughter, couldn't resist tugging at a lock of her hair and nodding at Vera, saying, 'You're an angel, so you are, missus. A true angel.'

'I'll give you what for in a minute!' Vera cried, giving Annie a playful slap.

'There yer are,' said Mike as he came puffing back into the room. 'Staff already lining up to come an' work for yer, so they are.'

'We'll be on our way now, Mike,' Vera smiled at him. 'I'll be back tomorrow with a couple of gentlemen from Dickens & Brown, where I used to work. They're going to look through the material and size up the sewing-machines.'

Mike said, 'Good enough. I'll be 'ere.' Then he cast a glance at Annie and asked, 'You coming back, an' all?'

Before Annie could answer, Vera spoke up. 'Maybe not tomorrow, but yes, she'll be coming back, you'll be seeing a lot of her soon, I hope. In the meantime, Mike, would you do your best to get some temporary lighting fitted up in the basement?'

He turned his head to look straight at Vera, and very seriously said, 'Don't trouble yerself, missus. I'll see to it I will, I will that, I will.'

Vera thanked him and they both hurried out.

Once they were out of earshot of Mike, Vera muttered, 'That one may be Irish through an' through but I'll tell you this, he knows how many beans make five. I've never laughed so much for ages. It isn't what he says, it's the way he says it. That and his voice. I've only got to hear it, and I want to start laughing.'

Annie grinned. 'It's mainly his accent. You don't need many guesses to know where he was born. But I do think he will turn out to be a Godsend to you.'

'Oh, I'm aware of that fact, so I am, yes, I am that,' Vera replied, laughing.

Annie punched her shoulder. 'Oh get on with you! You can mock all you like, but you can't imitate his accent. Besides, I know you already think the world of your Mr O'Halloran.' They were still laughing together as they linked arms and walked towards the tube station.

Chapter Thirty-four

RHODA WAS BREATHING HEAVILY as not only her granddaughter and her husband entered her house but also Doris and Frank Smith. 'Come on, out with it,' she demanded in a hoarse voice, once they were all standing in her living-room. 'Something bad must 'ave 'appened to bring all of you round here in the middle of the afternoon when most of you should be working.'

Jack leaned forward, his hands gripping both of Rhoda's and in a heavy voice he told her, 'The school sent for Annie. Mary's gone missing.'

'What do you mean – she's gone missing?'

'Just what I say. Though we've found out from young Ronnie that there's a lot more to this than we've been told.'

Rhoda took a deep breath and looked at her grand-daughter, then Doris and Frank, who were standing looking out of the window, and for a moment it appeared that she was lost for words. Then pulling herself together she quickly said, 'Annie, go and put the kettle on and the rest of you sit yourselves down. For God's sake, you, Jack, start at the beginning and tell me straight what is going on and then perhaps we can decide what we're going t'do about it.'

Annie did as she was told and took herself off into the scullery.

Jack didn't move, but stood looking about the room. Everything was much as it had always been, the furniture brightly polished, lace doilies laid on tops of small tables, a pot-plant in a pretty bowl dead centre of the big table. He had been happy living here. Rhoda hadn't said much, but in her quiet way had always let it be known that she knew how lonely he must have been and how she was only too glad to be able to provide him with a home, even if it were only on a temporary basis. Nothing would wipe out the fact that he no longer had a family, and during those days there hadn't seemed much point in looking to the future.

Not for the first time he felt he could well imagine what Ronnie and Mary must be going through. He was a grown man, and he'd found it hard to come to terms with the knowledge that there wasn't a soul that you could say was related to you, far less was responsible for your well-being. For two small children to live day by day with that knowledge must be heartbreaking.

Rhoda's voice brought him back, louder now. 'Look, are you going t'tell me what is going on or not?'

'All right, all right! I just had to gather me thoughts and get them into some kind of order. It seems nobody missed Mary until it came to the dinner break. The teacher sent for her brother and he swears that they came to school together and entered the building also together. After that they split up and went to their own classrooms. The headmaster was informed. He questioned the children who were normally close to Mary but not one remembered seeing her today. Yet the teacher says she answered to her name when she called the register.'

Rhoda, holding on to the back of a high chair as if for support, now turned and cut in, 'Have the police been called?'

'Yes, they have now, but Annie had already asked if she could speak to Ronnie on his own, and it's what she got out of him that is worrying all of us the most.'

As a foot kicked at the door, Doris moved quickly to open it and let Annie in with a tray of tea-things. As she put the tray down on the table, Rhoda almost shouted at her, 'Leave the tea for the moment, or let Doris pour it out. I'm waiting to be told what Ronnie had to say about all this.'

'Gran, I'm so sorry. I've known for a couple of days that all was not right with him, and I truly meant to get him on his own and make him tell me, but he can be as slippery as an eel when he wants. At the school he had no choice but to tell me.' Annie had to take a deep breath and make a great effort to stop her tears. 'Ronnie's story is that one day last week he found Mary in a corner of the playground all by herself, and she was crying her eyes out. It's all about this calling of the register each morning. Agnes Hill is bigger than most girls in the class and therefore takes it upon herself to be the leader. Having cornered Mary, she got several girls to form a ring around her and then demanded to know why she was known as Mary Wilson.'

'Oh Annie, no!' Rhoda was facing her squarely now. 'I can guess what you're going to tell me next.'

'Sadly, I expect you've guessed right, Gran. Mary's been

heard to tell her best friends that she's got a mum *and* a dad now. This Agnes heard her own parents talking, and added two an' two t'make five. She taunted Mary with the fact if that were the case, her surname would be Higgins, 'cos all kids have the same surname as their mums an' dads. It seems she also took great delight in adding: You're Mary Wilson whose mum is dead and yer dad run off an' left yer. Mr an' Mrs Higgins only look after you 'cos you ain't got no one else.'

'Christ almighty! Kids can be really cruel, can't they?'

Annie sighed. 'Yes, I'm afraid you're right, Gran. Not hard to imagine how Mary must have been feeling. But we have tried, truly we have, to make it plain to those children that both Jack and I really do love them and want them to go on living with us for ever, not just for a while.'

'I know you 'ave, luv. You've nothing to reproach yerself for, and as for Jack, well, he's been a brick where those kids are concerned, and no mistake.'

At that point the telephone rang. The loud shrillness of it made everybody jump. 'I'll get it,' said Frank, which was sensible, as he was sitting nearest to the door. There was utter silence as they listened and heard him say, 'Hallo. What? Oh, it's you, Sid.'

Then silence, during which they all stared at the floor until Frank called out, 'Annie, come to the phone. It's good news! Sid's got Mary there, an' he's gone to fetch Flossie to talk t'you.'

The sigh of relief was unanimous as Annie ran out. By now they had all crowded into the narrow passage where the phone was, listening intently to the one side of the conversation. There was a touch of hysterical laughter in Annie's voice as she repeated for the third time, 'And you're sure she's all right?' It didn't matter that they couldn't hear Flossie's answer, because suddenly Annie's face was wreathed in smiles and they heard her say, 'Get ready for an invasion, 'cos we'll all be over in less time than it will take for you to boil a kettle.'

Having replaced the receiver, Annie bowed her head and sent up a silent prayer of thanks. 'I'd never have forgiven myself if anything had happened to that dear child,' she murmured.

Jack said something to Frank, and the pair of them turned to Rhoda. 'I'm making no promises,' Jack told her, his voice thick with emotion. 'But it won't be for want of trying if I can't sort this problem out once and for all. Those kids are with Annie and me because we both love them as if they were our own. Frank's just suggested that I see a solicitor and try to make it legal, and that's exactly what I'm going to do. First thing tomorrow morning.'

Annie cried, 'Oh, Jack! Do you really mean that? You would adopt them both?'

'I do so. I'll do me damnedest. Now, for God's sake stop that crying. You too, Doris.'

'Leave them be for a moment,' Rhoda ordered. 'We won't bother ourselves with that tea now,' she nodded towards the tray that lay untouched on the table. 'It will be well and truly stewed. If I've learned anything in all the years that I've lived in the East End, it is that you'll go a long way an' not find a better cup of tea than that which Sid and Floss make in their café. So let's go and fetch the child back home and get ourselves a good cuppa at the same time.'

The men looked at each other, not sure whether to laugh or to cry, while Doris and Annie were leaning against each other, laughing now while endeavouring to dry their faces.

After a moment, Rhoda said, 'Come on now, you girls, go and wipe your faces over and let's get going. I suppose it's too much to 'ope for that you've got your car outside, Jack?'

'You're right, I haven't, but Frank has got his, an' seeing as how it's a much better model than my Ford you'd better ask him nicely if he'll take us all to Sid's.'

Frank rose quickly from the chair, and he and Rhoda stood silent, smiling at each other. Then, making a crook of his arm and taking Rhoda's hand, he tucked it through, saying, 'It will be my pleasure to escort you, Rhoda.' And like that, with the others following, they all left the house.

In various ways they were saying to themselves that it was a short happy journey they were about to make. But each knew it could have turned out to be so very different. Only Annie was asking herself: What now? How in God's name do I find the words that will really reassure Mary that she is loved and, above all else, wanted?

Sid was piling fried potatoes on a plate that held two fried eggs and three rashers of bacon when the door to his café opened and Rhoda led her troop in. He gave her a grin and nodded towards the back of the café. 'Upstairs, take 'em all up. Flossie's making a fuss of young Mary an' there don't seem t'be much 'arm done.'

'Thanks, Sid, I'm much obliged to you. We all are. God knows what might 'ave 'appened if she 'adn't found 'er way 'ere.'

'Never mind all that. Came 'ere looking for Annie,

that's what she did. Go on, Flossie's got the tea on, an' I'll be up t'join yer as soon as I can.'

They all congregated into the big front room immediately above the shop. Mary was sitting on Flossie's lap, her face buried in her ample bosom. Flossie nodded to them all, saying, 'Everything is all right, I'm happy to say. Sit down, all of you. Would you like some tea?' She struggled to get up, setting Mary down on her feet.

Suddenly the child was across the room, her arms round Annie's waist, her face only just level with Annie's stomach, and she was crying bitterly. 'Now, now,' Flossie said, patting her shoulders. 'You promised no more tears. No one is going to be cross with you.' Then turning to Annie, she said, 'Why don't you take her into the bathroom, give her face a little wash and by the time you come back we women will have the tea all set out.'

'Oh, Annie, I didn't . . . I couldn't find you,' Mary hiccuped.

Annie got down on her knees, looked at the child's red, puffy eyes, and her heart ached. She lifted Mary up, glanced first at Rhoda, then at her husband, and having received a reassuring nod from each of them, she held Mary even more tightly and left the room, all the time whispering, 'It's all right, Mary luv, don't cry. It's all right. I'm here now.'

With a soft sponge and lukewarm water she tenderly bathed and rinsed Mary's face several times, all without saying a word. 'I don't want t'go t'school no more,' Mary blurted out.

'Never mind about that. I want you to tell me all about the way Agnes Hill has been getting at you.'

Wide-eyed, Mary looked up at her. 'How d'you know about that? She tells all me friends they shouldn't talk t'me.' Her face was still flushed, but the words were now tumbling out almost as if the child was relieved to be able to talk about was hurting her. 'They pinch me in class, an' if I tell them it 'urts, they only giggle.' Annie stayed quiet. She was sure there was more to come. 'I told Daisy, she's me best friend, that it was lovely at 'ome now that we 'ave you and Jack all the time. Not that it wasn't when Gran came, but . . . well, it's nice when one of you tucks me in bed an' it's ever so good when we come downstairs in the morning an' we all 'ave breakfast together – that's if Jack ain't gone t'work.' She had to stop talking; her small chest was heaving, tears were never far away.

Annie kept hold of her hand, all the while thinking to herself that Mary looked like a woebegone Alice in Wonderland in her short-skirted navy blue drill slip. It showed her thin legs, and socks that were now all wrinkled around her ankles. What she really wanted to do was crush her in a very tight embrace and swear that she would never again allow anyone or anything to hurt her, although she knew what a hopeless and futile promise that would be. Nobody in this world could promise a child that much. 'Come on,' Annie said. 'Let's go into Flossie's bedroom and I'll brush your hair, tidy you up a bit, then we'll go and have some tea.'

Seated on a stool facing the mirror of the dressing-table, Mary was able to see the reflection of Annie, who was standing behind her. Slowly and gently Annie ran the brush through the long fair hair that a few minutes ago had been a sort of tangled mess. It felt relaxing, and in a few moments Mary ventured, 'Annie, I didn't do anything wrong when I told Daisy that I now 'ad a mum an' a dad, did I?'

Annie answered her question with a question. 'Mary,

have you ever come across a little boy or girl that has been adopted?'

'No, I don't think so,' she said, giving Annie a puzzled look.

'Do you know what the word adopt means?'

'Well, sort of . . . Miss Newman read us a story that was about this girl whose muvver an' farver died in an accident and she said two people went to the 'ome where the girl 'ad been sent and they chose 'er to be their daughter. Then they took 'er 'ome with them.'

'That's about right, pet. You've explained that very well. That is exactly what adoption is all about.' Annie paused, but went on steadily brushing Mary's hair. At the same time was thinking: I have to be so careful here. One thing I must not do is to make the child any promises that I might not be able to keep. 'That story is almost the same as what has happened to you and your brother. Don't you think so? Jack and I have chosen to keep both of you with us because we don't have any children of our own, and even if we do in the future, it won't change our love for you. We'd still want to keep both of you.'

'Well, it's not quite like what the story was,' Mary muttered and the sound of tears was back in her voice.

'How do you mean? Come on, luv, you tell me what the difference is.'

Mary hesitated. 'Miss Newman said that the two people changed the name of the little girl so that everyone would know that she belonged to them. I think they 'ad t'go t'the police station to do it. You ain't changed our names. Even Ronnie said you ain't, 'cos I did ask 'im. If you want t'keep us, why 'aven't yer?'

Beneath her breath Annie prayed, God give me strength! She laid the brush down on the dressing-table, licked two

411

of her fingers and ran the crumpled length of ribbon through them. It didn't get all the creases out, but it did look somewhat better. Bunching Mary's tresses together, she wound the ribbon round them twice before finally tying it in a bow. Then, looking straight at their reflection in the mirror, she said, 'There, that wasn't so bad now, was it?' She felt utterly guilty as Mary got down from the stool, turned round and looked her full in the face, waiting for an answer. Suddenly Annie's mind was made up. 'The truth is, Mary, only your mother is dead. Before Jack and I can ask the authorities to allow us to adopt you and Ronnie, we would have to have permission from your father.'

'Well, he don't want us.'

The way the child made that statement had Annie herself in tears. 'This is very difficult for all of us, Mary,' she replied, her voice trembling, 'but this much I can promise. Jack is going to see someone who deals with things like this, and if at all possible we shall adopt you, and then we'll change your surname and you'll be able to tell the whole world that we chose you.'

Mary winced before saying, 'An' 'ow long will all that take?'

Annie knew that this wasn't doing either of them any favours, and to prolong it was only piling up trouble. So her answer was honest. 'I really have no idea, but surely you trust Jack to do the very best he can for you both? Tell me one thing, Mary. Do you believe that Jack and I do love you?'

'Yes,' came the muffled reply.

'Well, then, will you try and be patient? And will you also promise not to run off from school any more?'

'All right,' was Mary's answer, said so low that Annie only just caught it.

'Good.' She took hold of Mary's hand, kissed her cheek, and said, 'Let's go and get ourselves some tea before the others eat it all up.'

She was rewarded by the first smile she'd seen on Mary's lips that day.

Chapter Thirty-five

VERA SAT UP ABRUPTLY in bed, her chest heaving. She'd been dreaming about the workshop and the four staff she had taken on. Such a vivid dream, everyone's face clear as a bell. Besides Maudie Williams and her daughter she had been lucky to find Connie Jones and Elsie Cooper, both experienced machinists. Elsie had even worked with Maudie Williams at Bronnerley's for quite a few years. In these hard times with so many unable to find work, they were all grateful because she had offered them employment. Vera frowned. It was a great responsibility. On the other hand, everything was going so well.

Too well! It worried her. She had as much work as she could cope with. Several orders were in the book. Dickens & Brown were falling over backwards to help her. They even let her have the use of one of their vans one afternoon a week, *and* they supplied the driver.

As for Peter, he seemed to have taken on a new lease of life. He hadn't made a miraculous recovery, of course he hadn't, but there was now a meaning to his life. He had a job, a reason to get up in the morning and to face the day knowing that he was doing something useful. They were working for themselves, beholden to no one. Hardly ever did he venture down to the basement, but he had made the cutting-room his territory, coming in to work at least two days a week.

At first he had merely watched the two lasses who were responsible for cutting out the curtains, which, if the length and weight of the material demanded it, were spread full length on a trestle table or on one of the heavy benches. But one day, as he sat watching, Maureen Williams had suggested he move closer. 'Look an' learn' was what she'd said, and that was exactly what he'd done. Maureen had also taught him to tack every seam rather than only pinning it before sending the work down to the basement to be machined. That way, there could be no costly mistakes.

Vera often wished Peter could use a machine. It seemed so much more of a man's job, but there was no chance of that, not with his gammy leg. Still, he had his own apron with the huge patch pocket, and the two pairs of scissors he had claimed for his own were his pride and joy.

From the beginning she had tried to take it slowly. Better safe than sorry, she kept telling herself. The luck she had had with employees was outstanding. Both Mrs Williams and her daughter were gems, equally as good as they had promised. In fact all four of the women were proving to be a good investment.

It frightened her sometimes just how well things were going. Would it last? She tried to get rid of this doom and gloom mood by snuggling down again in bed but it was hard to get back to sleep. Her thoughts turned to this house. They were so lucky that Annie had fought and saved their home for them. God knows how Peter would have fared if he had been taken back to live in Roehampton Hospital. Annie really was a great girl. Vera loved her as if she were her own daughter. Life wasn't that smooth for Annie, though. Not that she wasn't happily married – she and Jack had been made for each other. Happy as the day was long, those two were. It was a shame about their problems.

Jack had made it known that he had been to see a solicitor about adopting Ronnie and Mary, but he hadn't been at all happy with the outcome of that first meeting. It wasn't simply a matter of stating what both he and Annie would like to do, but more a matter of listening to a load of legal jargon that, when boiled down, only seemed to make their position almost impossible. Vera sighed. Outwardly, Ronnie seemed to cope quite well; it was young Mary's emotional problems that caused everyone concern.

Annie and Jack had made it plain that they had room in their hearts and in their home for both of these children. They were a caring couple, good friends, going out of their way to help her and Peter, and she would dearly love to be able to help them in return. Try as she might, and she had discussed the matter at length with Rhoda and with Doris, there did not seem to be any short way round this complicated adoption system. Of one thing she was sure; no matter how great the problem became, Annie and Jack would never turn their back on Ronnie and Mary. The fact that no one else seemed to want the responsibility for them made their need that much greater. It was sad for Jack and Annie, and even worse for the children. Vera was only glad that she didn't have the task of answering the questions that the kiddies came up with from time to time.

That wasn't the only problem the newly-weds had on

their plate. The first and second floors of this house were still without a tenant, and although Annie argued that she could well afford to repay the monthly instalments on the bank loan, it just didn't seem right to let the place stay empty like that. An idea had been rattling around in Vera's head for some time, and suddenly she made up her mind. She was going to be very bold and put it to Annie outright. After all, she could say No if she didn't take to the idea, and nothing would have been lost. Rhoda won't be best pleased if Annie does act on my suggestion, she said to herself. She'll more than likely be downright furious with me. The following Sunday they were all to meet at Annie's house for Sunday lunch, and that's when I'm going to tackle her, she decided.

Come Sunday, God was good. The weather was fine, and Vera and Annie were sitting alone in the garden peeling the vegetables. Jack and Peter had taken the children with them in the car to pick up Rhoda, and Doris and Frank had not yet arrived. Vera decided there would never be a better time to broach the subject and so she jumped in with both feet. 'Shame you've had no luck in letting the first two floors of your house,' she began.

Annie stopped scraping a carrot and said to Vera, 'You're not still worrying yourself over that, are you? The agent told me only a couple of days ago that a few people were after the flat, but it's too large and the rent is too high.'

'My thoughts exactly,' Vera stated. 'Pity you didn't think about it when the alterations were being carried out.'

'We can all be clever after the event,' Annie retorted. 'If we had made it into two flats, they would have been let by now, but the cost would have been so much more and the size of the rooms would have had to be altered just to make another bathroom and kitchen.'

'That would have been a shame,' Vera said sadly. 'As they are now, it is a really good set of rooms, what with that large front room that has such a smashing view of the common and in the distance you can see the River Wandle.'

'I couldn't agree more,' Annie told her. 'It's the three rooms on the second floor that are the bugbear. I don't really want tenants with several children.'

Vera nodded her head in agreement and then made her suggestion. 'Why don't you and Jack move out of the East End and take the two floors for yourselves?'

Annie's jaw dropped, and she stared at Vera with raised eyebrows. 'Me, move south? What d'you think me gran would say? And what about Jack? His livelihood is tied up with the river.'

Vera dropped a potato into the pan of cold water with such a plop that it made the water splash up into her face. She roared with laughter. 'Annie Higgins, you really do take the biscuit! No one's asking you to desert the East End, and the Thames won't alter its course just because you move to the other side of it. Just you think about it. You'd 'ave loads more room, which would be a great help if you decided to start a family of yer own. Ron and Mary could both go to new schools, and they'd 'ave the garden and the common to play on. You should at least think about it.'

Annie felt her cheeks flush. That was what she was longing for. Oh yes, she'd give a great deal for Jack and her to have a baby of their own.

Vera broke in again before Annie's thoughts could run

too far along those lines. 'It would make sense. You'd have no rent to pay, seeing as how you legally own the house. No more outlay than the loan you have at the moment,' she said practically.

Annie smiled at that. But yes, it did make sense. The renovations had really transformed the house, and she loved it. It was one thing having Vera and Peter living in the garden flat, for they were careful tenants, and the same thing could be said of the young couple who rented the two top rooms. They were quiet, considerate tenants, both out at work all day, saving hard to buy their own place. She didn't want a big family occupying the other two floors, maybe destroying the newly decorated rooms, even perhaps causing damage that would devalue the property.

'Yes, all right, I'll think about,' she promised Vera, and was rewarded with a hug.

It was late in the evening before Annie got Jack on his own. Slowly but surely she outlined the proposal that Vera had put to her that morning. Much to her surprise, he was all for it.

'What about me gran?' Annie was quick to ask. 'There would be plenty of room for her to come with us. You wouldn't mind, would you?'

'Of course I wouldn't. We could fix her up with her own sitting-room, but I don't think it will happen.'

'Why not?'

'You'd have a job persuading Rhoda to move out from the East End of London,' he replied cynically. As it turned out later, that was the understatement of the year.

'But, Jack, *you* don't seem to mind the idea,' Annie persisted.

'It's different for and me you.' He smiled at her lovingly. 'We are young enough to make a fresh start. The past is gone. I've come to realize it's no use trying to hold on to what used to be. The future is there for us two, we hope. For Rhoda, it has to be different. She's lived all her life in the East End, and I think she'll end her days there.' Annie looked so downhearted that Jack had to laugh. 'It's not as if we'd be going thousands of miles away. From one side of the Thames to the other, that's all it amounts to. Rhoda has a telephone, and we could be with her in half an hour. Besides, do you really think she wouldn't visit us if we left here?'

He got out of his chair and went over to Annie. For a moment he considered saying that if she felt that badly about it, they'd forget the whole thing. Yet in his heart he knew the move could really be for the best, right in so many ways for all of them. 'Annie . . . Oh, Annie,' was all he was able to say. He pulled her to her feet and kissed her, a gentle, warm gesture just to show her how much he did love her. When they separated, he took her hand between both of his, saying, 'Come on, Annie, think about it. Wild horses won't keep your gran away from a Sunday dinner with her family. Just be careful how you put it to her. Don't let her think for a moment that we're deserting her.'

'All right, I'll do me best.' She sat up straight, gave him a look that was full of determination. 'I'll ask her opinion, won't let her think that we've decided anything. Don't you think that would be best?'

'Yes, I do. Great idea.' He kissed her again, this time a long, sweet kiss that said everything would work out all right. And as he straightened up, Annie smiled happily.

Jack turned away, his expression serious. What he was

thinking was: I'm glad it will be you that's putting it to your gran rather than me!

Suddenly Annie felt a twinge of guilt. There wasn't anything this man wouldn't do for her; his love and support since they had been married were far more than she had ever anticipated. Her voice dropped as she said, 'While we're discussing our future, wouldn't you like to tell me what happened at the solicitors?'

Jack frowned. This was one matter that he did not want to talk about. Not at the moment, anyway. He shook his head. 'There's nothing more to tell . . . At least, not anything you'd be pleased to hear. The authorities would have to contact Bob Wilson. Can you imagine what that will do to Mary if he turns up?'

Annie watched all kinds of emotion cross his face and she felt much sympathy for him. 'Jack, it couldn't have been all that bad.' She bit her lip. 'Please tell me about it.'

'I will. I will, Annie, if you're sure that's what you want. But I warn you it involves a lot more people and rules and regulations than either you or I ever dreamed about. Come and sit down again. It's very late, but I don't have an early start in the morning so perhaps now is as good a time as any to let you hear all the facts.'

Annie sat down beside him and said, 'I'm glad we have this opportunity to talk. I knew things hadn't gone well by the way you've been acting – all thoughtful-like.'

'Yeah, well, first off the man at the solicitor's office that I saw has dealt with a great many adoptions, mainly since the end of the war. He knows what he's talking about. James Oliver is his name, about forty-six years old, very business like. I liked him. To start with, he said, a social worker will want to interview both of us together, either here at home or possibly at their offices. You know, Annie, he couldn't believe that ever since your dad died it has been you that has been responsible for Mary and Ronnie. I explained that Rhoda had always been on hand, but it didn't make a bit of difference, he said. He also made it quite clear that it must have been an oversight on the part of the school not to have picked up that the children lived without what would legally be described as proper parents. Though he did add that such had been the case more frequently since the war, because neighbours had taken in children whose parents had been killed. Nevertheless, he said, the sooner we set the wheels in motion to make it all legal, the better for the children as well as ourselves.'

'So what you're telling me is the one thing I've dreaded right from the beginning. Stuffy do-gooders will come around here snooping, deciding if the place is kept clean enough to be a home for children. And if what they see and their opinion of us doesn't come up to scratch, they could easily recommend that the children be taken away and put into care.'

'Oh, Annie! That's the very reason why I haven't spoken to you about this before. You have to jump the gun! Mr Oliver was ready for that reaction when I murmured that it could drag on for months or even years, especially if their own father was to oppose it. He said the speed of response from the courts would largely be dependent on the value of our offer to adopt both children.' Jack paused, while he took in several very deep breaths.

'What the hell does "the value of our offer" mean?' Annie jumped in, quick with her question.

Now Jack allowed himself to smile. 'I was expecting you to ask that. In other words, if we seem to be a good bet as prospective adoptive parents, we are likely to get better and quicker attention. And before you go off the deep end again, Mr Oliver's view is that seeing as how both children have been with you and your grandmother for a great length of time would be points in your favour. Plus the fact that I courted you, knowing that if I married you, we would start off with a ready-made family. Having made our decision to be partners for life, we had not discarded Ronnie and Mary, but had provided them with a good home life and upbringing, which hopefully the reports from their school will confirm.'

'So you think we may be in with a chance?' Annie sounded less doubtful.

'Yes, I do, honestly I do. But that won't hasten things along. You will just have to prepare yourself for a long-drawn-out session. But having said that, I did get the feeling that Mr Oliver was of the opinion that we would make excellent adoptive parents and also that he would do his best to help.'

'Well, I suppose that is something, and at least now you've told me a bit more, I'll be more prepared to meet these social workers and answer their questions.'

For the umpteenth time she wondered how Jack really felt about having not only married her but taken on the children as well. Each time the matter came up he did his best to reassure her that this was what he wanted. She hoped and prayed that every word was true and that reasonably soon they could settle down in the knowledge that they were a proper family. The possibility that Mary and Ronnie might be taken away from her was far too cruel for Annie even to contemplate.

Chapter Thirty-six

ANNIE HAD CONSIDERED HAVING Doris there when she tackled her gran about moving, then decided not to. Much better if there were only the two of them. That way, if they got into an argument, said things they didn't really mean, no one else would hear.

'That was a lovely piece of ham,' Rhoda declared across the table. 'I really enjoyed it. But you should know by now, my girl, I'm nobody's fool. You don't purposely ask me round for a midday meal in the middle of the week unless you've something on your mind that's worrying you, or you want something. So, come on. Spit it out, whatever it is.'

Annie took a deep breath. This was going to be every bit as hard as she'd imagined. A determined expression came to her face as she began to outline the idea that she and Jack might move to Tremaine Road and take over the middle two floors of the house. 'What do you think of the idea, Gran? It seems an utter waste to leave them lying empty, and the agents haven't had much luck in finding suitable tenants.'

Rhoda stared at her, aghast. 'You can't be serious, girl! Leave the East End and everybody you've known all yer life? You've grown up round 'ere – you'd be like a fish out of water.'

'Oh, Gran, why do you immediately look on the black side of everything? Why can't you think of all the advantages for a change?'

'I see. You aren't asking my opinion. You've all talked it over among yourselves, everything is already cut an' dried, is it?'

'No, it's not, Gran, it's not like that at all. Yes, Vera did put the idea into my head and I discussed it with Jack, but nothing more than talking has taken place. I am asking you to be fair, think about it for a minute, weigh up the pros and cons, and give me your advice.'

After a silence, Annie eventually said, 'Come on, Gran, talk to me. Whenever have I gone ahead with anything that really mattered without first asking what you thought about it?'

Rhoda huffed, crossed her arms, and glowered at Annie. 'That's all in the past. You're a married woman now – you don't need my approval for anything.'

Annie couldn't help laughing. 'Going t'play the hurt bit now, are we? The poor lonely old woman left all on her own because her kith an' kin don't want her any more?'

'That's about the truth of the matter, isn't it? I've served my purpose, an' now you think I should be put out to grass. Well, you go ahead. Move lock stock an' barrel. No one will ever be able to say that I stood in your way.'

Annie sighed. 'This isn't the way Jack said you would react.'

'Oh?' Rhoda sounded really surprised. 'And just what did Jack Higgins have to say on the matter?'

'He said we'd only be moving from one side of the river to the other. And although there would be plenty of room for you to come an' live with us, he didn't for a moment think you would.' Rhoda looked as if she was about to explode, but Annie rushed on. 'He said you had earned your independence, but wild horses wouldn't keep you from visiting us. As for Mary and Ronnie, they were your grandchildren in every sense of the word and nothing and no one would keep you from seeing them. Even if we were moving to the North Pole, he added, the facts would remain the same.'

Again there was a lengthy silence during which Rhoda seemed to be considering what Annie had just told her. So, striking while the iron was hot, Annie said, 'We'd still expect you to help with the Sunday dinner! Jack would fetch you in the car, and during the winter when it gets dark so early you could always stay the night, and Jack or Frank would take you home on Monday morning. Mary would love it if her gran stayed overnight.'

Those last few words got to Rhoda. Her old eyes glistened with tears, something Annie hadn't seen in a very long time. She jumped to her feet, threw her arms around her gran's shoulders and held her tight, murmuring, 'As if I could manage without you, or any of us, for that matter. Honest, Gran, Jack said no matter where we lived, Sunday wouldn't be the same if Rhoda wasn't there to cook the dinner. You are part an' parcel of our lives. You were the mainstay for David and me when our mum died. You gave Jack a home when he came out of the Navy. He tells everyone if it hadn't been for you, he would have gone mad when he came home and realized he had no home and no family. Then there's Mary and Ronnie. Sometimes I don't think they know what to call me – or Jack, for that matter, but have you ever heard either of them refer to you as anything other than Gran? You've been a rock in their lives ever since their own parents deserted them.' Now, very cleverly, Annie turned the tables. 'I think it's ever so unfair of you, Gran, to think that we would just go off and abandon you, as if we didn't give a hoot for you.'

Rhoda took the bait. 'Annie, luv, I didn't mean it, not like that! Given time, I think I'll be able to see the benefits. As long as you're all settled and 'appy, that's what counts.'

'No, Gran, what counts is that we stay together. Always loving each other, no matter what.'

Rhoda laughed, but it was a lost, lonely sound. 'That's just it. We aren't all going to stay together, are we?' she murmured with a pained expression on her face.

Annie sighed, now on the verge of tears. 'Honest to God, Gran, why won't you listen to what I'm telling you?'

Rhoda slumped in her chair and said brokenly, 'I just never in my wildest dreams imagined you'd up sticks and leave me. With David gone and your father dead, I thought at least I'd always 'ave you around till the end of me days.'

Annie's next words came softly, with a lot of emotion. 'Gran, if you feel that strongly about us moving, then we won't go. I'll stay near you, I promise.'

Her words were spoken with such sincerity that they made Rhoda want to cry with despair. She knew she was being utterly selfish, yet she couldn't keep her big mouth shut. This beautiful, kind granddaughter of hers deserved a life of her own. Hadn't she herself prayed to the good Lord to send a decent man into Annie's life? Until Jack, Annie had been trapped in a situation that was not of her making, devoting her life to another woman's children. Now that she was asking for a chance to break away and start a whole new life, I should be glad for her. I know I should, but won't I miss her! All this is happening when I thought everything in the garden was rosy. Even David had got in touch, and there had been talk of them all going on holiday to Plymouth to see him and meet his young wife. Now this. Why was it that life's never easy?

Annie could tell that her gran was struggling with her conscience. 'I'm sorry I've upset you.'

Rhoda brushed angrily at her eyes, 'No, luv, it's me that should be saying sorry. I'm a mean-minded old woman. But I'll do me best t'get used to the idea.'

They both got to their feet. Rhoda pulled Annie into her arms, holding her tightly. As Annie breathed in the scent of her, she felt as she always had done with her gran, right back for as long as she could remember, safe and secure. As a child, she would cuddle her, read her bedtime stories, kiss a wound better if she fell over. Tears were still prickling at the back of her eyes. What would she have done without her grandma over the years, she didn't know. No matter what had happened, and there had been some had been hard knocks and sad losses, she had always been there, ready to help and comfort. Suddenly it was she who was doing the hugging, holding on to her gran as if her very life depended on it.

Rhoda kissed her gently, smelling the nice shampoo she always used, all the time thinking she's nought but a young girl herself, and I shouldn't be adding to her troubles. She's had enough as it is, what with one thing an' another. She pulled away, smiling sadly. 'You and Jack go ahead, make your plans. I'll fit in with whatever you decide.'

Annie smiled. 'Don't suppose we could persuade you to come with us?'

'No chance! So don't push yer luck. Born an' bred round 'ere, and far too old to alter me way of living now.'

'That's exactly what Jack said you would say. But honestly, Gran, we won't desert you. I promise we won't. It'll all turn out for the best, and we shall see just as much of you when we're living in Tremaine Road as we do now when you're only round the corner.'

Rhoda sighed. 'I'll put the kettle on, shall I? Nice cup of tea will make us both feel better.' As she busied herself in the scullery, she was thinking, talk comes cheap, and the road to hell is paved with good intentions. See as much of them and the children as I do now? I'd like t'think that was going to be the case, but I wouldn't bank on it. We'll just have to wait and see.

Chapter Thirty-seven

ONE GLANCE AT ANNIE'S worried look, and the fact that two strange women were seated at the table with all sorts of forms and documents spread out in front of them, made Jack size up the situation immediately. 'Hallo, Annie luv,' he said. Then there was a slightly awkward pause as he turned to face their visitors.

'I'm Sarah Fowler.' The short, neat, blond-haired lady, aged about thirty, stood up, smiled, and held out her hand. Jack decided she looked friendly enough.

Shaking her hand, Jack said, 'I presume you are social workers come about our application to adopt the two children who are already part of our family?'

'That's right, Mr Higgins. My associate is June Gower.'

This lady was a different kettle of fish entirely. For one thing, she wore a wedding ring. In her late forties, grey-haired, tall, thin and bony. He shook her hand, saying, 'It would have been better had you advised us in advance of this visit so that I could have made arrangements to be here to meet you.'

Mrs Gower's eyes were cold as she said scathingly, 'The whole object of our visit is to view the home without prior warning.'

Jack's heart ached for Annie. 'Please make a pot of tea, luv, while these ladies bring me up to date on what has gone on.'

Annie left the room reluctantly.

'Mr Higgins,' Sarah Folwer began, 'we shall ask you in a minute to show us round the rest of your house, after which we shall make our report. You and your wife will then be invited to attend a series of preparation group meetings, probably six to eight sessions over a period of two months.'

Without giving Jack time to comment, June Gower told him, 'Sometimes your performance at these group meetings may be used as a formal assessment.'

When Jack shot her a look so intimidating that it penetrated even her hard shell, she had the grace to look ashamed, but he was not about to let the matter drop. What kind of a person was this June Gower? Surely not someone whose sole interest should be finding a happy home with loving parents for unwanted kiddies or even kiddies whose parents had both died. This woman appeared to be as hard as nails, and although he had made her acquaintance only a few minutes ago, everything about her set his teeth on edge.

Annie had her ear glued to the door, her mind in turmoil. I knew we should never have got involved with social workers, she said sadly to herself as she carried in the laden tea-tray. The next twenty minutes seemed a lifetime to her as she listened to feet tramping through the upstairs rooms.

When at last the women gathered their papers and files,

she tried to get some sort of answer from Sarah Fowler. 'Isn't there any way to shorten all these formalities? These children have lived with me for a considerable time now, and nothing untoward has happened to them.'

Sarah shook her head, well aware of Annie's distress. 'We'll do our best to speed things up. That's a promise.'

'I hope you mean that, for Mary's sake,' Annie murmured, more to herself than to Sarah.

'Is there something I should know about Mary?' Sarah asked kindly.

'Well,' Annie hesitated and looked across at Jack.

'Much better if you put us in the picture,' Sarah urged.

'It's just that Mary gets very upset when the children taunt her at school. They tell her that if Jack and I were really her parents she would have the same surname as us. It bothers her more than she lets on.'

Jack nodded his head vigorously and turned to Mrs Gower. 'Surely you can understand the way the child feels? The quicker we make the adoption legal, the quicker we can change the children's surname.'

The woman acted as if she had not heard Jack's comments. 'Everybody's application goes through the usual channels. There are no short cuts.'

Jack put his arm over Annie's shoulders as they followed the women to the front door and watched Mrs Gower unlock a small car. Sarah Fowler hesitated, and came back to Jack and Annie. 'Everything will be all right, really it will,' she told them, adding with a small laugh, 'June's bark is far worse than her bite! You are nice people and you have a lovely comfortable home.'

Annie hung on to that remark as Jack led her back inside. The whole meeting had exhausted her, left her feeling apprehensive. 'Come on, luv, I'm starving! How about we have a whacking great fry-up? I'll cook it all if you lay the table and cut the bread.'

'Oh, Jack,' Annie cried, sounding a lot more cheerful than she had so far. 'What the hell would I do if I didn't have you?'

'Question doesn't arise, my darling. For better or worse, you're saddled with me for life.' Taking her gently in his arms, Jack hugged her. 'Things will get sorted. Nothing and no one will take Ronnie and Mary away from us. Not if I can possibly prevent it.'

Then he had a twinge of anxiety. Was he making promises he'd never be able to keep? To him, Annie was perfect. Whatever she wore, she looked immaculate, her thick dark hair always shone, and . . . he couldn't describe that certain quality that set her apart from other women. She had that quiet dignity, that certain way of letting folk know that she was sincere. Now she was upset, and it showed in her big brown eyes. Doing his best to lighten her mood, he laughed, saying, 'I love you dearly, Annie, but I won't if I don't soon get something to eat!'

Annie giggled. 'I love you too, Jack. You're a good man.'

What was the world coming to? Jack wondered as he busied himself cooking their meal. Here we have two children who are perfectly happy, well loved and cared for, yet it was left to social workers to decide whether they could stay with us as a family or be taken into care, as they put it!

Those kids *will* stay with us, he vowed to himself, or I'll know the bloody reason why.

Annie was returning from the greengrocers when she saw

a small stout woman standing by her front gate. Coming nearer, she asked, 'Can I help you?' When the woman took a deep breath but did not answer she spoke louder, 'What's wrong? Has something happened to you?' She could see that the woman's face was white and strained.

'Are you Annie Bateman? 'Cos if you are, I need to talk t'you.'

Looking puzzled, Annie answered, 'I was Annie Bateman but I'm Annie Higgins now. I married.'

'Please, do you mind if we go inside?' There's so much I want t'tell you an' I can't stand 'ere for long – me legs are giving me gyp.'

Annie led the way and ten minutes later they were seated at the table with steaming cups of tea in front of them. Annie waited until the woman had taken several sips of her tea, all the while doing her best to control her curiosity, before saying, 'Perhaps a good start would be to tell me your name.'

'I'm Phyllis Wilson, Robert Wilson's mother, and before you jump to any daft conclusions, please, hear me out. By the way, I got your name and address from Bill Webb.'

Annie wrinkled her forehead. 'I don't think I know a Bill Webb.'

'He owns a number of lorries, his firm is William Webb an' Sons. My Robert used to work for him – well, in a way, he still does. On an' off, you might say.'

Suddenly it dawned on Annie. In her mind's eye she could picture Mr Webb as clear as anything. He'd gone out of his way to help her, and so had his son. She remembered they both had a shock of reddish hair. Mr Webb had spoken to her sternly but kindly. He it was who had insisted that Robert came down from Scotland to meet her and to see his children. Not that his visit had done much good! Still, she had a lot to be grateful for when it came to talking about Mr Webb, and if this woman had been sent by him, she had nothing to fear.

Phyllis Wilson watched the different emotions flit across Annie's face and wondered how she should begin her tale. It was seeing the picture of Ronnie and Mary in a frame on the mantelshelf that made her decide what to do. If this young lass were willing to listen, then she would start at the beginning, tell her the truth, everything, the good and bad things that were in her heart.

'I was in a 'ome until I was fourteen,' she began. 'Then I was turfed out, found a place in service and left to get on with my life as best I could. As far as I knew I hadn't a living relative anywhere in this world, and as for boyfriends and suchlike, I was as innocent as they come. For two years I slogged from early morning till far into the night for that family, where the only kind words I ever got came from the cook. Family members scarcely ever looked at me, let alone spoke to me. All my orders came from the butler. Then one day I fell down a flight of stone steps and the youngest son helped me up. I thought he was *so* kind.'

She sipped her tea before continuing. 'For two whole months I was seeing him on the quiet. Yes, and I was daft enough to believe that he loved me. God, the shemozzle when the missus found I was pregnant, and I thought she was going to kill me when I told her I'd been with no one but her son! My feet weren't allowed to touch the ground. I was out of that house before you could say Jack Robinson. I had the baby, a boy. The unmarried mothers' 'ome let me stay on and work there for six months. Then, because I wouldn't agree to 'aving the baby adopted, I was once again kicked out. Anyway, I rented two rooms and

I managed. Some of the jobs I did in order to keep us both you don't want to know about. When Robert was coming up to school-leaving age I wasn't well – went funny in the 'ead, if you must know – and ended up shut away in a nut 'ouse.' She laughed bitterly. 'Robert, that's the name I gave him, came t'see me once a week, on a Sunday afternoon, for the first two months. Then he stopped coming. When I was finally discharged, an old neighbour let me lodge with her. She had been very good to me over the years. For months on end, day in day out, I tried to track down my boy. He'd gone. Disappeared, left not a trace. Well, later on I met a man, a good man, and we decided to live together. Never got married, though. Then one day we were reading the local paper and the outcome of that was I discovered my son was in Wormwood Scrubs. After making a lot of enquiries I also learned that he'd been married and that I 'ad two grandchildren. The rest I found out from the newspapers.'

Phyllis looked drained, and Annie's heart went out to her. 'Even as a lad he had a temper,' she continued. 'I should know, 'aving been on the receiving end of his fists many a time. Seems he nearly killed the bloke his wife went off with. And assaulted one of the policemen.'

Annie now felt compelled to ask, 'What has brought you to me? All this happened a long time ago.'

Phyllis told her, 'Didn't bother to follow it up until my Andy died, and then I suppose I was feeling sorry for meself. Kind of lonely, yer know. Thought 'ow great it would be if I could see me grandchildren and maybe me daughter-in-law. Even thought she might turn out to be friendly. 'Cos at that time I didn't know she was dead.'

'Such a sad story, isn't it?' Annie said patiently.

'Yes, poor lass. Seems she wasn't any better than she

should be, but all the same no one deserves to die the way she did. That lover of hers cleared off as soon as they got chucked out of the pub. Dorothy was too drunk to walk and she fell down. Poor soul wasn't found until the next morning. Terrible! Choked on her own vomit. When I read that, I felt for her.'

'I know,' Annie agreed. 'No one deserves to die like that.' Then she decided she didn't want to listen to any more; she thought she had put all this behind her. Swiftly she picked up the cups and saucers and headed for the scullery, saying, 'I'll make a fresh pot of tea.'

Phyllis got to her feet and followed, stopping in the doorway. 'All I really wanted was to find out what had happened to the children. I traced me son to Webb's, and they gave me his address in Scotland. I made that journey, for all the good it's done me.'

Annie turned her head sharply. 'You mean you've met up with Robert?'

'Yeah,' she paused and sighed heavily. 'He didn't wanna know. Settled all right with a woman named Pauline . . .' She half smiled. 'I felt sorry for her. Thought she was onto a good thing when my son took her and her twin boys on, so she told me. Found out different, ain't she? Seems my Robert is all right when he's working, but he likes the drink too much. When I finally got to where they were living, he wasn't there. He was in 'ospital, something wrong with his liver. I went to that 'ospital to see him, but he told me not t'come again. I went back to their 'ouse, thinking that Pauline might at least be friendly towards me. Couldn't 'ave been more wrong. She didn't even ask me into the 'ouse. Kept me standing on the doorstep. I asked about me grandchildren, an' all the answer I got was that they were nought t'do with her.'

'I have the children with me, you know,' Annie said.

'I do know that now, and if young Mr Webb had told me that in the first place I need never 'ave gone all the way to Scotland.' Phyllis stared around the living-room, thinking to herself, this is a lived-in room, homely, warm, and comfortable.

'You still haven't told me why you've come to me. Are you thinking of making a claim on your grandchildren?'

Phyllis looked shocked. 'Oh no, my dear. No, it's nothing like that. I'm in no position to care for them. Too old, for one thing. Only got a one-bedroom flat. When I got back to London I went to Webb's again and this time I was lucky to catch Mr Webb himself. It was his son that gave me Robert's address in Scotland. Mr Webb told me of your visit and how you had met my son, but I expect you've already guessed as much. He told me you were a kind, caring young lady, that he was one hundred per cent sure that the two kiddies were being well cared for, living with you. Right as rain, was how he put it.'

The kettle came to the boil and Annie made another pot of tea. Setting it aside to brew, she walked over to the window. 'I thought your son was a selfish, miserable man with no thought for anyone except himself. I'm sorry, but it's the truth. He didn't give a hoot about his children. Wouldn't even have bothered to tell them their mother had died if I hadn't insisted that he did so.'

Phyllis nodded. 'One thing I 'ave t'tell you . . . He declared outright that he was not the father of the little girl.'

Annie swung round to face her. 'I had a feeling you were going to bring that up,' she said angrily. 'What kind of a man is he? Poor little mite; he was openly hostile when he saw her, and that was only very briefly. Mary her name is, and it wouldn't have hurt him to have shown a little kindness towards her. She has never been a burden to him, fostered out, pushed from pillar to post until my father brought Dot Wilson to live in our house with her children. Anyway, he'd have a job proving he's not her father. It's his surname that is on her birth certificate, and I'd hate anyone ever to tell her any different.'

Phyllis held out her hands and nodded solemnly. 'I understand what you're saying, an' I couldn't be more sorry. I'll forget he ever told me that. Honest, I will. As far as I'm concerned I 'ave two grandchildren, and I'm hoping against hope that you'll let me 'ave some contact with them. Maybe see them . . . just once now and again?'

Annie thought about this old lady. She was neatly but poorly dressed, and if what she had said was true, she hadn't had much of a life.

'You've made me feel a bit guilty. I have to tell you that my husband and I have applied to adopt Mary and Ronnie.'

Phyllis pulled out a handkerchief and wiped her eyes. 'What on earth 'ave you got to feel guilty about?' she sniffed. 'You're about to offer them a new life, a good one, from what I've learnt so far. You've cared for those kiddies even though their mother went off and left them. Some women should never 'ave children. As for their father! I found my son, but I wasn't impressed. I had no good feelings toward him. In fact I wasn't a bit sorry that he told me not to keep in touch with him.'

'Are you saying that you'd have no objection to my husband and me adopting your grandchildren?' Annie's voice was full of disbelief.

Phyllis laughed. 'None at all. In fact I think it is wonderful!'

Annie's sigh was one of utter relief. 'You do realize that legally you have more right to them than we do?'

'Look, luv, I've already told you I didn't come 'ere looking for what's legal or to claim me rights an' all that. I tried to find first me son an' then me grandchildren, an' that's all. When you've been brought up in a home, no relatives to send birthday cards to or spend Christmas with, you get a bit lonely as you get older. And, believe you me, there's nothing worse than loneliness. I'm all for your adopting them if you and your 'usband agree. Let the kiddies 'ave this chance, as I said. A new life, and I hope it's a happy one for all of you. Kids can bring you joy, if they're treated properly. Though there's no telling 'ow they're gonna turn out.'

There was a long silence, each deep in thought, until Annie broke it by saying, 'Would you be prepared to tell the court that you are fully agreeable for the adoption to go ahead?'

With a sob in her voice, Phyllis answered, 'I've learned a lot by coming here today. Yes, Annie, I swear to you that I think it would be very much in the interest of my grandchildren to have you for their mother.'

Annie walked forward and embraced Phyllis. 'Thank you! I'm so glad you *did* come here today.'

They were both wiping away their tears when the front door opened and Rhoda called out, 'Jack's just gone to the paper shop. He said to tell you to put the kettle on.'

At the doorway, Rhoda stood still. Annie saw the startled look in her eyes, and grinned. 'Come on in, Gran,' she said lightly, making the introductions. 'This is Phyllis Wilson and this is Rhoda Bateman. You both have something in common: namely two grandchildren who will, please God, soon be registered under the names of Ronald and Mary Higgins.' Annie thought she had never seen such stark emotion on two elderly ladies' faces, and as she turned away to give them a minute to compose themselves, she saw that her husband had come in.

'Oh, Jack, you'll never believe this!' Annie's voice betrayed so much happiness that he quickly answered, 'I hope I shall.'

Going to the dresser, Jack brought out the bottle of whisky and four glasses. Then he held his hand out to Phyllis. 'I'm Jack Higgins, and if you are who I think you are, than I really am very pleased to meet you.'

Annie could contain herself no longer. 'Her full name is Phyllis Wilson, and Ronnie and Mary are her two grandchildren. Not only is she willing for us to become their parents, but she is willing to tell the court exactly why she feels the way she does.'

Jack, who had been standing with one arm across Rhoda's shoulders, now put his other arm round Phyllis and drew her close. 'Seems I shall have to watch me step. Be like having two mothers-in-law to cope with!'

Phyllis gave a great sob, and her whole body shuddered. Rhoda broke free from Jack and stood in front of her. 'Whatever is the matter? Please don't get so upset. Just tell us what's wrong, an' we'll see what we can do.'

It was quite a while before the poor woman could control her crying and bring herself to speak. When she did, her words were barely audible. 'You're all being so kind. Taking me at face value. Asking no questions. It's as if you're letting me belong and . . . I've . . . I've never 'ad a family before. Never.'

Annie was all of a fluster. 'I made another pot of tea. I'll pour it out.'

'Not since I came in you 'aven't,' Rhoda declared

442

loudly. 'So, if you did, it must be well an' truly stewed by now.'

'Tea is not what anyone one wants,' Jack stated, breaking the seal on the bottle of whisky and pouring out four good measures. When they were all seated they sipped their drinks, each smiling, unsure how to proceed.

Annie watched the woman who had just come into her life and said a silent prayer of thanks. She felt sure she could trust her, even become friends with her, maybe even love her – the poor woman hadn't had much love in her life up till now. She got to her feet, saying, 'I'm just going to make a few sandwiches.'

'I'll give you a hand,' Jack volunteered.

Closing the door, Annie began to relate what she had been told. However, because she was so excited her words were jumbled – confused to say the least.

'Ssh, ssh, ssh.' Jack took his wife into his arms. 'Time enough for all the explanations later on. I've grasped the main points that Phyllis is the children's grannie and that she is all for us going ahead with the adoption.'

'More than that, Jack, she's willing to tell the court that their father wants nothing to do with them.'

'All right, hold yer horses. I'm really glad she's turned up, but, please, Annie, don't let's start counting our chickens before they are hatched.'

'Don't you think the court will listen to her?'

'That remains to be seen. She's in an awkward position, is Phyllis Wilson, between the devil and the deep blue sea. All will be fine as long as her son doesn't decide to be awkward.' Then, giving her no time to argue, he bent his head and covered her lips with his own.

When finally they got round to making the sandwiches and taking them through to the living-room, Rhoda and

Phyllis were chatting away as if they had known each other all their lives. With her hat and coat now removed, Phyllis looked nice. Her hair, once dark brown, was now much of it grey and coarse. Her eyes were brown and round, very much the same as Ronnie's. Her mouth was her best feature, the lips full as if ready at all times to smile. She was certainly short and stout, but not fat. Motherly was the word for her. Against all odds she had done her best to hold on to her son and be a good mother to him until he was the age to leave school, and then look what had happened to her! Shut away in a madhouse with no one to visit or even care if she never came out. It didn't bear thinking about. Now all she was asking was the right to see and love her own grandchildren.

They were all quiet while eating, until Rhoda said, 'It's been quite a day of revelations, hasn't it?'

'Yes, it certainly has,' Phyllis replied.

'Will you mind telling the court how your son feels about his children?'

Annie drew in her breath sharply. Her gran shouldn't be asking that kind of question. Phyllis considered for a moment before she said, 'No, I think the way he has behaved towards them is utterly disgusting. What his wife did was not right, but two wrongs don't make a right either. Throughout life we're all confronted with decisions at one time or another. Most of them are never simple. You look back on them and you think you should have done this or that, but at the time, I suppose, we all do what we think is best. Looking back now, perhaps I should have had Robert adopted. I was never able to give him much of a life. He never knew the joy of having a father. But I never for a moment let him think he was not wanted. All those years I worked and kept him with no help from anyone.'

She nodded her head as if to assure them it was true, and then went on, 'If only I hadn't got ill, if only . . .'

Now Rhoda jerked her head at Jack. 'Pour us another drink, lad. I think we all need one.' Then, quickly turning her attention to Phyllis again, she said, 'Well, what about it? Are you willing to take all of us on? Because you've let yourself in for something good an' proper. You know that, don't you?'

They stared at each other. Phyllis's expression was sad, but Rhoda's at that moment was jovial as ever as she added, 'There are more of us than what's in this room. There's Doris an' Frank, two lonely ducks at one time, now married very happily and, by the way, they adore the children. So do Peter and Vera, another pair of good friends they are. You'll get on well with Vera. Yes, two of a kind I'd say you were. Then there's neighbours by the dozen, number one being Gladys Dawson, heart of gold she 'as. Do anything for young Ronnie and Mary.'

'Stop it, Gran,' Annie pleaded. 'You'll frighten Phyllis so much she won't want to come here again.'

Phyllis's face lit up. 'Don't you believe it, Annie. I suppose ye could say I ain't 'ad much luck in me life, but coming 'ere today was meant to be. The good Lord was on my side for once.' With that, she got up and added, 'Don't want to wear me welcome out, though. I wrote me name an' address down just in case you were out. I was gonna push it through yer letterbox.' Taking a sheet of notepaper from her bag she handed it to Jack, saying, 'I mean it. Anything I can do to help, I will.' Once again the poor woman wasn't far from tears.

Jack took it. 'Come on now, dry your eyes. Before we go any further, we all want you to come and meet Ronnie and Mary. Don't we?' he said, turning to Annie and Rhoda.

Both women were by now tearful, but managed to nod their heads in complete agreement.

They were grouped together on the doorstep when Jack made his final suggestion. 'Phyllis, why don't you come to us for Sunday dinner? Rhoda here is famous for her roasts. Every Sunday almost it is the gathering of the clans, and Rhoda gets here nice an' early in order to take charge.'

'Oh . . . I couldn't impose . . . not like that.'

'Why ever not?' Rhoda asked.

'Of course that's the best idea,' Annie declared. 'Give us time to tell the children all about you. They will be thrilled to bits to know they've got another grandma. Please, Phyllis, say you will come.'

'I'll fetch you in the car,' Jack volunteered.

'I would certainly love to come,' Phyllis said, 'but only if you're sure, and you mustn't think about coming for me. I can get a bus easily enough.'

'That's all right, then,' Jack told her. 'Come as early as you like. I promise Ronnie and Mary will be on the lookout for you.'

Rhoda went back indoors, her heart too full to watch the poor soul go up the road. Jack and Annie remained until she reached the corner, where she stopped, turned and waved her hand. They waved back.

Then, rubbing her eyes, Annie said, 'I love you, Jack.' Her arms came round his neck and pulled his head down and it was she who delivered the sweet lingering kiss. Finally he broke away and stood still, stroking her hair. Suddenly she murmured, 'Want to know something, Jack? I'd die if you stopped loving me.'

He murmured in answer, 'Then you'll live to be a very old lady, because I aim to live for a very long time and always with you by my side.'

Chapter Thirty-eight

DURING A SLEEPLESS NIGHT Annie had tossed and turned, her mind crowded with doubts. Had they done the right thing in asking Phyllis Wilson to spend the day with them? She badly wanted to believe that if she were to become part of the children's lives, it had to be for the best. She knew there were some good people in this world, kind and concerned and compassionate, and then again some who have been ill used, and are alone with their troubles and pain. Was Phyllis one of the good people, in spite of falling into the second category?

Even after such a short meeting, Annie felt she was a lovely person despite all the hard knocks life had dealt her. But would Ronnie and Mary feel the same way? A few days earlier she and Jack had sat the children down and told them about their grandma's visit. Ronnie had listened attentively, as he mostly did. Mary had been on the verge of tears and had hardly spoken since, despite all their efforts to reassure her. It was a blessing that the children were still on their summer holiday; it would

447

give them time to get used to the idea of having a new grandmother before they had to return to school.

Now Sunday had arrived and it had to be faced. Although it was only six o'clock she decided to get up, make a cup of tea and start thinking about getting the dinner. She'd been downstairs only about ten minutes when the door opened and Jack said, 'There wasn't any need for you to get up so early. I know what's worrying you, and it's daft. It's an ordinary Sunday with just one more for dinner, and you'll have plenty of help as you always do. Nothing will go wrong.'

'How can you say that, Jack? We haven't a clue as t'how the children will react, Mary in particular.'

'Well, Phyllis Wilson is used to being snubbed. If the worst comes to the worst, she'll take it all in her stride.' He came and sat beside her at the table, took her hand, and held it tightly. They sat together like that for a while, until he said, 'You're meeting trouble half-way, imagining that all sorts of things will go wrong today, and that's silly. There will be enough of us here and everything will go smoothly. I promise.'

'You can't make that promise. You know no more than I do about how Mary will react.'

'That's true. But sometimes we have to go along with our instincts. I admit we really know nothing about Mrs Wilson except what she's told us. To me, she came across as a decent human being, a truthful caring lady with qualities that mean a lot. She admitted that although the children's father is her son, she has never been married, but by God she's not come through this life unscathed. That much I'm sure is true. She's an old lady now, lonely, and it strikes me that if she is willing to make a commitment and help us in our efforts to adopt Ronnie and Mary, she deserves to be allowed to try and form a relationship with the children. Ronnie we know will accept her, willingly and cheerfully, because he is that kind of lad. As to Mary, of course she's going to be wary, even scared. You represent stability to her, she clings to you because you are the only person in her short life that has shown her constant love. Her fears and problems are deep-rooted. We have to give her time. Just be there for her. Impress on her that no one is going to take her away from us.'

All the while he had been talking Jack had held her hand. Now she leaned towards him. 'What would I do without you? I'd worked myself up into a right old state.'

'Yeah, well, have a bit of faith in yourself. You make everyone feel welcome, you always have. Now come on. We'd better get dressed before our guests start arriving.'

Annie knew immediately that her gran was looking forward to having Phyllis Wilson join them for the day. She supposed that over the years she had acquired a second sense about Rhoda's different moods, and she recognized she was in a very good one this morning. Having gone to the front door to bring the milk in at the same moment as her gran arrived, they had kissed and all the cheerful signs were there. She dearly wanted this Sunday to be a happy, carefree day. It could be a turning point in all of their lives.

'I don't know why you had to do all the vegetables yourself,' Rhoda said, smiling, as she took off her coat and came into the kitchen. 'I always help you, don't I?'

'Yes, you do,' Annie answered quickly, 'but I'd been up since the crack of dawn and I needed something to fill the time. You don't mind, do you?'

'No, of course not.' Rhoda took an apron from her

bag, tied it round her waist and moved towards the big table, obviously anxious to start mixing the batter for the Yorkshire puddings and to make the pastry for her famous apple pies.

'Shall I pour you a drink or will you wait until Jack gets back? He's gone to pick up Phyllis, thought it would be a nice gesture, took the kids with him. By the way, we've invited Gladys Dawson to join us. Her daughter Phoebe and her family are away hop-picking – they'll be gone for about six weeks.'

'Hop-picking? I didn't think that started until the autumn.'

'Well, what's this if it's not the autumn? We're already in the first week of September. It's been a gorgeous summer, both the children are as brown as berries, but I think they'll be glad to go back to school when the new term starts next week.'

'My goodness, how this year has flown by! Anyway I think it was kind of you to invite Gladys. She's been a good friend and neighbour over the years.'

Annie laughed. 'I had an ulterior motive, Gran. I thought if Gladys learned first-hand about the children's grandmother turning up, we might put it to some good.'

'How d'you mean?'

'Well, hopefully she'll get on well with Phyllis an' she'll spread the word. Give her a good report, and you know how quickly word will spread. I'm kind of hoping that maybe the kids at school will hear from their parents that Mary really does have some proper relations and not tease her so much.'

'Why, you crafty old thing! But I agree, Gladys gets on well with most folk, and get her on Phyllis's side an' we're 'ome an' dried.'

At the sound of the front door opening and heels clicking along the linoleum of the passage, Rhoda and Annie looked up from what they were doing. It seemed that almost everyone had arrived at the same time.

Doris opened the living-room door and ushered Phyllis Wilson in, cheerfully saying, 'Morning, Annie, morning Rhoda! We all met up outside, and Gladys was standing at her gate. She called out that she'll be along in a few minutes.'

Annie immediately threw her arms around her, saying, 'You look great.' She felt better already. With Doris here she had a friend and a true ally, besides which, Mary trusted her.

'Thanks, I feel good, it's such a lovely day,' Doris responded, smiling her usual sunny smile.

'I must say you don't look so bad yourself. I told you that dress would suit you. Sage green goes so well with your hair. Aren't you glad you bought it?'

'I didn't have much choice; you pushed me into it!'

They both giggled and turned to where Rhoda and Phyllis were chatting away to each other. They were both grandmothers, but looked totally different. Rhoda carried her years well, seventy-two, yet seemed years younger. She was a tall handsome woman even if her face did always look so weather-beaten. Phyllis Wilson looked so much more serious. Short and stout, shabby by comparison. Annie felt a wave of sympathy for her. Even the life she had been forced to lead was not remotely similar to Rhoda's. Her father had certainly provided well for them. The house they were thinking of moving into was set in a nice area south of the river, the money from his insurance policy still mostly lay in the bank, and the cash they had found in his tin box had been very useful to her, Ronnie and Mary until Jack had become master of the house. Yes, each one of them had a great deal to be grateful to her father for, and none more than Vera and Peter, who were the only ones who hadn't arrived yet.

A hearty laugh from Rhoda broke into Annie's thoughts. Gran's attitude to life was spontaneous, outgoing, filled with a love that was infectious. She was never happier than when she had company to care for, felt wanted, and it wasn't only family that it applied to; she had that effect on everyone.

Today was probably going to be very difficult for Phyllis. She had never known a loving family. It must have taken guts for her to set out on a mission to find her son and then get only rejection, but to continue with the quest for her grandchildren was more than most would have done. Perhaps we shall become the family she's never had, Jack and me and Ronnie and Mary.

At that moment she noticed that Phyllis was bending down and speaking earnestly to Mary. The child wasn't looking at her, but down at the floor. Then, without any warning, Mary gave the old lady a push which sent her reeling backwards, turned and ran across the room to bury her face in Annie's lap. Seeing that Jack and Frank were helping Phyllis to get up, she took Mary by the hand and led her upstairs. She closed bedroom the door, sat Mary on the bed and drew a chair up close for herself.

'Mary,' Annie began, 'you're being very naughty and I don't know why. Are you going to tell me?'

The little girl ground her teeth and Annie knew without a doubt that she was feeling unwanted. She wanted to scoop her up in her arms and hug her tight. I mustn't, she vowed to herself. If I give in to her now, she'll never take to her gran. What am I supposed to do? She felt tears pricking her own eyes. Impatiently, she rubbed them away, swallowed hard and said, as steadily as she could, 'You promised me you were going to be good.'

Mary looked up at Annie, her cheeks wet with tears, and it was all she could do not to take her in her arms and hold her close. 'Come on, Mary, tell me what's wrong.'

She shook her head so hard it made her beautiful fair hair swing. and took a long time to answer, but at last she said, ''Ow d'yer know that lady is really our grandmuvver?'

Oh hell, Annie muttered to herself, puckering her brow, don't pick this morning to find your voice and start asking questions. Have we been unfair, bringing Phyllis into the house, forcing the children to meet her? 'Of course she is, pet. Jack and I spent ages telling you all about her.'

'Where's she come from? What's she want?'

Annie willed herself to be patient. 'As we told you, she is your father's mother.'

'We ain't got no farver,' said Mary stubbornly.

'And who told you that?'

'Dunno.'

'You know that isn't true. After your mother died your father had to go away for a time, and that was when he found work up in Scotland and you came to live with us. Do you remember Uncle Jim?'

'Yeah, course I do.' Then with a sob she added, 'I wish he hadn't got knocked down an' killed. He wouldn't let 'er take us away from you.'

'Mary, I wouldn't lie to you or to Ronnie. No one is going to take you away. You are going to stay here living with Jack and me. It is true that Mrs Wilson is your grandmother because she is your father's mother.'

'Then why don't she live near 'im? Your mum lives near us. We see 'er all the time,' said Mary logically.

Annie's mouth tightened. She would give anything to make this child trust her. 'It hasn't worked out like that. Mrs Wilson was ill for a long time, and by the time she got better, your dad had moved away to Scotland and they'd lost touch with each other.'

'Oh,' she murmured, 'you mean she was in a 'ospital?'

'Yes, she was. For a very long time.'

'Is that really true?'

'Cross my heart, Mary,' said Annie looking deadly serious.

'And me dad never went t'see 'er?'

'Well, he did at first.'

'You mean he stopped going, an' he ain't seen 'is muvver for a long time?'

What could Annie say to that? 'I'm afraid that's about right,' she finally managed.

'Oh,' Mary said again, then her voice faltered. 'Just like me an' me bruvver.' Her voice was barely more than a whisper.

'What do you mean?' Annie asked, dreading to hear the answer, but knowing that she must.

'Me dad don't want 'er any more than he wants us.'

'Out of the mouths of babes and sucklings' was the thought that came to Annie. Now she groaned as she picked Mary up and gave her a cuddle. 'You're too wise for your own good, young lady,' she told the frightened little girl as she wiped her face with a clean handkerchief. 'It doesn't matter too much about your dad. You and Ronnie have me, Jack, Gran and a whole host of aunts and uncles. In fact you have a nice big family. Isn't that right?'

'Suppose so,' Mary smiled uncertainly.

'Well, poor Mrs Wilson hasn't got anybody. We've invited her to come to our house today and share our dinner. It could turn out to be a very happy day if only you would try and be kind to her. That isn't too much to ask, is it?' Mary hesitated, then shook her head. 'Good girl. Now I'd better brush your hair again an' we'll go downstairs and see what everyone is getting up to.'

'Will she be cross 'cos I pushed 'er over?' Mary asked cautiously.

'I think she would be pleased if you were to tell her you were sorry,' said Annie solemnly.

Mary set her small shoulders back firmly. 'Well, all right then, an' I'll tell 'er I won't be nasty to 'er no more.'

'That would be a very nice thing to do,' Annie agreed, giving in, hoping that from now on she'd be able to keep a peaceful atmosphere.

Rhoda had the situation in hand. 'Come along, Mary,' she said, grasping the child by the hand. 'Yer Aunt Vera an' Uncle Peter 'ave arrived; come and say 'allo t'them. Jack has poured you out a lemonade.'

Annie decided she was going to leave them all to get on with it. But first to Phyllis, she nodded her head and smiled, and this time her smile was one of reassurance.

Then she turned to Doris. 'Want to help me lay the table? We'll have to put the extra leaf in today.' She picked up the cutlery tray and led the way into the front room.

'How many are we going to be for dinner?' Doris asked.

'About a dozen, I think. Let's see, there's you an' Frank, Vera an' Peter, Gran an' Phyllis Wilson, me, Jack and the two children, an' we mustn't forget Gladys. I guess that makes eleven altogether.'

'Pity we couldn't find another stray, make it a round dozen.'

They laughed, and Annie said, 'I think we've got more than enough to contend with as it is.'

'I think you're right. All I can say is, thank God your gran's doing most of the cooking.'

Annie grinned at the expression on her friend's face. 'I know what you mean. Luckily Gran is in her element when she's got a crowd to feed.'

'Will we be able to get everything on the table?'

'I thought we'd set up the vegetable dishes on the sideboard. Just put the meat and Yorkshire puddings on the plates, with the roast potatoes, gravy boats, horseradish, mustard and the cruets on the table, then you and I can pass the other dishes over one at a time.'

Doris nodded, but did not say anything for a few minutes, just stood staring into space. There was a funny expression on her face. Eventually, she said, 'I've been right puzzled these last few days. I just couldn't believe all you told me about Mrs Wilson. The way she's been treated! But now, having met her, I don't think it has made her bitter. I hope the children will accept her and take to her.'

Annie walked round the table and gave Doris a hug. 'You really are a good friend, and a marvellous auntie to Ronnie and Mary. You do think Jack and I are doing the right thing in applying to adopt them, don't you?'

Doris gave a heartfelt sigh. 'Oh, Annie, what do you want me to say? From the beginning I thought you had been pushed into a terrible situation. Bad enough that their mother went off and left them both in your house. It wasn't so bad when your dad was alive. But then . . . a young girl, two kids that were nothing t'do with her, not many would have stood for it. You – you took it in yer stride. Honestly, I think the way you've coped has been fantastic. Nobody could have done more for those kids than you have.'

They stayed quiet for a while, until Doris said, 'An' I'll tell you another thing. Frank and I feel great being part of this family. Everything has worked out so well for all of us. Look at Jack! Dead lonely he was, and with good cause, wouldn't you say? Most folk lost someone in the war, but he had his whole family wiped out. You two were made for each other, and yes, Frank and I, we're right behind you in this adoption business.'

Annie turned what Doris had said over in her mind, then, with a light laugh, said, 'We'd better get a move on with setting this table and we've got to bring some odd chairs down from the bedrooms.'

Doris picked up a pile of paper serviettes and began to fold them in half. Annie was filling two salt-cellars when Doris said, 'It's all going to go off really well, Annie. This Sunday dinner is going to be the best, and the happiest, we've ever shared.' She uttered the words with such conviction that Annie believed her.

Very late that night when she climbed into bed and snuggled up to Jack, she was truly grateful that Doris had made that prediction. It had been one hundred per cent true.

Chapter Thirty-nine

ANNIE LIKED JAMES OLIVER the minute she walked into his office. He looked so fit. Tall, well built, but by no means overweight, with dark eyes, dark wavy hair and a pleasant face. Almost immediately, she felt at ease with him. He obviously knew what he was talking about, was totally in command of the situation, yet he had a quiet, reserved manner which gave Annie complete confidence. At last, she felt there was hope that the adoption would go through. With Mr Oliver in charge and Phyllis Wilson prepared to tell the court that she was in full agreement, there surely wouldn't be any more ifs and buts.

'Thanks for coming in at such short notice,' he said as he shook hands with Jack. 'And it's very nice to meet you, Mrs Higgins.'

Once they were seated, Mr Oliver sat facing them behind his desk. He was very good at breaking the ice, making people feel comfortable. Looking at Annie, he said, 'We've had an amazing stroke of luck. I've managed to get you a hearing at the assizes for the thirteenth of February.'

Annie's face dropped a mile. 'February? But that's nearly six months away.'

'That's not very long, Mrs Higgins,' he assured her, smiling. 'With so many adoptions coming up before the courts, the wait can be as long as two years. All I need today is for both of you to sign these papers, and then I can proceed.'

Annie cast a dismayed glance at Jack, but before she could say a word, he exclaimed, 'Time will soon pass, and at least we now know that things are on the move.' Annie couldn't think of a reply.

Mr Oliver asked some more questions about the first meeting she had had with Robert Wilson and just how the children had reacted to his visit. Annie told him. He mentioned the fact that their mother was dead, and Annie said that the children hadn't been aware of that until she had insisted that their father tell them.

Jack listened to them talking, occasionally joining in. Then Mr Oliver, as if bringing the serious business to a close, said to Annie, 'Your husband tells me you are going to move, going south of the Thames to a big house.'

'Yes, we are. A week today, actually. The children will be starting at their new school and they'll each be able to have a bedroom of their own.'

He nodded. 'Well, that will be another point in our favour when the application is heard.' He got to his feet. After handshakes again all round, he promised to let them know every step of the way what was taking place, and with that Annie had to be content.

They stood on the pavement, undecided as to what to do. The meeting was over much quicker than either of them had anticipated. 'What say we pay a visit to Vera and Peter?' Jack said out of the blue. Then, seeing the puzzled look on Annie's face, he quickly added, 'I don't mean go to the house. I know you an' Gran have been going there almost every day, but how long since you went to their workshop?'

'Oh, I dunno. Ages, I suppose. But Vera knows how busy we've been, hanging curtains, seeing the right floor-covering was laid in the right rooms, being there when the gas-men brought the cooker, besides all the packing we've had to do at home.'

'I wasn't criticizing you. It was just something I heard Vera telling Gran last Sunday that made me think we ought to take more of an interest in what they were doing.'

'What d'yer mean? What was she telling Gran?'

'It sounded to me like they were thinking of expanding a bit. Anyway, we can't stand here all the morning, you want to go or not?'

Annie grinned. 'You know very well wild horses wouldn't keep me away. I'm dying to find out what their plans are. I do feel a bit guilty – haven't given much of my time to Vera lately.'

'I didn't tell you to make you feel guilty, and I'm sure Vera understands only too well the pressure you've been under. Anyway the car's only just round the corner, so shall we get going?'

Holding hands, they broke into a run, laughing like a couple of children who were hopping the wag from school.

Even before they got their feet in the doorway Vera was letting them know how pleased she was to see them. 'All the work is going on downstairs, but come and see the

461

difference we've made to what you called a hall, Annie, when you first saw it.' Vera led the way.

Minutes later the three of them stood in the middle of the long room with tall windows which, as Annie remembered, looked out on a peaceful country lane. Surveying the work that had been done by a local builder with the added help of Mike O'Halloran, and the pretty drapes that hung around the walls, Annie exclaimed excitedly, 'I can't believe it, Vera!' She looked around, taking everything in. 'You have done wonders!'

Vera looked very pleased with herself. 'Remember the room we worked out had been a works café during the war?'

'Yes, and all the cupboards stacked with china,' Annie answered.

'Come through an' see what we've done in there.'

'Hang on a minute,' Jack interrupted. 'I think I'm gonna leave you two to natter on together. Is Peter in today?'

'Yes, he's downstairs. Since we've had special handrails built on to the walls, he finds it much easier to manoeuvre himself down there. Mike has taught him a lot. Mostly how to do minor repairs to the sewing-machines if the girls have a problem. Go on down, he'll be pleased to see you.'

With Jack gone, Annie started to walk around the long room which was now so very much more than just the cutting-room. 'D'you mind me prowling round here first?' she asked, nodding towards the new shelves that held lovely pieces of china, glass candlesticks and the most gorgeous tablecloths and serviettes that Annie had ever seen.

'Of course I don't. Take your time.'

At the far end, the settings changed. Annie gathered that the front end of the room held accessories for dining-rooms. This area was for bedrooms. Satin-edged blankets, linen sheets and pillowcases, not plain white, which had been the only thing available for years and then only mainly on coupons, but these goods were in the prettiest of pastel colours. There were small lamps with frilled shades made of the same material as the lovely bedspreads on display. Then there were the window curtains. Some hung from brass rails, some from mahogany poles, tied back with silk ropes from which dangled heavy tassels. Lloyd Loom wicker armchairs held plump cushions, some made to tone in with the colours of the curtains, others matching exactly.

'All this is fabulous!' Annie cried out, 'but how has it all come about? Surely you haven't made enough money to buy all this stock already, have you?'

'Of course I haven't, an' t'be truthful it wasn't my idea.'

'Well, do tell me how it's happened, because I'm like the cat – my curiosity is killing me.'

'All right.' Vera then began to laugh. 'It started because my feet were killing me. No, don't look at me as if I've gone mad; it's absolutely true. Word got about that we were making good curtains, and before we'd time to look around we had more orders than we could cope with. But the snag was, they were all well-off folk that wanted us not only to make their curtains and go to their homes and hang them, but all the matching trimmings that went with such an order. Honest, Annie, you wouldn't believe the traipsing about I was doing. Finding silk tassels, fringes and cords, an' 'alf the time when I took them to the house, the customer would complain that they weren't exactly what she had had in mind.' Vera took a deep breath, and Annie cut in.

'You certainly let yourself in for more than you bargained for, didn't you?'

'I was on the point of packing it all in. Then, I was in the haberdashery department of Bon Marché at Brixton one morning when the floor walker said the manger of the software would like a word with me. I almost told him t'get lost 'cos I couldn't spare the time, but ain't I glad I didn't! Mr Parnell turned out to be a very good businessman. He told me he'd noticed how often I was coming into the store to buy accessories and that he'd made enquiries as to what line of work I was in. Then he asked if I'd join him for a cup of coffee, because he had a proposition to put to me. To cut the story short, all this is down to him and the owners of Bon Marché. It don't cost me a penny. They show their goods off in our premises, we're able to give our customers a choice of what goes with the curtains we're making for them. We pass on their special orders and the store even pays us commission. An' the best bit is, it saves my poor feet. There, what d'you think of that?'

'Wonderful! Everything is so different, unusual.'

'Yes, and the beauty of it is that the folk who order hand-made curtains from me can afford these things. Expensive is not a word they have to think about. After the austerity of the war years with nothing but plain blackout curtains in every room, who can blame them?'

Annie looked thoughtful. 'Aren't you in danger of putting all your eggs in one basket?'

'Peter an' I did talk about that and decided there was no risk. We do still have customers who bring their own material which they've bought elsewhere and come to us to have it made up. They are able to browse through the accessories we can now offer. We also still sell material that we buy wholesale from Dickens & Brown. Bon Marché benefit because they have no needlewomen on the premises. They sell the material and put the making up out to home-workers, but not always with satisfactory results. There is no one in their homes to supervise the work. Promised delivery dates are not always kept to. This way they sell the material, recommend us for the making and, if the customers like all the additional trimmings they see here, the store benefits, and we receive commission as well as getting paid for making the curtains and whatever else they choose to order.'

Annie shook her head in disbelief and Vera laughed at the expression on her face. 'Didn't think I'ad it in me, that's what's going through yer mind, ain't it?'

'That's not it at all, Vera. It's just that it's all happened so fast. But then again you and Peter had your run of bad luck, it was about time that some guardian angel appeared and balanced the books.'

Vera punched her playfully, 'I like to think along those lines, an' all. There were times when I began t'think that we'd reached the end of our tether and God alone knows what 'appened, but I ain't complaining. The difference all this 'as made to Peter is enough for me t'get down on me knees at night and thank the good Lord. But come on. Let's go through to what was the canteen. You'll see a difference in there.'

'I can't believe it!' Annie cried once again. 'This room was all white, cold and bare-looking before.'

'I know. It's kind of cosy now, don't you think?'

'It's more than that, it's really lovely.'

The walls had been painted in the palest yellow, and

there were six small tables which would seat two or three persons. The tablecloths were sage green, as were the upholstered seats of the high-backed chairs, and the curtains at the windows were in a combination of both colours.

'The chairs and tables were absolutely grotty when we bought them at a second-hand shop,' Vera informed her. 'Peter cleaned them off and gave them two coats of paint. The girls made the curtains down in the workroom, *and* they 'and-covered the chair seats.'

'You're not intending to open this as a café, surely?' Annie asked, still not quite able to take it all in.

'Looks that way, don't it?' Vera laughed. 'In a way, it's true, only there'll be no charge. It was Peter's idea to let the customers sit down in comfort. Don't let them feel they have to make a decision in a 'urry. And while they're looking through the swatches and pattern-books, give them tea, coffee or a cold drink if they prefer. Some we'll even butter up by offering them cakes or scones an' cream, you never know!'

'Why, you crafty old thing! Talk about set a sprat to catch a mackerel.'

'We're going keep the big kitchen that's through there. Staff can warm up their lunch or cook if they feel like it. Come the winter, we might even offer our customers hot soup and a crusty roll.'

Again, Annie said, 'It's unbelievable. A great idea. It will keep the customers here longer, encourage them to choose more of the lovely things you have out on display.'

'Yes, and the best part is that Peter got himself so involved. He says the heavy-duty cooking stove is an absolute gem.' Vera paused and grinned. 'You'll never believe it. He's ordered a big refrigerator, so I'm not looking too far ahead as to what else he has in mind.'

'You mean he might be planning to serve hot meals later on?'

Vera shook her head. 'We haven't got as far as talking along those lines yet.'

With a smile, Annie said, 'I think it's great. I love it.'

'Well, would you like to come downstairs? We haven't done many alterations down there, but it's working well and that's where the money is made.'

Vera led the way. The boarded-up windows had been uncovered, their frames newly painted white. The stair-well had also been painted white, as had the edge of every tread of the stairs. The handrail was bound with non-slip rubber, and that too was white. Because of all the whiteness, the way down to the basement was no longer dark and dingy but airy and light-filled.

'All this is down to Mike O'Halloran,' Vera told her. 'He told Peter the tins of paint fell off the back of a lorry!'

Even the workroom had been totally remodelled and given a new appearance. Maudie Williams and her daughter Maureen called a cheery greeting to Annie, and Peter came forward, smiling broadly, and kissed her.

'I thought you only had four women working here?' Annie asked.

'The extra lady is a relation of Elsie Cooper; we're aiming to keep it all in the family,' Peter grinned. 'But tell me, Annie, what do you think of us so far? Not that we're running before we can walk, I hope.'

'Oh no,' Annie quickly protested. 'You've done marvellously. The things you're showing upstairs are different, unusual. Such goods haven't been in the shops for years.

Everyone is fed up to the teeth with drab colours and the plain old things that used to be all people could buy.'

'Those were my thoughts, too, when Mr Parnell suggested it,' Vera told her. 'Now I think I'm going to bring in a few cheaper lines for the folk that are less well off.'

'Are you? First I've heard of it.' Peter sounded pleased.

'We get plenty of remnants left over from the good curtains that are ordered, so I thought when we get slack periods the women could use them up. Make cushion covers, runners and even short curtains that could sell very cheaply. We could still display them nicely in a different part of the room, and with them we could feature pretty soaps, coloured candles, candlesticks. Perhaps even lavender bags and small bottles of lavender water. Poor people like nice things as well, you know.'

Jack looked at Annie, and they both burst out laughing. 'What's so funny?' Vera demanded.

Annie couldn't stop laughing, so it was Jack who told her. 'For a little woman getting on in years, and from the East End of London at that, you're talking as if Selfridges themselves will have to look to their laurels or otherwise you'll be pinching half their trade.'

Now Peter had joined in the laughter, and Vera, hands on hips, stared at them. 'Go on, laugh all you like, but with the war scarcely over and everyone doing their best to pick up the pieces and make a new life out of the shambles that's left, a bit of colour and a few pretty things ain't gonna go amiss. While I'm on, Jack Higgins, not so much of the getting on in years or I'll box your ears, so I will.'

Applause! They all turned. The women sitting at their sewing-machines were clapping. Suddenly everyone in the room was laughing.

'Sorry, Vera,' Jack said, still grinning. 'I'm just so pleased about what you and Peter are taking on. All your ideas are splendid. I just know you're going to do well. And it'll give you both a new lease of life.'

'It already has,' Peter spoke quietly. 'And when you come to think about it, it's all mainly up to Annie. She could have said, No, she hadn't got the money to buy the house her father had so generously allowed us to live in, instead of fighting our corner. If she hadn't introduced us to the bank manager and Mr Ferguson, well, who knows where we would have ended up. At best I'd have been back in Roehampton Hospital and Vera probably be renting two furnished rooms.'

'I agree,' Vera added quickly. 'But it's more than just the business we're grateful for. You two have made all the difference to our lives. Until we found Rhoda and Annie, we had no one. We got by – we existed, but that was about all. Peter and I mean everything to each other, you know that, but we were sorely in need of help. Now we count our blessings. We have a family. Rhoda and Annie took us on, and now we 'ave you, Jack, and the children and Doris and Frank. You've all been so good . . . we'll never be able to repay you.'

Annie saw that her eyes were brimming and she heard her swallow hard. 'It works both ways,' she told her. 'We have you and Peter, and remember what me gran is always telling us? You're as rich as the number of friends you've got.' Vera could only nod.

Peter looked at his watch. 'It's getting on for one o'clock. Shall we go upstairs and I'll rustle us up some lunch in our café? It's the best offer you'll get today because it's the only free café I know of.'

'But he won't show you a menu. You'll eat what he

469

gives you, or go without,' Vera pointed out. She linked arms with Annie, smiling now, and Annie, as she walked back up the stairs, was thinking what a happy day this was turning out to be.

Chapter Forty

IT WAS A COLD Saturday morning, the first one in November, and with it had come the first snap of frost. Annie felt she couldn't complain, as their move to Tremaine Road had gone very smoothly. The weather during October had helped a great deal. It had been so mild. Real Indian summer weather. Sparkling days, sunny, with bright blue skies. The way things had worked out, Annie had been sure that for once God was on their side. Her gran and Phyllis Wilson must have been feeling exactly the same on this cold but glorious morning. The fact was that they were neighbours now.

Jack had come back from taking Phyllis home, utterly appalled at the conditions in which she was living. He had hardly entered the house before he was describing her flat to Annie and Rhoda. 'The only time I've ever been further than the front door, and if I have my way I'd never set foot in that flat again. Bad enough all those flipping stone stairs she has to climb to get there. Filthy they are, and the walls! The whole building stinks of urine. But the inside!

Gloomy! I don't know, I haven't the words to describe that place. You want to go and see it. I'll tell you one thing, though. I'd stake my life that there's many a farmer in this country whose animals are housed better than the tenants of those flats. Damp doesn't half-way describe it. Even the inside walls are running with water.'

As soon as Jack's tirade had come to an end, Rhoda had said, 'Bad as that, is it, lad?'

'Worse. Honest, Rhoda, you would not believe it. I asked Phyllis if I should light her fire for her and know what she said? I'll see to it, Jack. I've the coal to fetch up first.'

'Fetch up from where?'

'Exactly the question I asked. Then I made it my business to find out. Coal bunkers are round the back of those tenements. Rows of them, out in the open in a yard. Can you imagine what it must be like for her lugging a full scuttle up all those stairs in all weathers?'

Rhoda had been quiet all through the rest of that evening, and as Jack was helping her on with her coat, she had said, 'I think I'll do as you say. Take meself up there tomorrow. If it's as bad as you describe, maybe we should do something about it.'

'Oh, Gran,' Annie had exclaimed, 'will there ever come a time when you stop worrying yourself over other people's problems?'

Rhoda had made a face. 'Blooming old busybody is 'ow you see me, is it?'

Jack was going up the passage, calling, 'I'll start the car up. It's too late for you to walk home.'

'See, I've only a few minutes' walk an' I'll be in me own comfortable warm 'ouse, yet that lad is going to run me 'ome, see me safe an' sound indoors. Phyllis

472

Wilson ain't got a soul in the world t'give an eye t'er well-being.'

Annie had looked very thoughtful and as she was kissing Rhoda goodnight, she'd murmured, 'You're up to something. Going to tell me what it is?'

'Not tonight, luv. I'll sleep on it. Then tomorrow I'll go and see Phyllis, and from that visit . . . well, we'll see.'

And see they had. Rhoda Bateman had never been one for letting the grass grow under her feet, but this time she had exceeded herself. She had actually persuaded the landlord to give the tenancy of Annie's house to Phyllis Wilson. Whether Phyllis would be able to afford the rent had raised a serious question. When told just how much that was, twelve shillings and tenpence per week, Phyllis had smiled before answering, and her answer had had them all falling about laughing.

'Good gracious! That's eighteen pence cheaper than what I'm paying now,' she had declared, and just to make sure, she'd looked at Jack, saying, 'That's right, ain't it? I pay fourteen shillings an' fourpence now.'

'That's right. You'll be one shilling and sixpence a week better off,' Jack had assured her when everyone had stopped laughing.

And so the big day had arrived. Annie had stood in the road and watched her own furniture being brought out of the house and packed into the removal van. Since she had got older she had come to appreciate that little house. She was going to miss it. She would also miss the friendly neighbours and the district. Lytham Street was short, the pavements cobbled, with terraced houses on both sides. There was Ma Turner's grocery shop on the corner – not only a grocers, 'cos she sold everything from candles to a clothes-line. For those truly in need, goods on the slate were available, but try conning Ma and you'd never do it twice. Turn right, and before you came to the embankment there was a big piece of waste ground where, when she and David had been going to school, all the kids met to play, the girls with their skipping ropes, the boys with their iron hoops and whips and tops. Sadly even that had changed since the war had ended. It now held quite a lot of Nissen huts that the council were using to house folk who had been bombed out. She couldn't forget Joey, 'Any 'ole rags, bottles or bones', his usual cry. She doubted that a rag-and-bone man would come pushing his barrow round the area they were moving to. She hoped to God they were doing the right thing in leaving the East End.

Just then another removal van had turned into the road and stopped, and the van-driver had lifted Phyllis down from the tail-board, where she had travelled in style sitting in one of her own fireside chairs. Just to see the smile on Phyllis's face as she had stood on the pavement gazing up at the small windows, where the curtains were still hanging and the starched white lace ones as well, was enough to tell Annie that it was a good move all round. Jack had suggested they leave quite a few bits and bobs behind for Phyllis, because coming from that poky little flat, she hadn't much in the way of furniture to bring with her.

Rhoda had been waiting on the doorstep to welcome Phyllis and to help her settle in. Vera and Doris had taken the day off to be at Tremaine Road to do the same for Jack and Annie. Ronnie and Mary had not yet started at their new school, and their excitement at being told they could climb up into the removal van and travel with the furniture had been infectious. Yes, looking back, Annie felt she could say it had been a very happy, if tiring, day.

Now, more than a month later, she was absolutely sure they had done the right thing. Jack didn't seem to mind his to journey to work a bit, and at the end of each shift he declared it was wonderful to come south of the river.

The children had gone to the Saturday morning pictures and she and Jack were going to do the weekend shopping. Having finished washing up the breakfast dishes and putting them away in the cupboard, she turned to leave the kitchen when her eye fell on the photographs the children had brought home yesterday. They were typical school photos. Ronnie looked exactly as you would expect, his big brown eyes dancing mischievously, his lips stretched in a broad grin showing the gap where he'd recently lost a tooth, looking every inch the lovable lad that he was.

It was the one of Mary that she stared at the longest. Jack, coming into the room, saw her concentration and asked, 'What's wrong?'

'Nothing, but Jack, it's uncanny really. Look at this school picture of Mary again an' tell me what you think.'

He did so, smiled, and said, 'I think she looks great. Extraordinary, really.'

'That's it exactly. She does look so different. Look, I fished these out of the drawer – they're old photos taken some months ago back in the summer, probably about the time she was having all that trouble at her old school.'

Jack looked over her shoulder. 'Good God,' he muttered, 'doesn't look like the same little girl. In these, she looks so serious, and it's a strange thing to say, but she looks older in them than she does now.'

'That's what I thought. These new ones show her as much younger. Years younger, in fact. It's as if all the things that were worrying her have slipped away. Lovely picture, isn't it? She looks really happy.'

'She is, can't you tell? She doesn't have those quiet moods any more. And most of it is down to you.'

Annie looked at him intently. 'Are you being honest?'

'Yes. Truly I am. You've done wonders with both Mary and Ronnie and I'm sure in years to come they'll show you their appreciation.'

'Jack, it's not only been me. You've been marvellous, and so have Gran and all our friends. Everyone has done their best to show those two that they really are wanted, and it shows in these new photos. We have made them happy, haven't we?'

Jack's hand caught hers and held on tightly. 'Oh yes, Annie, I'm sure we have.'

Annie gave him a kiss, just a peck on the cheek, but, as they say, actions speak louder than words. Each of them was thinking, all we need now is for the adoption to go through without a hitch.

'Come on, let's get going,' Jack said, putting his arm into the sleeve of his overcoat and shrugging it on to his shoulders. 'There's not many more shopping days left before Christmas, and we've a good many presents to sort out yet.'

At the door, Annie stopped and faced him. 'Do you think we could send something nice to David and Marion this year?'

'That's a funny question. Whatever brought that to your mind?'

'Well, ever since David wrote that first letter to Gran, we've all been exchanging letters. Even you have written to him.'

'Course I have. Rhoda suggested it, and I was happy to do so. Had to tell him that I'd married his sister and that we both hoped to meet him and his wife before too

476

long. Why d'you ask now? You read the letter before I posted it.'

'I know, and I even got the children to write him a little note letting him know they were still with me. It's just that he's been on my mind for days now, and I don't really know why.'

'Didn't Marion, his wife, say they were hoping to move into a flat of their own early in the new year?'

'Yes, she did. And from what I gathered they were ever so pleased. Can't have been much fun starting life in two rooms of your parents' house.'

'Well, I don't see what's bothering you, but we can't just stand here all day or we'll never get the shopping done.'

A couple of hours later Jack made his suggestion. 'I think we've bought enough for now – we're absolutely loaded down with parcels. Don't know about you, but I'm for heading for the pub. I'll make short shrift of a pie and a pint.'

Annie thought that sounded good. It was getting very cold wandering from stall to stall in the big open market. Shivering, they hurried the few yards to the pub and thankfully went inside.

A blowsy type of woman with blond hair and far too much make-up was playing the piano, and customers were standing round her, singing loudly. The bar was thick with cigarette smoke and the air smelt of stale beer, but it didn't matter, for it was coming up to Christmas. Whether East End of London or down here in the south, the people all had the same idea. Shortages were coming to an end and the feeling was of good-will to all men.

Jack came back from the bar with two enormous steak and kidney pies, a pint for himself and a glass of port for Annie. 'Thought that would warm the cockles of yer heart better than anything else today,' he said as he sat down beside her. Then he suddenly remarked, 'We've really no idea of your brother's circumstances, have we?'

Annie sighed. 'If you mean financially, no, no idea at all. An' t'be honest I feel a bit guilty at times.' Jack didn't answer, so she added, 'You what I mean. My dad left everything to me. Even his insurance policy, and I've never been able to work out why.'

'What you're trying to say is that you'd like to share some of it with David?'

'How come you can always read my thoughts, Jack? Maybe he doesn't need it, but if he did . . . you wouldn't mind, would you?'

'You know you've no need to ask me that question. We're both of us sitting pretty. Better off than we could ever have imagined we would be. Just look at the house we're living in now, never mind my good job and the money we've got in the bank. If your brother needs help, then I'm all for us giving it.'

'But how do we find out?'

'That's a question I can't answer. As soon as the weather improves, maybe Easter when the kids are on holiday, we'll go down to Plymouth, have that holiday I suggested, and then we can judge for ourselves how he an' Marion are doing. Meanwhile, think what Frank was saying last weekend.'

'Frank? I'm not with you.'

'He was on about how busy they were at Fortnum & Mason's this year. Said they're taking on a lot of temporary staff in the packing department to deal with the Christmas hampers. First time they've done them since 1939, so he said.'

'Yeah, I remember hearing all that, but what's that got to do with my brother?'

Jack laughed. 'Let's be posh for once. Send a hamper of goodies to Marion an' David. Even if they are doing all right, a present like that isn't going to cause embarrassment.'

Annie squeezed his arms. 'Oh, you're great, Jack, you really are. A hamper from Fortnum & Mason's! No Christmas present could be nicer.'

'That's settled, then? Thank goodness.'

'This will be our first Christmas in our new home. Loads of room, Gran an' Phyllis are gonna stay. Vera and Peter only downstairs, and Frank an' Doris to swell the numbers. The kids will have a great time. I only wish . . .'

'I know exactly what you're going to say. You wish the children really were ours.'

'Well, don't you feel the same?'

'You know I do. But on the other hand I feel very privileged to be given the chance to have a hand in bringing them up. In a funny sort of way I feel I am paying back some of the kindness your gran showed me when I came back to no one with no home to go to. Plus the fact that since then you've become my whole life. When you said you'd marry me, I knew damn well just how lucky I was.'

Despite the fact that the pub was crowded, the singing even louder on this busy Saturday, Annie hugged him and he whispered in her ear, 'Try and be patient. Mr Oliver has everything in hand. Trust me, it won't be too long now and those kids will be telling their teachers at school that their surname is Higgins. Now I'm going up to the counter to get us another drink.'

As he walked away, Annie was thinking, 'Please God, let that be true. Please.'

It was as they were crossing the busy high street that they caught sight of Ronnie and Mary disappearing into Solly's Bazaar. When safely on the other side, they stood at its entrance and peered in. Very popular place was Solly's. Many items he sold were tuppence, for sixpence there was a wide choice, and getting into the more expensive bracket his price always took some beating.

'Very difficult to spot them,' Jack muttered.

'There they are, over there,' Annie said, pointing a finger. 'Let's see if we can get a bit nearer without letting them see us.'

When they were half hidden behind a huge display of Christmas annuals, they were able not only to observe the children but listen to what they were saying.

'Oh, why ever didn't it occur to me?' Annie murmured.

Ronnie was telling his sister that she hadn't got enough money to buy the pretty hairbrush she was holding. 'But Gran would love it,' Mary was protesting loudly.

'Come away,' Jack urged, tugging at Annie's sleeve. 'Let's go before they see us.'

Once outside the store, he heaved a great sigh. 'You ask why you didn't think of it, what about me? I give them a few coppers pocket money every week, and Frank an' Peter regularly give them a penny or so, but I should have thought that they'd want to buy Christmas presents. Thank God we did come across them.'

'What will you do?' Annie asked.

'Not quite sure yet. Can't let them know that we've

seen them, let alone overheard what they were saying. But I'll think of some way to give them extra money.'

It was six o'clock on Monday evening before Jack got his chance. Their evening meal was over and everything cleared away. The fire was well banked up, flames shooting up the chimney, and Mary was sitting at the table colouring her Christmas cards that Annie had helped her to cut out from sheets of pretty cardboard. Ronnie was stretched out on the hearthrug with a couple of comics.

Jack went to the dresser drawer, pulled out four buff-coloured envelopes and held them up high. He shook them, and both children and Annie also, looked up in surprise as they heard the sound of coins rattling.

'Everyone come and sit round the table,' Jack ordered, grinning. 'It's pay-out time.'

Ronnie scrambled to his feet, saying to his sister, 'Move some of that stuff.'

'I don't see why I should. It ain't 'urting you,' said Mary defensively.

'You can be a right little 'orror sometimes,' Ronnie told her.

'Now, what's all this about?' asked Annie casually. 'There's plenty of room for all of us round the table.'

'Not with all the stuff she's got spread out, there ain't,' Ronnie protested.

'Well, ask her nicely to tidy her work into a couple of neat piles, and I'm sure she won't mind, will you Mary?'

'Not if you want me to.' Mary's fingers were moving swiftly, snatching her cards away out of the reach of her brother.

Jack made no comment. He knew it was a storm in a

481

tea-cup, best ignored. They wouldn't be normal children if they didn't have a tiff now and again. 'Anyone want to guess what's in these envelopes?' he asked when they were finally all seated.

'Dunno,' said Mary.

'It's my opinion there's money in 'em,' Ronnie stated, still sounding a little peeved because Annie had taken sides.

'Well, I'm pleased to tell you, young man, that your opinion is absolutely right,' Jack told him.

'He ain't always right.' Mary rolled her eyes.

Annie covered her mouth to smother a laugh. She daren't look at Jack.

'There's one of these packets for each of us,' Jack said, handing out the envelopes.

The children stared as he opened his and shook out silver coins and several pound notes. Then Annie did the same.

'Crikey! You've got all that money,' said Ronnie. 'Where'd it come from?'

'Well, I didn't rob a bank, so you can take that look off your face,' Jack told him. 'Every week all the year round I put a bit by out of my wages, 'cos everybody knows that you need a bit extra when Christmas comes. This year, instead of giving you two youngsters a bit more pocket money every week, I saved for you as well. Go on, open up, count what you've got.'

'You ain't 'aving us on, are you?' asked Ronnie.

'Course I ain't having you on,' said Jack.

'Jack,' Mary hesitated, eyeing him carefully, ''ow about me?'

'Just the same, my love. The money in there is yours to do what you like with.'

Ronnie ripped his open while Mary slowly slipped her finger beneath the flap and very tidily slit it free. Brother and sister looked at each other, and at a nod from Ronnie tipped the contents on to the table.

There was a ten-shilling note, one two-shilling piece, two single shillings and two sixpences. 'Cor, blimey! Fifteen bob! Jack, I dunno what t'say, 'onest I don't.'

'I've got the same. Look, Annie, I've got a load of money as well. Isn't Jack kind?'

Jack was choked as Annie gave Mary a loving cuddle, and even more so as Mary knelt up on the chair in order to kiss him.

Ronnie hesitated, not at all sure how to show his appreciation. Getting to his feet he held out his hand, his voice kind of muffled as he said, 'You're a great bloke, Jack. Me an' me sister would be 'aving a very different time of it if it weren't fer Annie an' you. Fanks. Fanks ever so much.'

That was too much! Jack pushed his arms out and drew the boy towards him. Holding him tight, he murmured, 'You ain't such a bad lad yerself.' It was a while before anyone spoke again.

Adults and children alike were busy with their own thoughts, and none more than Jack. Life had turned around for him. He remembered that first Christmas after he had been demobbed. He had never felt so lonely in the whole of his life. He had had no one and had felt that no one had wanted him. Now look!

He reckoned he'd begun to live again because of Annie. She was goodness itself, that's what she was.

Chapter Forty-one

NEITHER ANNIE NOR JACK could remember a Christmas like it. It began at half-past five in the morning when the children burst into their bedroom, shouting, 'Annie, Jack, wake-up, look what Father Christmas has brought us!'

'Well I never!' Annie's voice was full of laughter as she nudged Jack to move over and make room for Mary to climb in beside her. Ronnie was stretched out across the foot of the bed hugging a box of Meccano to his chest.

'Come on, give me a cuddle for Christmas,' she said, pulling Mary closer to her side.

Jack leaned forward, saying, 'I'll give you wake us up at this ungodly hour!' Then he started to tickle Ronnie unmercifully, which made him giggle and protest loudly.

'You're worse than they are!' Annie exclaimed. 'You'll wake the whole house up between you.' Laughing and shaking her head she climbed out of bed, pulled on her dressing-gown and went down to make tea for everyone.

Christmas day had started off really well. By midday

the table was groaning under the weight of all the food. But it was late in the afternoon when Rhoda said, 'Well, between us all, we've done justice to that meal.'

Vera came into the room and set a large tray down on the table with a clatter, saying, 'I bet there's not one of you that will say no to a cup of tea or coffee. I've made both.'

The women looked at each other and burst out laughing. 'She's trying to sober us up.'

Doris said, 'Suppose we have got through a few bottles.' She pointed to the sideboard. 'But never mind, Christmas comes but once a year.'

Jack and Frank were stretched out on the floor, helping Ronnie to assemble a big fort and line up the two sets of soldiers that Vera and Peter had bought for him. Mary was dressing her new doll and laying it down in the perambulator that had been their gift to her.

Suddenly Peter said quietly, 'It's been a lovely Christmas day, hasn't it? I've never seen everyone so relaxed. I think it's because we've all been together.'

No one answered him for a moment, then Rhoda raised her eyes and looked at the ceiling and in a thoughtful voice she said, 'I expect on the quiet we've all drunk to absent friends, I know I have. But when it's all boiled down we 'ave t'make the best of life. Even when my 'usband and my son were alive we missed our parents, but that didn't stop us from being gay and laughing. We never forget the past, but we have to live in the present and look to the future. If you've got friends to share it with, so much the better.'

Annie turned to Phyllis. She, too, looked relaxed as she held the doll still while Mary tied its bonnet on. She never imagined that the children would grow fond of her so quickly, but they had. Indeed, over the past few weeks everyone had come to like this small plump lady, who had been so kind and thoughtful when they had sat discussing the children's future. Annie was sure now that the general opinion was that she was in need of friends but, given that friendship, she would repay it tenfold.

Phyllis broke into Annie's thoughts. 'I know I've never experienced a Christmas like this. I've always dreaded this time of the year. But today has been . . . well,' she went on in a hesitant way, 'different. There's been companionship, an acceptance. I'm . . . I'm sorry.'

Mary raised her head, put out a hand and laid it on Phyllis's. 'What's amatter, Gran? Don't be sad. It's still Christmas, an' you ain't got t'go 'ome ternight, 'as she, Annie?'

'Of course she hasn't, nor the day after.' Annie pulled herself together. 'I think it's time we played some games. See all those parcels still lying round the tree? They're prizes, so who's for trying to win one?' She was beside Phyllis now, shaking her two clenched hands between her own. She could see her eyes were bright with unshed tears.

'I'm all right, really I am. It's . . . It's just because I'm so happy . . . Annie, you'll never know what you've done for me. All of you. You've made me feel wanted.'

'You are, Phyllis, you really are. Look how fond of you the children are already and it's not only them. All of us feel that way.' Annie pulled out her handkerchief and dabbed at her own eyes as she said, 'You're stuck with us now for better or worse. You're only seeing the good side of us – we can be a bad-tempered lot at times, oh yes.'

'Go on with yer, lass! Nobody is perfect. I'll put up with all that, dear, if you'll put up with me.'

'The bargain is struck,' Annie told her, moving out of the way so that Mary could climb up and sit on her Grannie Phyllis's knee.

During the whole of the holiday Annie had kept her mouth shut and her thoughts to herself regarding the letter that had arrived on Christmas eve. Now for the umpteenth time she withdrew it from the envelope and started to read it. It was headed:

THE ADOPTION OF CHILDREN (SUMMARY JURISDICTION) RULES, 1936. TAKE NOTICE OF AN APPLICATION FOR AN ADOPTION ORDER in respect of two infants named Ronald Arthur Wilson and Mary Louise Wilson IN THE COUNTY OF LONDON

THAT an application has been made by, Jack Alfred Higgins and Anne Margaret Higgins his wife for an order under the Adoption of Children Act 1926, authorizing them to adopt the said infants, being one infant of the male sex, aged eleven years and one infant of the female sex, aged eight years resident at 48, Tremaine Road, Wandsworth Common, London.

THAT the said application will be heard before the Juvenile Court sitting at Wandsworth on Friday, the . . . 13th . . . day of February 1951, at the hour of 10.30 in the forenoon and that you are required to attend before the Court.

Dated the 20th day of December 1950.

'Hey, remember me? I'm still here.' Jack interrupted her thoughts and brought her back to the present. He got up and moved his chair so that he could sit beside her. 'Annie, listen to me.' She raised her head, and his heart ached as he saw the worried look on her face. 'I know, I know, it's been a long time, but it's almost over now. Come here,' he said, smothering her in his strong arms.

Minutes passed, and when he spoke again his voice was choked with emotion. 'It's New Year's eve, there'll be friends dropping in this evening. Try not to think about the court order. We'll make it a happy day, even though it will be a quiet, probably dull, day. Perhaps I should have booked up somewhere, taken you out.'

'Oh, Jack.' Annie laughed quietly before adding, 'Quiet? Apart from everything else, I don't know who could be dull when the kids are about . . .'

The children had been invited to a luncheon and entertainment afterwards in the church hall. As it turned out, Annie liked having a quiet lunch, just the two of them. She liked their evening dinner, too, with the children prattling on about the magician who had made birds and rabbits appear from out of a top hat. In fact she was feeling very relaxed and happy as she sipped her coffee. Outside, a gale was blowing and the freezing rain was coming down in torrents. It was a laugh really, because for weeks Rhoda had been going on about a white Christmas, how the garden would look great covered in snow, and big oak logs would be crackling away in the grate inside. The bit about the fire was the only thing that had come true. Now, a week later, and if anything the weather was worse. The wind could knock you off your feet, and the cold was biting enough to get inside your bones.

Jack had just remarked that you couldn't expect folk to turn out on a night like this when the phone rang. He answered it, and looked across, shouting, 'Here you are, kids, it's your two grandmas. Come and wish them both "Happy New Year".'

Ronnie took the phone, shouting down the line before handing it over to Mary. Now it was Annie's turn. 'Hallo, Gran. All the best for the New Year. But you should be here, you know, Phyllis an' all. Still, with the weather as it is . . . I'm glad to hear that Phyllis is spending the night at your place. Yes, we all love you, too. See you soon.'

There was great excitement when Vera and Peter came up from downstairs bringing a bottle of brandy. They only stayed for an hour. Peter was looking very tired. Frank and Doris phoned, teasing the kids that it was freezing hard and swearing that by the morning the rain would have turned to snow. By eleven o'clock the kiddies' eyelids had begun to droop. Jack carried Mary up to bed and Annie followed to tuck up the pair of them.

So there were only the two of them standing together when the New Year was announced on the wireless. 'A happy New Year, my darling.' 'And to you, Jack.'

They embraced, and Jack's tenderness brought a lump to Annie's throat. This was what she had always dreamed of. A kind and loving man to care for her as she cared for him. They were about to raise their glasses, when Jack very quietly said, 'Here's to an eternity of loving you, Annie.' Her heart was full.

Then there came a ring on the doorbell. 'God almighty! Who the hell is mad enough to have ventured out tonight? No, Annie, stay where you are. I'll go . . . I tell you, I'll go!' He pushed Annie back into her chair and went out of the front room, across the landing and down the stairs to the front door. When he opened it, he squinted at the sight of the two figures standing there sheltering under a huge umbrella.

'You must be Jack. I'm David, and this is my wife Marion,' said the tall, dark-haired young man.

'Well, well, well! Come on in. Your sister will be over the moon.' He caught David's hand in both of his and shook it vigorously before turning to shut the door. He put a hand gently on Marion's arm saying, 'She'll be really glad to see you both. She really will. Come on, I can't wait t'see the look on her face.' He led the way upstairs, then thrusting open the front-room door, he called out, 'You'll never guess who's here.'

Annie was already standing in the middle of the room racking her brain as to who this late-night caller might be. Suddenly she froze. Her feet wouldn't move. David came towards her, saying, 'Happy New Year, Sis! Hope I'm your first footing, an' that I'll bring you good luck. I've brought a lump of coal with me.'

'Oh, David! I can't believe it. Oh, David.' For a long moment they stood close, arms round each other.

David broke away, smiling, and said, 'There's someone I want you to meet. Marion, this is my sister Annie, and Annie, this is my wife Marion.'

Quickly Annie took the few steps over to her sister-in-law, and in a trice they too were hugging each other close. 'You're frozen,' Annie said. 'Come near the fire. Come and sit in this armchair. Here, give me your coat. Oh, your hands are cold. Where have you been? It's the middle of the night. How did you get here?'

David and Jack looked at each other and laughed. 'She hasn't altered much,' David declared. 'Asks questions, but never waits to hear the answers. We came by car of course.'

'Then I can't understand why you're so cold. Don't you have a heater in your car?'

'Of course we do, Sis, but we've been sitting outside for ages waiting for midnight, and you can't keep the heat on in a stationary car.'

'Oh, you pair of fools,' Annie cried, playfully punching her brother's arm.

'Let me take David's coat and get them both a hot drink, and then you can ask him any amount of questions. But let them get warm and settled before you start the bombardment.' There was a smile on Jack's face as he turned to their visitors. 'A hot toddy would be in order, I think. Is that all right by you?' They both nodded their heads.

'Have you had anything to eat?' Annie asked with concern.

David looked at his sister and then at his wife before shaking his head. 'We left home hours ago, and we'd eaten all our sandwiches by the time we got through Somerset. There wasn't a café open anywhere. To tell you the truth, I think we're both starving.'

'That's no problem. I'll rustle you up a hot meal while you drink your toddies.'

As Annie went out, Jack said, 'I'll come and give you a hand with the trays.' It was as if at this moment he was at a loss as to what to say to this young couple unless Annie was there too.

Less than twenty minutes later, David was saying, 'Thank you both ever so much. Hope we haven't put you to too much trouble?'

It was then that Marion found her voice. Warmed by the hot toddy, her cheeks had reddened. 'David has been on about coming here for weeks,' she said.

'And were you for coming as well?' Annie asked.

Marion looked directly at Annie, with a grin on her

face that showed it could easily spread into laughter, as she said, 'I've heard so many tales about you that wild horses wouldn't have kept me away!'

Annie returned the grin. She was thinking that David's wife was an extremely smart young woman who looked to be in her mid-twenties. She was plainly dressed in a navy blue skirt and a heather coloured twin-set, but her clothes were good – expensive was the word that came to Annie's mind. Her face was lovely and had a kind gentle look to it; with laughter in her eyes. She hoped they would become good friends.

Jack swallowed hard as he listened to what Annie was saying to her brother.

'How have you been making a living?'

'Well, I did various jobs when I first arrived in Plymouth, mainly in the shipyards. I wrote and told you. But since the shortages have eased off I kinda fell on my feet.'

That statement had her feeling a bit edgy and she glanced at Jack, but took no notice of his frowning look.

'Not still ducking an' diving, are you? I'd have thought you learnt your lesson years ago when you tried a few of our father's tricks.'

'Annie, give me some credit! I'm a married man now.' The look he exchanged with his wife did wonders for settling Annie's mind. It was like a charge of electricity, and left her in no doubt that he had found the right woman to spend the rest of his life with.

'They run a sweepstakes in the dockyard. It's an ongoing thing, only pays out once a year, and I was lucky enough to win it.' David was looking more at Jack as he began talking. 'I had the money invested until I got on friendly terms with a cousin of Marion's. The outcome is we pooled our resources and now we're partners, all legal and above board. There were so many buildings and whole streets demolished in Plymouth during the war that it will take years even for the demolition work to be completed. We can't compete with the big firms on clearing sites and rebuilding, but we can repair and make good decent well-built properties that were caught by the blast rather than severe bomb damage. We're a private firm, we employ ten men, all specialists in their own field, and we're never short of work.'

Jack watched him as he raised his glass and drained it. He came across as a decent honest young man and he was pleased that he had taken the trouble to come first footing tonight. When Jack remained silent, David noticed that his wife and sister were holding their own friendly conversation, and said, 'There's so much unrest down in the West Country that I count myself lucky to be my own boss.'

'I know what you mean,' Jack quickly agreed. 'It's much the same in London, believe you me. Lads coming home to find no houses and not much work aren't going to take it lying down. Not this time.'

David nodded. 'Seems t'be the state of the country as a whole. It's unbelievable. The workers aren't asking for the moon, yet the unions seem set on bringing them out on strike. If they get them an extra shilling or two, the bloody prices of food and suchlike will go up, and they'll be no better off. I gathered from your letter that you work for yourself?'

'Well, more or less. I've me own lighter and can afford to be pretty choosy about what jobs I take on. Though if you rely on the Thames as I do, and you're not afraid of hard work, you've no need ever t'go short of a bob or two.'

'Are you two going to talk all night?' Annie cut in on them briskly. 'David, you are aiming to stay a while, aren't you?'

'Well, yes, that's if you can put up with us.'

'Oh, David, I still can't believe you really are here. Can't wait to see Ronnie and Mary's reaction in the morning.'

'Get on, Sis! I think it's wonderful that you've kept them with you all this time, but they won't even remember me.'

'Oh, won't they, Mr Clever-clogs? They wrote to you, didn't they? Just you wait and see. By the way, where's your suitcases?'

Marion got to her feet. 'They're in the boot of the car. The icy rain was so bad we just ran to the front door.'

'I'll come with you to get them,' Jack volunteered. 'Any beds made up?' he asked Annie.

'Yes, I made up the big bed in the back room in case Gran decided to come and stay. I'll fill a couple of hot-water bottles and pop them between the sheets.'

David's face turned scarlet. 'I've yet to ask about Gran. Her letters to me and Marion have been friendly enough, but how will she take to us turning up like this?'

Annie laughed. 'Since when could you do any wrong in Gran's eyes? She'll probably hug you both to death, and it's sure she'll say you need feeding up and she'll start cooking enormous meals.'

'I think I'd better put a stop to all this,' Jack cut in. 'Marion looks as if she's out on her feet. Let's get your cases and see you both set up nicely for the night. There'll be plenty of time all week for questions and answers, and more than a few surprises, I bet.'

Annie went off to fill the hot-water bottles and a few minutes later Jack and David returned with the suitcases.

Annie led the way to the bedroom, where David hugged her and told her again how good it was to see her. She gently put her arms round Marion, whispering, 'Sleep well. I'll see you in the morning.'

Jack shook hands with David and kissed Marion on the cheek, then left them alone together.

Annie's last thought before she finally dropped off to sleep was what a wonderful way to start the New Year. Not only her brother but her new sister-in-law, whom she already felt she would grow to love, were lying in bed not yards away.

Chapter Forty-two

THE HOUSE SEEMED SO empty, so quiet. Jack had gone to work and the children to school. Annie wandered about her living-room, watering what had been her Christmas cyclamen, snipping off dead heads and withered leaves. After three weeks of snow the weather had turned gusty, the strong wind helping to clear the messy slush that had gathered in piles, and the spring-like sunshine was a joy to behold. As a parting gift Marion had bought a bowl of primroses, their pale yellow faces and delicate green leaves so lovely. It's lasting very well, she thought as she moved the bowl to the centre of the table. It seemed ages since they had stood on the top step waving, promising to keep to the arrangements that they and the two grandmas would travel down to Plymouth by train and stay for two weeks during the children's Easter school holidays. By then, Marion had assured them, she and David would be in their new house and they'd sort the sleeping arrangements out somehow.

Ronnie and Mary had talked of nothing else, especially

Ronnie, because David had promised to take him out on the sea in a motor-boat. That was almost a month ago. Ten days they had stayed, and every day had been so good. The children had made a fuss of David, and Marion had become a favourite with everyone.

Annie sighed heavily. All good things must come to an end. Oh, it was going to be such a long day . . . She had stripped the beds, run the carpet-sweeper through every room, dusted and polished every bit of furniture, scrubbed the kitchen floor and got through a huge pile of ironing and it was still only a quarter to one.

I'll make myself a cup of tea, she decided. Then she changed her mind as she went through to the kitchen. I'll have coffee. She took a mug down from the dresser, one that Jack preferred, made the coffee, and took it across to the living-room. With the poker, she stirred the fire to life. As the flames shot up, she carried the mug to the settee, piled three cushions at one end, and curled herself up with her feet tucked beneath her. On the opposite wall was a photograph of the children. She gazed at it intently. She loved both Ronnie and Mary as if they were her own. There was no doubt in her mind about that. Warm and snug, she began to recall the various happenings that had led to her becoming responsible for them both.

She finished her coffee, laid down the mug, reached for the rug that lay folded over the back of the settee and settled down on the cushions with the rug tucked tightly around her. She closed her eyes. Please, God, be on our side when we have to go to court.

It couldn't have been more than five minutes before the door bell rang. Throwing off the rug, she got to her feet to answer it.

Her gasp of surprise was quickly smothered as she was

pressed close to Flossie Owen's ample bosom. It was a minute or two before she was able to say, 'Oh, this is a lovely surprise!'

Big Sid Owen's ruddy face beamed as he roared, 'Well if Mohammed won't come to the Mountain, then the Mountain has to come to Mohammed.'

'Sid!' Annie breathed as she stood on tiptoe in order to kiss his cheek. 'How come you two are out together? Who's minding the café?'

'We've retired,' Flossie told her, grinning from ear to ear.

'Ave we gotta stay on this blinking doorstep, or are you ever gonna ask us inside?' Sid was still holding Annie as he pushed the front door wide with his foot.

'Oh, I'm sorry.' She led the way, saying over her shoulder to Flossie, 'I don't believe for one moment that you've given up the café just like that. Whatever will you do with yourselves all day?' Without waiting for a reply, she added, 'I'll put the kettle on.'

'No, you won't.' Sid handed her a bag. 'A small offering, since it's the first time we've been in your new home.'

She took the bag and automatically looked inside. 'Sid, you shouldn't have! Take your coats off and I'll fetch some glasses.'

'The whisky is for Jack, the sweets are for the kids, the chocolates are for you and the Champagne is for us to drink now. I hope that's to your liking.' Sid grinned as he pulled the gold-topped bottle from the bag that Annie was still holding.

'I don't know what to say,' Annie mumbled, coming back with three glasses. She turned to Flossie. 'You haven't really retired, have you?

Flossie had sunk down in the corner of the settee and was watching her husband as he dealt with the bottle and glasses. He brought a glass each for her and Annie, then he collected his own and sat down in the armchair opposite. He raised his glass. 'Cheers! Here's to a long and happy life in this house.'

'Thanks, Sid. Thanks, Flossie,' said Annie.

They drank, and Flossie began to talk. 'We thought it was about time we eased up a bit. Had a bit more time together instead of working all the hours that God sends. So Sid 'as leased the café to Bill Whatley, good customer in his time. You must remember 'im, Annie?'

'Of course I do. Annie said. 'Good-looking bloke, loved the ladies even though he had a wife and two children. But he worked on the docks. What does he want with a café?'

Sid looked up, turning his glass in his hands. 'Sad story. Peggy, his wife, died. There was no one to look after those young kiddies, and the odd hours on the docks didn't help. Long an' short of it is, he's moved in over the café, runs the business and all in all it's made his domestic arrangements a good deal easier.'

Annie tactfully waited a little, until she felt bound to ask, 'Have you had any lunch, 'cos I can soon make us some sandwiches.'

'No. If you've finished yer drink, we're going to take you for a pub lunch. What time do you meet the children from school?'

'Not until half-past three for Mary, and Ronnie doesn't come out until a quarter to four.'

'That's all right, then. 'Ow they doing at this new school?'

'Fine. They really are. I've just thought: do you know

500

that the date is set for the court hearing of the adoption application?'

Flossie looked a bit sheepish as she said, 'Yeah, we dropped in to see Rhoda a fortnight ago, an' she told us. You don't mind us knowing, do you, Annie? You know we wish you well, all of you.'

Annie took hold of Flossie's hand. 'Mind? Of course I don't! I must say though that I shall be damned glad when it's all over.'

'Well, if you two 'ave quite finished with catching up on the news, how about we get going for something to eat?'

Sid's gleaming new car took them to the Surrey Tavern, and as soon as they were settled with a hearty ploughman's lunch each, he asked, 'Annie, 'ave you got anything planned for tomorrow?'

'Why?'

''Cos there's racing at Kempton Park and I thought me an' Flossie might like to see the gee-gees run for a change rather than just pick their names out of the paper. We'd like you to come with us.'

Flossie nudged her. 'Go on, say yer will. Life is altering for all of us, so it's about time we began to enjoy it. We'll make sure we're back in time for you to meet the children from school.'

Seeing that Annie was wavering, Sid said, 'I could tempt you with the promise of a real slap-up meal, an' even a few tips as to a winner.'

Annie smiled, then shrugged her shoulders. 'Why not? A day out with you two has got to be just what I need. You're an amazing pair, you know that!'

'So we've been told.' Flossie had the last word.

* * *

It was twelve noon. Jack, Annie and Phyllis Wilson were standing at the foot of Lavender Hill having walked down from the law courts. 'The thirteenth. Lucky for some,' Annie murmured.

They had waited so long for this hearing, and now it was over. Just like that! The moment she had walked into that court room and spotted the panel of child-care experts and doctors who were sitting there to deliberate on the future of two small children, her heart had sunk into her boots. It hadn't been half-way as bad as she had imagined. Mr Webster smiled encouragingly at her. She knew him to be a more senior social worker because it was he who had made the last visit to their home. He was a thin man, aged about fifty. He had a kind face, and a manner that put one at ease, although he looked very formal.

If anything, it had been poor Phyllis who had to answer the most questions. Did she really approve of strangers adopting her two grandchildren? Could she shed light on the fact that her son had given his written permission for the adoption to go ahead? She had told them exactly what she knew and felt. Her words had come from the heart. The following silence had been unbearable.

Then with a smile Mr Webster requested Mr and Mrs Higgins to come forward and face the bench.

'Are you saying that you approve of us?' Annie had interrupted the posh-speaking gentleman.

'Ssh! Listen, dear, he hasn't finished yet.' Jack, obviously moved, spoke gently.

Annie couldn't remember a word that had been said after that. The end had come suddenly. It appeared that the reports on them and their home-life had been quite satisfactory. They were approved as adoptive parents.

Now she broke the silence that had settled between

them since they had left the court. 'Phyllis,' she began, 'you were so good. You seemed to know exactly what they wanted to hear. How can we ever thank you?'

Phyllis looked sadly at both of them. 'If they had refused the adoption, it would have been a dark day for those children.' She shook her head as though she felt bewildered. 'Ronnie might have weathered being taken into care, he's a tough little nut. But being parted from his sister would have been the disaster for him. Not so, young Mary. I know something of what that child has been through, her feeling of rejection must have been unbearable at times. My son made it plain to her that he neither liked her nor wanted her. Young as she is, she sensed that, and she found it impossible to come to terms with.' Her eyes were moist as she looked at Jack. 'Many a time that's what's prevented her from showing her real feelings. How do I know all this when I've only been around for a short time? Remember, I've been there! Besides, Mary talked to me. It took some doing, but I really believe she's come to trust me.' She drew in a deep breath and said, 'I don't suppose she'll 'ave much to say when you tell her, but watch her face. You do that. I think her expression will speak for her.'

Jack took each of them by the arm and led them up the front steps and through the big glass doors of *Arding & Hobbs*, saying, 'We'll get arrested if we stand on that corner any longer. I'm going to treat you both to a slap-up lunch.'

'Oh? I thought we'd go straight to the school.'

'Hold your horses, Annie,' Jack said. 'We'll be at the school gates the minute they come out, never fear. I want to tell them just as much as you do, but now we are going to have something to eat. You had no breakfast at all.'

'Jack, will you do me a favour?' Phyllis asked when they were all seated in the restaurant and the waitress had taken their order. 'Would you take me home before you go to meet the children, or at least drop me off at Rhoda's so I can tell her the good news?'

'We'll all go an' tell me gran – we've got plenty of time,' Annie cut in. 'But why don't you want t'come to the school with us?'

'Well, I don't think it would be right. Just you two, that's 'ow it should be. You and the kids 'ave waited long enough.'

The day was brilliant, the air sharp, the sun weak, but to Annie as she stood beside her husband at the school gates it wouldn't have mattered if there had been a gale blowing. They were here to meet their children.

When Mary came running across the playground, her cheeks were pink. Her legs, below her navy blue coat, were skinny but strong. Her satchel was slung over her shoulder, her long blond hair flying in the wind. In not many months she'd be going up to the senior school.

Ronnie, lean and still fairly tanned, overtook his sister and skidded to a halt. There was no cheeky grin today as he squarely faced Annie, his eyebrows raised questioningly. She half-smiled and nodded her head. His satchel was flung to the ground and his arms were round Annie's neck. She held him close, and heard him, with great difficulty, swallow the lump that had risen in his throat.

'I don't usually get a hug when you come out of school,' Annie said, doing her best not to cry.

'I don't mind givin' you a hug, now an' again,' he retarted, blinking hard to keep his tears at bay . . .

'Especially today, eh?'

'Yeah, especially today.' Annie had to turn away to hide her emotions as she watched Mary, who by now was being held high in Jack's arms. He put her down, and she came to Annie and asked, 'Is everything proper-like now?'

'Yes, Mary, my luv. Everything is sorted and proper now.'

'You said if it was all right I could ask some of the girls in my class to tea.'

'And I meant it,' Annie assured her. Then delving into her handbag, she brought out a packet of pretty cards. 'See, I've bought the invitation cards for you to write.' She bent her knees so that her face was on a level with Mary's, and taking out one card she said, 'See, you fill in the girl's name that you want to invite on the top line and you put your own name on the bottom line.' Mary didn't answer, but studied the card. Annie straightened up and waited.

Mary stepped back a space. 'Ta, Annie. I do love you.'

'I love you too, pet. Is there something you want to ask?'

Mary looked at her brother, who was standing tall and silent beside Jack. Then she asked quietly, 'Can I write me new name?'

'You most certainly can,' Annie told her. 'You can tell the whole world if you like.'

Still Mary looked undecided. Then suddenly she took a deep breath and the words came out in a rush. 'Then I'm not gonna call you Annie any more. Ta, Mum.'

It was hard to tell who was the most moved. As Annie hugged Mary close to her, Jack turned to Ronnie. 'We went into the dockyard on our way down here, and I registered my son as a would-be docker when he's passed all his exams and is old enough to leave school. The harbour-master said to say "Congratulations" to you.'

Ronnie just stared at Jack. 'Maybe you won't want to be a docker. With an education under your belt you could still work on the docks but as a white-collar worker. The choice would be up to you, son.' Jack put great emphasis on the last word.

'Fank you.' Ronnie was having trouble getting his thoughts into words. 'Jack . . . What I mean is, can I . . . will it be all right . . . if I call you Dad?'

'You'd jolly well better, after all the trouble your mother and I have gone to!'

All the mums standing around, meeting their own children, sighed happily as the four members of the Higgins family came together in a bunch with arms entwined.

Minutes later the children were racing towards the car, when Annie tugged at Jack's sleeve. 'Hang on a minute, Jack, I've something I want to tell you.' He stopped in his stride. 'What's that then?'

'I went to the doctor's a week ago.'

'And?'

'Do you really need to ask?'

'No,' he said with that lovely smile of his that said everything.

'Aren't you going to tell me how pleased you are?'

'Wait until we're in bed tonight. Actions speak louder than words.'

'Oh, you're beyond help, you are!'

'Not quite,' he answered, giving her another wonderful smile. 'But right now I have to get our children and my pregnant wife home.' He bent to kiss her.

As Jack concentrated on driving, the kids, in the back of the car, were singing, 'Show me the way to go 'ome.'

Annie was saying to herself, 'Who said dreams don't come true?'